# The One Who Got Away

*She was so beautiful.*

Nate needed to get a grip. He needed to get his head screwed back on straight, needed to remember that tonight was about catching up on old times.

Nothing more.

Andi's face, which was already a little flushed, went pink. And still, she took his breath away. "You ready to head over to the Tavern, Andi?"

Without waiting for her response, Nate reached for her hand to take her away. To have her all to himself.

She looked down at his outstretched hand, not taking it right away, and he swore he could see the pulse at the side of her wrist fluttering just beneath the skin.

Finally, she put her hand into his and the shock of her skin against his made him wonder how he could have possibly waited ten years to touch her again.

# Home Sweet Home

## BELLA RILEY

FOREVER

NEW YORK   BOSTON

This book is a work of fiction. Names, characters, places, and incidents are the product of the author's imagination or are used fictitiously. Any resemblance to actual events, locales, or persons, living or dead, is coincidental.

Forever
Hachette Book Group
237 Park Avenue
New York, NY 10017
www.HachetteBookGroup.com

Forever is an imprint of Grand Central Publishing.

The Forever name and logo are trademarks of Hachette Book Group, Inc.

The publisher is not responsible for websites (or their content) that are not owned by the publisher.

Printed in the United States of America

First Edition: October 2011

10 9 8 7 6 5 4 3 2 1

*To Paul.*
*You took me to the lake fifteen years ago,*
*and I fell in love.*

# Acknowledgments

First and foremost, I couldn't have written this book without the support of my awesome husband and kids! To my agent, Jessica, thank you for the endless hours of brainstorming and reading and then more brainstorming and more reading. The past seven years we've been working together have been a blast. To my editor, Michele, and everyone at Grand Central Publishing and Forever, it's a huge thrill to be working with you on my Emerald Lake series. I've wanted to write these books for a very long time, and I'm glad our vision matches so well! To all of my friends for our lunches, the endless laughter and support, the constant phone calls and texting, you know who you are... and that I adore each and every one of you.

And last but in no way least, thank you to each and every person who reads romance! I have read (more like devoured) romance novels my entire life, and I am constantly stuffing my bookshelf and e-reader with new ones. Romance readers are the best!

*Home Sweet Home*

# Chapter One

Home.

Andi Powell couldn't believe she was back home.

During the five-hour drive to Emerald Lake from New York City, Andi had felt her stomach tighten down more and more with each mile she covered, each county line she crossed. She'd pulled up in front of Lake Yarns on Main Street five minutes ago, but she hadn't yet been able to get out of the car. Instead, she sat with her hands still tightly clenched on the steering wheel as she watched people on Main Street. Mothers pushed strollers, shoppers moved in and out of stores, and happy tourists walked hand in hand.

Through her car window, Andi could see that the warm days of summer had already given way to a crisp, cool fall. She would have had to be blind not to notice that the thick green trees around the waterline were transformed into a dazzling display of reds and oranges and yellows.

No wonder why everyone on Main Street looked so happy. Utterly content. Emerald Lake was picture-perfect: the sky was blue, the lake sparkled in the sunlight, and the white paint on the gazebo in the waterfront park looked new.

But Andi wasn't here to become a part of *picture-perfect*. She had a job to do. Which meant it was time to unclench her chest, to untangle the knots in her stomach, and to get down to business.

The sooner she dealt with Emerald Lake, the sooner she could head back to the city.

Pushing open her car door, she grabbed her briefcase and headed toward her family's store. The Lake Yarns awning was bright and welcoming, and the Adirondack chairs out front welcomed knitters to sit for as long as they had time to spare.

She smiled her first real smile of the day, thinking of how much love and care her grandmother and mother had put into this store over the years.

The shiny gold knob on the front door was cool beneath her palm, and she paused to take a deep breath and pull herself together. Entering a building that had practically been her second home as a little girl shouldn't have her heart racing.

But it did.

Opening the door, the smell of yarn was what hit her first. Wool and alpaca, bamboo and silk, cotton and acrylic all had a specific scent. Although Andi hadn't touched yarn in almost two decades, somehow the essence of the skeins lining the walls, in baskets on the floor, knitted up into samples throughout Lake Yarns had remained imprinted in her brain.

She hadn't come back to Emerald Lake to play with yarn, but as Andi instinctively ran her hands over a soft silk-wool blend, thoughts of business momentarily receded. The beautiful blue-green, with hints of reds and oranges wound deep into the fibers, reminded her of the lake and mountains on a fall day like today.

From out of nowhere, Andi was struck by a vision of a lacy shawl draped across a woman's shoulders. Strangely, the woman looked like her.

"Andi, honey, what a lovely surprise!"

Andi jumped at her grandmother's sudden greeting, dropping the yarn like she was a thief who'd been about to stuff it into her bag and dash out the door.

What on earth had she been doing thinking about shawls? This creative world where women sat around and chatted and made things with their hands had never been hers.

She let herself be enveloped by her grandmother's arms. At barely five feet, Evelyn was eight inches smaller than Andi. And yet it never ceased to surprise her how strong her grandmother's arms were. Warm, too. They were always warm.

"Your father's commemoration isn't until next weekend. We didn't expect you to come home a week early." Her grandmother scanned her face for clues as to why she was back in Emerald Lake.

Andi forced a smile she didn't even come close to feeling. Lord knew, she certainly had practice pretending. In the year since her father's sudden death, she'd been going into the office every day with that same smile on her face, working double-time to make sure her work didn't suffer in the wake of her grief.

But it had. Which was how she'd found herself about to lose her biggest client ever in a meeting a week ago.

The Klein Group wanted to build beautiful vacation

condominiums in the perfect vacation town. They'd shot down every single one of her proposals—Martha's Vineyard, Nantucket, Cape Cod. Her boss, Craig, had been frowning at her the same way for three months, like he didn't think she could hack it anymore, and as panic shook her, Andi's mind had actually gone completely blank. That was when her phone had jumped on the table in front of her, a picture of Emerald Lake popping up along with a message from her mother.

*It's beautiful here today. Makes me think of you.*

Before she knew it, Andi was saying, "I have the perfect spot."

Just that quickly, the old energy, the excitement she used to feel during pitches, rushed through her as she pulled up one beautiful picture after another of Emerald Lake on her computer in the middle of the meeting.

No pitch had ever been easier: The condos would have a spectacular view. There was an excellent golf course close by. And best of all, their clients would be only hours away from New York City, close enough to take a break from the stress of their real lives but far enough removed to get away from it all.

Andi would never leave the city, but that didn't mean she didn't see how magical Emerald Lake could be for the right kind of people. The Klein Group had agreed.

The previous Wednesday, she'd been ecstatic, but now that she was back in her hometown, all she could think was, *What have I done?*

In lieu of going into a detailed explanation about her sudden appearance, Andi asked, "Where's Mom? I was expecting her to be in the store with you."

"Carol had some errands to run in Saratoga Springs and

won't be back until late tonight. Will you be able to spend the night before heading back to the city? I know how much your mother would love to see you."

What a huge understatement that was. Andi's mother would be heartbroken if her daughter came and went without seeing her, but Evelyn had never believed in guilt. She had never once pressured Andi into coming home more often or sticking around for longer on the rare occasions when she did visit. When Andi heard her coworkers talk about how their families were forever pressuring them to move back to their hometowns, she was glad her own family was so hands-off with her. They would never try to convince her to come back to the small town she'd grown up in. They respected her goals and plans too much to ever bombard her with hints that they missed her.

Wasn't she lucky to be so free?

"I'll probably be here a week. Maybe two." And then she would leave again, returning back to the city life she'd chosen as soon as she'd graduated from Emerald Lake's small high school. "It's a bit of a working vacation actually."

Fortunately, her grandmother had never been interested in talking business—yet another way they were different.

"Two weeks?" Evelyn looked like she'd won the lottery. "What a treat to have you here, especially when we're having such a beautiful fall."

As a sharp pang of guilt at not seeing more of her family settled in beneath Andi's breastbone, she followed her grandmother's gaze out the store's large front windows to the lake beyond the Adirondack chairs on the porch.

"Fall was always my favorite time of year at the lake," she admitted softly.

Andi's career as a management consultant in New York City meant she'd barely been back to Emerald Lake for more than a weekend, even over holidays. Growing up watching her father do such great things for so many people as senator had fueled her to want to follow in his footsteps. Not as a politician, but as someone who worked hard, cared deeply, and felt joy at a job well done. After graduating from Cornell University with both an undergraduate degree in economics and then an MBA, she'd chosen Marks & Banks carefully based on their commitment to the environment and the fact that they did more probono work than any other consulting company out there.

Her father had always encouraged her to "go for the brass ring," and even if some nights she fell onto her bed fully clothed and woke up the next morning with mascara smudged around her eyes and her stomach empty and grumbling, that was exactly what she'd done for the past ten years far away from her teeny, tiny hometown. Emerald Lake was barely a speck on the map, a blue stretch of water surrounded by rolling mountains.

Andi pulled her gaze away from the sparkling lake. "The store looks great, Grandma."

Evelyn frowned as she scanned the shelves. For such a tiny woman with a sweet, pretty face, her grandmother could be one of the most blunt people Andi had ever come across. The polar opposite of Andi's mother Carol, actually, who simply didn't believe in confrontation. But they were both small and gently rounded. Andi had always felt like a giant around the tiny women in her family.

"I just don't know about the changes your mother made."

Seeing the way her grandmother hated to move even a couple of skeins of yarn from one side of the store to the other, had Andi second-guessing her project for the Klein Group again.

Why couldn't she have blurted out any other Adirondack town than Emerald Lake? Still, she was glad for her grandmother's unintended warning to tread carefully. The condos were bound to be more change than this town had seen in fifty years at least.

Taking the time to notice the changes in the store, Andi said, "Actually, I think the changes help liven up the place." And then, more gently, "It's still your shop, Grandma. Just a bit shinier now for the new generation of knitters."

"That's exactly what your mother said. Two against one."

Andi didn't want her grandmother to think they were ganging up on her. Just as she would have approached a potentially disgruntled client, she took another tack. "What have your customers said?"

"They love it."

Andi had to laugh at the grudging words. "Good."

"Well, since you're going to be home for so long, I'll be expecting you to finally pick up the needles again," her grandmother shot back.

Barely holding back an eye roll, Andi said, "We both know that isn't going to happen, Grandma."

"You used to love to knit when you were a little girl. I'm telling you, it's not natural to quit knitting one day and not miss it."

"Are you calling me a freak of nature, Grandma?" Andi teased. Only way down deep inside, joking about not belonging didn't really feel like a joke.

Instead, it felt like a reality that she'd tried to pretend hadn't hurt all her life.

Evelyn picked up a few balls of yarn that were in the wrong basket. "I'm saying I think you must miss it." She looked thoughtful. "Perhaps it's simply that you haven't found the right reason to start knitting in earnest yet."

"I just don't like knitting, Grandma. Not like you and Mom do." Andi hadn't thought about knitting, hadn't been into another yarn or craft store for nearly two decades. Clearly, the yarn addiction hadn't passed through to the third generation.

"You know, my mother tried to get me to knit for years before I really fell in love with it."

"You're kidding me?" Andi assumed her grandmother had been born with knitting needles in her hand. "What changed?"

Evelyn sat down on one of the soft couches in the middle of the room. "I met a man."

"Grandpa?"

"No. Not Grandpa."

Andi's eyes went wide with surprise as she sank down beside her grandmother.

Evelyn reached into a basket beside her seat and pulled out a half-finished work in progress. As if she was hardly aware of the movements of her hands, she began a new row.

"Everyone was doing their part for World War II. I wanted to help the soldiers, and I was always good with knitting needles. I knew our socks and sweaters were giving joy and comfort to men, strangers I'd never meet, but who desperately needed a reminder of softness. Of warmth."

Andi thought about the tiny caps and booties her grandmother had always made for the new babies at the hospital. Andi had made them, too, when she was a little girl. She'd loved seeing a little baby at the park wearing something she'd made. But her grandmother was right. That hadn't been enough to keep her knitting.

"So it wasn't just one man who made you love knitting," Andi said, trying to keep up with her grandmother, "but many?"

"I knit for the cause, but that's all it was. A cause. It wasn't personal. Not until *him*. Not until I made his sweater." Evelyn's eyes rose to meet Andi's. "Every skein tells a story. As soon as a person puts it in their two hands, the mystery of the story is slowly revealed."

Andi's breath caught in her throat as her grandmother said, "Hold this, honey." Since she didn't know how to knit anymore, Andi laid the needles down awkwardly on her lap.

"Those fibers you're holding can become anything from a baby blanket to a bride's wedding veil," Evelyn said softly. "But I've always thought knitting is about so much more than the things we make."

Andi looked at her grandmother's face and saw that Evelyn was a million miles away.

"Sometimes yarn is the best way to hold onto memories. But sometimes, it's the only way to forget."

Andi found herself blinking back tears.

This was exactly why she never came back to the lake. There were too many memories here for her. Memories of people that had meant so much to her.

The walls of the store suddenly felt too close, the room too small. She needed to leave, needed to go someplace where she could focus on work. And nothing else.

"Grandma," she said as she stood up, "I need to go." The needles and yarn fell from her lap to the floor.

Frowning, her grandmother bent to pick them up, but suddenly she was racked with coughs. Fear lancing her heart, Andi automatically put an arm around Evelyn and gently rubbed her back as if that could make the coughing stop.

Her grandmother tried to say, "I'm fine," but each word was punctuated by more coughs.

Evelyn Thomas was a small-boned eighty-eight-year-old woman, but Andi had never thought of her grandmother as frail or fragile. Until now.

As her grandmother tried to regain her breath, Andi couldn't believe how translucent her skin had become. Evelyn's hands had always been one of the most impressive things about her with long, slim fingers and nails neatly rounded at the tips. So strong, so tireless as she quickly knitted sweaters and blankets, the needles a blur as she chatted, laughed, and gossiped with customers and friends in Lake Yarns.

"You shouldn't come to work if you have a cold." Fear made Andi's words harder than they needed to be, almost accusing. "You should be resting."

Mostly recovered now, her grandmother waved one hand in the air. "I told you, I'm fine. Just a little coughing fit every now and then." At Andi's disbelieving look, she said, "Things like that happen to us old people, you know."

Andi hated to hear her grandmother refer to herself as old, even though she knew it was technically true. It was just that she couldn't bear to think that one day Evelyn wouldn't be here, wouldn't be living and breathing this store, the yarn, the customers who loved her as much as her own family did.

A twinge of guilt hit Andi even though there was no reason for her to feel this way. Her mother and grandmother had always run Lake Yarns perfectly well by themselves. Nothing had changed just because Andi was going to be in town for a couple of weeks.

Still, she couldn't help but feel that she should have been here before now. What if something had happened to her mother or grandmother while she'd been gone? Just like it had happened to her father.

"Have you seen Dr. Morris yet?" Andi asked, immediately reading the answer in her grandmother's face. Sometimes Evelyn was too stubborn for her own good.

Andi grabbed the cordless phone and handed it to her grandmother. "Call him."

"I can't leave the store unattended."

"I don't care about the store, Grandma. I care about you. That cough sounded awful. You need to get it checked out, make sure it isn't something serious."

When Evelyn didn't take the phone, Andi decided to take matters into her own hands. "Hello, this is Andi Powell. My grandmother Evelyn has a terrible cough and needs to see Dr. Morris as soon as possible." After a moment of silence, where she listened to the friendly receptionist's questions, Andi shot Evelyn a look. "She isn't calling herself because talking makes her cough. Yes, she can be there in fifteen minutes." She put the phone down on the counter. "He's squeezing you in."

"I won't put a closed sign up in the middle of the day on my store. I've been open rain or shine for nearly sixty years."

Andi found her grandmother's purse behind the counter

and forced her to take it, just as Evelyn had forced her to take the needles and yarn. "I'll watch the store."

"You?"

Evelyn's disbelief was right on the edge of insulting. "Yes, me. How hard can it be?"

One neat eyebrow moved up on her grandmother's pretty face, and Andi realized how insulting her response had been.

"I didn't mean it like that, Grandma. Look, the register is the same one you had when I was a kid. I couldn't have forgotten positively everything about knitting. If I don't know something, I'll figure it out. I promise."

"Well, if you think you can handle it for an hour..."

The challenge in her grandmother's voice had her saying, "After your appointment, I want you to take the rest of the day off. I'll close up."

But after Evelyn left, the bells on the door clanging softly behind her, Andi stood in the middle of the store wondering what the heck she'd just signed up for. With all the money Andi made in skyscrapers and on corporate campuses, she had absolutely no idea what she was doing in a place like this.

Still Andi told herself there was no reason to panic.

Anyone with half a brain could run a yarn store for a few hours on a Monday morning.

A few seconds later, the front door opened and a gray-haired woman walked in.

"Hello," Andi said in an overbright voice. "Welcome to Lake Yarns."

"Thank you. I've heard such good things about your store that I drove all the way from Utica to come take a look."

Andi's eyes widened. "You drove an hour and a half to visit this store?"

The woman gave her a strange look. "Yes, I did. Several of my friends simply rave about your selection and customer service."

Andi hoped she didn't look as horrified as she felt. This woman had traveled one hundred miles to shop here…and she was getting stuck with someone who didn't even know how to knit.

Sorely tempted to run down the street to call her grandmother back, Andi told herself she was being ridiculous. How much help would someone need in a yarn store? If you were a serious knitter, shouldn't you already know everything?

With another wide smile, Andi finally said, "Be sure to let me know if you need anything."

She stared down at the ancient register, not really remembering how to use it at all, and wondered if there was an instruction booklet somewhere under the counter. She didn't want to look like an idiot in front of her first customer.

"Excuse me?"

Andi straightened up from her fruitless search for a manual. "Yes? Is there something I can help you with?"

The woman held up a skein of yarn. "It says this is superwash, but I'm a fairly new knitter and I don't know whether I should trust the label or not. Can you tell me how this actually washes? Does it pill or felt if you leave it in the dryer for too long?"

Andi carefully studied the label as if "100% Superwash Merino Wool" meant something to her. If she said she had no idea how it washed because she didn't knit or know the first thing about any of the yarns in the store, the woman would be—rightly—disgusted. But if she lied and said it would wash well and then it didn't, Lake Yarns would have lost a customer for life.

She'd never thought she'd have to think so fast standing in the middle of a yarn store.

How wrong she'd been.

Quickly deciding the truth was her best option, Andi said, "Actually I've never used that particular yarn."

The woman frowned. "Is there anyone here that has?" she asked, craning her head to see if there was some yarn guru hiding in the back of the store.

"I'm sure there's some information online about that brand. It will just take me a minute to look it up."

Thank god she never went anywhere without her tiny laptop. Unfortunately, it seemed to take forever to start up. She felt like she was standing in front of one of her clients who wanted answers about their project and wanted them now. Andi usually worked double-time not to be put in this kind of position.

But her grandmother really had sounded terrible. Watching the store was the right thing to do.

"I'll just find an Internet connection and then—"

Shoot. All of the nearby wireless providers were locked tight with passwords. Working not to let her expression betray her, Andi reached for her phone. But after what seemed like an eternity of trying to pull up her search page, all she got was a message that said, "Cannot connect."

She couldn't believe it. She was being beaten by a yarn store.

Shooting her clearly irritated customer a reassuring smile,

she said, "I'll have the information for you in another few moments," then picked up the cordless phone and local phone book and went into the back.

Flipping through the pages, she found another yarn store in Loon Lake and quickly dialed the number. "Hi, this is Andi Powell from Lake Yarns. I have a quick question for you about—" The woman on the other end of the line cut her off. "Oh yes, of course, I understand if you're busy with a customer. Okay, I'll call back in fifteen minutes."

But Andi already knew that fifteen minutes would be way too long. Desperate now, she walked out the back door and held her cell phone out to the sky, praying for bars.

"Thank god," she exclaimed when the word *searching* in the top left corner of her phone slowly shifted to the symbol that meant she had a wireless connection. Typing into the web browser with her thumbs, she actually exclaimed "hooray" and pumped her fist in the air when the information she'd been looking for appeared.

A moment later, greatly relieved to find her customer was still in the store, she said, "Good news. It seems that everyone who has used that yarn is really happy with how well it washed. Plus it evidently doesn't itch in the least."

The woman nodded. "Okay."

Uh-oh. That was less than enthusiastic.

Hoping that talking about the woman's intended project might reengage her earlier enthusiasm, Andi asked, "What were you thinking of knitting with it?"

"A baby blanket for my new granddaughter."

The woman pulled a picture out of her purse. The baby was chubby and bald and smiling a toothless grin.

"She's beautiful," Andi said softly.

The woman nodded, her previously irritated expression now completely gone. "I learned to knit for her."

Just like that, Andi suddenly understood what her grandmother had been talking about: this baby was the reason this woman was falling in love with knitting. As Andi instinctively ran the yarn's threads between her thumb and forefinger, a shiver of beauty, of sweet, unexpected calm suddenly moved through her.

At long last, the knot in the center of her gut came loose, and she told the woman, "I think it will make a really beautiful baby blanket."

Andi wasn't trying to sell the woman anything anymore.

She was simply saying what she felt.

# Chapter Two

Nate Duncan heard the phone ringing on his way out of his office at city hall, but he didn't want to be late to pick up his sister, Madison, from school. He was waiting on a call from the Adirondack Council about funds for an important riverbed restoration project, but he didn't believe in mixing work with play.

His sister was the most important person in his life. The people of Emerald Lake who had rallied around him when he needed them most came next. Everything else could sit on the back burner, if necessary.

Before jumping into his truck, he made sure the canoe, paddles, and fishing poles were secure. It was time for their first fall fishing trip.

Madison swore she hated fishing, that she'd rather be doing anything else. Nate smiled, thinking that her complaints didn't change the fact that his ten-year-old sister was one hell of a fisherwoman. A picture of Madison holding the sixty-pound pickerel she'd caught last winter when he'd taken her ice fishing hung above their mantel at home.

Pulling up outside the elementary school, he saw his sister talking animatedly with her best friend, Kayla. Her friend's mother, Betsy, smiled along with the girls.

As soon as he walked up to the group a minute later, his sister hit him with, "Nate, can I sleep over at Kayla's house tonight?"

"It's a school night. Besides, we're going fishing."

"But Kayla's my partner in natural science, and we were going to work on our wildlife project together. It will be so much easier to do it at her house. And Kayla's mom was going to feed me, too. I can easily get there in time for dinner after fishing. Please, Nate, can I sleep over at her house?"

Betsy gave him an apologetic smile. "I'm sorry, Nate, I shouldn't have planted the idea in their heads. I just thought they could work on the project. Would it make things better if I fed you dinner, too, Nate?"

He and Betsy had so much in common. She was a single mother, and he had been a full-time parent to his sister since she was a month old. Plus, Betsy was an attractive blond, always smiling, always happy to take Madison for the night if he needed help. She looked great in her jeans and sweater, like a woman who was comfortable with herself. He loved that he could count on Betsy to look after his sister when she was with Kayla.

But no matter how much he wanted Betsy to be his type, she wasn't. For some reason Nate couldn't understand, he hadn't yet managed to fall for her, even though she was a sweet, attractive woman.

"Thanks for the offer, but I'll have to take a rain check on dinner."

He didn't want to give Betsy false hope. She was too

nice to get tangled up with a guy who didn't have anything to offer her.

"But I can go to Kayla's tonight, right, Nate?"

On the verge of saying no, Nate looked down at his sister's pretty face, her hopeful eyes, and saw himself for the sucker he was.

"Fine. But you're not ditching out on fishing with me first." He looked between the girls, who seemed positively gleeful about their new plans. "And you both have to promise to go to sleep at a reasonable hour."

Madison and Kayla both nodded and said, "Of course we will," at the same time, but he'd been raising this little girl for long enough to know better.

"I'll drop Madison off in a couple of hours if that's all right, Betsy."

He could tell the woman was smiling through her disappointment. "Great. And if you change your mind about dinner, there will be plenty."

Feeling like an idiot for not wanting something any other sane guy would have, he said, "Good day at school?" as he and his sister walked to the truck.

"Yup," she said, tucking her backpack under the passenger seat before she climbed in and put on her seat belt.

Used to be, he couldn't get her to stop talking. Four, five, and six had been the chatty years, when he thought his ear was going to fall off from the long, winding stories she would spin for him day after day. Lately though, getting anything out of her was like pulling teeth.

"Anything exciting happen?"

She didn't say anything at first, and when he looked over at her, she was blushing. "There's a new kid."

"What's her name?"

She shook her head, just like Nate had suspected she would. "It's not a girl."

Working to ride the fine line between interested and neutral, he asked, "What's his name?"

"Jaden."

Nate was split. On the one hand, he thought it was cute that his sister had her first crush on a boy. On the other hand, she was only ten. He hadn't thought they'd be getting into boy-girl stuff for at least a couple of years.

He'd thought he'd get her all to himself for a little while longer.

"Cool name," he finally said. "So where's he from?"

"California." The floodgates suddenly opened, and she told him, "His parents are scientists from Stanford who are studying stuff in the Adirondacks. But he's only going to be here for one year."

Nate's hands tightened on the steering wheel. It figured that neither he nor his sister could do things the easy way, didn't it?

Instead of falling for people who were going to stick around, they couldn't stay away from the ones who were inevitably going to leave.

But he could tell she was dying to talk to him about the kid, and he'd always vowed to be there for her. So he said, "Tell me more about him, Mads," and for the next fifteen minutes, he heard more than he'd ever wanted to know about a ten-year-old boy. Fortunately, by the time they paddled out onto the cool lake, his sister seemed to be all out of Jaden fun facts.

Floating on the lake, surrounded by the patchwork colors of the mountains, hearing a loon calling out to its mate a hundred yards away was the perfect way to spend a fall afternoon, especially when Madison reeled in another good-sized bass with a grin.

"I'm on fire today!"

Nate recast his line. "Got any tips for your big brother? If it weren't for your success, I'd swear nothing was biting."

"Yeah, I was thinking it was weird that you're not catching anything. What's up with you today?" Madison suddenly frowned. "Hey, you know what I've just realized? You haven't done your fall speech yet."

She lowered her voice and imitated him. "*Look around, Mads. You see the leaves changing on those trees? You feel the nip in the air? It's fall and there's magic everywhere. Anything is possible.*"

Laughter rumbled through him, joining with Madison's to skip across the surface of the still water. Of course he'd had hopes and dreams that he hadn't been able to see come true. He'd never been able to play college football. He'd never experienced carefree dating. He never got the chance to live in a big city and be surrounded by all that speed and light and sound and excitement.

But getting to laugh with his happy sister, being able to see that pretty smile on her intelligent face, was easily worth any sacrifices he'd had to make during the past decade.

Finally he felt a nibble on his line. He gave a quick yank to set the hook and reeled the fish in.

"Wow." Madison's eyes were huge as she looked at the huge pickerel flopping around on the bottom of the canoe. "I think that might be bigger than the one I caught last year."

Nate didn't even have to think about it as he carefully

unhooked the two-way spinner from the fish's toothy mouth. This might be the biggest fish he'd ever caught, but there was no way he was going to beat his sister's record.

"This guy looks like he's got a lot of life still left in him. Want to bring a little fall magic to his life and help me throw him back in?"

His sister cocked her head to the side. "You really are acting weird today, you know." But she picked up the back half of the fish, and they threw him back in the lake on the count of three.

As they watched the fish float there for a few seconds before abruptly coming back to life and swimming away, Nate actually envied the fish his second chance...and found himself hoping that the fish managed to escape the lure the next time it flashed before him, so shiny and tempting.

\*     \*     \*

Finally alone again, Andi tried to focus on tidying up the yarn displays throughout the store. But it was difficult to keep her focus on yarn when she knew she was only avoiding the inevitable.

Nate Duncan was the town's new mayor and, as such, head of the architectural review board. Andi should have already called him to set up a meeting, but every time she'd picked up the phone, something had stopped her. Nerves that didn't make any sense. Along with memories that were too clear, almost as if she'd said good-bye to him yesterday instead of ten years ago.

Instead of getting the job done like she always did, Andi had let the idea of coming back to the lake—back to Nate—completely unravel her.

No. She wouldn't—couldn't—let that happen.

Resolved to take care of business as efficiently—and with as little emotion as possible—Andi quickly found the phone book and looked up the number for the mayor's office. If she was at all relieved that her call went to voice mail, she would never admit it to herself.

"Hello, you've reached Nate Duncan at city hall."

Relief didn't last long, however, not when the sound of his voice immediately had her palms sweating and her heart pumping hard in her chest. It had been so long since she'd spoken to him, and in her head he was still the same boy he'd been at eighteen. Not a man with a deep voice that rumbled through her from head to toe before landing smack-dab in the center of her heart.

"Nate, it's Andi. Andi Powell. I'm back in town for a little while and, well, it's been a long time, and I was hoping we could catch up on old times and get current with each other."

Pushing aside the little voice inside her head that told her she should be more up front with her reasons for wanting to meet with him, she quickly said, "I'm free tonight, if there's any chance that would work for you. My cell phone reception is pretty spotty, so if you want to call me back, could you try me at Lake Yarns?"

She knew she should hang up already, but now that she was finally—almost—talking with him again, she couldn't bring herself to sever the connection so soon. "I'll leave you a message at home, too. Hope to hear from you soon!"

Feeling like a thirteen-year-old who'd just left a rambling, somewhat embarrassing message for the boy she had a secret crush on, Andi forced herself to quickly make a second call to his house. When she finally hung up, she had to take a few moments to try and regain her composure.

*What was wrong with her?*

Anything that had happened between her and Nate a decade ago was water under the bridge. They'd thought they were in love, but really they'd just been childhood sweethearts who couldn't have possibly known what real love was yet. Besides, everything had worked out perfectly for both of them, hadn't it? She was a successful management consultant now, and he was mayor.

Everything would work out fine.

\*    \*    \*

After dropping Madison off at her friend's house and going for a punishing run up a narrow mountain trail, Nate was about to crack open a beer when he saw the blinking red light at the bottom of his phone.

*Something had happened to Madison.*

This was why he hated letting her stay over at a friend's house, why he knew he sometimes hovered over her.

He couldn't stand the thought of something happening to his sister. Almost ripping the phone off the wall, he dialed his voice mail code, but it wasn't Betsy's voice that came over the line.

It was Andi's.

Even after ten years, he would know the slightly husky voice—so at odds with her polished veneer—anywhere.

Nate's relief that everything was okay with his sister was quickly replaced by surprise—and alarm—that Andi was calling him out of the blue to get together and catch up on old times.

Instead of slowing down, his heart rate sped up even more.

For ten years he hadn't heard from her. Not a birthday call or a Christmas card. Why would she be calling him now?

Even though something told him it would be smarter to keep his distance, the truth was, Nate simply couldn't resist the thought of seeing Andi again.

He picked up the phone and dialed Lake Yarns.

# Chapter Three

By 5:25 that night, mere hours after Andi had made the bold—and incredibly foolish—offer to watch the store for her grandmother, her heels were killing her feet and she was dreaming of a hot bath and a bottle of wine. Scratch that, two bottles.

All afternoon she had been running around the store, helping customers, searching for colors, needles, patterns. How, she suddenly wondered, did her mother and grandmother do this six days a week?

With only five minutes until she could lock the front door and collapse on one of the couches in the middle of the room, two women came in through the front door, laughing and carrying big felted bags.

"I'm sorry," Andi said, although she was anything but sorry about kicking them out. "I'm afraid the store closes in a few minutes."

The two women shot each other a look, but Andi was too tired to worry about being rude anymore. The yarn would be here tomorrow. They'd just have to wait until then.

The store's phone rang and Andi grabbed it. "Lake Yarns. How may I help you?"

"Andi, it's Nate."

Oh god, she'd been so frazzled for the past few hours that she'd actually forgotten she asked Nate to call her here. Now, with her guard completely down, the sound of his low voice in her ear had her reaching for the counter to steady herself.

"Hi." She couldn't say anything more for the moment, not until she caught her breath, not until she pulled herself back together.

And then he said hi back, and ten years fell away so fast it made her head spin.

She was a teenager again and they were on the phone and she was so happy to be talking to Nate even though she didn't have the first clue what to say.

"So, about tonight." He paused and she actually held her breath. "That sounds great."

"It does?" She cringed at her clearly flustered response.

"How about we meet at the Tavern at seven thirty?"

If she left right now, she would have time to take a long shower and change and redo her makeup before heading out to the Tavern. Looking down at her previously pristine black dress and sheer nylons, she noticed that she was covered head to toe with little threads of color from the yarn she'd been handling and brushing up against all day long.

"Seven thirty is perfect."

"See you soon, Andi."

She put the phone down and was reaching for her bag when she realized she wasn't alone. The two women she'd spoken to at the door were sitting on the couches in the middle of the room looking like they planned to settle in for the night.

Didn't they know she needed to get out of here to get pretty so Nate wouldn't think she'd turned into an old hag in the past ten years?

"I'm sorry, but I really do need to close the store."

The older woman with bright red hair nodded. "Of course you do. Our knitting night is about to begin."

*Oh no.*

How could she have forgotten about the Monday night knitting group?

Her plans to go home to shower and change before her meeting with Nate went up in smoke. Andi looked down at the tiny threads of cotton and wool stuck to her sweater.

Oh well, Nate wouldn't care what she looked like. It wasn't like they were going out on a date or anything. Tonight was simply two old friends catching up with some business tacked on to the back end.

Scrambling to cover her gaffe, she said, "It's been such a busy day in the store that I almost forgot it was Monday night." The women just stared at her as she babbled unconvincingly. "Can I get you two anything?"

The slightly younger woman with shiny gray hair laughed. "Not to worry, honey, we always come prepared."

The women produced four bottles of wine along with a big plastic container full of big chocolate chip cookies. Andi's stomach growled as she tried to get her exhausted, overwhelmed brain to remember where the glasses were.

Fortunately the knitting group regulars were way ahead of her as they opened the small doors of the coffee table and began to pull out mismatched tumblers for the wine.

More long-buried memories came at Andi, joining all the others that had been scrambling into her brain all day. It had been her job, after everyone had gone, to wash out the glasses in the kitchen sink and dry them and put them back under the coffee table. Her grandmother always told her how important her role was, that wine made people comfortable, that it let them talk about the secrets they shouldn't be holding inside.

The Monday night knitting group had been going on as long as her grandmother had owned the store. Evelyn always said the group was as important to her as family—and that they were responsible for keeping her sane more than once over the years. As a little girl, Andi had loved sitting on the floor, listening to the women talk, laugh, and cry. But by ten she had grown out of it. Not just the knitting group, but anything to do with yarn or the store.

Andi still remembered her last ever Monday night at Lake Yarns. She had been sitting next to Mrs. Gibson and only half listening to her complain about her swollen ankles to the woman next to her. Andi swore Mrs. Gibson was always pregnant. One of her kids was in Andi's fifth-grade class, and John had five younger siblings already.

Andi had been working on a scarf for her father in a zigzag pattern, but she kept screwing it up. Bad enough that she needed help unraveling it and then getting it back onto the needles so she could fix her mistakes. Her mother and grandmother were both busy helping other people, and she had no choice but to turn to Mrs. Gibson.

*"Of course, I'll help you with this, honey,"* the woman had said. *"You know, it's no surprise you're having trouble with this scarf. John told me how smart you are. You're*

*going to go out there and do big, important things like your daddy. You really don't belong here with us knitters, do you?"*

Andi was pulled back to the present as she heard a throat being cleared and looked up to see that the red-haired woman was holding out a glass of wine, saying, "I didn't know Evelyn and Carol had hired anyone new."

Andi gratefully took the glass and was about to respond with her name when the woman said, "Wait a minute. I need to put my glasses on." Later, after a few moments of peering, she said, "Andi? Don't you recognize me? It's Dorothy. Dorothy Johnson."

Andi suddenly realized why the woman looked so familiar. It was her hair that had thrown Andi off, red instead of dark brown, and the fact that she seemed to have shrunk several inches in the past decade.

Dorothy introduced her to Helen who had moved to Emerald Lake five years earlier.

"I would have eventually guessed who you were," Helen said. "You really are the perfect combination of Evelyn and Carol."

"I look more like my dad," Andi said automatically.

"I can see Richard in you certainly, but if you ask me, you take after the women in your family more. I'm so sorry about his passing, honey. We all were."

It was hard to hear her father's name on a stranger's lips, harder still to be reminded that he was gone.

Andi briskly smiled. "Thanks. Please don't hesitate to let me know if there's anything else I can help you with," she said before moving to the door to welcome in more Monday night knitting group members.

Fifteen minutes after six, the wine was flowing with

nary a needle in motion when one final woman pushed in through the door.

"Sorry I'm late."

"Brownies will make it all better," another woman said. "You do have brownies don't you?"

"Why do you think I'm late?" the latecomer replied with a laugh, but to Andi's ears it sounded forced.

She put the tray of brownies on the table, then looked up in surprise. "Oh. Andi. I didn't expect you to be here."

Andi hadn't seen her old friend in years. Now, as she took a good look at Catherine, she almost didn't recognize her.

Andi remembered her as being a cute blond, not a mousy brunette whose once fit frame now carried around an extra thirty pounds.

"Catherine, how are you?"

Andi wasn't prepared for her onetime friend to look her straight in the eyes and say, "Apart from divorcing my rat bastard husband, I'm all right."

The women all around them still chatted as if everything was perfectly normal. Andi scrambled to find an appropriate response. But really, there wasn't one.

Catherine shrugged, a show of nonchalance that Andi didn't buy.

"Welcome home," Catherine said before going and sitting down on a couch in the opposite corner.

Andi hadn't even known Catherine had been married. Then again, she hadn't gone to any of their high school reunions or registered at any social networking sites.

Dorothy tapped her wineglass several times with a knitting needle. "Everyone," she said authoritatively, "please say hello to Andi, Carol's daughter." The woman's eyes twinkled. "Even if you already know each other from her years growing up here, be sure to tell her something unique and memorable about yourself."

Andi looked up from her spot behind the register. She'd hoped to be able to sit there and hide out for a couple of hours while the knitting group did their thing. But when Dorothy scooted over on the couch and patted the seat beside her, Andi knew she was cornered and cornered good.

"Andi and I have already met," Helen said, "but just to be sure you don't forget me, you should know that I have never so much as stuck a toe into the lake and never plan to."

Andi was so stunned by Helen's admission that she completely forgot her manners. "Why not?"

"I had an unfortunate incident with a swimming pool when I was a child," Helen said with a shake of her head.

"But swimming in the lake is incredible."

From the time Andi could walk, she'd loved to run off the end of her parents' dock and cannonball into the water, whether eighty degrees at the height of summer or somewhere in the sixties in the late spring and early fall.

Andi was surprised by a fierce—and sudden—urge to run out of the store, strip off her clothes, and go running off a dock, any dock, just so she could experience that glorious moment when she hit the water.

Being surrounded with floor-to-ceiling yarn all day had clearly started to make her go a little nuts.

"I'm sure it is," Helen said regretfully before turning the table over to the middle-aged woman sitting next to her. "Your turn, Angie."

"I have four little monsters at home, and were it not for the fact that I knew I was going to be able to escape to this group after a weekend when none of them would stop screaming, I might very well have had an unfortunate incident of my own in the lake. On purpose."

Everyone laughed, but Andi struggled with knowing what the right response was. It had been years since she'd known the comfort of being around other women. At work, she was primarily surrounded by men, and given her rule about no emotional entanglements in the office, Andi spent the bulk of her time with people who were pretty much just professional acquaintances.

Catherine was next. "Andi and I go way back. She doesn't need to hear me bore her with stories about how things have gone since high school."

Andi might not have been particularly well versed in girl talk in recent years, but she had a pretty good sense that Catherine wasn't thrilled with her being back in town and running tonight's knitting group.

Fortunately right then, another woman, who Andi judged to be around her same age, smiled and said, "I'm Rebecca. I help run the inn on the lake, and it is such a pleasure to meet you, Andi. I just adore your mother and grandmother."

The pretty woman with the long, straight golden-brown hair and startlingly green eyes looked down at the diamond ring on her finger, drawing Andi's gaze down to it.

"And what about you, my dear?" Dorothy asked. "What brings you back to town?"

Andi froze. She didn't want to lie to these women, but she needed to sit down and talk about her project with Nate first. He would know the best way to present her building plans to the townspeople. Perhaps if she'd come back to town more since high school, it wouldn't seem so strange that she was here now, but the constant demands of her job had always come first.

"Fall on the lake is always so peaceful, so quiet. This seemed like a good place to focus on a big project at work."

"Quiet?" Dorothy and Helen both laughed. "Emerald Lake is a hotbed of excitement and intrigue."

"Okay, who's got gossip?" Rebecca asked, obviously trying to change the subject and take the focus off of Andi, who felt more and more out of her element with every passing second.

"Not so fast," Catherine said. "Andi hasn't told us something unique about herself yet."

Andi felt another rush of blood move up to her cheeks. She dearly wished Catherine hadn't drawn attention to her, not when she was trying so hard to fit in seamlessly with these almost strangers.

"I can't think of anything," she said, but she was met with a wall of raised eyebrows. Realizing they weren't going to move on until she gave them something, she said, "I can't knit."

Oh no, she hadn't just blurted that out, had she?

Dorothy scrunched her face up as if she was trying to access some long-lost information. "Wait a minute, I remember a little girl who looked like you sitting right here and knitting many, many years ago."

Andi held up her empty hands in an effort to defend herself. "I haven't knit since I was nine or ten. I seriously doubt I remember how." She certainly hadn't earlier in the day with her grandmother.

"Nonsense," Dorothy said as she reached into her canvas bag for some large needles and soft blue yarn, so much like the skein Andi had been admiring earlier that morning. "It's like riding a bicycle. You never forget how to knit, no matter how long it's been. Take these."

Keeping her hands firmly on her lap, Andi said, "Thanks, but you don't need to give me your—"

"Take them."

Andi immediately responded to the firm note in the older woman's voice. "Okay."

She sat awkwardly with the things on her lap when Rebecca took pity on her.

"I can show you how to cast on if you want."

Wishing she could be anywhere but Lake Yarns on a Monday night, Andi nodded. "Thanks."

Rebecca deftly wound the yarn around the needles. "Any idea what you'd like to make?"

Andi began to shake her head, but then she realized that if she had to sit here all night, she might as well start something she might use when she was done with it.

"A shawl." The one she'd been wearing in her earlier vision.

Rebecca nodded. "Good idea. With the size of these circular needles and gauge of the yarn, it should knit up really quick and look great. How about a simple triangle pattern? You'll only have to do a yarn over at the beginning and end of every other row with all the other rows being a simple knit stitch."

After Rebecca quickly showed her how to do the alternating rows, Andi softly said, "You don't know how much I wish you'd been here this afternoon when I took over the store for my grandmother. You would have been so much more helpful than I was at answering customers' questions."

"I'm sure you did great," Rebecca said kindly, "but definitely call me next time you need help. I can run over from the inn."

*Oh no.* Andi had learned her lesson and learned it well. There wasn't going to be a next time for her at Lake Yarns. From here on out, she was going to focus on her real job and leave the yarn to people who knew what the heck to do with it.

For the next hour or so, while the women in the group tackled their works in progress and talked about people she didn't know anymore, Andi worked diligently on a shawl she'd never planned on making. She wasn't a real member of the knitting group, and yet it was sort of nice to be in a room with a group of women relaxing together.

Suddenly Nate's name came up in conversation. "I hear things didn't work out with the woman from Albany."

Andi's heartbeat kicked up. They'd broken up so long ago that it shouldn't matter to her if Nate had recently been involved with someone. Then again, nothing had made sense since the moment she crossed into the Adirondacks.

Maybe it was all the fresh air, all the beauty that was mucking with her system after a decade of pollution and recycled office building air?

"I don't think she was too gung ho about having a ten-year-old girl around all the time."

"Then I say, good riddance. Besides"—Dorothy made an invisible ring around her mouth with her fingers—"she wore too much lipstick. That boy is a saint. Raising his sister, holding his family together after what happened with his parents. He deserves better."

It was a forceful reminder to Andi that Nate was far

more than just a loving older brother to his younger sister. He was eighteen years old when his mother died giving birth to Madison, and his father had shot himself one month later. From that moment on, Nate had been solely responsible for things like getting his sister to bed on time and taking her to the doctor for shots. Andi couldn't begin to imagine how he had done it.

Catherine singled Andi out again. "Didn't you and Nate go out for a while?"

Oh no. Why did Catherine have to say that? Especially when she knew darn well that she and Nate had been an item.

Knowing there was no way to get out of it in front of everyone, Andi nodded and forced another one of those smiles. "We did."

Helen's mouth was an O of surprise. "How could you have ever let a man like that get away?"

"Nate is great," Andi said slowly, not wanting to say more than she absolutely needed to. "But we were just kids."

"So, do you have a new man in your life?" Dorothy clearly didn't believe in bothering with subtlety.

"No."

Andi refused to feel bad about it, either. She had a lot going on at work right now and didn't have time to focus on a relationship, too. She hadn't actually had time to focus on one since heading off to college.

Dorothy shook her head. "You girls all wait too long nowadays to look for a husband. No wonder your eggs are all drying up. If you ask me"—which Andi hadn't—"you should take a page from Rebecca's book. She's marrying Stu in the spring."

Thrilled by the chance to—finally—turn the focus away from herself, Andi asked, "Stu Murphy is your fiancé?" When Rebecca nodded, Andi said, "Congratulations! I'll have to stop by and offer him my congratulations, too."

Glancing up at the clock, Andi saw that it was almost 7:30 p.m. On the one hand, she was dying to get out of the shop—and away from the knitting group.

On the other, she was downright nervous about the thought of finally seeing Nate again.

Finally, women started putting their needles and yarn away in their bags. Andi put her knitting on the table and said to no one in particular, "I need to close up the register."

It was such a relief to step away from the group—and their prying questions—that she nearly groaned aloud.

"See you next week, Andi," Dorothy said as she and Helen came by the register to say their good-byes.

Andi found herself smack-dab on the spot again. She couldn't insult Lake Yarns's customers by telling them she'd rather do a swan dive into a boiling oil pit than sit through another Monday night knitting group.

"Mmm," she said in a perfectly noncommittal tone.

As she waved good-bye, Angie joked, "Back to the monsters." Catherine disappeared before Andi could say good night.

Rebecca hung back in the empty store, picking up the wineglasses and heading into the bathroom to wash them out in the sink.

"They also hit me with twenty questions when I first started coming to the group," Rebecca said, empathy behind her words. "Why did I leave sunny California? How did I find Emerald Lake? Why wasn't I married with a stroller full of kids yet? And then they proceeded to list the attributes of every unattached male below retirement age."

Andi couldn't help but laugh at Rebecca's account of the trials and tribulations of being a newcomer in a close-knit small town. She was right. Andi shouldn't take their questions and comments as a personal attack.

And she shouldn't be worried about meeting with Nate, either. Just like she had said to Helen, they'd just been kids. A couple of high school sweethearts who'd gone their separate ways after graduation.

She and Nate would talk about what they'd been up to for the past ten years, maybe laugh over old times, and then she'd run her plans for the condos by him.

No big deal. It would go fine.

# Chapter Four

Nate was halfway down Main Street when he saw Andi step off of Lake Yarns's front porch toward a group of women chatting outside.

*She was so beautiful.*

He needed to get a grip and was glad he had another thirty seconds to try and get used to looking at her. Unfortunately he needed to do a heck of a lot more than just get used to looking at her. He needed to get his head screwed back on straight, needed to remember that tonight was about catching up on old times.

Nothing more.

"Nate!" His next-door neighbor Dorothy called out to him, pulling him into the group with a firm hand. "Did you know your old girlfriend was back in town? Isn't she lovely?"

Andi's face, which was already a little flushed, went pink. And still, she took his breath away, just as lovely as Dorothy had said. In any case, how the heck had Andi already hooked up with this crowd? And how did Dorothy remember that he and Andi had once been an item?

"We're just meeting for a drink actually," he told his extremely nosy but well-meaning neighbor. "You ready to head over to the Tavern, Andi?"

"You're a dark horse," Dorothy whispered in Andi's ear, loud enough for everyone to hear. "You didn't mention you had plans tonight."

Without waiting for Andi's response, Nate reached for her hand to take her away from the crowd. To have her all to himself.

She looked down at his outstretched hand, not taking it right away, and he swore he could see the pulse at the side of her wrist fluttering just beneath the skin.

Finally she put her hand into his and the shock of her skin against his made Nate wonder how he could have possibly waited ten years to touch her again.

\*     \*     \*

Andi felt stupid.

So incredibly stupid.

How had she thought she could come back to Emerald Lake, see Nate again, and not feel anything? And why hadn't she connected that new, deep voice on the phone to the fact that she should have prepared herself for the positively breathtaking man holding her hand?

Nate had been good-looking at eighteen, but his shoulders were so much broader now, his dark hair trimmed shorter, and the faint lines around his eyes and mouth gave proof to the fact that he smiled easily and often.

He wasn't a boy anymore. Not even the slightest bit. A man stood in front of her, one who'd overcome more challenges in the past ten years than most people would during their entire lives.

*And she'd let him go.*

The thought shook her, almost as much as how good it felt to hold Nate's hand now.

Panic had her suddenly pulling her hand away from his. For a split second, Nate didn't let her go. But then, as he released his grip, Andi thought she must have imagined his hold on her.

Ten years. It had been ten years since she'd seen him. Since he'd held her hand. And now that he was here in the flesh, as they walked together toward the Tavern, she didn't have the first clue what to say to him—or how to say it.

"I forgot just how small a small town can be, but the Monday night knitting group just brought it all home," was the first thing that popped into her head, unfortunately. In a light voice that she hoped belied her nerves, "Parts of it were fun. It's just when they get personal, they really get personal."

His voice was just as light, just as easy, as he asked, "What did they want to know?"

"Oh, you know, the usual things," she said. "Why I'm not married with babies yet. If I'm dating anyone." The words slipped out before she could stop them.

She felt him grow still beside her, but then that easy smile was back and she knew she was imagining things again. The only problem was, his smile had always had the power to rock her world. Clearly, judging by the way her heart raced and her skin flushed, growing up hadn't made a lick of difference.

Still, for all his easy charm, when he asked, "Are you?" his voice held a slightly rough edge to it that sizzled over her skin.

If only she was actually seeing someone, she wouldn't have had to give such a pathetic answer. "Nope."

Andi didn't need to ask him. She already knew about the girl with the lipstick. About how he deserved better. And Dorothy was right. Nate deserved to be with someone amazing. Someone who would be there for him the way he was always there for everyone else. Someone who would love his town as much as he did, a woman whose dreams included high school football games and little children, who had Nate's eyes, running on the beach. One day, probably in the very near future, there would be a wedding on Emerald Lake where Nate would slip a ring on someone else's finger...and promise to love that woman forever.

Andi's step faltered as he held open the bar door and she stepped inside.

Once upon a time she'd thought she could be that woman. But she should have known better, should have known the fairy tale wasn't in the cards for them. She just didn't have it in her to wait in the tower for the prince's kiss to wake her up, didn't have the first clue how to act the part. Not when she'd always known exactly what she wanted and refused to wait for it or to compromise on her plans.

Her stomach clenched into a tight little ball, and Andi practically bounced off of a man's chest. Nate's large hands came around her waist, pulling her against him to keep her from falling. But instead of feeling steady, Andi felt shakier than ever being so close to him.

"Andi," Nate said, "I don't know if you remember Henry Carson."

The owner of the large general store had been a friend

of her father's, and she found herself pulled into a warm hug. She smelled wood fire and sawdust on Henry's shirt, reminding her of how proud her father had been of his latent blue-collar skills. It seemed that whenever he was in town he would spend half his time chopping wood and lighting it on fire. She'd wanted so badly to be a boy back then, for her father to hand her an ax rather than telling her to get back inside before she got hurt.

"Andi, I'm sorry about Richard's passing."

Not wanting to get caught in the well of grief that always bubbled up in her when her father was mentioned, she forced herself to say with another one of those fake smiles she was really starting to hate, "Thanks. It's nice to see you again, Henry."

"You planning on sticking around town for a while?"

Her night with the curious—and meddling—knitting group took the edge off of Henry's very direct question. "I'll be here for a couple of weeks at least."

Nate stiffened at her side in what she assumed was surprise.

"Good. Your father would be glad to know you're home with your mother and grandmother," Henry said. And then to Nate, "I've got the new blueprints you said you needed. You'd better put on your football pads for the next architectural review because I am going to come at you with everything I've got. This time, I'm not going to take no for an answer."

"You'll keep getting a no until your building fits in with the historical architecture of the town," Nate said in a firm but friendly voice.

Henry raised his eyebrows at Andi. "Hard to believe us old folks are the ones who get blamed for resisting change. If I didn't know better, I'd think this guy wanted to live in the Middle Ages."

Andi forced a smile, but frankly all of this talk about architectural review committees—and Nate's surprisingly firm stance—sent new shivers of unease up her spine. Up until now, she had hoped Nate would be as excited about her project as she was. But as they headed for the only open table, a very private, very small booth in a dark corner of the room, she suddenly wondered, *What if she was wrong?*

But she couldn't hold onto the question, not with one of Nate's hands still resting on the small of her back, creating a patch of heat that burned up through the rest of her. Not when she was remembering a hundred times when he'd held her like that, so gently.

With such love.

"What would you like to drink, Andi?"

"Club soda and lime."

"Just because I don't drink, doesn't mean you have to abstain," he said softly, but there was a slight edge to his words.

"I had a couple of glasses of wine with the knitting club. That's my limit," she insisted.

In high school, when everyone else was experimenting with beer they'd smuggled out of their parents' basement, Nate had always stuck with Coke. His father hadn't been a nasty drunk; he'd just always had a can in his hand. Solidarity—along with the fact that cheap beer was disgusting—made her stick with Coke, too. More than a decade later, it was instinct not to drink when she was with Nate.

After Nate returned from the bar with their drinks, they

sat down and both took a sip from their glass. Silence reigned until Nate said, "You look great, Andi," and when her obvious response came, "So do you, Nate," it was like she was watching the two of them sit awkwardly together from a distance.

Two people who had once been so close.

Two people who had no idea what to say to each other anymore.

Because they were two people who had left too many things unsaid for too long.

Suddenly Andi understood that all the hours, all the years, she'd spent trying to convince herself that she and Nate were nothing more than childhood sweethearts, that their past was water under the bridge, were just lies she'd told herself so that she could move on with her life. So that she could try to forget him.

But she hadn't forgotten him. She saw that now. How could she possibly forget when the past was still holding them so tightly together?

Andi hadn't been planning on having a big conversation about their past. But if they were going to have any chance of working together successfully on her condos, she knew they needed to have it. Now. Before things got any more awkward and stilted.

"I know we've never really talked about what happened with us. But maybe we should talk about it now."

Nate's expression didn't change one iota. "There's nothing to talk about, Andi. Not on my account anyway."

She wanted to believe him, but she was too perceptive not to notice the way his fingers had tightened around his glass, white beginning to show beneath the knuckles.

"It's just that I've always felt bad about the way things

ended, and I guess I thought that if we cleared the air, then maybe—"

"We were just kids, Andi. Besides, what teenage romance ever works out anyway?"

Andi couldn't do anything but nod and say, "You're right. Never mind."

She should be glad that he was letting her off the hook. But the truth was it hurt to know for sure that a relationship she'd thought had been so important didn't actually mean anything to Nate at all.

No, it didn't just hurt.

It was brutal.

\*   \*   \*

Nate could see that his response had hurt Andi—and he hated seeing that flash of pain in her eyes, regardless of what had gone down between them when they were kids. Still he just didn't think it was a good idea to go there.

Not when talking about their past was a one-way ticket to a potentially bad situation.

Really bad.

Still she needed to know that he hadn't been sitting around for the past ten years nursing his resentment. "Look, Andi, things are good now. Real good."

He didn't want to look backward, didn't want to have to see that kid who had struggled to recover from losing every single person he'd ever loved.

Anyone else would have dropped the whole thing by now, but he knew Andi too well, knew how persistent she was, and he braced himself for more prodding, more poking.

Instead, she said, "I'm really glad to hear it, Nate. And

I'm so glad you made time to see me. How's Madison doing?" Andi's expression softened as she asked about his sister. "I'd love to hear about her."

Nate usually loved to brag about his sister. He should have been relieved that Andi was doing exactly what he wanted her to do. She was dropping the whole subject of their breakup. And what had caused it.

But where relief should have been came a disappointment that didn't make any sense, and he found himself gripping his drink hard. Too hard. As if he could somehow get glass to bend if he only worked at it long enough.

Slowly unwrapping his fingers from around the glass, he said, "Madison's in fifth grade now. She has lots of friends, loves ballet and dancing. She hates fishing, but she humors me and does it anyway." He smiled thinking of his sister. "She's just a really happy kid."

Andi was smiling now, too, and he realized it was the first real smile he'd seen yet.

"Do you have a picture of her that I could see?"

He pulled out his wallet and showed her Madison's latest soccer photo, the one where one of her pigtails was falling out and she was missing a tooth on the right side of her big smile.

"She's beautiful."

She was staring at the picture of the little girl that meant everything to him, but Nate was looking at Andi when he said, "I know."

Andi looked back up at him, her eyes big and full of emotion. He remembered when she used to look at him like that.

"Madison looks so much like you did in fifth grade. I can't believe it."

Her smile turned to a grin, and he saw a flash of the old Andi, the fun Andi, the sweet Andi. The Andi he'd been head over heels in love with.

"Now I know what you would have looked like with pigtails."

Nate couldn't hold back his own grin. It was nice, really nice just to be with her like that again. Just for one short moment to be like they used to be.

"Congratulations on being elected mayor," she said suddenly. "How do you like the job?"

Disappointment flared again at how brief their moment of connection had been. But he knew she was right to move past it as quickly as she had. It would be better for both of them to keep things bobbing along the surface, rather than diving deep.

"I'm enjoying the challenge of the job. It's definitely a change from being out there on the football field with the kids every day."

"Do you miss the kids you used to work with?"

"I do, although I help out with the team whenever I can."

"What about being in an office all day? Has that taken any getting used to?"

"You know, I thought I'd be stuck behind the computer more. But I'm dealing with open-space issues so often, I've got to keep a pair of mud boots in my truck. Your grandfather was mayor. Did he ever talk much about it to you?"

"I was too little to talk town politics. But I do have vague memories of his coming home looking worn-out."

Nate laughed at the funny little face she made when she was talking about her grandfather. From what Nate could remember, Arthur Powell had been a really easygoing guy, the perfect match for Evelyn who could be, well, spunky at times.

"Probably all the damn meetings."

"I know all about those," she joked back. "But you enjoy it, don't you?"

"I wanted to find a way to pay everyone back for what they did for me and my sister after my parents died. And I've always loved this town. I've always figured that if you love something enough, there's got to be a way to make it a priority."

Andi looked away and shifted slightly in her seat, and he felt like a jerk for saying all of that.

She was trying to keep things light. He had no reason to start hitting below the belt. His mother's death, his father's suicide, Andi leaving had all happened so long ago.

He was over it. All of it. And his life was great. He had everything he wanted, everything but the right woman beside him. He would find her eventually. But only if he made sure to remember that this woman sitting across the booth from him could never be that woman.

Still, remembering didn't mean he couldn't still feel Andi's pain, that he couldn't see the way she'd flinched when Henry had brought up her father.

"I'm sorry about your father, Andi. I know how much you loved him."

"I—" She swallowed hard. "He—"

God, he wanted to take her in his arms, wanted to hold her and tell her that if anyone understood what she was going through, he did. But he couldn't do that.

Once they'd been best friends. Lovers.

Now they were little better than strangers.

Seeing how close she was to crying—and knowing how much she'd hate it if she cried in front of him—he swiftly shifted back to the small talk they'd been making.

"How's life in the city, Andi?"

"The city is good."

"You're a management consultant, right? How do you like it?"

"I love my job. Especially when I've got a new project to work on."

"Sounds exciting. Tell me about it."

She took a sip of her drink before answering, giving him enough time to wonder how they had come to this, two strangers sitting in a bar together?

All those years he'd loved her, Nate had never thought things would end this way.

But they had.

# Chapter Five

Andi had come here tonight planning to tell Nate all about the Klein Group. She had the initial drawings and plans in her bag, but that was before she'd realized things were going to cross over into memories and emotions. She couldn't shake the thought that her well-thought-out plans had backfired a little. More than a little, actually.

It seemed strange to turn the conversation over to business now. And the truth was, she'd only just realized—or rather, let herself acknowledge—how starved she'd been for information about Nate. She'd never let herself google him, had only heard that he was mayor through her mother and grandmother during one of the times she wasn't able to steer the conversation away from Emerald Lake.

And then there was the fact that she'd wanted to throw herself in his arms and sob her eyes out about her father.

But she couldn't. All she could do was answer his question—and try to pretend that her heart wasn't breaking all over again at the realization of just how wide the chasm was between two people who had once meant everything to each other.

Still despite his clear interest in her work and the fact that he'd given her the perfect lead-in, she had a moment of hesitation. No, it was more like a bad premonition that this whole condo on Emerald Lake thing was a bad idea, that it had been a bad idea from the moment the words "I know the perfect place" had burst from her mouth at the meeting on Wednesday.

"You don't want to hear about my work, Nate. We don't have to talk about it. Not tonight."

Her boss was going to kill her, but Andi needed more time, needed things to be more comfortable, more normal—and way less emotional—with Nate before she launched into her sales pitch.

"Andi, I've wondered about what you've been doing for ten years."

Her breath caught in her throat. Not just because she wasn't the only one who had been wondering from a distance, but because she was seeing something in his eyes she hadn't thought to ever see again.

Not just curiosity. Not just simple interest in her and her life.

No, what had her breath coming in fits and starts was the fact that he was looking at her like he cared. Really and truly cared.

"Tell me about your job. Please."

"I've worked with my client, the Klein Group, for a couple of years," she began slowly. "They're great with their employees, both in terms of benefits and corporate culture; plus they're almost completely green."

"And here I was thinking all big companies cared about was ripping off the little guy."

She thought he was teasing, was almost sure of it, but

all of her sensors were off tonight, spinning around wildly inside her brain and body.

And heart.

"Not all of them," she tried to joke back.

Now. She had to tell him about the condos now; otherwise it would be like lying to him.

And really, why was she worrying? How could he possibly complain when the project was so perfect for the town, when there were so many obvious benefits for the townspeople?

Andi reached into her bag, realizing her hands were sweating against the soft leather as she fumbled for her proposal. "Actually, I have something I want to show you."

"What's that?"

She pulled out the papers, slid them out across the table. "The Klein Group would like to build beautiful new residences here where the old carousel sits."

Everything about the moment—the way Nate stared unblinkingly at the plans, the fact that she could hear each and every one of her breaths over the music playing on the jukebox—told her she was saying the wrong thing the wrong way.

It was just that nothing about today had gone as it should have. Her grandmother shouldn't have been coughing. Andi shouldn't have spent the day running Lake Yarns. And she and Nate shouldn't have been sitting in the Tavern with a huge black cloud of memories hanging over them.

Unfortunately now that she had opened the door, it was too late to shut it. Way too late to go back to that moment when he'd been looking at her like she still meant something to him.

Trying not to let her hand shake, she moved a finger across a drawing. "They'd also like to put in a new public baunch loat." *Oh god, what had she just said?* "I mean a new public boat launch."

Nate was dangerously silent, and she felt her skin go hot all over.

Oh no, why hadn't she drawn out the pleasantries a bit more, asked him more about his sister, about everyone in town before jumping straight into business?

But small talk wasn't her way. She'd always believed in being direct with people rather than trying to charm them into anything.

*Perhaps,* she thought as Nate's silence continued, *a little more charm, a bit of friendly banter wouldn't have been out of place in this discussion.*

Using every ounce of poise she had to continue her pitch, Andi said, "These are only preliminary sketches. I plan to work closely with their architects and designers to make sure everything fits in smoothly with the classic Adirondack architectural styles and the surrounding buildings on Main Street."

"Now the truth comes out."

There was none of the warmth that had crept into his voice anymore.

"I knew there had to be an ulterior motive here somewhere. Ten years have gone by, and you haven't wanted to catch up on old times. I'm such an idiot. I should have known there had to be a reason you wanted to get together now. You knew I could never say no to you. Hell, you probably thought you were going to walk in here and charm me into rubber-stamping these plans, didn't you?"

The breath she hadn't realized she'd been holding

whooshed out of her as if he'd sucker punched her in the gut.

Because he just had.

"No! God, no!" She couldn't believe he'd said that to her, that he was accusing her of trying to use an old relationship to suit her own purposes. Not wanting to let herself believe that he was at all right, either, she said, "How can you even think that about me?"

His jaw was tight, and his eyes narrowed in anger. She knew that look, had never been able to forget it when that was her very last memory of Nate, burned forever into the back of her mind.

"What the hell am I supposed to think, Andi? You come in here looking like that—"

"Looking like what?" She gestured down at her simple black dress still covered in yarn. She hadn't had time to go home and clean up, to get even the slightest bit pretty. She couldn't have dressed less provocatively.

"—All of your curves on display in that dress, and those high heels that make your legs look a hundred miles long to mess with my mind and distract me when you start saying you want to clear up things from the past—"

"I wasn't trying to distract you!"

"—And then you hit me with"—he moved his hand in the direction of the drawings, making them flutter and scatter across the old wooden table top—"this garbage."

The word *garbage* was a gauntlet that had her anger finally rising to meet his. "My project isn't garbage, Nate."

Each word came from between her teeth, but even though she was seeing red, she knew this wasn't the way to get him to see reason. She needed to calm down. They both did.

"Look, why don't you take these with you tonight? We can talk more tomorrow after you've read through my entire plan."

He shot a disgusted glance at her presentation. "I've already seen enough." He threw some money down on the table as a tip. "Good to finally *catch up on old times* with you, Andi."

Forgetting all about the importance of never, ever touching him again if she wanted to hold onto what was left of her sanity, she grabbed his arm as he got up to leave.

Heat scalded her palm, searing between his skin and her hand. He stared down at her hand on his arm, a muscle jumping in his jaw.

"Please, Nate, at least hear me out. I don't want you leaving now making assumptions. Just give me five more minutes." She was panting as if she'd just sprinted around a track. There just wasn't enough oxygen in the room anymore, barely enough to say, "Please just let me explain."

Her entire career rested on the success of this project. She couldn't fail now. Especially not with Nate, not when her relationship with him was already her biggest failure to date.

Finally, thank god, he shifted back into his seat. "I'm listening."

"I was looking at some pictures my mom had sent on my phone when I realized just what an incredible spot the carousel is sitting in. No one even uses it anymore. I'll bet parents are afraid to let their kids goof around on it like we used to because they don't want them to get hurt on a shard of metal or risk the chance that it might collapse altogether. But the land it's on is the perfect spot for families who want their children to know what it's like to grow up playing on the beach and fishing in the lake. It's the perfect spot for couples who are finally ready to relax and enjoy their retirement. That's why I pitched it to the Klein Group."

"Hold on a minute. Are you telling me this was completely your idea? That the company didn't just bring you in because they knew you had ties here?"

The way he said "you had ties here" rankled. She'd grown up here, too. Emerald Lake was her hometown. Her family went back generations.

"Of course, it was my idea," she said, realizing too late that she was snapping at him. "That carousel is sitting on prime waterfront real estate. If it's not me coming in here with this company to build, it's going to be someone else. It might not be for a few years, but I guarantee you it's going to happen."

"There are plenty of other towns that would welcome this kind of development. Go there."

"I can't. It has to be here."

"Why?"

She shook her head, knowing she couldn't tell him how close she'd been to being tossed out on her ass, even after ten years of working it off for Marks & Banks. She couldn't tell him that failure was so close for once that she could almost taste it. She was only as good as her last deal. She might have been screwing up since her father's death, but she still knew how to read a client. She'd sold the hell out of Emerald Lake, and now that was what they wanted. Not some substitute lake town down Route 8.

"You won't understand, Nate. It has to be here. It has to be."

"You just don't get it, do you, Andi?"

"Tell me your concerns, Nate, and I'll address them."

"I'm not one of your clients that you can wow with a PowerPoint presentation," he said, his words hard. Bitter. "You want to know what my biggest concern is?"

She didn't like the tone of his voice and knew she wouldn't like what was coming any better. But she was the one who'd insisted they talk about the project tonight.

She had to say, "Yes."

"You're not from here anymore." As she worked to process his horrible words, he hit her with, "Coming to me with this crap makes me think you were never from here."

Andi felt as if he'd slapped her across the face and couldn't stop herself from lashing back at him.

"Well, you're so stuck here that you don't see what could happen to this town. But I do. So if you don't mind my being just as blunt, if you're not careful, your antiquated rules and policies will drive companies out of Emerald Lake. Businesses won't be able to survive here, not without a chance to make some money."

His face was stubborn. But still heartbreakingly beautiful.

Why did they have to be having this conversation? Why did they have to be at each other's throats?

It wasn't what she wanted. Not at all.

"People who want to stay, stay," he insisted. "If you're tough enough, you find a way to make it work. And you know you've earned the right to be here."

There was a subtext here, she was sure of it, that went something like, *If you'd really loved me, you would have stayed.*

Working to keep her focus on their debate over the condos rather than the emotions whipping around them, Andi said, "Are you even listening to yourself? Saying how tough you have to be to stay. Instead of celebrating how hard it is to stay afloat in Emerald Lake, why don't you try a little harder to make it easier for the people who elected you mayor?"

"One building leads to more, leads to problems you can't even begin to foresee. What I know for sure is that the people who stay are the ones who really love Emerald Lake, just the way it is. They want to be able to swim in the lake, to know that it's clean and that too many boats and too many tourists haven't polluted it. They want to be able to hike in these mountains without facing bald hills logged to make a couple bucks."

"Do you really think I'd bring in a company that would pollute the water or destroy the forests?"

"Everything we do has consequences, Andi. Even if they're unintended."

She couldn't argue with him about consequences. Not when one simple meeting with him was spinning off into consequences, one after the other.

"You want promises. I'll give them to you. I'll make sure the building is done by local people. That the money coming into Emerald Lake stays here. And that the building process is totally green."

"I know all about your promises, Andi. Don't kid yourself. This is all about your career."

She gasped, actually sucked in a mouthful of air and choked on it. But even as her heart felt like it was drowning, her brain still tried to stay above the waterline.

"Wouldn't you rather have somebody who actually cares about Emerald Lake be involved?"

"You're right about that at least. I'd like to be dealing with someone who cares about this town, someone who cares about more than just her latest deal."

Working even harder to push down the hurt building up inside of her, to tell herself he couldn't really mean any of the horrible things he was saying, she said, "I'm not going to deny these condos are a good career move, but they're also for the town. My father always wished more people knew about Emerald Lake. At the end of the day, he supposed there wasn't enough here to bring them in. These small changes could be enough."

"Do you really sleep at night telling yourself those lies?"

Just like that, the hurt won.

"How dare you tell me that there was nothing to talk about, no old wounds to heal between us, when all along you've been hating me with every single breath. When all along, you've been resenting every single second we spent together. When all along, you knew you'd never, ever forgive me for not giving up my entire life to come back here and take care of you and your sister."

She was up and out of the booth before he could stop her.

Away. She needed to get away from all of the horrible accusations he'd made. She needed to stop seeing the anger, the betrayal, the fury in his eyes as he looked at her like she was a traitor who didn't understand him. He acted like she had never understood him.

He acted like she hadn't loved him with every piece of her heart.

"Andi, wait!"

She heard him calling out to her, heard his footfalls on the sidewalk behind her, but she didn't stop.

Only, Nate was faster than she was, and at the end of Main Street where the grass began, his arms came around her waist, pulling her against his back.

Oh god, that heat, it pulled her into him despite herself. Despite what he'd said in the bar, despite how he'd said it.

Despite the fact that she wasn't even sure he liked her.

"Andi, I didn't mean to hurt you."

"But you did."

"Andi." Her name was a breath of heated regret breaking through the cold fall night. "You caught me off guard. I shouldn't have said any of those things."

Every heartbeat was excruciating when all she wanted was to rewind back to that moment when he'd said, *"I've wondered about what you've been doing for ten years."* She wished they could step back in time so that she could tell him how much she had missed him, that she'd thought about him every single day for ten years, even though she hadn't wanted to.

"You were right, Andi. We do need to talk about what happened."

"Not tonight." She couldn't yet bear to move her cheek away from his warmth. If things had gone differently, this warmth could have been hers all along.

Not when she was feeling as weak as she ever had. She would need to be strong for that conversation.

Andi forced herself to pull out of Nate's arms. "I need to go."

And this time, he let her.

\*    \*    \*

Her mother was waiting up for her when Andi got home.

"Oh honey, it's so good to see you." Andi had never

needed Carol's hug more than she did right that second. "Your grandmother said that you were planning to stay for a few days this time. Is that true?"

"Actually I'll probably be here a week at least. Maybe two." She took a deep breath before saying, "My project is here in town. That's why I'm back, to oversee the development and building of some beautiful residences on the waterfront."

She waited for her mother's reaction, but Carol was the woman she had always been: thoughtful and quiet, gentle even when concerned.

"I'm sure you'll do a fantastic job with it, honey."

"Do you think I'm wrong to even be thinking about building condos here, Mom?"

Andi didn't know where the question came from, didn't know why she was asking her mother to give her opinion about a business situation.

Carol frowned and shook her head. "I don't know, honey. The only thing I know for sure is that change is hard. Good or bad."

That was when Andi noticed how Carol's usually vibrant blue eyes were smudged with dark circles beneath her lower eyelashes. She knew how hard her father's death had been on her mother. How could it have been anything but hard to have him right beside her one moment at an end-of-summer cocktail party, laughing with their friends—and then gone the next, a heart attack taking him so suddenly? Too suddenly, and utterly without warning, without giving anyone a chance to save him.

Andi knew that Nate's parents' deaths had been just as unexpected. He'd lost his mother first when she gave birth to Madison and bled out. One month later his father pulled out a gun and shot himself. But Nate had survived, had even told her how happy he was with his life tonight. She and her mother would not only figure out a way to survive, too, but they'd learn how to be happy again, wouldn't they?

Andi felt her mother's hand on her arm. "Thank you for making your grandmother go see the doctor."

"What did Dr. Morris say?"

"Evidently it's just a cold that she's let go a little too long. Nothing that a little rest won't take care of."

"Thank god. I was really worried about her today."

"I know, honey. But you know how strong your grand-mother is. And we both really appreciate you looking after the store today. Especially on a Monday with the knitting group showing up."

Andi forced a smile. "It was no big deal. Really. Every-one was great." Well, mostly anyway. Catherine had been a little weird, but Andi was trying not to take it personally.

Her mother looked fondly at her across the table. "You always had such a wonderful eye, honey. The store used to look so much better after you rearranged things. I'm sure you've got a lot of ideas for us about how to make the place better."

Andi frowned at her mother's compliment. They both knew she was a numbers girl and not the least bit creative or artistic.

"I was just a little girl playing with yarn. And the place looks great already, Mom. You know that."

And the surprising truth was, considering her mother and grandmother had no formal training in marketing or sales, the store really was very well optimized. Everything from the layout to the displays to the selection was spot-on.

Knowing her mother would find out soon enough, Andi forced herself to say, "Anyway, Nate and I met tonight. To catch up." The words were catching in her throat. "And to talk about my project."

Her mother looked at her more carefully. "You two haven't seen each other in quite a while. How was it?"

All her life, whenever she'd had problems, Andi had gone to her father for advice. Of course, her mother had always been there with cookies and Band-Aids and hugs and bedtime stories, but Andi had just never felt as connected to her mother. Not when they were so different.

Tonight, for the first time, she wanted to blurt out everything that had happened with Nate. She wanted to cry on her mother's shoulder. She wanted to ask for help, for guidance, for some salve to patch the old wound in her heart that had just been reopened.

But she couldn't. Her mother was still grieving, still reeling from her father's death, one year later. Andi didn't need to dump her problems on Carol, too.

"It was fine, but I'm exhausted." Andi yawned. "I haven't spent that much time on my feet in a very long time. I think I'll head to bed now."

Up in her childhood bedroom, she changed into her pajamas, sat down on her bed with her open laptop, and tried to focus on answering the dozens of e-mails that had come in during the day. But she was hard-pressed to focus on work with all of the things Nate had said zinging through her mind.

*"You knew I could never say no to you."*

*"You're not from here anymore."*

*"I know all about your promises, Andi."*

*"Do you really sleep at night telling yourself those lies?"*

No, she thought, as she began to reply to an e-mail from her assistant. It was unlikely that she'd be getting any sleep tonight.

# Chapter Six

Nate couldn't stop thinking about Andi. About the things he'd said to her at the Tavern.

As mayor, he often peacefully disagreed with friends and neighbors over issues. But he never lost it. Never.

So then, as soon as Andi had pushed those condo plans across the table to him, why had he all but blown apart?

She wasn't the one who had made it personal. She'd been all business. He was the one who'd taken their discussion from condos to their screwed-up past.

And to the fact that he didn't trust her anymore.

Jesus. He should have seen it coming, but he hadn't. He hadn't known Andi would still have the power to rock his world as much as she ever did. He should have known that the first shock of seeing her, talking with her, touching her was going to be bad, but like a fool with his head stuck in the sand, he hadn't.

\*　　　\*　　　\*

*"Andi, he's dead."*

*"Nate? Is that you?"*

*He sat in the dirt outside his trailer. He'd wrapped his baby sister in a blanket and had the phone propped up against his shoulder. He could hear the sounds coming from Andi's dorm room at Cornell, music and laughter, so different from the almost perfect silence that surrounded his trailer by the lake, a silence only broken up by an occasional frog . . . and his sister's whimpers.*

"Wait a minute," Andi was said. "I can't hear anything. My roommate's stereo is up too loud. Let me go out into the hall. Darn it, it's even louder out here. Hopefully my cordless will reach outside."

*He could hear her walking past people, who were saying hello. Her college life was a whole other world he knew virtually nothing about.*

"Okay, silence. Finally. That's better. I'm so glad you called, Nate. I was just thinking about you. I was just missing you. Can we start this call again?"

"He killed himself, Andi. He put a bullet through his brain."

"Nate? What are you talking about?"

*He knew he wasn't making any sense, but it was hard to make sense after what he'd seen.*

*After the way his life had just imploded.*

"My father. He shot himself."

"Oh god. Oh no."

*All Nate wanted was for Andi to be here with him. To have her arms around him. To tell him everything was going to be okay. To see her and know that they'd figure things out together.*

"I left to get some groceries and diapers, and when I came back, he was on the floor and there were brains—" *He almost threw up again, barely swallowing down the bile.*

*"Madison was in her crib. She was crying. Her diaper was dirty."*

It was still dirty. He needed to get back inside and grab the diapers he'd bought to change her. But he couldn't. He couldn't go back inside.

*"Have you called the police yet?"*

*"No."*

He'd needed to call Andi first. Needed to know that there was still someone left who loved him, that there was still someone left that cared about him, that wouldn't leave him when the going got too rough.

*"I'm going to hang up right now, Nate, so that you can call 911 and tell them what happened."*

*"I need you, Andi."*

*"I know. That's why I'm coming right now. Right away."* He thought he heard a sob in her voice right before she said, *"I love you, Nate. Be strong and wait for me. I'll be there soon."*

She hung up and he called 911. He knew the paramedics and police would help him and his sister. His neighbors would help.

But Andi was the reason he would make it through.

As long as she was by his side, he'd be okay.

\*     \*     \*

Nate woke up from his dream, sweat coating his skin, the sheets kicked off. He was sitting up in bed, cradling his pillow like it was his baby sister while his heart pounded almost through his chest.

He had to force himself to look around his bedroom, to see the house he'd built on the lake four years ago. He wasn't that kid anymore whose whole life had changed in

an instant. He wasn't the boy waiting in the dirt for someone to come save him.

Still he couldn't stop thinking about those first hours
after he'd discovered his father on the floor of the trailer.
Right after getting off the phone with him, Andi had
called her family, and Carol had come right away to take
him and Madison to the empty cottage behind their big
house. By the time Andi had arrived in Emerald Lake, the
trailer had been closed off by the chief of police to ensure
there was no foul play.

Andi had run to him, held him, rocked him in her arms.
Nate could see how badly she wanted to help, only he was
already way beyond help.

But somehow seeing her only made things worse, only
reminded him of all the things he could no longer have.

Because from the moment he found his father lying
on the floor, everything had changed. His sister became
his number one priority, and any dreams that he'd had for
himself—for a life with Andi—had to be stuffed away.

He didn't remember falling asleep on the couch between questioning from the police and practically being
force-fed by Andi's mother. All he remembered was waking up to the sounds of his sister's wails—and seeing Andi
calmly changing Madison's diaper, even though he knew
she'd never done much babysitting around the lake. There
was baby poop all over both of them, and she should have
been freaking out, but she wasn't.

She was calm and collected and methodical about it all.

And Nate knew he couldn't do any of this without her.

Over and over he'd told himself not to ask her to stay. It
wasn't her life that had exploded. It wasn't her mess that
needed to be dealt with. But in that moment, it was less

courage than desperation that had him asking.

Begging.

*"Stay with me, Andi."*

She had looked at him with such shock, as if what he was asking her was so utterly unexpected, that he knew he shouldn't say anything more. He should have told her never mind, that he didn't mean it, that it was the exhaustion—and grief over losing his father—that was making him say crazy things.

But he hadn't done or said any of those things. Instead, he'd decided it was a test.

A test to see if she really loved him. Or not.

*"Defer college for a semester. This is all such a big mess. Help me with Madison. Help me get my feet on the ground. I don't know if I can do it without you."*

She'd stared at him, then scanned the four walls of the cottage as if she could find an escape route if she looked carefully enough.

*"Of course, you can do it,"* was what she'd told him.

She didn't need to say anything more. Those six words made everything perfectly clear to him. But he'd still pushed.

Still hoped.

*"I need you, Andi."*

He watched the care, the love, with which she carefully laid his clean and dry sister down in the donated crib and covered her with a blanket, kissing her on the cheek. Madison waved an arm in the air and Andi caught it, holding onto it with a smile for the little girl.

Hope had flared in his chest one last time as he watched the sweet interplay between the two people he loved most in the world.

But then Andi turned to him and he read the truth on her face.

She wasn't going to stay.

*"Of course, I want to help you. I'm going to come home and visit you whenever I can, on weekends and school breaks, to help you through this."*

*"I thought you loved me."*

*"I do love you, Nate. Of course, I love you. But you know I can't stay here. I can't live in Emerald Lake. And if I defer a semester, I'll get so behind I might never be able to catch up. I've waited for this moment my whole life, to get away and become something. Please don't ask me to give it all up now."*

Reality hit him then, like fists pounding all over his body, and a deep rage took over, so swift and strong, that he could no longer stop himself from giving into it. Tears had been right there about to fall. And yet at the same time, he wasn't sure he would ever be able to feel anything again.

*"Just fucking go!"*

He'd yelled the words so loud that he startled his sister out of her sleepy state, and she started to whimper from her crib. But that didn't stop him.

He'd sneered, *"You'd better hurry back to school or you might miss an important test."*

Andi had come toward him, her arms outstretched. *"Please don't be like that, Nate. Please don't push me away."*

He'd gone to the door and opened it. *"I need to concentrate on Madison right now. Not a long-distance relationship."*

*"So this is it? You're breaking up with me?"*

*"You're the one who was already leaving, Andi."*

A few seconds later, she left. Heading back to a life that had nothing to do with him.

Memories, snippets of words they'd said to each other came back at him all morning as he showered, dressed, made breakfast, then got in his truck to head to the important meeting he had in a town a half hour away.

Betsy had taken Madison and Kayla to school this morning after their sleep-over. There was no reason for Nate to drive past the school.

Instead, he sat outside the building and let his brain play tricks on him. He and Andi had gone here together. He'd pulled her pigtails, and she'd knocked him off the monkey bars. They'd been too young to admit their real feelings for each other back then. Their first kiss wouldn't come until they were sixteen.

Seeing Andi again was a big deal. A huge deal. All of his old feelings for her were much closer to the surface than he wanted them to be. Not just his latent anger with her, not just the fact that he still desired her, but the fact that he still felt a strong emotional connection to her, even after all this time.

He'd let down his guard in the bar for a split second, had let himself forget anything but her sweet smile and soft laughter, had even let himself give rise to the secret hope he'd held on to—that one day they'd meet again and it would all work out.

*Boom!* That was when she'd come in with her plans.

He'd felt so burned, so crushed, like such an idiot for letting himself start to fall again when he knew better.

Andi had wanted to clear the air last night and now he knew she was right. There was no question that they needed to say whatever needed to be said, to let bygones be bygones. And when they were done settling the past back in the past where it belonged, then they could have a rational discussion about her condos.

The rational discussion they should have had last night.

\* \* \*

Andi woke up on top of her covers, her laptop teetering precariously on her stomach.

With the sun streaming in over her pillow, she had no choice but to drag herself into the shower. She stood beneath the warm spray, but none of her muscles relaxed. Not when she'd been a ball of nerves since the moment she'd seen Nate. Earlier than that actually. She'd been wound up like a tangled ball of yarn since the moment she'd blurted out to the Klein Group that the condos should be built at Emerald Lake.

Work. She needed to focus on work. It had always saved her before. It would save her again now.

And lord knew, after losing the previous day to Lake Yarns, she had a ton of work to tackle today. Especially, she thought with a frown as she toweled off, given Nate's enormous objections to her project.

Andi was reaching for a pair of jeans and a long-sleeved T-shirt when she realized that dressing down in the middle of a workday was exactly what she shouldn't do. She wasn't here for a vacation—she was here on a business trip.

She selected a navy-blue dress from her garment bag, and by the time she had her earrings in, her hair done, and heels on, Andi felt a little better, like she was wearing the proper armor.

Downstairs the kitchen was quiet, and she guessed that her mother was already at Lake Yarns, opening it up for the day. As always, Andi was drawn to the leather chair by the fireplace where her father used to read his stacks of newspapers. She ran her hand over the high back remembering how, when she was a little girl and he would be gone for weeks at a time in Washington, D.C., she used to curl up in his chair with a blanket and fall asleep because it was the closest thing to being in his arms. And when he was there, she'd spent hours sitting beside his chair while he was on the phone, wanting to be with him but knowing she had to be quiet and not disturb his work.

Uncomfortable with the memory, she headed for the screened porch at the front of the house. As she opened a door, the high-pitched squeak that echoed into the front hall made Andi suddenly realize just how lonely it must be for her mother to live in the large house by herself.

Still despite its huge scope—the whitewashed, two-story home was one of the oldest and biggest in town—Carol was good at making each room homey. The screened porch with its whitewashed wooden planks and the bright reds and yellows and blues on the furniture's upholstery was a bright retreat even on rainy days. And of course, there was the basket of knitting in the corner by the couch and a similar basket in every room. Knitters, she knew from a childhood of being surrounded by them, loved to start projects but loved finishing them a whole lot less. Thus, the piles of works in progress near every comfortable chair in every room.

Every time she came home for a visit, Andi was struck by how different her childhood home was from her city loft. Much like her father's apartment in Washington,

D.C., she'd always tended toward minimal color, mostly blacks and whites, whereas this house was stamped with her mother's eye for design and color. Fabrics that would have been out of control in anyone else's hands looked just right together the way Carol had arranged them.

Andi felt simultaneously comforted—and completely out of her element.

She hadn't come home for more than a night or two in ten years, but as she turned around to look out at the rising sun sparkling over the blue water, memories rushed over her.

Waking up to go meet Nate out on the beach to pick blueberries for her mother's blueberry pancakes. Warm summer nights in front of a bonfire, roasting marshmallows with Nate, digging deep sand tunnels and laughing when adults who walked by in the dark fell into them. Saturday afternoon sailing races in her Sunfish on perfectly still days where she and Nate practically had to paddle their way around the buoys. Sitting out on the end of the dock on Adirondack chairs, watching the sun fall behind the mountains, making up stories about the images they saw in the clouds.

She'd expected her father's memory to assault her at every turn. But amazingly, apart from the leather chair in the living room, she saw Nate in the house around her more than she saw her father.

Nate was the one who she had always gone to after her father left again.

Nate was the one who had comforted her, soothed her.

Her heart squeezing, she exited the porch and headed around to the back of the house, across the lawn that led to her grandmother's cottage behind the big house. Andi saw the top of a large straw hat in the field of yellow and white chrysanthemums before she saw the rest of Evelyn.

Her grandmother looked just right among the blooms, as pretty as any of the flowers, as much as part of this land as it was part of her.

*"You're not from here... you were never from here."*

Nate's words whiplashed through her head again. She shook it to try and get them out, but they were already lodged way too deep.

"What's wrong, honey?"

Last night Andi had decided she would work things out on her own. But it turned out she was defenseless against her grandmother's very real concern. Feeling like a little girl coming to cry on her grandmother's shoulder with a skinned knee, she said, "Nate and I had a big blowup last night."

Her grandmother handed her the shears, and Andi was glad to turn her focus over to the beautiful mums for a moment rather than her too-strong feelings for Nate.

"I know how much you've always cared about him. Do you want to talk about it?"

No. She wanted to pretend none of it had ever happened.

"I'm working on a new project. It's the reason I'm here actually. I have a client who wants to build some residences on the lake. Nate doesn't think they'd be good for the town."

"And you do?" There wasn't any judgment on her grandmother's face.

Andi dropped the stems into the basket on the grass. "Very much so. Not just because of the money they will bring the town, but because of the new life it will give to the waterfront. That old carousel is nothing but an eyesore."

Evelyn stiffened. "I thought you were talking about some new buildings. What do they have to do with the carousel?"

Suddenly Andi had that same feeling from the night before with Nate. The one that told her she should not just tread carefully, but probably not tread at all. But yet again, she'd already said too much to turn back.

"That's where my client will be building the condos, Grandma. Where the carousel is sitting."

"No, they can't do that. Absolutely not."

With that, her grandmother turned and walked away. Stunned, confused, Andi picked up the basket of flowers and ran after her.

"What's wrong, Grandma? It didn't seem like you were upset about the condos until I mentioned the carousel." Worse, she had looked disappointed, as if she expected better from her own granddaughter.

"Buildings, shmildings. Go ahead and build whatever you want. But why would you even think about removing that carousel? Don't you realize how important it is to everyone?"

What was her grandmother talking about?

"Nobody has even gone over and looked at that thing in twenty years."

"*That thing* is important and magical."

Andi felt the power of conviction behind Evelyn's words. But that didn't mean she understood where it had come from.

Trying to be gentle despite the fact that she had no idea why her grandmother was getting so wound up, she said, "I'm sure it used to be really magical, Grandma, but it's in such a bad state now that I'm afraid it would take a great deal of money to restore it." And there was no way she was going to be able to get the money to do that out of the Klein Group, not when putting in a new boat dock made a whole lot more sense for the town and for the people who would buy the condos.

The set of her grandmother's face was stubborn. "Well, then you'll just need to figure out a way to make it work. Isn't that what you do?"

Maybe it was something in the water around here that had everyone acting so nuts. Andi would have to remember to stick to bottled.

"I'll talk to the builders," she said, careful not to make any promises she couldn't keep. "But honestly, I doubt they're going to get behind the idea of incorporating the carousel into their plans."

She couldn't picture it, couldn't see a way to make it work. Not when the whole point was to move the town forward rather than back into the past.

"It has to work, Andi."

"Why is the carousel so important to you? What is so magical about it?"

"Yesterday when we were in the store, I told you about falling in love with knitting. Do you remember?"

"Of course I do, Grandma."

"I didn't just fall in love with knitting. I fell in love with Carlos, too."

"Carlos?"

Her grandmother smiled. "Why don't you follow me to my cottage, and we can sit down and relax a bit while I tell you a little story."

\*     \*     \*

*Emerald Lake, 1941*

*Evelyn was coming home from a planning meeting for the new exhibit at the Adirondack Museum when she first noticed the man talking to her father.*

*He had jet-black hair, a little too long, just starting to curl at the base of his neck. He looked strong, his muscles a little too big. His skin was dark, and one more breathless glance told her his eyes were blue with thick, dark lashes.*

*He was quite simply the most beautiful man she'd ever set eyes on, even in his ratty sweater that was starting to unravel at the wrists and the neckline.*

*The wind blew colorful leaves down from the trees, but although it was a strangely cold fall day, Evelyn felt overheated.*

*She guessed the man was one of the jack-of-all-trades who had come into town to see if anyone had work. The locals had likely sent him to her father, who was building a new wing on their mansion on the water. Evelyn knew her father was paying these men pennies and that they were glad to have this money.*

*The man suddenly looked at her over her father's shoulder, and a powerful current, a rush of something she didn't understand, passed between them.*

*Her father shifted, clearly sensing someone was behind him. Evelyn tucked her head down and moved swiftly toward the house. Her mother intercepted her just as Evelyn stepped into the kitchen and started taking off her hat and gloves and jacket.*

*"Oh, there you are, honey. I was thinking, it's such a cold day, and the men out there are working so hard.*

*Would you mind putting together some sandwiches and hot drinks for them?"*

*Evelyn nodded, responding with a calm, "Of course, Mother," even as her heart raced.*

*Maybe she would find out his name. Maybe she'd get to speak with him.*

*Thirty minutes later the tray of snacks and drinks was ready. Putting her jacket and hat and gloves back on, she headed out of the house and across the wide stretch of grass that led to the construction area. There were usually a half-dozen men working, but there was only one there now.*

*The beautiful man in the ratty sweater.*

*A sudden vision came at her of a new sweater, one she would make for him, a complicated Fair Isle made up of blues and whites to pick up the color of his eyes.*

*She'd been full of anticipation about the chance to see him up close, but now that it was just the two of them she was nervous. Skittish. Normally composed and sure of herself, Evelyn was thrown off by her own uncertainty around this stranger.*

*"Hi." The one short word sounded squeaky to her ears. She cleared her throat to try and fix it. "You looked cold. I thought I'd bring out some coffee. Some food, too, if you're hungry."*

*She put the tray down on a makeshift table made out of plywood, then stepped back.*

*The man's blue eyes darkened for a moment before he simply nodded. "Thank you."*

*She let his low voice rumble through her as she watched him move to the tray and pour himself a cup of coffee. His hands were big but not rough like a laborer's would be.*

*Why, she suddenly wondered, was he here doing this work? And where had he come from?*

*She felt his eyes on her again, just before he said, "You look cold. You should run back inside."*

*It was true—she was getting cold. But it was the way he'd said "run back inside" that had her stubbornly staying right where she was. She wasn't a little girl with pigtails. She was eighteen years old, old enough to get married and have her own house if she wanted to.*

*Certainly old enough to carry on a conversation with one of the men working for her father.*

*Shrugging, she said, "I've spent all day inside. It's nice to be out here. And so beautiful." She looked up at the thick canopy of the maple tree above them. "Look at that tree, at those amazing reds and yellows." She took a deep breath of the sweet, crisp air. "And the air smells so good."*

*"How long have you lived here?" The slightly rough edge in his voice was tempered by something smooth that whispered over her skin.*

*"My whole life. Why do you ask?"*

*"You act like you've never seen your own land before."*

*Evelyn's back immediately went up again. First he had treated her like a child. Now he was implying that she didn't pay any attention to her surroundings. Worse still, she didn't know how he kept managing to ruffle her feathers—everyone knew she was unruffleable!*

*"I'm busy with school and helping my mother's charities. There are a lot of needy people out there who need my help. I can't waste my day staring at trees."*

*"Ah." He nodded, his eyes darkening, his full mouth going taut for a split second. "Charities." But then, as if he was trying to be kind to the poor little rich girl, he*

looked out over the lake in front of her house and said, "You're right. It really is beautiful." His eyes met hers again. "Almost more beauty than a man can take in."

There was no reason she should think he was talking about anything but the trees and the lake.

But for a moment it felt like he was talking about her.

Not knowing how to deal with a sudden flare of attraction that was so much bigger and brighter than anything she'd ever felt before, even as her cheeks flamed, she found herself admitting, "I really should get out more."

"So what's stopping you?"

That was when she realized that something had shifted between them. Instead of treating her like a little girl, instead of letting her get away with her previous excuses, this beautiful stranger was actually forcing her to dig deeper.

And he acted like he cared about her answer.

She shook her head, realizing she didn't have a good answer. "I don't know. It just never fits into my plans, I guess."

"Or maybe," he said softly, his blue eyes even darker now, "something out here scares you?"

That was when she jumped to her feet. Because even though she instinctively knew this man would never harm her, her reaction to him was scaring her.

"I think I hear my mother calling."

His mouth quirked up into a smile that didn't reach his eyes. "You'd better run back to her, then."

She was almost on the grass when she had to turn back around one more time. "I don't know your name."

He remained silent for a long moment. Finally he said, "Carlos."

*It wasn't until she was back in the house, closing the door on the trees and the lake and the mountains again, that she realized she hadn't told him her name.*

*Her sisters, Celeste and Rose, were sitting in the living room giggling over something when she walked in. Dazed, Evelyn tossed her hat onto the love seat, then promptly sat down on it.*

*"You look funny," Rose said as Celeste tried to yank the hat out from beneath her rear end.*

*Celeste, the mother hen of the group, put her hand on Evelyn's forehead. "You're hot. You should lay down."*

*Evelyn would have pushed her sister away, but she was still too caught up in thinking about the man outside.*

*Carlos. His name was Carlos.*

*Still, Evelyn hated being told what to do. "I don't need to lay down."*

*Unfortunately, Celeste hated not being listened to just as much. "Remember what happened the last time you got a fever?"*

*Instead of responding to her sister's question, Evelyn said in a slightly higher pitched voice than normal, "I'm going to make a sweater."*

*Her sisters looked at each other in surprise. "But you don't like knitting. Why would you want to make a sweater?"*

*Evelyn stood up and walked into the sewing room. She quickly found several skeins of blue and white yarn and her mother's book of knitting patterns. Her heartbeat kicked up as she imagined the beautiful man wearing something she had made with her own hands.*

*"He needs this sweater."*

*Evelyn didn't know her sisters had followed behind her*

*until she heard Celeste say, "You're making a sweater for Arthur?"*

*Arthur Powell was from the most well-to-do family on the lake, even wealthier than they were. He was a perfectly nice, good-looking guy, but she didn't love him.*

*Evelyn had always told her sisters everything before. But now, for the first time ever, there was something she wanted to keep all to herself.*

*"Could you talk me through this Fair Isle pattern?" was what she finally said, a knot of guilt forming in Evelyn's stomach as her sisters stared at her, then nodded.*

*Together, Celeste and Rose talked her through the difficult first few rows of the sweater that would keep Carlos warm—and make his blue eyes seem even bluer.*

*Evelyn had never had the patience for handiwork like this, had never enjoyed needlepoint or quilting. But here she was, sweating it out over counting stitches and alternating colors for a sweater that she wasn't sure she would ever have the guts to actually give to a stranger.*

*A stranger she suspected just might steal her heart.*

# Chapter Seven

Could I have a glass of water, honey?"

Andi was so riveted by her grandmother's story that it took her a moment to respond. "Of course, Grandma. I'll be right back with it."

At first it had been a little bit of a shock to realize Evelyn had been head over heels in love with someone who wasn't her grandfather. But then, Andi suddenly thought, with a strange sense of kinship to her grandmother, maybe everyone had a Nate in their past, a man they wanted but couldn't have.

Still, none of this helped her understand why her grandmother was so attached to the carousel.

Coming back in with the water, Andi waited until Evelyn finishing drinking as if she'd been walking through the desert. But then suddenly the glass fell to the ground and shattered as her grandmother began to cough, deep hacking coughs that wracked her small frame.

"Grandma!"

Their earlier roles in the garden now reversed—Andi was the one trying to comfort her grandmother this time—

she rubbed Evelyn's back, noticing as she did so just how much the bones in her grandmother's ribs and spine pressed into her palm.

Andi hated feeling palpable proof of the fact that the woman she loved so much was losing more and more of the flesh every year that had once protected her from falls, from illness.

Fortunately this coughing fit wasn't nearly as prolonged as the one in Lake Yarns had been, and a moment later Evelyn managed to say, "The water went down the wrong pipe."

Andi made sure none of the glass had pierced her grandmother's skin before she knelt down carefully on the ground to pick up the shards of glass.

"You shouldn't have tired yourself out with all that talking."

"But you had to know, didn't you?"

Didn't her grandmother realize she hadn't yet got to the part about the carousel, hadn't yet told her why it was so important? But Andi knew she couldn't ask her now. Not today. Not when Evelyn shouldn't be doing anything but resting. Especially not revisiting such emotional territory.

After last night in the Tavern with Nate, Andi knew firsthand how fiercely all of those lost dreams and hopes ripped at your heart.

"I want you to see the doctor again, Grandma."

"Pfft. I told you. The water went down the wrong pipe. Besides, your mother needs me to help her with the inventory today. I need to head in soon."

"No way. I'm going to go help Mom with the store again so that you can stay here. In bed."

Andi refused to leave until she had her grandmother

tucked in beneath the soft covers of her bed with a couple of books and another glass of water on the bedside table.

Her project workload would just have to wait again. Lake Yarns was calling.

\*          \*          \*

Carol was helping a customer when Andi walked into the store. "Andi, honey, would you mind coming over here to give us your opinion? We're trying to figure out the best color combination for a blanket."

Andi walked over to the table where a dozen skeins of various colors were set up in three different groupings. She quickly pulled a skein out of each grouping. "These."

The customer said, "Perfect! Now why didn't we see that?"

"My daughter has a great eye," Carol said with pride, and Andi wondered for half a second if it was true. She never had any problem putting together her presentations, but that seemed less about design than content.

After Carol finished ringing up the yarn, she came over to where Andi was sitting in the back, booting up their old computer.

"I'm going to take over for Grandma today if that's okay with you. I went over to her cottage for a visit this morning." *And she told me all about a man named Carlos.* Something told Andi not to bring that up with her mother, who most likely wouldn't appreciate hearing that Grandpa wasn't Evelyn's one true love. "She started coughing again, so I sent her back to bed."

"You know I love having you here," her mother said again, her big smile sending off more of those pangs of guilt in Andi's chest. Carol pointed to the computer screen. "Everything look okay?"

"Actually, I've been looking at your ordering and inventory systems, and I can't help but think everything would run more smoothly if you upgraded a few things."

"You're the expert. We trust you to do what's right for the store."

Andi's fingers stilled on the keyboard as she remembered Nate's pointed questions from last night, the way he'd said she was only thinking of her career, not of her own town. Of course, the condos were going to be good for the store. Her mother's trust wasn't misplaced. Andi would never do anything to hurt Lake Yarns.

Although, truth be told, she was beginning to worry about how her mother and grandmother were going to cope with running the store by themselves in the coming years. Was there anyone they trusted to take over one day as manager?

"Mom, do you and Grandma have many employees?"

Her mother pulled up a chair and sat down. "A few ladies who come in part-time now and again. Jenny is probably here the most. Why do you ask?"

Not wanting to tread on her mother's toes—after all, she'd been running this store with absolutely no help from her daughter for decades—Andi proceeded carefully. "With Grandma starting to slow down, I can't help but think running Lake Yarns alone has got to be a big burden for you." She gauged her mother's expression before continuing, "Have you ever thought about hiring a manager? Perhaps one of the women who already works here?"

"I've been trying to get Evelyn to agree to hire a

manager, but so far your grandmother refuses to even consider it."

Andi found herself staring at her mother practically openmouthed in surprise. This was the first time she had heard anything about problems at the store. The irony wasn't lost on her: her job was fixing companies that were breaking.

And yet, her own mother hadn't thought to come to her for help with their family business.

"How long have you been talking about this?" Andi asked her mother.

Carol sighed. "Awhile now. But Evelyn says the store should be run by family, not a stranger who is only working for a paycheck. That it's about love and personal connection, not money. You know how she is. There's no talking to her about anything. Her way or the highway." She smiled. "You've always reminded me a lot of her."

Barely biting back a *how?* Andi wasn't the least bit reassured by her mother's answer. Not when the only family member left to manage the store was her—and they all knew the last thing Andi was going to do was give up her job and move back to Emerald Lake to run Lake Yarns.

\*     \*     \*

Later that afternoon, Andi caught Carol yawning for what had to be the hundredth time. It was one thing to worry about her mother from a distance, but it was another to watch her barely make it through the day.

"Haven't been sleeping well?"

"Oh honey, it's just that ever since your father passed away, the bed has seemed too big."

Andi was a breath away from noting that her father had

rarely been there, even when he was alive, but she knew that wasn't what her mother needed to hear.

"Did you take any time off, Mom? After?"

"It's better to be busy."

Andi knew she should agree. After all, hadn't she done the same thing? Gone to her father's funeral in Washington, D.C., one day and been back at her desk in New York City the next.

"But you seem really tired." Andi was reminded of the way her mom would be in the weeks after her father went back to D.C. "Maybe I should just kick you out, just like I did with Grandma yesterday."

Carol's eyelids were drooping, but she still insisted, "Oh no, you've already done too much."

Was her mother kidding? Two days in the store wasn't even close to "too much." Sure, Andi was neglecting her own job. But her family needed her right now.

"Please, Mom. I'm happy to take care of closing up."

"Well, if you're absolutely sure."

"Positive."

Heck, she'd already made it through a day and a half at the store. She was feeling pretty proud of herself and of the fact that she could almost talk about yarn and patterns with customers like she had half a clue what she was saying.

Andi didn't see Nate standing just inside the doorway until Carol moved to go get her things.

"You're a good daughter," he said softly to her, right before Carol went to say hello to him. Andi moved over to the register and tried to act really busy, even though she knew there was no escaping him.

She shouldn't want to escape him. Or should she?

Would it be better for both of them? Would it be easier if she just turned around and went away again? If she had never come back at all?

Nate walked Carol out, then came up to the counter and leaned against it, looking even better by day than he had last night. Andi had always loved the way his dark hair curled a little bit at the nape of his neck, the faint hint of stubble that always magically appeared at 5 p.m., the amazingly long eyelashes on such an otherwise masculine face.

And here she'd thought she would be better prepared to see him now that the first shock was past.

Good one.

"Andi, I'm glad you're here."

He ran a hand through his hair, leaving the soft dark strands sticking up just enough that she had to grip the edge of the cash register to prevent herself from reaching out and smoothing them down.

"I was sitting in an Adirondack Council meeting today, and I was missing pretty much everything I needed to hear because I couldn't stop thinking about you. Because I couldn't stop thinking about the things I said to you. I was out of line, Andi. That's why I needed to come here today, needed to see you again to make sure that you don't hate me."

"I still don't like the things you said, but I don't hate you." How could she possibly hate someone she'd once loved so much? She forced herself to meet his gaze head-on. "But that doesn't mean I'm backing down on the project."

He looked as tired as she felt. So much for the peaceful lake town where you could let your cares drift away. Not one of them was getting any sleep in Emerald Lake.

"I know you're not," he said. "Here's the thing. I know we didn't exactly see eye to eye last night."

She raised an eyebrow at that stupendous understatement. "There was practically blood, Nate."

He winced. "Again, I'm a total asshole."

"Don't be so hard on yourself," she said with a small smile. "*Total* might be taking it too far."

It was good to see him start to grin, and despite the words that had been shot out across a scratched-up table at the Tavern, Andi knew she wasn't ready to lose him as a friend. Not when she'd only just found him again.

"You were right. I can see that now. We've got to talk about what happened between us. We can't pretend nothing happened when we were eighteen." He shook his head. "It's just that I honestly didn't realize things had affected me like that."

Appreciating his honesty, she found herself admitting, "Me, either."

"Once we've hashed through everything, said whatever needs to be said, we can leave the past in the past. Where it belongs. You weren't the one making things personal last night. It was me, Andi. I shouldn't have done that. I won't do it again."

Boy, he sounded so sensible now. So different from the man who had been coming at her last night, all emotion and unavoidable feelings.

Andi knew she shouldn't be wanting that intense, difficult Nate back.

But she did.

Because then at least she'd known he cared.

No. That was crazy. Of course, she was happy that they weren't at a total impasse. Of course, she was thrilled that he was willing to discuss the condos with her in greater detail without it becoming a big, heated fight where one of them ended up storming out.

He cleared his throat, looking more than a little nervous. "So I was thinking, what if we each get one night to try to make our point about the condos?"

*One night.*

Her brain—and body—immediately spun off in the worst possible direction, away from condos and proposals and sensible discussions to other nights full of kisses and sweet caresses from their past.

The same past that Nate was so bound and determined to put to rest. The same past she knew she needed to let go of too.

Andi licked her lips, hating her own nervous gesture, but not knowing how to stop the nerves when Nate was this close, his warmth radiating out at her from across the counter.

"I want one night to remind you of everything that's good about Emerald Lake. What do you say? Will you give me one night, Andi?"

Was that really yearning in his voice? Or was she just imagining it was there because that was what she suddenly wanted to hear?

"When?"

"How about I'll take tonight and you take tomorrow night?"

The longing to be with him swelled within her, swift and overpowering, pulling all of her emotions to swirl around inside her chest, right behind her breastbone.

Still she tried with everything she had to tell herself it was the businesswoman saying, "You've got yourself a deal," and not the flesh and blood woman inside.

# Chapter Eight

As nervous as Andi was about spending another night with Nate—especially knowing that they were going to be having "the talk"—she had to smile when she realized where he was taking her.

"I haven't been to a football field since high school," she told him. The new coach was already putting the kids through their paces when she and Nate arrived at the field. "Funny, it looks exactly the same."

Nate grimaced. "No kidding. We're in desperate need of an overhaul. But hey, it still does the job. And the kids still love it. The town still shows up every Friday night. One day we'll get there with something a little shinier."

Looking more carefully, she saw that the bleachers had seen better days, way better if the rust stains on the seats and beams were anything to go by. The goalposts were pretty darn beaten up, too. The seed of an idea flashed into her mind, and Andi made a mental note to think more about it later.

She took a seat on the least dented row only to jump up with a small shriek. It was like sitting on an ice cube. The wind had picked up since they'd left the store, too, and she barely held back a shiver.

"I didn't expect it to be that cold."

"Let's try this instead." Nate laid out the blanket he'd brought onto the seat. "I should have known you'd be cold, that you wouldn't be dressed for the weather."

Sitting down on the blanket, Andi suddenly felt self-conscious, like her dress was all wrong, the same dress she'd put on that morning for an extra dash of confidence, to try and ground herself in who she really was. Only now she was a greenhorn who didn't know how to be "dressed for the weather."

"If I'd known this was where we were going, I would have changed into something else."

Obviously reading between the lines, Nate said, "You look really pretty, Andi. I've always loved you in blue." But even as he complimented her, he looked irritated. "It's my fault. I should have thought this through better."

He tucked the blanket up and over her shoulders and around her lap, until she was completely cocooned in thick wool.

"Fortunately I did think to bring this." He pulled a thermos of hot cocoa out of his bag and poured her a cup.

When was the last time a man had worried about her? she found herself wondering as she burrowed one hand out from under the blanket to grab the cup. When was the last time a man had cared about something as simple as whether she was warm or thirsty?

"Hey Nate, awesome to see you out here!" one of the kids called out. "Any chance you can come run some drills with us?"

Nate grinned. "Howie, meet Andi."

The teenager said hi, and she remembered being that young once, when the entire world was her oyster.

Neither she nor Nate had any idea that it would all implode in the blink of an eye.

"We're just here as spectators tonight, Howie," Nate told him. "I'll work with you guys later in the week, okay?"

But the truth was Andi needed a little space, a little time to catch her breath and figure out an ironclad way to control her reaction to Nate.

"Go run drills," Andi said.

Seeing the way the boy's eyes lit up—Nate was clearly his hero—made her feel even more confident that she was doing the right thing by sending him out onto the football field.

"I'm here for you tonight, Andi. Not them."

But she didn't want to hold him back. Not when she knew that these kids were far more important to him than she could ever be.

"I'm fine. Really. It'll give me some quiet time in the great outdoors. With helping out at the store, I haven't had much of that since I've been back."

Heck, she hadn't had much of that since she'd left at eighteen. She spent most of her time inside either her office or apartment, usually in front of a computer.

For the next hour she watched Nate yell, laugh, and run with the team, and for a moment she was seventeen again, watching him, so young, so beautiful, as he would catch a touchdown pass, grinning up at her in the bleachers as she sat just like this, under a blanket with a thermos of hot chocolate.

But she wasn't seventeen anymore. And not only was he a man who had weathered far more than he should have—she was also making the mistake of finding him a thousand times more beautiful.

She loved the way he focused completely on the kids, singling them out one by one, clearly forgetting that she was sitting in the bleachers. She loved watching how the boys almost seemed to grow bigger from Nate's attention, whether it was his hand on their elbow as he corrected a throw or because he'd just showed them exactly how to evade the defense.

Nate had a very rare, very special gift: he made you feel like he cared. Her father had done that, too; every politician did, but it was different with Nate.

Andi didn't like the way her thoughts were going, didn't like admitting to herself that her father's attention almost always came with an ulterior motive. Whereas Nate simply cared because of who he was.

That was why she had fallen in love with him so long ago.

And why she was having so many problems with her feelings now.

Because how was she supposed to resist the one person who had always been irresistible? Even when they were kids, Nate was the only person who had ever made her think about staying in Emerald Lake. He was the only one who could have made her even consider giving up her dreams.

She shifted so suddenly on the bleachers that the blanket half fell off of her lap.

*Oh no.* That's what this feeling was. It was happening again. All over again. Just one night with him at the Tavern—a night where he hadn't even liked her very much—had her crumbling, about to deviate from her carefully laid plans.

No, she couldn't go there. Falling in love with him the first time had been easy, so natural.

But doing it again would be beyond crazy.

Losing him once had hurt bad enough.

It would destroy her if she let herself fall back in love and then lost him again.

It was just a matter of mind over heart. She needed to make sure she thought with her head, not with the erratically pulsing lump behind her breastbone. She just needed to remember that if this project for the Klein Group went well, she would not only keep her job but might even have the chance of making the leap to partner in the near future.

Still, when practice ended and Nate jogged back over to her, the wild urge to leave, to run, to flee took her over. She could be on the road in minutes, leave her bags behind in her mother's house, head back to the city and never come back to Emerald Lake. She could bury herself in work and forget all about *one night*.

This was precisely why she rarely came back to Emerald Lake. Once she drove across that thin blue line into the Adirondacks it was as if everything inside of her twisted up, turned inside out.

*Calm down, Andi,* she told herself, taking control of her runaway heart with an iron fist. *He doesn't want anything from you anyway. Especially not your heart.*

Nate reached into his bag and pulled out containers of food. "Courtesy of the diner."

She eyed the food suspiciously. "How can that be from the diner? It actually looks good."

He laughed, the sound warming her more than she wanted it to. "Janet took it over a few years ago."

"You're great with those kids."

He raised an eyebrow. "Didn't you hear all the yelling I was doing? Bet the little punks are real happy they asked me to run drills tonight, huh?"

"They were. They know that you yell because you love them."

"I remember when I took the job. I thought I was just there to teach them sports. But that ended up being the smallest part of it. Mostly they just want someone to talk to—or to care about them enough to tell them they're acting stupid. Not all of them have someone at home to expect great things from them."

Silence fell between them, but she didn't reach for the food. Neither did Nate.

"Look," he said, and she knew what was coming. The dreaded talk. "I'm really sorry for what I said to you that night when we were eighteen, Andi. You were just trying to help, and I—" He shook his head. "I shouldn't have lost it like that."

She knew exactly which night Nate was talking about, right after his father had died and she'd rushed home to be with him. The night he'd asked her stay and she'd told him she loved him, that she would help him any way she could, but she just couldn't stay.

And then he'd yelled at her and said they were through.

Shocked that the memory could hurt just as much now as it had then, all Andi could say was, "I'm sorry I wasn't more helpful, Nate. I wish I had been. You don't know how much I wish that things had been different."

"Me, too, Andi. I wish they'd been different, too." He paused, then said, "Can I say one more thing, Andi?"

She wasn't sure she could handle one other thing. Not when it was just the two of them out here under the stars, and he smelled like soap and freshly mowed grass and Nate, and she was holding the blanket in a death grip so she wouldn't reach out for him and tell him that she was still scared and hurt and sorry she'd let him down, but that he'd let her down, too.

"What's that?"

"Thanks for giving me another chance tonight."

Was that what this was? A second chance? For her to pitch her idea to him? For them to save their friendship? Or was it something bigger than either of those things?

"Same here."

"Well, that wasn't too hard, was it?" He couldn't mask the sound of relief in his voice.

Unable to shake that unsettling feeling that the reason it wasn't hard was because they'd barely scratched the surface of their past, Andi made herself smile back.

"Okay then, I'm ready to hear your side of things on the condos. After all, this is your night to convince me I'm wrong."

Only expecting words, she was surprised when he took the cup of cocoa from her hands. "Close your eyes."

She just sat there, not able to follow his instructions so quickly. Not when there was so much trust involved in his simple request to close her eyes.

She'd always trusted him. The problem was, she wasn't sure she trusted herself anymore.

"Here," he said, moving so that he was sitting on the row behind her. "I'll make it easy for you." His hands came down over her eyes.

Warm. He was so incredibly warm.

"Breathe, Andi," he said, his voice low as it whispered across her skin. "I just want you to feel."

Oh, she was feeling all right. Too much, in too many forbidden, off-limits places. And with her sight temporarily taken away, all of her other senses came into high alert.

"I never forgot this smell," she admitted softly. She took one breath and then another, letting the fresh, sweet night air fill her lungs. "Fresh cut grass. The sap on the maple trees. The wind blowing in off the lake."

She wasn't stupid. She knew this was part of his plan, to make her feel everything she'd pushed out of her life. She just couldn't see the point in lying about how much it affected her. Everyone had always thought she was so smart, whereas they'd been fooled by Nate's big muscles, his charming smile. But Andi knew firsthand just how smart he was.

Smart enough to come at her not with facts and figures but with sensation. And emotion. And memories.

The same memories she was trying to close off, shut down.

"I always liked knowing you were in the stands," he said from behind her. Her eyes were closed now, but he didn't pull his hands away from her face. "What do you bet one of those boys on my team has a crush on one of the girls in the stands? From one generation to the next."

Danger. They were heading straight for the danger zone. She could feel it, skin on skin, his heart starting to beat against her back as he leaned into her and said shockingly simple things that played havoc with her insides.

She put her hands over his knuckles to slide his hands

away from her eyes. But even though she was trying to put space between them, she found herself lingering over his touch a moment longer than was strictly necessary.

\*        \*        \*

Nate knew he was overstepping the line, but his problem with resisting Andi was getting worse, not better. He hadn't brought her here tonight so that he could touch her, so that he could bring it all back to the two of them again. But he hadn't been able to help himself. Not when she was so easy to be with. Not when she was so adorable, looking out at him from beneath the big blanket.

Damn it. He needed to stop this insanity. Hell, he should have known he was still lying to himself again this morning when he had told himself they could put the past behind them and keep their focus on the condos tonight. Not to mention what he'd said—or hadn't—at the Adirondack Council meeting that morning. When they asked him if there were any building plans the council should be aware of, he'd said no. He hadn't even told his assistant, Catherine, about Andi's plans yet.

For some reason, he couldn't stop himself from protecting Andi. Even though he was damn sure it was going to come back to bite him in the ass later.

Moving off the seat behind her, making sure to put her out of reaching distance, he said in a gruff voice, "Tell me about the store. Tell me how it's been working there these past couple of days."

"It's surprisingly engaging."

"Why surprising?"

"You know I never planned to have anything to do with the store as an adult," she said. She held up a hand and added, "But before you jump all over me again with the whole 'You're not from here anymore' rant, the truth is there are so many more facets to running Lake Yarns than I ever realized."

"I'm an ass, Andi," he said again, wishing he'd never said those things to her.

"Yes, we've already established that," she said in a crisp voice. "Sorry. I didn't mean to bring it up again." She shook her head. "Okay, I'm officially over it. For good."

He didn't believe her, not when he could still see hurt flickering in her eyes.

"Tell me about the facets."

She almost seemed surprised by her smile, by the laughter that bubbled out of her mouth. "You're so good at acting interested."

"It's not an act. I am interested."

And he was. Anything and everything she said mattered to him. They could have been talking about paper towels, and he had a feeling he'd be sitting here rapt, hanging on her every word.

"Well, beyond inventory and ordering, there's this whole layer of interaction with their customers. Not just on a business level but on a personal level." Her eyes warmed. "My mother and grandmother really care about these women, about what they're going through with their marriages, their kids, if they're trying to go back to school, or if their husbands are looking for work. And somehow the yarn has a place in all of that."

"I've never knit, but I can see how it would be something to pull people together." He gestured to the field. "Like football."

She nodded, her face glowing. Nate wondered, did she have any idea how excited she became from talking about her family's store?

She licked her lips again. And didn't she know she needed to stop doing that already before he went and helped her out with it? Because, damn it, it was so damn tempting to just give into the urge to kiss her. He'd wanted to do it from the first moment he'd seen her standing outside the yarn store, had been dying to know if she still tasted the same as she had at eighteen, as sweet as sugar.

And then she was looking at him the way she always used to, her mouth slightly open, her lower lip damp from where she'd licked it, and he couldn't stop himself from shifting closer and—

One of the kids ran by blowing a whistle, and both he and Andi jumped apart.

"Gotcha, Nate!"

But Nate wasn't laughing at the too-close save.

He hadn't come here to try and woo Andi back into his life. He'd come here to remind her of why this small town was so great. So simple and pure. He'd come to make the girl who didn't want to feel, feel. He'd thought he was smarter than this, that there was no way he was going to allow himself to be swept back up into her.

Suddenly, though, Nate wasn't sure he had it in him to keep holding out. Which wasn't a good thing at all, because thanks to his brilliant suggestion earlier, he still owed Andi a night. *One night* that just might break every vow he'd made about staying away from her in the past ten years.

"It's getting pretty cold out. I'll take you back home."

But as she helped him clean up the food and neatly

folded the blanket into a perfect square, even as he tried to tell himself that he was glad they'd escaped potential danger, he couldn't push back the regret at how her previously open expression—when she was talking about her family's store, when she was waiting for him to kiss her— was completely shut down again.

And he couldn't deny that being this close to her and yet so far away made him miss her more than he ever had before.

Minutes later, he parked in front of her house and got out to walk her inside.

"You don't have to walk me to the door."

"Of course I do."

Didn't the guys she dated walk her in at the end of the night?

The thought stopped him cold: one, because this wasn't a date; two, because just the thought of Andi going on a date with some stranger made him sick to his stomach.

*She should have been his.*

"Nate."

My god, he thought, as he looked at her face in the moonlight. She was so beautiful when she smiled like that, a little nervous but so determined to be strong anyway.

"Your night." She gave him a half smile. "It was a good one. Thank you for sharing it with me. And I wanted to let you know, it would be great if your sister came with us tomorrow night. You've already been away from her the past two nights. I need to get my project details ironed out, but I understand that you have a family, Nate."

Andi was right. He didn't ever spend this much time away from his sister. But the truth was, he knew Madison liked having her own space from time to time, especially as she was getting older. He had just never been able to give it to her before.

He'd had to hold on extra tight because she was all he had.

"Madison has choir late tomorrow night. My next-door neighbor can stay with her until I get back."

"In that case, if we leave early, we can get home early so you don't miss too much time with her. Will five o'clock work?"

She was sweet to think of his sister. So damn sweet it was hard to remember all the reasons why kissing her was such a bad idea.

"It's perfect."

"Great. See you tomorrow night." Her voice was cool, calm, but her hand was shaking as she opened the door and went inside.

He shouldn't have been glad to see that the girl no one could ever fluster still wasn't immune to being with him.

But he was.

\* \* \*

Andi's mother was curled up under a blanket on a couch in the living room when she walked in. The lamp beside Carol was still on and there were needles and yarn on her lap. Andi was about to say hello when she realized her mother's eyes were closed.

When she was a teenager, her mother would wait up for her like this. So many times, Andi had come home from a midnight bonfire to find her mother right there on the couch, knitting, waiting.

Suddenly Andi realized what a comfort that had been.

To know that she was coming home to someone who cared about her.

She'd only been home a couple of nights, and yet her mother was right there.

Caring about her.

Wanting her mother to know she was back safely, Andi knelt down in front of her mother and put a hand over hers. "I'm home, Mom."

Carol's eyes fluttered open, a smile moving onto her lips when she saw Andi. "Did I fall asleep?"

Andi nodded, then gently said, "You don't have to wait up for me anymore."

But her mother just shook her head. "I know you're all grown up now, honey, but you'll always be my little girl."

And that was just how Andi felt, like a little girl who needed her mommy. And when her stomach grumbled and Carol offered, "How about I make you a snack before bed?" Andi decided to let the warmth of being home wrap itself around her like one of her mother's knitted blankets.

Just for a little while.

# Chapter Nine

Determined that her "one night" would be as good as the one Nate had given her, Andi was hard at work on her laptop early the next morning. She pulled up data on tourism in the Adirondack Park, on its residents, their career options, and spending patterns. She made phone calls and set up appointments.

Knowing she should be glad to finally get a productive day in, Andi found that her mind kept wandering. Not just to Nate, but to Lake Yarns, too. This was the first day she hadn't spent in Lake Yarns, and strangely she kept wondering what was going on in the store.

Saving her file, she decided to drop by the store with coffee, say hello to her mother and grandmother, and then come back and work some more. First, though, there was one call she needed to make.

Her boss picked up on the first ring. "Andrea. How's life in the backwater?"

She winced at Craig's words, even though she'd always referred to Emerald Lake like that.

"Good. I'm progressing on the project, but I want to

run something by you before I call the Klein Group. A new boat launch is great, and I still think they should do it, but I think there's something else that will be even better for the town: a new high school football field, lights, stands, locker rooms."

A very intelligent man—ruthless, some might say, when it came to making money—Craig said, "You're having trouble convincing the town."

"Small towns operate differently from the rest of the world. High school football is practically a religion here."

"I'll take your word for it," he said, and she could tell he was already moving past their conversation. "Just do whatever you need to do to make it happen. We're all counting on you here."

\*     \*     \*

Andi walked into Lake Yarns carrying a tray of hot coffee to find the place packed with kids.

"The fifth graders are paying us a visit today," her mother said with a smile when she gratefully took a cup from Andi.

"Where's Grandma?"

"She decided to take it easy again today."

Worry about her grandmother's health rose up again. "You should have called me," Andi told her mother. "She should have called me."

"You've already done so much."

"You know I haven't. Tell me where you need me."

Five minutes later, Andi had a girl on each side of her, correcting their cast ons, laughing as the boys pretended their knitting needles were swords. She hadn't spent much time with kids, not since her babysitting days. Children had no part in her world in the city.

"I just can't get it," one of the girls in the back corner cried, throwing her needles and tangled yarn onto the ground.

Andi was already heading over there when she realized those were Nate's eyes looking back at her in defiance. This was the little girl with the pigtails and the missing tooth. This was the little baby whose diaper she had changed.

Andi nearly stumbled as she reached for the seat beside Madison and slid into it.

Forcing herself to take a deep breath, Andi said, "I was really frustrated, too, when I started."

"Knitting is stupid."

Andi wasn't about to tell her it wasn't. Not when she'd spent two decades thinking exactly the same thing.

"Why would anyone waste their time on this kind of stuff?"

Andi shrugged. "I guess they like it."

"Why?"

Andi settled back into her chair, looked around the store at the laughter, the concentration, the colors, the creativity. "I suppose knitting makes them feel good."

"Good how?"

When had Madison become interested? Andi suddenly wondered. For that matter, when had she?

Knitting had never been her thing. She was sure of it. But then, up until she was Madison's age, hadn't she been there every Monday night, knitting blankets for her dolls or a scarf and mittens for winter?

"It can be fun to use your hands to make something," Andi said slowly. "It's not just how soft the yarn is, how pretty the pattern is, it's the magic of it."

"Magic?"

Andi startled at that. Had she really just said that knitting was magic?

She thought about the way her grandmother always looked happiest when she was knitting. Her mother, too. Anything that could make someone feel that good had to be magic.

Andi nodded. "Yup."

"I guess you could show me how to do it," Madison said grudgingly, even though Andi hadn't offered.

Hiding her smile, Andi said, "Sure."

\*     \*     \*

Andi was heading back toward her mother's house to get ready for her night with Nate when she heard voices coming from her grandmother's cottage.

She didn't know whether to laugh or cry when she opened the cottage door. Her great-aunt Celeste was concentrating on the lettering of her SAVE THE CAROUSEL sign. Dorothy and Helen from the knitting group were there, too.

"Grandma, what are you doing?"

"Just what it looks like," she said matter-of-factly. "Getting a jump on our campaign. This is just the start. Everyone in town that we've told about the carousel wants to help."

Andi pushed down the hurt that rose up at the realization that her grandmother had so little faith in her, not to mention the fact that she hated knowing they were on opposite sides of her proposal: first her and Nate, now her and her grandmother—and all of these women.

A sharp pang landed smack-dab in the middle of her chest. It felt like they were all against her.

The insiders versus the girl who had never belonged.

There were so many things she wanted to say to Evelyn, but she made herself stick to her grandmother's health first.

"You're supposed to be resting."

"I'll rest when we're done here."

Fine. Andi would skip right to point two.

"I told you I was going to talk to my client about the carousel, Grandma. You don't need to do all of this." Not yet anyway.

"You gave me no guarantees, honey, and I've always thought it's better to take things into one's own hands."

And the truth was, Andi couldn't help but be impressed with how quickly her grandmother and her sister and friends had put everything together. A part of her wanted to jump in and help...but she couldn't fight this battle for her grandmother. Not when it would mean fighting against herself, her client, and her future with her consulting firm. Not when it would be one more step toward failing—and away from the brass ring she'd always gone for.

"Don't feel bad," Dorothy said, finally looking up from her computer where she was doing god knows what. "We know you're just doing your job."

Andi bit back a reply. Of course, she didn't feel bad. This project was going to be great for the town. Totally great.

Realizing she wasn't going to be able to stop these women—they were clearly relishing their task too much—she decided instead to see if she could get some more background on the carousel, something she could share with her clients that would help them understand why it was so important for Emerald Lake.

"Tell me about the carousel. Tell me what it means to each of you."

Her great-aunt Celeste looked up with a smile. "Rosie used to love riding on it so much, didn't she, Evie?"

Andi's grandmother nodded, smiling at the memory. "Our little sister would always try to stand on top of the horses like she was in the circus."

"Mother thought it was too dangerous, but Rosie never fell. Not once."

"Every time I walk by that carousel I think of her," Celeste said softly.

Andi had never met her great-aunt Rose. She had disappeared a long, long time ago in the 1940s when she was twenty. No one had ever heard from her again.

Andi noticed that Dorothy had stopped typing on her laptop. "What about you, Dorothy?"

"We were very poor when I was little girl."

Andi was surprised to hear it. Dorothy looked so classy and put together.

"We didn't have money for any extras, barely had enough to keep ourselves clothed and fed. Remember, Evelyn?"

"You used to wear my old shoes."

Dorothy snorted. "Old? You'd barely worn them before you told your daddy you needed another pair, and he bought them for you."

"Did you hate me for it?" Evelyn asked. Everyone in the room stopped and turned to Dorothy, waiting for her answer.

Andi could see them so clearly—two girls in school together, two friends who came from such different backgrounds, who had such different things. For a second, she was reminded of the way she and Catherine had once been.

"Sometimes."

"I hated you sometimes, too," Evelyn said, shocking all of them. "You had so much freedom."

Dorothy smiled. "Well, more than you lot, anyway, with all of your fancy money and expectations. But you were asking about the carousel, weren't you, Andi? Not the history of two old friends."

Andi worked to bring herself back to the carousel, but it was hard when she couldn't stop wondering about what her grandmother had said about freedom. What hadn't Evelyn felt free to do? Love Carlos instead of the man who had become Andi's grandfather?

"It was five cents for a ride, but one day a year it was free."

"The Fall Festival," Celeste said.

"We would finish our chores early and run over to get in line to ride it over and over."

"Why was riding on the carousel so great?"

Andi vaguely remembered enjoying carousel rides as a little girl, but she couldn't imagine that would be a cherished memory in her eighties.

"You have to understand," her grandmother said, "we didn't have roller coasters or TV. Just the sand and the sun and the lake. And the carousel."

"If it was so important to all of you, then why haven't you tried to fix it up or get it running before?"

Andi's grandmother looked her right in the eye. "You're right. We should have done something about the carousel long before now. But sometimes it takes almost losing something to realize just how much it really means to you."

"I have to confess," Andi said. "I still don't completely get it."

"Maybe that's because listening to our stories isn't the same as telling one of your own."

Andi shook her head, quickly saying, "I don't have a carousel story."

But then one came at her, spinning back into her conscious mind as if it were the present, not the past.

She was five years old and her kindergarten day was over. She walked outside onto the playground expecting to see her mother. But—oh my!—her father was there instead.

*"Ice cream, Andi. We're going to get ice cream."*

She was excited, so excited she ran away from Nate and Catherine without saying good-bye. She got a double scoop of rainbow sherbet, but she was so intent on holding her father's hand that it kept almost falling over in her free hand.

Her father had wanted to sit and eat their ice cream on the carousel. He held her cone while she got on one of the matched pairs of horses, then he climbed onto the other. She'd loved this, just the two of them. The carousel didn't even run anymore; it hadn't been running since long before Andi was born. But it was fun to sit on it and pretend with her father. So much fun she could hardly believe it.

He was smiling, a bigger smile than she'd ever seen before. *"Always go for the brass ring, Andi. No matter what the obstacles are, always go for what you want and don't give up."*

Andi started in her seat. That had always been her father's mantra for her, but until now, she hadn't realized that was the first time he'd said it to her.

"Andi, honey, are you all right?"

She looked up at her grandmother. "How old was I when Daddy won his first election?"

Evelyn thought about it for a moment. "You must have been around five."

Andi worked to keep her expression clear. All these years, she'd thought her father had been so happy because he finally got to spend the day with her.

Now she knew, that was the day he had become senator.

He'd chosen her to celebrate with him. But only that once. After that, he'd been busy in Washington, D.C., always gone when she needed him.

Was this the reason she hadn't cared about getting rid of the carousel? Not just because it was falling apart, but because instead of associating joy with it, there was pain.

The pain of being left behind.

Uncomfortable with not being able to put everything into a nice, neat little box, Andi turned back to her grandmother with the intention of asking more pointed questions about the actual worth—rather than the unquantifiable emotional worth—of the carousel.

But Evelyn had that faraway look in her eyes...the very expression Andi suspected she herself wore whenever she fell back into her loving memories of Nate.

# Chapter Ten

1941

Evelyn had never been happier to be outside. After a week of straight rain, she'd all but begged her mother to let her head to the train station to pick up the special ordered napkins for the museum gala. Anything to get out of the house...a house that suddenly felt stifling.

Waiting on the side of the train tracks for the freight train to arrive, she closed her eyes and turned her face up into the bright fall sun. She was finally relaxing, soaking up the precious rays of warmth, when goose bumps suddenly popped out all across the surface of her skin.

Quickly opening her eyes, she whirled around, only to look straight in the face of the man she'd gone out of her way to avoid for weeks.

Carlos.

But just because she had succeeded in avoiding him, didn't mean she'd been able to stop thinking about what he'd said to her.

He had point-blank called her a scared little girl.

*The worst part of it all was the fact that she'd contin-*
*ued to work on his sweater. No amount of reasoning with*
*herself had gotten her to put it down yet.*

*Not when Carlos had made her feel more alive and yet,*
*at the same time, more confused than she'd ever been.*
*Scared, too.*

*Darn it.*

*"Hello, pretty girl."*

*She blushed, even as she tried to respond in a stern*
*voice, "My name is Evelyn."*

*"Hello, pretty Evelyn."*

*She didn't want to smile, but it was really hard to keep*
*her lips from turning up. Still, she wasn't going to get*
*into another conversation like the one at the building site,*
*wasn't going to walk away from Carlos with her stomach*
*all twisted in knots again.*

*She turned her gaze away from him to stare down the*
*length of the railroad tracks at the approaching freight*
*train. She simply needed to ignore the continuing prickles*
*of awareness all across her body—and inside her chest,*
*where her heart was beating way too fast, way too hard.*

*"You ever just hopped on one of these things and seen*
*where it takes you?"*

*"No." What a ridiculous thought. "Of course not."*

*But oh, how quickly did that ridiculous thought become*
*tempting as she collected her package and started to turn*
*away.*

*"Come on, pretty Evelyn. Let's have an adventure." He*
*hopped into the open freight car and held out his hand to*
*her.*

*Evelyn had a moment of panic at who could be watch-*
*ing them, at who might report this back to her parents. But*

*amazingly, they were the only two people on the platform today, the only two people waiting for a delivery from the train.*

*Still she shook her head. "Are you kidding? They'll chase us off. We can't just hop on and take a ride without buying a ticket and knowing where we're going."*

*He didn't argue with her, and she was unaccountably disappointed. Stupid girl, she should be glad that he was letting her off the hook this easily.*

*The train started to move, but instead of walking away, instead of heading back home where her mother and sisters were waiting for her, Evelyn couldn't take her eyes off of Carlos as he pointed to the moving wheels.*

*"Oh no, it's happening. Do you see that?"*

*She had no idea what he was talking about. All she could see was the rolling of the metal wheels against the iron track.*

*"What?" she finally snapped, as the train started to pick up speed. "What am I supposed to be seeing?"*

*He gestured to the world around them. "Life is passing you by."*

*She felt it then, a sudden surge of anger mixed with something even wilder. An urge for freedom, for adventure, for passion, for everything she'd dreamed of for so long but had been too scared to reach out for because none of that was part of the master grand plan for her life.*

*Before she realized it, she was running after the train.*

*"Jump and I'll catch you. I promise."*

*And then she was jumping, and he pulled her into the freight car with him, both of them crashing together onto the wooden floor. As the two of them laughed, she felt so free, free enough that none of the rules she'd lived her life by until now seemed to matter anymore.*

*But then, as their laughter died down for a second and she got her bearings, Evelyn realized she'd never been this close to a man before, never found herself in a tangle of limbs and heat before.*

*For propriety's sake at least, she moved away from him, straightened her skirts, and sat up in as dignified a manner as she could given the circumstances.*

*"I've been waiting to see that smile, pretty Evelyn. To hear you laugh."*

*His words, the way he was looking at her made it hard for her to breathe and to say, "This is crazy."*

*"And life is short."*

*There was a darkness in his eyes as he said this, and she couldn't stop wondering again about where he'd come from and why he was working for her father.*

*Oh god. Her father. He was going to kill her. She felt her skin grow hot and then cold as she thought about what he'd do, the way he would yell, if he ever found out about her impromptu—completely unladylike—train trip.*

*"We need to get off at the next town." Her voice sounded way too shaky for her liking, and she forcefully steadied it before adding, "I shouldn't have done this. I know better."*

*The train slowed down at the next stop, and she was more than a little surprised when Carlos helped her climb off, even more surprised to find him getting off right behind her with both of their packages in his hands.*

*He looked at the timetable posted on the wall. "The next train back won't be here for an hour."*

*She tried to tamp down on it this time, that itch in the back of her neck, that wild yearning coming over her again. But one taste of adventure had given her a craving for more.*

*She wanted "more" so badly that she could taste it on her tongue, almost as if someone had given her one short lick of the sweetest lollipop before wrapping it back up and putting it away—out of her reach but where she could still see it and long for it—for good.*

*"Well," she found herself saying, despite the fact that she knew better. "If we're going to be stuck here anyway, I might as well show you the waterfall."*

*His beautiful mouth quirked up slightly at the corner, and when he raised his eyebrows, she raised hers right back. This adventure might have been his idea, but now it was her turn to show him things he hadn't seen.*

*Fortunately the waterfall was only a few minutes' walk from the train station through the pretty red covered bridge. Soon they were standing in front of a cascading wall of water that arched off the rocks toward them. Warm from their short walk, feeling more confined than usual by the tight long sleeves of her dress, Evelyn moved closer to the cool spray of water.*

*Carlos's warm voice caressed her. "Have you ever seen the back side of water?"*

*She frowned. "What are you talking about? Water doesn't have sides."*

*"Sure it does. The back side looks completely different. Come here and I'll show you."*

*But this time, she knew better. Heck, it was her stupid wild yearnings that had gotten her here, wasn't it? Carlos was dangerous. She'd known that from the start, right from that first conversation when he had started unraveling her control as if she was simply a strand of tightly wound yarn.*

*"I can see it just fine from here, thank you."*

*"It's okay to be scared, pretty Evelyn. But life is unpredictable. Don't wait too long to take a risk."*

*"Stop calling me scared!"* She turned on him in sudden fury, not just for constantly goading her, but at herself for all the things she wanted but was so scared to want, so scared to let herself feel. *"I'm here, aren't I? I got on that freight train, didn't I?"*

*"Yes, pretty Evelyn, you did."*

But she could hear what he wasn't saying. That just because she'd taken one step didn't mean there weren't more in front of her, just waiting for her to decide if she was brave enough to take them.

*"Fine. Show me the back side of water."*

And this time when he reached for her hand, she wasn't distracted by the movement of a train, wasn't breathless from running...and she felt his touch all the way down past her skin, past her bones, past the blood that moved in her veins.

She felt his gentle touch all the way down into her heart as he carefully led her over slippery rocks to the small bank of dirt between the waterfall and the rock wall.

*"Do you see it now?"*

The water was a thick wall of movement, mesmerizing as it poured down from the rocks above their heads. It was nature's misty curtain falling with such grace and ease.

*"You're right."* She breathed in wonder. *"Everything does look different from the other side."*

She could feel Carlos's eyes on her, knew he wasn't looking at the strange shape of the trees, the sky, the mountains through the water. Her mouth tingled in anticipation of the kiss she knew was coming.

But then he was saying, "Come on, pretty Evelyn, let's get you out of here before you get too wet," and that was when she realized, just as he hadn't forced her to get on the train with him, he wouldn't force her to kiss him, either.

If she wanted a kiss from Carlos, she'd have to be the one to take that step.

To choose not just his kiss...but him, too.

## Chapter Eleven

Nate was miles beyond impressed with the night Andi had set up for them. She'd taken him to Loon Lake, another Adirondack town thirty minutes down Route 8. As soon as they'd parked the car, she started to introduce him to families who had bought into the condominiums that had been built on the lake a handful of years ago.

Again and again, men and women told him how thrilled they were to actually be able to own a small piece of property in the Adirondacks. For some of them, it was an escape from the pressure of their real lives. For others it had been a chance to start over again, to build a new life.

She took him down the main street, busy and beautifully lit even on a weekday in fall, and introduced him to store owners who told him how glad they were to be able to keep their doors open all year-round rather than having to rely on a big summer and winter to sustain their bottom lines.

She pointed out how careful the town had been with its expansion, showed the ways in which the people had been very firm about staying away from chain stores, restaurants, and arcades.

According to Andi's research, Loon Lake was making a name for itself as not just the perfect weekend getaway from nearby cities but as an ideal place to summer and retire and start new businesses as well.

"Loon Lake embodies everything I've been talking about. Development without going in the wrong direction. No casinos. Not too many tourist shops. The only thing about it that isn't really ideal is the fact that the lake is so small. They can't have any motorized boats on it or even the bigger sailboats."

She turned her gorgeous eyes to him, a small smile on those beautiful lips. "You've had a good time tonight, haven't you? Talking to everyone, learning about their town."

"I have. I should have done it before," he admitted. "You're a very impressive salesperson, Andi."

She'd made reservations at a restaurant on the lake and they'd stepped out onto the porch with their drinks. Clouds had come in during the past hour, completely covering the moon. Nate could smell rain in the air.

But the weather wasn't the only thing shifting. The mood between them was shifting, too, as they both let themselves sink more and more back into the comfort—and pleasure—of being with one another again.

"I met your sister today at Lake Yarns." Andi turned to look at him, so beautiful in the faint moonlight that his breath hitched in his chest. "She's fantastic."

He didn't bother to hide his pride. "Madison is a really good kid. I got lucky with her."

"And she got lucky with you." Andi's voice was soft, filled with emotion she didn't bother to conceal.

Nate couldn't stop himself from moving closer, not even when Andi nervously tried to put the conversation back on safer ground by saying, "I realized the other night that it's been a long time since I've been in the lake. Any lake."

He moved a little closer again, unable to keep his distance after such a good night with the woman he'd once loved. "How long?"

"Years maybe."

He didn't think, just plucked her glass from her fingers and put it next to his on the rail of the porch. "Let's go."

She laughed that beautiful laugh he loved hearing so much and took a step back. "Maybe next summer when it's warm again."

"No." He took her hand in his. "Right now."

He had her halfway down the stairs to the beach before she could react, before she could protest and say it was too cold to be doing this, that they had reservations and they were going to get all sandy. He took her partway down the beach away from the eyes of the people inside the restaurant.

"The water will probably feel better with your shoes off," he teased.

"You were always full of ideas."

"You forgot to add the word *good* in that last sentence."

"No I didn't."

God, he loved this. Teasing her. Her teasing him back. Hearing the laughter in her voice.

"If you're really going to make me go through with this," she finally said, "I'll need to roll up my jeans."

"No one could ever make you do anything you didn't want to do, Andi."

He felt her hand tense in his a split second before she said, "You're going to have to let go of my hand so I can take care of my pants."

He grinned in the dark, glad that she was going along with his impromptu change in her plans for the night, glad that she was embracing adventure again. Even a small one like walking into a freezing cold lake.

After they had both kicked off their shoes and socks and rolled up their pants, she looked out at the water and said, "It's going to be cold."

He held out his hand for hers again. "We'll get cold together."

He felt rather than saw her hesitation before she took his outstretched hand. Finally she slipped her cold fingers through his. Together they walked into the lake, and he heard her quick intake of breath at the feeling of the icy water.

"Refreshing."

He laughed out loud at her sarcasm. "That's definitely one way of putting it."

"Do you remember, we all used to dive into the lake after football games? We were crazy."

"The kids still do it, you know."

It was so dark he could barely see the white flash of her smile. "You're kidding? Do you ever go in with them?"

"After every game." He could swear there was something vibrating through her hand to his, an unspoken desire to go even deeper than their shared memories. "Come to the game this Friday, Andi. Jump into the lake with us."

"No way."

"Chicken?"

"More like old enough to know better. In fact"—she

tried to pull him back out of the water—"my feet are knowing better right now."

But instead of getting out, he pulled her in deeper and she gasped. "Nate! What are you doing?"

He would have told her if he knew, if he had a clue just what he was trying to get himself into, but before he could respond, fat drops of water started falling down on them. Moments later the sky opened up Noah's ark–style.

"I saw a boathouse over there," Nate said, pulling her down the beach.

"Shouldn't we head back to the restaurant?"

"The boathouse is closer."

Sixty seconds later they were out of the storm, taking shelter in the small covered boathouse with one faint lightbulb hanging from the ceiling. Rain was lashing out across the dark lake and the wind had kicked in big-time.

Andi wiped her hair away from her eyes. "Oh my god, we're soaked."

Her clothes were plastered to her, her thin, wet sweater and form-fitting black pants leaving very little to the imagination. Too little for Nate's peace of mind.

"This wasn't at all what I had planned for the rest of the night," she said frowning.

"It's been good, Andi. Real good."

She shivered and he scanned the boathouse, finally finding what he was looking for in the corner.

"Here," he said, wrapping the towel around her back.

"Thanks." She wrapped it all the way around her. "Isn't there another one?"

"Nope."

"This one is big enough for us to share, Nate."

There was nothing he wanted more than to get in there

with her under the towel, pressed up against her, her heart beating against his.

"That's probably not a good idea, Andi."

"You're wet. The wind is blowing. It's a good idea."

No, it wasn't. But there was no denying her.

Or himself.

He moved closer, and she held open the corners of the towel to let him in. He stifled a groan as her arms came around him, closing the towel around both of them. She was tall, but he was taller, and her head fit against his shoulder. Just like it always had.

"Better?"

He could feel her breath against his skin, was burning up from the heat of her warm body against his. He could barely get the word out, the word that was both complete truth and a complete lie all at the same time.

"Better."

And then she looked up at him, and the desire sliding across her features, along with a deep, elemental yearning he saw in her eyes, had him damning the consequences.

"Do you have any idea how badly I want to kiss you, Andi? Right here. Right now. Just one kiss so I can finally know if you taste as sweet as you used to. So sweet I've never been able to find anything else like it."

It was the only out he could give her, the chance to get the hell out of this boathouse and back to the safety of her mother's big house on the lake.

Instead of running, her eyes dropped to his mouth, the pulse in her throat beating a wild rhythm.

"Just one kiss," she echoed in a breathless whisper.

And then before he could kiss her, her hands were in his hair and her mouth was slanting across his.

Her mouth was soft, warm, sweet. She moaned softly into his mouth, and he uncovered the lemon and bubbles of the drink she'd been sipping outside the restaurant.

She was sweet. So sweet.

All these years he'd kept away from alcohol, not wanting to risk falling into the trap his father had. But Andi's mouth was more addictive than anything he'd ever known.

*She was the biggest risk of all* was the only sane thought left in his head, but this wasn't about sanity. This was about taking everything he'd wanted, needed for so long, from the only woman who had ever really mattered to him.

He cupped her jaw in his hands, holding her steady for his onslaught, and Nate lost track of his surroundings as he made love to her mouth, nipping at her full lower lip, tasting the corners where her lips came together with the tip of his tongue. Moving his mouth temporarily away from those sweet lips, he ran kisses across her jawline, then down into the hollow of her neck to taste that pulse point that beat so wildly for him.

Andi gasped with pleasure, her chest rising and falling against his, and more than a decade of self-control shattered inside Nate as he kissed her.

"Andi, sweetheart," he whispered against her skin. "We need to get out of here."

"Nate?"

His name was a soft question on her lips, but when he reached out to brush the hair back from her face and her eyes locked with his, instead of desire, he saw panic move in.

"Nate. Oh no." She inched away from him, but they were tangled up so tightly against each other beneath the towel that she couldn't make any headway. "I shouldn't have…we shouldn't—"

*Damn it.* He let loose a long, harsh breath.

"Don't you think I know that, Andi?" Her eyes widened at his words, at the touch of his hand on her chin as he tilted her head back up to his and forced her to meet his eyes, to see the truth of his feelings for her on his face. "But do you really think either one of us can help it?"

She sucked in a shaky breath. "It was just supposed to be one kiss."

He should have stopped. He'd felt her vulnerability in the way her lips trembled beneath his. He knew he couldn't afford to lose his heart to her again when she was going to be leaving the lake soon.

It was the inescapable anger at himself for losing control—not just giving into his physical desire for Andi, but worse, giving into the emotions for her that had never gone away—that had him spitting out the words, "Trust me, I don't want to be feeling this way about you any more than you want to feel it about me," before he could grab them back.

And this time when Andi's eyes met his, there wasn't any heat in them anymore. Only an icy cold that reminded him of that night so long ago when he'd told her to leave.

# Chapter Twelve

Andi didn't have to push out of Nate's arms because he'd already let her go.

How could she have done that? How could she have so recklessly—so stupidly—kissed him?

She hadn't been able to help herself, had been utterly incapable of standing so close to Nate without wanting to get closer. He was contentment. Comfort. Warmth. Familiarity.

But none of those things had made their relationship work in the past. Didn't she know better than to think comfort and warmth—or incredible kisses—would make things work out for them now? Facts were facts. They were two very different people with very different goals. Just like her mother and father had been.

Andi definitely didn't want to repeat her parents' marriage—one person staying and waiting, one person going and doing, even as they both professed to love each other.

Now, although it was still cold in the boathouse, as they stood in their wet clothes and faced each other down, Andi couldn't stop hearing his words on repeat in her head.

*"Trust me, I don't want to be feeling this way about you any more than you want to feel it about me."*

Every part of her was smarting, and she barely noticed the towel falling off her shoulders as the hurt, the anger, came bubbling up.

"Go ahead, Nate. I want to hear you say it this time. I want to finally hear the truth of what you really think of me."

His face was tight. Harder than most people had ever seen it. "Don't push me, Andi. Not here. Not now. We both need to calm down."

Something inside her chest tightened, locking back down where it had been about to crack open. She knew Nate so well, knew how hard it was to push him past the charming, easygoing guy that he was at his core. She also knew him well enough to hit him right where it hurt.

"I'm sick and tired of being calm, of trying to pretend there isn't a huge abyss between us, that it isn't overflowing with all the things we aren't saying to each other. It's time for both us to come clean. Here. Now. We don't leave until this is over." She crossed her arms over her chest. "Go ahead, Nate, hit me with your best shot."

"You want my best shot, Andi? How about the fact that you betrayed me. You were the one person I knew I could count on. When everything went to hell, I knew, *knew* that you were going to be there for me. You always said we could survive anything. But when anything came, when life wasn't just a big garden of roses, you were out of there so fast it made my head spin."

He didn't yell the words at her, but they were almost more powerful for the lack of volume. They might have caught her off guard, might have crushed her, if she hadn't already covered herself in a suit of invisible armor, the same suit she'd been wearing for ten long years.

Ever since the boy she'd loved had been just one more person to tell her that she didn't belong in his world.

"I left because you sent me away, Nate. You told me I was in the way, that you needed to focus on your sister and not a long-distance relationship. How can you blame me for going when you were the one who didn't want me there?"

She'd only seen him look at her like this once—when he'd told her to get out of his life.

"Hell, Andi, you say you want to get it all out once and for all, but you're not actually going to admit culpability for a damn thing, are you?"

She wasn't eighteen anymore. She was going to stand up for herself this time. "Give me one reason to accept the blame and I'll take it."

"I was losing it, Andi. My dad had just shot himself in the head. I was still grieving over my mom. I didn't know how the hell I was going to be able to take care of Madison, or if they were even going to let me keep her. You should have known all those things. You should have known I didn't mean it when I told you to go. You should have known I was scared. You should have known I needed you. But you didn't. You were the only person I had left that loved me, and you walked away."

Reeling from the weight of his enormous expectations, Andi shot back, "I was eighteen years old! What did you expect from me? I loved you, and I was hurting for you so bad that it felt like my pain, too. Of course, I wanted to help you. Of course, I wanted to be there for you. But did you really think I was going to drop all of my dreams, that I was going to give up my entire life before it even began?"

Nate looked flat-out disgusted with her. "No, Andi. You're right. None of it is your fault. It's mine. You were never going to sink so low as to actually end up with the trailer trash you said you loved, were you? Not when you had such big plans to go take care of. Not when you had so many big dreams to go achieve."

No. No way. She wouldn't let him go there.

"How dare you say that. I never thought you were trailer trash."

"You sure about that, sweetheart?"

Oh god, no, he couldn't be calling her that now. Not when he'd once used the endearment with such love and now the word was underwritten with sarcasm.

"Don't call me that." And she wouldn't let him rewrite history, either. "We were going to achieve our dreams together, Nate. You were saving money to come out to be with me in the city. You were taking classes at night. I never planned to do it without you, you knew that."

"Don't try to rewrite history, Andi. You spent one month at that fancy college and you started changing. Not just your clothes, not just your friends, not just the way you talked or the things you talked about. You saw bigger things, the things your father had always taught you to want, the things you were already chasing. Fact is, you've never been able to stop and enjoy what you already have because you're always looking ahead for the next thing."

Each beat of her heart was a throb of pain. Still, Nate could say whatever he wanted to about her, but bringing her father into it was stepping over the line. Way over. "Don't you dare talk about my father like that. Don't you dare try to bring him into our mess just because you were intimidated by my goals and dreams."

"Not intimidated, Andi. Just not interested."

"Don't lie to me, Nate. You were going to play college football in Syracuse until your mother died, and you put it off temporarily to help your father with the baby. And then it was all ripped away from you. Don't you know how much I wanted your chances back for you? Don't you know how much I wanted you to have the same opportunities that I did?"

All the while as she spoke, Andi waited for Nate's expression to change, for him to bend a little bit, but clearly she was going to have to keep waiting.

"You haven't changed at all, have you? You still think you know what's best for everyone else, still think you know what everyone else should do. It was your plan, Andi. Always your plan. I loved you, so I figured I could bend for you, figured I'd find a way to make my dreams work around yours, figured eventually you'd bend for me, too. But you were never going to bend, were you?"

Somehow the words *I loved you* made everything he was saying even worse. "You never gave me a chance to bend, Nate. You never gave me a chance to even try to be there for you. Yes, you're right, I didn't insist on staying when you told me to leave. But you didn't come after me, either. You didn't come tell me all those things you just said about being tired and scared."

The truth of it all finally hit her. So hard, she would have lost her breath if it hadn't already been gone.

"I wasn't the only one who wanted to be free, was I, Nate? You wanted to be free, too."

"Ah," he said quietly, more regret than she could have

thought possible lying beneath that one short syllable. "So now the truth comes out. We never should have been a couple in the first place, let alone try to do it again now."

Now that the red-hot flames of anger and resentment were gone, Andi didn't know what to say anymore. She just felt drained.

Empty.

"But it was for the best, wasn't it, Andi? You got to go back to bright lights, big city without a heavy chain attached to your ankle. And I was able to really settle into the town I love, a place where I can breathe clean air and listen to the birds in the trees when I wake up in the morning, the call of the loon when I'm watching the stars."

His words were softer now, as if she'd managed to wring all the anger out of him.

She couldn't make herself agree that it was all for the best. Not knowing what else to say to him, her heart feeling as raw and chafed as it ever had, she did what she'd done a thousand times before to try and hide her hurt and made herself shift the focus to business.

"Before we go, I have to know. Has seeing Loon Lake changed your mind about the condos?"

She felt his answer before he said it.

"No. I still think Emerald Lake is different. Special. That it's going to mean something years from now that there were never condos on the waterfront. Even if it ends up being a little harder in the present."

"That's what I thought," she said, forcing herself to nod, to keep her voice steady, even though the dam holding back her tears was finally about to break. Because there were no more excuses to be this close to Nate.

Not a single one.

For the first time ever, she knew that they were completely over.

*One night* had been a mistake. A mistake she'd been unable to keep herself from making, a mistake she'd justified by saying it was business, that she had to spend the night with Nate at Loon Lake for the sake of her project.

*One kiss* had been more than a mistake, though, more than a heady reminder of the innocence and excitement of young love.

*One kiss* had destroyed them completely.

\* \* \*

This time when Andi saw the light in the living room from the front porch, she was tempted to slip in the back door. One look at her was all her mother would need to see what a huge wreck the night had been.

Last night, spending time in the kitchen with Carol had been warm and comfortable. Tonight, Andi knew that same comfort, that warmth, would be the final straw in breaking apart the tenuous hold she had on herself.

Andi poked her head into the room, planning to let her mother know she was heading straight up to bed. But that promise of the comfort that had been lacking from her life for so long, too long, was so irresistible she actually found herself moving into the room instead.

"Mom, I—" she began, knowing she was on the verge of spilling it all out, when Carol looked up as if Andi had startled her.

"Oh honey, there you are." Her mother looked sad. And a little nervous. "Could you give me your opinion on something?"

"Sure."

"I wanted something special for your father's com-memoration on Sunday. I thought I could make us scarves in his favorite color." Andi noticed Carol's hands were shaking as she held up the beautiful autumn-red yarn. "Do you think that's silly?"

Guilt ripped through Andi, nearly buckling her knees, and she had to sit down on the edge of the couch facing her mother.

Here she'd been all twisted up over Nate, feeling sorry for herself, sure that no one had ever been in this much pain. But looking at her mother's face told her just how wrong she was. Carol hadn't just lost a boyfriend.

She'd lost her husband of over thirty years.

"No. It's not silly, Mom. I think he'd love it."

Finally her mother smiled. It wasn't a big smile, but at least she wasn't crying. Andi had never been good with tears. Not hers or anyone else's.

"I'm not quite done with this one if you'd like to put in some stitches, honey."

Andi shook her head quickly. "I'd probably only just mess it up." She stood back up. "I think I'm going to get these damp clothes off and take a shower before bed."

Carol frowned. "Why are your clothes wet?

"I took Nate to Loon Lake to show him a few things. But it rained." Andi pressed a kiss to her mother's cheek. "Good night."

Andi went upstairs to her bedroom and pulled out her laptop, but instead of opening it up and getting down to work, instead of blocking out everything but her goal, she couldn't stop thinking about her mother and grandmother, the store, the women in the knitting group…and an old romance that should have never been revived.

# Chapter Thirteen

Knowing for certain that she wasn't going to get Nate's vote as head of the architectural review committee, Andi dug down extra deep into researching Adirondack building laws as Thursday slid into Friday, looking for loopholes, making endless calls, and sending dozens of e-mails. Reading through Adirondack Council and Nature Conservancy meeting reports, Andi learned just how hard Nate had fought development in the Adirondacks, not just since he'd become mayor, but even before that. For some strange reason, though, he wasn't fighting very hard against her.

Nonetheless, it was time to stop playing with what-ifs, to stop losing herself in fantasy, to stop mucking around at Lake Yarns, and to do her job.

Her real job.

The Klein Group confirmed the addition of the football field to their plans. Not surprisingly, they rejected the carousel retrofitting.

Andi felt bad for her grandmother, but again, romanticizing memories and dealing with the real world were two very different things.

She barely looked up from her computer until flashes of bright-colored light in the sky drew her to her bedroom window. Friday night fireworks at the high school football game were a town tradition, going back as far as her grandmother's teenage years. And even though they were usually simple, inexpensive sparklers and fountains of color, they were always thrilling nonetheless.

Was Nate there? Was he out on the football field with the team, looking for her in the stands? Was he going to jump into the lake tonight after the game and think of her?

Her cheeks itched, and she brushed at them without thinking, shocked when her hand came back wet.

\*　　　\*　　　\*

Nate stood on the public beach just off Main Street and watched as the members of the high school football team ran down the dock one after the other and jumped into the cold lake on a holler. Amped up from winning the game, they hardly felt the cold, Nate knew.

But even without jumping in, Nate was frozen.

Wednesday night at Loon Lake, he'd let himself hope again. Big enough that he'd said, "*Come to the game this Friday, Andi. Jump into the lake with us.*"

Of course, she hadn't been in the stands tonight. For all he knew, she'd left town after their explosive kiss had disintegrated into a raging argument in the boathouse.

He shouldn't still be able to taste her sweet lips, shouldn't still be able to feel the soft imprint of them on his own lips. And he definitely shouldn't miss her tonight.

But he did.

They'd finally told each other the truth Wednesday

night. All of it. He knew now that they'd both hurt each other. Badly.

And yet, it wasn't the accusations they'd hurled at each other that lingered. Strangely he almost felt better for what he'd gotten off his chest.

No, what grated was what he'd said to her, that their breakup had been "for the best."

Because no matter how hard Nate had tried to convince himself that it was true, he just couldn't.

*     *     *

Thirty-six hours later, after burying herself in work all of Saturday, too, Andi woke up to the Sunday she'd been dreading. The Fall Festival...and her father's commemoration.

Her father's official funeral in Washington, D.C., one year ago had been a blur. Although Richard Powell had actually been buried at Emerald Lake in a plot next to the one her mother would one day be in, only she and her mother and grandmother had been there to watch his casket being lowered into the ground in the graveyard behind Main Street.

Today was the day Emerald Lake would finally get a chance to celebrate his life as the town dedicated a playground in Richard Powell's name—at the Fall Festival, her father's favorite celebration. And now, the one-year anniversary of his passing.

Exhausted from two almost sleepless nights—sleeping left her brain, her soul, too vulnerable to Nate's accusations—Andi knew she needed to put on a good face.

It was another day of putting on the perfect dress as armor, the perfect makeup and hair and jewelry and shoes.

As if any of that could prevent her—or protect her—from feeling. And hurting.

A knock sounded at her door. "It's time, honey."

Andi took a deep breath and opened up her bedroom door, only to be immediately confronted with her mother's concerned gaze, the very gaze she'd been running from for the past two days. Longer if she was being honest.

"Here's the scarf I made for you."

Andi didn't realize her hand was shaking until she reached for the red scarf. "Thanks. It looks great. Perfect for fall."

"Are you sure you're going to be all right today, honey? I don't want you to give the speech if you don't feel up to it." Carol almost seemed to grow taller, stronger before Andi's eyes. "I can do it."

"No, Mom. Of course, I'll give my speech."

She couldn't possibly let her mother suffer through giving the speech at his commemoration.

"This is what I do. I'll be fine."

Only, thirty minutes later when they were standing beneath the EMERALD LAKE FALL FESTIVAL sign, Andi realized that no speech she'd ever given as a management consultant had ever been this personal. This difficult.

As a little girl, Andi had loved the Fall Festival. Every year, the town green was transformed into an autumn wonderland. From morning until late into the night there was food and fun, laughter and music, a hundred lanterns hanging from the large gazebo in the center of the waterfront park, the lights blinking and swaying in time to the beat of the band.

Andi was never sure which booth she was going to stop

at first, her wad of dollar bills jammed into the pocket of her jeans. She always bought one of Mrs. Johnson's mini–berry pies while they were still warm. A slightly burned tongue was worth the way the berries exploded one after the other in her mouth, only to be chased down by the sweet brown sugar on top. But what next? Should she go play one of the festival games, like dunking the football coach in the tub of warm water? Should she let the music from the band in the gazebo pull her in until she was breathless from dancing with her friends?

But then in the end, the decision was easy. Because the best thing about the Fall Festival was simple. Her father was always there, regardless of how busy he was in Washington, D.C.

For Andi, there was nothing better than holding his hand, large and warm around her smaller one, as they stood together in the middle of the park. Even if the rest of her friends were off running around, calling to her to join them, even if the band was playing her favorite song, she was happy just to stand there beside him as he talked to the other adults about boring things.

Throughout the day, Andi would pop in and out of the Lake Yarns booth to bring her mother and grandmother food, something warm to drink, sometimes to even help the littler kids with their first knit stitches when they needed another set of knowledgeable hands. But mostly, she would stick by her father's side as long as he would let her, until his discussions grew more serious and he inevitably started working for his constituents again.

That was when she'd find Nate. Her best friend—and then boyfriend—would make her laugh and dance and feel loved.

"It really is lovely for the town to dedicate the new playground in your father's memory."

"He would have loved it," Andi agreed, unable to mask the scratch of emotion behind her words when being at the Fall Festival without her father—and without Nate waiting in the wings—felt so wrong.

Carol drew Andi into her arms as they waited for Evelyn, who had come from the store, to slowly walk across the green to join them. It made Andi's chest even tighter to notice that her grandmother already had the red scarf on.

Evelyn reached for Andi's hand on one side and Carol's on the other. "Shall we?"

Andi was amazed by how much stronger she felt from just the simple touch of her grandmother's hand.

After getting Carol and Evelyn seated on the gazebo stage, Andi closed her eyes and took a deep breath to steady herself. A heartbeat before she turned to step up to the podium, she felt a hand on her arm.

Nate's heat hit her first, his innate strength second. But it was the hurt and the love that were all mixed up together whenever she looked at him—whenever she even thought about him—that hit her hardest of all.

"I'm going to be right behind you if you need me."

"You're here?"

She couldn't believe Nate was waiting for her. That after everything they'd said and done to each other, *he was here anyway.*

"Of course I am, Andi," he said gently. "Where else would I be?"

Andi wanted to fall into his arms, to have him hold her and know that he was never going to let her go.

Instead, she forced herself to move away and walk up to the microphone.

"Richard Powell wasn't born in Emerald Lake. He came to town by way of a local girl."

Andi turned and smiled at her mother and saw that her eyes were already wet, although no tears had spilled down her cheeks yet.

Steeling herself to make it through her speech in one intact nonsniffling piece, just like she'd promised her mother that she would, Andi continued, "But he loved Emerald Lake as much as any born-and-bred local."

*     *     *

"Come," Evelyn said to her daughter and granddaughter when the commemoration was over and people had finished paying their respects. "Let's see who we can hook with our needles and yarn in our booth."

No question, Evelyn knew both Carol and Andi needed to lose themselves in something right now. Knitting would help them the way it had always helped her. Knitting had always soothed her, even when she'd been an eighteen-year-old girl who hadn't known her own heart or mind any more than her granddaughter—and that boy she'd always been so in love with—did.

But Andi simply shook her head. "I'll be over in a bit, Grandma," she said before heading off by herself, away from the crowds.

Carol stayed right where she was, staring down at the beautiful plaque Nate had given her from the town. *In memory of Richard M. Powell.*

"I want him back, Mom."

"I know, honey. Of course you do."

When Carol finally looked up, there were fresh tears in her eyes. "Not just for me, but because Andi needs her father. She's always needed him." One tear slid down across her cheek, then another. "I know she's seen Nate a couple of times since coming home. Something must have happened between them, but she won't talk to me. And I don't know how to ask. We see each other in the kitchen, in the hallway, in the store, but she won't tell me what's bothering her."

"It's not you, honey." Evelyn patted her daughter's hand. "Andi doesn't know how to put into words what she's feeling yet."

"If her father was here, she'd feel safe enough to confide in him."

Evelyn shook her head. "No," she said softly. "I don't think she would."

Not when Andi's father—and the things he'd taught his daughter to believe in—were an integral part of her struggle.

Richard Powell had been a good man, although not always the world's best father or husband, Evelyn thought with a narrowing of her eyes. Too busy, too often gone saving strangers to see much of his own family. And yet, when he did find the time to come home, he made every minute fun and exciting. That charisma, that honest love for life, was what had made his reelections almost a given. Richard Powell had been a man who was impossible to resist.

Evelyn knew firsthand about those kind of men. Both she and Carol had fallen for men who, rationally, they should have stayed away from. Men it didn't make any sense to love. Men whose love came with as much pain as pleasure.

It made perfect sense that Andi would follow in their footsteps.

She was one of them, after all. Three peas in a pod whether her granddaughter ever realized it as the truth.

"She'll come to you," Evelyn predicted. "When it's time."

A few minutes later they were settled into their booth, and as children and adults made their way over to knit and laugh, Evelyn was glad to see the lines of fatigue, of grief and confusion eventually settle out of Carol's face.

Periodically Evelyn scanned the festival grounds for her granddaughter, because even though she truly believed the three of them were, at their cores, strong and unbreakable, she also knew that it might take Andi a little while to find that well of strength and learn how to draw from it.

Just as it had taken Evelyn some time to find it for herself so many years ago.

*       *       *

Andi was halfway across the park when a man she didn't know stopped her. "Are you the one bringing those condos into town?"

Her brain couldn't compute the man's words, not when she was lost in thoughts of her father. Her body couldn't keep up, either, and she stumbled to a halt as she said, "Excuse me?"

The man repeated himself. "You're in charge of the condos, right?"

Stunned that someone was actually bringing this up— at her father's commemoration of all places—it was all she could do just to nod.

"You're going to have a fight on your hands, you know."

She rubbed her hands over her eyes. "If this is about the carousel—"

"I don't give a damn about the carousel." The woman beside him looked deeply uncomfortable. "This place is meant to be forever wild."

Andi had spent enough time poring over building restrictions to know that he was talking about the congressional meeting at which the fourteenth amendment, the Forever Wild clause, was created. Concern for the importance of the watershed was one of the driving forces for creating the Adirondack Park.

Trying to get her brain to start functioning again, Andi said, "I'm just as concerned about protecting the water sources as you are, and I can assure you that the proposed development will not in any way alter it."

"You don't live here anymore, do you?"

She had to shake her head. "No, but—"

"Then if you'll excuse me for being perfectly frank, you are not anywhere near as concerned as I am."

"I'm not an outsider," she finally protested. "I grew up here, spent eighteen years living my life in Emerald Lake. My mother is here. My grandmother is here. This is where I'm from."

"Look, I'm not trying to hurt your feelings. I'm just trying to make you see what I see when I drive outside the Adirondack Park. More and more open space converted to developed land. New homes being built faster than people can occupy them while the old ones fall, neglected and rotting. Roads that shunt rainwater and snowmelt and pollution into streams at accelerated rates. I'm just saying you're probably used to all that in the city. I don't think you can see how important this is as clearly as someone who's actually here can see it."

Another time she might have taken out her phone and made notes. She would have scheduled a meeting to address this man's concerns. But right now she was just too tired—and too full of a heart-deep sadness—to do anything more than say, "Okay."

The man's wife tugged on his arm. "George, this isn't the time for this." The woman lowered her voice. "*Her father.*"

The man grunted. "There will be a town meeting for this, won't there?"

Andi nodded. "Yes." She almost had everything she needed to turn in the paperwork. "This coming Thursday."

"We will see you there. And I sure hope you'll have thought about what I said by then."

Stumbling away from the couple, Andi realized she was standing beside the carousel. Needing to hold onto something—anything—she climbed onto it.

The paint had mostly chipped off, giving way to large patches of bare metal and porcelain. The red-and-white awning was faded to pink and gray, and the whole thing rocked dangerously as she stepped onto it.

As much as an inanimate object could project an emotion, the carousel looked desolate. Forlorn.

She hadn't cried in the boathouse with Nate. She hadn't cried at the commemoration. But hearing that stranger point out all the ways she didn't belong, all the ways she couldn't possibly be a part of a town that had raised her, finally had tears of grief and loss spilling down her face.

Straddling one of the horses, she leaned her head against the pole that held it to the splitting ceiling boards above, her tears soaking the scarf her mother had made in her father's memory.

*          *          *

It had been Nate's idea to build the new playground in Richard Powell's name. But watching Andi stand in front of the town—trying to be so brave, so strong when she was only a heartbeat away from breaking as she gave her beautiful speech—had him wondering if he'd been wrong to force Andi to revisit her father's death again in such a public forum.

Lord knew he owed Richard Powell a great deal for his help in keeping Madison from going to a foster home when she was a baby. But nothing was worth adding to Andi's grief, damn it.

And when she'd fled the festival, and he'd seen the couple corner her, he'd had to follow her, had to go to her.

Nate was too late to intercept the man who had barged into his office earlier that day to demand answers about the condos. But by god, despite the words they'd thrown at each other in that boathouse on Loon Lake, whether he liked it or not, whether it was easy or not, Andi was a part of his soul.

And she needed him.

He'd spent the past three days trying to wade through what had happened between them in the boathouse. Not just the kiss, but what had been said. And what he'd been amazed to find out was that simply getting it all off of his chest had really made him able to take a look at their past with clear eyes.

When they were eighteen, they'd both screwed up. Badly. Did he wish they could have done things differently? Hell, yes. But they hadn't. And while neither of them was blameless, no one was more to blame than the other, either.

In the end, Nate knew one thing for sure: Both he and Andi had paid the price for their anger, for their pride in not wanting to admit fault, and for their stubborn desire to be the one to hear "I'm sorry" first. And the price had been high, way too high.

Because he'd missed her like crazy for the past ten years.

And he didn't want to have to miss her anymore.

Andi didn't look up when he approached. "Go away. I just want to be alone."

Nate wasn't surprised she tried to push him away. He'd be more surprised if she didn't.

Climbing up onto the merry-go-round, he lowered himself down beside the horse she sat on.

"I know it feels like that, but I'm not going to let you push me away. You need somebody right now."

"I'm fine."

He didn't answer her lie, just stayed there and watched her tears drip onto her scarf until he couldn't take it anymore.

Softly, he told her "It gets easier, sweetheart."

Finally she looked at him, her cheek still pressed against the pole, her beautiful blue eyes glassy with tears.

"When? When will it ever get better?"

With anyone else he could have told the lie she needed to hear. But he couldn't lie to Andi anymore.

Never again.

"The truth is that it won't ever go away completely." Another sob rocked her—and the old porcelain horse she was sitting on. "But it will fade, and you'll wake up some mornings and actually be able to convince yourself that you're okay."

"But what if—" He had to get closer, had to practically press his ear to her mouth to hear the raw whispered words. "What if I get too okay and forget him?" Pain clawed at each word. "What if I'm already forgetting the way he smells and the way his eyes crinkled when he laughed and the way he used to drive me crazy by humming 'God Bless America' all the time?"

With each word, Andi's breath came out shakier, the words barely coming through her tears. She was tearing his heart apart one soft broken word at a time.

"Your father loves you, Andi, and wherever you are, believe me, he knows how much you love him. You don't have to mourn forever to prove that to him. Or to yourself. Your father wants to look down and see you smiling. Laughing. Forgetting."

Nate was ready for her to rail at him for making things worse. He was ready for her to scream at him to go away. The only thing he wasn't ready for was her whispering through her tears, "Why didn't you tell me?"

Not sure what she was asking him about, he gently asked, "What did you need me to tell you?"

"How much you needed me. When your parents died." She didn't wait for him to reply. "I left you. I know I left you. But I swear I didn't know what it felt like, not until Daddy died, Nate. If I'd known, I would have been there for you." He couldn't keep up with the tears streaming down her cheeks, couldn't wipe them away fast enough. "I would have been there, Nate. Please believe me."

She was crying harder now, his strong Andi no longer

strong, and it was breaking the last part of his heart that hadn't been broken out in the boathouse on Loon Lake.

"Shhh, sweetheart. Not now. We don't have to do this now."

"I'm just so sorry for what happened. For what I did."

"I know you are. And I'm sorry, too. I wasn't there for you, either. Not when you needed me the most. Let me be there for you now."

She shook her head, tears launching from her cheekbones and landing on his skin, searing him with her pain.

"I don't want to hurt you more than I already have, Nate. I don't ever want to hurt you again."

"Come here." He knew she needed arms around her. His arms. "Just a hug, I promise."

And then she was in his arms, his chin on the top of her soft hair, her face buried in the crook of his shoulder as she cried, the wind taking the end of her scarf and wrapping it around him too.

# Chapter Fourteen

The following night, Andi wasn't exactly sure what she was doing walking in the door of Lake Yarns. After her experience the previous Monday, she'd planned to stay as far away from the knitting group as she could. Only she couldn't stand the thought of another second alone in her bedroom with nothing but her computer for company.

But when she walked inside and heard the words, "Andi, honey, you came," a dozen smiling faces turned around with smiles. Dorothy said, "I knew you'd be back. Didn't I say that, Helen?" Helen poured her a glass of wine. "Here you go, my dear." Andi knew exactly why she'd come here tonight.

Nate's arms around her as she cried on the carousel at the Fall Festival had confused her more than ever. She desperately needed comfort, and she'd known deep inside that there would be laughter here. Not only softness from the yarn, but the true warmth of other women who'd surely loved and lost before, just like her.

Catherine walked in just as Dorothy asked, "Do you have your shawl?"

Andi didn't want to admit that she'd been so flustered by the end of the previous Monday night, she couldn't remember what she'd done with it. Wishing she didn't feel so uncomfortable around her old friend, Andi suddenly wasn't so sure that being a part of the Monday night knitting group was such a good idea after all.

Flustered all over again, she said, "Actually, I'm not sure whe—"

Rebecca handed the shawl to her. "I must have accidentally grabbed it last week when I was packing up my things."

Andi thanked her with her eyes.

"Honey, I didn't know you were working on a shawl." Carol looked simultaneously pleased and maybe a little bit hurt that Andi hadn't mentioned knitting something to her at any point that week.

Evelyn patted the seat next to her. "Come sit next to me. Just like you used to when you were a little girl."

Andi did as she was told, taking a deep breath and trying to get comfortable. She was just about to make her first knit stitch when her grandmother said, "I was telling everyone about how we're going to save the carousel."

Her heart skipped a beat or two before it went down like a heavy rock. She hadn't planned to lead with the bad news but not telling her grandmother now would feel like lying.

"I talked to my client about the carousel, Grandma."

"Of course, they're not going to save it." Evelyn patted Andi's knee, giving her a moment to recover from her surprise. "I never thought they would. Not when there isn't a dime to be made from it."

"Actually," Andi made herself say, "I was hoping to

talk with all of you about the details of my project tonight. That is, if you don't know already." She could feel Catherine's eyes on her. Not angry. Not cold. But watchful. Knowing her old friend worked as Nate's part-time assistant at city hall, Andi chose her words extra carefully. "I'm working with a builder to build several beautiful residences on the waterfront," she began. She knew the women who had been at the group last week, but there were several faces she didn't recognize. "In addition to bringing in additional revenue to the town and the store owners, they are also going to add in some wonderful extras."

"Like what?" one of the women asked.

"A new boat launch." When no one looked particularly excited about that, she was glad she had something else to give them. "And a new football field—lights, locker room, bleachers—the whole nine yards."

The woman who had looked so unimpressed before suddenly smiled. "That's wonderful. My sons are both on the team." She turned to the woman next to her and said, "Isn't that great news?"

Andi silently breathed a sigh of relief as the conversation blew off course for a few minutes as several women started talking about the team's chances at a championship this year. No one was freaking out. In fact, it was abundantly clear that the football field might end up being the tiebreaker.

Catherine leaned across the coffee table. "Can we talk in the back?"

Andi put down her knitting and made an excuse about getting another bottle of wine before following Catherine into the back room.

"I've been trying to keep my mouth shut, but I can't anymore." Catherine's voice was quiet but determined.

"If you're upset about my project, I'd be happy to meet with you tomorrow morning to discuss it."

"I don't care about your project," Catherine said, her mouth pulling into a tight line. "I want to know what you're doing with Nate."

Andi felt the remaining color leave her cheeks. "I understand that you care about him, but my relationship with Nate is private."

Catherine crossed her arms across her chest. "I don't know what happened between the two of you last week, but I know something is wrong. He's not himself."

Pain flared behind Andi's breastbone. Catherine was right. She should have never let things get as far as they had.

*She should have never come back.*

"I think it's wonderful that you're so concerned about him," Andi said in as even a voice as she could manage. "But what's between me and Nate is just that. Between the two of us." Andi turned to leave.

"I know your type."

That stopped Andi cold. "My type?"

"I was married to one of you."

Andi couldn't keep her eyebrows from going up, her arms from adopting the mirror image of Catherine's defensive crossed position in front of her chest.

"Are you comparing me to your 'rat bastard' ex-husband?"

Catherine's eyes narrowed. "Seems sometimes like you think you're too big, too important for a place like this."

"I grew up here, Catherine," Andi reminded her. She'd

expected to take some flak tonight at the knitting group, but about the project, not this personal attack. "We used to be friends. Why are you so angry with me?"

"The fact that you don't know why says it all."

"Are you in love with Nate?" Andi guessed, even though the pieces didn't quite add up.

Catherine laughed, but there was no humor in it. "Don't you think I wish I could have fallen in love with him instead of—" Her mouth wobbled slightly around the corners.

"I'm sorry," Andi said softly. And despite the way Catherine had just attacked her, she was.

But the other woman wasn't interested in her apologies. "Do you have any idea how hard it was for Nate after his father killed himself? All of us were there for him, babysitting, bringing over food, cleaning up that dank trailer the best we could, teaching him how to deal with a baby. But not you, Andi. The one person who should have been there wasn't."

"I was wrong." Andi knew that now, had always known it. "If I could make it up to him, I would. I care about him, Catherine. More than you know."

More than he knew.

"If you care so much, then you should stay."

"Here?" It wasn't until the word had left her mouth that she realized just how insultingly incredulous she sounded.

"Yes, here." Irritation flashed again on Catherine's face.

"No," Andi said, shaking her head. "I couldn't stay here."

Catherine raised an eyebrow. "Why not?"

"My job, my apartment, they're in the city."

"So get a new job and sell the apartment."

"It's not that easy."

"Sure it is."

"You know I never wanted to settle here, Catherine. Emerald Lake is a great town and everything, but I'd go crazy here if I knew I couldn't get out. It's too small. Too quiet."

"So let me see if I get what you're saying," Catherine said slowly. "Emerald Lake is fine for quieter, smaller people, but not for you because you're too big for it?"

"It isn't personal, Catherine."

Only, every word between the two of them since Andi had returned to town had been deeply personal. Hurtful.

"Why can't you see that I'm not trying to hurt anyone? I'm just trying to be true to who I am."

"I'll tell you exactly who you are," Catherine said. "You are a woman who was damned lucky to be loved by one of the best men I've ever known. You are a woman who's about to throw it all away again for a bunch of flashing city lights. You are a woman who's too damn scared to even give love a chance." Catherine's gaze was stony. "Whatever you've been telling yourself all these years, that's who you really are, Andi."

Andi could feel how hot, how red her face must be, and she only just barely stopped herself from covering her cheeks with her hands.

She wanted to deny everything Catherine was saying. But how could she when the truth was that the glamorous life her father had lived, the very life she'd aspired to, hadn't really been all it was cracked up to be? Long nights in the office. Friends she never really got close to because she didn't have enough time to form strong bonds.

And yet, it was those very truths that had her fighting

what she was feeling. Because realizing that her feelings for Nate hadn't gone away, realizing that her life in the city wasn't as fulfilling as she'd thought it would be, made her feel weak. Like she wasn't as strong as her father. Like she was somehow letting him—and herself—down by allowing herself to get too comfortable at Emerald Lake.

Andi opened her mouth a couple of times to respond to what Catherine had said, but the words wouldn't come. She didn't know what to say.

Because she didn't know what to feel.

A moment later, her mother started screaming.

\*     \*     \*

Everything moved in slow motion for Andi from that moment. As they rushed back into the main part of the store to find Evelyn lying on the floor in Carol's arms, Andi could hear Rebecca calling 911, her calm explanation that Evelyn had started coughing, then had passed out coming through Andi's ears as if through a long, thin tube. Andi was barely aware of dropping to her knees and putting two fingers on Evelyn's pulse, finding a faint heartbeat.

She heard someone say, "Please, god. Not her. Not yet," and only barely realized that it was her, that she'd been the one begging for her grandmother.

Andi didn't know how much time passed on the floor, just that every second felt like an eternity until they heard the sirens of the local volunteer ambulance crew, the only crew that could get there quickly. And then like magic, Nate was there with another volunteer paramedic, both totally focused on her grandmother, getting her up on the gurney and taking her vitals.

Andi held onto her mother as they watched them roll

Evelyn into the back of the ambulance. Andi couldn't think of where she'd put her car keys so they could follow them to the hospital.

Nate returned to Andi and her mother. "Evelyn needs both of you right now."

He led them out to the ambulance, and it was a tight fit in the back, but Andi had never been so glad to be squeezed in. She held onto one of her grandmother's hands while her mother held the other.

In a calm but not at all detached voice, he asked them for whatever details they had about Evelyn's health.

Andi looked at her mother, saw that she couldn't possibly speak with the tears rolling down her cheek one after the other. "She's been coughing a lot. I sent her over to Dr. Morris. She said he told her to rest." Andi was fighting back her own tears. "I should have gone and talked with him myself to make sure she wasn't just hearing what she wanted to."

Nate's hand was warm on her shoulder. "It's good that you had her see him, Andi. And even good doctors like Dr. Morris sometimes miss things." Obviously sensing she was desperate for reassurance, he said, "Syracuse General isn't a big hospital, but it's a great one with doctors that have trained at all of the best schools.

She knew he was trying to allay her concerns about taking her grandmother to a bunch of hick quacks. Still, Andi couldn't stop thinking that if they were in the city, they would already be at the nearest hospital.

Evelyn's lungs moved up and down as she took in the oxygen through the mask they'd put over her mouth and nose, and Andi couldn't stop asking herself, when was the last time she'd sat with her grandmother? With her mother? Talking or eating or knitting rather than just dropping in for a few minutes before flitting away to take care of her "important" life. Even this week, she'd been hiding out from them. Too afraid that they would look into her soul and see everything that was wrong with it.

It shouldn't have taken her grandmother in an ambulance to pull them together.

*But it had.*

Andi was sorry, so sorry that she hadn't been there more. She knew she would never forgive herself if the last real conversation she'd ever have with her grandmother had been last week in the cottage about the carousel, when Andi had been impatient to get going, to send e-mails, to convince Nate that she was right about everything she wanted to be right about.

*　　　*　　　*

Nate stayed with them as the doctors saw Evelyn. Carol still hadn't spoken, but she took the cup of coffee he handed her. When Andi shook her head, he gave her water instead and watched to make sure she drank it all down.

Carol's suffering, her fear, was written all over her face, in the slump of her shoulders, in the shadows under her eyes. Andi was clearly hurting, too, but she'd obviously assigned herself the role of holding it together.

He wanted to pull her aside, tell her he'd hold it together for her.

He couldn't take the burden of strength off of Andi's shoulders—he'd been there, knew just how heavy it was—but he could bring her food, he could sit with her, he could watch over her.

And he could pray.

# Chapter Fifteen

A doctor came into the waiting room. "Evelyn Thomas's family?"

Andi asked, "What happened?" just as Carol said, "Is my mother going to be okay?"

The doctor sat down with them on the blue padded chairs. "Evelyn passed out because her lungs were almost completely full. From our first round of X-rays and tests, it seems that she's been walking around with low-grade pneumonia for weeks, if not months. Oftentimes this kind of infection can go on for a while before flaring up and causing big problems. We're waiting for the results of a few more tests to see how her organs have been holding up."

"Her organs?" Andi asked. "I thought you said her lungs were the problem?"

"It's just a precaution to make sure the lack of oxygen hasn't done more damage. But I have to tell you, that is one strong lady in there with us. She's been sucking in oxygen through a very thin tube. Most people half her age would have collapsed long before she did. We'll be keeping her sedated and on oxygen for the night at least to give her body a chance to rest while it takes in the first round of antibiotics. As far as you know, is she allergic to anything?"

Andi looked at her mother for the answer. "I don't know," Carol said, her words barely above a whisper. Her voice quivered as she added, "She was never sick. Not until recently." Tears came again. "I thought she had a cold. She told me she had a cold."

The doctor handed Carol a Kleenex from the box on the side table before standing up. "We're going to keep her in the ICU until we have a better handle on her situation. You're welcome to stay with her there for as long as you like."

\* \* \*

During the hours Evelyn went in and out of sleep in the hospital bed that dwarfed her, she heard many voices: Carol's, Andi's, the doctor's, the nurse's, a man's voice that she recognized but couldn't place. She tried again and again to find the surface, to awaken completely, but her lungs felt so heavy, like trying to breathe with a hundred pound weight strapped across her chest. Her eyelids were as heavy as her limbs.

Slowly she began to lose the thread of where she was, and then something cool flooded her veins and it was easier just to let herself settle deeper into the recesses of her mind.

Into her memories.

Seventy years disappeared, erasing everything but Carlos.

\* \* \*

*1941*

*It had been one week since their trip on the freight train. Seven days. 168 hours. 10,080 seconds.*

*Too long.*

*It wasn't just the kiss she hadn't been brave enough to give him that hung over every one of those seconds... it was learning something about herself that she hadn't liked learning.*

*Namely that she wasn't anywhere near as brave as she'd always thought she was.*

*Somehow she needed to figure out a way to see Carlos again. To be alone with him again.*

*And to finally be brave.*

*But after a full week where she hadn't been able to find any way to be with him, she finally realized just how precious their stolen moments had been.*

*Every Friday night in fall, her family went to the high school football game. A onetime star when he was younger, her father would be out there with the team on the field, helping the coaches, supporting the players, while she and her sisters and mother enjoyed the evening under thick blankets with cups of hot chocolate to help keep them warm.*

*That Friday night she was surprised to look out from the bleachers and see Carlos at the edge near the trees looking back at her.*

*"Mom, I think I just got my period. I've got to head back home."*

*"Maybe one of your sisters should go with you," her mother replied.*

*Seeing that her mother was still half focused on the*

*game, Evelyn said, "No, I'll be fine biking home with the full moon out tonight."*

*Evelyn's heart raced with delicious anticipation as she rode her bike through the crisp night air. Assuming Carlos would be waiting for her at her house when she approached the park at the edge of the downtown strip, she was surprised to see him leaning against the carousel.*

*For a moment she felt like a little girl as she dropped her bike onto the grass. But then as she walked across the stretch of green and saw his eyes on her, dark blue eyes that were full of the same need she was feeling, Evelyn felt her first real rush of feminine power. And pleasure.*

*Finally she reached the carousel, and it was hard to breathe as she put her hands on one of the horse's flanks and stepped up onto the platform. Running her fingers along the painted beasts, she slowly moved to the two-person sleigh being pulled behind a pair of horses and sat down.*

*She watched him as he made his decision. Watched him as he climbed up onto the carousel.*

*Her heart raced. She was scared, frightened of the strength of her feelings, the strange sensations that had taken over her body inch by inch from the first moment she'd set eyes on him.*

*Carlos, her Carlos, was graceful as he moved toward her. And then he was kneeling in front of her, ignoring the open seat next to her.*

*"Pretty Evelyn."*

*She took his face in her hands, the solid lines of his jaw firm against the flesh of her palms, the dark stubble across his chin rough against her skin.*

*Just as the fireworks that marked halftime at the foot-*

*ball field exploded in the sky above them, she pressed her lips against his... and knew that she was his forever.*

*Nothing—no one—would tear them apart.*

*Not without tearing her apart, too.*

\*          \*          \*

The whole time she held her mother in her arms on the floor and in the back of the ambulance, as they waited for news in the hospital, Carol hadn't stopped thinking how right the needles and yarn had looked in Andi's hands.

*Andi was knitting a shawl.*

And then there was Nate. Carol had known him his whole life, knew what a good boy he'd been, what a wonderful man he'd turned into.

These past hours she'd watched him watching her daughter and saw what her daughter hadn't dared tell her.

*The love between them had never gone away.*

Nate loved her little girl with such devotion, such purity, it simply took Carol's breath away.

Did Andi know? Did Nate?

And even if they did, would it matter? Would it change anything for her beautiful daughter?

Even as a child, Carol had marveled at the fact that Andi was actually half hers. Not so often when she was a little girl, when they would bake together or play with yarn or fabric or make sand castles on the beach, but later when it seemed as if Andi was going out of her way to grow up too fast. When the only thing that mattered was what her father thought. When her sole purpose was getting out of Emerald Lake.

Carol had loved her husband, even if she hadn't always understood him. But now she was afraid that those things she hadn't understood—the pressures he had always put on his only child, the way he'd repeatedly told his beautiful daughter that she had to be more, bigger, stronger—had only been magnified in his death.

Carol was afraid that Richard Powell now loomed larger over Andi from the grave than he had as flesh and blood.

She was afraid that just as she'd never known how to be the kind of mother her daughter really needed as a child, she didn't know how to help her as an adult, either.

She worried that Andi's return to Emerald Lake would only make those demons that ate at her daughter's heart and soul stronger.

But most of all, she worried that this time if her daughter left for the city again, she wouldn't be coming back.

So many questions, so many worries, too many for this hospital room full of beeping machines and bright lights.

But through it all, she held onto that picture of Andi with the barely begun blue shawl on her lap...and how right it had looked. Like her daughter was finally coming back to a home she should have never left.

"Thank you for being here with us, Nate," Carol said. "You should go home and get some sleep. Andi, you too."

Her daughter looked surprised. Then stubborn. Always so stubborn.

Even when something as beautiful as true love was staring her straight in the face.

"I'm staying here. With you. With Grandma."

But for all that Carol had rarely pushed her daughter to do anything she didn't want to do, she wasn't afraid to do it now.

"Since the day your grandmother opened Lake Yarns,

her store has been open Monday through Saturday. Not once in fifty-five years have the doors been locked shut. We're not starting now. Not when she's counting on us. The doctor and nurses have already told me that I can stay here with her as long as I need to." Carol gestured to a pullout couch that had been supplied with a pillow and blankets. "You've got to get some sleep with what's left of the night so that you can run the store."

Andi's eyebrows raised in surprise. Carol held her breath as she waited for her daughter's reply to see if she tried to call her bluff.

She worked to hide her relief when Andi nodded. "I'll do whatever you need me to do. Anything, Mom. You know that, don't you?"

"Of course I do, honey," Carol said in a softer tone, letting go of her mother's hand long enough to hug her daughter.

When Carol turned to hug Nate, he whispered, "I'll take care of her," into her ear.

"I know you will, Nate."

*But would Andi let him?*

\*     \*     \*

Nate drove Andi back to Emerald Lake in the car his ambulance chief had left for him, but when they pulled up in front of her mother's house, her legs didn't want to move.

"Don't worry, there's no way you're going back to that big house all alone."

How had he read her mind?

She didn't trust her voice as Nate came around her side of the car and opened her door. Taking her hand, he said,

"We're going to pack a bag for you, and then you're coming back with me. To my house."

Somewhere in the back of her mind, she knew it wasn't a good idea, that she should be strong enough to sleep in her mother's empty house. But god, how she didn't want to. Which was why she threw some clothes into a large shoulder bag, along with her toothbrush, and got back into his car.

Nate parked behind his house, and this time she got out of the car by herself, but instead of heading into his house, her feet took her, almost like a sleepwalker, down to his dock, not stopping until she was standing out over the lake.

Her mind wasn't racing anymore. Instead it was blank. Completely empty.

All that remained was a deep ache in her chest, her stomach.

She didn't hear Nate come up behind her, didn't know he was standing right there until he said, "That one looks like an elephant."

Her brain tried to restart, but it was like an engine without any oil. The key had turned, but all it could do was sputter before dying out again. And then his hand slipped over hers, and she curled her fingers into his and held on for dear life.

Warm. He was so warm.

"The one over to the right looks like a headless horseman."

She finally realized he was looking up at the sky, up at the clouds. She couldn't believe it when her mouth almost found a smile.

This was a game they'd played as kids, lying out on

the end of the dock watching the clouds change shapes.

Her heart and her head were both glad for the chance to focus on something that didn't hurt. She finally found her voice. "That one's a witch on a broom."

Nate moved closer, pointed up at the sky again. "And she's being chased by three little witches."

Maybe it was the fact that she knew she didn't have to try to fall asleep in her mother's big, overly quiet house, maybe it was the relief that Nate was always there right when she needed him, or maybe it was simply how he always found a way to make her smile, but as the clouds moved apart in the sky and covered the moon for a split second, her heart also split open for the second time in as many days.

As Nate's arms came around her, holding her tight, she cried for her grandmother, for her mother. She cried for herself. For everything she didn't understand.

And for everything she wanted but had never let herself have.

When her tears dried, Nate led her back up the dock and into his house. She barely noticed Dorothy getting up off the couch and saying "How is she?" barely heard Nate's reply. And then he was taking her into his bedroom and helping her pull her sweater off over her head. He took off her shoes, her jeans, and settled her into a large bed.

He was pulling the covers over her, whispering, "Good night, sweetheart," when panic settled over her.

"Please," she said. She couldn't be alone. Not now. Not anymore. She was so tired of being cold. So tired of feeling empty. "Please don't go."

Her eyes closed of their own volition before she heard

his response, but she was still awake when the bed dipped. She sighed with relief, finally letting herself fall all the way into blessed darkness just as his body found hers and pulled her back into his chest.

For the first time in a long time, she wasn't alone.

# Chapter Sixteen

Andi woke up as the first, faint rays of light began to brighten up the sky outside the bedroom window. She hadn't slept many hours, but they'd all been good ones, safe in Nate's arms.

She shifted slightly beneath the soft covers, wanting to sink deeper into the mattress. Into Nate.

He pulled her closer, his arm tight over her waist, his hand curling into her rib cage. Holding her breath, she listened to his breathing. It was even, and she assumed he was still asleep, that his reaching for her had been completely unconscious.

A week ago, she would have been up and out of his bed in seconds, throwing on her clothes and getting in his rowboat, speeding across the lake as fast as her arms could take her to make sure she put distance between them.

But last night, he'd been there for her in a way no one ever had. He'd been there for her mother, too, taking care of both of them in the ambulance and in the hospital.

Somewhere between then and now, between that moment when he'd come rushing into Lake Yarns with the paramedic crew and pointing out cloud formations on his dock, between how she'd trusted him to strip her clothes off to put her into his bed and slept all night curled up in the safety of his arms, she realized a new truth: no matter what happened out in the real world, whether there were condos built or not, if they lived in cities or small towns, she could always count on Nate.

They had always been in it together, best friends and playmates practically from birth. He'd been the boy in sixth grade who had taken her to the office for ice when they'd been playing kickball and the ball had nailed her straight in the nose. He'd been the teenager who had asked her to dance in eighth grade at their first real after-school party when she'd been standing all alone in the corner. He'd been the one to pull her out of the way of the propeller when she had fallen out of the speedboat in tenth grade, letting her cling to him long past when she'd stopped shaking.

And he'd been her first lover at seventeen, the night she'd outdebated him over "doing the right thing," tackled him in the backseat of his beat-up old car, and made him take her virginity.

As the magnitude of her realizations, coming one after the other, brought her more and more awake, she realized Nate's breathing was no longer even and there was a slight tension in the arm slung across her.

Last night had been pure comfort, without even a hint of sexuality between them. But this morning, with his muscles hot and hard against her skin, she had another epiphany.

Not only was making love again with Nate a given.

It had always been a given.

Not if.

*Now.*

And even though the voice of common sense screamed inside her head, trying to get her to listen, to stop before things went any further, something much strong than common sense had her silencing that voice and moving her hand over Nate's to thread her fingers between his.

Slowly she brought his hand up over her stomach, her rib cage, losing her breath as she took him between the valley of her breasts, not stopping until she held his fingers against her lips.

She pressed a kiss against his fingers, the small hairs on his knuckles brushing against her lips as she followed up with another kiss and then another.

Against her hips, she felt the growing proof of his arousal. It was pure instinct to shift herself into him. His low groan came from behind her and that one sound, combined with the incredibly sensual pleasures of finally being so close with Nate, had her skin prickling with awareness.

With unabashed need.

It was the most natural thing in the world to turn around, to put her arms around his neck and press her mouth against his. Not breaking their kiss, a heartbeat later, his heavy weight was completely over her, pressing her down into the bed. His tongue found hers, and as a soft moan of pleasure found its way from her chest to her throat and out her mouth, her legs moved apart for him so that he could press deeper against her.

She'd never had another lover like Nate, never wanted to run her hands and mouth everywhere at once. But she already knew he wouldn't let her mouth go, not when he was holding her a willing prisoner with his, so she used her hands instead. She wanted to go fast, but she made herself go slow, running her hands down from his neck, across his broad shoulders, then down his back.

Her hunger was even stronger for the memories of how good it had been between them so long ago, stronger for the sure knowledge that it was going to be even better— so much better—after denying herself for so long.

She didn't want anything between them, not even the thin cotton of his T-shirt or hers, so when she found the rim of his shirt, she gripped it in her fists and pulled it up, letting the edge of her fingers, her nails, rake lightly across his skin. His muscles rippled beneath her hands, and she felt him suck a breath in deep as he lifted himself high enough that she could take the shirt all the way up and off.

There was enough light in the room now for her to see him, to stare at his incredible beauty.

Perfect, he was perfect, his muscles rippling as he held himself in place for her inspection. And when she looked up at his face again in absolute wonder at finally being here with him, she saw the same wonder in his eyes tangled up with such heat she lost what was left of her breath.

"Now you," he said, but she couldn't wrap her brain around his words, not until she felt his fingers skimming her belly as he slowly lifted her shirt up across her sensitive skin. His fingers caught against the curve of her lace-covered breasts, making her shake with need.

He took his time looking at her, his dark, hot eyes burning a sizzling path across her skin that had her trembling. He'd seen her without her clothes before, but ten years had passed between then and now. She wasn't a girl anymore. And he definitely wasn't a boy.

And then he was lowering his head and she felt the soft press of his mouth on the upper swell of her breasts, first one and then the other, and she forgot all about the lost years. They were just kisses at first, until his tongue began to lave her skin, dipping into one cup of her bra.

Andi's memories of making love with Nate had been so sweet, so good. But the truth was it had never been like this between them. Andi arched into him, desperate for more, and he groaned at her obvious pleasure before moving his mouth to her other breast. She was turning to liquid pleasure, melting as his mouth came down over the other sensitive peak.

She couldn't remember a single reason why she'd ever denied herself Nate.

"Beautiful," he said as he pulled back to look at her, and she cried out not just from the delicious physical sensations, but from the look in his eyes, the emotion that he wasn't trying to hide from her anymore.

And the fact that being together like this felt so right.

So perfect.

Her bra was gone a moment later, his large hands cupping her flesh so that he could run kisses over both breasts at once. Her head fell back against the pillows as she tried to take it all in, pleasure so deep she thought she'd burst. Just when she thought she had found a way to deal with it, he was moving away from her breasts, his mouth kissing a path down her rib cage, his tongue finding the hollows in between her ribs.

Somewhere in the fog that had taken over her mind, she knew what was going to happen, that he was going to kiss her *there*, but she was already so far gone that when she felt his fingers slip into the side of her underwear, she needed his help lifting her hips so that he could slide them off.

As he pulled that final piece of her clothes off, she waited to feel shy, expected to be embarrassed at how her body had changed from a skinny girl's to a woman's, complete with a little cellulite on her thighs.

But those feelings never came.

Only a sweet anticipation that told her how long she'd waited for this.

"You are so beautiful," he said against her stomach between kisses, and then his fingers were moving over her, across the slick patch of skin between her thighs. "More beautiful than ever."

She lifted her hips into the soft press of his hand over her mound, groaning as he cupped her, begging silently for more. He must have heard her silent plea, because the next thing she knew, his mouth was there, over the aroused swell between her legs. She cried out as his mouth covered her, peaking and falling beneath his mouth.

It was too much, so much more than she'd ever felt with anyone else. She couldn't remember anything or anyone that came before Nate, couldn't possibly think about what would come after.

She'd never felt so soft, so womanly as he moved his mouth down over her thighs, kicking the covers off so that he could press kisses against her knees, her shins, her ankles, the tops of her feet.

Only with Nate had she ever felt this much love.

And now, she thought as he laid back on the bed and pulled her over him, it was her turn to show him with her body, with her mouth, with her hands, all the things she could never say.

*       *       *

Straddling his hips, looking down at him with such satisfaction, Andi was soft and naked and so beautiful Nate could hardly breathe, could hardly believe she was finally here with him in his bed.

He hadn't been a saint in the past ten years, but being with Andi again made it painfully clear that she wasn't just his first, she was also the only one who mattered.

All week, ever since he'd seen her outside the yarn store, he had been warning himself about keeping his distance, and this was why. He wouldn't have had to warn himself to stay away if she hadn't been so important.

Nate couldn't escape from the fact that he was going to have to stop and figure this all out soon, too soon. But later, not now, not while Andi, *his sweet Andi*, was soft and sweet and giving herself to him so openly. Not when he never wanted to stop loving her, not when he could listen to the sound of her coming apart beneath his mouth, his hands, over and over for a hundred years and never tire of hearing it.

Her hands were splayed flat across his chest. "I don't know where to start," she said, almost as if she were talking to herself.

"Anywhere, sweetheart."

And then she was leaning down over him, her soft hair blanketing his chest, his shoulders, as her mouth ran a path across his skin from his arms down to his hands, loving each finger separately before she moved back up to his shoulder, to his neck.

He couldn't keep from stealing a kiss, from capturing that sweet mouth and tangling his tongue with hers. She tasted so good. Everywhere he tasted her.

She continued her sensual assault down his chest, over his abs. He tightened his stomach muscles, fighting for control as her tongue slid into the hollows. Finally she removed the last barrier between them, his boxers joining the rest of their clothes on the floor.

It killed him to have to shift away from her for even a second to get a condom out of his bedside table. All the while she was pressing kisses against his face, his neck, his shoulders, and chest. With a groan, he ripped open the package and shoved the condom on.

And then, she was wrapping her legs around his waist and guiding him into her, gasping with pleasure until he was finally right where he belonged.

He looked into her eyes and saw wonder in them—along with pure joy—and he knew that only emotion could have them wanting each other so much, so badly. Only love.

"I love you, Andi."

Before either of them could really react to the words he hadn't planned on saying, nature was taking over, their tongues slipping and sliding against each other as their hips did a similar dance. He had dreamed of this moment a hundred times. A thousand. But being with her, as adults, was so much better than it had ever been when they were kids.

All he knew, all that mattered, was that Andi was finally his again.

*Sweet Andi.*

And then she was saying, "Please, Nate, now," and he

was lost, his body joining hers in an explosion of pleasure more incredible than anything he'd ever thought to feel.

When it was all over, he rolled back onto the mattress, taking her sweat-slickened body against his. She was already asleep by the time her head found his shoulder.

The sun was almost up completely, and Nate knew it was time to get his sister ready for school. First, though, he'd steal another sixty seconds with Andi.

And say his prayers for another sixty years.

# Chapter Seventeen

When Andi woke up again in Nate's bed, she wasn't the least bit shocked by what had happened. How could she be, when making love with Nate, when being that close again, had simply been inevitable?

And yet what had made being with him so amazing, the real reason his every kiss and touch took her breath away, was because of their connection. Even ten years apart couldn't break the strong emotional current that had always run between them.

She frowned as she sat up in his bed to look out at the lake through the window.

Unfortunately recognizing the steady strength of their bond didn't help anything else make sense, and it didn't mean that things between her and Nate could work beyond one beautiful sunrise.

She was reeling, not just from the most explosive love-making of her life, not just because Nate had dared to say "I love you" to her, but because being with Nate meant being a part of his sister's life. Being with Nate meant being a part of Emerald Lake; it meant she would be tied down, tied here, to one person and one little town. Being with Nate meant letting go of the brass ring and giving up all of her dreams for something bigger, dreams that her father had helped to nurture.

And all of those things terrified her.

Fully awake now, Andi knew she needed to call over to the hospital to check on her grandmother and mother. Unable to find a phone in his bedroom—so different from how she normally slept with her cell phone on the mattress beside her—she found a robe on the back of his door and put it on.

She hadn't felt shy when they were making love, but as she stepped out into his kitchen wearing his robe, she did.

"Good morning."

Nate looked up from the stove where he was turning over pancakes with a smile. Madison sat at the breakfast bar reading a book and said, "Hi Andi."

It was a little bit of a shock to be greeted so casually by the young girl. Was Madison so used to having women spend the night with her brother that she barely reacted?

Jealousy rode Andi like an out-of-control Mustang hell-bent on escaping its pen.

"Your grandmother is doing great, Andi." Nate's voice was warm. His eyes were even warmer as he took in his robe over her naked skin. "I spoke to Carol a little while ago, and she said Evelyn was awake and asking for her knitting needles."

Andi instantly forgot all about her stupid jealousy. Of course, Nate wouldn't parade women in front of his sister.

Relief flooded her as she leaned against the island. "I wish I could head straight back to the hospital to see her," she said, but they both knew she'd promised her mother she would run the store today.

"I'd like to come with you tonight to see her, if you don't mind."

Andi wanted to throw herself on him, plant kisses all over his face. But he'd already given her so much. Too much. More than she had any right to deserve.

And she was scared. So damn scared.

Andi was about to say something like *Oh no, I know you're busy* when Madison said, "Can I come too?" She shoved another huge bite of pancake into her mouth before adding, "I really like Evelyn. She comes into our class sometimes to read us books."

How could Andi say anything but "Of course, you can come. I'd love that. And I know Grandma will be so pleased to see you, Madison."

Still feeling horribly awkward in their cozy family kitchen, like she was the only piece that didn't fit in an already-finished puzzle, she started backing out of the room.

"If you don't mind, Nate, I'm just going to go take a quick shower, and then I'll be out of your hair."

But Nate was already sliding a plate of steaming pancakes on the counter.

"Sit first. You need to eat."

She would have denied it in her effort to get the heck out of there, but her stomach confirmed the truth of its emptiness with a loud growl before she could. Leaving her no choice but to sit down on an empty stool and pour syrup over the pancakes.

"I'm really sorry about your grandmother not feeling good," Madison said as she forked up another bite. "Nate told me she was coughing a lot. I had pneumonia once when I was a little kid, and it was really awful."

"Oh, that's really nice of you," Andi said stiffly, feeling as far out of her element as she could be in the too-big robe with bed hair, eating pancakes in Nate's kitchen with the sister he'd raised alone from a baby.

Trying to think of something, anything to say, she asked, "How's the knitting going?"

She was surprised by Madison's crooked smile. What a pretty girl she was. And so lucky to have a brother like Nate.

"It's going okay."

Frankly, Andi was shocked to hear that Madison had continued at all given how rough her beginning had been.

Nate's face lit up with pride. "She's almost finished a scarf."

"Nate." Madison's voice held a note of warning. Clearly she was embarrassed.

"Wow," Andi said casually, not wanting to make too big a deal out of it but wanting Madison to know how impressed she was. "That's awesome. I'd love to see the scarf when you're done."

Andi took a bite of her pancake. "Oh my god. This is amazing." She licked her lips again, closed her eyes as she took another bite. Her mouth was half full as she said, "I've never had pancakes this good."

Nate was smiling at her when she opened her eyes back up, but his eyes were full of heat.

And the love he'd professed less than an hour before.

Madison finished her last bite, slid off her seat, put her plate into the dishwasher, then walked out of the kitchen, leaving them alone. Wanting to look anywhere but at

Nate, Andi swept her glance around what she could see of his kitchen, living room, and dining room.

Nate's home was classic Adirondack with two stories, a large screened-in front porch, and a shingled front. The windows were framed in red, and the rails of the stairs and the porch were beautiful, glossy logs.

"You have a beautiful house, Nate."

It was the perfect home in the perfect setting. Andi couldn't help but think Nate's house was far more in keeping with the lake and the Adirondack Mountains than her mother's big white house could ever be.

"I dreamed about building this place for a long time."

Nate had always said he was going to build his own house one day. He'd done it, creating a real home for himself and his sister—so different from the cramped, dingy trailer he had grown up in.

She lifted her eyes to tell him this, and that's when she realized he hadn't taken his eyes off of her for one single second. The edge of darkness, the throb of heat—and love—in his gaze, ran little bolts of electricity down her spine. At which point Andi's heartbeat kicked up so hard and fast she dropped her fork, the tines clanging loudly on the edge of her plate.

\*     \*     \*

"Are you okay?"

Nate could see Andi trying to run from him again, trying to put back distance where they'd just erased it in his bed with the sunrise shining in on them.

"Nate, you were amazing last night. Thank you for being there. Not just for me, but for my mother and grandmother, too."

"You don't have to thank me for anything, sweetheart. Not one single thing."

He saw the flare of pleasure in her eyes at the endearment, along with the way it quickly morphed into panic.

"And what happened this morning"—she paused—"it was incredible, but—"

He put a finger over her mouth. "Not yet, Andi. Don't overthink it. Not yet."

"We have to think about it," she finally said, her voice barely above a whisper. "About what we're doing. About the fact that it can't possibly work."

Sitting beside her in his kitchen, watching her pull away from him, feeling it in her every word, every panicked glance she shot him, Nate should have finally seen proof of everything he'd thought was true. That nothing had really changed from when they were kids. That she wasn't going to stick through the hard stuff this time.

Only there was one big difference this time around: he wasn't going to make the mistake he'd made ten years ago.

The second time around, Nate simply refused to lose faith in the one woman he'd always believed in.

His life had never been easy. Hell, in those early days, weeks, years after losing his parents, he hadn't known how things were going to work out. All he'd known was that if he gave up faith in being able to take care of his sister and himself, then he would have been lost.

He had to believe he and Andi would work things out, too. He had to believe that together they'd find their way back to love. To a bigger, better, stronger love than they'd had before.

Because not believing it—and having to let her go again—would destroy him.

That was why he was going to believe—and let himself love her the way he always had, every single minute since they were kids.

"Let's take it hour by hour, sweetheart. Day by day."

That sweet hope flared in her eyes again before she tamped down on it. "But everything that happened between us—"

"Is all in the past now. You know it is, Andi. We don't have to go back there again."

From that moment he'd pulled her into his arms on the carousel, when she'd sobbed out her pain against his chest and they'd both honestly apologized to each other, he'd known that they were done having to go back to eighteen. Back to a place where neither of them had been anywhere near mature enough to know how to love the other person right.

He could see Andi didn't want to believe him. And that she was frightened by the thought of not using their past as an excuse to keep them apart.

"But in the boathouse didn't we agree that you have wide open skies and I have flashing city lights? That isn't changing, Nate."

"I may have the open spaces of this town, but I also have an empty space inside of me that no amount of blue skies could ever fill. Only you can do that, Andi." He put his hand on her cheek. "When I'm with you, I don't feel empty anymore."

"And you make me feel warm again," she whispered.

Her eyes opened wide with alarm, as if she had only just realized what she'd said.

Yanking herself back from his touch, she said, "It's still a mistake, Nate." Her beautiful blue eyes were sad. Resigned. "Being with you again was beautiful. And even though I should, I can't make myself wish it didn't happen." She slid off her stool, picked up her plate, and held it up like a shield between them. "But none of that changes the fact that making love is still a mistake we can never repeat."

# Chapter Eighteen

Dorothy and Helen were sitting on the Lake Yarns porch when Nate dropped Andi off on the way to Madison's school.

She thought she saw Dorothy's eyes widen a bit, seeing the two of them together in the light of day, but fortunately the woman was far more interested in how Evelyn was doing than the state of Andi's love life. Inviting them inside the store, she worked to get Lake Yarns ready for customers as she filled them in on Evelyn's situation.

That first day she'd had to take charge of store she'd been so lost, had been so far in over her head. A week later she felt that she would be well able to take on another day at Lake Yarns, start to finish.

The only problem was, she couldn't concentrate. She could barely think about anything but the slow slide of Nate's hands and mouth across her body, could barely focus on anything but that sweet emotion in his eyes as they finally came back together. And she couldn't stop remembering how many times she'd called their love-making a mistake.

As if saying it over and over could somehow make it true.

"You're a good girl, taking over the store for your mother and grandmother."

Andi looked up from a box of unspun alpaca hanks that she was unloading onto the shelves. She knew she needed to shake off her morning with Nate if she was going to get through the day. But it wasn't like shaking off a bad business deal so she could make another pitch to another client.

This was her life—her own heart—she was trying to shake off.

"I'm sorry?"

Dorothy put a hand on her arm. "I know how exhausted you must be, honey. I was just saying I know how pleased Evelyn and Carol both are, knowing you're here keeping the ship afloat."

The warmth of the woman's touch helped melt the ice that Andi had forced herself to swallow down in Nate's kitchen.

"It's not exactly a hardship, you know, hanging out with knitters all day."

Her grandmother's friend laughed. "My how things have changed. And how quickly. You should have seen your face at that first Monday night knitting group."

Andi was surprised by her own grin and so glad for a reason to do something other than cry. At least for now. "I'm glad I could provide some laughs to the group."

"Now," Helen said, "tell us about Nate."

Andi felt a telltale flush move across her cheeks. "He was great last night."

Oh god, she thought, may they not realize there was

more to "last night" than a trip to the hospital in an ambulance and a friend's couch to sleep on. But she knew better than to even hope that these women would let it go.

They were knitters. They could execute complicated stitches that made Andi's head spin just to look at the pattern.

And they could read a blush like a book.

They both leaned in. "Do tell."

"He stayed with us in the hospital and really took care of me and Mom."

Both women stared at her with knowing smiles. "I always wondered what he was waiting for," Dorothy said. "Why he wasn't married yet."

Helen nodded. "Now we know."

Andi's mouth fell open. "No. He—I—We—" She forced herself to shut her damn mouth before she made herself into even more of a fool.

"You've had a difficult night. We shouldn't be teasing you." Dorothy and Helen each put a hand over hers. "Give your grandmother our love when you go visit her tonight."

Before Andi could find her feet again—not that she'd been on them from the first moment she had set foot back in Emerald Lake a week ago—the door opened again. For the next hour, Andi reassured Evelyn's friends. And when customers from out of town came in, her grandmother's friends were right there helping them to find yarn and needles, helping to explain confusing patterns, giving their experience to new knitters.

Nate had been there for her last night. Today it seemed everyone in town was joining in.

The stack of get-well cards she had to deliver to Evelyn

kept growing, becoming tall enough that she needed to co-opt one of the store's shopping baskets for them. Through it all, Andi was amazed at the outpouring of love.

Jenny, a pretty middle-aged woman who worked about ten hours a week in the store and had the quickest fingers Andi had ever seen with needles and yarn, came in carrying an enormous vase of flowers. "I ran into the UPS guy outside."

She put them down on the counter, and after Andi had given her the update on Evelyn, Andi remembered to ask, "How did your son do on the math test he was so worried about?"

Jenny was happy to brag about her kids for a while. "He got a 90 percent. And Susie got the lead in the school musical."

"They're great kids." Andi had met Jenny's son and daughter the previous week when they'd dropped by the store for a few minutes after getting milk shakes at the diner.

"Susie wants to have a formal knitting lesson with you soon, by the way. She keeps asking me if I've talked to you about setting it up."

"But you're a much better knitter than I am."

"I'm also her mother. Trust me, she's better off learning from you."

Andi couldn't hide her pleasure at the request. "Tell her I'd be thrilled to teach her what I know."

"You're great with kids, you know. You have the same touch Carol and Evelyn do. All of you are effortless teachers."

Surprised yet again by the positive comparison to the women in her family, Andi honestly replied, "I'm just trying to keep from running all of my mother and grand-mother's customers away while they're gone."

Evelyn's doctor had made it perfectly clear that her grandmother would not be able to resume her regular hours at the store. No question, Evelyn's days of running Lake Yarns were over.

"Actually Jenny," Andi said, "I really need to find someone to manage the store. Are you interested?"

"Very part-time is pretty much all I've got right now." Jenny frowned. "But what about you? I thought maybe you were..."

Andi knew her expression must have been one of ab-solute horror because Jenny stopped and put her hand on Andi's arm.

"Sorry. I know you've got a big job in the city. I was just hoping that you'd started to think about sticking around. Especially with you and Nate being together."

"Nate and I aren't—"

Andi cut herself off before the lie could drop com-pletely. She and Nate *had*.

"How could people be talking about us?"

"You've been spotted around town together. At the bar. In his car." Jenny shrugged as if it was no big deal. "Look, if people are indeed talking about you, who cares?"

Andi opened her mouth to explain all the reasons she cared, but nothing came out.

"Nate's an amazing guy. You're a wonderful woman. If anything, people are going to be thrilled to find out that the two of you are a couple."

Until she left him high and dry. Again. Then she'd be the villain. Local girl gone bad. It was just what she'd wanted to avoid, part of the reason she had tried so hard to resist Nate. In a town like Emerald Lake, gossip was as much a part of the local infrastructure as the historic buildings.

Wanting desperately to turn the conversation away from her and Nate, Andi said, "Well, if you think of anyone who would be a great manager, could you let me know?"

"Sure, Andi. I'll help out any way I can. You know that. But for the record, I still think you're the best choice. No pressure, of course."

Considering that pressure was her middle name lately, Andi had to force a laugh she didn't really feel.

She felt guilty about leaving her family's store in a stranger's hands by going back to her job in the city. She felt guilty leaving her company in the lurch by being here in her family's store.

She'd been pulled in so many directions since returning to town—from Nate, from her family, from the store, from her job, from her new friends—she felt dizzy with it.

Jenny said, "You look beat. How about you let me take over for a few minutes while you get out of here and find something to eat and drink?"

Andi nodded gratefully. Her throat felt raw from the constant talking all morning, the tears the night before, and the in-between when she'd been unable to hold back the honest sounds of pleasure at how sweet it was to be back in Nate's arms.

She bent over to pick up her bag and a folder slid out.

Her heart stilled.

How could she have forgotten for even a second the entire reason she'd come back to town?

In order to make the architectural review deadline for the month and be a part of the town hall meeting this

Thursday, she needed to file the papers today. She looked up at the clock in horror.

The town clerk's office closed in ten minutes.

The taste of betrayal filled her mouth. This morning she'd been in Nate's bed. And even if it had been a mistake precipitated by a moment of weakness, even if she'd made it perfectly clear to him that there wasn't going to be a repeat performance, it didn't make filing the papers to get the condos under way just hours later feel any less wrong.

Nate would think she was using the condos to lash out at him, to push him away. He would think she was using the condos to make sure he didn't get too close.

He wouldn't understand that the condos had nothing to do with what she felt for him, that it was all her own deal. He wouldn't understand that she'd worked too hard to fail now, that she couldn't stand the thought of waking up and seeing that everything she'd given up for her career might all be for nothing.

"You dropped this," Jenny said, handing her the thick folder.

Andi stared at her project plans for a long moment before taking it.

\*     \*     \*

The town clerk's office was on the other side of Main Street from Lake Yarns. Every step Andi took was heavier than the one before it. And still she continued on, past the grocery store, past the art gallery, past the ice cream shop. She came to a stop at the mayor's office and looked up at his window.

Never more than at that moment did she wish that she

and Nate weren't on opposite sides of her building project. They'd had to overcome so much from their past just to get to where they were now.

A few seconds later she pushed open the heavy front door to the town clerk's office and practically walked headfirst into Catherine.

"Andi, I'm glad to see you."

She was? Andi wasn't at all sure she managed to mask her surprise in time. Where was Catherine's cold glare from knitting night when they'd been going at each other in the back room of Lake Yarns?

"I've been wanting to come by the store all morning to ask about Evelyn. Nate told me she was awake and wanting to knit this morning, thank god. Any other updates?"

"She's still on oxygen, but the nurse let her talk to me for a minute." Andi had to smile at what Evelyn had said to her. "She wanted to make sure I could handle the store on my own."

"Sounds like the Evelyn we all know and love."

As they stood together on the sidewalk chatting, Andi could almost think they were friends again. But then Catherine looked down and saw the folder in her hands, the KLEIN GROUP PROJECT tab facing out in bold, black letters.

Catherine's smile fell. It was perfectly clear to Andi just how disappointed she was. "You're still going through with your plans?"

Andi took a deep breath. "I am."

"Everyone in town is going to be at the town hall meeting, you know. And they aren't going to care that you grew up here." Catherine didn't look angry anymore, not the way she had last night at the knitting group, but she obviously wasn't thrilled in the least with what Andi was doing. "It isn't going to make them any less honest about what they think."

Andi had loved town hall meetings as a little girl, the way the adults would often yell at each other for what seemed like absolutely no reason. But she'd never thought she'd be one of those adults.

What other choice did she have? If she didn't file the papers, she'd lose her job. And the truth was, Andi still believed the condos could be good for Emerald Lake. Just as she told Nate that first night at the Tavern, she'd make sure they were.

Finally Andi said, "I'm sorry you're so upset with me."

Catherine's gaze didn't waver. "I am, too."

As she walked away, Andi had to put her hand over her breastbone. It felt like something sharp was digging into her chest, piercing her skin, trying to get all the way into her blood and guts.

Ten minutes later she was back out on the sidewalk, holding an empty folder.

# Chapter Nineteen

Nate and Madison walked into Lake Yarns as Andi was ringing up her last customer of the day. Madison showed her brother all the yarns she liked while Andi closed up. It should have only taken Andi five minutes to clear out the register and put away the order forms she'd been filling out, but the collage of images of her and Nate together in his bed, then in his kitchen, all the words they'd said—*"I love you"* and *"it's still a mistake"* and *"you are so beautiful"* and *"please, Nate, now"*—made her slow and clumsy and confused with the money and papers.

Finally when the three of them were all in his truck together, Madison asked, "How old were you when you learned to knit, Andi?"

More glad than she could ever say to have Nate's sister as a buffer between them, Andi screwed up her mouth and thought about it.

"Honestly, I can't remember not knowing how."

"Babies can't hold knitting needles."

Andi had to laugh at that. "You're right. I wasn't a baby. But I couldn't have been more than four or five."

There hadn't been any formal training, just years of sitting at her mother's and grandmother's knees, of being like any normal girl and wanting to do what they did.

Until that day she'd realized she wasn't like them, that she didn't fit in, that she wasn't girlie enough or good enough with her hands. She was good with numbers and arguing. She wasn't soft and small and rounded. She was tall and lean and dark like her father.

"Andi even made me a scarf once."

She looked at Nate in surprise. "I did?"

"Do the words Christmas and first grade mean anything to you?"

A vision of a lumpy, putrid-green mess full of holes jumped into Andi's brain, and she had to groan. "Unfortunately yes."

"So you weren't always really good at it?"

Andi suddenly realized why Madison was asking her these questions. She must not be feeling she was good enough at something. She must not be confident that she could ever learn how to get things right.

Boy, she was certainly coming to the right person on that one.

"Honestly, I'm still not really good at it." Andi shifted as far as she could from beneath her seat belt to meet Madison's eyes. "But if I wanted to, with enough practice and dedication and focus, I know I could get really good at it."

"So, the only reason you're not good at knitting is because you don't want to be good at it?"

Andi had to take a moment with that one. And then it was the craziest thing, but she found herself saying, "You want to know the truth?"

"Yes."

Nate's eyes were still on the dark road, but Andi could feel his focus on her now, too, as both he and his sister waited for her answer.

"I'm not good at knitting because I quit too young. I got frustrated, and instead of working through it, I told myself it was stupid. I told myself I didn't like it."

But she had. She'd loved sitting with her mother and grandmother making easy hats while they made the more difficult mittens and booties for newborn babies.

"And you know what I wish?"

"Yeah," Madison said easily. "You wish you hadn't totally lied to yourself."

Andi barely kept her mouth from falling open. "Pretty much."

Speaking of lies, Andi couldn't stand keeping what she had done from Nate another second longer. Thankfully that was when Madison put her headphones on.

Still, even with his sister listening to music, Andi wanted to be careful. How many times had she sat there with her headphones on, listening in on her parents' conversations, to things she shouldn't have heard? Her mother offering to come back to D.C. with Andi for an extended trip but not really meaning it. Her father looking almost relieved at telling her to stay at Emerald Lake.

"I filed the papers today." She waited for Nate's reaction, for a telltale sign of his anger.

"I know."

It killed her that she couldn't read him. "If I could have waited even one more day—"

"You wouldn't have made the deadline today if you had."

Knowing he couldn't have possibly seen the final plans yet, she had to say, "I convinced my client to throw in a new football field, too." Hoping to cut off the objections she was sure had to be coming, she quickly said, "I didn't do it to try and buy your support. I just thought it would really help the town."

He sighed then. "I appreciate you giving me a heads-up about the project, but the way I see it, there's the condos and politics and football fields. And then there's you and me. Just us, Andi."

She felt like she'd been so clear with him about the fact that "you and me" wasn't going anywhere, wasn't going past one night of giving into the need to hold each other for just a few precious hours. Why was he so determined not to listen?

If she could have, she would have reminded him about their *mistake*, that last night was a one-time-only thing. But she couldn't, not with his sister in the seat behind them.

Somehow Andi was going to get through this visit to her grandmother, focus all of her energy on the woman she loved so much, and then in a couple of hours, she'd be back in her mother's house again. Just her and her computer, no Nate there to tempt her.

Yes, in just a couple of hours, she'd be perfectly safe.

And completely alone. Again.

\*      \*      \*

Evelyn could see there was something different between her granddaughter and the mayor the second they walked in with his sister. Their bond was strong again, the air between them fairly crackling with electricity.

Andi was especially tense. Nate was particularly watchful.

Madison ran over first and hugged her—so young, so fresh, so happy because of all her brother had done to give her a good life.

Andi dropped a basket of cards onto a nearby table. "Grandma! It's so good to see you sitting up. You look great."

Over Andi's shoulder, Evelyn kept her eagle eye on the project Carol was knitting.

"Carol," she rasped out, "too tight."

"Mother?"

Evelyn looked at Carol. "Give. Andi. Finish."

Carol held up the barely begun project in her hands in clear confusion. "The Fair Isle? You want me to give it to Andi?"

Evelyn nodded and Carol frowned. Evelyn nodded again, and Carol gave the barely started sweater to a very bemused Andi, who had watched their exchange in confusion.

"You. Make this."

Evelyn suddenly realized why she'd had to start another Fair Isle sweater in the exact pattern she'd made for Carlos so long ago on the day that her granddaughter had arrived back at Emerald Lake. She had thought it was because of the memories, because age and her dreams were taking her closer to him all the time. But now she knew the real reason.

The sweater was Evelyn's second chance at true love.

A chance that meant so much more because it wasn't for her.

*       *       *

Nate was aware of Andi's nerves during the whole drive home from the hospital. She didn't fidget. Instead she was strangely still. Too still.

And then finally, they hit the only stop sign in town. Left to her house, right to his, and he still hadn't figured out a way to try and convince Andi to stay with them again. Not when he could practically see her building walls—complete with reinforcements—every minute they were together.

Right then, Madison asked, "Do you like spaghetti?"

Andi practically jumped out of her seat. "Spaghetti?"

"Yeah, 'cause Nate makes the best spaghetti in the world."

Andi's mouth opened, closed, as she blinked between him and his sister.

His beautiful, wonderful, brilliant sister.

"You're coming home with us again, right?" Madison asked. "Since your grandma and mom are in the hospital still?" Without waiting for Andi to answer, Madison added, "'Cause I was kind of hoping you could help me finish my scarf. There's a word for it, right? When you tie it all up at the end?"

Finally Andi found her voice. "Binding off. It's called binding off."

Nate knew that was what she'd been planning to do with the two of them tonight. Bind them off. Tie everything up. So that she could walk away again.

Didn't she realize yet that he was going to fight like hell for her this time?

"So can you help me bind off my scarf?" Madison blushed. "I'd like totally die if I gave it to Jaden, and it unraveled."

Andi's eyebrows raised at the boy's name. She shot Nate a quick look. "Don't worry. I promise Jaden won't have a chance of unraveling your scarf."

Nate wanted to just make the right turn, but he couldn't make the decision for Andi. He couldn't let his sister make it for Andi, either.

"My house, Andi? Or yours?"

She paused for long enough that he was afraid of what her answer would be. She was obviously warring with herself.

Finally she said, "Your house, Nate." She smiled back at Madison. "We've got a scarf to bind off." She didn't quite meet his eyes as she added, "And spaghetti to eat."

When they were all inside his house a couple of minutes later, Andi stood awkwardly in the kitchen. "Can I help with dinner?"

"Nope. Go ahead and knit. I'll let you know when it's done."

He could see them from the stove, Andi's dark head and Madison's blond hair, bent over their needles. He knew how easily his sister could get frustrated, was listening for telltale sounds just in case he needed to intervene, but all that floated back to him were two soft voices and clicking needles.

He didn't mean to stare, but he couldn't help himself. Now that Madison was working solo again, Andi had turned her face to the side to look out the window at the moonlit lake.

He drank in her beautiful profile, his body tightening—his heart swelling—again in anticipation of another night with her. He wanted to kneel beside her and take her face in his hands, tell her he loved her again, then kiss her until she was breathless and begging him to take her back to his bed.

But all that would have to wait for spaghetti and looking over homework—and for him to figure out a way to convince her being together wasn't a mistake.

He watched Andi reach into her bag and pull out a soft blue-and-white bundle. Evelyn's knitting passed on through Carol in the hospital. She unfolded a piece of paper and frowned at it, her eyes scanning the page as she read it over. She reached into her bag again and pulled out a mini-laptop.

He heard her ask his sister, "You have wireless, right?"

"Yeah." Madison barely looked up from her scarf. "Why?"

"This pattern my grandmother gave me is ridiculously difficult to follow."

Madison took the pattern from Andi and made a face. "It's like another language."

"No kidding. Thank god for the Internet. I just found out this week that you can watch videos to learn how to do this kind of sweater."

"Cool. Can I see?"

They shifted closer together as Andi moved her fingers over the keyboard and brought up a video of a woman's hands.

The two girls he loved most in the world were sitting together, working side by side on his couch, in the home he'd built with his own two hands. Happiness flooded him, pushing around his insides.

And then from out of nowhere, he had a vision of Andi in a sleek white dress, holding a bouquet, walking down the aisle to say "I do," the most beautiful bride in the world.

Nate ran a hand over the lower half of his face, sucking in a breath, working to push the vision aside. But he couldn't do it.

Not when he wanted to make that vision real more than he'd ever wanted anything.

He had to reach out to the counter and hold on tight as he watched them. It wasn't until he heard the sauce sputtering in the pot and felt a hot splash of it against his cheek that he finally moved back to the stove.

Turning down the heat, stirring his sauce with a wooden spoon, he said, "Come and get it."

"I'm starved," Andi said as she took her seat at the dining table. She ran her fingers over the polished-wood top. "Did you make this, too?"

"He makes tons of stuff," Madison said. "All of my friends' mothers are constantly asking him to come over to help them with things."

Andi raised her eyebrows. "Really?"

He thought he saw a flash of jealousy in her pretty blue eyes. Good. Maybe realizing she didn't want anyone else to have him would help her realize that she did.

They all ate in silence for a while, and then like he did every night, Nate asked Madison if there was anything she needed help with on her homework before bed.

She shook her head, proudly telling him, "I got 100 percent on my spelling test today."

"Awesome."

They high-fived, and Nate realized Andi had stopped eating and was staring at them, her eyes full of longing.

"May I be excused?" Madison asked.

Nate looked at Madison's plate. She'd eaten more than half, which was pretty good.

"Sure. Go get ready for bed. I'll be in soon."

His sister pushed her chair back, put her plate into the sink, and was practically out of the room when she turned back.

"Thanks for showing me that stuff on the computer and also how to finish the scarf, Andi. I hope it's cold enough for Jaden to wear it soon."

Andi smiled. "You're welcome. It looks awesome. He's going to love it."

When he heard the bathroom door close and the water turn on in the sink, Nate said, "She likes you."

"It's mutual."

Nate couldn't stop the visions of more dinners like this, lunches and breakfasts, too.

He knew he was moving too fast, that he'd barely gotten the woman he loved back into his bed. Who knew what it would take to get her to agree to white lace and school plays? But he'd waited so long already.

Ten years was just too damn long. He didn't want to wait another hour.

"You really are a fantastic cook, Nate. Where did you learn?"

He forced his brain back to the here and now. "All around the lake." Hoping to see that spark of jealousy again, he said, "Women kept inviting me over for cooking lessons."

"Any excuse to have you over," she muttered right on cue.

He had managed to keep his hands off of her until now. But now that it was just the two of them, alone in his dining room, after she'd made the choice to stay another night with him, he was done controlling himself.

Scooting his chair closer to hers, he reached over and slid a lock of her hair around his index finger. "Jealous?"

She pulled away. "No."

"Liar." He stood up. "I need to go kiss Madison good night."

"And then I'd really appreciate it if you drove me home."

Nate knew better than to respond, knew she was itching for an argument, to have a concrete reason to have to leave. He simply stacked their plates and took them into the kitchen on his way to Madison's room.

But before he headed down the hall, he looked back into the dining room. Andi was still sitting in her seat, the lock of hair he'd wound around his finger, wound around hers now.

A surge of pure male satisfaction rode him. He liked that his touch, even the barest, lightest one, could make her lose her place, could stop her cold for at least a few seconds.

Tonight he planned to make her forget everything.

Everything but how perfectly they fit together.

# Chapter Twenty

Full of nervous energy, Andi cleaned off the table, loaded the dishwasher, and washed the dishes. When the countertops were so clean she could practically see her reflection in them, she walked back over to the couch and sat down next to her knitting.

How could her grandmother have possibly thought she had the knitting skills to finish this sweater? She hadn't even known what Fair Isle was until she'd looked it up with Madison.

And yet, Andi couldn't stand the thought of letting her grandmother down. Helping out at the store for a few days was one thing. Tackling this sweater, she could already see, was another thing entirely. Andi knew how to run a business, but dealing with multiple strands of yarn while trying to knit them into an intricate pattern...well, that was going to take some serious concentration.

Normally, Andi thought as she picked up the needles and pattern and tried to make sense of them again, she was a master of concentration. But when Nate was around, her

thoughts ended up fluttering around like little lost butter-
flies.

She looked down, realized she was clenching the needles and yarn tightly in her hands. He had gently accused
her of not telling the truth earlier about being jealous of
the women who swarmed around him. He was right. She
wasn't normally a liar. It was just that these feelings were
confusing.

As soon as he finished putting Madison to bed, Andi
needed to head back to her own bed, too. If she were
smart, she would get out of his house right now, swim
across the cold lake if she had to, before she did something stupid again. Before she made another—bigger—
mistake by giving into feelings that couldn't possibly
make rational sense.

But she couldn't leave without at least saying thank
you for dinner and good night, could she?

The train of her thoughts was too dangerous for her to
keep following them. This impossible sweater on her lap,
for all its difficulty, was much safer.

Carol had marked where she'd left off on the pattern
in the hospital, and Andi forced herself to begin there, to
take one stitch and then another.

She couldn't let herself look any further than one stitch
ahead. She couldn't let herself worry about getting to the
end. She couldn't worry about making sure the sweater
turned out perfectly. Because if she did any of those
things, she might as well save herself time and frustration
by stuffing the yarn, needles, and pattern into the garbage
can right now.

"Seeing you with those needles makes me realize how
much you look like your grandmother."

Nate's warm voice caressed her spine, made her skin tingle all over.

How long had he been standing there by the door, staring at her with those dark eyes? She'd been so focused on the pattern, on trying to pull in the correct strands of yarn, that she hadn't realized he'd come in.

His large hands were hooked into the pockets of his jeans, and a small shiver ran through her, a shiver filled with the foolish anticipation of having those hands on her again.

And that dark, sinful gaze shining with love for her as she came apart in his arms.

"Your eyes must be playing tricks on you," she finally replied. "I don't look anything like them."

"Do you really not see it, Andi?"

"My mother and grandmother are so small and feminine," Andi found herself saying. "They've always been able to make the most beautiful things with their hands. Not just with yarn, but with paint and fabric. I've never fit in with them, you know."

She loved her grandmother, her mother, but she'd always felt a world apart from them.

"They're so soft. They bake and sew and cook."

Not only did Evelyn and Carol have curves she never got, but they'd always chosen to live happily on a small scale, whereas she'd never stopped shooting for big. For bigger. Just like her father.

"You have your grandmother's eyes." Nate knelt down in front of her, his knuckles brushing against her cheekbone. "Only yours are in sharper focus. Brighter." He brushed the pad of his thumb across her lower lip. "You have the same mouth as your mother, only your lips are plumper." He slid his thumb down to her chin. "But this chin is all your own, sweetheart. So stubborn." He brought his mouth closer to hers. "So sweet."

A lump had formed in her throat at everything he saw, all the things no one else ever had. "You know just what to say," she whispered against his mouth. "And just how to say it."

"No, sweetheart, I don't."

She lifted her eyes to his in surprise.

"If I did, I'd know what to say to get you to stay for more than one night at a time. For more than a week or two before heading back to the city."

The air grew still between them, the tension riding high at his words, at their barely banked desire for each other, at the control she was constantly trying to put over it.

She knew she had to pull away, walk away from this. From him. She needed to do it right now. She should have done it last night, when they were in front of her house and she could have gone up to sleep in her cold, empty bed.

Andi couldn't lie to herself and call this a hometown fling. Not when being with Nate was so much more than that. It was why she'd stayed away from him for so long. Because she'd known that if she ever let her defenses down, he'd be right there, stealing even more of her heart than he already had.

But hadn't she been strong for years? Hadn't it eaten through her soul to be that strong for so long? She'd spent so long worrying about complications. Couldn't she have one more night with Nate? One final night where he was hers and she was his?

She'd have to be strong again soon, she knew that, but with her grandmother in the hospital, with her career suddenly having more to do with yarn than Fortune 100 business development, with Nate's eyes seeing things no one else ever had, as her fingers curled with tension into the sweater in her lap, suddenly all she could think was, *One stitch at a time. No looking forward. No worrying about making it to the end.*

And that was when she finally said, "I'm here now."

*For one more night.*

A second later, Nate's arms were around her rib cage and beneath her knees, and he was lifting her off the couch, her knitting sliding off her lap onto the cushions.

"I don't want to waste one more second with you, Andi," he said, and then he was making good on his words by kissing her as he took her back to his bedroom.

Once inside, he pushed the door shut with his shoulder, then turned them so that her back was to the door. As she slid down his body, back to her feet, every inch of contact caused a slow burn across her body.

"I swore I was going to do this slow," he said as he pulled her shirt off, along with her bra. "I told myself I was going to have some control this time."

But Andi was sick to death of control.

"Please," she whispered as she helped him slide off her jeans and panties. "Love me, Nate. Just love me."

His dark eyes dilated to black, and then her hands were tugging at his pants, at his boxers and T-shirt, and it was the most natural thing in the world for him to put his hands on her bottom and say, "Wrap your legs around me," and for her to trust that he would hold her.

To trust that he wouldn't let her fall, no matter what.

And then he was pushing into her and she was pushing back, wanting all of him. She buried her head in the crook of his shoulder as he filled her so completely that her breath left her lungs in a whoosh.

She lifted her head, had to look at him, had to say, "Nate."

He held her body still around his, his arms strong. Steady.

"I love you, sweetheart."

That was all it took for the dam to break. She'd never felt so wild, so strong, so good. She could feel her inner muscles squeezing him as she got closer, so close to that sweet spot where nothing mattered but how good he made her feel, where there was no past, no future.

Only a stunningly beautiful present.

And then he was moving them to his bed and his mouth was moving across her forehead with slow little kisses. She breathed him in as he ran kisses down across her temple, down over her cheekbones, her closed eyelids, the tip of her nose.

With each sweet press of his lips against her skin, she felt herself coming back alive, inch by sensual inch. His body was a wonder, his shoulders and arms corded and rippling with muscles, his chest broad, his abs defined by the deep shadows between them, all of it tapering down to slim hips.

"I can't believe I'm here. With you. How do you do this to me? How do make me feel so much?"

His low chuckle was full of sensuality. Full of such deep desire—and love—that she didn't know how to take it all in.

"Sweet, Andi. You're so sweet."

No one but Nate had ever called her sweet. As far as she knew, no one had ever thought it.

A heartbeat later everything stopped, her breath, her heart, her thoughts as she came apart beneath him. And then he was calling out her name, holding her hips completely still as he exploded into her.

She couldn't open her eyes, couldn't move a muscle. Not when she was still reeling from the passion between them. But then she felt him shift as he brushed a lock of damp hair away from her face.

"I've never known anyone as beautiful as you."

And she had never felt as beautiful as she did when she was in his arms. But before she could find the breath to say the words aloud, sleep came at her like a runaway freight train.

Andi was only barely aware of his words of love, of his lifting her and sliding her beneath the covers, warm and safe against his body before she fell asleep.

# Chapter Twenty-one

Andi woke up alone in Nate's bed. At 2 a.m., the room was dark and all she could hear was the slow push of waves on the shore outside his bedroom window.

The bed felt empty. Way too empty.

Where was Nate? And why had he left the bedroom in the middle of the night?

Slipping out of his bed, she wrapped his robe around her naked body. Making sure to keep her footfalls quiet so that she wouldn't wake Madison, Andi went down the stairs and looked into the kitchen and living room. They were both empty, and she was frowning when she heard the creak of a chair out on the porch.

She pushed open the front door, and the cold fall air hit her as she stepped outside.

"Nate?"

He looked surprised to see her and then glad, so glad that her heartbeat kicked into double-time.

"Come here, sweetheart."

He pulled her onto his lap, covering them with a nearby blanket.

No one had ever held her like this, no one but Nate. He settled her more firmly onto his lap, and it was the most natural thing in the world for her to lay her head against his shoulder. Even in only a long-sleeved T-shirt and jeans on the cold porch, he was warm.

Sitting on the porch with Nate, curled up safe and warm in his arms, looking out at the fall moon, felt like a home she'd only thought existed in fairy tales.

She wanted to sink into it, wanted to let herself believe that she really was home. She wanted to pretend that he could make her dinner every night and she could teach Madison to knit on the couch, and then later, when the sun fell and the moon rose, she could lose herself in Nate's kisses, his heat.

And yet, even as he pulled her closer, she knew she couldn't let herself get used to this feeling.

Emerald Lake wasn't home for her, no matter how good being with Nate was.

She lifted her head from his chest and her heart squeezed at his tormented expression.

"Why did you leave the bed, Nate?"

He shook his head. "It doesn't matter."

And then his mouth was on hers, demanding and giving all at the same time, and for a few long moments, she wasn't able to do anything but submit to his need—and her own.

It took every last ounce of self-control to pull away.

"It matters, Nate," she said softly. "Talk to me. Please. You wouldn't be out here if something wasn't wrong. Tell me what's wrong."

"I'd rather tell you what's right. You're here, Andi. Have I told you how much I love having you here?"

She smiled at his words, even though she knew he was stalling. "You weren't sleeping?"

He shifted beneath her, and she could feel his discomfort at her question. "No." He looked out at the lake, anywhere but her.

"Why?"

A muscle jumped in his jaw. "Old demons, Andi. That's all they are."

She reached a hand up to his face, soothed the tight muscle, wishing she could take his pain away. She knew she should leave him alone, that she wasn't going to be here for much longer, but the pain she felt vibrating through him wouldn't let her go.

"Is it us?"

"No. I told you our breakup was behind us, and I meant it."

She knew what it had to be, then. "It's your parents, isn't it? You have nightmares about what happened to them, don't you? About what happened to you?"

His thigh muscles were so tight beneath her hips she was almost afraid to move.

"Andi."

Her name was a warning, and her chest squeezed as she realized just what deep pain he must be in, deep enough that he was afraid to share it with her.

Had he shared his lingering grief, his suffering, with anyone? But she already knew the answer, because he'd even hidden it from her, and would have kept hiding it if she hadn't spent the night.

Thanking god that she was actually here for once when he needed her, Andi wrapped her arms around him. Because for all her fears about being with him, despite the fact that she knew forever was never going to be theirs, she still wanted so badly to give him comfort, to smother his demons with love until they couldn't live and breathe inside of him anymore.

Hugging Nate was like hugging a brick wall, but she didn't let go, couldn't let go of him.

Over and over he'd been there for her, had helped her and her family, and if holding him here in the dark was her only option, it was what she would do.

And then suddenly, there was a little give beneath her hips and his arms weren't so stiff anymore. Slowly she felt him soften beneath her hug.

"I still dream about it, Andi. Walking into the trailer and seeing my dad there. The trailer was quiet, too damn quiet, and I knew something was wrong before I even opened the door."

Andi didn't loosen her hold on him, not even at the stark pain in his voice, so at odds with the beautiful sound of the waves lapping at the lakeshore in front of his porch.

"I knew he was taking my mom's death hard. I knew he was having a hell of a time trying to take care of a newborn. I knew he was drinking more than he usually did. But I didn't know he could ever do something like that."

Andi could feel Nate's heartbeat racing against her chest, could feel him tense up again. She wanted to tell him he didn't have to say anything else, that he didn't need to relive it all for her, but she couldn't get the words out. Because something told her that it was, strangely, just the opposite.

Nate needed to finally talk, and she could feel him opening up word by word, sentence by sentence. It meant more to her than anything ever had before that he trusted her with his pain.

"There was blood everywhere. So red and thick it looked like someone had broken a ketchup bottle all over the floor, the walls, the couch, with bits and chunks of something. I threw up, Andi. Right there in the middle of it all, I threw up."

*Oh god.*

She'd thought she knew the story, but she hadn't been inside his trailer that weekend—and he hadn't ever gone into the details of what he'd seen. She hadn't been brave enough to ask for details, either.

She shivered at the awful picture and pulled herself in closer to him. She could tell by the rigidness of his body beneath hers that he was lost in his memories of that night he'd found his father.

"Nate, I'm so sorry." Andi couldn't stop her tears from falling. "You were so young. You never should have had to see something like that." He never should have had to live through it, either.

His eyes were on her, but she didn't think he saw her. Instead she knew he was seeing his old trailer, bloody from his father's suicide.

"I don't even know how I got to Madison, how I made it through that mess to her crib. But she was crying. And from that moment on, I vowed to do whatever it took to take care of her. Anything."

Madison was why he had stayed at Emerald Lake. Not just because he loved the town. Not just because he felt he owed the people here a lifelong debt for helping him when he needed it most.

It was all for Madison.

Although Andi had left Emerald Lake as soon as she could, she understood why he wanted to raise his sister in this small town. Emerald Lake was a place where people took care of each other, where Dorothy watched over Madison as a grandmother would have, where Andi's own mother and grandmother showed their love with yarn and hugs and cookies.

Nate wasn't just a good man. He was a magnificent man. And she would never ask him to choose her over the welfare of his sister. It didn't matter what she felt for him. She would never ask him to leave Emerald Lake. It didn't matter that her heart was going to break a hundred times over when she left without him at her side. She would never again question his decision to stay here.

Tonight all that mattered was finding a way to help him heal, to clear away the darkness from his soul so that he could sleep at night, so that lingering pain didn't hide behind his smile, pulling him down when he deserved to soar.

"Who knows what you've just told me about what you saw, about how bad it really was?"

"The police chief. The paramedics. They kept it quiet. People knew my father shot himself, but none of them dared ask me to paint them a picture."

"So you've never seen a therapist to talk about your nightmares or a—"

He cut her off. "No."

"You just picked up the pieces and moved on?"

She felt him tense again. "I did what I had to do."

"But I saw how angry you were, Nate. That first weekend when I came back from college after you called to tell me what happened, you were so angry."

"I told you, Andi, I'm not upset with you anymore."

"No, Nate, even before we had our blow up you were

angry. And how could you not be? If your father had given one single thought to the kind of life he was leaving his kids to deal with, then you wouldn't have had to—"

His hands came around her waist fast and hard, lifting her off of his lap so that he could stand up and leave.

Deep, heavy regret pulled at her, made her wish she could have kept her mouth shut. For so long, she'd been a master at holding everything inside.

The one time she let her real thoughts and feelings loose, look what happened. She hurt the very person she never wanted to hurt again.

"I'm sorry, Nate. I shouldn't have said it like that."

But instead of leaving, he said, "How could I have been angry with my father, Andi? He was depressed. He couldn't control what he did."

Andi had a big decision to make. She could give in and stop talking about his father and maybe salvage some of the night. Or she could risk whatever was left of their confusing relationship and push him all the way to where he needed to go.

But the truth was, there wasn't any decision to make.

If helping Nate meant risking everything—even the love she didn't know how to return—that was what she had do.

It was what she *wanted* to do.

Tonight, out on his porch, she saw all the shades of the boy she'd known, the man she was discovering. Nate Duncan wasn't just an incredibly great guy that she'd adored as a girl. He wasn't just a protector of his little sister. He wasn't just mayor of a town that he deeply cared for. He wasn't just sexy, wasn't just funny, wasn't just loving, wasn't just a man who made her heart race every time he was near.

He was also a man who had been working like crazy every minute of his life to contain a deep well of anger and sadness and pain.

Going to where he stood staring out at the lake, she was shaking as she pressed herself against his hard muscles.

"You were such a great son, but you had already been dealing with your father's depression for years. Isn't it one thing to be empathetic with someone who's got problems and another thing entirely when they take an action that's guaranteed to hurt you? With everyone else you can be Mr. Hero, swooping in to save your sister and the town, but even though you really are a hero, it doesn't mean you can't take some time to deal with your own demons. So that you can finally move on."

She rested her cheek in the center of his broad back, felt his heart beating strong and fast.

"You can pretend with everyone else, Nate, but you don't have to pretend with me. You've always taken care of everyone around you. You've looked so strong for so many years. But has anyone ever taken care of you the way you need?"

"The town was there for me, Andi. Henry from the general store used to send over packages from out of the blue—pipes would be delivered just in time to fix bathroom plumbing, paint cans would show up right when the front porch was peeling through. He even gave me new windows after a tree limb broke through during a nasty storm, telling me it was part of an order that his guys had screwed up for someone else and what were they going to do with one window. Catherine would babysit. Your mom was constantly dropping off food."

Yes, she could see that so many people had helped him with the details.

But had anyone been there to heal his heart?

*She should have been there.*

He'd said the past was behind him, that he wasn't angry with her anymore, but that didn't mean she wasn't still angry with herself.

Andi knew she couldn't turn back the clock, couldn't redo what was already done. But she was here now with a few precious hours before the sun rose to try and heal the man who didn't deserve to still be hurting.

\*          \*          \*

As Nate slowly resurfaced from the darkness, he realized Andi was soft and warm against his back.

Out there on the porch, it felt like she was trying to break though his armor. Armor he had barely acknowledged he'd covered himself with for the past ten years.

Everyone had long ago assumed he was over his parents' death. No one knew he continued to have nightmares about finding his father dead on the carpet.

Nate turned around to come face-to-face with the woman he loved. He needed to take her into his arms to find his balance.

Even though she'd just sent him careening.

Hadn't he known all along that it would come to this, that letting Andi in, even part of the way, meant she wouldn't stop until she'd yanked off every last layer of armor?

This armor had gotten him through the worst moments of his life. When she'd been nowhere to be found.

But the armor was heavy.

And he was sick of wearing it.

Faith.

He had faith in Andi. Faith that her caring about him this much tonight meant that she wouldn't just be here for him tonight . . . but that despite having told him she wasn't going to stay, in the end she just might choose to stay forever this time.

Without saying another word, he picked her up and opened the front door without letting her go.

"Nate?"

He didn't speak as he walked through the house with her, didn't say a word until they were back in his bedroom. "Thank you for helping, sweetheart."

"But I didn't—"

"Yes"—he cut off her soft protest with a soft kiss— "you did."

And it was amazing just how much lighter he felt, that just giving voice to his nightmares could erase so much of the junk that had been eroding his soul for so long.

And then Andi leaned in and kissed him softly, so softly he had to groan against the slow sweep of her tongue as it slid against his.

This kiss was different than her other kisses. Sweeter, steeped in pure emotion.

He slid her down to her feet, and she stepped back from him, holding his gaze all the while, her eyes full of heat and something he wanted to believe was love as she slipped his robe off of her shoulders.

He drank in her naked body in the stream of moonlight. Her beautiful face looked different, too, softer, more vulnerable.

She took the hem of his long-sleeved T-shirt into her hands, pulled it up his torso, off his arms, over his head.

He forgot how to breathe, forgot almost everything but the light scratch of her fingertips against his skin as her hands found the button of his jeans next, deftly undoing it and then the zipper.

She was stripping his clothes off, but it felt like so much more, like she was stripping away the layers, the defenses he'd built up around him so many years ago.

And then before he realized it, she was on her knees.

"You don't have to do this, Andi," he managed in a voice so low he wasn't sure she would hear him. But she was already taking him into her hands and then her mouth, and he couldn't do anything but thread his hands into her hair, couldn't hold back a groan of deep pleasure.

He knew what she was doing, that she was trying to replace his nightmares, trying to destroy his demons with the feel of her skin, her hands, her mouth.

If he were a better man, he would make her stop, tell her that he could deal just fine on his own. If he were a stronger man, he'd pull himself away from her sweet lips and take care of her pleasure first.

But Andi had always been his weakness.

And then he lost the thread of his thoughts, everything except the "I love you" that came a heartbeat before he could no longer form words. The muscles in his arms and legs were still shaking when he reached down and pulled Andi up off of her knees, dragging her tightly against him.

Her lips were tilted up into a wicked little smile. "That was fun."

He couldn't believe he was grinning, couldn't believe he was actually feeling playful on a night when the nightmares had come.

He picked her up and plopped her back on the bed, her

laughter choking off midstream as she realized what he was planning. "You didn't think you could get away with that only going one way, did you?"

Her eyes were big. Aroused. He didn't wait to let her answer before putting each of her legs over his shoulder and dipping his head down between her thighs. Her breath came out in gasps as he took her where she'd just taken him.

But it wasn't enough. He needed all of her. Beneath him. Wrapped all around him.

Moving up to the side table to pull out a condom, he felt her hand on his arm.

"Please. I don't want anything between us. I'm safe, Nate."

Even though he knew she had to be talking about her body as she reached for him, her arms coming around his neck, her legs around his waist, he wanted to believe that the word *safe* had another far deeper meaning.

And as their kiss began at the same moment that he slid into her, as every touch, every kiss, every slow slide of his body against hers felt like pure, sweet love, Nate told himself he was doing the right thing having faith in her.

Andi would keep his heart safe this time. She had to.

Because even though he'd somehow managed to live without her for ten long years, Nate could no longer imagine how he'd done it...he simply couldn't imagine any other world, couldn't even think of his life, his sister's life, her mother's life, her grandmother's life without Andi in it.

Somehow, some way, he had to believe they'd find a way to make it work.

# Chapter Twenty-two

The following day Andi was on the verge of throwing down the Fair Isle sweater she was about to murder, when Dorothy walked into Lake Yarns.

"Just looking at Fair Isle gives me the hives."

Assuming she was there to ask about her grandmother, Andi said, "Grandma is doing lots better. The doctor said he expects her to make a full recovery."

"I'm so glad to hear it," Dorothy said. "I'll have to give her a call when I get back home to let her know how well you're doing on the sweater."

Dorothy picked up the sleeve Andi was obsessively working on, running her fingers over the surprisingly even stitches.

"My mother made me try Fair Isle when I was a little girl. In retrospect, I can see that I was far too young for the challenge."

Andi felt strangely possessive over the pain-in-the-ass sweater. She wanted to pull it out of the other woman's hands when Dorothy didn't let go of it soon enough.

"You know, now that I think about it," Dorothy said,

"there's something to be said for a challenge, isn't there? Perhaps I should try again. Perhaps I should refuse to give up before I get it right."

It was the same thing Andi had said to Madison, reinforced from one generation to the next and then the next again.

"It isn't nearly as difficult as it looks," Andi said. "Believe me, I panicked when I first read the pattern."

"It always surprises me how much life is like knitting." Dorothy's hand was soft and warm across Andi's. "How things always seem so much more complicated than they really are when you finally sit down to work them out."

After Dorothy bought a bagful of yarn, leaving Andi to sit behind the register in the strangely silent and empty store, she couldn't help but feel unsettled by Dorothy's words.

Andi looked around Lake Yarns, amazed that one weak moment in a meeting had turned her life upside down and brought her here. Two weeks ago she'd been in an office building, wearing a suit, crunching numbers; not helping women select knitting projects, not ordering new yarn off the Internet because she couldn't resist the colors and recommendations from other knitters, not obsessively working on her grandmother's Fair Isle sweater whenever she had a free minute to herself...and definitely not reliving every moment in Nate's arms.

Andi had always known what success meant to her. A big, important job with a big, important company. But being with Nate had her rethinking her definition of success. Not just with regards to her career, but to her entire life.

She was uncomfortable with the kind of thinking she'd started to do in the hours after he'd said "I love you," didn't like the idea that the way she'd lived her life for so long could possibly have been wrong.

Because it wouldn't just mean she was failing during the last couple of weeks.

It would mean she had always been failing.

The threads of thoughts inside her head all tangled up, Andi bent her head back over her grandmother's sweater. Thankfully a welcome feeling of relief came by the end of the row. By the time she'd done half a dozen rows, everything fell away but a picture inside her head of Nate wearing this sweater.

*      *      *

"Did you guys used to date when you were kids?"

Sitting in the passenger seat of Nate's truck as they headed off to the hospital again that evening, Andi jumped at Madison's unexpected question.

Nate's hands tightened slightly on the steering wheel, but he was smiling as he looked back at his sister in the rearview mirror.

"We sure did."

"So why did you break up for so long?"

Andi's heart all but stopped at the implication that they were no longer broken up. Oh god, she knew she'd let it go on for too long. She was afraid enough of breaking Nate's heart again when she left. It made her sick to think she was going to break Madison's too.

"Well," Nate said slowly, "sometimes it takes two people a long time to see things clearly."

Andi's breath caught in her throat. She knew he would never try to trap her into staying in Emerald Lake with him, and yet even that one sentence made her feel like the bars were coming down in front of her. Made her feel like the lock was being turned on a prison she hadn't meant to set foot inside.

And then Madison was saying, "Everyone is wondering why you want to get rid of the carousel, Andi."

*Boom!*

So that was what being kicked in the stomach felt like.

"I don't want to get rid of it, Madison."

Nate's sister frowned in confusion. "But aren't you trying to build something over it?"

Wow, neither Nate or the guy who had cornered her after her father's commemoration had made Andi feel this bad about the condos, like she was dirt on the bottom of a boot for even suggesting bringing these buildings to Emerald Lake. Clearly, guilt was much more effective when it was created completely unintentionally.

And darn it, what was it about sitting in Nate's truck with the two of them that always messed so badly with her insides?

"I thought it was just a piece of junk," Andi finally admitted.

"You're kidding, right?" Madison couldn't seem to wrap her head around Andi's statement.

"Unfortunately no, I'm not. When I decided on the building site, I didn't realize how important the carousel was to people."

"Me and my friends love it," Madison told her. "That was always our special rainy day place when I was little."

Nate's lips moved up in a smile at the memory. "Rainy days with a four-year-old." He mock-shuddered. "That carousel was a lifesaver."

"We always stayed dry on the merry-go-round because

of the awning," Madison explained to Andi. "We would pretend we were in the circus, that we were stunt riders on the horses."

Then she said to her brother, "Hey Nate, if Andi gets rid of the merry-go-round, can we put it in our backyard?"

"No, Mads," he said, his love for the little girl in the backseat rounding out every short word. "We cannot put it in the backyard."

But Madison's idea got Andi thinking. What if they moved the carousel? Sure, she couldn't foresee having the money to actually rehab it—not yet, anyway—but maybe they could find a good home for it, at least. Someplace kids could still play with it and pretend that they were in the circus, just like Nate's sister and Andi's long-lost great-aunt had.

Stuck at a surprisingly long light in Lake George, Madison's eyes got big as she looked out the window at a huge entertainment complex. "Look, they have an arcade!"

The blinking lights blinding her, Andi said, "No kidding. I'll bet they can see that neon sign up in space."

"Can we stop here on the way home from the hospital?"

Nate snorted. "No way. You still have homework to do."

Madison's mouth went flat and her arms came across her chest. "I wish we had an arcade at home. It's so boring sometimes." She shoved her earphones into her ears and cranked the music up loud enough that everyone in the car could hear it.

Feeling Nate tense beside her, Andi tried to comfort him by saying, "It's perfectly natural for any kid to want what they don't have, Nate. You know, the grass is greener and all that." When he didn't respond, she added, "You're doing the right thing, raising her at the lake where everyone knows and loves her."

"I know I am. But one day she's going to be old enough to make her own decision about where she wants to live. And it breaks my heart to think it might not be here with me."

Andi wanted so badly to make him feel better by saying, "*She'll choose the lake. She'll want to stay with all of her friends, with you.*"

But she couldn't. Not when she hadn't chosen that path herself.

And not when she knew that Nate couldn't possibly control his sister's desires and dreams. Those would have to be all her own, even if Madison's choices sometimes hurt the man who had given up so much to raise her.

\*      \*      \*

The three of them knocked softly before walking into Evelyn's room, and when they didn't hear a response, Andi's heartbeat kicked into overdrive as she automatically assumed something must be wrong.

But when she flung open the door, her grandmother was sitting up in bed with a finger over her lips.

"Your mother is sleeping," she whispered.

Andi would have swapped places with her exhausted mother in a heartbeat. But she knew how important it was to Carol that she stay close to her mother. It was better for Andi to run the store.

Still, there was one big reason to celebrate: Evelyn's fingers were flying with her needles again. Which had to mean she was feeling better.

After they had all given her a kiss, Madison immediately focused in on her knitting. "What are you making, Mrs. Thomas?"

"Something very special."

Andi had never seen a pattern like the one Evelyn was making, a long oval that almost looked like fabric it was so painstakingly created. It wasn't a scarf or sock or the front or back of a sweater. Andi supposed it could be a strangely shaped shawl, but even that didn't seem quite right.

Madison moved closer and Evelyn put the intricately knitted white silk yarn into her small hands.

"Wow, it's like a spider's web. How did you ever figure out how to do this?"

"It isn't nearly as difficult as it looks," Evelyn said. "However, it does take a great deal of focus. You can't give up on it when the going gets rough."

She was talking to Madison but looking at Andi.

Andi filled her grandmother in on the comings and goings at Lake Yarns, taking out her phone to make some notes on various issues that had crept up in the past couple of days. When the nurse poked her head in to tell them that visiting hours were over for the night, Andi went to kiss her grandmother good night.

Nate moved to her grandmother next, whispering something that had Evelyn's eyes widening, her cheeks crinkling into a wide smile.

A few minutes later when they were back in the truck and Madison had her headphones back on, Andi said, "It was so good to see Grandma smile. What did you say to her?"

"I'll tell you later, Andi. I promise."

Andi drank in the perfect lines of his face, the shadows of stubble across his chin that had darkened throughout the evening. She couldn't remember a time she hadn't wanted to be with Nate. Five or fifteen or nearly thirty, she had always been drawn to this man sitting beside her.

"Tell me what you said, Nate. Tell me why she smiled like that."

His eyes were on the dark road, lit only by his headlights, and yet she could feel his entire focus on her as he said, "I told her I knew exactly what she was knitting. And who she was knitting it for."

Within seconds, Andi felt her throat close up, her breath getting caught inside her chest. Because suddenly, she knew exactly what her grandmother was knitting in her hospital bed out of the finest white lace.

*Grandma Evelyn was knitting a wedding veil. For her and Nate.*

Clearing her throat, trying to focus on something else—anything but that white lace that Andi swore she could almost feel coming down over her head—she said, "The town hall meeting is tomorrow night. Everyone's going to get a chance to give their opinion about my project. Including you. Why don't we talk about it now while we have the time?"

"The town hall meeting can wait until tomorrow night."

"But we have time to talk about it now. And we haven't discussed the project since—" She swallowed hard. "Since Loon Lake."

"You're not going to back down, Andi. I know that. I have never underestimated you. I'm not starting now. I know you're going to give a hell of a presentation to the town. And I know you're going to wow a good number of them, too."

How could she find any space to put between them when he wouldn't even let her cut the ties that bound them together with an issue that they were on the opposite sides of?

And that was what had her finally saying what she should have said all along. "I need you to take me to my house tonight, Nate."

She had to end this.

Now.

\*       \*       \*

Nate didn't argue with her; he just took her home. Madison was already asleep in the backseat, and Andi didn't know what to do, what to say when they pulled up in front of her house.

"Nate, I—"

"You need time, Andi." His eyes were dark as he undid his seat belt. "Take it."

He came around the car, a gentleman as always, and opened the door for her. Knowing she shouldn't feel as if he was kicking her out of his truck—not when she'd been the one to insist on coming back to this big house she'd grown up in—she climbed out on shaky legs.

But even though she knew the smart thing would be to walk up the brick pathway to her mother's front door and close herself off inside the big, empty house, Andi couldn't stand the thought that she was being a coward and running from him.

She'd been a coward before, she saw that now. She couldn't stand it if she repeated history.

"Nate," she began, not knowing what to say or how to say it. "You're my best friend. You've always been my best friend. And making l—" She faltered, not used to taking about sex.

Taking a shaky breath, she tried again. "Making love with you is wonderful." No, that wasn't good enough. Not even close. "Beyond wonderful. Better than I remembered. So much better. But I can't do this. I can't be what you need me to be."

And she couldn't say the three words he needed to hear, couldn't possibly admit to loving him again.

"I shouldn't have stayed with you that first night. I should have been strong enough to sleep alone."

"Andi, sweetheart, I wouldn't have let you sleep all alone in that big empty house that first night."

She took a breath to try and corral her thoughts so that she could make sense of them. But he was so close. Too close. And his words were soft in the fall chill, wrapping around her like a warm blanket, the warmth she'd been craving so long.

"I can't control myself around you anymore, Nate. It's not fair for me to keep pushing you away every morning just because I'm not strong enough to resist sleeping with you every night."

"Do you really think this is just about how much we want each other? Do you really think this is just about sex?"

She tried to breathe. "Nate, please—"

"I loved touching you, Andi. I could kiss you for hours and never, ever want to stop. The sounds you make when I'm loving you are the most beautiful I've ever heard. But this thing between you and me isn't even close to just being sex."

She worked to suck in any oxygen she could. No one else had ever talked to her like that.

*No one else had ever wanted—or loved her—this much.*

He closed the small distance between them, brushing her bangs away from her eyes. "Don't you know that I can see how you feel whenever you look at me, sweetheart?"

He laid his hand over her heart, and she felt it race beneath his large palm.

"Don't you know I can feel it in the way your pulse moves whenever I'm around?"

And then his mouth was a breath away from closing in on hers again as he whispered, "Don't you know you give away your true feelings with every one of your kisses?"

His mouth was a soft breath of emotion against hers, his lips barely grazing hers, just enough to make them tingle.

But instead of kissing her, he pulled back and said, "All day long I've thought about what you said to me last night, Andi. I grieved when my mother died, but when my dad shot himself—"

"Oh god, Nate, I hate that I made you go back there."

"No. You're right. I was too mad to grieve. Not just for what he did to me, but for what he did to Madison. Our lives were never going to be the same. She was never going to have a normal childhood with two parents. All she had was a big brother who went from being a kid to being her everything in the pull of a trigger. All through my childhood I told myself no one needed to know the truth about what was going on at home. But last night you helped me see that it's long past time for me to still be pretending. No one has ever seen inside of me the way you do, Andi. You're barely back here a couple of weeks, and you're making me face things no one else wants to acknowledge. Because you care about me. Because you want me to be happy. So take time to do that thinking I know you need to do. And know that I'll be waiting for you, Andi. All you need to do is come with your heart. You can leave the rest to me, sweetheart."

"I've told you so many times that I'm leaving. How can you have faith in me like this?" she asked him, her words barely a whisper in the night.

She swore her heart was beating in time to his as he said, "I'm not going to lie to you, Andi. It hurts that you're so hell-bent on leaving."

She had to reach out for him then, had to put one hand on his beautiful face, his stubble scratching against her palm.

He covered her hand with his own, his warmth seeping into her pores, into every cell.

"But no matter what, I'm not going to stop loving you. I never stopped loving you, Andi. Not even when the past had me wanting to. Not even now when the past isn't a reason anymore, and I know you're going to be sitting in your mother's house tonight making a list of all the reasons why you don't think the future will work, either."

And then he was gone, leaving Andi alone with the lake and the moon and the lonely call of a loon desperately looking for its mate.

# Chapter Twenty-three

Evelyn had kept busy her whole life. Busy with the store. Busy with her husband and daughter. Busy with her town. These past few days in the hospital were the first time she'd had to do nothing but sit and think for nearly seventy years. She was knitting, of course, but for once the constant movement of her hands wasn't nearly enough to keep her in the present. To keep her away from Carlos.

It wasn't just being idle that had her mind—and heart—returning again and again to her first love. It was her prayers for Andi and Nate that had her fingers stilling over her lacework and her memories coming back once again.

\*    \*    \*

*1941*

*Friday nights were theirs.*

*It was surprisingly easy to find an excuse to sneak away from the football game or to skip it altogether. The bike ride out to the carousel had her heart flying in her chest every single time.*

*She and Carlos could have met somewhere else, some-where safer where there would be no threat of discovery, but Evelyn knew that was part of it.*

*A part of her was hoping they'd be discovered.*

*Every Saturday through Thursday, she remembered the way his mouth had felt, slanting against hers, the slow, hot press of his tongue against hers, his big, strong hands cupping her as he pulled her closer on the carousel. Restless, unquenched need made it hard for her to fall asleep, and every morning when she finally rose, she felt like a sleep-walker until she finally settled herself down on the porch with his Fair Isle sweater on her lap, thoughts and dreams of Carlos making up the heart of every stitch.*

*Dropping her bicycle to the ground, she threw herself into his arms and covered his face with kisses. "I love you."*

*The words pressed from her mouth to his, and that was when he pulled away.*

*"Evelyn. My pretty Evelyn. You're so innocent."*

*"Did I do something wrong?"*

*"No. You're perfect." He ran his hand over her long hair, threading the dark strands through his large fingers.*

*"But something is wrong, isn't it?"*

*"Your father's project is going to be done soon."*

*She had been trying to pretend it wasn't true, but every time she looked at the new addition, there was a new wall, a new window, a new door.*

*"There's always more work," she insisted.*

*"Yes, but not here. Not for me."*

*He'd had a life before her. She knew that. But it had been easier to believe that time was standing still for them. Until now she'd let herself focus on laughter and kisses and adventure.*

*Tonight she knew what he was telling her: Just as she'd had to be the one to reach for their first kiss, she would need to decide about their future. And soon.*

*Only, before she could make any decisions about her future, she needed to understand his past.*

*"Why did you come here?"*

*"There was a fire. My wife. My son. I lost them both."* His voice was a raw scratch of pain. *"And my business. The books I printed. They all burned."*

*"Oh, Carlos. No."*

*Pain ravaged his usually playful face. There had always been a fire inside the man in her arms, a fire that had sparked her own inner flames to life. For the first time, they were extinguished.*

*"I came to Emerald Lake because I had to leave Chicago."* His eyes found hers, held them with such intensity she almost had to look away. *"And then I found you."*

*She opened her mouth to express her sorrow for him, to say how sorry she was for all that he'd lost, but in that moment she knew that her words could never be enough.*

*"You made me feel again, Evelyn, for the first time in a year of feeling nothing at all. That's why I tried to push you away that first day you brought me coffee. That's why I tried to scare you with the freight train ride so that you'd run away. You're too sweet, too pure, too young for a man like me. You deserve someone who can love you without a past holding him back. You have your whole life ahead of you. Mine is already behind me."*

*He brushed her tears away, but they were falling too fast for him to get ahead of them. "You should be smiling. Always smiling. I don't want to be the man who makes you cry. That isn't how I want to remember you, pretty Evelyn."*

*He needed her, had always needed her, from that first moment she'd seen him on the lawn talking with her father, from their first sparring conversation over hot coffee. She saw that now, how even as he teased her for her innocence, he needed something to remind him of hope. Of unquenchable dreams.*

*But what about her love? Could her love replace all that he'd lost?*

*And could she possibly be strong enough to heal him?*

*Evelyn wanted to be right there waiting with open arms. She wanted to be his shelter from the storm. She had always thought that love would be fun and exhilarating, not difficult.*

*But the truth was that as Evelyn wrapped her arms around the man she'd fallen in love with, she simply didn't know if she was strong enough to be his cure. Because if she hadn't even had the guts to tell her sisters—let alone her parents—about her relationship with Carlos, then how could she possibly be strong enough to be the medicine he needed?*

*"I don't want you to leave" was all she finally said.*

*But both of them knew she hadn't asked him to stay, either.*

*They held onto each other until they heard the telltale sounds of the football game ending.*

*When she was finally back in her room later that night, Evelyn sat on top her bed, intent on finishing the Fair Isle sweater. One of her hairs had fallen into the yarn, but instead of pulling it off, she knitted it in.*

*Looking at her hair threaded into the sweater she'd made with such love, Evelyn finally made her decision.*

# Chapter Twenty-four

Nate picked his sister up out of the backseat, warm and smelling faintly like the Oreos he had given her as an after-dinner treat. She stirred slightly in his arms, putting her arms around his neck, her blond head settling in beneath his chin.

When had the little baby he'd been so afraid of breaking turned into a big girl he had to use muscles to lift?

Madison curled up on top of the bed as he removed her shoes. Nate was usually strict about things like toothbrushing, the amount of TV she watched, and bedtimes. Not wanting to wake her up, he decided she could brush for four minutes instead of two in the morning to make up for tonight's cookies and pulled the blankets up over her.

He kissed her on the forehead. "I love you, little sister."

Her faint response, slurred with sleep, came as he closed the door. "Love you, too."

He'd just closed her door with a soft click when he heard it, the sound of tires on the gravel behind his house.

Andi.

He was waiting for her on the porch when she walked

over. Every instinct he possessed had him wanting to pull her against him, but he knew he needed to let her lead tonight.

"I needed to come back, Nate, to talk to you, to explain things."

He'd known Andi, his sweet Andi, was too brave to hide out in her house all night. He'd known she would come right back here, that she'd be unable to resist something neither of them should have been resisting all along.

"Madison's asleep. How about we talk out on the dock?"

The two of them walked silently across the sand, then out to the end of the wooden dock. But unlike the hundreds of times they'd come out to the end of a dock together since they were little kids, Andi didn't immediately sit down and swing her legs over the edge.

Instead, she turned to face him, looking as serious as he had ever seen her. "I'm not going to stay," she said softly. "And you're not going to leave."

"Distance, miles, those are things we can live with over time, Andi. Those are things we can figure out together. As a couple. A team."

"You make it sound so easy, but I know better. Growing up, whenever my father was around, it was as if my mother was floating on air. She was so happy. But when he left—and he always left—she'd deflate like a balloon. She didn't want me to see it—I know she didn't—but how could I not? You and me tried it already, Nate. We tried having that commuter relationship like my parents had. With one person at point A and the other at point B." That sad, resigned look firmly lodged in her beautiful blue eyes, she continued with, "I know we were young, that we couldn't have possibly been equipped to deal with what happened, but I still don't think our relationship would have worked, even if things had been more normal. And now," she shook her head, "I just couldn't stand to be the one coming to the lake for a long weekend here or there. I couldn't stand to always feel like I was leaving you behind."

"Neither of us want that, Andi." And it was true, he wanted the woman he married, the woman he had his children with, to be there with him every night, curled up in his arms. "But just because it was like that with your parents, just because we couldn't pull it off when we were kids, doesn't mean it has to be like that now."

"Listen to me, Nate. It's more than location and place and distance. It's the fact that you and I are two very different people. You're so easygoing, so happy to just be out in your canoe with a fishing pole and I'm so type A, always reaching, just like you said."

He had to smile at her then, at the fact that she really was going down her list of reasons why not, one bullet point at a time. But he was fighting for Andi, fighting for his own heart, and he had his own lists of all the reasons love was going to work this time.

"Don't you know that's one of the things I love about you? The fact that you're never going to let things stay static? I need you to pull me forward, and you need me to sit you down beneath the stars and hold your hand while we wait for them to start shooting. Together we can make those wishes, sweetheart."

She looked up at the sky then, almost as if she were waiting for a shooting star to make a wish on. Too soon she looked away. "I grew up with two people who should never have fallen in love with each other. They wanted different things, different places, different lives. My mother should have had a half-dozen kids to bake chocolate chip cookies for. My father went off to live the life he needed to live. And I honestly don't think he regretted being gone so much." Softer now, almost to herself, she said, "He hurt my mother by leaving all the time. Badly."

Nate almost couldn't stop himself from reaching for her then. Just as he couldn't stop himself from saying, "It's not just your mother who was hurt, sweetheart. He hurt you, too."

She shook her head in denial. "I always knew he loved me."

Her soft words pierced her heart. But he'd been there for all of those moments when she'd needed to look into someone's eyes and know how much she was loved.

"Richard was a great senator; he gave everything he had to strangers, but he wasn't there for you enough. Not when you were giving speeches and singing in the choir and learning to swim."

Her beautiful face was stubborn now. "My father had an important job helping people. And when he was home, he was great. He was the best father in the world."

"Yes, Andi, he was great," Nate agreed. "When he was here." He paused, weighing his words again, not wanting to hurt her, but also knowing there couldn't be anything left out this time. "But it wasn't enough. And now you're so afraid of loving and being left again that you're grasping at any reasons you can find to push me away first."

Her eyes widened at the truth of his statement. Resolve came quickly on its heels. "I'm not grasping at reasons, Nate. My father said he loved my mother, acted the part in front of the crowds, in front of me, but when it came right down to it, he never really let her be a part of his life. I know you want me to say I'll try to make things work with you, but how can I, when I know that we'll be heading down the exact same path?"

"Has your mother told you that's how their relationship was? Have you actually asked her if that's what was going on with her and your father?"

Andi's stubborn chin set even more firmly into place. "He's only been gone a year. I'm not going to hurt her by asking a question like that."

"Is that really why you aren't going to ask her for the truth? Or is it because you're afraid of her answer? Are you afraid she won't let you use her marriage as a reason not to risk loving me all the way?"

The words were barely out of his mouth when it hit him that it was time to admit something big to her. And to himself.

"I'm scared, too, Andi."

Not once in the past ten years had he said those words. He hadn't ever let himself think them because he'd thought that admitting fear meant he wasn't strong enough to take on everything that he had.

Only now, as he and Andi stood on his dock beneath a clear fall sky, he could finally see that the truest strength of all was admitting he didn't want to be alone anymore...and that he'd always needed support. Andi's support.

Andi's love.

"I'm not afraid of loving you, sweetheart. The only thing I'm afraid of is what it would be like to try to make it through another day, another week, without you. I've already done it for ten years. I know how bad it is, how long and dark the road can be."

"But I'm not good for you, Nate. You let me file those papers at city hall for the condos without a fight. We both know you'd be fighting harder if it weren't me. I've read all about your stance on development in the Adirondacks. If a stranger had come in with this proposal, you'd be going after these condos with everything you've got."

She stepped away from him, and he felt the separation as keenly as if their connection had been cut with a knife.

"You're putting aside your own moral code for me, Nate. What if someone in town thinks I'm sleeping with you to win you over to my side?"

He hadn't wanted to get angry tonight, had promised himself he would calmly listen to all of her arguments. But he hadn't expected this one.

"Anyone who would think that clearly wouldn't have a very high opinion about you or me."

"What else could they possibly think, Nate?"

"They're going to think I love you. They're going to think I can't help but want to protect you because you're mine. *Mine*, Andi. They're going to think I'll never be able to hurt you. Never, no matter what."

"But shouldn't the person you're with, the person you love and who loves you back, make you a better person rather than make you compromise your values? Rather than making you hurt yourself to keep them from being hurt?"

"You're the smartest person I've ever met, sweetheart, but you're dead wrong on this. We could sit here and debate those condos for the next sixty years, but at the end of the day, they're just buildings. As far as I'm concerned, there are only two things that matter in any of this." He cupped her face in his hands and made sure she was looking at him. "You and me."

"But it isn't just you and me, Nate," she protested. "Madison is the most important person in your life. And she should be. I would never want to do anything to hurt her, Nate. Because I love her, too, right from the minute I held her after your father died. Every time I saw a little girl her age on the street, I'd think of her, wonder how she was doing. And I'd always know that she was fine. Because I knew you were taking care of her better than anyone else could have. I can't risk hurting her, Nate. I can't risk saying I'm going to stay and then realize later that I can't. I can't risk hurting an innocent little girl. Not when I know exactly how much being left behind hurts."

"If the other choice was living without you, sweetheart, if it meant I'd fall asleep with you in my arms every night, if it meant I'd wake up holding you every morning, I'd deal with a city. I'd find a way to make it my home. And I'd make sure Madison was happy there. We both would."

Her eyes opened wide with anguish. "Please, don't ever leave Emerald Lake for me. It would kill me if I did that to you. To Madison."

"Andi, it's not black and white. Leaving doesn't have to mean cutting ties."

But he could see she didn't believe him.

"That's exactly what it means. That's exactly what we did, Nate. We cut ties. *I* cut them."

"We were young. Both of us, Andi, not just you. We can make it work this time, I know we can."

He'd been working like hell to give Andi her space, to

give her the room to let it all out, but now he had to move closer.

"You picked Emerald Lake for those condos for a reason, Andi."

"I pitched Emerald Lake because I knew it would be a sure thing for my client. I was going to lose my job, Nate."

He watched her eyes widen with shock at what she admitted to him. She had never liked being vulnerable, not even with him, not even when she should already know he was the one person she could be vulnerable with.

"My boss hadn't actually said anything to me about my job performance, but I could tell he was watching me. Waiting for me to screw up. After my father died, I couldn't concentrate. Not like I had before."

Nate had promised himself he wouldn't stop her from going down her list of reasons why not. He'd thought they needed to get everything out there, every bit of pain, every last protest, to make sure there wasn't anything left between them to keep them apart. To keep them from forever.

But when he saw her eyes grow glassy with tears, the final hold Nate had on his control snapped in two.

\*     \*     \*

The minute Nate's arms came around her—warm and steady, comforting and loving—Andi realized she was all out of objections. All out of protests.

He had broken through all her defenses, one after the other, everything from the past to the future.

So then, why was she still so scared?

She could feel herself shaking in his arms. She'd always been strong. Had always taken care of herself.

But maybe instead of being one hundred percent of something hollow...maybe she could be one-half of something whole.

"Andi. Sweet Andi." He pulled her closer, stroked her back with his hands, working to calm her. "Everything's going to be all right. I promise."

"How?" Her throat felt like she had swallowed fire. "How can you make that promise?"

"Because I believe in us. In you. In me." He kissed her softly. Gently. "Baby steps, Andi. That's what we'll take."

"Baby steps," she repeated hollowly. He made it sound so easy, made it sound like there weren't a dozen things that could go wrong along the way.

"Come home with me tonight, sweetheart. Not because you don't want to go back to your mother's big house. But because you're choosing this. Because you're choosing me. Because you want what's mine to be ours."

And despite all of her vows to herself to be strong, instead of holding firm to her resolution to cut Nate loose once and for all, for his sake, she took his hand and led him up the dock, across the sand, and through his front door.

# Chapter Twenty-five

Andi felt shy with Nate, shyer than she should have after their past two nights together. It would have been easier if he had reached for her, if he'd kissed her first and eased her into their lovemaking. But just as he'd needed her to make the choice to come inside with him, she knew he needed her to make this choice, too.

To make love to him not simply because she couldn't resist...but because he was what she wanted. Past. Present.

And future.

She put her arms around him and buried her face in his neck. He was so strong. So steady. So warm.

She could feel how much he wanted her, but he held himself perfectly still, letting her lead their dance this time. She pressed her lips against his skin, kissing him where his pulse had leaped to life. She moved her hands to his shirt, pulling it free of his jeans, and as she ran her fingers over his rippling abdominal muscles, she could feel his growl of pleasure rumble up from his chest.

Both of their clothes were soon gone, leaving them to ride a wave of pure instinct, no thinking, no second-guessing, just a man and a woman who couldn't get enough of each other. She relished every touch, every brush of his lips against hers.

Everything she wanted was right here, right now, in his arms.

Pulling him down with her to the bed, she was so glad to be pinned beneath the hard heat of his body. And then he was filling her until she was bursting with him, with all the emotion she couldn't manage to hold back. She cried out into his mouth as he kissed her, just as they both reached the peak, then fell long and hard.

And when it was over, when she was on the verge of falling asleep in his arms one more time, she heard him say it again.

"Andi, sweetheart." He pressed a kiss to her forehead. "I love you."

\*       \*       \*

*Andi was out on the carousel. It wasn't old or peeling or cracking. The horses were shiny and new, and it was spinning around and around, circus music playing as she rode a big white horse.*

*Holding on to the gold bar that moved up and down in time with the music, Andi wondered how the carousel had gotten fixed up so quickly and why she was out here alone riding it? But the thought wouldn't stay in her head. Not with the music playing, not while she was spinning.*

*And then a moment later, she was sitting on the sleigh behind the matched pair of horses, holding knitting needles and yarn. The his-and-her horses shared a tender look as they ran forever in front of their sleigh.*

*Her heart warmed as she thought about how happy*

*Evelyn must be to have her beloved carousel looking brand-new again, to know that children would be able to experience the joy that had been such a big part of her childhood.*

*And then Andi looked down and realized her hands were moving. She was knitting something out of yellow yarn, the perfect color to match the marks on the carousel horse directly in front of her.*

*For a moment, her hands looked so much like her grandmother's that she got confused. How could that be? She and her grandmother had so little in common.*

*Nate's words floated into her brain. "Seeing you with those needles makes me realize how much you look like your grandmother."*

*He would never lie to her, she knew that even out on a spinning carousel, so maybe it was true.*

*Maybe she was more like her grandmother than she'd ever realized.*

*As the shock of how quickly, how surely, her hands were moving over the needles and yarn receded, she looked closer at what she was making. Somehow without needing to think about it, without needing to consult any kind of pattern, she cast off the final stitches.*

*She had never felt like this, so completely out of her body, almost as if she was floating.*

*No, that wasn't true. Every time she was in Nate's arms, every time he loved her, she had no choice but to let go of the thread that connected her to who she thought she was.*

*Being with him was like flying, floating on a cloud of pure pleasure.*

*And boundless love.*

*She looked down again and saw that her hands were moving again, draping the garment she'd knitted over the horse's mouth. The bridle was a perfect fit as was the knitted saddle that magically appeared on the horse's back.*

*When she looked more closely at the carousel, she realized all of the horses were wearing knitted bridles and saddles.*

*Who had made them? She still barely knew how to knit and was far too slow to have done all of this. Had the women in the knitting group done this to surprise her grandmother?*

*The carousel suddenly stopped, so suddenly that she had to grip the horse beside her so that she didn't fall down.*

*A moment later everything started to fade, the horses disappearing one by one until the carousel was gone completely and she was left standing in the middle of the building site, still holding her needles and yarn and the bridle and saddle, but not needing them anymore.*

\*     \*     \*

"Andi, sweetheart, it's just a dream. You're okay now. I've got you."

She woke up to feel Nate's hands stroking her damp hair back from her face. She worked to catch her breath as she came back to reality, naked and warm with Nate in his big bed.

She'd been dreaming about the carousel.

She pressed her palm against his chest, letting herself be comforted by the strong, steady beat of his heart. She felt so safe with Nate.

More safe than she knew it was possible to be.

"Every time you touch me," she whispered, "I forget everything. Everything but how you make me feel."

"Tell me how I make you feel, Andi."

His eyes were filled with so much love in the moonlit room that even though she knew better, she had to whisper, "You make me feel pleasure like I've never known before."

She closed her eyes, relishing the simple touch of his hands on her skin, the way his thumb had begun to brush lightly across her lower lip. "You make me feel comfort. Warmth. Happiness."

She opened her eyes again and met his intense gaze. "And love. So much love, Nate."

Suddenly, so suddenly that it took her breath away, she realized that holding back the words from Nate didn't make them less true.

"I love you."

His chest stilled beneath her hand, even as his heartbeat jumped. "Tell me again so I don't think I'm dreaming it."

Fear hit her like a sledgehammer, but this time instead of pushing Nate away, she worked to push the fear away instead.

She placed her hands on either side of his face, her mouth on his, and she kissed him. He was so warm, so real, the most solid man she'd ever had in her life.

"You were right all along."

She didn't realize she was crying until he began to kiss away the wetness over her eyes, across her cheeks.

"I'm scared, Nate. I don't know how to do this. I don't know how to be a partner, how to put anyone but myself first."

Now that the floodgates had opened, she couldn't stop

talking. "You're my best friend, and I'm so afraid of losing you again. Of losing our friendship forever this time. I tried to stop myself, tried to tell myself we could be lovers without ruining everything, but it was the biggest lie I've ever told myself."

"Just tell me again, sweetheart. That's all you need to do."

She took a shaky breath, the words on the tip of her tongue. But now that she knew for sure just how big the floodgates of emotion were that came with them, renewed terror kept her silent.

"Saying it the first time was the hardest part," he told her in a gentle voice. "We've got all night for you to get there again," he teased.

It was when the hint of a smile slid onto his lips, just visible from the faint moonlight coming through the window, amazing her that it could come when she was almost paralyzed with terror, that she realized he was right. She could do it.

He needed her to do it, to say the words aloud again.

"I love you, Nate."

His mouth found hers, stealing what was left of her breath. "I'm never going to get tired of hearing you say that, Andi."

It was easier this time, as if she knew how to unlock the keys to the prison the words had been locked up in for so long.

"I love you, Nate." The three words settled down deeper into her as shock began to recede.

"Do you know how long I've waited to hear you say that again?"

"Two days?"

His laughter moved across her skin. "Ten years. And before that, twenty."

Only Nate could have her confessing her love in one breath and laughing in the next.

"You've been waiting for me to say that since we were infants?"

He moved his lips across her face, dipping onto her mouth and then down her neck, her shoulders, the tops of her breasts.

"Longer than that."

His mouth closed over the tip of her breast, and "I love you" came out of her mouth again, this time on a gasp of pleasure. His tongue rewarded her admission, and she arched her back into his mouth, her hands threading through his soft hair. He moved to lave her other breast, and she said it again, amazed by how much easier "I love you" was every time she said it.

And as they came together one more time, as he slid into her and took her breath away just as he always did, when he bent down to kiss her, the "I love you" she whispered against his mouth was all either of them needed to jump off the edge.

Together.

She was still scared, still twisted up, still knocked as far off center as she'd ever been, still completely uncertain about how they were going to work out a future together, but at least here, in the private cocoon of his bedroom, the love Nate gave her temporarily overpowered her doubts.

# Chapter Twenty-six

Good news, honey. I'm coming home today."

Andi whooped with joy behind the Lake Yarns register, not caring that she'd just startled a customer into dropping a handful of yarn on the floor.

"I'm so glad you're all right, Grandma."

Maybe everything was going to be okay after all.

All morning Andi had been on pins and needles waiting for the other shoe to drop. Because it couldn't possibly be that easy as two childhood sweethearts falling back in love with each other, could it?

No, she told herself for the hundredth time that day, she was just being silly. Trying to throw roadblocks up on an otherwise smooth track.

Still, before her grandmother had called from the hospital, Andi had been preparing for the town hall meeting. Her notes were spread out all across the counter, her laptop open so she could make last-minute changes to her presentation. But she hadn't been able to concentrate on her presentation. Heck, she had barely been able to concentrate on her job—the one thing she usually gave everything to—for the past week.

That lack of focus had her saying, "I had the strangest dream, Grandma, about the carousel. I was knitting bridles and saddles for the horses."

"Andi, honey, you're a genius! What a perfect way to raise money to move and restore the carousel."

Andi had spent her entire career making other people money, but this time she couldn't see where it was going to come from. "I don't get it, Grandma."

"We'll have a knitting contest. People will pay a fee to enter."

"You know what?" Andi had to smile at the excitement in her grandmother's voice—and in her own. "That might actually work."

"Of course, it will work," Evelyn said in a no-nonsense voice. "In any case, I'm glad to hear it's finally happened."

"What's finally happened? Apart from me losing my mind, that is."

"You've found your reason to knit. I thought maybe falling in love would take you there. But this makes much more sense."

"Nothing is making sense anymore," Andi muttered into the phone.

She'd never dreamed about knitting or anything else even slightly artistic. She'd always been one of those people who dreamed about tests and school.

"This does. Of course, you would have to knit toward a goal. Something tangible like saving the carousel. Have you started making a saddle yet?"

"Of course I haven't," Andi all but snapped. Even though the truth was that all morning she'd been looking at different skeins wondering how they'd knit up for the horses, fighting the urge to pick up a pair of needles to try and knit a saddle. "How could I possibly knit something like that without a pattern?"

"Well, if you don't think you're up to the challenge, honey, I understand."

Feeling cornered, Andi came back at her with, "You're not much for subtlety, are you, Grandma?"

"I'm too old for subtlety. Speaking of which, how's that boy who's so in love with you doing?"

Andi didn't bother to deny it. What was the point when her grandmother obviously saw everything? Even the things Andi had tried so hard not to see.

"He's fine." That same dark premonition she'd been trying to run from all morning weighed back down on her as she said, "We're going to be facing off against each other tonight at the town hall meeting."

"I sure wish I felt up to attending, honey. I'd like to see the fireworks. Be sure to drop in to the cottage tonight to tell me all about it. And I'll let my friends know about your knitted saddle idea so that we can get started on them right away."

Andi was still staring at the receiver wondering how her life had managed to get so crazy in such a short time when Rebecca walked in.

"I've been meaning to come by for the past few days, but things have been crazy at the inn."

Andi smiled or tried to anyway. "Don't worry about it. Things have been nuts with me, too." She thought about Nate, about her dream, about her grandmother knitting a saddle for a carousel horse. "Really nuts."

"It's not your grandmother, is it?"

"No," Andi said quickly. "She's coming home from the hospital today."

"That's great news." Rebecca gave her a half smile. "You should know, rumor has it that I'm a great listener if you ever want to talk."

Andi had never really had a girlfriend who she could talk about dating or guys with. Not since she and Catherine were kids actually. Now, for the first time, she found that she desperately wanted to sit down with another woman and talk about her...feelings.

But before she could take Rebecca up on her offer, the door opened and Catherine walked in. "Here's the schedule for the town hall meeting tonight." She dropped a printout on the counter before turning to Rebecca with a smile. "Hey there. How are you?"

"Good. Taking a much needed break."

Jenny walked in next. "Sorry I'm late, Andi. Blood and kids is all you want me to say about it."

"Are your kids okay?"

"They're fine. Just stupid. Hi Rebecca, Catherine."

"I was just going to get a cup of coffee at Moose Cafe," Catherine said to Rebecca. "Care to join me?"

"I'd love to. Andi, come with us."

Before Andi could gracefully decline the invitation, Jenny jumped in with, "You've been chained to the register all week. Even for those of us who were born with knitting needles in our hands, all this wool and alpaca can start to make you crazy after a while. I can man the store solo for a while. Go."

Andi knew when she was cornered. Not just by Jenny gently kicking her to the curb, but because Rebecca clearly wanted to try and mend things between her and Catherine.

And yet as she followed after the other women, she was surprised to realize that she wasn't overcome with relief at getting a chance to escape Lake Yarns.

The truth was, she liked working in the knitting store, liked talking with women, liked helping people with something fun that truly got them jazzed. And then there was the yarn itself, which she'd fallen head over heels in love with too.

The three of them ordered their drinks, then sat down at a table by the lakeside window.

Looking out at the blue lake, the patchwork quilt of colored leaves spread across the mountains, Andi said, "It really is beautiful here."

"Don't bring those condos in and change everything," Catherine suddenly said.

As Andi turned her gaze from the water to her old friend's face, Rebecca jumped in again. "I'm sure she didn't mean it like that, did you, Catherine?"

But Andi knew she had and found herself saying, "I always admired you so much when we were kids, Catherine. You were never afraid to say what you thought. What you really meant."

Catherine blinked at the unexpected compliment. "Neither were you."

But Andi was just starting to know better than that. "It may have looked like that, but lately I've been wondering if I was just trying to make everyone happy."

Her father, of course, but she hadn't stopped there. She'd spent years trying to please every teacher, every boss.

When, she suddenly wondered, had she tried to please herself?

Catherine's face softened slightly, just as Rebecca

murmured, "It's pretty darn easy to fall into that people-pleasing trap."

Andi shifted her gaze to her pretty, new friend just as Rebecca twisted her diamond engagement band. Maybe one day soon she would feel close enough with Rebecca, comfortable enough doing the girl-sharing thing, that she could ask Rebecca about her relationship with Stu. And if everything was okay.

Andi picked up her cherry-red mug but didn't take a sip. "I never meant to come back here and upset everyone. So many times I've wondered if I did the right thing coming back at all."

Andi expected Catherine to jump all over her admission, to agree with her that she shouldn't have come back to town, to maybe even pack her bags and drive her back to the city to make sure she really left.

Instead the woman said, "I know I told you that you coming back into Nate's life has been bad, but I'm not sure I got it completely right. It's more that he's been different since you've been back."

"Different how?"

"After years of seeing someone be up and energetic all the time, you sort of forget they're ever any other way. These past couple of weeks, it's like his outer layer has started to drop away. Sometimes he looks terrible in the morning. And other times it's like something has changed inside of him, way down deep, like I'm finally seeing the real Nate Duncan." Catherine shook her head. "I'm more than a little ashamed that I didn't realize he was covering part of himself up all this time. You touch him, reach him in a way no one else has, Andi. In a way no one else ever could."

Andi was afraid everything she felt for Nate was written on her face. She started to try to contain it out of sheer habit, but then it hit her: What was she doing? Why was she always trying so hard to hide from what she really felt? Where was the gain in that?

"I love him, Cat." The childhood nickname slipped out right alongside her true feelings for the man they'd both been friends with as children.

Surprise flashed across Catherine's face a split second before she said, "I know you do." She paused, almost as if she was giving Andi time to catch her breath. "So, what are you going to do about it?"

Andi gripped her mug tighter, tried to still the panic rising inside of her. "I'm going to try to make it work."

She'd never moved forward on anything without a plan. Not until Nate had touched her. Not until Nate had kissed her. Not until they'd made love as adults.

But the truth was, she simply hadn't had a choice. Not in any of it.

Because she loved him.

When Catherine's voice came again, it was softer. Gentler. She reached out her hand, put it on Andi's arm, regret mingling with shame in her pretty eyes.

"I'm sorry I've lashed out at you so many times. I had no right to say those things I said to you at the knitting group on Monday night."

Andi looked down at Catherine's ragged nails, a Band-Aid wrapped around her thumb, the same friend who used to spend hours on her manicure in high school.

"You're Nate's friend," Andi said slowly. "You just want what's best for him. I can understand that."

"Just because I'm his friend doesn't mean I should

be acting like this. Not when I know firsthand how hard love is."

Andi could almost see the olive branch being extended out across the table. It was habit to proceed cautiously, to make sure she didn't connect too closely with anyone— and to make sure she didn't let Emerald Lake or the people in it reach out and grab hold of her. Of her heart.

But she didn't want to live that way anymore.

"What happened, Catherine?"

"I married the wrong guy is what happened."

Andi frowned. "When did you figure it out?"

"When I found him in bed with another woman, that's when."

"Men suck."

Catherine raised her eyebrows at Rebecca's statement, obviously just as surprised by it as Andi was.

"What are you talking about, Rebecca?" Catherine asked. "Stu's the perfect fiancé. You couldn't have found a nicer guy if you'd tried."

Rebecca looked so uncomfortable that Andi dove in to save her with, "I've got to tell you guys about my crazy dream."

She never would have guessed it was possible from the way their coffee break had begun, but soon the three of them were discussing contest ideas and possible patterns for knitted saddles and bridles for carousel horses over their emptying coffee cups. And Andi was enjoying herself. More than she'd ever thought she would with two women that she had nothing in common with save living in the same town and knitting.

She wanted to believe she could have more than one afternoon like this, chatting over coffee with girlfriends.

"Wow, those dark clouds came from out of nowhere." Rebecca pointed out the coffee shop window out toward the lake. "There's definitely going to be a storm tonight."

Andi shivered even though the café was perfectly warm. She shouldn't be afraid of a little storm.

But she was.

# Chapter Twenty-seven

Andi hadn't been to a town hall meeting in a decade. The din of voices in the huge, old red barn hit her first. Every seat was full, and people were lined up all along the walls. They were all chatting easily with one another, passing thermoses of hot drinks and baskets of brownies and cookies back and forth, but she'd been to enough town hall meetings to know that the mood in the room could—and often would—change on a dime.

What had she started?

She looked up and saw Nate standing up on the stage that had been erected in the front of the barn. Her breath shouldn't have left her at nothing more than a glance at the man she loved, not after knowing him for as long as she had. But it did.

Sensing her presence, he looked up at her from the stage and smiled. Her lips actually tingled in response, as if he'd managed to send her a kiss from all the way across the barn.

A hand brushed her arm, and she pulled her gaze away

from Nate to see who was trying to get her attention. Her eyes widened in surprise.

"Mr. Klein?" My god, when had the president of the company she was here to represent decided to show up? "How are you?"

"This is quite a lively town you've got here."

She nodded and worked to compose herself. Ever since her grandmother had ended up in the hospital, Andi had been living in jeans and long-sleeved T-shirts. Tonight, thank god, she'd run home from the store to change into a suit, fix her hair, and put on makeup and heels.

"Are you planning on spending the night, Mr. Klein? If so, it would be my pleasure to give you a tour of Emerald Lake tomorrow."

Andi cringed at what that tour would entail. *Here's our general store. Here's the grocery store. Oh, look, here's my family's yarn store. And of course, here's the lake. Isn't it pretty?* And then after those thirty minutes were up, she'd have to start dancing around like a circus animal to keep her client entertained.

The differences between the city and the lake had never hit home quite so hard.

"Yes, I'll be at the inn tonight. It was dark by the time I arrived tonight, but I'm certainly looking forward to getting to know Emerald Lake and the Adirondacks better. Be my guest for breakfast."

Andi knew she'd better get her lips up into a smile and fast. "Breakfast sounds great."

"Before the meeting begins, Andrea, I wanted to give you something to sleep on. Back in the office, we've been tossing around the idea of acquiring at least one of the old buildings on Main Street to put our own stamp on it. Some people want new, some people want something that's been here for a while. It's the perfect way to appeal to both audiences. Of course we will assist the current stores in finding excellent nonlakefront locations. Perhaps you can give some thought tonight on which buildings would be best to target."

Andi felt her smile falter, but she couldn't manage to fake a positive response. Not when she hated her client's idea with every fiber of her being.

History was history.

Now she knew how she was going to use her time the next day. She was going to have to use every skill she had in her arsenal to convince her client to keep his hands off of the historic buildings.

And yet how could she be angry with him? He wouldn't have even known about Emerald Lake if not for her. And she was the one who hadn't cared about the history of the carousel.

Her stomach roiled at the thought.

What had she done?

Just then, her mother moved to her side. "There you are, honey."

They'd spoken earlier in the day after her grandmother had been settled back into her cottage. Helen was with Evelyn now so that Carol could attend the meeting without worrying.

"Mr. Klein, I'd like to introduce you to my mother, Carol Powell."

His attention shifted to her mother so completely that Andi almost felt as if she'd disappeared.

"How do you do?"

Instead of simply shaking her mother's outstretched

hand, he took a more old-fashioned approach and bent over her hand to press a light kiss to it.

Andi couldn't believe her mother's reaction, her blushing cheeks, along with the light that jumped into her eyes. She was clearly exhausted from her days in the hospital with Evelyn, and yet a stranger was making her look prettier than Andi had seen her in a very long time.

"It's nice to meet you, too," Carol said softly before turning back to Andi. "I wanted to let you know I've saved you a seat if you need one."

Still stunned by the clear chemistry between her client and her still-grieving mother, Andi somehow managed to say, "Thanks, but I believe I'll be sitting up front on the stage so that I can give my presentation and answer questions."

Looking almost shy, her mother shifted her gaze back to Mr. Klein. "In that case, would you like to sit with me?" A small smile moved onto Carol's lips. "If you're not used to it, these town hall meetings can sometimes be a little overwhelming."

"I'd like that very much, Carol. Thank you." Before they walked away, he said, "I'm looking forward to hearing your presentation, Andrea."

Andi forced what she hoped was a believable smile, then watched with more than a little alarm as her mother led her very rich, very distinguished client over to a crowded bench of Emerald Lake locals. Within seconds he was the focus of everyone's attention. Andi grimaced and wondered if she should go over there and save him.

Nate's eyes were still on her when she looked back up at the stage.

Her heart squeezed. She missed him.

Rationally she knew it had only been a handful of hours since she'd last seen him, since she'd last been in his arms, but rational thinking fled every time he was near.

*She loved him.*

A warning flag went up in her as she instinctively moved toward him. She wasn't used to leading with her heart rather than her head. Not to mention that the strength of what she saw in Nate's eyes scared her enough to make her almost lose her footing as she walked up the stairs to the small stage.

Nate was right there to help her, to make sure she didn't fall. Just like always.

"You look beautiful."

She wanted to kiss him, but they were standing in front of three hundred people—some friends, some foes to her project.

The podium hid their hands from the crowd as he reached out to take hers. He rubbed his thumb across her palm.

"The only reason I'm not kissing you right now is because I know you'd kill me if I did."

She shivered at his touch and the love in his eyes. "You're right. I would."

"Soon, Andi, it won't matter what people think. Because they'll know that you belong to me. And I belong to you."

Her stomach tightened even as she said, "My client is here."

But Nate didn't look away from her at her small warning.

"The man sitting with your mother?"

"I didn't know he was coming." She frowned. "I hate surprises."

His low laughter warmed her skin. "Have I mentioned I love you lately?"

Her eyes flew to his. Didn't he know they couldn't be flirting like this in front of her client—and practically the entire population of Emerald Lake? "Nate!"

"And that you're the most beautiful woman I've ever seen?"

Flustered, she worked to turn his focus, along with her own. "I should be reviewing my presentation. I haven't done nearly as much as I should have today."

"Why not? Was the store particularly busy?"

"Not really."

"Then what had you so preoccupied?"

She couldn't miss the loving gleam in his eyes, the heated grin playing around the corners of his mouth. "You know what."

"Tell me."

Just as he'd needed her to say "I love you" last night, she knew he needed this from her now. So even though she knew better than to flirt with the mayor in front of the entire town not five minutes before going head-to-head with him on her building project, she said, "You, Nate. You're what has me so preoccupied."

The air between them shot off with electricity. She had never wanted anything more than she wanted to reach out and pull him into her, to kiss him, to lay her claim to his love in front of everyone. Even the warning flags waving all throughout her brain couldn't find a way to stop her from moving closer.

She was almost there, could almost taste his mouth,

could almost feel the warmth of his hard chest pressed up against hers, his strong arms holding her, when Catherine cleared her throat—loudly—beside them.

"The natives are getting restless." She purposefully didn't look down at their linked hands. "We should probably get started."

Andi dropped Nate's hand and took an awkward step back. "Thanks, Cat."

Fortunately Catherine wasn't acting like anything strange was going on. "Here, I'll put your jacket in the back room just beyond this door. Anything I can do to help you set up?"

Andi reached into her bag and pulled out her laptop. "All I need is the cable to hook this up to the projector."

Catherine efficiently untangled the cord so that it would reach Andi's computer. Andi had been giving these kinds of presentations for so long she rarely got nervous anymore. But this time everything felt different. Probably because she'd known everyone in the audience since she was in diapers.

And because she didn't want to let them down.

Especially the one person who wasn't there. Her father wasn't out in the audience, but she could still feel him there. Watching her. Telling her not to give up, no matter what the hurdles.

At this thought, her fingers went numb and she dropped her power cord. Andi could feel Nate's concerned glance on her even though he was speaking with someone off to the side of the stage.

Catherine quickly moved to pick up the power cord and plugged it in. "Are you okay?"

"No." Andi started at her too-honest response. "I mean, yes. Of course. I'm fine."

Catherine uncapped a bottle of water. "Drink."

Andi hadn't realized just how dry her mouth was until she put the plastic bottle up to her lips.

"Seriously, Andi, you're white as a sheet."

"I was just thinking about my father. About the fact that he isn't here tonight."

"He expected a lot of you, didn't he?"

The plastic bottle shook in Andi's hand. "Of course he did." *The brass ring. That's what he had expected her to grab. Every time.* "What parent doesn't expect the best from their child?"

"Don't forget, I've known you for three decades. Well, the first two, anyway. I used to see that look on your face whenever you knew your father was watching you do something."

Andi couldn't believe she'd been so transparent. Guilt had her saying, "My father was wonderful."

"He was. And imposing. A little scary, too."

"I wasn't afraid of him," she protested. He had never raised a hand to her. Or his voice.

"But you were afraid of disappointing him. How could you not be? Heck, we all were afraid of disappointing the senator. I can't imagine how hard it must have been to be his daughter."

Andi's throat felt tight. Nate's words from his dock came back at her. *"He hurt you, too."*

And the truth was, she'd never realized how strong her fears had been. Not just of disappointing her father.

But of disappointing herself.

Her entire identity had been her success, first at spell-

ing bees and then with what colleges she went to and then
with her career. Somewhere along the way she'd replaced
her father's voice in her head with her own, and she'd
drawn a world around herself where there was black and
white but nothing else. None of the soft rainbow of colors
lining the Lake Yarns's walls.

She'd wrapped herself up tightly in that identity to try
and keep herself warm. But without the heat from Nate's
eyes, from his kisses—from his love—she'd been cold
anyway. Somewhere along the way she had forgotten how
to do anything but go for the brass ring. Even when it
turned out to be so chilly and lifeless in her hand every
time she managed to grab hold of it.

Andi felt her friend's hand on her arm. "I'm sorry.
I know you need to concentrate right now. But if you
want to talk more later"—Cat paused, looked at Nate, then
squeezed Andi's arm—"about anything at all, you know
where to find me."

"Thanks, Cat."

"And good luck. I'm not a fan of the condos, but I
guess I get how things are a little better between you and
Nate now. He just wants what's best for you, even when it
might not be best for him." Cat shook her head and gave
Andi a lopsided grin. "It was easier when things were
black and white. When I could just focus on hating you."

Andi was glad for the sudden laughter that sprung to
her lips. "Yeah. That *was* a lot of fun."

Cat laughed, too, and it was amazing how much it felt
like old times—and how much she liked their renewed
connection. Girlfriends weren't something she'd focused
on much for the past ten-plus years. There had been no
place for them on her master plan.

Nate moved back toward them. "I'm about to open the meeting. Are you ready?"

No. She wasn't ready for any of this. Not for the way her hometown, the people of Emerald Lake, the store—but especially Nate—had all crawled in underneath her skin.

Into her heart.

Still, right this second, with her client waiting for her to blow him and the rest of the audience away, there was only one answer. Only one response to Nate's gentle question.

"Ready."

Nate frowned at her false smile before turning so that his back was completely to the audience. "I don't want you to forget for one single second that I love you, Andi. Always. Forever."

With that said, he turned back around, stepped up to the microphone, and opened the town hall meeting.

# Chapter Twenty-eight

Nate kept his opening statement short. After filling in the crowd on the progress the road crew had been making on the main highway into town and the recent library fund-raiser, he got down to the real reason everyone was there.

"I've invited a special guest to our meeting tonight. Most if not all of you know Andrea Powell. Her mother and grandmother have owned and operated Lake Yarns for many, many years, and her late father was a valued member of our community, as well as the entire state of New York. Andrea, thank you for coming to speak to all of us tonight."

She didn't look the least bit nervous, regardless of what she was really feeling. It didn't matter in the least that they were on opposite sides of her project. He was proud of her.

He would always be proud of her.

Graceful and elegant, she rose from her seat and approached the podium. "Thank you, Nathan."

He almost laughed out loud at the way they were both

using each other's legal first names. They'd been Andi and Nate to each other for so long, it almost felt like a private joke they were sharing with each other amid the seriousness of the night.

She began her presentation, and as she took them through her excellent maps, drawings, and photographs of the proposed building site, he admired the way she spoke to the crowd. Not as if she was above them, but as if she was one of them. Which she was.

He had been a damn fool to say those harsh things in the bar that first night when she'd showed him her initial plans. He knew that now. And he would never stop making each and every one of those cruel words up to her.

The town remained focused and silent until she came to the end of her presentation. "Thank you, Nathan, and everyone who came out tonight, for this opportunity to speak with you about the project."

She paused, looking down at her notes as if she was trying to make a decision. She folded them up and looked back out at the audience.

"This isn't a part of what I planned to say, but I can't help but feel as if my father is here tonight with all of us."

It was the first time her voice shook all evening, and he watched her try to draw strength from her mother. Carol was right there for her daughter, just like she always had been, with a smile and a small nod.

Nate knew he wasn't the only one who was choked up as Andi continued with, "As all of you already know, my father loved Emerald Lake. Many times, he told me that he wished more people knew about all our town has to offer, the beauty and nature. And the peace of mind just being here brings."

Had she realized what she'd said? *Our town.* She was no longer talking about Emerald Lake as if it were an anonymous town that she wanted to bring additional revenue into.

Nate almost lost the fight to get up out of his chair and put his arms around her, to kiss her in front of everyone like he'd wanted to all evening, to drop to his knees and pledge his love to her in front of the entire town.

No, not just tonight. He'd wanted to claim her as his for nearly thirty damn years. Even when they were kids he had looked at her on the playground and thought, *Mine.*

Andi took a deep breath, lifted her chin, and looked out into the crowd, brave and ready for whatever was going to come her way tonight. "And now, I'd like to take your questions and address any concerns you may have about the proposed project."

Several hands went up, but Mr. Wilcox spoke up without waiting to be called on. "I think we'd all like to hear what our mayor has to say about this."

Andi moved slightly away from the podium so that Nate could stand beside her. He took her hand in his behind the wooden podium and squeezed it.

Despite the fact that they were standing in front of hundreds of people, the only person he was aware of was her. The vision came at him again of getting down on one knee, up on this stage, proposing to her in front of the entire town.

Someone in the audience cleared his throat and rational thought managed to push back into Nate's brain.

"Andrea has made some excellent points about our town and about how all of us could benefit from growth. Unfortunately I don't believe that condominiums are the best way to go about growing Emerald Lake. To me, what makes us special is our personal touch. Every building, every store, every park is unique. Coming to visit Emerald Lake is not like going anywhere else. And living here, as all of us know who are fortunate to call Emerald Lake home, is a true privilege."

Nate called on one of the women who had her hand up. "Mrs. Wagner, do you have a question for Andrea?"

"I'm not sure how I feel about the condos, but I sure do like the idea of a new football field. Is this something we'll be able to do without the builder's money?"

Andrea leaned into the microphone. "I was thrilled by how quickly the Klein Group came on board with the football field. They immediately understood how important sports teams are to all towns, big and small. That being said, I believe that's a question for Nate."

Nate was glad to hear her switch back to the shortened version of his name rather than the overly formal Nathan. Taking her space at the microphone, he said, "You all know how important football is to me." Everyone laughed. "But in answer to your question, Mrs. Wagner, I've taken a fairly detailed look at the city's finances, and I'm pleased to say that a new football field might not be as far off as I once thought, and I'm planning on having a series of brainstorming meetings over the next few months to see if we can make it happen."

Mrs. Graystone, an elderly woman who had lost her husband to cancer a year earlier, raised her hand. "I'd like to ask you about affordability, Ms. Powell. Without my husband here to help maintain our house, I'm starting to realize that my house is getting to be too much for me to take care of. Especially with winter coming. Knowing there were other options besides leaving Emerald Lake for an old folks' home in Albany would be really comforting."

Andi smiled at the woman, her blue eyes warm and reassuring. "I'm so glad you brought up the issue of cost. My client intends to make sure there are floor plans in a range of sizes and prices. Granted, the units with the water views will be more expensive, but I'd be happy to show you the current blueprints if you'd like to see where the more affordable units are situated."

Mr. Radin jumped up next. "I, for one, would like to know what some city girl is doing coming into our town with her fancy buildings? Not only would your father not be behind these condos, but to my way of thinking, he would be ashamed to call you his daughter."

Nate felt Andi's world rock beside him as gasps of shock ricocheted through the crowd. But before he could grab the microphone, Andi's mother was on her feet.

"Settle down, Ellis. If you have a question, ask it. But don't you dare say something like that to my daughter again or you'll have me to answer to."

Knowing exactly where Andi got her strength from, Nate told the crowd, "None of us came here tonight to give or listen to personal attacks. Andi is here on good faith to talk to our town about her proposed building project. If anyone else comes at her like that, I'll shut this forum down for good."

He was so angry he barely felt Andi's hand on his arm. She said, "It's okay, Nate."

She shoved his hip aside with her own to speak into the microphone. "I'm very sorry to hear that you feel that way, Mr. Radin."

Her voice was steady. *Too steady,* Nate thought. Almost as if she was systematically shutting down chunks of her heart to get through the evening.

"All I can tell you is that I had the town's best interests in mind when I put together my proposal for the Klein Group. As to what my father would think of it, perhaps you're right and he wouldn't have approved. I wish he could be here tonight with us to speak his mind as much as you do."

Nate knew how hard it was for her to speak of her father, and yet there wasn't a hint of emotion behind her words any longer. He wanted to pull her away from this stage, this barn, and yank down all of those walls she'd just rebuilt.

The heavy silence in the barn was broken by Dorothy's voice. "I don't have any problem with the condos, but I would like to know what the Klein Group plans to do with the historic carousel? Not only is it an important piece of this town's history, but I believe if we could all work together to find a way to restore it, the next generations of children would enjoy it as much as I did when I was a child."

Nate was glad to feel Andi soften slightly beside him.

"Thank you so much for bringing up the carousel, Dorothy. Admittedly, restoring it was not part of my initial project plan. But in speaking with you and my grandmother and my aunt and so many others whose memories are so strongly tied to the carousel, I have revised my plan. Nathan is right—this town is special. Very special. And the carousel is one of the elements of Emerald Lake that make it uniquely beautiful."

She paused to single out her clearly surprised client. "I

promise to work closely with the Klein Group to ensure we are doing everything we can to find a new home for the carousel so that present and future generations of Emerald Lake children will be able to enjoy it as much as you did."

She paused again and seemed almost surprised by herself as she added, "Actually, we'll be announcing a knitting contest soon from which all proceeds will benefit the Carousel Fund. Anyone who wants to find out more can come and talk to me or my grandmother, Evelyn, at Lake Yarns."

A younger woman stood up, new enough to town that Nate didn't know her yet. "Look, this isn't a personal attack, but I specifically moved to Emerald Lake because there were no motel chains on the water or condos clogging up the town. I can't believe I'm sitting here listening to this. Not just from her but from our mayor. From everything I'd read and heard about this town before moving here, I expected you to take a much harder line on something like this. What's going on?"

Andi stiffened again and tried to pull away from him, but Nate wasn't planning to let go of her hand any time soon.

Not when he needed her just as much as she needed him.

"Welcome to town and thank you for your feedback. My door is always open, and I'd be happy to speak with you more one-on-one about any concerns you have about both the town and my role as mayor. As for taking a hard line on these condos, while I've made my personal feelings about them clear already, it's not up to me to run Emerald Lake alone. My decisions and my choices are not—and should not be—law."

He ran his eyes over the people in the room, the men and women who had always been such a big part of his life, even before he'd needed their help keeping his family together after his parent's deaths.

"In fact, before we go any further I'd like to see a show of hands. All of those for the condos?"

Nate was surprised to see more than a few hands go up.

"All of those against?"

Again many hands went up, but not nearly as many people were opposed to the condos as he had expected.

"All of those who would like to continue the discussion before making a decision?"

Half of the people in the barn held up a hand.

Interesting. He'd always trusted his own biases to lead the town in the right direction. Suddenly he wondered if he should have been talking less and listening more. Asking people what they did—and didn't—want, even when it went against what he himself thought was right for them.

If not for Andi coming into town and shaking things up, would he ever have learned this incredibly valuable lesson?

More questions came, and he and Andi fielded them, her hand in his the entire time, until Catherine finally gave him the signal to close the floor.

"Thank you to everyone for attending our town hall meeting.'

On final person stood up, Jerry, who had gone to high school with both of them and was now raising his young family in Emerald Lake.

"I have one last quick question that I know a few of us are wondering about."

Nate didn't want anyone leaving the meeting feeling like they hadn't had a chance to speak their mind or get their questions answered.

"Sure, Jerry, go ahead. We have time for one more quick question."

"So, with you and Andi being a couple, do either of you really think it's possible to be objective about these building plans? Isn't there an inherent conflict of interest here? Look, what I'm asking is, should we think about bringing in a third, totally impartial party to assess the implications of this project?"

Andi's hand went stiff and cold in his. He tried to keep his hold on her, but she was already slipping free. He saw Andi's horrified gaze shoot to where her client was sitting beside her mother and watched a dozen different emotions cross her beautiful face—all of them grounded in fear—and even before Andi leaned into the microphone, Nate knew what she was going to say, knew what she was going to do.

And he also knew that there was no point trying to stop her. Because he couldn't hold onto someone who wasn't ready to be held.

Nate had to accept that, in the end, no amount of faith in the world could make love between two people work if only one of them had faith.

"Thank you for giving me a chance to clear things up, Jerry. Yes, Nate and I were a couple back in high school. But I assure you, we are both totally able to be objective now."

She didn't say they were a couple again. She didn't say they weren't a couple. Andi was the perfect politician, just like her father, hedging her bets, playing both sides.

Jerry looked confused. "So, you're saying you're not in a relationship with Nate? And that personal issues won't affect your objectivity? For either of you?"

The barn was utterly, perfectly silent as everyone waited for Andi's reply. Nate knew he shouldn't be waiting along with everyone else. Only a fool would wait for something that was never going to come.

"No," she finally said, her response barely a whisper into the microphone. "We're not in a relationship, and personal issues won't affect our objectivity for either of us."

As soon as Andi stepped away from the microphone, the crowd stood up to gossip over the strange twist the meeting had taken while her client made a beeline for the stage.

Even as darkness stole through him, Nate couldn't take his eyes off of Andi. She was standing a foot from the microphone, looking tormented.

Horrified.

Her hand moved over her mouth and her eyes were big as she turned to him.

"Nate."

His name was a plea. But he couldn't talk to her here. Now.

"Don't, Andi. Just don't."

Nate knew it wasn't fair to blame the silver-haired man for any of this, but in that moment, he actually hated the stranger. Simply because his presence tonight had forced Andi to admit the truth of her feelings—and to make her choice—not just in front of Nate, but before every single person at the town hall meeting.

She hadn't just denied being with him; she'd simply

failed to be the one person he needed in his life to make him whole. He had invested so many hopes and dreams and promises in her, in the future he envisioned for them, and in the end—the end where he'd thought everything would work out eventually—she just wasn't there, wasn't ready to step up to the plate and *try*.

He'd reached for her again, for the second time since he was a teenager...and she'd pushed him away.

Nate heard her say, "Mr. Klein, thank you again for coming tonight," as if through a thick barrier.

The man's reply barely funneled through Nate's brain. "I'm not sure what to say, Andrea. I'm more than a little confused about this carousel business and what a knitting fund-raiser could possibly have to do with our project plans?"

Nate couldn't stand there and listen for one more second. Not when everything he'd thought was finally his wasn't.

Not when he needed to get out of there and start figuring out how to pick up the pieces.

Again.

\*    \*    \*

"Nate, please wait!" Andi had followed him through the back door to the small room behind the stage.

Nate felt broken. All used up. Emptied out.

And still, he couldn't make himself leave. Not when Andi was still so close.

Not when her voice was breaking with tears—and fear.

"I shouldn't have said that to Jerry. My answer was a mistake. I heard the question and saw the look on my client's face and freaked out. I wouldn't have said what I said if I didn't have to. But I didn't mean it. You know I didn't mean it, Nate."

Jesus, he hadn't felt this sick to his stomach since that moment he'd walked into the trailer and saw his father's body. Nate's throat was so tight he could hardly get any words out, and Andi was blurring in front of him where she stood.

"Your boss was there," he told her, unable—unwilling—to keep the sarcasm from his tone. "You had to protect your job."

And they both knew the only reason she'd had to save her butt was because she was going back.

Because Andi had never had any intention of staying.

She was coming toward him, her hand outstretched. "No, Nate, I just messed up. I messed up so badly."

He could see the tears in her eyes, but for once, he knew he couldn't let them move him.

"I can't believe I said that. I was just acting out of habit, giving the kind of answer I've had to give a hundred times when a deal is going bad."

He moved out of her reach, and her eyes flashed with deep pain.

"Please, Nate, listen to me. I swear, I'm going to figure out a way to make it right. I'm going to tell everyone I didn't mean it."

All these years, the horrible memories of his father's suicide had darkened Nate's dreams, along with that vision of Andi walking away from him. He'd had to fight like hell not to guard his sister like a crazed man, not to imprison her with his fears. But he'd made sure to imprison himself, to keep what was left of his soul safe.

Until these past two weeks. Until Andi returned to him... and he'd let himself love her again.

Wouldn't you know it, all of his fears had come back to nail him right in the middle of his heart, tearing out chunks, piece by piece, until he wasn't sure how there could be anything left beating inside his chest anymore.

"I always believed in you, Andi. I know all those years came between us, but we were both just kids then, immature and full of pride. But we're not those kids anymore. You didn't think you were strong enough to deal with coming home and worrying about my sister and helping your mother and grandmother and loving me, but I knew differently. I knew you were. I had faith in you."

"Then give me another chance." She wiped away her tears with the back of her hand. "Because nothing has ever hurt more than this—than knowing I had a second chance at love and I blew it. Please, Nate, believe in me one more time. Just one more time."

God, it was all he wanted. To hold her in his arms and kiss away her tears. But he couldn't keep pretending that would be enough.

Because it wouldn't be. He knew that now.

"I figured something out tonight, Andi. Something I didn't want to see." His throat felt like he'd swallowed fire. "It doesn't matter what I believe. You've got to believe it, too. And I don't know how to make that happen."

She looked at him with those big blue eyes, tears falling one after the other as the words he had to say gutted him, body and soul.

"I thought it was about you admitting your love for me, Andi, I thought once you did that everything would be okay, that you'd be able to happy. I thought we could finally be happy together. But now I can see it's not about me at all. It never was. You were always loving me the best you thought you could. You still are."

*And it wasn't enough.*

"You said what you said tonight to drive me away." He made himself hold her gaze, even though just looking at her hurt. "Congratulations. It worked."

Nate picked up his bag and made himself walk to the door, even as she said, "I thought you were going to love me forever, Nate. I thought you said you'd love me no matter what this time. Wasn't that what you told me?"

Loving his mother hadn't stopped her from dying too young. Loving his father hadn't stopped him from killing himself. Loving Andi hadn't stopped her from leaving at eighteen. And it wouldn't stop her from leaving now.

He thought he'd broken through the final shred of fear in his soul. But now he knew that he couldn't survive being left again by someone he loved.

Looking at her over his shoulder, he said, "I meant it, Andi. I will always love you."

And he would. Forever.

Even though he had to be the one who left this time.

The door closed behind him with a soft click.

# Chapter Twenty-nine

Out.

Andi needed to get out of the barn, out of the room where she'd made her biggest mistake ever.

Leaving her bag behind, she ran down Main Street. The wind was whipping through the trees, her hair was flying, and goose bumps were running up and down her limbs. It wasn't until she was past all of the stores and restaurants that she realized it was raining, too.

The storm had come. And she'd been right to be afraid.

She ran until she was out of breath. Until she couldn't run anymore. And that was when she looked up and realized she was standing in the middle of the town cemetery.

She hadn't planned to run here. To run straight to her father. But she had nowhere else to go for answers.

Tears and rain made it hard for her to find her father's gravestone. Finally she saw the contours of her father's name etched so carefully into the granite.

"I've missed you, Daddy." She dropped to her knees in the wet grass. "So much you wouldn't believe it."

She knew he wasn't actually there in front of her, but

she felt that he was listening all the same. And that was why she knew she had to be honest. More honest than she'd ever let herself be.

"I tried to grab the brass ring, Daddy. I gave it every-thing I could." She bowed down over his grave, her sobs heaving in her chest, her entire body. "But it was too hard. It took too much out of me. And I failed."

She'd never wanted to have to admit to anyone that the reason she'd always worked so hard was not so much be-cause there was something vitally important that she needed to achieve...but simply because she was terrified of failing.

"Do you know that I never really felt like I fit in, Daddy? I was so busy chasing after you, after your ap-proval, that I never really let myself focus on the people who were here all along."

She'd always felt like an outsider looking in. Searching for her place. Last night in Nate's arms, when she'd finally confessed her love, she'd wanted to believe that she'd found her place. But she hadn't.

"Now that I've come back, so many of them hate me. I don't want to be an outsider anymore. But I am. And it's all my own fault."

Even in the city she'd kept herself from forming strong attachments to anyone. Not just men—she'd known deep within herself that no one could ever take Nate's place in her heart—but even with the women who had made over-tures toward becoming friends.

"I'm still in love with Nate, Daddy. He was in love with me, too, and he gave me a second chance." The magnitude of everything she had just lost sent shooting pains through her, cramping her belly. "But I ruined that, too. I threw his love away. For a job."

Oh god, how could she not have realized until now—until it was too late—that losing her job was absolutely nothing compared to losing Nate?

"I should have never come back home. Why did I think these condos would fix everything?"

Not just her career. But her past with Nate. Somehow she'd thought if she did enough good with her job, it would make choosing her career over him ten years ago all worth it.

"I know you loved me. I know you raised me to be strong. And I tried, Daddy. I did just what you said and gave it everything I could. But I don't think I have anything left to give this time."

Nothing but losing Nate ten years ago had ever hurt this bad. Not even, she now realized, her father's death.

She felt her phone ring inside the pocket of her suit jacket. *Please, let it be Nate. Please, let it be Nate!*

But when she went to pull it out, she could already see it wasn't Nate's name on the bright screen. It was her boss, Craig.

Grief came at her doubled as she dropped the phone back into her pocket.

\*     \*     \*

Nate could hear laughter coming from inside Betsy's house when he knocked on her front door.

"Oh Nate, hi!"

She had on a sparkly hat the girls had made her. Behind her the house looked warm. Happy.

"Thanks for having Madison over for dinner while I was at the town hall meeting. I really appreciate it." He tried to smile, but he couldn't. "I can take her home now."

"Nate?" Betsy moved closer to him, pulling the door closed partway behind her. "Is everything okay?"

Uncomplicated. That's all he could think as he looked at the woman standing in front of him. Loving Betsy would have been so uncomplicated.

"It's been a long night."

Her eyes were full of concern. "You look like you need a drink." She gave him a little smile. "I've got an open bottle of wine that I'd be happy to share with you."

Betsy wasn't the kind of woman who would break his heart. She would always be there, waiting for him with a smile, with open arms. She'd take on his daughter without blinking an eye, without worrying for one second if she had what it took to help raise Madison.

"You're getting wet. Come inside, Nate."

And for the first time ever, Nate went in.

# Chapter Thirty

Andi knew her mother would be waiting for her when she got home. She found her elbow deep in flour and chocolate chips.

Her mother had always baked when she was upset, had once told Andi that the process of watching separate ingredients come together into a cohesive whole always gave her hope that things would make sense in the end.

Carol stopped kneading the dough the minute Andi walked into the kitchen.

"Honey, I've been worried sick about you."

Her mother was across the room in a heartbeat, her sticky hands reaching around Andi's shoulders. But even her warm arms couldn't erase Andi's deep chill.

"You need to take off those wet clothes and dry off."

"It doesn't matter, Mom. I'm fine like this."

Andi didn't think she would ever feel warm again. Not even after she'd changed into dry clothes. Because her chill wasn't skin deep.

She'd yanked out her own heart tonight and replaced it with a block of ice.

"What happened, honey?" Her mother's pretty face was ravaged with concern.

Andi had just come from telling her father everything. But she'd never known how to confide in her mother like that. She still didn't.

"I can't stand to know that you're in pain, honey. I know I haven't been the best mother to you, and I know I'll never be able to replace your father, but if you'll just give me another chance—"

Andi finally found her voice. "How can you say you weren't a good mother to me? You were always there for me. Always."

"Not in the ways you needed me to be. I knew how to bake muffins and do your hair, but I never believed I knew how to guide you in the direction you seemed to want to go. Which was why I left that all up to your father." Carol's face was awash with regret. "I left too much to your father. I see that now."

"Were you happy with Daddy?"

Andi hadn't ever planned to ask her mother that. She'd been too afraid of pushing her mother even further away with the pointed question. But weren't all those fears the reason she was hurting so bad now?

"Yes, honey, I was happy with your father."

Any other night, Andi knew she would have taken her mother's response at face value, simply because it was what she wanted to hear. But she couldn't do that anymore, couldn't twist everything up so it fit into a neat little box.

"How can you say that when he was gone all the time? How can you say that when he never included you in his plans unless he needed his pretty, smiling wife at his side to look good?"

Carol's eyes glittered. "Oh, honey, I'm so sorry to hear you say that. To know you think that. I should have sat down with you before now to talk about our relationship. To explain about our marriage."

"What's there to explain? It's obvious that he thought he was too big, too busy for you."

*And,* she couldn't help but think, *for his own daughter.*

Her mother moved around the kitchen island to take Andi's hands in hers, flour and chocolate forgotten. "Come. Sit down. Please."

Andi let her mother lead her over to the kitchen chairs.

"You already know that I met your father when we were both at the university in Washington, D.C., and we lived there until we had you."

"Until he dumped us into the backwater and started his political career."

Andi was as surprised as her mother by the resentment in her own voice. Just like Nate, she hadn't wanted to admit how angry she was with her father for the way he'd treated his own family, like they were second-class citizens to his constituents.

"No, honey, he didn't want to leave me here. And he definitely didn't want to leave you here."

"Then why did he?"

"Because I refused to go back to the city. I refused to leave my family to live on a street full of strangers. I refused to let my daughter go to schools where I didn't know every single teacher by name. Deep in my heart, I believed that you needed to grow up in Emerald Lake. And I loved having you here with me, loved knowing you were surrounded by people who loved you, who looked after you to make sure you stayed safe."

"Are you kidding?" Andi tried to push down the sob that rose up and failed. "Did you see what happened at that meeting tonight? Everyone here hates me. I've never fit in. Never."

Her mother reached over to wipe away her tears then, the same thing she'd done when Andi was a little girl. "Oh, honey, no. People might hate the idea of condos, but they could never hate you. You've always been the town's golden girl, the one everyone has been so proud of since that first spelling bee you won when you were eight. How could you not know how proud we all are of you?"

"I went for the brass ring, Mom. I thought I had it. But I wasn't strong enough to hold on. Daddy always told me to be strong, but I couldn't do it."

"Honey, you've always been strong. Always. And if you'd seen more of your father maybe you would have known what going for the brass ring meant to him. That it didn't just mean success. It meant family and love and happiness."

Andi reeled from what her mother had just told her. Had she really been wrong her whole life about her father's mantra? And how would she ever know for sure without him being here so that she could ask him?

"Oh, Andi." One lone tear rolled down her mother's cheek, quickly followed by another. "All this time I wanted to think that my way was right, that I did the best I could, that I made the best decisions I knew how to make. Instead, I held you captive in a town you couldn't wait to get out of. Your father tried so many times over the years to try and get me to change my mind, but I wouldn't bend." Carol covered her mouth with her hands. "I just wouldn't bend."

So many things didn't make sense tonight to Andi. "Are you saying that you and me living here without him was your decision?"

Her mother looked surprised by Andi's question. "Yes."

"And you stood up to him again and again?" At Carol's frown, Andi said, "All this time I thought you were going along with whatever he wanted because he was so strong and you were—"

"Weak."

"No!" Andi almost shouted the word at her mother. "Gentle. Warm. Because you loved him too much to stand up to him and tell him what you really wanted."

"I still love him," her mother said softly. "Every second of every day."

"But you were so unhappy sometimes," Andi said, unable to forget those bleak hours after her father left again for D.C., when both she and her mother knew he wouldn't be coming back for weeks. "Didn't you ever wish that you had married someone who wanted the same things you did? Someone who would be there every morning and every night?"

"I'd be lying to you if I said no. But what I felt for your father was bigger than where we lived. Or how much time we were able to spend together. My only regret about loving your father is the toll it took on you not always having two parents in the same place at the same time." Carol wouldn't let Andi evade her gaze. "Is that what's holding you back with Nate, honey?"

"I never stopped loving him, Mom. He told me he loved me, too. That he forgave me for leaving before. I had everything I ever wanted." She had to close her eyes against the pain. "And I blew it tonight when Jerry asked that question. I tried to explain, I tried to apologize, but Nate wouldn't forgive me. Not this time. And why should he? I left him before. I almost left him again." She tried to breathe, but couldn't find any oxygen. "But he left me first."

Carol scooted her chair over and put her arms around Andi. "Give him time, honey. He never stopped loving you and he won't stop now, I can guarantee that. Real love doesn't have anything to do with perfection. Real love is what happens when everything isn't perfect...and you love each other anyway." Carol pulled back, tilted Andi's face back up to hers with her index finger. "Promise me, you'll give all of this some time. Not just for Nate, but for you, too."

Andi had never looked at her mother as anything more than a politician's wife, a mother, and a small knitting store owner. She could never understand why her mother hadn't wanted more. But now, as she sat and talked with her mother—finally connecting the way they should have years ago—Andi finally saw the truth: Through her innate gentleness, through her baking, through her presence at Lake Yarns, Carol had always made a difference in people's lives. Perhaps it was on a much smaller scale than what her father had been able to accomplish as senator, but that didn't mean it was any less important to the lives her mother had touched.

Had she been looking to the wrong person for lessons in strength all along? Instead of her father, should she have been giving the credit to her mother and grandmother, to all of the incredible women she'd connected with at the yarn store, women who were strong enough to triumph over anything life threw into their paths? Women who had all of the strength but none of the glory?

"I know this has been a hard night for you, honey, but your grandmother has been waiting up for you to tell her about the meeting tonight. I don't want her to worry that something happened to you."

But Andi couldn't leave yet. Not until she said something she didn't say nearly enough.

"I love you, Mom."

Her mother's eyes were awash with tears. "I've never loved anyone more than I love you, honey."

They hugged for a long time, both of them crying. Finally Andi pushed her chair back and was halfway out of the room when she realized there was one more thing she needed to say.

"Thank you for offering to sit with Mr. Klein tonight. I didn't expect him to attend the town hall meeting."

Again there was that surprising spark in her mother's eyes, a slight flush in her cheeks. "It was no problem at all, honey. Actually he was very nice."

"It's okay, Mom."

The words were hard to force out, but that spark that had been missing from her mother's eyes made it possible to get them out. And to know that she was doing the right thing.

"It's okay if you want to see Mr. Klein again."

Her mother stood up so fast she almost knocked over her chair. "Your father—"

"Is gone. But you're still here."

"No. Really. I couldn't possibly be with another..."

"I'm not saying you have to marry the guy. But if he asks you out—and I really think he will—can you at least think about saying yes?"

Her mother took a deep breath. "Maybe."

Just then, Andi's phone rang again. She cringed at the hope in her mother's eyes.

"It's not Nate."

"Please, just look, just in case."

The hope in her mother's eyes was almost enough to spill over into her, but when Andi looked at the screen, she simply confirmed, "It's my boss."

She had made a trade, love for a career. But even that had gone wrong.

For Craig to be calling her again and again on a Thursday evening meant she'd screwed up in a big way at the town hall meeting.

She hadn't just lost Nate, she was going to lose her job, too.

Blinded by the tears that were coming again, tears that just kept coming, Andi didn't see a bag that was on the floor until she had stepped on it. Bending down to pick the bag up, she realized the Fair Isle sweater she'd been obsessively working on was inside.

*       *       *

Lightning continued to light up the sky when Andi knocked softly on her grandmother's bedroom door. She wasn't surprised to find her grandmother sitting up in bed knitting.

Knitting the wedding veil.

Andi's gut twisted hard enough that she had to stop, had to take a deep breath to recover before crossing to her grandmother's bed.

"Grandma, I'm so glad you're better. And that you're finally back home."

Andi almost forgot she was soaking wet as she went to go hug her grandmother.

"Give me a kiss first, and then after you've put on something dry of mine, we can have a good long hug. There's a nightgown in your size folded up in the left corner of the armoire."

Andi pressed her lips to her grandmother's soft cheek, then took out the soft nightgown. As she unfolded it, she realized just how old the fabric was.

"This is beautiful, Grandma."

The workmanship was incredible with hand-sewn lace along the neckline, wristbands, and hem.

"I made it for your aunt Rose. Go. Put it on."

Andi was extremely careful with the soft, thin fabric as she changed out of her wet clothes in the bathroom.

"Beautiful," Evelyn said when she emerged. "You remind me so much of Rosie sometimes."

"I wish I could have known your sister."

"Maybe someday you will."

Her grandmother had never given up hope that the sister who'd disappeared so many years ago would someday reappear, even though there had never been so much as a hint that Rose was still alive.

"Now come give me that hug."

Andi should have been there to take care of her grandmother. But as soon as Evelyn's strong, slim arms came around her, Andi knew that it was exactly the opposite.

"Everything is going to be all right, honey. I promise you it's true."

Andi didn't say anything, just let her grandmother stroke her hair. Finally Evelyn pointed to Andi's bag.

"Is that the Fair Isle?"

Andi pulled out the sweater. She didn't know why she'd brought it to Evelyn's cottage.

"I knew you'd do a wonderful job with it, honey."

"What made you think I could figure it out? Especially when I've never seen such a complicated pattern before."

"You can do anything you set your mind to."

"I used to think that was true," Andi said softly.

"Tell me what your first thoughts were when you first saw this pattern?"

"I'm not sure you want to hear those kind of words, Grandma."

"You kids think you invited dirty words. And sex." She pinned Andi with a wicked look. "You most definitely didn't."

Not sure she wanted to picture her soft, sweet grandmother having wild monkey sex with anyone, Andi quickly said, "The pattern looked like another language. One I couldn't see the point of figuring out."

"But you did."

"I had some help." From Madison. While Nate had made them spaghetti.

"You could have given up."

"No, Grandma. You wanted me to help you make it. I couldn't have given up."

"I've wanted you to do a lot of things, honey. But you've always moved to the beat of your own drummer."

Andi blew out a breath. "Look, I figured if a blue-haired retiree could figure it out, so could I." Knowing how terribly judgmental that was considering all of the wonderful knitters she had met in the past two weeks, Andi said, "That isn't fair. I take it back. All I'm saying is that I've accomplished some really difficult things in my career. I couldn't stand the thought of a sweater being the thing that broke me."

"But it didn't break you, did it?"

Andi looked down at the partially—perfectly—finished sweater on her lap and found another smile. "Not even close."

Suddenly Andi remembered the conversation she'd had with Madison about giving up knitting when she was a girl.

*"I'm not good at knitting because I quit too young. I got frustrated, and instead of working through it, I told myself it was stupid...I told myself I didn't like it. And you know what I wish?"*

*"You wish you hadn't totally lied to yourself."*

Andi had thought she was only talking about knitting. But she wasn't. She saw that now. She hadn't just lied to herself about her reasons for quitting knitting, she'd also lied to herself about her reasons for leaving Emerald Lake—and her family, too.

She'd always loved both the town and the people in it, but she'd been afraid they wouldn't love her back.

So she'd run.

"Pull out one of your hairs, honey. A long one."

Andi frowned. "What? Why?"

Her grandmother didn't reply, she simply waited for Andi to do as she asked. Andi reached into her hair and separated it until she was holding one long strand. It came out with a quick tug, probably nine inches long.

"Wrap that hair around the blue yarn."

Still not understanding what was going on, Andi did as her grandmother directed.

"Now knit a row."

Even though she was still wondering what was going on, Andi followed Evelyn's directions once more. Her grandmother didn't say anything else until she made it to the end of the row.

"There's a knitting superstition that if you knit one of your own hairs into a garment it will bind the recipient to you forever."

Andi had never believed in superstition, only what she could see with her own eyes, only what she could hold in her two hands. So then why were chills running through her?

"But I'm already bound to you, Grandma."

"We both know you haven't been making this sweater for me. Just as we both know you're strong enough for any challenges that come your way."

Her grandmother was right about one thing at least. Every stitch Andi had made had been for Nate.

"Do you remember the story I was telling you about my first love?"

"Carlos. You were making him a sweater." Andi suddenly remembered something else. "That first day I was home in the store you told me it was a Fair Isle, didn't you?"

"Yes, honey, it was. That very pattern you've been working on actually." Evelyn's eyes grew cloudy with memories. "Our first kiss was on the carousel on the chariot behind the matched pair."

"So that's why you love the carousel so much?" Andi said softly. "What did he say when you gave him the sweater, Grandma? Did he like it?"

Evelyn's light blue eyes flashed with pain. "I never got the chance to give it to him."

"What happened, Grandma? You loved him, didn't you? Didn't he love you back?"

"Yes, honey, he loved me. So much that he left only hours before I was going to give him the sweater, before I could tell him I'd made my choice to be with him, no matter the struggles ahead of us."

"But if he'd really loved you wouldn't he have stayed? Wouldn't he have given you the chance to choose him?"

Evelyn sighed. "I've thought about that question for seventy years. And I still don't know what the right answer is. Until Carlos, I thought love was all fun and kisses. And then I learned about his past and thought I was in way over my head."

"What kind of past? Was he a criminal on the run?"

Her grandmother laughed, but it quickly fell away. "No, honey. Before Carlos came here to work for my father, he lost everything in a fire. His wife and son. His business."

Andi's hand moved over her grandmother's. "That's horrible." And not all that different from what Nate had dealt with ten years ago. "So Carlos came to the lake to start over?"

"No. I don't think so. I think he came just to try and figure out how to make it through another day."

"And then he met you." Andi squeezed Evelyn's hand. "What a light you must have been for him."

"Do you know, honey, that's exactly what he said to me. That I was the light in his dark world." Evelyn looked down at the lace veil in her hands. "But I was so afraid, honey. So afraid that I'd fail him. So painfully aware of the two different worlds that we lived in."

"I know exactly how you must have felt," Andi murmured softly.

"I never said those words to him, but he knew me well enough to look into my eyes and see the truth of my feelings. The morning after he told me everything on the carousel, he was gone."

"He left without saying good-bye? How could he have done that to you? Especially if he loved you, too?"

"Because he saw me for exactly what I was: a young, frightened girl."

"You would have learned how to be strong, Grandma. You're one of the strongest people I've ever known."

Andi suddenly wondered why she'd never seen the strength in her mother and grandmother so clearly until now.

"I waited for him, honey. Waited even when my mother tried to convince me that it was all for the best. Waited even when my father tried to threaten me into marrying Arthur. I wrote letters and never heard back. And I knit. Every free moment I had was spent with needles and yarn. Knitting was the only way I could stay even the slightest bit sane. And you're right, somewhere in all that stubborn waiting and knitting, I grew strong. And knew that if I ever got the chance to get love right, I wouldn't quit until I'd loved with everything in me, I wouldn't give up because I was afraid or because I didn't think I was strong enough. I would just love."

Despite the fact that she was pretty sure she already knew the answer, Andi had to ask, "What happened to him, Grandma?"

"I scoured the casualty list in the newspaper every week for his name, but I knew he wouldn't be on it. Until the day that I knew he was." Her grandmother's eyes had never looked so sad. "Carlos was killed in active duty."

"That's just so awful. So unfair. I wish you'd never gone through any of that, Grandma."

"Oh no, honey, even knowing how it ended, I would have done it anyway. I would have loved Carlos." She squeezed Andi's hand, surprising her with a smile. "But don't worry, I loved your grandfather, too. Strong and true."

Andi was afraid her grandmother was only saying that because it was what she wanted to hear.

Obviously reading her mind, Evelyn said, "At first it was a different kind of love. Your grandfather went to fight in the war, too, enlisting not long after Carlos. All through those years that they were gone, I found solace in knitting for the war effort. That was when Lake Yarns first became a reality."

"But I thought you didn't open the store until the fifties?"

"Oh, I wasn't anywhere near having a fancy shop back then, not until after I'd had your mother and she started school, but that didn't stop me and your aunts and my friends from meeting every Monday night in my bedroom to knit."

Andi quickly did the math and realized the Monday night knitting group had been around even longer than the store. Seven decades.

Amazing.

"When Arthur finally returned from the war, I was still grieving over Carlos, but even then I could see that your grandfather had left a boy and come back a man. Just as I'd been a girl when he left, and he'd returned to a woman.

I think he'd always been a little bit in love with me, only now he was confident enough to prove it to me. I kept trying to push him away, but he was there with flowers and laughter and kisses. Oh, they were wonderful kisses, Andi."

Her grandmother smiled a secret smile that Andi wasn't sure she'd ever seen before. Or if she had, she hadn't understood it.

"But what about Carlos? Weren't you still in love with him?"

"You wouldn't believe how long I spent telling myself that I couldn't possibly love Arthur because I'd already given my heart away. It took Arthur never giving up on loving me for one single second for me to see that loving Carlos had actually opened up my heart so that I could love Arthur fully and completely. If not for Carlos, I might have spent my whole life running scared from love."

But Andi still had to know. "What happened to the sweater you made for Carlos, Grandma?"

"At first, I held onto it because it was my only true link to him. But then after he died, it wasn't something I could give away to anyone else. Especially not your grandfather." Her grandmother gave her a small smile. "I thought about unraveling it a thousand times, but I just couldn't. Because first loves are something special. And even though I found love again with your grandfather, I still believe that if you can make that first love work, you should give it everything you've got."

Evelyn's words rocked through Andi. She'd had a second chance at first love, but she'd been scared, too scared to realize just how precious it was.

"I know you're looking for answers, honey. But maybe

all you really need to know is that you left Emerald Lake a girl, but you came back a woman. Strong and loving."

Andi looked down at the wedding veil on Evelyn's lap, then at the sweater on her own, at the precise way she had wrapped her dark hair around the blue yarn, making sure it never came unthreaded from the sweater.

So many strands woven together. Alone they could be easily broken, but together they were strong.

"I love you, too, Grandma," she whispered, but when no response came, she looked up and realized her grandmother had fallen asleep.

Tiptoeing out of Evelyn's cottage, she was on the small front porch when the cell phone in her pocket rang again.

The time had finally come to answer it.

\* \* \*

"Hello, Craig."

"Jesus, Andrea, I got a call from Mr. Klein, and it sounds like there's quite a shit storm going on in that little town of yours." She could hear his irritation, his frustration at watching one of his trains derail from a distance. "Look, I don't know what happened tonight, but we're going to need a bulletproof plan to fix it. There's no room for error this time, Andrea, no second chances to try to get it right."

Andi didn't interrupt her boss. But with every word he spoke, it became more and more clear to her that of all the things that had gone wrong tonight, trying to keep the Klein Group on board was not the thing she needed—or wanted—to fix first.

"Craig, I can't leave my family's store. Not with my grandmother still recovering from pneumonia. And not without a good manager in pl—"

She stopped herself short on the final word. She was doing it again. Trying to take the easy way out. Refusing to make any declarations about her real feelings because she was afraid of disappointing her boss.

Because she was afraid of being a failure.

"Look, Craig, that's not the real reason I'm not coming back. My heart's not in the game anymore. And I think we both know it hasn't been for a very long time."

"What the hell could you be heading off to do that's better?"

"I'm going to manage my family's yarn store."

Sure, she could get another job in the city, but not only did her family need her to run the store...she also didn't want to leave Emerald Lake. Even though it would be so much easier to run from Nate again, to go back to the safety of her city life.

"You're serious, aren't you?"

Andi waited for embarrassment, for defensiveness to kick in, but neither came.

"I am."

\*     \*     \*

Andi tossed and turned for a couple of hours in her old childhood bed before she gave up on sleep. She'd gotten too used to Nate's warm body beside her, to his arms wrapped around her waist, to feeling his warm breath against the small hairs of her neck as she spooned into him.

Realizing the rain had finally stopped falling, Andi slipped on her shoes and wrapped a warm blanket around her shoulders. Now that the storm had cleared, it was one of those perfect full-moon fall nights, the kind they put in movies and posters that made people want to come to the Adirondacks to forget their cares. The same people that the Klein Group hoped would buy a condo on the waterfront.

Picking up a flashlight, she left the porch and headed for the dock. After uncovering the rowboat and putting on her life vest, she used the oars on the sandy bottom of the lake to push away from the shore.

The lake was empty and slowly, surely, Andi rowed out into the middle of it. Her breath came faster as blood rushed through her system to try and keep up with the rapid beating of her heart. She had never needed a gym while she'd lived here, just the grass and mountains and lakes as she'd grown up running and hiking and swimming and sailing.

She propped the oars in the boat and let herself float. She leaned back to look at the stars, and as the sky darkened, they appeared before her one by one. She took a deep breath of the sweet, cool air, then another and another. And then she finally rowed herself around to face the opposite shore to see if there was a light on across the lake.

And if someone was out there missing her as much as she missed him.

But there was only darkness. The darkness she'd longed for just a night ago because she'd been so afraid of the flaws and cracks that the light would reveal.

Shivering, Andi knew she needed to get back to the dock before her frozen fingers were unable to hold onto the oars.

She was halfway turned around when she saw something flicker on Nate's porch from the corner of her eye.

A single light turning on.

# Chapter Thirty-one

The next morning, Andi sat down across from her client in the inn's dining room. Rebecca's eyes were full of concern as she placed steaming teapots on the table. Andi was glad to know she had a friend's shoulder to cry on. Later. First she needed to have a difficult discussion with her client.

"I'm glad you're here, Mr. Klein, so that I can give you the news in person." She paused. "I resigned my position with Marks & Banks last night. I will no longer be working on your project."

"I'm very sorry to hear that, Andrea. Although your mother was telling me that you've been a great help at her store."

She hadn't always been sure that she was doing a great job at Lake Yarns during the past two weeks, but she'd done the best she could. And she was proud of what she'd learned about running a knitting store.

"I've enjoyed myself more than I knew I would," she finally said. But she wasn't here to talk about her plans to run Lake Yarns. "Although I won't be working with you any longer, I still feel compelled to give you my honest opinion about your plans to renovate the historic buildings. Stores like my family's yarn store that are in historic, preserved buildings, even the old carousel in the park, are all extremely important for small towns like Emerald Lake. Not just for my family, but for the generations of people who know that they're part of a real strong community. That is why I'm afraid I cannot endorse your newest plan to continue your development into the historic buildings."

Strangely Mr. Klein didn't look upset by her opinion. More thoughtful.

"Do you know what I did this morning, Andrea? I woke up early and spent some time walking down Main Street, looking into the windows of local shops. You see, you sold me so thoroughly on the allure of the Adirondacks, I had to come and see it for myself. I had to come see what I was missing."

He smiled at her, and she was surprised to find herself smiling back.

"Last night I sat in that barn and listened. Really listened. What I didn't understand about the workings of a small town, your mother explained. The conclusion that I came to, by the time I got back to my room at the inn, was that the only way our project could work for all parties involved is if all parties are actually involved." Andi could see the excitement in his eyes as he said, "I want this to be a first for our company, a community-based project that will set the stage for future growth that benefits real people, not just the corporate bottom line."

"I'm thrilled to hear you say all of this." And she was, even if she wouldn't be working on the project anymore.

"I thought you might be. I had the utmost faith in you to lead us into a brand-new way of doing business, Andi." He gave her another smile. "I still do."

It was the first time her client had ever used her nickname. He never would have known she had a nickname if he hadn't come to the town hall meeting, if he hadn't seen her surrounded by people who had known her—and loved her—her entire life.

"Is there any chance I could convince you to do one more project?" he asked. "I know you're needed at your mother's store, but perhaps since you'll already be working from Emerald Lake, there would be a way for you to oversee our project. A new one, Andi. One that will be good for everyone. For the locals who need to downsize, for the city folks like me who desperately need a quiet place to go, for my company. And for you, too."

Everything had felt so black and white the night before. Nate and the lake and the yarn store versus her job and the city. And she had made her choice when she'd resigned her job.

But perhaps Nate had said it best: *"Andi, it's not black and white. Leaving doesn't have to mean cutting ties."*

She'd always assumed that moving back to Emerald Lake would mean giving up every last part of her life in the city. But was that assumption also wrong?

"I need some time to think about it, Mr. Klein. Honestly, your offer sounds wonderful, but I can't put myself first this time. I just can't."

"I understand that, Andi. And I'd be lying if I said I wasn't envious that you get to stay in Emerald Lake." Mr. Klein's expression changed slightly. "I'm hoping to come back for a visit in the very near future."

Andi immediately understood what he was asking. "I'd like that very much. Just be sure to let me know you're coming next time. My mother is a wonderful cook, and there's nothing she likes to do more than to make sure people feel welcome."

A grin lit up his handsome face. They stood up and shook hands. "I'm looking forward to hearing back from you on my offer. I'll be seeing you very soon, Andi."

"I'll be looking forward to it, Mr. Klein."

"John, please."

Noticing that the glow in his eyes mirrored the one she'd seen in her mother's just last night, Andi was glad to be beyond formalities.

"John, it is."

\*　　　\*　　　\*

Andi left the inn and headed out across the waterfront park. Unlike last night when she'd run blind from the town hall meeting, she knew exactly where she was going today.

The carousel.

She didn't just climb on board and sit down on one of the horses this time; instead she really studied the merry-go-round that had been such a big part of so many lives at Emerald Lake.

The red-and-white striped awning all around the top was matched by the red paint all along the trim. The carousel animals were graceful, realistic. The carvers had obviously paid enormous attention to anatomical detail, the painters' renderings of every nuance of the animals' coloration were exquisite. The three-row machine carried twenty-nine horses and a chariot behind a matched pair.

There were also giraffes, goats, deer, and a lion and a tiger.

Walking around the carousel, Andi ran her fingers over the horses, stopping behind the chariot where her grandmother had her first kiss with Carlos. She wanted so badly to find something important, some sort of sign or secret message that Evelyn's first love had left for her before he disappeared.

But if there had ever been a message there, it was now covered in decades of paint.

Thinking how lovely it would have been to find something from Carlos, Andi waited for the disappointment to settle down over her. But the image that appeared before her instead was one of her grandmother and grandfather holding hands out on the porch in the years before he passed away.

Evelyn didn't need a secret message from her lost love to be happy. She'd made her peace with the past, knew that everything that had happened had only made her stronger.

Andi was looking into the rusted mirror, the image of the blue lake shining out from behind her, when an epiphany slammed into her so hard that she had to sit down on the chariot: not only were there no secret messages, no symbols or signs engraved in the paint...but just as her grandmother didn't need them, Andi didn't need them, either.

With Nate's love, through spending time with knitters at Lake Yarns, by observing her mother and her grandmother and finally talking to them the way she always should have, she had finally learned just how much strength and fortitude it took to be the one that stayed, to be the one who kept the home fires burning. Future answers would come from everything she'd learned about her small hometown, about her mother and grandmother, about the man she loved. And especially, her own heart.

All her life she'd given her all for whatever goal she was shooting for. Now she realized all that hard work had been practice, training her for the ultimate goal, for the ultimate achievement.

For love.

She wanted Emerald Lake. She wanted Lake Yarns. She wanted to be near her family.

And Nate.

She wanted Nate.

\*     \*     \*

Andi was climbing off the carousel when Madison's words from Wednesday night suddenly came back to her. *"Nate, if Andi gets rid of the merry-go-round, can we put it in our backyard?"*

Andi's hand was still on a cold metal pole, and with one of the horses looking up at her with something that looked like a smile, just like that, Andi knew exactly what she had to do.

And this time she was going to follow her own heart all the way there.

# Chapter Thirty-two

For the next four days, Andi was either on the phone, sending an e-mail, knocking on a door, or demanding answers and papers and official stamps from government offices. Her mother and grandmother helped with her plan where they could, but mostly it was a matter of digging into old papers at the library, at the courthouse, or on the Internet. She hadn't yet given John Klein his answer, but that could wait.

Absolutely exhausted by Monday morning, she was glad to spend a few hours surrounded by the busload of women that had come by as part of their annual Knit into Fall yarn crawl.

Andi was warmed by the knowledge that she was finally in the right place. After all these years of searching, she had managed to find it right where she'd started. Her family, her friends, they were all a part of Lake Yarns. They always had been; she'd just been too blind to see it until now.

She and Jenny were beginning to set up the store for the Monday night knitting group when the UPS truck parked outside the store. A minute later Andi held the certified letter she had been waiting for in her hands. Hands that were shaking.

Jenny told her, "I can handle the rest of this."

Andi looked up at her friend. "I've never been this nervous before." Maybe because nothing had ever been this important.

She never would have admitted her nerves to anyone before. Not when she'd been too afraid to admit her fears even to herself.

Jenny gave her a hug. "For courage. Now go."

\* \* \*

For the past four days, Nate had spent more time with his ax in the forest behind his house than he had in the past four years. He and Madison now had a pile of firewood to last them into the next decade at least.

It was times like this when he wished he was a drinker. But that was exactly what his father had done—and when trying to drown his sorrows in alcohol hadn't worked, he'd opted for a bullet instead.

After a weekend of too much hard physical labor and not enough sleep, Nate felt worse than he had in years. Not since that weekend when he'd lost everything but his sister. He even felt guilty for walking into Betsy's house Thursday night, for giving the nice woman any hope at all that he was ever going to come around. She'd poured him a glass of wine, but he hadn't stayed to drink it. Instead he'd grabbed his sister and gotten out of there as quickly as he could.

Madison walked into his office without knocking. "Hey Mads, don't you have after-school art today?"

"It was canceled." Madison sat down on the couch against the far wall and started playing with her shoelaces. "Mrs. Riggs threw up."

A pang of guilt hit Nate as he realized his sister was upset about something. He'd been so wrapped up in his own misery that he hadn't paid enough attention to her lately.

"Everything okay?"

She shrugged. "Sure."

Uh-oh. He knew that shrug. Knew that *sure*. Working like hell to pull it together for his sister, he got up out of his chair and walked over to the couch, all the while trying to figure out what she might be upset about.

It hit him right as he sat down.

"Did you give Jaden the scarf you made for him?"

She shook her head. "No. I'm not going to give it to him."

"Why?"

"He's not going to stick around. If I really let myself like him, I'll just feel bad when he goes back to California. I was thinking it would be better if I just kept it or whatever."

Suddenly Nate knew why he'd been chopping wood until his palms started to bleed, why he'd been unable to sleep.

And it wasn't because Andi had hurt him by not having the guts to claim him as hers during the town hall meeting. She'd asked him to forgive her afterward. She had explained her momentary panic from standing in front of her client. And she'd begged for a chance to do it over and get it right this time.

No, damn it, her behavior wasn't the reason he couldn't look at himself in the mirror in the morning.

The reason he couldn't live with himself was because he'd screwed up again.

Andi had made one little mistake, and he'd lost his mind, then come up with a hundred ways to justify it.

Just like he had ten years ago.

"Jaden might be leaving next fall, Mads, but he's here now. Do you like him?"

"Yeah, he's pretty cool."

"Then give him the scarf. Because you know what I had to learn the hard way?"

She blinked up at him, her green eyes so big and innocent. "What?"

"There's a chance you might regret listening to your heart now, but you'll definitely 100 percent regret it later if you don't."

\* \* \*

"Hi Cat."

Catherine was clearly surprised to see Andi entering Nate's domain. Concern was only a beat behind.

"How are you doing? I've been so worried about you. I would have been over to the store before now, but I left town right after the meeting on Thursday and only got back a couple of hours ago."

"It means so much to me to know you care," Andi said softly, meaning every word, more glad than she could ever say that their friendship had managed to survive the years after all. "And I promise I'll talk your ears off about everything soon, but right now I really need to see Nate."

Cat nodded. "He needs to see you, too, Andi. Madison's in with him."

Andi took a deep breath and gripped her slim package

tighter in one hand as she turned Nate's doorknob with the other.

Nate and Madison were sitting on the couch together, but as soon as he saw her, he stood up.

"Andi?"

She drank in the beautiful sight of him, the way his hair was sticking up on one side like he hadn't remembered to comb it, the dark stubble growing along the bottom half of his face.

The urge to apologize all over again for screwing everything up—and to beg for another chance—hit her so hard her knees almost buckled from the force of it.

Swallowing hard, she made herself take a step toward him and then another. She held out the slim package, waited for him to take it from her shaking hand.

"It's yours now."

He looked down at the express envelope, then back up at her. "What is this?" But he was already reaching into the envelope and pulling out the official notarized sheet.

"The carousel?" He looked down at the paper again, then back at her. "You're giving the town the deed to the carousel?"

Madison grabbed the page from him as Andi explained, "When I was doing my research for the Klein Group, I learned that the carousel wasn't already owned by the town like I'd always assumed. A company in Rochester owned it, Nate. Along with the land around it. I knew if they ever realized they still owned a patch of prime Adirondack waterfront, they'd put it on the market. Something Madison said to you one of the nights we all drove to the hospital made me realize that I couldn't live with the risk of someone coming in and buying it."

"Andi, where did you get the money for this?"

"It isn't important."

And it wasn't. He didn't need to know that she'd emptied out her bank account for the carousel.

"All that matters is that the carousel—and the land it's sitting on—is safe now."

She knew she should leave before she did something stupid like crying or pleading for him to take her back, knew she couldn't possibly expect Nate to still love her after all the chances she'd already had, knew even giving the carousel to the town wasn't a big enough gesture to win him back...but it was so hard to go. Not without saying just one more thing to him while she knew he was listening.

And even though Madison was in the room with them, this time Andi didn't use his sister as an excuse to hold anything back.

"Over the years we were apart, I went back to eighteen all the time, Nate. And I always swore if I had the chance to love you again, I'd love you right." She couldn't stop her tears from falling, wasn't sure she'd ever be able to again. "You'll never know how sorry I am that I didn't."

Running had never been the answer; she knew that now. But when Nate didn't say anything, when he simply stood and stared at her as if he was seeing her for the very first time, there wasn't a single other thing she could do but turn.

And run one last time.

# Chapter Thirty-three

Lake Yarns was the only store on Main Street with its lights still on at 6:30 p.m. on a Monday night. As Nate and Madison walked up to the front door, he could see the women laughing together inside, toasting each other with mismatched wineglasses, passing skeins of yarn and needles and works in progress back and forth. Strangely, they looked like saddles.

He knew that Andi had kept herself from being a part of a group of women for so long. He was glad, so damn glad, that she'd finally let them in.

He hadn't wanted to wait this long before coming to find her, but he'd had to go back home to pick something up. Something important.

The din of voices was so loud it reached all the way out to the sidewalk, and at first none of them noticed him walking in. Rebecca saw them first.

"Nate? Madison?"

Everyone's heads turned to face them, their questioning, interested gazes eating up the situation.

But Nate only had eyes for Andi.

*His sweet Andi.*

Dorothy and Evelyn drew Madison over to them, and then without even realizing he had moved across the room, Nate was down on one knee in front of Andi.

"Nate?"

"It's not the deed to the carousel that has me here, Andi."

He needed her to understand that before he said anything else.

"It's you. All you, sweetheart. I would have been here anyway. After the town hall meeting, I was hurt. Upset."

"I'm so sorry, Nate. If I could go back in time and change what I said, I would."

He wanted to stop, kiss her, tell her he loved her right then. But first he needed her to know how sorry he was for what he'd done.

Reaching for her hands, he said, "For ten years, Andi, I haven't let anyone get close to me. And then you came back to town and even as I was telling myself that I had faith in us to get it right this time, I was waiting for you to leave. I was looking at the condos like a test that I was daring you to fail. But it wasn't you failing, sweetheart. It was me."

"You've never failed me, Nate. Never."

"We both know I did. And we both know we'll disappoint each other again, that over the next seventy years one of us is bound to mess up again." He brushed a lock of hair away from her beautiful face. "Remember when we were kids and we'd go out sailing and one of us would blow it and we'd end up in the lake?"

"Laughing," she said softly, pressing her cheek into his palm. "We were always laughing."

"It was an adventure. And it didn't matter that we'd screwed up because we knew we were going to climb right back on that hull and keep sailing."

Her eyes were huge, beautiful, shining with tears that were on the verge of falling.

"There's no one else I'd rather take an adventure with, Andi. No one else I'd rather go sailing off into the distance with. It's always been you, sweetheart. You take away the darkness. You fill all my empty spaces. And I'll take you any way I can get you. Any hours you can spend here with me, whatever part of your life that you've got to share. I can't promise I won't keep asking for more, because we both know that I will, but if it's a choice between losing you or getting to love even a little bit of you, I choose love, Andi. I choose you. I don't care how we do it—if I move to be with you or you move to be with me or even if we have to put new tires on our cars every six months from all the miles we're burning up to be together as often as we can. All that matters is that we're together."

"You could never live like that, Nate." Her words were raw. Shaky. "Neither of us could."

Nate's heart all but stopped. His eyes closed involuntarily, just as they would have the second before he slammed into a brick wall. But then, her hands were moving to his face and she was tracing the line of his jaw with her fingertips.

When he finally was able to open his eyes again, he saw that she was smiling through her tears.

"I'm not going back."

He could barely process her words until she smiled again. Bigger, stronger, steadier this time.

"I'm moving back to Emerald Lake. I'm going to run Lake Yarns with my mother and grandmother."

Everyone in the room, especially Evelyn and Carol, gasped with happiness, but Andi never turned her gaze from Nate's.

"I would have stayed just for you, Nate. You know how much I love you, don't you?"

"I do, sweetheart."

He was vaguely aware of her shifting slightly to reach into a bag beside her. Something soft brushed against his knuckles, and he looked down to see a beautiful sweater draped across her lap.

"I have something for you."

She held it up for him to push his hands and arms and head through. The sweater was a perfect fit.

"I knit one of my hairs into this sweater. Do you know what that means?"

He had to kiss her. "You ran out of yarn?"

She gave him that wicked little grin that he hoped to see for at least the next seventy years. "It means you're bound to me now."

He kissed her again, longer, even sweeter this time. "I've always been bound to you, Andi."

Nate pulled the ring that had once belonged to his mother out of his pocket. "Marry me, sweetheart."

And a moment later when Andi said yes and he slid the engagement ring onto her hand, a room full of knitters cheered.

# *Epilogue*

Y ou guys were right," Andi said to Nate and Madison. "This really is the perfect spot for a rainy day."

The three of them sat on the carousel beneath the red-and-white striped canopy, sipping hot chocolate and looking out at the lake. Andi and Nate were on the chariot behind the matched pair of horses while Madison rode one of the horses pulling the sleigh.

The winter snow was just starting to give way to spring rains, and they could hear the sounds of construction on the new condos that were being built on a wooded lot with lake access within walking distance from Main Street. Andi had really enjoyed working part-time with the Klein Group on the new residences over the winter. Smaller and more affordable than her original plan, the units were still beautifully designed and crafted.

From where they were sitting, she could look across the street, could see her mother and grandmother through the Lake Yarns window helping customers. Over to the right at the inn, she knew Rebecca was inside making guests smile.

Andi had finally caught that brass ring she'd been reaching for her whole life. Family. Friends.

Love.

"I know we're planning on getting married at next year's Fall Festival." She smiled a secret little smile. "But all that planning is giving me a headache."

"You?" he teased. "Not wanting to plan?"

She shrugged, hardly able to keep herself from blurting it out. "How do you feel about a shotgun wedding instead?"

Nate's eyes got big. Really big. He swallowed hard. "Andi? Are you—"

She reached for Nate's hand, intertwined their fingers, then laid them both over her stomach. "Yes."

Rebecca Campbell was set
to marry her best friend, continue
working at his family's beautiful,
historic inn, and enjoy a happy life.
Then one moment—and one man—
changed everything...

Please turn this page
for a preview of

# With This Kiss

# Chapter One

You are such a beautiful bride."

Rebecca Campbell smoothed out the cuff of Andi Powell's long-sleeved silk wedding gown and smiled at her friend in the full-length mirror. Emerald Lake, still mostly frozen and lightly dusted with snow from last night's short storm, reflected through the large-paned window into the mirror.

Andi's eyes met hers in the mirror, full of excitement and anticipation for her wedding day. "I know I've said it a hundred times already, Rebecca, but thank you so much for everything you've done to help with my wedding. I could have never pulled this off so quickly or so beautifully."

Rebecca was extremely pleased by how smoothly the wedding preparations had come together. Her final walk-through downstairs a half hour ago confirmed that the Emerald Lake Inn had been completely transformed into a tasteful, elegant wedding venue. She had done it before, of course, but it meant more to her this time, knowing that she was an integral part of Andi and Nate's special day.

Still, she had to tease her friend. "We both know you could have planned a dozen last-minute weddings in the past two weeks, Andi, and probably gotten a spread in *Brides* magazine while you were at it."

Andi grinned before tossing off, "That was the old me, before I decided to start playing with yarn all day instead."

Rebecca was happy to let Andi say whatever she wanted. After all, this was her wedding day. But both of them knew that moving back to Emerald Lake and becoming engaged to Nate hadn't changed the core of who she was. Andi had always been driven, brilliant, and on top of that, she also happened to be one of the most loving, caring people Rebecca had ever had the good fortune of knowing. Business at Lake Yarns was more brisk than ever now that Andi had taken over the store for her mother and grandmother. Not just because Andi was a great businesswoman with a background in management consulting but because she was truly passionate about knitting—and the women who patronized her store.

As Andi turned back to look into the antique mirror in the inn's "wedding prep" room, Rebecca noted that her friend seemed surprised by her own appearance: the wedding gown, the soft curls brushing against her collarbone, the pretty makeup.

"I never thought today would come," Andi said softly. "But I always wanted it." She lifted her gaze to meet Rebecca's. "I've loved Nate my whole life."

Rebecca blinked quickly to push away the tears that had been threatening to fall all morning just thinking about Andi and Nate's wedding.

"You deserve it." She could hear how scratchy her words sounded. She had to work to swallow away the lump that had formed in her throat at Andi's confession of love. "You and Nate both deserve the love you've found again. Especially since this time it's forever."

She shot a knowing glance at Andi's slightly rounded stomach, the lump in her throat replaced with the joy of knowing there would soon be a new baby to cuddle and kiss and spoil.

Rebecca refused to acknowledge the envy that tried to steal through her as her friend's slender fingers automatically spread across the growing life inside her in a gesture of instinctive protectiveness and nurturing. But she couldn't hide from the concerned look on Andi's face in the mirror as she obviously noticed her heightened emotions.

"A little more blush," Rebecca said quickly, letting her long light brown hair hide her face as she bent down to pick up the makeup bag.

She knew she'd just given too much away. She always did. Some people had poker faces. Her best attempt at trying to fake one would cause her to lose everything in the casino because she didn't have the first clue how to play the game.

And it was true. Rebecca had never figured out how to play the game. Not with love, that was for certain. And not with jobs, until she had landed here at the inn and realized she'd finally found something she was good at, something she loved.

Even though they both knew her makeup was already perfect, Andi let Rebecca brush a tiny bit more powder over her cheekbones, just until her friend regained her composure.

But then, before Rebecca could step away again, Andi reached out and put a hand on her arm. "You know you can talk to me, don't you? Anytime." Her gaze softened. "My groom isn't going anywhere," she said with perfect confidence. "I've got all the time in the world.

Knowing that the last thing she should do was dump her fears and hurts and baggage all over Andi on her wedding day, Rebecca was intent on finding a way to deflect her concern. "I always get emotional at weddings. You should have seen me at each of my sisters' ceremonies. I cried buckets. The guests in my row were all wishing for raincoats so I wouldn't soak them." She smiled a crooked little smile, hoping to lighten the mood. "This time I've tucked some under the seats next to mine as a precaution."

But her friend, the woman she'd helped see through such a difficult time the previous fall, didn't so much as crack a smile.

"You don't have to pretend with me, Rebecca." Regret flashed across Andi's pretty features. "Ever since I got pregnant, my brain has been fuzzy and I just want to sleep all the time. That's got to be why I didn't see it all more clearly before." She shook her head. "We shouldn't have scheduled our wedding for this weekend."

Andi said her words softly, and while there wasn't pity behind them, Rebecca believed that was only due to the close friendship they'd forged during the last six months.

Unfortunately there was no escaping the fact—not with Andi or anyone who was going to be downstairs at the wedding and reception—that Rebecca was supposed to have been the one about to get married this weekend. Instead of wearing the gown and saying "I do," she was going to be sitting in the audience, watching two wonderful people make their vows of love to each other.

The truth was that it hadn't been easy walking down

Main Street these past three weeks, going to the grocery store, passing people she knew on the cross-country ski trails thinking—knowing—they were whispering about her. Sure, they still smiled, still exchanged the same pleasantries. But she knew they had to be either feeling sorry for her... or they were trying to figure out just what horrible thing she'd done to make Stu call off the wedding.

And disappear from Emerald Lake the very next day without a word to anyone.

Only the women at Lake Yarns's Monday night knitting group had remained the same as always. Warm. Gossipy. And yet, utterly unjudgmental. No matter how busy she was, Rebecca made sure to keep every Monday night open for drinking too much wine and usually doing more talking and laughing than knitting.

She felt like she'd found her home in Emerald Lake and liked to imagine growing old on an Adirondack chair on a dock while she watched her future grandchildren playing in the blue water.

She hated to think that she'd only been accepted by the locals because she was engaged to Stu Murphy, whose family had lived in Emerald Lake for generations. She wanted to believe she belonged here on her own merit. Because people liked her and thought she contributed something valuable to the community.

But regardless of how off-kilter she felt, she absolutely refused to taint Andi's wedding in any way.

"You know I absolutely loved being able to put on this wedding for you and Nate. And really, it worked out perfectly. You needed a wedding venue right away, and I had one all ready to go." Rebecca already had the tables and chairs and glasses and food ordered for her own spring wedding at the inn, so Andi and Nate were able to use them without having to try to pull everything together at the last second. "It was meant to happen this way, Andi. I'm certain of it. I absolutely love knowing that I'm a part of your happily ever after."

Anyone else would have stopped talking there, would have held something back, would have hidden the rest of her feelings, but Rebecca had never known how to do that. Especially when a dear friend was looking at her with such deep concern. Besides, she had finally stopped lying to herself about her ex-fiancé three weeks ago. So what was the point in trying to hold back the full—painful— truth with anyone else now?

"You know Stu and I weren't right for each other. Not as anything more than friends. The truth is, I enjoyed putting the finishing details on your wedding far more than I ever enjoyed working on it when it was my own." She shook her head. "I guess that should have been my first clue that something wasn't right. It was seeing you and Nate together that showed me what real love was supposed to look like."

"You never told me that," Andi said, clearly surprised by what Rebecca had divulged. Awareness dawned suddenly in her blue eyes. "Oh my gosh. Three weeks ago. That's when Nate and I came in to ask about squeezing in a shotgun wedding here at the inn."

Rebecca nodded, feeling like a diary that had fallen open with a splat. "You two were supposed to be flipping through a booklet of cake toppers. Instead your foreheads were together and you were staring into each other's eyes."

She hadn't been able to tear her gaze away from them,

not even when Nate cupped Andi's cheek and gently kissed her.

That was what real love looked like. Deep and true love.

*Forever love.*

Just like that, Rebecca had known she couldn't go through with marrying Stu. Not just for her sake, not just because she wanted that kind of love for herself, but because it wasn't fair to Stu, either. He deserved forever love, too.

"I don't know what to say. I hate to think that I caused your breakup. But—"

Rebecca shook her head, wanting to still the remorse, the guilt that was emerging on Andi's face. "You didn't cause anything. You just helped me see the light." Finally. Long after she should have seen it on her own. "I'll be forever grateful to you for that."

Andi hugged her tightly, and even though Rebecca longed to tell her friend more—it simply wasn't her nature to hold things back and the secrets she was keeping were eating her up inside—there was one thing she couldn't tell anyone.

Specifically what had happened three weeks ago when she went to break her engagement off to Stu after seeing Andi and Nate so in love.

# THE DISH

*Where authors give you the inside scoop!*

♥ ♥ ♥ ♥ ♥ ♥ ♥ ♥ ♥ ♥ ♥ ♥ ♥ ♥ ♥ ♥ ♥ ♥ ♥ ♥ ♥ ♥ ♥

*From the desk of Bella Riley*

Dear Reader,

The first time I ever saw an Adirondack lake I was twenty-three years old and madly in love. My boyfriend's grandparents had built their "camp" in the 1940s, and he'd often told me that it was his favorite place in the world. ("Camp" is Adirondack lingo for a house on a lake. If it's really big, like the Vanderbilts' summer home on Raquette Lake, people sometimes throw the word "great" in front of it.)

I can still remember my first glimpse of the blue lake, the sandy beach, the wooden docks jutting into it, the colorful sails of the boats that floated by. It was love at first sight. My mind was blown by the beauty all around me.

Of course, since I'm a writer, my brain immediately began spinning off into storyland. What if two kids grew up together in this small lake town and were high-school sweethearts? What if one of them left the other behind for bright lights/big city? And what would their reunion look like ten years later?

Fast-forward fifteen years from that first sight of an Adirondack lake, and I couldn't be more thrilled to introduce my Emerald Lake series to you! After thinking she had left the small town—and the girl she had once been—behind forever, Andi Powell must return to help run Lake Yarns, her family's knitting store on Main Street. Of course everyone in town gets involved in a love story that she's convinced herself is better left forgotten. But with the help of the Monday night knitting group, Nate's sister, Andi's mother and grandmother, and an old circus carousel in the middle of the town green, Andi just might find the love she's always deserved in the arms of the one man who has waited his entire life for her.

I hope you fall as much in love with the beauty and people of Emerald Lake as I did.

Happy reading,

*Bella Riley*

www.bellariley.com

P.S. That boyfriend is now my husband (Guess where we honeymooned? Yes, the lake!), and four years ago we bit the bullet and became the proud owners of our very own Adirondack camp. Now, just in case you're tempted to throw the word "great" around, you should know that our log cabin is a hundred years old...and pretty much original. Except for the plumbing. Thankfully, we have that!

♥ ♥ ♥ ♥ ♥ ♥ ♥ ♥ ♥ ♥ ♥ ♥ ♥ ♥ ♥ ♥ ♥ ♥ ♥ ♥ ♥ ♥

*From the desk of Jane Graves*

Dear Reader,

In HEARTSTRINGS AND DIAMOND RINGS (on sale now), Alison Carter has been stuck in the dating world for years, and she's getting a little disillusioned. In personal ads, she's discovered that "athletic" means the guy has a highly developed right bicep from opening and closing the refrigerator door; and that a man is "tall, dark, and handsome" only in a room full of ugly albino dwarves. But what about those other descriptions in personal ads? What do they *really* mean?

"Aspiring actor": Uses Aussie accent to pick up chicks

"Educated": Watches *Jeopardy!*

"Emotionally sound": Or so his latest psychiatrist says

"Enjoys fine dining": Goes inside instead of using the drive-through

"Friendship first": As long as "friendship" includes sex

"Good listener": Has nothing intelligent to say

"Likes to cuddle": Mommy issues

"Looking for soulmate": Or just someone to have sex with

"Loyal": Stalker

"Old fashioned": Wants you barefoot and pregnant

"Passionate": About beer, football, and Hooters waitresses

"Romantic": Isn't nearly as ugly by candlelight

"Spiritual": Drives by a church on his way to happy hour

"Stable": Heavily medicated
"Young at heart": And one foot in the grave
"Witty": Quotes dialogue from *Animal House*

Alison finally decides enough is enough. She's going to hire a matchmaker, who will find out the truth about a man *before* she goes out with him. What she doesn't expect to find is a matchmaking *man*—one who really *is* tall, dark, and handsome! And suddenly Mr. Right just might be right under her nose...

I hope you'll enjoy HEARTSTRINGS AND DIAMOND RINGS!

Happy reading!

*Jane Graves*

www.janegraves.com

♥ ♥ ♥ ♥ ♥ ♥ ♥ ♥ ♥ ♥ ♥ ♥ ♥ ♥ ♥ ♥ ♥ ♥ ♥ ♥ ♥ ♥ ♥

*From the desk of Eileen Dreyer*

Dear Reader,

I love to write the love story of two people who have known each other a long time. I love it even more when they're now enemies. First of all, I don't have to spend time introducing them to each other. They already have a history and common experiences. They speak in a kind of shorthand that sets them apart from the people around

them. Emotions are already more complex. And then I get
to mix in the added spice that comes from two people
who spit and claw each time they see each other. Well, if
you've read the first two books in my Drake's Rakes series, you know that Lady Kate Seaton and Major Sir Harry
Lidge are definitely spitting and clawing. In ALWAYS A
TEMPTRESS, we finally find out why. And we get to see
if they will ever resolve their differences and finally admit
that they still passionately love each other.

Happy reading!

*Eileen Dreyer*

www.eileendreyer.com

♥ ♥ ♥ ♥ ♥ ♥ ♥ ♥ ♥ ♥ ♥ ♥ ♥ ♥ ♥ ♥ ♥ ♥ ♥ ♥

*From the desk of Amanda Scott*

Dear Reader,

St. Andrews University, alma mater of Prince William and
Princess Kate, was Scotland's first university, and it figures significantly in HIGHLAND HERO, the second book
in my Scottish Knights trilogy, as well as in its prede-
cessor, HIGHLAND MASTER (Forever, February 2011).
The heroes of all three books in the trilogy met as students
of Walter Traill, Bishop of St. Andrews, in the late fourteenth century. All three are skilled warriors and knights
of the realm.

Sir Ivor Mackintosh of HIGHLAND HERO—besides being handsome, daring, and a man of legendary temper—is Scotland's finest archer, just as Fin Cameron of HIGHLAND MASTER is one of the country's finest swordsmen. Both men are also survivors of the Great Clan Battle of Perth, in which the Mackintoshes of Clan Chattan fought champions of Clan Cameron. In other words, these two heroes fought on opposing sides of that great trial by combat.

Nevertheless, thanks to Bishop Traill, they are closer than most brothers.

Because Traill's students came from noble families all over Scotland, any number of whom might be feuding or actively engaged in clan warfare, the peace-loving Traill insisted that his students keep their identities secret and use simple names within the St. Andrews community. They were on their honor to not probe into each other's antecedents, so they knew little if anything about their friends' backgrounds while studying academics and knightly skills together. Despite that constraint, Traill also taught them the value of trust and close friendships.

The St. Andrews Brotherhood in my Scottish Knights series is fictional but plausible, in that the historic Bishop Traill strongly supported King Robert III and Queen Annabella Drummond while the King's younger brother, the Duke of Albany, was actively trying to seize control of the country. Traill also provided protection at St. Andrews for the King's younger son, James (later James I of Scotland), conveyed him there in secrecy, and wielded sufficient power to curb Albany when necessary.

We don't know how Traill and the King arranged for the prince, age seven in 1402, to travel across Scotland from the west coast to St. Andrews Castle. But that sort of mystery stimulates any author's gray cells.

So, in HIGHLAND HERO, when the villainous Albany makes clear his determination to rule Scotland no matter what, Traill sends for Sir Ivor to transport young Jamie to St. Andrews. Sir Ivor's able if sometimes trying assistant in this endeavor is the Queen's niece, Lady Marsaili Drummond-Cargill, who has reasons of her own to elude Albany's clutches but does not approve of temperamental men or men who assume she will do their bidding without at least *some* discussion.

Traill's successor, Bishop Henry Wardlaw (also in HIGHLAND HERO), founded William's and Kate's university in 1410, expanding on Traill's long tradition of education, believing as Traill had that education was one of the Church's primary duties. Besides being Scotland's first university, St. Andrews was also the first university in Scotland to admit women (1892)—and it admitted them on exactly the same terms as men. Lady Marsaili would have approved of that!

Suas Alba!

*Amanda Scott*

www.amandascottauthor.com

# VISIT US ONLINE

@ WWW.HACHETTEBOOKGROUP.COM

## AT THE HACHETTE BOOK GROUP WEBSITE YOU'LL FIND:

# THE COCOA CONSPIRACY

## A LADY ARIANNA REGENCY MYSTERY

# ANDREA PENROSE

AN OBSIDIAN MYSTERY

OBSIDIAN
Published by New American Library, a division of
Penguin Group (USA) Inc., 375 Hudson Street,
New York, New York 10014, USA
Penguin Group (Canada), 90 Eglinton Avenue East, Suite 700, Toronto,
Ontario M4P 2Y3, Canada (a division of Pearson Penguin Canada Inc.)
Penguin Books Ltd., 80 Strand, London WC2R 0RL, England
Penguin Ireland, 25 St. Stephen's Green, Dublin 2,
Ireland (a division of Penguin Books Ltd.)
Penguin Group (Australia), 250 Camberwell Road, Camberwell, Victoria 3124,
Australia (a division of Pearson Australia Group Pty. Ltd.)
Penguin Books India Pvt. Ltd., 11 Community Centre, Panchsheel Park,
New Delhi - 110 017, India
Penguin Group (NZ), 67 Apollo Drive, Rosedale, Auckland 0632,
New Zealand (a division of Pearson New Zealand Ltd.)
Penguin Books (South Africa) (Pty.) Ltd., 24 Sturdee Avenue,
Rosebank, Johannesburg 2196, South Africa

Penguin Books Ltd., Registered Offices:
80 Strand, London WC2R 0RL, England

First published by Obsidian, an imprint of New American Library,
a division of Penguin Group (USA) Inc.

First Printing, December 2011
10  9  8  7  6  5  4  3  2  1

*For Saybrook College,*
*a fabulous community of students, scholars, and Fellows*
*whose camaraderie and intellectual curiosity is a source of*
*constant inspiration*

# ACKNOWLEDGMENTS

While writing a story is a very solitary endeavor, the making of a finished book requires the hard work and dedication of a number of people. I'm very lucky to have an amazing support group who listen patiently to my questions, endure my querulous whining, offer sage advice ... and help me keep the Muse well supplied with chocolate!

As always, I'm profoundly grateful to Gail Fortune, my agent, for all the brainstorming chats, and to Sandy Harding, my editor, for all her incredibly thoughtful suggestions and criticisms.

And no author could wish for more wonderful—and brilliant—friends! That they are willing to sit up into the wee hours of the night parsing the arcane little details of history and sharing their expertise is not only amazingly enlightening, but also provides a modicum of reassurance that I am not the only one who finds the past fascinating. So I raise a glass of wine (well, maybe two) to offer special thanks to Ammanda McCabe, Lauren Willig, Tracy Grant, and John Ettinger. You guys are the best!

"*Where there is mystery, it is generally suspected there must also be evil.*"

—George Gordon Byron

# 1

## From Lady Arianna's Chocolate Notebooks

### Spanish Colonial Brownies

¾ cup olive oil, plus more to grease pan
⅓ cup cocoa powder
½ cup plus 2 tablespoons boiling water
2 ounces unsweetened chocolate, finely chopped
2 large eggs
2 large egg yolks
1 teaspoon vanilla extract
2½ cups sugar
1¾ cups all-purpose flour
¾ teaspoon kosher salt
2½ ounces bittersweet chocolate, coarsely chopped
2 cups shredded sweetened coconut
Fleur de sel, *for sprinkling*

1. Heat the oven to 350 degrees. Lightly grease a 9-by-13-inch baking pan.
2. In a large bowl, whisk together the cocoa powder and ½ cup plus 2 tablespoons boiling water until smooth. Add the unsweetened chocolate and

whisk until the chocolate has melted. Whisk in the olive oil. Add the eggs, yolks and vanilla, and continue to whisk until combined. Add the sugar, whisking until fully incorporated. Using a spatula, fold in the flour and salt until just combined. Fold in the bittersweet chocolate pieces.

3. Pour half the batter into the prepared pan and smooth with a spatula. Sprinkle 1 cup of the shredded coconut on top of the batter. Pour in the remaining batter and smooth. Top with remaining coconut. Sprinkle with *fleur de sel* and bake until just set and firm to the touch, about 25 to 30 minutes. (These brownies solidify as they cool, so inserting a toothpick to check for doneness will not work; it will not come out clean.) Transfer the pan to a wire rack and allow to cool completely before cutting into 2-inch squares.

The book's binding was crafted out of dark, fine-grained calfskin, its richly tooled embossings age-mellowed to the color of . . .

"Chocolate," murmured Arianna Hadley. Removing her gloves, which were still sticky from foraging through the food stalls at Covent Garden, she traced the delicate leaf design centered beneath the gilded title. "How lovely," she added, and then carefully opened the cover.

Dust motes danced up into the air, tiny sparkles of sunlight in the shadowed corner of the alcove. As she shifted a step closer to the diamond-paned window, the scrape of her sturdy half-boots on the Aubusson carpet momentarily disturbed the hush that hung over the ornate bookcases.

Her heel snagged, and to her dismay she realized that a streak of mud—and something that looked suspiciously like squashed pumpkin—now marred the stately pattern.

*Hell and damnation.*

Arianna gave a guilty glance around, but the room appeared deserted. The only stirring was a small flutter of breeze wafting in through the casement. It teased over the polished oak, mingling the scents of beeswax, ink, paper and leather.

*The smell of money.*

A wry smile twitched on her lips as she turned her attention back to the book. Set discreetly within the marbled endpapers was a small slip of paper that noted the price. It was expensive. *Very expensive*—as was every volume and manuscript offered for sale by Messrs. Harvey & Watkins Rare Book Emporium.

But then, Arianna could now afford such luxuries.

She slowly turned the pages, savoring the feel of the creamy, deckle-edged paper and the subtle colors of the illustrations. With her new husband's birthday fast approaching, she was looking for a special gift. And the intricate engravings of *Theobroma cacao* were, to her eye, exquisite.

"Chocolate," repeated Arianna, pausing to study the details of a criolla tree and its fruit. Her husband was, among other things, a serious scholar of botany, and cacao—or chocolate—was his particular field of expertise. The text was Spanish, and the date looked to be—

A sudden nudge from behind nearly knocked the book from her grasp.

"I beg your pardon." The deep voice was edged with a foreign accent.

Arianna turned, about to acknowledge the apology with a polite smile, when the man gave her another little shove.

"I beg your pardon, but that book is *mine*," he growled. "Hand it over at once."

Sliding back a step, she instinctively threw up a forearm to parry his grab. "I'm afraid you are mistaken, sir. It was lying on the display table, free for anyone to choose."

"I assure you, there is no mistake," he replied. "I must have it."

*Turn over her treasure to a lout who thought to frighten her with physical force?* Her pulse kicked up a notch, its hot surge thrumming angrily in her ears.

"Sorry, but I saw it first."

Her husband had jestingly warned her that serious book collectors were an odd, obsessive lot, and this one in particular sounded slightly deranged. *Or demented.* But, be that as it may, Arianna was not about to be intimidated by his bullying tactics.

"You will have to look around for something else, for I intend to purchase it," she added, and not just for spite. She had already decided that the engravings were the perfect present for her husband.

"You can't!" he exclaimed in a taut whisper.

*Oh, but I can.*

Closing the covers, Arianna hugged the book to her chest.

As the man edged closer, a blade of light cut across his pale face. Sweat was beading his forehead, and several drops hung on his russet lashes. "I tell you, that book is meant for *me*."

"Then you should have asked the clerk to put it aside." She gestured at the other volumes arrayed on the square of dark velvet. "Come, there is no need to squabble like savages. You have plenty of other lovely choices."

He snarled an obscenity.

"Be advised, sir, I know plenty of worse words than that," responded Arianna with a grim smile, and she added a very unladylike curse to prove it.

His eyes widened for an instant, then narrowed to a slitted stare. "Give me that book," he repeated. "Or you will be sorry."

His strike was quick—but not quick enough.

Her reactions honed by half a lifetime of fighting off drunks and pimps, Arianna caught his wrist and pivoted, twisting hard enough to draw a grunt of pain. "I wouldn't wager on that."

"Poxy slut." Breaking away, the man clenched a fist and threw a wild punch at her head.

She ducked the blow and countered with a kick that buckled his knee. "True—if I were a real lady, I would be falling into a dead swoon." Her jab clipped him flush on the chin. "But as you see, I'm not. Not a lady, that is."

Staggered, the man fell against the display table, knocking several books to the floor. His curses were now coming in a language she didn't recognize, but the edge of panic was unmistakable.

*What madness possessed him?* It was only a book, albeit a lovely one.

Arianna glanced at the archway, intent on making a strategic retreat. The last thing she wanted to do was to ruffle the rarified feathers of Messrs. Harvey & Watkins by brawling among their rare books. Such a scene would only embarrass her husband, who, ye Gods, had suffered enough gossip on her account ...

*Bloody hell.* A glint of steel drew her eye back to her assailant.

His fumblings inside his coat revealed not only a book hidden in the waistband of his trousers but a slim-bladed knife.

"Try to use that on me, and you'll find your cods cut off," she warned softly.

He blinked, looking torn between anger and fear.

The sliver of silence was broken by the sound of hurried steps in the adjoining room. "Is someone in need of assistance?" called a shop clerk loudly.

Her assailant hesitated for an instant, then whirled and darted for the archway, bumping into the other man as they crossed paths.

Smoothing the wrinkles from his sleeve, the clerk frowned at Arianna. "This is *not* a place for sordid assignations, miss," he chided, looking down his long nose at her chipped straw bonnet and drab serge gown. As his gaze slid to the fallen books, he added a sharp sniff. "I must ask you to leave—immediately. We cater to a very dignified clientele who expect an atmosphere of decorum when they visit us."

*Ah, no good deed goes unpunished,* thought Arianna sardonically. On her way home from the rough-and-tumble markets, she had stopped her carriage on impulse to browse through the fancy books. Better to have waited until she had swathed herself in silk and satin for the requisite morning calls in Mayfair.

"First of all, it is *madam*," she corrected. "And secondly, I am quite aware of what sort of patrons frequent your shop."

The clerk winced at the word "shop."

"However, you might want to take a closer look at the so-called Quality you allow through your door," Arianna continued, assuming an air of icy hauteur. "That man was certainly no gentleman. He had a knife, and was probably cutting prints out of your precious volumes." Her husband had explained how some unscrupulous collectors sliced up rare books for the maps or prints, which were sold individually to art dealers for a much higher profit.

The clerk's look of disdain now pinched into one of horror.

"He also stole a book," she added. "I saw it hidden under his coat."

"B-but he has made several purchases recently, all properly paid for," protested the clerk. Another glance, another sniff. "You must be mistaken. By all appearances, he is a perfect gentleman; no matter that he is a foreigner."

"Well he's not," shot back Arianna. "You may take my word for it."

His mouth thinned. "And who, might I ask, are *you*?"

"The Countess of Saybrook." Arianna held out the chocolate book. "Now, before you toss me out on my arse, kindly wrap that and write up a receipt. And do make it quick. My carriage is waiting and the earl does not like for his prime cattle to take a chill."

# 2

## From Lady Arianna's Chocolate Notebooks

### Coconut Hot Chocolate

2 tablespoons unsweetened cocoa powder
$\frac{1}{3}$ cup boiling water
1 15-ounce can coconut milk
$\frac{1}{4}$ cup dark brown sugar
Pinch kosher salt
1 ounce bittersweet chocolate, chopped (about $\frac{1}{4}$ cup)
1 teaspoon vanilla extract

### For the meringue (optional)

1 large egg white
3 tablespoons superfine sugar

1. Whisk cocoa into $\frac{1}{3}$ cup boiling water.
2. In a saucepan, combine coconut milk, brown sugar and salt. Simmer, stirring, until sugar is dissolved, about 2 minutes. Whisk in hot cocoa and chopped bittersweet chocolate until smooth. Stir in vanilla.
3. In bowl of an electric mixer, beat egg white on

medium speed until it begins to foam, about 1 minute. Add superfine sugar tablespoon by tablespoon as mixer is running. Beat until egg white stiffens to soft peaks and is shiny, 5 minutes. Dollop onto cups of hot chocolate.

❧

Heels clip-clopping over the black and white marble tiles of the entrance hall, Arianna crossed to the side table and tossed down her bonnet. It was, she admitted, a hideous head covering. But until now, she hadn't noticed the smudge of green slime on the peak of its poke.

*No wonder the shop clerk continued to eye me suspiciously, even after I passed over a large wad of banknotes to pay for the book.*

"You are looking very fetching, my dear."

As she turned abruptly, several hairpins slipped free, loosening a lopsided spill of curls across one cheek.

"And is that a new perfume you are wearing?" Alessandro Henry George De Quincy, the fifth Earl of Saybrook, gave an experimental sniff. "Eau de Rotten Cabbage, perhaps? Or is it turnip?"

"Oh, please. Don't ask."

"Very well." His gaze moved to the neatly wrapped package tucked under her arm. "What have you there?"

"Never mind," she said tartly to her husband. "It's a surprise."

He made a face. "I am not overly fond of surprises."

*Neither am I.*

"This one is perfectly harmless," Arianna assured him. Anxious to change the subject, she gestured for the maid who had accompanied her on the shopping expedition to take the baskets of fresh produce down to the kitchens. "Elena, tell Bianca that there were no cèpes to be had," she instructed. "Though I do think she will find the goat cheeses a perfect match for the Seckel pears she purchased yesterday."

Her husband raised a teasing brow as he surveyed her disheveled appearance. "Did you have to battle a regiment of Soult's cavalry for the last wedges?"

"The market was crowded this morning," she answered evasively. "I know I look a fright."

"You would look ravishing wearing a burlap grain sack," he replied with a grin. "Still, you may wish to change before joining Charles and me in the library for tea."

"Your uncle is coming by? Good Lord, then I'd better hurry."

Saybrook coughed. "Actually, he arrived just a few moments before you did."

It was only then that Arianna noticed the tall, elegantly attired figure standing in the shadows of the marble staircase.

"Forgive me for intruding without notice at this early hour." Charles Mellon stepped forward and bowed over her hand.

*Some perverse imp of Satan must be intent on making mischief for me today.*

"Nonsense, sir. You know that you are always welcome here." Despite the quick assurance, her smile was a little tentative. She suspected that Mellon was not very pleased about her recent marriage to his nephew, though he was too much of a gentleman to be anything but scrupulously polite in her presence.

"Thank you, milady," he replied with grave formality.

That he hadn't approved of her at the beginning of their acquaintance was no secret. *And with good reason,* Arianna thought wryly. At the time, she had been a fugitive from justice, and because of her, Saybrook had been drawn into a tangled web of corruption and conspiracy. It was only by the grace of God—and their cleverness—that they had escaped with their lives.

"It is always a pleasure to see the two of you," Mellon went on.

More than a few men may have been less sincere in such sentiments. After all, with the earl's demise, the Saybrook title and fortune would have passed to Mellon. However, Arianna had never doubted the affection that the older man had shown for his nephew.

"I won't take up too much of your time," he finished.

"It's nearly noon—you must join us for nuncheon," she said. "Bianca will be bitterly disappointed if you miss her special Serrano ham."

"Tempting." Mellon allowed a faint smile. "But a meeting at the ministry demands my presence. I cannot stay for long. I've simply stopped by to ask a favor . . ." His pause was barely perceptible. "Of you both."

"Anything—" began Saybrook.

Mellon cut him off with a quick wave. "It's never wise to agree to a proposal before knowing all the details. I would rather that you and your wife hear me out before giving an answer."

"I've already rung for the refreshments, my dear," said Saybrook, an oblique reminder for her to make haste.

"I shall only be a few minutes in freshening up," promised Arianna.

Taking the stairs two at a time, she couldn't help but wonder what help her uncle-by-marriage could possibly need from her. For the most part, they moved in very different circles. A senior diplomat in the Foreign Ministry, Mellon spun effortlessly through the gilded splendor of London's haute monde. While she preferred . . .

*No use speculating.* Arianna expelled a harried sigh. She would find out soon enough.


"Attend a country house party?" Saybrook stirred a pinch of grated nutmeg into his cup of hot chocolate. "For a fortnight?"

Mellon nodded. "I am aware of how little you—both of you—like such frivolous entertainments. But the Marquess of Milford has kindly consented to hold a shooting party at his estate in Wiltshire. There will be a number of foreign diplomats present, including a delegation from Spain."

"I see," murmured Saybrook.

His expression, noted Arianna, gave nothing away. As a former military intelligence officer attached to the staff of Arthur Wellesley—now the Duke of Wellington—during England's Peninsular campaign to drive Napoleon's armies out of Spain, he was well trained in keeping his thoughts to himself.

"Given the upcoming Peace Conference in Vienna, our government is, of course, anxious to work in harmony with all of our wartime allies," continued Mellon.

"And, of course, it would be a help to know what the Spaniards are thinking," said Saybrook.

Another confirming nod. "That your mother was a Catalonian noblewoman will be a great mark in your favor. As will the fact that you have spent your childhood summers in their country and so are at home with their language and their customs."

"A mark in my favor," repeated Saybrook, a note of sarcasm edging his voice. "How ironic that my own countrymen see my mixed heritage as a stain on an ancient and venerable title." Seeing Mellon frown, he quickly went on, "Oh, come, Charles, you know I've heard the whispers behind my back—how could the old earl have tainted the precious De Quincy blood by producing a mongrel as his heir?" He took a long sip of his drink. "A new batch of spice?"

"Yes," said Arianna, knowing the question was directed at her. "I discovered a small shipment from the isle of Grenada at the market. Along with a sack of coffee from the Blue Mountains of Jamaica."

Her husband took a moment to savor another taste. "It's slightly more piquant than the nutmeg from Martinique."

"Sun and altitude," she pointed out. "Which do you prefer?"

Saybrook smiled. "As you know, I tend to choose bold over mild in most things." Adding a pinch of powder from a dish on the tea table, he continued. "The mace looks to have a bit of bite as well."

Mellon waited patiently for the discussion of food to

end. "My palate is not nearly discerning enough to sense such nuances and how best to blend them together," he remarked when they were done.

"Your expertise lies in judging the complexities of character, and how best to convince a group of conflicting personalities to come to a common consensus," said Saybrook.

"It is all a matter of training, I suppose," replied Mellon.

"And passion," said Arianna softly. "I believe that one must care deeply about something to do it well."

Mellon regarded her for a long moment. "I know your opinion of Society, Lady Saybrook—"

"It's the same as mine," interrupted Saybrook. "We both abhor the mindless conformity, the vicious gossip, and the gleeful attacks on anyone who dares to defy the petty-minded rules."

His uncle expelled a sigh. "I—"

"But that said," Saybrook went on, "we will be happy to attend the Marquess of Milford's party, if you feel that our presence will be of any help to you and your negotiations."

"It would be extremely helpful," answered Mellon, looking much relieved. "Don Pedro Gomez Havela de Labrador, Spain's envoy to the Conference, is a very proud man, and quick to take offense at any imagined slight. He and Lord Castlereagh, our representative, don't rub together very well."

"So in other words, if an English lord who happens to understand the quirks of Castilian character could manage to flatter Labrador's vanity, he might be more amenable to supporting our government's proposals."

"Clearly you understand politics just as well as you do cuisine," replied his uncle.

"More than I care to," muttered Saybrook, threading a hand through his dark hair. "When should we be ready to leave for Gloucestershire?"

"In two days," said Mellon apologetically. "It wasn't until yesterday evening that we received final word that the Spaniards had consented to come."

"It doesn't matter. We have no other plans," Arianna

lied. The trip to visit a noted botany expert and his conservatory of rare tropical plants in Cornwall would simply have to be postponed to a later date, no matter that Saybrook had been looking forward to it. "If you send over the list of expected activities, I shall have Maria begin packing our trunks."

"Oh, it will be the usual array of superficial entertainments," replied Mellon. "The men will spend much of the day slaughtering birds on the marquess's grouse moors while the ladies will amuse themselves indoors. There will be riding, picnics and scenic walks. And at night, there will be endless eating, drinking and dancing."

"Put that way, how can we resist?" she said.

Mellon let out a brusque chuckle. "Quite easily, I imagine. Nonetheless, I am very grateful." He rose. "In truth, you might not be as bored as you think. With such an international array of guests, the interlude is bound to offer some interesting diversions."

"I shall cancel next week's appointment at Kew Gardens," said Arianna, looking up from her list as Saybrook returned from seeing his uncle to the waiting carriage. She then added another notation. "And I shall write to Professor Turner and tell him we must put off our visit."

"I would much rather be scrabbling in the dirt of his hothouses than dancing attendance on a crowd of overfed aristocrats," groused Saybrook as he settled into his favorite armchair and propped his booted feet on the hassock.

"As would I."

"And what about my manuscript?" he said. "I need to consult some of Turner's reference books to complete the current chapter." Drumming his fingers on the worn leather, he scowled up at the ceiling. "How the devil can I write a book when I have such distractions?"

Arianna remained tactfully silent, as did the painted putti overhead.

He expelled a harried sigh. "But I couldn't very well refuse Charles, could I?"

"Have another cup of chocolate," she suggested. "Perhaps it will help sweeten your mood."

A laugh rumbled in his throat. "Forgive me. I've been in a sour frame of mind all morning, and my uncle's request was like . . . a splash of vinegar."

"Is your leg hurting you?" she asked.

Saybrook had suffered a serious saber wound during the Battle of Salamanca. Invalided out of the army, he had been a morose, opium-addicted specter of his former self when first they had met. It was Mellon who had suggested that his nephew rekindle some interest in life by helping the Ministry of State Security investigate the attempted poisoning of the Prince Regent—though she suspected that he had quickly come to regret it.

*The best laid plans of mice and men* . . . Arianna repressed a rueful smile. She had been the prime suspect, but luckily for her, Saybrook was one of those rare individuals who valued truth over expediency. Smelling a rat, he had refused to rush to judgment. Together, they had formed a wary alliance to pursue a common enemy; no matter that at first, they each had far different reasons and far different notions of justice.

Mistrust had slowly softened into respect, and then . . .

Her husband shifted and stood up. "It's not my leg," he quipped. "It's the prospect of a fancy house party that's a pain in the arse." Moving to the sideboard, he spun the *molinillo* in the chocolate pot and poured himself a fresh cup. "As you see, my limp is gone—and I shall soon be losing my manly figure as well if you and Bianca keep stuffing me with sweets."

"She thinks you are still far too thin."

"Ha! Between the two of you, I fear I will grow as fat as Prinny and have to wear a corset."

Arianna rolled her eyes. His long, lithe frame had fleshed out considerably since their initial encounter, but it was all lean muscle and whipcord sinew. "I should think twice about that, if I were you. Corsets are horribly uncomfortable. And they creak."

"Ah, well, the sound would simply be another quirk added to my list of eccentricities."

"In that, we are two peas in a pod." She made note of yet another errand to be done and then looked up. "Is there any other reason you are in such an oddly maudlin mood?"

The dark fringe of his lashes hid his eyes. "Is it that obvious?"

"Only to me."

Saybrook shuffled to the bank of leaded windows and stared out over the gardens for several moments before answering. "A letter arrived from my sister Antonia this morning."

"Has something happened?" she asked quickly. "Is she unwell? Unhappy?"

"On the contrary, she sounds quite cheerful." He, on the other hand, did not. "She is enjoying her tour of the Lake District with Miss Arnold, and is looking forward to the new school term."

"You must not feel guilty. For the moment, this arrangement is probably the best for her."

"I know, I know," he muttered. "And yet it seems cowardly to let her believe I am merely a distant relative, who takes a casual interest in her well-being." It was only a year ago, on the death of the old earl, that Saybrook had discovered he had a younger sister. "Damn my father for never explaining the situation to me. Whatever was he thinking, to leave such important matters unspoken?"

"He undoubtedly thought he had time to do so," answered Arianna. "He did not expect to fall from his horse during a fox hunt."

Saybrook replied with an exasperated oath. "Having lost both his first wife and second wife—or lover—to sudden illness, he, of all people, should have understood how quixotic life can be." His mouth thinned to a grim line. "If he was indeed married to Antonia's mother, why did he keep the relationship a secret, and hide her away in a school after her mother's death, instead of acknowledging her as his legitimate daughter?"

"We can only speculate as to his motives," said Arianna softly. "I imagine that at first he was worried about how English society would react. Your mother was of noble birth, and still she was not accepted by many in the *ton*. Antonia's mother was a commoner, and according to the notes you found among his papers, the ceremony took place in a small Papist chapel, rather than an English church. It seems that he meant to straighten things out, and prove it was a proper marriage. But"—she heaved a sigh— "fathers often keep secrets from their children."

Her own father had been a prime example of that, she reflected. A brilliant but mercurial man, the late Earl of Morse had been forced to leave England with his young daughter after being accused of cheating at cards. He had been innocent of that crime, but his murder, and her subsequent quest to clear his name, had led to unexpected revelations.

"Whether it is out of guilt or shame or some emotion that eludes words, they don't know how to explain their actions," Arianna went on. "Your father may have feared that you would resent a sibling, or think her unworthy of the family name."

"I should have been delirious with delight to discover I had a sister," he said gruffly.

Arianna nodded. "I know that." She paused, recalling the horrors of her own adolescence—an orphaned girl, alone and unprotected . . .

"I would be more than happy to have Antonia come live with us, if that is what you wish," she assured him. "No matter what the gossips might whisper."

Saybrook blew out his breath. "No, much as I hate to admit it, you were probably right to suggest that it's best for her to remain in school. For now, that is."

"It would be different if I were more familiar with Society." She made a rueful face. "But until I learn how to navigate through the treacherous waters of the *ton*, I might only sink her chances of acceptance." She breated a sigh. "We have another year until she is of age to be formally introduced. I shall start practicing with my oars."

The statement drew a reluctant laugh from her husband. "Learn the waters? I thought you didn't give a damn for drawing room society."

"I don't. But it would be fun to tweak their noses." After a moment she smiled. "Besides, I think your great aunt Constantina would love helping to orchestrate a debut Season for Antonia. Her connections would open most every door in Mayfair."

"That's because most every hostess would fear that the old battle-ax would kick the door to splinters if an invitation wasn't forthcoming," growled Saybrook, but he too was smiling. The dowager, a great favorite with both of them, had a *very* sharp tongue to go along with her shrewd wit.

"True." Arianna bit back a laugh. "And God help any fortune hunter who tries sniffing around your sister's skirts."

His brows arched. "You think me unable to guard her from rakes and reprobates?"

"Hardly. But you have to admit that Constantina is even more frightening than you are when her temper is roused."

"She says the same thing about you," replied Saybrook drily.

"Beast." After making a face at him, she went back to her writing. A comfortable silence settled over the room, each of them lost in their own musings.

A quarter hour ticked past before Saybrook finally turned away from the window and set down his cup. "Perhaps we ought to have a brandy to fortify us for the coming ordeal."

Arianna made a last notation and then rose. "Actually, I had rather keep a clear head. There is much to do if we are to leave for a fortnight."

"I have been thinking . . . it might be possible to cry off," he said hopefully. "I could tell Charles that we suddenly remembered a previous commitment." His eyes lit. "With an elderly scholar, whose health is failing."

She shot him a skeptical look. "And what would your conscience say to that?" Saybrook was the most honorable man she had ever met—which was both a blessing and a curse.

"Damn," he muttered.

"I had better get Maria started on packing the trunks." Arianna sighed. "I suppose that I shall have to make a visit to Madame La Farge and order a few ball gowns. And you must stop by Weston and select a silk for a new waistcoat."

"Must I?" Saybrook grimaced.

"You claim that the floral pattern I chose makes you look like an organ grinder's monkey," she reminded him.

"Oh, very well." He began to gather up his papers. "Milford is the sort of fellow who has a wine cellar stocked with superb vintages of port, and a library offering naught but dreadfully dull volumes from the last century. So let us be sure to pack plenty of books. Otherwise we shall be bored to perdition."

# 3

## From Lady Arianna's Chocolate Notebooks

### Gateau Reine de Saba

#### For the cake

12 tablespoons (1½ sticks) butter, more for pan
6 ounces bittersweet chocolate, chopped into small pieces
3–4 drops almond extract
2 tablespoons strong coffee
4 large eggs, separated
Pinch of salt
1 cup sugar
1¾ cups finely ground almonds

#### For the glaze

2 tablespoons sugar
1 tablespoon corn syrup
¼ cup water
4 ounces bittersweet chocolate, chopped into small pieces
1 tablespoon butter

1. Heat oven to 325 degrees. Butter a 9-inch spring-form pan, and line the side wall with parchment paper. In a heavy-bottomed pan, combine 12 tablespoons butter, 6 ounces chopped chocolate, almond extract and coffee. Melt over low heat, then transfer to a bowl and allow to cool.

2. With an electric mixer, whisk egg whites and salt until soft peaks form. Slowly add ½ cup sugar until thick and glossy. Set aside.

3. In a separate bowl, whisk together egg yolks with remaining ½ cup sugar until thick. Fold in the melted chocolate mixture. Add ground almonds and mix well. Whisk in a dollop of egg whites to lighten mixture. Using a rubber spatula, gently fold in the rest of egg whites, keeping batter airy.

4. Scrape batter into pan and bake until cake is dry on top and a bit gooey in center, 30 to 40 minutes. (After 30 minutes of baking, check center of cake with a tester or toothpick. If center seems very wet, continue baking.) Cool cake on a rack for 20 minutes, then remove side of pan. Allow to continue cooling. Top of cake may crack as it cools, but glaze will cover most cracking.

5. In a small saucepan, combine 2 tablespoons sugar, the corn syrup and ¼ cup water. Bring to a boil, then remove from heat. Add 4 ounces chopped chocolate, swirl pan to mix, and allow to stand until melted, about 3 minutes.

6. Whisk 1 tablespoon butter into icing, then pour evenly over cake. Use a spatula to ease icing out to edges of cake. Allow icing to cool and set before slicing.

A dappling of sun filtered through the tall mullioned windows, its honeyed hue deepened by coming twilight. Overhead, a myriad of candles flickered in the chandeliers, highlighting the rich fabrics and opulent furnishings that graced the Marquess of Milford's formal salon. Glass-paned doors at the far end of the room opened on to a terrace overlooking the gardens. The scent of lilac and roses drifted up from the ornamental plantings, the subtle fragrances swirling with the lush floral perfumes and spicy colognes of the guests who had gathered for champagne before the welcoming dinner.

Flowers needed no artifice to enhance their natural sweetness, thought Arianna as she paused in the archway to regard a group of bejeweled ladies clustered near the marble display pedestals. The same could not be said for the *fauna*. Plunging necklines, decorative lace, sparkling sequins—there was an old adage about gilding the lily . . .

*Ah, but I am one of them now,* she thought ruefully, smoothing a hand over the lush silk of her gown. And yet, she still felt like an imposter, a wild weed sprung to life among a garden of cultivated blooms. A single pearl from the lustrous strand woven through her upswept hair would have fed her for a year in her former life.

"Smile, my dear," counseled Saybrook, slanting a sidelong glance at her expression.

"Very well," she replied under her breath. "But please don't ask me to simper."

His mouth twitched.

The buzz of conversation grew louder as yet another small group made its way into the room.

"That is the party from Paris," said Saybrook. Like them, most of the guests had arrived at the country estate that afternoon. "Beaulieu, an old Royalist, will be part of Prince Talleyrand's delegation in Vienna. But he has come to London to confer with our Foreign Ministry and the émigré leaders here in London before traveling on to the Continent. To his right is Flambert, a former colonel in Napoleon's Imperial Guards."

"Sandro, you must remember that I was raised in the West Indies, where Europe and its wars seemed very far away," replied Arianna. "I need some help in understanding the complex politics and alliances. Royalists, émigrés, Talleyrand—you must explain to me what they all stand for."

"Sorry," he said with a wry smile. "I shall try to explain things simply. You know, of course, that in 1789, the French people rose up in revolution and beheaded King Louis XVI and his queen, Marie Antoinette, several years later, along with a great number of the old aristocracy. The Bourbon dynasty had ruled France since the 1500s, but now it was gone in a wink of steel. A democratic republic was declared, which frightened the rest of Europe, and so France was attacked by a coalition of its neighbors. For over two decades, the continent has been torn by conflict, and once Napoleon came to power in France and declared himself emperor, the wars escalated. Now that he has finally been defeated and exiled to the isle of Elba, there is a complicated jockeying for power, both within France and across the Continent."

"I see," she murmured. "Perhaps I should be taking notes."

"It does get rather complicated," said Saybrook. "The Royalists are those who remained loyal to the Bourbon dynasty, and are now happy that it has been restored to the throne of France. In general the émigrés—that is, the French who fled here to England to escape the Revolution—are Royalists. But the former supporters of Napoleon aren't happy that the Bourbon dynasty has been returned to power. They would like to see a different form of government established, one where the people have more of a voice."

He took a look around the room before going on. "That is just one of the many issues that will be decided at the upcoming Peace Conference in Vienna. Prince Talleyrand, the current Foreign Minister of France, will be leading the negotiations for his country. He is clever, cunning and a master of diplomacy. The other main powers at the Conference will be England, Russia and Austria. You will meet some of their representatives here tonight."

"I shall endeavor to keep all of this straight," said Arianna. "Though in truth, I find politics an ugly game." Her gaze shifted to an extremely handsome gentleman who had just turned away from Beaulieu and Flambert in order to bow over their hostess's hand.

"Who is Adonis?" she asked, finding it hard not to stare. Like a Greek god, the man possessed striking classical good looks—curling ringlets of golden hair framed chiseled cheekbones, a straight nose and a full-lipped, sensuous mouth.

"Le Comte de Rochemont." Saybrook paused. "Who, like you, believes that he is blessed with Divine Beauty. Along with a cleverness that puts Almighty God to blush."

"I take it you don't like him," she murmured.

"I think that he's a bloody, brainless ass," responded Saybrook.

Seeing as he felt that way about most of the *haut monde*, Arianna took the assessment with a grain of salt.

"He's considered an influential member of the French émigré community here in London, on account of his family, a very prominent and well-connected member of the old nobility," continued Saybrook. "But as far as I know, the comte spends most of his time gambling or bedding other men's wives."

"So does most of the English aristocracy," Arianna pointed out.

*"Pas moi,"* muttered Saybrook.

"Not every man is capable of matching your prodigious skills in the . . . kitchen."

He choked down a laugh. "Some men might be offended by that remark."

"But not you, for you know I adore your chocolate confections." She placed a gloved hand on his sleeve. "Now come, we might as well go feed ourselves to the lions."

"You mean the carrion crows." He looked at the flock of black-coated diplomats with distaste. "Who plan to peck away at a war-ravaged Europe, in order to feather their own nests."

"Try not to be so cynical, Sandro."

"That is rather like the pot calling the kettle black."

"True, but we promised your uncle to help create a mood of international camaraderie." The reminder was as much for herself as for him. "So we must make the best of the situation while we are here."

"Yes, yes, you are right, of course." And yet he looked a little unsettled. A little on edge.

*Why?* Arianna considered herself very skilled at reading people, and now that she had settled into marriage, she felt that she was learning to interpret the nuances of his moods. But this one was puzzling her. She couldn't quite put a finger on what was troubling him. A glance at his downturned face was no help. The light from the gilded sconces couldn't penetrate the fringe of dark lashes shadowing his eyes.

However, further reflection was interrupted by Saybrook's uncle, who stepped out from one of the side salons.

"Ah, there you are, Sandro." Mellon acknowledged her presence with a small nod. "Milady."

She repressed an inward sigh. The fortnight was already promising to be a long and tedious affair.

"I trust that you had a pleasant journey from London," Mellon went on politely.

"Quite," she responded.

"Excellent." Mellon's eyes had already shifted to Saybrook. "Might I steal your husband away for a moment? The Spanish diplomats have just arrived and I would like to make the introductions."

"Of course. You need not worry about me, sir. I can fend for myself."

Mellon's mouth twitched slightly, but whether in annoyance or amusement, it was impossible to discern.

Arianna guessed the former. The allusion to her less than ladylike past was not apt to elicit a chuckle.

Saybrook shot her a look of silent apology and then gestured for his uncle to lead the way. "I shall do my best to appear *simpatico*."

As the two men moved off, Arianna turned toward one

of the colonnaded alcoves and began perusing the collection of oil paintings hung on the oak-paneled walls.

*I would be happy to blend into the woodwork,* she mused. The superficial pleasantries of Polite Society always seemed to stick in her throat . . .

"Ah, the elusive Countess of Saybrook."

Arianna didn't need to turn around to recognize who was speaking.

"Why does it not surprise me to find you skulking in a dark corner?" Lord Percival Grentham asked, his voice deceptively soft as he glided a step closer to her.

She turned slowly, refusing to flinch. The Minister of State Security, Grentham was feared by most people in London. And with good reason. He was said to be utterly ruthless and remorseless in pursuing those whom he considered a threat.

*A threat to what? King, Country, or his own overweening pride?*

He looked at her as if horse droppings had suddenly befouled his elegant evening shoes.

She returned the stare with equal disdain. *I don't like you much either.*

A master of manipulation, Grentham liked being in control of people. To him they were pawns, insignificant pieces to be sacrificed without a second thought to serve his own purposes. And so he harbored a simmering enmity for her and Saybrook, despite their having saved him from considerable embarrassment by unmasking a dangerous conspiracy. Their refusal to play by his rules had resulted in a veiled warning that he was watching . . . and waiting to pounce if they made the slightest slip.

As their gazes locked, a glint of malice lit in his eyes. "I trust you are not here to cook up any new trouble?"

"No, I shall leave making a hash of things to you, sir." She smiled sweetly on seeing a tinge of color rise to his cheekbones.

"A hash calls for dicing a slab of flesh into mincemeat, does it not?" replied Grentham. "I prefer a more sophisticated style of cuisine. One that requires delicate carving skills . . ." His well-tended fingers flicked at his lapel. "Rather than a few heavy hacks with a cleaver."

Arianna had stabbed a man to save Saybrook's life, and the minister knew it. But she would be damned if she let him guess that the memory still gave her occasional nightmares.

"Ah, yes," she riposted. "I've heard that you have a great deal of experience in roasting a man's cods, and then slicing them into *amuse-bouches*." It was, she knew, childish to provoke him. But she couldn't help it. "Tell me, do you spice them with oregano or rosemary? Or do you serve them plain, with naught but a sprinkling of salt?"

"You have a clever tongue, Lady Saybrook," replied Grentham softly. "Have a care that it doesn't land you in a vat of boiling oil."

He moved away without further comment as a shadow fell across the recessed corner.

"Was that self-important prig harassing you?" demanded Saybrook in a low growl as he came up behind her.

Arianna shook her head. "The minister and I were simply exchanging pleasantries."

Her reply elicited a phrase unfit for the elegant surroundings.

"There are ladies present," she cautioned. "Not that such language offends *my* ears. But I daresay that the others would fall into a swoon were they to overhear you."

He chuffed a disgruntled sigh.

"Speaking of ladies, I can't help but be curious—is Lord Grentham's wife here?" She wondered what sort of female could live with such an unrelenting lack of humor.

"I believe he's a widower," replied Saybrook.

Arianna suspected that the minister was standing on the other side of the tall *Chinoiserie* curio cabinet, and couldn't resist a parting dig. "Ha. My guess is he either tortured the poor woman in some foul dungeon. Or"—the pause was deliberately drawn out—"she simply expired from boredom."

Saybrook gave a chuckle.

"Honestly," she went on. "Does the man think of nothing but work, and how he can persecute the people around him?"

"It's his job to be a nasty, nosy son of a bitch. And he does it extremely well." Her husband disliked the minister even more intensely than she did. He hadn't revealed the reason, but she guessed it was very . . . personal.

"Forget Grentham," muttered Saybrook. "Come, let us mingle with the other guests and be polite."

Rochemont, the French Adonis, was engaged in conversation with the Duke of Ellis and two military officers from the Horse Guards. As she passed close by, Arianna heard him describing a hunting trip to Scotland.

"The Paragon of Masculine Beauty appears to speak perfect English," she observed.

"The comte has lived in London for nearly two decades," answered her husband.

"He must be delighted to see Napoleon exiled and the House of Bourbon restored to the throne of France," she mused.

Saybrook shrugged. "I would imagine it all depends on how power shifts. No one likes to lose his position of influence. The British government treated the émigré community in London as an important ally. Now that there is no Napoleon to fight against, Rochemont and his followers might become irrelevant."

"I hadn't thought of it in that light." Arianna pursed her lips, finding it hard to understand the allure of the political world. As Saybrook said, it must all come down to a craving for power.

*While, I, on the other hand, satisfy my innermost desires with chocolate.*

"What has stirred such a cat-in-the-cream-pot smile?" inquired Saybrook, arching a dark brow.

"I was giving thanks to God that we will not have to be involved in all the sordid machinations."

"Amen to that," replied her husband. He plucked two

glasses of champagne from the tray of a passing waiter and handed one to her. "A toast to the quiet life of cooking and scholarly study."

The wine's effervescence prickled against her tongue. "You are sure that it's not *too* quiet?" she asked softly. "I sometimes fear that you miss having a complex conundrum to solve."

"I don't miss whizzing bullets and slashing steel," he quipped.

And yet, she wondered . . .

"Ah, there you are, sir!" Their host, the Marquess of Milford, flashed a genial smile at Arianna. "Lady Saybrook, would you allow me to take your husband away to the terrace for a moment? Mellon tells me he knows something about plants, which is a godsend. The Spaniards are asking me all sorts of questions about my ornamental gardens, and I haven't a deuced clue as to the answers."

"His Lordship is indeed an expert in botany," she replied. "I'm sure he'll be able to help. In the meantime, I won't wilt while he's away."

"Wilt . . . Oh, ha!" The marquess gave a bark of laughter. "Clever gal you've married, Saybrook."

"Yes," said Saybrook drily. "Isn't she?"

Left alone once again, Arianna looked around, wondering if there was a familiar face among the guests. Other than Saybrook's uncle—and the odious Lord Grentham—she had seen naught but strangers.

The marquess's wife had led a group of ladies into the adjoining salon and Arianna decided that it would be rude not to join them. Steeling herself for a detailed discussion on the state of the weather, or whether cerise or plum was a more fashionable color for autumn, she started to make her way across the room.

"Please forgive the demands on Sandro." Mellon appeared by her side and offered his arm. "His attentions will make the Spaniards happy, though it rather leaves you in the lurch."

"You need not keep apologizing, sir. We are here to help

you foster the bonds of international friendship." She dutifully smiled at a passing foreigner. "If there is anything I can do, you have only to ask." Knowing his reservations, she decided to confront them head-on. "I can behave like a perfectly proper lady when I put my mind to it."

His arm stiffened beneath her gloved hand.

*Apparently I was much mistaken.* A proper lady would have known better than to express such frankness . . .

To her surprise, Mellon actually chuckled. "I imagine that you could do just about *anything* that you put your mind to."

"I'm not sure if I should take that as a compliment," replied Arianna lightly. *Or perhaps as an olive branch?*

Mellon had no chance to reply for he was accosted by a very large and very plump gentleman with the most extraordinary set of side-whiskers that Arianna had ever seen. The wild frizz, heavily sheened with Macassar oil, covered all but a scant strip of smooth flesh at the tip of his chin. It gave him the look of a slightly demented bear.

"For shame, Mr. Mellon! You are taking unfair advantage of your foreign visitors." The heavily accented English was punctuated by a waggling finger. "Do you mean to keep your lovely relative all to yourself?"

Mellon acknowledged the accusation with a courtly shrug of surrender. "Not now that I've been caught out, Grimfeld. But can you blame me?"

*"Nein,"* responded the Bear with an appreciative look her way. "I would do the same if I were in your sows."

*"Shoes*, Heinrich, not *sows*," corrected one of his companions. "Sows are *schwein*."

"Lady Saybrook," said Mellon, keeping a straight face. "Allow me to present Herr Grimfeld, who is part of the Prussian contingent visiting London, and Count Kostikov, who represents His Imperial Highness, the Tsar of Russia."

Both gentlemen bowed low over her hand.

"May I also have the honor of introducing my countryman," said Kostikov as he straightened and stepped back to permit the third member of their group to approach. "Mr.

Davilenko has served this past year as our government's attaché in London, but he will be traveling with me to Vienna as part of our peace delegation."

"What a great pleasure it is to make your acquaintance, madam," said Davilenko, moving quickly to perform the gentlemanly ritual of brushing a kiss to her glove.

Arianna stared in mute shock at the top of his head. *The curling russet-colored hair, the bald spot on his crown, the jug-shaped ears . . .*

For an instant she wondered whether she had drunk too much champagne for the floor suddenly seemed to be spinning beneath her feet.

"It is a privilege to be in the presence of such a lovely English rose," Davilenko went on.

*And yet last time we met, you called me a poxy slut.*

Ending his gallantries with a flourish, he clicked his heels and looked up.

Arianna held her breath in her lungs.

"A rose," he repeated, his broad smile mirroring the up-turned slant of his cheekbones. "And one of the most ex-quisite, enchanting blooms of this island's beauty."

*Apparently, beauty was in the eye of the beholder,* she thought sardonically, realizing that he didn't recognize her. Tonight she was swathed in costly silks, with a king's ran-som in emeralds dangling just above her décolletage. While during their previous encounter in Messrs. Harvey & Wat-kins Rare Book Emporium she had been wearing a drab bonnet and ill-fitting work gown.

Looking somewhat bemused by her wide-eyed silence, Mellon gave a discreet cough. "A very pretty compliment, sir."

"Yes, how kind of you, sir," she murmured, roused from her initial shock by the gentle reminder. Quelling the in-sane urge to laugh—and then give the leering Russian a good, swift kick in the crotch, Arianna fluttered her lashes. "Have you an interest in plant life, Mr. Davilenko?"

"I consider myself a connoisseur of beautiful blooms," he replied jovially, oblivious to her subtle barb. Casting an appreciative glance at her bosom, he added, "If you would allow me to escort you to the refreshment table, we might discuss the subject at greater length."

Accepting his arm, she let him guide her around an arrangement of potted palms.

"I have noticed that English ladies are very fond of flowers," said Davilenko. "Have you a favorite, Lady Saybrook?"

"Actually I tend to favor more exotic species of flora. Like *Theobroma cacao*."

His smile turned a trifle tentative. "Oh? I am not familiar with such a plant."

"No?" said Arianna. Another little flirtatious flutter. "And yet you seemed so very anxious to get your hands on the volume of *cacao* engravings I was buying for my husband."

His jaw went slack.

Recalling the embarrassing incident set off a fresh spark of indignation inside her. "Steal any more books lately?" she asked tartly.

The blood drained from Davilenko's face.

"Oh, yes. I saw the other one tucked inside your coat," she said in a low whisper. "I don't imagine your embassy would be happy to hear that you engage in petty thievery."

Pivoting on his heel, he hurried away without uttering a word.

"Barbarian." The comment came from just behind her.

Arianna gave an inward wince, realizing that the exchange must have been overheard.

"*Ja*, the Russians have a well-deserved reputation for boorish behavior," chimed in another voice. "Do come join us, Lady Saybrook. We promise to be more congenial company."

She turned slowly, forcing a smile as she found herself face to face with three diplomats whom she had met earlier in the evening.

"Stealing books?" Le Notre, a member of the French

émigré community in London, raised a questioning brow. "Why, whatever did you mean, Lady Saybrook?"

"It was more of a misunderstanding." Arianna had no intention of explaining what had really happened at the book emporium, and quickly deflected the conversation to a more mundane topic. "I understand that the marquess's estate offers some of the best shooting in Gloucestershire. Do you gentlemen enjoy hunting?"

"Indeed," said Enqvist, the Swedish military attaché. "I am particularly fond of grouse . . ."

Henkel, an aide to the embattled King of Saxony, followed the paean to birds with a lengthy tale of a Black Forest boar hunt. Then, to her relief, Saybrook reappeared and saved her from further stories by asking for her company on a stroll out to the terrace.

"If you will excuse us, there are some plants that I know my wife will find very interesting," he explained.

"But of course." Le Notre gave an apologetic bow. "Forgive us, Lady Saybrook. I hope we haven't upset your delicate sensibilities with all our talk of bloodshed."

Covering his amusement with a small cough, the earl offered Arianna his arm. "Thank you for your concern, gentlemen. However, I am happy to report that my wife is not nearly as fragile as she looks."

Arianna waited until they passed the refreshment table before responding to her husband's quip.

"And yet, we all know that looks can be deceiving."

# 4

## From Lady Arianna's Chocolate Notebooks

### Tropical Milk Chocolate–Banana Pudding

*5 ounces milk chocolate, finely chopped*
*3 tablespoons sugar*
*2 tablespoons unsweetened cocoa powder*
*2 tablespoons cornstarch*
*Pinch salt*
*2 egg yolks*
*1½ cups whole milk*
*½ cup heavy cream, plus 1 cup whipped*
*1 teaspoon vanilla extract*
*2 large bananas, thinly sliced*
*14 whole chocolate wafer cookies, plus 4 crushed,*
*for garnish (see note)*

1. Place chocolate in a bowl. In a separate large bowl, sift together sugar, cocoa, cornstarch and salt; whisk in egg yolks and ½ cup milk until smooth.
2. In a large saucepan over high heat, bring remaining 1 cup milk and ½ cup cream to a simmer. Pour

over chopped chocolate and whisk until smooth. Whisking constantly, slowly pour hot chocolate mixture into egg mixture until completely incorporated and cocoa is dissolved.

3. Return custard to saucepan. Cook, stirring constantly, over medium heat, until thickened, about 10 minutes. Do not let mixture reach a simmer. If custard begins to steam heavily, stir it, off the heat, a moment before returning it to stove top. Strain through a fine-mesh sieve. Stir in vanilla.

4. Spread several tablespoons pudding evenly into an 8-inch square pan (or a glass bowl). Top with an even layer of bananas; arrange whole cookies on top of bananas. Cover with remaining pudding. Top with whipped cream and sprinkle with crushed cookies. Chill at least 3 hours or overnight before serving.

(Note: Nabisco Famous Chocolate Wafers work very nicely.)

Saybrook laughed. But then, on seeing Arianna draw in a lungful of garden-scented air as they passed through the French doors, he eyed her askance.

"*Are* you feeling a trifle faint?" he asked. "You look as though you have seen a ghost."

"A specter," she replied, avoiding his gaze.

"Would you care to elaborate?"

"Not at the moment." Arianna essayed a smile. "I—I shall explain it all shortly."

"That has a rather ominous ring."

"No, no," she assured him. "It's quite the opposite, actually."

His dark brows angled up. "Now you have me intrigued."

As a gust of wind ruffled through the ivy vines, a sudden chill teased down her spine. Shaking off the sensation, she turned abruptly and braced her palms on the stone railing. "Don't be silly."

The earl came to stand beside her. "I'm sorry," he said softly, after taking a sip of his champagne. "I should have guessed that Grentham would be here." The set of his jaw betrayed his inner tension. "If you wish, we can find a reason to leave. A sudden illness is a perfectly plausible excuse."

"You need not worry, Sandro. Grentham doesn't frighten me."

"He should," replied Saybrook tersely.

Yet again, she wondered what private clashes had provoked such a tone of loathing. She had a sense that he was holding something back.

*But so am I.*

"We may have piqued his insufferable pride, but he has no real reason to do us harm." Arianna shrugged. "Besides, I am not certain what weapon he could wield, even if he wished to. You said yourself that he has agreed not to talk about my sordid past in return for you keeping silent about his own shortcomings. He is pragmatic . . ." She paused for a fraction. "As well as a being a prick. So I doubt he will be any trouble."

He allowed a grudging grin. "I suppose you are right."

"I confess, it may be petty, but I rather enjoy tweaking his nose." She smiled. "It turns a ghastly shade of puce when he is angry."

"All jesting aside, don't push him too hard. I, for one, don't underestimate him. He is a diabolically cunning man, and if he wishes to exact revenge, he will figure out a way to do so."

She lifted the wine to her lips. "I shall be careful."

Whatever he was about to say was swallowed in a harried sigh. "It seems any moment of privacy will be all too fleeting," he said under his breath as footfalls on the stone announced that someone was approaching.

"Sandro, might I take you away again?" Mellon lifted his shoulders in apology. "Labrador has a question . . ."

"Of course," replied Saybrook.

"You need not worry that your lovely wife will be left alone in the dark, Lord Saybrook." Rochemont stepped forward with a gallant flourish. "I told Mr. Mellon that I should be delighted to keep the countess company."

"How kind of you," drawled Arianna.

"Indeed," muttered the earl. Setting down his drink, he let his fingers graze her glove before turning and following his uncle across the shadowed terrace.

Rochemont watched them for a moment, then assumed Saybrook's place at the railing.

Arianna quelled a flare of annoyance as he sidled closer. *Temper, temper.* For Mellon's sake she would do her best to be polite.

Tilting his head to the light, he ran a hand through his hair, leaving the blond curls artfully tousled. "Will you and your husband be traveling to the Peace Conference in Vienna, Lady Saybrook?"

*Oh, well done, sir.* She wondered how many hours it had taken to perfect the deliberately careless gesture.

"No," she replied aloud. *Actually, I would rather be dropped into the hottest hole in Hell.* "My husband and I have no interest in politics."

"Ah, but it promises to be a spectacle, the likes of which the world has never seen before." The torchieres danced in the evening breeze, gilding his face with a reddish gold glow. "Kings, emperors, archdukes, margraves—why, with all the bejeweled splendor and dazzling finery, Vienna will sparkle brighter than the heavenly stars. Every night there will be dancing and feasting." He looked up at the night sky. "And of course, flirting."

"It sounds . . . delightful."

"Demand that your husband take you there, milady." Rochemont smiled and winked. "A newlywed man does not dare deny a beautiful bride a heartfelt request."

"Really?" She let the question dance away on the breeze before asking another one. "Are you married, sir?"

"But of course." He shrugged. "However, it is—as you

English so delicately phrase it—a marriage of convenience."

Which most likely meant the lady's family gained the prestige of allying with an ancient and august title, while the comte gained a great deal of money.

As for the lady herself, no one much cared whether or not she benefited from the arrangement. She was simply a pawn.

"How convenient for you," she murmured.

"That is how I look at it." His gaze slid down to her cleavage. "All very civilized, *n'est pas*?"

"That all depends on how you choose to define the word," she replied.

"Ah, a lady who is interested in philosophy. How very intriguing." His handsome mouth curled up at the corners. "Pray, how would you describe your marriage, Lady Saybrook?"

*As something infinitely more complicated than the bartering of wealth and power.*

Arianna decided to deflect his intimate probings with a show of humor. "It is still so new to me that I've not yet had a chance to form any definite opinions."

His laugh was low and throaty, a sound suggestive of rumpled silk and whispered passions. "You," he said slowly, "are a fascinating female. Pray, tell me more about yourself."

*What would you like to know? That my father was a disgraced earl who was forced to flee from England to the West Indies? That from the age of fourteen I had to fend for myself, working as an actress with a traveling theater troupe, a cutpurse, a cardsharp and a faux French chef?*

She brushed an errant lock of hair from her cheek. "Really, sir. We ladies live such boring lives. The rules of Society allow for little adventure."

"Don't tell me that you haven't ever wanted to break the rules, Lady Saybrook," he teased.

Arianna was quickly growing bored with his blatant flirtations.

Rochemont interpreted the meaning of her silence in a far different way. "Come to Vienna," he urged with a flash of his pearly white teeth. "I promise that you will enjoy yourself."

"A tempting offer." Lifting a gloved hand, Arianna slowly uncurled a finger and turned his chin. "However, you will have to look elsewhere for amusement. I've no desire to travel at the moment—I am quite satisfied with my life here in London."

"A pity." He captured her hand and with a lazy grace, turned it palm up and brushed his lips over the soft kidskin. "But life is . . . how do you say . . . quixotic. One never knows when things may change, *non*?"

The echo of his question gave way to the silvery sound of a bell, signaling that it was time to move into the dining salon.

"Enjoy your stay in Vienna, Lord Rochemont," said Arianna, coolly disengaging herself from his hold and steering the conversation to a blandly impersonal subject. "I wish you luck in your diplomatic dealings."

The oblique rebuff seemed to take him by surprise. Light winked off his lashes, gold sparking with gold as he narrowed his eyes. Clearly he was used to women falling in worship at his feet.

His hubris, however, quickly reasserted itself. "I am always eager to pursue a new challenge, Lady Saybrook."

"I imagine you will encounter more than enough of them in Austria to keep you satisfied." It was her husband who responded to Rochemont's assertion. Amusement shaded the earl's voice, along with a sharper undertone that Arianna couldn't quite identify. "Are you ready to go in to supper, my dear? Charles has just informed me that you will be seated between Herr Grimfeld and Colonel Lutz of the Bavarian delegation."

"Are they friend or foe? I confess, it is hard to keep track of all these German factions," she said drily.

He chuckled. "Perhaps we should have our host hand

out a primer on all the European rivalries, along with the menu."

"Ignorance is bliss," she said under her breath.

And with that, they returned to the glitter and gaiety of the stately manor house.

"*Dio Madre*, I thought the evening was never going to end." Stepping through the door connecting their bed-chambers, Saybrook unwound his cravat and stripped off his coat.

As was their habit at home, they had dismissed their valet and maid, preferring to undress themselves at night.

"You, at least, enjoyed a bottle of superb port with your cigars, while I and the other ladies were served tea." Arianna tossed her shawl on the dressing table. She was very fond of the Portuguese wine, so it rankled that ladies were never permitted a taste in Polite Society.

Her necklace followed.

Saybrook winced slightly. "My great-great-great-grand-mother was given those baubles by Queen Elizabeth. After passing through wars and pestilence unscathed, we should try to keep them in one piece to pass on to the next generation."

She watched the candlelight play across the faceted gems. "Your uncle seemed to unbend just a little tonight. I wonder, do you think he will ever come to like me?"

"He doesn't dislike you," said Saybrook, taking a seat on her bed.

She was still getting used to habits of the English aristocracy. It was *de rigueur* for husband and wife to have separate bedchambers, both at home and when visiting.

*Especially* when visiting, she thought a little sardonically. The discreet name cards on all the doors were apparently to help late-night trysts go smoothly.

"No, he simply disapproves of your marriage," replied Arianna.

"He"—her husband seemed to be searching for words—

"worries about the family. He has no children, and I have no brothers, so—"

"So he thinks me unfit to continue the line?" Tired and tense from the evening's complicated social demands, she interrupted more sharply than she intended.

"I didn't say that," he answered calmly.

His reasonableness somehow made her even pricklier. "You didn't have to."

Silence greeted the reply

*Family.* When they had first met, Arianna had envied Saybrook and his relationships. His grandmother's journals, brimming with chocolate lore and her earthly observations on life, had been a source of solace during his illness, while a loving uncle and aunt had provided the affection and support of surrogate parents.

But perhaps being all alone was easier, she thought sardonically. One could be supremely selfish.

*The world is so much simpler when seen only through the prism of one's own needs and desires.*

"I am sorry," said Arianna, her voice still a little rough around the edges. "It should have occurred to me when you offered marriage that you would expect an heir." An uneasy pause. "I—I should have thought to inform you that ... I may not be able to produce a child." She sat down, and as she began combing out her hair, she tried to catch his reflection in the looking glass.

But he had withdrawn into the shadows.

Retreated into himself. They were both very private people, who kept their feelings well guarded.

"I have had a previous liaison, one that went on for nearly a year, and I never conceived." Oh, this was damnably hard. "I should have told you."

"Why?" he replied calmly. "I never felt obliged to discuss my previous life or relationships with you. How we lived and what we did before we met is not an issue in our marriage."

"But it is," insisted Arianna. "You had a right to know of any flaw before entering into a bargain."

"I was not making a purchase at Tattersall's," he said softly.

"Your peers would disagree," she said with a brittle laugh. "That's exactly why aristocratic gentlemen enter into marriage—they need a bride to use as a brood mare."

"I think you know by now that my views on life rarely march in step with those of my peers."

"Oh, God." Arianna put down her brush and felt tears prickle against her lids. The conversation had taken a strange turn, leaving her feeling confused. Conflicted. "I'm sorry."

"Don't be."

Arianna looked down at her hands, feeling awkward and unable to articulate her sentiments coherently. In the flickering candlelight, the glint of the gold ring was like a dagger point pricking against her conscience. "No wonder your uncle had reservations about such an impetuous marriage. You should have refused to be rushed. I should have insisted that you take time to consider the ramifications."

"Arianna, nobody held a pistol to my head," he said drily.

*True.*

And yet, Arianna couldn't help feeling that circumstances had forced his hand. For all his cynicism, the earl had a stubborn streak of chivalry when it came to damsels in distress. His offer of marriage had saved her from Lord Grentham's wrath.

It had been a purely practical solution.

Love?

The word hadn't been mentioned during the discussion of her options.

No, they weren't in love—they were both too pragmatic, too dispassionate for that. Trust didn't come easily, for at heart, both she and Saybrook did not wish to be vulnerable. They did, however, have a great deal in common—a cynical sense of humor, an open-minded curiosity, a love of chocolate . . .

"Arianna." Saybrook had come up behind her. His

hands settled on her shoulders and as his long, lithe fingers began kneading her tense muscles, she felt her anger start to melt away.

A pleasurable heat spread through her as his palms chafed against her bare skin. Physical attraction was not a problem between them. Her lips quirked as she watched his movements in the looking glass. That part of their relationship seemed to be going smoothly. They both enjoyed the intimacies of marriage, finding the fleeting joining of their bodies eminently satisfying.

As for a meeting of minds . . .

Arianna let out a silent sigh, finding it hard to explain.

Somehow it chafed to be beholden to someone else's whims. It felt as though she had lost some small but essential piece of herself.

As for Saybrook, she sensed a detachment in him. A distance. As if, at times, he was miles away. He was a complex man, hard—nay, maybe impossible—to understand. *Layers within layers.* It was not easy to peel away the protective covering around his innermost emotions.

He was prone to black spells of brooding.

*As am I,* she admitted. *Like Sandro, I can be difficult. Prickly.*

"Let us not quarrel." His words interrupted her musings. After brushing a light kiss to the nape of her neck, Saybrook straightened and tugged off his shirt. Light dipped and darted over the chiseled contours of his chest, accentuating the sculpted muscles, the coarse curls of dark hair.

"Come to bed," he murmured.

She did so.

And yet, even after the tension had been coaxed from her limbs, Arianna lay awake for a long time before falling into a troubled sleep.

# 5

## From Lady Arianna's Chocolate Notebooks

### Chocolate Pistachio Fudge

*12 ounces 70 percent dark chocolate, chopped, or 12 ounces
semisweet chocolate, chopped
1 14-ounce can condensed milk
Pinch salt
1 cup shelled pistachios*

1. Melt the chopped chocolate, condensed milk and salt in a heavy-based pan on low heat.
2. Put the nuts into a freezer bag and bash them with a rolling pin, until broken up into both big and little pieces.
3. Add the nuts to the melted chocolate and condensed milk and stir well to mix.
4. Pour this mixture into a 9-inch square foil tray, smoothing the top.
5. Let the fudge cool and then refrigerate until set. Cut into small squares.

Arianna watched the morning mists drift in low, leaden skirls over the heathered moor. The sun had not yet broken through the clouds, leaving the hills looking a little sullen and bruised.

"So, the gentlemen are leaving early for their shooting?" she asked, turning away from the breakfast room windows.

A chorus of masculine voices rose in assent from the long table.

"Splendid morning for birds," said Enqvist as he wolfed down the last bite of his shirred eggs.

Arianna gave silent thanks that she was not venturing out of the marquess's well-feathered nest. Judging by the puffs of breath rising from the group of ghillies waiting with the gun wagons, it was quite chilly.

*"Jawohl,"* agreed Lutz, and his comment was quickly echoed in several different languages.

The prospect of gunpowder and blood seemed to have stirred a convivial mood, despite the early hour. From outside came a flurry of barking as the kennel master and his assistants led the pack of bird dogs across the lawns. Several of the men quickly finished their coffee and pushed back their chairs, eager to get under way.

"Enjoy your day," she said as Saybrook and Mellon joined the group trooping out the door.

The earl shrugged. He had come down earlier and was already looking bored. "I can think of better ways to spend my morning," he murmured.

"As can I," added his uncle. "However, I feel we must show the English flag, so to speak."

"I doubt the poor grouse give a fig for what nationality is blasting them out of the air," she replied. "Though given the amount of spirits that were consumed last night, the aim of the hunters might be a bit erratic."

"Yes, and the flasks of hot coffee will be fortified with brandy," said Saybrook. "So it's not likely to improve."

Mellon chuckled.

"Have a care," she joked.

"You appear to be alone," observed Mellon as Saybrook

gathered up their hunting coats. Arianna was the only female who had come down to breakfast. "I fear that most of the other ladies won't appear until noon."

"I have plenty to keep me occupied," she assured him. "I have brought a notebook of Dona Maria's chocolate recipes to transcribe."

Saybrook's late grandmother had spent years researching the history of *Theobrama cacao*, and her collection of historical documents pertaining to the plant was a treasure trove of fascinating information. The earl was writing a history of chocolate and its various uses, from ancient Aztec times to the present, while she was compiling a cookbook.

"However, it's deucedly difficult to work out the proper measurements," she went on. "Especially when the ingredients are written out in German."

Her husband quirked a sympathetic look. "Ah, I take it you have brought her journal on Austria and the Holy Roman Empire?"

"Yes, and I am learning that Charles VI and his daughter Maria Theresa were immensely fond of chocolate. She had her personal chef experiment with adding a number of flavorings, including the essence of certain fruits."

"Chocolate was very popular among the Hapsburgs," explained Saybrook to his uncle.

Mellon nodded abstractly.

"Don't let me keep you," said Arianna, thinking the poor man was growing tired of their constant commenting on cuisine. "The wagons look ready to set off." Gathering her skirts, she seated herself at the table and signaled for tea. "After my breakfast, I intend to curl up in a cozy spot with my *flora* while you men pursue your *fauna*."

Saybrook slapped his hands together in mock enthusiasm. "Indeed, the age-old masculine rite of spilling blood should put everyone in a jolly mood for the rest of the day."

She shot him a look of silent reproach.

With that, the two men moved off, leaving her alone with the sumptuous smells wafting up from the line of silver chafing dishes.

*A fortnight of playing aristocratic games?* An unappetizing thought, especially as she dared not upset convention by asking if she might spend some time in the marquess's kitchens, experimenting with the contessa's Austrian recipes.

*Highborn ladies do not soil their dainty little hands with manual labor.*

Arianna cracked her knuckles. Thank God she had brought plenty of books to keep herself occupied.

The sudden whir of wings filled the air as a brace of birds exploded from the thicket up ahead.

"Lord Saybrook?" Rochemont, who had been paired with the earl for the morning beat, cleared his throat with a low cough. "I believe it is your turn to shoot."

*"Hmmm?"* Saybrook lifted his gaze from the patch of mossy ground beneath his boots. "Ah, sorry. I was distracted . . ."

The ghillie carrying the cartridge bags gave him an uncomprehending look before squinting into the hide-and-seek sunlight. "A plump pair," he said somewhat accusingly. "But no matter, milord. The beaters will flush more." He shaded his eyes. "The line of the hunt is shifting, sirs—we had better move to keep our proper place in line."

"Are you not enjoying the shooting, milord?" asked Rochemont. "Your skill with a firearm is quite evident, and given your military background . . ." He let his voice trail off as he gave a Gallic shrug.

"As you say, I've spilled enough blood—the thrill of the hunt no longer seems exciting." The earl hesitated, and then suddenly handed his fowling gun to their grizzled guide. "You go ahead and take my shots, Rochemont. I've just spotted an interesting species of mushrooms and wish to have a closer look. I shall catch up with you shortly."

The comte raised a brow. "Mushrooms?"

"An uncommon variety for this part of England. I should like to examine the soil and surroundings, so that I may make proper note of the details," answered Saybrook.

Shaking his head, the ghillie uncocked the gun and blew

the priming powder from the pan—along with a few mumbled words about aristocrats being queer in the attic.

"Good hunting," said Rochemont, his voice mildly mocking as he stepped over to take the earl's position. "I shall try not to disgrace myself in your stead."

Saybrook was already hunched over a patch of mossy ground, carefully picking away at a tangle of damp, decaying leaves. "Yes, yes," he said absently. "I won't be long."

As the two other men moved off, he dug up one of the small speckled mushrooms and wrapped it in his handkerchief. "*Morchella esculenta*," he murmured to himself. "And given their preference for limestone-based soil . . ." He swung around to survey the surroundings.

*Bang. Bang. Bang.*

The shooting party had moved well past the copse of trees that fringed the denser strip of forest growing up the hillside. Placing the specimen in his pocket, he began to pick his way through the brush, intent on examining the mulch beneath the canopy of leaves and pine needles.

*Bang. Bang. Bang.*

As he paused to unsnag a twist of thorns from his coat, a movement on the far side of the moor caught his eye. Flitting in and out of the gorse was a man, heading in a hurry for the dark shadows of the trees.

It appeared that someone else found the bird shooting as boring as he did. And yet . . .

Saybrook quirked a frown. There was something strangely furtive about the man's movements.

The earl watched for a moment longer, then continued on his own way—but quietly, his steps lighter, his gaze sharper, his senses on full alert.

Like all the hunters of their party, the man was wearing a thick tweed shooting coat and oilcloth hat. The collar was turned up and the broad brim tugged low, making it impossible for Saybrook to make out his quarry's identity.

Whoever he was, the figure suddenly looked around and then quickened his steps. Ducking low, he disappeared beneath the branches.

"*Dio Madre*, Arianna's talk of specters has me imagining the worst," muttered Saybrook under his breath.

The leaves stirred in the breeze, the dark greens going gray in the shifting shadows.

"Don't be a birdwit. The fellow simply prefers privacy for a call of nature." He straightened from his crouch, feeling a little foolish.

*Bang. Bang. Bang.*

Recalling that he had promised to join Mellon at the next break for refreshments, Saybrook reluctantly decided there was not enough time to explore the woods. Turning away, he started to make his way back to where Rochemont was stationed.

And yet, the earl remained on edge. Every few steps, he paused to look back at the dark tangle of trees.

"Any luck with your *champignons*?" asked the comte, stumbling slightly as he turned to look at Saybrook.

"I found one interesting specimen," he replied gruffly, turning to steady Rochemont's footing. "I plan to come back for a closer look at the woods behind us—"

The glint of sun on steel lasted only an instant as the barrel of a gun shifted ever so slightly within the gray-green foliage.

On instinct, the earl shoved the Frenchman down and dove for cover, just as sharp *crack* rent the air.

A gorse branch shattered close by his face, the splinters nicking his cheek.

"Damn," he grunted, clapping a hand to his shoulder as he rolled up against the thorns. His fingers came away sticky with blood.

*Silence.*

And then the sound of running footsteps thrashed through the bushes. "Sandro!" Mellon must have seen the earl fall, for he had cut away from his place in the shooting line and was rushing to help.

"Get *down*, Charles," he ordered, grabbing his uncle's legs and pulling him to the ground. "You too Rochemont. Don't move."

The comte gave a dazed moan. A purpling bruise on his forehead showed that he had struck his head on a rock. "My face, my face," he whined. "I fear I shall have a permanent scar."

"Stop squirming," snapped Saybrook. "And stop mewling, unless you wish to draw another round of fire."

"What the devil—" wheezed Mellon as the comte froze.

"Stay here." Slipping a long-bladed knife from his boot, Saybrook scrambled to his feet and set off at a run.

Arianna didn't linger long over her tea and toast. Discreetly avoiding the main drawing room, where her hostess was busy organizing a shopping trip to the nearby village, she hurried up one of the side staircases and took refuge in her chambers. Looking at lace or plumes held absolutely no interest for her. Feminine frills were more often than not a cursed nuisance. She much preferred the freedom of men's garb—breeches and boots—rather than yards and yards of suffocating skirts and delicate slippers.

Arianna thought longingly of her buckskins back in Grosvenor Square, and the many times in her previous life that she had ventured into public dressed as a boy. Ha! The other guests, both male and female, would most likely swoon on the spot if she were to gallop across the marquess's manicured lawns riding astride.

Not that she would give rein to any such unladylike urges. She had vowed to herself that Mellon would have no cause to regret his invitation.

Still, her spirits were brightened by the mere notion of shocking the *ton*.

Humming a cheerful Bach fugue, Arianna began gathering up her projects. There was Dona Maria's journal, with its deucedly difficult German script to decipher—not to speak of measurements and ingredients that sounded even more foreign. Without a kitchen close by for constant experimenting . . .

Huffing a sigh, Arianna set the notebook aside in favor of starting with a simpler task.

*Coward,* she chided herself.

But she quickly assuaged all twinges of guilt by reminding herself that tomorrow was Saybrook's birthday, so it made sense to take advantage of his absence and wrap his gift now.

Perhaps the magnificent engravings of the cacao fruit would help assuage whatever ill was plaguing him, she mused. Chocolate was, after all, considered to have potent medicinal benefits. Even Saybrook's good friend Basil Henning, the highly skeptical Scottish surgeon, conceded that its effects on both body and spirit were intriguing.

Taking up her purchase from the rare book shop, as well as a colorful pasteboard box, scissors and ribbon, she carried them to the escritoire.

Once the brown paper wrapping had been stripped off the leather-bound volume, Arianna paused to once again admire the exquisite detail and subtle hues of the colored illustrations. They were truly lovely works of art, and she looked forward to seeing Saybrook's expression when he opened the cover—

Her own face suddenly fell as her fingers touched upon the inside of the back binding. A corner of the marbled end paper had come loose.

"Damnation," she muttered under her breath. It must have been snagged during the scuffle.

Setting the book down on the blotter, she angled it to the light and smoothed at the rough edge. The damage appeared to be minor, so perhaps if she could find a glue pot in the marquess's library . . .

*How odd.*

There seemed to be a bulge beneath the decorative paper. She took a moment to check the front cover.

*Yes, yes, there is a distinct difference.*

Frowning, Arianna fetched Saybrook's silver book knife from the adjoining room. Sliding the slim blade into the opening, she ever so gently worked it up and down.

A bit more of the paper popped up.

Sure enough, she could now see that several sheets of

folded paper had been tucked inside the binding. Slowly, slowly, she eased the sharpened metal down the edge of the marbling, loosening the glue. When finally the gap seemed big enough, she gingerly extracted the hidden papers.

*Secret chocolate recipes?* A smile tweaked on her lips. Oh, wouldn't that be a delicious discovery. Or perhaps it was a pirate map, with a skull and crossbones marking buried plunder. Or . . .

*Or perhaps I should stop reading Mrs. Radcliffe's horrid novels.*

The reality would likely prove much more mundane. A packing list, a notation of expenses, tucked away for safekeeping during a trip.

A faint crackling teased at her fingertips as she unfolded the sheets. There were three in all—two were grouped together, while the third was on its own. Sitting back, she skimmed over them quickly.

"Oh, bloody hell."

Arianna closed her eyes for an instant, and then read them again. "Bloody, *bloody* hell."

Like the hapless grouse flushed into flight on the moors, all notions of a peaceful country interlude had just been blasted to flinders.

Saybrook crossed the clearing in a flash and darted into a stand of oaks. Pressing up against a gnarled trunk, he held his breath and peered into the gloom, looking and listening for any sign of movement within the grove.

He detected nothing, save for the silent, shifting shadows. The air was very still, the earthy musk of damp decay tinged with lingering traces of burnt gunpowder. The earl waited a moment longer before heading deeper into the trees.

Leaves crunched softly beneath his boots, punctuating the whispery brush of the pine boughs against his coat. He stopped every few steps and listened for footfalls up ahead, but heard only the distant cackle of a raven and muffled cracks of gunfire out on grouse moor.

"Damn." After surveying the tangle of underbrush and the dense thickets ahead, he swore again.

"Sandro?"

"Over here, Charles," he answered. As Mellon crashed through the brambles, the earl added an exasperated warning. "For God's sake, man, try not to rouse the dead."

"Sorry." Mellon stumbled up beside him, gasping for breath. He had lost his hat and his normally impeccably groomed hair was standing on end. "I haven't as much experience in this sort of thing as you do."

"Which is exactly why I ordered you to stay where you were," snapped Saybrook.

"What the devil is going on?" Mellon's expression pinched in shock. "Christ Almighty, you've been shot!"

The earl touched his shoulder. "It's naught but a scratch."

"It is hard to believe a poacher would be so bold—or stupid—to be shooting with our party close by."

"It wasn't a poacher, Charles. A poacher would not possess a rifle," replied Saybrook grimly. "Such a weapon is very expensive."

"H-how do you know it was a rifle?"

"The sound. It's quite different from that of a musket."

"But who . . . ?" Mellon left the rest of the question unsaid.

"I haven't a clue." The earl swung his gaze back to the forest. "And there's no point in trying to chase after the fellow. He'll have no trouble losing himself in the forest."

Mellon blinked, suddenly noting the blade in Saybrook's hand. "You were going after the fellow armed with naught but a *knife*?"

"As you say, I am experienced in warfare." He shifted his grip on the hilt. "You, on the other hand, have no such excuse."

"I couldn't very well let you charge off into danger on your own," muttered Mellon.

"We'll argue the fine points of battlefield strategy later," said Saybrook. "Come, let us return to the hunt."

But as he edged back to let his uncle go first, his eyes

narrowed. "A moment," he murmured, angling another look through the overhanging leaves. Several quick strides took him over a fallen tree and through a screen of young pines. An outcropping of weathered granite rose up from the center of a tiny clearing. It was the spattering of bright crimson on the gunmetal gray stone that had first caught the earl's gaze. However, as he came closer, he saw what had caused it.

Crouching down, Saybrook placed a finger on the side of the man's slashed throat. "No pulse," he murmured as Mellon came up behind him. "But the flesh is still warm."

Mellon closed his eyes and, repressing a gag, quickly looked away. "Why would someone deliberately shoot at you?" he croaked, once he had recovered his voice. "Have you been stirring up any trouble?"

"Not that I know of." Saybrook sat back on his heels. "And yet, trouble seems intent on rearing its ugly head." Expelling a grunt, the earl went on to explain about seeing a man sneak into the woods just before the shot.

"And you didn't recognize the fellow?"

Saybrook shook his head. "No, but I'm certain this is not him. The man I saw was dressed like a member of our shooting party, in heavy woolens and a broad-brimmed hat." He felt inside the corpse's moleskin jacket, and then made a check of the pockets. "There's nothing that might help identify him."

Mellon nudged the short-barreled gun lying half buried in the russet needles. "You were right about the rifle."

"Yes." The earl checked the firing mechanism and frowned. "And it's equipped with the latest mercury fulminate percussion caps." Flicking away a grain of gunpowder, he looked up at his uncle. "A design that is only available to our elite military regiments."

"Christ Almighty," whispered Mellon. "I fear something very sinister is afoot here."

"As do I, Charles. As do I." Thinning his lips, the earl wiped a bloody hand on his breeches. "You know, it might not have been me that the shooter was aiming at. Rochemont was right in the line of fire as well." He paused. "Is there any reason our government might be unhappy with the French émigré community in London? Rochemont is one of its leaders, and while they were a useful wartime ally, now that the monarchy has been restored to France, their loyalty will lie with a foreign sovereign and a foreign country." A pause. "So perhaps they are no longer viewed as a friend."

Shouts rose from the edge of the grove before his uncle could answer.

"I sent our ghillie to raise the alarm," explained Mellon. He stood and called an answer to the group.

A few moments later, a half dozen of their party were milling around the macabre scene, their shocked murmurs underscoring the agitated whine of the bird dog.

"Good God, what happened?" demanded a pale-faced Enqvist.

Mellon lifted his shoulders. "Someone shot at Lord Saybrook. We gave chase"—he shuddered—"and stumbled upon this."

"The devil take it, you're wounded, Saybrook!" exclaimed Bellis, one of Mellon's associates in the Foreign Ministry.

All eyes fixed on the dark stain spreading over the torn fabric of his coat.

"The bullet merely grazed me," replied the earl.

"I can't say that I blame you for slitting the cur's throat," muttered Bellis, casting a look at the knife in Saybrook's hand.

"No, no—Saybrook didn't kill him," protested Mellon. "As I said, we found the fellow with his throat already cut."

One of the men coughed. Several shuffled their feet.

"We'll need to bring the body back to the manor house," said Bellis. "The local magistrate will have to be summoned and an inquest arranged, seeing as there's been a violent death."

Mellon gave a brusque wave to the ghillie. "Go, man,

and bring back the cart, along with a few of your sturdiest fellows."

"Aye, sir."

The servant hurried away, and the others slowly followed.

Saybrook rose and carefully slid his blade back into his boot. When he looked up, it was to find Grentham watching him, a scimitar smile curled on his mouth.

"*Tut, tut.* You're getting a little careless, Saybrook," mocked the minister. "The last two times a man ended up dead from a knife wound, you made sure that no witnesses caught you at the scene red-handed."

The earl's expression remained impassive.

"If you recall, I did warn you to watch your step." Grentham dropped his voice to a whisper as he brushed by. "But it seems you have slipped. And now you and your sharp-tongued wife have nothing to barter. You are on your own."

# 6

## From Lady Arianna's Chocolate Notebooks

### Chocolate Date Pudding Cake

*6 ounces pitted dates, about 2 cups*
*¾ cup water*
*1¼ cups sugar*
*1 tablespoon pure vanilla extract*
*6 large egg whites*
*½ cup unsweetened cocoa powder*
*½ cup all-purpose flour*
*Confectioners' sugar, for dusting*

1. Preheat the oven to 375 degrees F. Spray a 1½ quart soufflé dish with nonstick spray.
2. Put the dates and water in a pot over medium-low heat. Cook and stir for 10 minutes until the dates are very soft. Transfer the softened dates to a food processor and puree until smooth. Add the sugar and vanilla, puree again until well blended. Scoop out the puree into a mixing bowl. Sift together the cocoa powder and flour and add to the date mix-

ture. Fold using a rubber spatula; combine gently until well mixed.

3. In a mixing bowl, whip the egg whites until they form stiff peaks. Fold the egg whites into the date mixture.

4. Pour the batter into the coated soufflé dish, spreading it evenly with a spatula. Bake on the middle rack for 25 minutes until the outside is just set. Cool to room temperature. Shake some confectioners' sugar on top and serve.

The flames licked up from the burning log, teasing, taunting little tongues of fire. *Do it. Do it.* The smoky crackle of the red-gold coals added their own siren song.

*Do it. Do it.*

Arianna stared into the hearth, mesmerized by the seductive light and heat. It would be oh, so easy . . .

Whirling away from the burning logs, she rushed to the window, and pressed her palms to the glass panes, willing the chill to cool temptation.

"No," she whispered.

*But who would know?* countered a devilish voice inside her head. She could consign the letters to the fire and nobody would know. *Poof*—the evidence would simply crumble to ashes.

The danger would disappear in a pale plume of smoke.

A papery sigh whispered as she unfolded the sheets yet again and read over the writing. Two of them contained naught but gibberish. It was the other one that raised a pebbling of gooseflesh up and down her arms.

There was—there had to be—a plausible explanation. However, in the wrong hands, the document could do great damage.

She drew in a measured breath, willing her heart to stop thudding against her ribs. In the past, the choice would have been a simple one for her. Concepts like right and wrong were mere abstractions when one was scrabbling hand over fist to survive. She would have done what was practical and pragmatic without a second thought.

But Saybrook was a man of unyielding honor, of unbending principle, she thought with a harried sigh. And strangely enough, she had come to believe in such platitudes.

*Though how and why, I can't explain—even to myself.*

The damnable documents posed more than a personal dilemma. Their existence indicated a far more insidious danger. Saybrook would say it was their moral duty to show the evidence to the proper authorities, no matter the consequences.

Arianna bit her lip. She was very good at hand-to-hand combat—but she hated wrestling with her conscience.

"I much preferred it when I didn't have one," she whispered wryly.

The sudden clattering of a horse cart rolling into the courtyard interrupted any further philosophical musings.

Her breath had fogged the windowpanes, so it took a moment to wipe away the vapor. Through the blurred glass she saw that a length of canvas was covering something in the back of the cart. Two ghillies jumped down from the backboard and the horse was quickly led away to the back of the manor.

Craning her neck, she watched the procession of grim-faced hunters come marching up the drive. In contrast to the casual camaraderie of the morning bantering, they appeared silent, subdued.

Saybrook was not among them.

Arianna turned away from the window, trying to quell a sense of unease.

A dog began barking in high-pitched yips that echoed sharply off the stately limestone walls.

Her nerves on edge, she nearly jumped out of her skin when an urgent knock suddenly sounded on the suite's entryway. Sliding the papers back inside the book, she rushed to open the door.

"Madam, there seems to have been an accident involving the earl. I was told to tell you that"—the agitated footman paused to catch his breath—"that you had best come quickly."

*Dio Madre.*

Arianna rushed to retrieve her shoes, which she had slipped off while sitting at the escritoire. As she shoved aside the chair, her gaze fell on the chocolate book and its hidden secrets.

On impulse, she carried it to the bed and shoved it beneath the mattress before hurrying down the stairs.

"There is no need to fuss, Arianna." Saybrook tried to fend off her hand. "It's naught but a scratch."

Ignoring his protest, she turned to a footman. "Have a basin of hot water, scissors, bandages and basilicum powder brought to the West Parlor—and quickly."

"Yes, madam!"

"And a vial of laudanum." Noting that her husband's face looked as pale as the surrounding Portland stone, she gestured at Mellon. "Charles, please assist His Lordship."

"I don't need any help," muttered Saybrook. But in truth, he looked a little unsteady on his feet as he started up the entrance stairs. "And I would prefer to go to my own rooms, if you please."

"The parlor, Charles," ordered Arianna. The bloodstain spreading over the singed wool was alarming.

Once inside the room, she had him strip off his coat and take a seat on the sofa. After propping a pillow behind his shoulders, she drew the side table closer and took up the scissors to cut away his shirt.

A hiss escaped her lips as she stared at the jagged wound. "You thick-headed man. Why, it's a wonder you didn't bleed to death! Did you not think to put a pad on the wound to staunch the bleeding?"

"I was . . . distracted," he answered.

Mellon, who had retreated several steps to give her room, cleared his throat. "What did Grentham say to you?" he asked tautly.

*Grentham.* Arianna felt a chill snake down her spine. "How is the minister involved in this?" she asked, carefully sponging the gore from Saybrook's shoulder.

"He was among the men who found us with the body," replied the earl.

*"Body,"* she repeated.

"A man was murdered in the woods near the hunt. We found him," replied the earl.

"Let us not read too much into Grentham's presence," said Mellon quickly. "Our ghillie raised the alarm, and the shooters closest to us came to investigate." He shifted his stance. "It was coincidence that the minister was among them."

"I don't put much faith in coincidence," she said softly. "Especially when it involves that bastard."

She felt Saybrook's muscles tense as she bandaged the wound. And yet, he remained stoically silent.

"Now, kindly explain to me exactly what happened," Arianna insisted.

Mellon gave a terse account of the action.

"Charles, will you please bring me a glass of brandy?" Arianna added a few drops of laudanum and handed it to the earl. "Drink this."

"I don't need any damnable narcotic," he growled.

"Ordinarily, I would agree with you." She considered opium a pernicious substance. "However, in this case, I've no ingredients to brew a more effective painkiller, and I want you to rest for a bit before I allow you to move."

"Bloody hell, I'm not at all tired. But I suppose it will be more trouble than it's worth to argue with you." Making a face, he swallowed the brandy in one gulp.

She made him lie down and arranged a blanket over his chest. Despite his protests, the earl quickly dozed off.

"It looks like he lost of lot of blood." Mellon looked

down at the crimson-soaked remains of Saybrook's shirt. "Is he in danger?"

"I know, it looks gruesome," replied Arianna. "But Sandro was right. It's just a flesh wound, though the bullet cut a nasty gash." She let out a pent-up sigh, thinking how close the bullet had come to splitting open his skull. "Thank God his soldier's instinct for survival is still sharp."

Mellon returned to the sideboard and poured himself a drink. "Amen to that." He held up the decanter. "May I offer you one as well?"

Arianna shook her head. She needed to think clearly.

He stared meditatively into the spirits before taking a sip.

"Charles, I . . ."

*I wish that I could coax a spark of warmth in your eyes. You are so cordial. And so cold. Is there nothing I can do to win your trust?*

"I . . . am concerned," she finished, deciding this was not the right time to broach their uneasy relationship.

"As am I." Mellon sucked in his cheeks. "Grentham is a dangerous enemy to have."

"I know that." Arianna hesitated. "Just as I know that I am the cause for the friction between them. I am sorry— you have every right to be upset with the situation." *And with me.*

It was several long moments before Mellon replied. "Sandro is a complex man. Most people find him hard to understand. He is intensely introspective—perhaps too much so. And prone to fits of brooding."

*Aren't we all,* she thought.

"But you seem to be drawing him out of himself. He seems . . . happy."

"Thank you," said Arianna softly. "I imagine that was not easy for you to say."

His mouth quirked. "A diplomat is trained to say the correct thing, regardless of his personal feelings."

*An oblique statement if ever there was one.* Especially considering the contents of the hidden letters. But negotiating any terms of a personal truce would have to wait for a less volatile time.

"We will need every bit of eloquence we can muster to counter whatever maliciousness Grentham has in mind," she said in reply.

Mellon's expression turned grim.

"Might I leave you to sit with Sandro for a short while?" she went on. "I have a few things I wish to arrange while he is napping."

"You sent for Henning? Blast it all, there was no need for that." Saybrook awoke from his nap in an irritable mood. "He's got patients who have far more need of him than I do."

"His friend Desmond can take care of them in his absence," answered Arianna. Their good friend Basil Henning was an irascible Scottish surgeon who held clinics for former soldiers too poor to pay for medical care. "There is no point in arguing. I have already sent a messenger, mounted on one of the marquess's fastest stallions."

She offered Saybrook a plate of cold chicken and rolls, knowing he tended to be snappish when his stomach was empty. "I've also dispatched our coach to wait in Andover. In order to save time, I've asked Mr. Henning to hire a private conveyance in London and travel with all possible haste to meet it there."

"Baz doesn't have much money," grumbled Saybrook after taking a reluctant bite of food.

"Along with the message about your injury, I included a note for him to give our housekeeper. Bianca will supply him with funds," replied Arianna. "I expect that he will be here by morning."

The earl shifted against the pillows. "You've already patched up the scratch. And if there is any need for further care, we could have summoned a local physician."

She carefully smoothed a crease from the blanket. "I would rather not trust a stranger to mix any powders or potions for you."

Saybrook muttered an oath.

"It's not simply a question of your treatment," Arianna continued. "Given what has happened, and the impending inquest, it is important to have Mr. Henning make a close inspection of the corpse."

"Your wife has a point," murmured Mellon.

Saybrook frowned but didn't argue.

"The angle of entry, the shape of the blade—Mr. Henning can give expert testimony that it wasn't your knife," she added.

"Don't be daft. Grentham is well aware that Baz is a friend and former army comrade of mine," countered the earl. "He'll do his best to discredit any such statements."

"Perhaps," she replied, ignoring his sarcasm. "But Henning is still a qualified medical man, and his observations, expressed openly in a public inquest, will force the coroner to take a closer look at the evidence. Murder is a very serious charge to bring against a peer of the realm."

His brows rose. "You have this all figured out?"

Arianna smiled sweetly. "As you once pointed out, I have a Machiavellian mind."

Her husband gave a grudging laugh. "And as you once pointed out, I should be extremely grateful for that fact."

"Yes." She stood up and brushed the crumbs from her skirts. "You should be."

Saybrook finished the last morsel of chicken and set the plate aside. "Thank you, my dear. But I think the threat is not as real as you think."

*Oh, yes. It is.* Arianna rose and handed him the fresh shirt brought down by his valet. "If you are feeling better, shall we go up to our rooms? I think you will be more comfortable there."

He didn't miss the subtle change in her voice. "Yes, of course."

"I should go dress for supper." Mellon stood up as well. "I shall see you later, then."

Once they were halfway up the guest wing staircase, and away from prying ears, Saybrook murmured, "I take it you have something pressing that you wish to discuss in private."

"Yes," replied Arianna. "And I fear . . ." *Fear.* The word raised a hot-and-cold prickling sensation at the nape of her neck. *Fire and ice.* "I fear you are not going to like it."

"Do go on," he said drily. "The bullet didn't kill me, but the suspense of waiting for this explanation might."

"Ha, ha, ha." She gave a weak laugh as they turned down the corridor to their rooms. "I don't mean to wax dramatic, but I've made a very disturbing discovery."

"What . . ." began Saybrook, only to turn the question into a growled oath. "What the devil?"

Up ahead, a footman was fumbling with the door latch of their suite. The carpet must have muffled their footsteps, for he whirled around at the sound of their voices, a spasm of guilt pinching at his face.

"Your pardon," mumbled the man.

To Arianna, he sounded more nervous than he should.

"I—I was told to bring these freshly starched cravats to your rooms, milord."

The sconce light flared and she saw that despite the coolness of the corridor, a thin beading of sweat rimmed his upper lip. She tensed, her senses on full alert. "Does not the Marquess of Milford have a large enough staff for the household to function properly?" The menial task of delivering laundry was the job of an under maid, not a footman.

"I—I wouldn't know, madam," stammered the servant. "I—I was merely doing as I was asked."

Arianna glanced at the folded linen that had fallen to the floor. "By the by, those are not His Lordship's cravats."

The footman crouched down to gather up the neckcloths. "They must have made a mistake downstairs. Forgive me for disturbing you." Crabbing back from the door, he rose hastily and fled without further word.

"Damnation," said Saybrook under his breath, staring for a moment at the stretch of shadows before following her into their suite.

The door fell closed with a soft snick.

"What mischief is afoot here?" he went on. "The cursed fellow was clearly up to no good. But why would he be stealing into our rooms? The emeralds are valuable." His mouth pursed. "But I would not have thought them worth the risk of murder."

"I don't think he was after the emeralds." Arianna took the volume of engravings out from its hiding place. "I think he was after this."

# 7

## From Lady Arianna's Chocolate Notebooks

### Bittersweet Chocolate Ice Cream

*2 cups heavy cream*
*1 cup milk*
*½ cup sugar*
*⅛ teaspoon kosher salt*
*8 ounces dark chocolate (preferably 72 percent cacao),*
*roughly chopped*
*1 tablespoon whisky or rum*

1. In a saucepan over medium-low heat, simmer cream, milk, sugar and salt, stirring occasionally until sugar dissolves.
2. In the bowl of a food processor, pulse chocolate until finely chopped. Add one cup hot cream mixture and process until smooth.
3. Transfer to a large bowl. Slowly pour in remaining hot cream mixture and the whisky or rum, whisking constantly. Place bowl in refrigerator or set in an ice bath to chill.
4. When cold, pour into the bowl of an ice cream ma-

chine and churn according to manufacturer's directions. Transfer to a container and freeze until solid, at least 2 hours. Let sit at room temperature for 5 to 10 minutes before serving, or in refrigerator for 15 to 30 minutes.

Yield: About a quart.

❧

"A book." Saybrook took it from her and thumbed through the pages before adding, "Quite a lovely book, in fact. But delicious as it is to us, *Theobroma cacao* is not something that ought to attract the violent interest of others."

"It's not the book, *per se*." Arianna drew a deep, unhappy breath, knowing her revelations were about to entangle them in a new web of secrets and lies. *Spiders and serpents.* Sinister, silent predators.

The thought of them made her skin crawl.

"But I had better start at the beginning." She quickly recounted what had happened in the bookstore, and the unexpected encounter with her assailant the previous evening.

"You didn't think an attack on your person was something I ought to know about?" he interrupted softly. "Or the fact that the man who assaulted my wife is present here?"

"The book was meant to be a special birthday present, Sandro. Any mention of the incident would have spoiled the surprise," she answered. "And besides, I thought Davilenko was simply one of those eccentric, obsessed book collectors that you mentioned to me. A boor and a bully, but not any real threat." The papers seemed to hiss and crackle beneath her fingertips as she pulled them out from behind the marbled endpaper. *Is it my imagination, or did a whiff of brimstone suddenly taint the air?* "Until I found these hidden in the binding."

Saybrook stared at the folded sheets for a long moment before reluctantly holding out his hand. "I take it they are not recipes," he muttered.

"Not unless you are looking to cook up chaos."

One by one, he carefully unfolded them, his face remaining expressionless as he read over the contents. The only sign of emotion was a tiny tic in the muscle of his jaw. But even that was quickly controlled.

Arianna waited for a reaction, but he simply reshuffled the sheets and appeared to begin a second round of study.

Finally, when she could stand the silence no longer, she cleared her throat. "Well, what do you think?"

The earl didn't look up. "If you are asking whether I think my uncle is capable of betraying his country, the answer is no, I don't."

"Nor do I," she said tightly. "But someone with access to his confidential files is."

"Renard?" During their previous investigation, they had uncovered a rumor about an elusive French spy called Renard. *The fox.* If the whispers were true, he was a very cunning individual who moved within the highest circles of Society.

"The name certainly leaps to mind when speaking of documents stolen from the inner sanctum of Whitehall." She paused. "Do you think he actually exists? We had only a criminal's word to go on, but . . ."

"As a matter of fact, I do believe Renard is more than smoke and specters," answered Saybrook slowly. "A few months after our investigation was over, I met with a former comrade in the upper echelon of military intelligence, who confirmed that the government had linked the name with several other instances of espionage. But then, Napoleon abdicated and the war was over, so I assumed that the threat had disappeared."

"And yet it's possible that Renard is still running free, teeth and claws as sharp as ever," said Arianna.

"Yes, it's possible," he replied. "But so are a myriad of

other speculations, ranging from the plausible to the absurd."

Arianna didn't blame him for sounding so sardonic. Regardless of his innocence, Mellon's reputation would be blackened by her discovery—or worse. The evidence was awfully incriminating. Two of the papers seemed to be written in a secret code, but the third bore the official stamp of the Foreign Office. Written in Mellon's hand, it summarized the progress of highly secret negotiations taking place with one of the German states. Knowing such privileged information would give any enemy of England a potent weapon at the upcoming Peace Conference in Vienna. The diplomatic jockeying for power would be intense as borders were redrawn, alliances reformed. And so, Europe was like a giant powder keg.

*Just one spark could ignite chaos.*

"Then we shall have to find solid proof of who is the real culprit," said Arianna. "Or . . ." She hesitated, wondering whether to admit that her thoughts had sunk to such a shameful depth. "Or deal with it in a different way. I confess, I was sorely tempted to throw it all into the fire."

That Saybrook said nothing was in itself eloquent of his own inner turmoil.

"It's something to consider," she went on in a near whisper. "We could warn your uncle of the danger, and together work discreetly on setting a trap for the traitor. Nobody else need be privy to the problem until the traitor's capture is a *fait accompli.* Think on it—in many ways it's the most logical tactic. The fewer people who know that the betrayal has been discovered, the better. A wary fox is harder to catch than one who thinks the henhouse is unguarded."

"Like your sinfully seductive confections, your well-reasoned arguments are tempting, my dear," replied the earl. He lifted his chocolate-dark eyes from the pages and she couldn't quite see what lay beneath the shuttered gaze. *A soldier must make himself impenetrable in order to survive,* she reminded herself.

"*Too* tempting," he added. "What you suggest would be

easy, and I fear that there is going to be nothing easy about this affair."

"Then what do you intend to do?" asked Arianna.

"I am not sure." Saybrook carried the papers to the leaded window and angled them into the light. "It depends partly on what I can learn from these coded pages that you found enclosed with the document written by Charles."

*Codes.*

She had guessed as much, but how the disjointed words could be turned into a meaningful message was its own puzzle. "They look like an opium eater's wild ramblings," she said. "It seems an impossible task to try to make sense of them."

"I am surprised that you think that." For the first time since he had returned from the moors, her husband allowed a small smile. "Codes are all based on a logical system. Some may be more complex than others, but the underlying principles are the same. As in mathematics, you simply have to see the patterns."

Arianna's father had been a mathematical genius, and she shared his knack for numbers.

"I hadn't thought about it that way," she murmured.

"You've had no need to," replied Saybrook drily. "I, on the other hand, spent some of my time on the Peninsula working with George Scovell on cracking Napoleon's military codes. The man was a veritable wizard." Moving to the escritoire, he set the papers down and absently smoothed at the creases. "Let us hope some of his magic has rubbed off on me."

She recognized the spark that had flared in his eyes. Like a moth drawn to a flame, the earl found a cerebral challenge impossible to resist. And danger seemed to make it only more alluring.

"They seem to be written in a different hand. Show me which one was folded together with the document from Charles's files. I'll start with that one."

"Change into your dressing gown," she ordered, after

doing as he asked. "While I fetch a blanket and shift one of the armchairs closer to the fire."

"I don't need to be coddled," he muttered.

"Go," said Arianna, cutting off his protest with a martial glare. "I shall send word that we won't be joining the party for the evening entertainments, and ask that a supper tray be sent up. But in return, you must humor me by not collapsing from loss of blood."

"Good God, a small scratch has never slowed me down."

"Pride goeth before a fall," she countered.

"Women." He surrendered to her demand with an ill-tempered grunt. "Hell, it is feminine fussing that will be the death of me."

"I profoundly hope not," she whispered, looking down at the rusty smudge on her apron and feeling her blood run a little cold.


The rhythmic tick of the longcase clock was the only sound stirring the deepening shadows. The embers in the hearth, silent specks of dying red, had burned down to naught but cinders, leaving the lamp as the lone flicker of light in the sitting room.

"It's past midnight, Sandro." Arianna tightened the sash of her wrapper against the chill. "Come to bed."

*"Hmmm?"* Another sheet of crumpled paper joined the growing pile on the carpet. "Yes, yes, in a moment."

"Yes, yes, and in the same space of time, pigs will spout wings and fly to Uranus."

He looked up. *"Hmmm?"*

"Never mind." Too restless to sleep, she padded over to the hearth and added a few fresh logs. Infused with new life, the fire sent up a blaze of bright flames, their cheery crackling a lighter counterpoint to the regimented marching of the minutes. "Any luck?"

He shrugged.

*A cryptic answer.*

After another quick jab at the coals, Arianna set the

poker aside and seated herself on the carpet beside his chair. "You're chilled," she commented, slipping a hand beneath the blanket and running her fingers lightly over his leg.

At that he looked up. "Are you trying to distract me?"

"I doubt that I could."

Saybrook chuckled. "Don't underestimate your powers." He flexed his shoulders and massaged the back of his neck. "I would far rather wrestle with your lovely limbs than these perverse little letters."

"Even though I often drive you to distraction?" she teased. Leaning in for a closer look at the papers piled on his lap desk, she took a moment to study the strange diagram he was drawing.

"What's that?"

"A Vigenère Square."

"It looks like the ravings of a lunatic."

His mouth twitched. "There is a method to the madness. As I mentioned earlier, all codes and ciphers are based on a logical system. One just has to be clever enough to figure them out."

"So it's a game of sorts." Arianna thought of her father and his delight in making numbers do his bidding—no matter that the equations had dire results. "A *mano a mano* match of Machiavellian minds."

Her husband gave a bark of laughter. "At times the challenge does feel personal. The code maker and the code breaker engage in an intellectual version of hide-and-seek. Competition can get fierce, for the stakes are often very high." His pencil tapped softly against the paper. "Mary, Queen of Scots, was executed because England's spymaster, Lord Walsingham, was able to decipher her secret correspondence with Babington and his group of Catholic conspirators. And then, of course, you have Scovell, whose skills helped Wellington drive the French forces from the Peninsula."

The life of a monarch, the fate of a country, the defeat of an army—strange how the fate of the mighty could be determined by a tiny, twisting hodgepodge of letters.

Resting her elbows on the arm of the chair, she settled into a more comfortable position. "If it's not too distracting, might you take a few minutes to explain your Square?"

"To begin with, there are all sorts of systems for creating codes," he answered. "A common form is a cipher code—that is, where one letter is replaced by another. Here is an example."

Placing a blank sheet of paper atop his notes, Saybrook wrote the words "The fox is in the henhouse." Above it, he lettered the alphabet in one line. "Now, I'll use a simple Caesar shift of three to encrypt the message, which means you take each letter of the original message and shift it over three positions." He quickly wrote out a line that looked liked complete gibberish—*wkh iua lv lq wkh khqkuvh*.

"The spaces are often omitted to make the text harder to decipher. Still, an experienced code breaker knows to use frequency analysis, a concept developed by the Arabs while we Europeans were mired in the Dark Ages. This helps determine what the real letter might be. For example, 'e,' 't,' and 'a,' are the most commonly used letters in English. So, one can begin by substituting a 't' for whatever letter occurs the most frequently in the encrypted letter. It's a matter of trial and error, of course. And the longer the message, the better the odds of the system working. Still, it helps one to make an educated guess."

"Fascinating."

"Yes, it is," he agreed. "But that's just the beginning. A code maker has all sorts of tricks to throw a code breaker off the scent. He—"

"Or *she*," remarked Arianna.

Saybrook smiled. "Point taken. I suspect you would be frighteningly good at this."

"Algorithms," she mused. "I can see where mathematical concepts come into play."

"Indeed. Mathematicians make excellent cryptographers. Oddly enough, so do poets. Chaucer was quite a good one. It has to do with imagination—which you also possess in spades." He smiled. "But as I was saying, the code maker can use other elements to protect his text. He—or she—can insert a code word, known only to the sender and receiver of the message, which is inserted as a 'blind' so to speak, in order to throw the frequency off. In cryptography, we call it a key."

Arianna made a face. "It sounds hopelessly complicated."

"Complicated, yes. The permutations of a complex cipher defy the human brain. However, keep in mind that a code maker can't get too clever or complicated. The receiver must also know the system being used."

"Ah, I see what you mean," she murmured. "And yet, what you were working on seems awfully complex."

"I thought it safe to assume that our enemy would be too clever to use a simple text cipher, so I'm trying out a few other schemes." He shuffled back to his original page. "A Vigenère Square seemed a good choice."

"What, precisely, is that?"

"A grid invented in the sixteenth century by Blaise de Vigenère, a French diplomat posted to Rome. It's a method for encrypting that offers a mind-twisting array of possibility."

He finished lettering in the alphabet both vertically and horizontally, forming two sides of a square. "You have twenty-six letters across, and twenty-six letters down, both of which begin with 'a.'"

She nodded.

"Then you begin the next row with 'b,' and then 'c,' and continue on like that until you have filled out the square. Now, you have twenty-six possible cipher alphabets. You can encrypt using two or twenty-two. Oftentimes, a code word is used to tell the receiver what rows to use. For example, say 'pen' is the code word. The receiver uses the row that begins with 'p' to decode the first letter of his secret message. For the second letter, he would use the row beginning with 'e,' and so forth."

Arianna blinked. "Ingenious."

"There are, of course, a multitude of other systems. Breaking a code requires intuition, patience, time—and most of all, luck." He made a wry face. "The odds of stumbling upon a solution for this cipher tonight are stacked against me. However, I am familiar with the way the French cryptographers think, and if our enemy is really a man named Renard, then perhaps I shall get lucky. In any case, it is worth a try."

"I should like to learn more about this," she mused. "I can see where mathematics would be a helpful skill. Probability and patterns—it's very much like gambling."

"An apt analogy," he commented. "As it happens, I brought along a book on the subject that was recently published by a don at Oxford. It is on my dressing table."

Arianna went into his room, returning with not only the book but also two glasses of brandy.

"What are you going to tell Charles about this?" she asked, watching his face from over the rim of her drink. Firelight swirled within the amber liquid, the play of molten sparks dancing along the ridge of his cheekbones.

His eyes remained shadowed. "I haven't yet decided." He looked tired. Pensive. "But come morning, I will have to make up my mind."

She fingered the wads of discarded paper, wishing that she could help. "Is there nothing I can do?"

Saybrook shook his head. "Not at the moment. I just want to test a few more ideas . . ."

The scratch of his pencil took up where his voice left off.

*Patterns and probabilities, intertwining with deceptions and betrayals.* The brandy burned a slow, sinuous trail down her throat. She had lived most of her life within the murky netherworld of secrets and lies. Which perhaps explained why the prospect of matching wits with a dangerous traitor was more tantalizing than terrifying.

*I suppose that Charles Mellon is right to think me a very odd sort of female.*

Taking another mouthful of the spirits, Arianna savored the heat of it against her tongue as she cracked open the book and began to read.

* * *

"Your pardon, milord." Saybrook's valet discreetly cleared his throat as he poked his head into the dawn-dappled sitting room. "But Mr. Henning has arrived. Shall I show him up?"

"God yes, before he wakes the house with his bellows." The earl yawned and stretched out his long legs. "He tends to be in an ill humor when he is hungry."

"Ouch." Arianna winced as she sat up. Her muscles were stiff and knotted with cold. "I shall likely have a bruise on my shin, though it probably serves me right for being such a nodcock as to fall sleep on the floor."

"You had better order up a big breakfast too, Hobbs," added the earl. "Eggs, gammon, kippers, along with plenty of rolls and jam. Henning isn't the only one who turns snappish when his bread box is empty."

"Wretch," muttered Arianna, tossing the sofa pillow at his head. "Please bring pots of coffee and chocolate as well, Hobbs."

"Yes, milady." The valet disappeared.

"I had better go and make myself presentable," she said, rising and retying the sash of her wrapper.

"An excellent suggestion," said her husband drily, waggling a brow. "You did summon Henning to make an inspection of naked flesh. However, I'd prefer it wasn't yours."

"As would I, seeing as most of the bodies he ogles are dead."

She returned—fully dressed—to find their friend Basil Henning warming his hands by the rekindled fire. His frayed clothing was rumpled and the expression on his angular face looked equally out of sorts—but that was nothing unusual. Henning always looked grumpy.

As if on cue, he gestured at the steaming silver pot set on the side table. "Auch, Sandro, ye roust me from a nice warm bed and drag my carcass halfway to Hades, only to greet me with naught but a puling cup of coffee?" The outspoken Scotsman had been a surgeon in the earl's army regiment, and the two men had formed a fast friendship during the long, brutal Peninsular campaign, despite the difference of wealth and birth. "Ye gods, man," he groused.

"It's me you should be raking over the coals, Mr. Henning." Arianna hurried over to brush a kiss to his leathery cheek. "Thank you for coming. We've ordered up plenty of hot food as well—eggs, gammon and your favorite kippers in cream sauce."

"Bless you, lassie," he said, patting his bony midriff. "A man cannot survive on Highland malt alone."

"The marquess has an excellent malt from Dornach in his cellars," said Saybrook. "I took the liberty of having a bottle sent up along with the coffee."

"Pour me a wee tipple," said the surgeon. "Then let us go see this body of yours."

"It is *not* Sandro's body," said Arianna.

"A mere figure of speech, Lady S."

"A cold corpse laid out on a slab seems awfully real to me," she countered. "I say we ought to have some sustenance before we begin the task."

"That might not be such a wise idea, considering what we're about to do," drawled Henning.

"I've a strong stomach," she replied. "And I think better when it is full."

"A frightening thought, considering how much you consume," quipped Saybrook.

"Yes, yes, I know I have an unladylike appetite—along with a number of other shocking habits."

"*Heh, heh, heh,*" chuckled Henning. "Are we about to have one of yer verbal fencing matches? It's always entertaining when you two cross tongues."

"Sandro has already lost enough blood without suffering any cuts from me," said Arianna. "In all seriousness, we ought not waste our breath on jests. Over breakfast, we have much to tell you."

# 8

## From Lady Arianna's Chocolate Notebooks

### Whisky-Soaked Dark Chocolate Bundt Cake

*1 cup (2 sticks) unsalted butter, softened, more for greasing pan*
*2 cups all-purpose flour, more for dusting pan*
*5 ounces unsweetened chocolate*
*¼ cup instant espresso powder*
*2 tablespoons unsweetened cocoa powder*
*1 cup boiling water*
*1 cup bourbon, rye or other whisky, more for sprinkling*
*½ teaspoon kosher salt*
*2 cups granulated sugar*
*3 large eggs*
*1 tablespoon vanilla extract*
*1 teaspoon baking soda*
*Confectioners' sugar, for garnish (optional)*

1. Grease and flour a 10-cup-capacity Bundt pan (or two 8- or 9-inch loaf pans). Preheat oven to 325

degrees. In microwave oven or double boiler over simmering water, melt chocolate. Let cool.

2. Put espresso and cocoa powders in a 2-cup (or larger) glass measuring cup. Add enough boiling water to come up to the 1 cup measuring line. Mix until powders dissolve. Add whisky and salt; let cool.

3. Using an electric mixer, beat 1 cup butter until fluffy. Add sugar and beat until well combined. Beat in the eggs, one at a time, beating well between each addition. Beat in the vanilla extract, baking soda and melted chocolate, scraping down sides of bowl with a rubber spatula.

4. On low speed, beat in a third of the whisky mixture. When liquid is absorbed, beat in 1 cup flour. Repeat additions, ending with whisky mixture. Scrape batter into prepared pan and smooth top. Bake until a cake tester inserted into center of cake comes out clean, about 1 hour 10 minutes for Bundt pan (loaf pans will take less time; start checking them after 55 minutes).

5. Transfer cake to a rack. Unmold after 15 minutes and sprinkle warm cake with more whisky. Let cool before serving, garnished with confectioners' sugar if you like.

Yield: 10 to 12 servings.

∾

"**B**loody hell, that's quite a lot to digest," muttered Henning as he pushed away his empty plate. "Theft, treason, murder." Shaking his head, Henning refilled his glass with whisky. "And here I thought ye were savoring the idea of a quiet, peaceful autumn."

"I seem to stir up trouble in His Lordship's life," observed Arianna.

"A toast to Trouble," said the surgeon, raising his drink in salute. "Ye have to admit, it keeps things interesting."

"If we have finished philosophizing, perhaps we could go have a look at my erstwhile assailant." Saybrook scraped back his chair. "The body is being kept down near the kitchens—in the game room, aptly enough, though the chef is apparently not happy about it sharing the space with his dead birds and skinned rabbits."

"Why?" quipped the surgeon. "The room's sole purpose is to hang carcasses until the flesh is ripe enough to peel off the bone."

"Thank you for the graphic explanation, Baz," said Saybrook, leading the way into the servant stairwell.

"No point in mincing words, laddie."

Arianna winced at the word "mince."

As they descended in the gloom, Henning checked that the small chamois bag of surgical instruments was well hidden in his coat pocket. "We'll just have a little poke around before the formal inquest begins."

"Nothing overt," cautioned Saybrook, as he peeked out from the landing to check that the corridor was clear. "I've enough to worry about without being accused of tampering with the evidence."

"Don't worry, laddie. I'm very good at what I do."

Moving quietly, the three of them slipped past the pantries and entered a dark, stone-floored chamber, taking care to close the heavy oaken door behind them.

"Light the lanthorn," whispered Henning.

Flint scraped against steel and a curl of smoke rose through the shadows. Arianna shivered as her husband shuffled forward and shone the beam on the dead man's face. Though bronzed by the sun, the skin had turned yellowish-white. A dull sheen made it look as if the death-softened features were carved out of candle wax.

"Big fellow, eh?" grunted the surgeon. The man laid out on the slab of granite was over six feet tall. "Bring the light closer." The surgeon leaned in and plucked up the corpse's eyelid.

*"Hmmph."* Next he drew back the dead man's lips and examined his teeth. Seemingly satisfied, he brushed his fingers on the front of his coat. "Lady S, would ye take charge of the lanthorn while Sandro gives me a hand in looking at the wound."

Swallowing hard, she watched as he and Saybrook gingerly peeled back the cloth hiding the slashed throat. *Perhaps breakfast hadn't been such a good idea after all.*

*"Hmmph."* After poking and prodding at the ghastly wound, the surgeon's only remark was a curt grunt.

Setting aside his scalpel, he took off his coat and rolled up his sleeves. "Help me remove his upper garments, laddie, and let us see what else we can learn about him."

Arianna closed her eyes for a moment, finding the soft whisper of cloth against the lifeless flesh faintly obscene.

"Well, well, well. What have we here?" Henning sounded a little surprised.

Her lids flew open.

"A tattoo," confirmed Saybrook. Like Henning, he was peering intently at the dead man's bicep. "A rather distinctive one. An eagle and a crown . . ."

"It's the mark of *Les Grognards*—the Grumblers," announced the surgeon after a closer inspection.

Saybrook swore under his breath.

Looking up at Arianna, Henning quickly explained. "That's the nickname of the First Foot Grenadiers Regiment. Along with the Second Foot Regiment, they made up the Old Guard, the most elite unit of Napoleon's Grenadier Guards."

"The Guards were Napoleon's personal favorites," added Saybrook. "A man had to have served in the army for ten years and distinguished himself in battle to win a place in their ranks."

"Aye. And every detail of their service was personally approved by Boney—their pay, their uniforms, their insignias," said Henning, slanting a meaningful look at the tattoo. "They were bloody good soldiers. Tough, disciplined, and fiercely loyal to their leader."

*"Dio Madre."* Saybrook peered more closely at the intricate design. "Are you sure about this?"

"At the Battle of Salamanca, I sawed off the arms of several wounded *Grognards* captured by our regiment. So yes, laddie, I am *quite* sure."

Arianna noted a grimness tighten her husband's expression, making the hollows under his eyes look deeper. Darker. "Can we please hurry?" she asked sharply. "It would be best if we weren't found here. And Sandro needs to get some rest."

"Arianna—" growled Saybrook

"Save yer breath te cool yer porridge. Lady S is right. Ye need te keep up your strength. Grentham has already bared his teeth and will be looking to go for the jugular." Henning chafed his palms together and spoke softly to the corpse. "*Alors, monsieur*. What else can you tell me about yourself, eh?" He palpated the chest, and then took up a thin metal probe to push back the hair around the ears and check inside the canal.

"Nothing usual."

"Save for his sun-colored face and forearms, don't you think?" remarked Saybrook. "It's been a very rainy summer here in England."

"A good point, laddie." Henning pursed his lips. "Have any of the locals been asked if they recognize the fellow?"

"Yes, several in fact," replied the earl. "The ghillies helped carry the body out of the woods. None of them had ever seen him before."

*"Hmmph."* Frowning, the surgeon cleared his throat and gestured for Arianna to look away. "Avert your eyes, Lady S, while we pull down the fellow's breeches for a moment."

She arched her brows but complied. "What in God's name do you hope to discover—or dare I ask?"

The surgeon bit back a chuckle. "Best leave no stone unturned, so to speak. Ye never know—perhaps he's part of some exotic sect of Eastern eunuchs. Or boasts a second tattoo on his privy parts that points—"

"Men and their schoolboy humor," Arianna gave the lanthorn an impatient shake. "Do get on with it."

Something metallic fell to the floor. "Damn." Henning quickly bent down. "It's just a coin," he muttered, shoving it into his pocket. A few more rustling noises, punctuated by the thud of flesh upon the stone slab.

"I'm finished here," he announced, putting away his instruments and donning his coat. "Let's be off."

The earl chose to lead them through the deserted scullery and out to the back lawns. The early morning air, heavy with the scent of the mist-dampened grass and the ripening apples in the nearby orchard, helped flush the dank smell of decay from Arianna's lungs. Breathing deeply, she tipped her head up to watch a skein of dark clouds scud across the sun. A gust ruffled through the leaves and tugged at her skirts.

"Rain is blowing in," groused Henning. "The bloody roads back to London will be mired in mud."

*London.* At the moment, the city and the sanctuary of their town house seemed very far away.

Arianna fisted the folds of flapping silk and held them close to her body. "So, what do you intend to do about the letters, Sandro?" she asked. "And Charles."

"Before ye answer that," said Henning. "Allow me te voice a few questions of my own, eh?"

The earl nodded for him to go on.

"Have ye considered that mayhap Grentham has planned all this? We know that he is diabolically clever. And when you look at how this web of intrigue weaves together, it's clearly been created by a cunning spider." Henning picked a loose thread from his sleeve. "He plants one of yer uncle's documents along with incriminating evidence of a traitorous plot, turning suspicion on your family while he continues to hand over secrets to England's enemy. Taking a shot at you only raises further questions about why someone would want you dead."

"You are forgetting that Rochemont may well have been the target," countered the earl. "That a *Grognard*—"

Henning cut him off with an impatient wave. "I grant you, it's possible that one of Napoleon's former officials has a grudge against Rochemont. He's one of the leading Royalists, and by all accounts has made a number of enemies with his arrogance. Not to speak of his flagrant dalliances. But bear with me for now, and let us stay focused on Grentham for the nonce."

"Very well," agreed Saybrook. "Your theory is interesting, and it's certainly devious enough for the minister's mind. But I don't really think it's plausible. There is no way he could know Arianna would buy that book. It was pure chance."

"It's known that you make regular purchases at that rare book emporium," countered Henning. "And how many rich aristocrats have an interest in chocolate?"

The earl didn't answer.

"You still think that Grentham may be conniving with the French?" Arianna made a face. In their previous confrontation with the minister, they had reason to wonder whether he was corrupt to the core. "I thought we had answered the questions concerning his integrity."

"As you have pointed out in the past, lassie, a smart criminal makes sure that his underlings never know the real truth about his involvement." Henning paused. "We have only Grentham's word that he was innocent of any wrongdoing. And that I take with a grain of salt."

She shivered in spite of the sunlight. "So you think the hidden papers may be a trap?"

"I don't think ye were meant te find them yerself. My guess is Grentham's plan would be to arrive at your town house with his lackeys from Horse Guards, and then make a show of discovering the hidden documents in the book. Catching you red-handed, as it were, would be a very clever ploy." The surgeon snapped his fingers. "*Voila!* The government would be convinced that the French threat is eliminated, leaving him free to play his filthy games. At the same time, the minister also gets his personal revenge on you for ruining his previous plan."

"Perhaps you ought to take up novel writing," said Saybrook drily. "You have a very vivid imagination."

"Which has saved our necks on more than one occasion," retorted Henning. "Look, as I was waiting in the side parlor for the footman to send you word of my arrival, I overheard the minister and his secretary as they were passing through the corridor. He mentioned you by name and said, 'The writing is on the wall.' "

"That is a common turn of speech," Saybrook pointed out. "I think you are reading too much into it. Don't forget, Grentham saw me crouched over a dead body, holding a knife." He fixed his friend with a level gaze. "I know your feelings about figures of authority, especially ones who are charged with keeping order." As a Scotsman, Henning was all too familiar with England's iron-fisted tactics of repressing dissent. "Take care that your loathing doesn't color your judgment."

The surgeon scowled. "My scenario may sound farfetched, but the fact is, we all know Grentham bitterly resents you for solving a mystery that stymied him," Henning retorted. "You showed yourselves to be very, very clever—and that may have him worried. If there is a highly placed traitor in the government, I say he is the most likely suspect."

"I can't help but wonder, Sandro . . ." Arianna could no longer keep from asking a question that had been bothering her for some time. "Mr. Henning makes a good point. If Grentham is not a traitor, the depth of his enmity is hard to fathom. Granted, we did not allow him to control us during the previous investigation, but in the end, we saved him from a great deal of public embarrassment."

The alteration of Saybrook's face was almost imperceptible. His expression didn't change—it simply hardened just enough to appear as if it were carved out of stone.

Ignoring the oblique warning to retreat, she pressed on. "Is there a reason I don't know about as to why the two of you dislike each other so intensely?"

"Yes," he replied curtly.

Arianna waited for him to go on.

"But at the moment, I don't care to discuss it. The details aren't really relevant."

His refusal hurt more than she cared to admit.

"Far more important are the questions concerning Charles and the incriminating documents."

"If the decision of how to deal with the damn papers were mine, I know what I would do," said Henning.

Metal rasped against metal as a gust of wind swung the lanthorn in her hand.

"Like Lady S, I'd be tempted to fight fire with fire, and turn them into ashes." The surgeon slanted a challenging look at Saybrook. "But then, my morals have always been a trifle more flexible than yours."

"And if they aren't a trap?" asked the earl.

"Auch, well, then I suppose the trouble is very real," conceded Henning.

"Trouble," repeated Arianna.

Saybrook appeared to be staring at some far-off spot on the heathered moors. His brow suddenly creased, and with a muttered oath, he turned abruptly, gravel crunching under his boots. "I must return to our rooms. I've just had an idea."


Arianna took yet another turn around the perimeter of the sitting room, taking great care to step as lightly as she could in order not to wake Henning, who was dozing on the sofa. Rain drummed against the windowpanes, echoing her inner turmoil. *Truth and lies.* Henning's cynical suggestions concerning their present predicament had stirred her own imagination to life. A pelter of possible explanations were spinning inside her head—none of them good.

*Did I push Grentham over the edge?*

Guilt nibbled at the edges of her consciousness. In the past, her temper and her tongue hadn't been cause for concern. She had been willing to suffer the consequences of her actions. But now, her decisions were no longer so simple. Like a stone striking water, they sent waves rippling out far from the original point of impact.

Which stirred an even more unsettling ripple in her head.

*Had marriage been an impetuous mistake?* The thought had been niggling at her for some time now. Having experienced the unfettered freedom of a vagabond nobody, she would never be entirely happy living within the gilded cage of aristocratic London. But she couldn't simply unlatch the door and fly away. She had obligations. Commitments. Responsibilities.

*Damn. Damn. Damn.*

Looking away from the gloom outside the glass, Arianna stared at the closed door of her husband's bedchamber. Not that Saybrook had any taste for the superficial glitter and glamour of Polite Society. He too seemed happier in his own private world.

A growl of thunder rumbled over the distant moors.

"Eh?" Henning opened an eye. "Did ye say something, Lady S?"

"The storm seems to be gathering force," she murmured. "I shall send down a request for a room to be made up for you tonight. I'll not have you traveling in such nasty weather."

The surgeon rubbed at his bristly chin. "I fear the atmosphere here may become even nastier."

She heaved a sigh. "You think I should have destroyed the documents?"

He shook his head. "Auch, let's not piss in that pot, lassie."

"Aye, hold your water, everyone." Saybrook emerged from his room and padded across the carpet, a sheaf of papers in his hands.

"Any luck?" asked Henning.

"Aye," replied the earl with grim satisfaction. "Luck, Chance, Fate—whatever you wish to call the fickle force, it has worked in our favor today."

In spite of her misgivings, Arianna felt a spark of excitement. "You mean to say you actually deciphered the code?"

"Aye," he repeated. "As I told you, intuition plays a key role in the process. Baz's discovery of the military tattoo and his mention of the Grenadiers at Salamanca got me to thinking. It seemed worth a try to test some of the basic ciphers used by Soult's forces during the last campaigns of the Peninsular War. I figured that a French operative would be familiar with that system, and likely to adopt it for his own use. After all, he had to train others, and coming up with a whole new system is no easy task."

"Clever lad." Henning swung his legs off the sofa, making room for the earl and Arianna.

"Unfortunately, cleverness is a two-edged sword." Saybrook sat down and dragged the tea table around for his papers. He spread them out, then traced a finger over the lines of jumbled lettering. "The encrypted message indicates that the person responsible for stealing the government document from my uncle's files is the young man he has been mentoring for the past several years."

Arianna felt her throat tighten. "David Kydd? The young man from Scotland?"

He nodded.

"But he seems so . . ."

"Incapable of betrayal?" suggested Saybrook grimly.

She stared down at her hands, recalling her encounters with the young diplomat at several of Mellon's soirees. Unlike many of the junior members of the Foreign Ministry, who seemed to think that being bland and boring was a virtue, Kydd had not been afraid to express his individuality. He was earnest, intelligent, articulate, and yet possessed a sly sense of humor. *Character and conviction.* No wonder he had been the only person she had actually enjoyed conversing with during the long and tedious evenings.

"To me, he appeared to be a man of lofty principles," Arianna finally answered. "His ideas and enthusiasms were interesting. And I got the impression that he admired Charles very much."

"Appearances can be deceiving," said Saybrook, echoing one of Henning's favorite sayings.

The surgeon grimaced. "You took the words right out of my mouth."

"*Merde,*" muttered Arianna.

"You too."

Saybrook quirked a humorless smile. "It is indeed a cesspool, and a foul one at that." Just as quickly, his expression tightened. "For along with passing on the details of Mellon's activities, Kydd also included a brief update on a meeting he had with a coconspirator. It says"—the earl picked up one of his note papers and read—"'*Met with R and all is going according to schedule. I've been appointed to the English delegation and our contact in Sx is also in place. Expect me in V by October. By the last week in November, the Deux will be dead. It will happen by the Night.*'"

He let the paper drop back onto the table, as if unwilling to soil his hand with it a moment longer than was necessary.

"R for Renard?" Arianna asked.

Her husband shrugged. "As we said before, it's possible. But we ought to be careful about making such an assumption." He looked at Henning. "Baz might say Grentham is merely being extra diabolical in eliminating my uncle's protégé."

The surgeon made a face. Shifting on the sofa, he shoved his hands in his pockets, then took them out again. "Aye. It's possible," he grumbled, fiddling with the coin he had picked up earlier. "It's . . ." His voice stopped abruptly as he stared at the markings on the coin. "Bloody hell."

"What?" demanded Saybrook.

"It's an old Scottish *Punnd Sasannach*," he said tersely. "One doesn't often see them here in the South."

"Unless . . ." The earl pursed his lips in thought. "Unless one has been paid by someone from the North."

Henning looked as if he wanted to protest but kept quiet.

"It could be coincidence of course," Saybrook went on.

"But Kydd is Scottish, and that he and our *Grognard* have something in common makes me even more inclined to think this is not a trap designed by Grentham."

A noncommittal grunt was the only sound from the surgeon.

Silence gripped the room for an uneasy interlude until the earl dispelled it with a shrug. "But forgetting Grentham for the moment, let us get back to the coded message and its meaning." Looking down at the paper, he reread the message aloud.

"V . . . 'In V,'" mused Arianna, quick to take up the challenge. "It sounds like a place—"

"Vienna," interrupted Henning. "Given the document stolen from your uncle's office, V has to mean Vienna."

The earl nodded.

"So the message seems to indicate that a murder is planned to take place at the Peace Congress in Vienna," the surgeon went on. He made a face. "But who, or why? '*The Deux will be dead. It will happen by the Night*' is hardly a helpful hint."

"A good question. And as yet, we haven't a damn clue." Saybrook paused. "Though 'Deux' in French means two, so maybe it's a double murder."

"*Dio Madre,*" murmured Arianna.

"Or it's simply a code name for the target," pointed out Henning. "Or one of a thousand other possibilities."

"A million," corrected Saybrook glumly. Leaning back from the table, he threaded a hand through his tangled hair. "The second note is penned in a different hand and uses a different code, one that looks to be more difficult. As of yet, I've made no headway on it."

"Ye have worked bloody miracles making sense of this," said the surgeon. "How your mind sees aught but gibberish is beyond me."

"Patterns, relationships . . ." The earl began to drum his fingers upon the table. "Kydd was educated at King's College, Cambridge," he continued after a pensive pause. "And everyone there agreed that despite his humble origins, he appeared to have a brilliant future in front of him. But it seems his background needs further scrutiny." His gaze slanted to the surgeon. "He is from Edinburgh, Baz."

Henning evaded eye contact, a troubled expression pinching at his features.

"So I am wondering—have you friends there who might do a little digging into Kydd's personal life? Most people have something to hide."

"Blackmail is the first thing that comes to my mind," offered Arianna. "A family scandal, perhaps? Or a gambling debt?"

Silence hung in the air for a long moment. The surgeon shifted and scratched at his chin before expelling an audible sigh. "Not necessarily. Seeing as he is Scottish, the first thing I would look at are his politics, lassie."

"But why?" she asked, perplexed by the suggestion. "Why would he betray England to the French?"

"Because you English—and your monarchy—are hated by a good many Scots," replied Henning bluntly. "The republican principles trumpeted by the French after their Revolution—*liberté, égalité, fraternité*—appeal to idealistic young men who believe that merit, not birth, ought to allow for advancement in Society."

"Regardless of sex," added Arianna under her breath.

"I am in complete sympathy with Mrs. Wollstonecraft and her manifesto for feminine equality," said the surgeon. "But alas, in that regard, you will find the Scots just as conservative as the English."

"Hypocrites."

Saybrook's lips quirked, but he quickly steered the conversation back to Kydd. "You think he might be a member of a secret political society?" Scotland was known to be a hotbed of radical idealism, especially among the university students.

Henning hesitated before answering. "Many bright, educated men are. And I can't say I blame them."

"If you would rather not get involved..." began the earl.

"I didna say that," shot back Henning. "Ye know where my loyalties lie."

"I do. I also know where your heart lies. I would rather not ask you to choose between the two."

"There is a difference between theory and reality. While I believe in a good many radical ideas, I think fanatics of any cause are dangerous. Fomenting change through violence and bloodshed is not something I espouse."

Saybrook held his friend's gaze for a long moment, and then looked away.

Arianna was loath to break the bond of silent camaraderie, but she couldn't help asking. "Wait—Napoleon has been banished to the isle of Elba and the monarchy has been restored to France. So while Kydd may have sympathized with the Republican ideals, why would his allegiance be to the new King?"

Henning blew out his cheeks. "It's not love of the French; it's about hate of the English. Many young, educated Scots feel that any enemy of England is a friend of theirs. They believe that working to weaken the British government will help further their own goals."

His voice tightened. "On my last visit north, I spent time with a cousin who blistered my ear with his radical ideas. Whitehall ought to be listening carefully—else it might find the bloody conflict isn't over just because Boney's been banished to some speck of rock in the Mediterranean."

"I agree with you," said the earl tersely. "But for now, let us stay focused on this particular powder keg. Arianna raises a very good point about France, and the spy we call Renard. During our previous encounter, there was little question that he was working for Napoleon. But now, the Emperor is gone, and the *Ancien Régime* has been returned to power. Which begs yet another round of whos and whys."

Saybrook pursed his lips and thought for several moments. "My work in military intelligence has taught me that in order to solve a conundrum, one must work with both fact and conjecture. I know that security in my uncle's office is very strict—there are guards, and special locks for sensitive documents. So I think it's fair to assume Kydd took the documents."

Arianna and Henning nodded.

"I also think it's fair to say he's not working alone. The documents indicate a complex plot that likely is based in Vienna. Again, it's a rational deduction, given the important Peace Conference scheduled to begin next month."

He paused before continuing his thought. "It's my conjecture that a group of Scottish radicals don't have the connections to put something like that together. It would take a more powerful network. Which is why I come back to Renard. We know that he is capable of weaving a sophisticated web of betrayal." The earl paused. "For now, logic dictates that he is the obvious suspect. And yet, it begs the question of who he is working for. And why he is still intent on sabotaging our dealings with the European powers."

Henning didn't hesitate in answering. "Not everyone is as principled as you, laddie. Renard probably doesn't give a fig for whose hand holds the ruling scepter. He's either loyal to his *terroir*—the sacred mother earth of France—in which case he sees England as his natural enemy." The surgeon picked up his near-empty whisky tumbler and spun it between his palms. "Or he's being paid obscenely well for his work."

Arianna watched as the few remaining drops in the glass blurred to a blink of gold.

"Look at Talleyrand, for God's sake." Henning gave a sardonic grunt. "He changes masters as easily as he changes his fancy silk stockings." Charles Maurice de Talleyrand-Périgord, the current French Foreign Minister, was known for dressing in the elaborate old style of the previous century—velvet breeches, starched satin cravats and jeweled shoes, topped off by a powdered wig. "He's served Louis XVI, the radical Revolutionaries, the Directoire, Napoleon, and now the newly restored King."   •

"Really?" asked Arianna.

"You don't know his history, lassie?"

She shook her head. "Remember, I grew up in the West

Indies." After the murder of her father, she had fought a tooth-and-nail struggle every day simply in order to survive. "I didn't have the luxury of studying the nuances of European politics."

Hidden by the shadow of his lashes, Saybrook's eyes were unreadable. "Like you, my dear, Talleyrand had an uncanny knack for survival," he murmured. "Though born into one of the noblest families of France, he somehow managed to keep his neck intact when so many other aristocratic heads were rolling."

"No doubt because he is willing to do a deal with Satan if it suits his purpose." Henning made a face. "He's an unprincipled rogue, a self-serving opportunist. Why, in France, he's called le *Diable Boiteux*—the lame devil, and not just on account of his deformed foot. It's well known he betrayed Napoleon's secrets to the Russians and the Austrians in '08."

She frowned.

"Claiming that he had become disillusioned with the Emperor's unrelenting wars," Saybrook pointed out.

The surgeon made a rude sound.

The talk of international intrigue was making Arianna's head spin. *Was the world naught but ever-twining concentric circles of lies and betrayals?*

"Let me see if I understand what you've both just said," she said slowly. "It seems we've now established that no matter who he works for, Renard is a threat to England. But why assume that he is in league with Talleyrand?"

"You are right—it's pure speculation. But there is solid reason on which to base it. Talleyrand is a master conniver. Although he represents the newly restored French King at the Peace Conference, you can be sure that he will be working on pushing his own personal agenda," said Saybrook. "And God only knows what that is."

"If Talleyrand means to deceive yet another master, then the presence of a Royalist minion like Rochemont in Vienna might be a nuisance," Henning observed. "How-

ever, as you say, all this is mere conjecture. At this point, we
are merely spinning in circles."

"Which brings us back to the question of Charles," said
Arianna reluctantly.

Her husband seemed to retreat even deeper into his
personal shadows.

"Are you going to tell him that Kydd has betrayed his
trust? Or do you mean to keep him in the dark?"

Henning seemed intent on playing the devil's advocate.
"*If* there has been a betrayal, I'll allow that what we've
come up with makes the most sense. However, I still say it's
not impossible that Grentham has orchestrated all of this.
He knows Kydd is your uncle's protégé. Perhaps the young
man is being sacrificed along with Mellon. The minister
may well view them as mere pawns, to be swept aside in
order to put Sandro in checkmate."

"That would require a cold-blooded ruthlessness rival-
ing that of Attila the Hun," remarked Saybrook.

"You think Grentham is all sweetness and light?" asked
Henning sarcastically.

"No." Saybrook began to sketch a doodle on his notepa-
per. "But nor do I think he is a twisted monster who has
become obsessed with personal vengeance."

Henning's response was a bristly silence.

"Be it an elaborate trap or a carefully constructed plan
to destroy England's political power, whoever has designed
this diabolical plan is an enemy we all should fear," said
Arianna.

Her gaze fell on the earl's paper, where his pencil was
just finishing the outlines of a fox. "Is it Grentham or Renard?" she went on. "I don't know, but it's my opinion that
whoever it is, we've already faced off against him once, and
were lucky to escape with our lives."

The surgeon waited for Saybrook to speak, but his only
reaction was to start another drawing. This one was of a
serpent.

"Grentham or Renard," repeated Henning. "Choose

your poison." A scowl pinched at his features. "If it's not our minister, I would wager it's Talleyrand who is behind this—there's a good reason Napoleon now calls him shite in silk stockings."

"I would tend to agree," said Saybrook, still intent on his artwork. He lapsed into a long moment of thought, drawing in a wicked set of curving fangs before going on.

"And it makes some sense when you think about the would-be assassin. My guess would be that the French Guardsman was simply a starving ex-soldier, hired because of his elite credentials to kill or wound me so that the conspirators could get the book back."

Arianna looked at Henning, waiting for his reaction.

"Or, much as we both give little credence to the concept, it could be coincidence," the earl went on. "The shooting may have been arranged by a jealous husband who has been cuckolded by Rochemont."

*"Dio Madre!"* exclaimed Arianna. "We could keep turning in circles, tying ourselves in knots. But the fact is, we can't afford to do that. We must decide on a direction and move forward."

"A pragmatic assessment, Lady S." The surgeon cocked his head. "So, laddie, what do you intend to do?"

*Choices. Choices.*

Arianna shot an involuntary glance at the coals in the hearth.

Saybrook finally looked up. "I plan to take the documents and what I have learned from them to the proper authorities."

"You are sure about this?"

"I don't see that I have the luxury of pondering over the choice of moral imperatives. The clock is ticking and we are in a race to see that the newly won peace in Europe doesn't explode in our faces."

# 9

## From Lady Arianna's Chocolate Notebooks

### Cranberry Chocolate Scones

1½ cups buttermilk
1 extra-large egg
1 teaspoon pure vanilla extract, preferably Madagascar Bourbon or Tahitian
3½ cups all-purpose flour
2 teaspoons baking powder
1 teaspoon baking soda
5 tablespoons granulated sugar
½ teaspoon kosher salt
1 teaspoon orange zest, about 2 oranges
½ cup unsalted butter, very cold and cubed
⅓ cup 65% chocolate, coarsely chopped
⅓ cup dried cranberries
¼ cup heavy whipping cream (used for brushing tops of scones)

1. Preheat the oven to 350° F.
2. Line the bottoms of two 12-by-18-inch sheet pans with parchment paper.

3. Combine the buttermilk, egg and vanilla extract in a medium bowl and whisk by hand until well mixed.

4. Sift the flour, baking powder and baking soda into the bowl of a stand mixer fitted with paddle attachment. Add the sugar, salt and orange zest. Beat on low speed until combined.

5. Carefully add the cold butter and beat on medium speed until the mixture resembles coarse meal.

6. Switch the mixer to low speed. Add the liquid mixture and beat until just combined.

7. Turn the mixer off. Add the cranberries and chocolate. Pulse until just incorporated. Do not overmix.

8. Turn dough out onto a lightly floured work surface, and press it into a flat square about ¾ inch thick. Cut into 2-inch squares and place onto the prepared pans, spacing them about 2 inches apart.

9. Brush the scones with heavy whipping cream. Bake on the middle shelves of the oven until the tops are golden and have a little spring when pressed with a fingertip, about 20 minutes.

10. Serve warm or let cool on the pans on wire racks.

"This way, Lord and Lady Saybrook." The footman escorted them through a set of double doors and down a vaulted corridor. "The minister is waiting for you in the library."

Arianna hung back a step, allowing Saybrook to enter the room first. She would allow the rituals of protocol and privilege to take precedence for now.

*Though only the Devil knows why.* The meeting was not likely to remain polite for very long.

Grentham had positioned himself in front of the soaring bank of diamond-paned windows. The storm had blown through and a watery light limned his elegantly attired figure, the glints of sunshine flashing like liquid silver through his carefully combed hair.

*Dear God—the man could probably contrive to cut out my liver without putting a crease in his coat.*

Hip perched on a display table, he watched them approach. It was hard to make out his features at first, but as she came closer, Arianna saw that he was looking supremely smug, as if anticipating that they had come to beg for mercy.

"You seem to have suffered no permanent injury to your shoulder," sneered Grentham. "Have you come to confess your crime in hope that I will help you save your neck?"

"If ever I was in need of help, I would know better than to seek it from you," replied Saybrook. "Though I daresay you do owe me a favor. As I recall, it was my wife and I who stepped in to pull your cods out of the fire."

A faint flush of color crept over the minister's cheekbones. "I'm assuming you didn't summon me here to exchange pleasantries, Lord Saybrook." So far he had studiously avoided acknowledging her presence. "Kindly get to the point of this meeting. I dislike wasting my time."

"I shall try not to bore you," said Saybrook, opening his notebook.

Grentham frowned slightly at the sound of crackling papers.

"Read this." The earl handed him the first coded sheet, along with the deciphered message. When Grentham looked up from the page, Saybrook handed him the second coded letter. The document from the Foreign Ministry he saved for last.

"Where did you get these?" demanded the minister.

"I shall allow my wife to explain," said Saybrook. He stepped back and crossed his arms.

"I shall try to keep it short." Arianna took the volume of engravings from under her arm. "I found this book on chocolate in the back rooms of Harvey & Watkins—"

"Is this some sort of jest?" demanded Grentham.

Ignoring the comment, she went on to tell of the stranger who tried to wrest the book from her grasp and the ensuing scuffle.

"Did the clerk at Harvey & Watkins witness this conflict?" interrupted Grentham.

"Not the actual blows. His arrival scared my assailant away," replied Arianna.

"I fail to see—"

"Allow me to finish, sir!"

Grentham snapped his jaw shut.

As quickly as she could, Arianna explained about her second encounter with Davilenko at the house party's welcoming reception and her accidental discovery of the papers hidden in the book's binding. "Given my husband's experience in military intelligence, he spent the night working on deciphering the codes. Which," she added with a note of triumph, "against all odds, he succeeded in doing with the first one."

The minister slowly read through the papers again. "This confidential document from the Foreign Ministry bears your uncle's signature," he said to Saybrook. "You know that, don't you?"

"Yes," replied the earl curtly.

Returning his attention to her, Grentham speared Arianna with a nasty look. "You discovered these yesterday?"

"Yes," she replied.

He pounced on her admission. "Then why didn't you bring them to me right away?"

Arianna assumed a pious expression. "My husband was shot, sir. He was feverish all night, and in no condition to discuss the matter. It was not my place to make any decision without his consent."

The minister's face went through a series of odd little contortions. If it hadn't been Grentham, she would have thought he was trying not to laugh.

"Quite right, my dear." Saybrook made no attempt to mask an insolent grin. "I'm sure His Lordship can find no fault with such proper wifely deference."

As the minister was fully aware of her utter disregard for the rules of Society, he couldn't help but know the comment was meant as a taunt, a slap in the face.

She slanted a silent warning at her husband. There was no point in goading Grentham to go for their throats. Not when he was already frothing at the mouth.

Saybrook paid no heed to her glance. "It appears you still haven't found your French traitor."

"Haven't I?" retorted Grentham, a malicious gleam flashing to life in his eyes. "A confidential government paper from Mellon's file, your wife observed in a clandestine meeting with a spy in the book shop—not to speak of her shady past." His mouth curled up in a cold smile. "Yes, I can easily imagine the newspaper story, can't you? Like father, like daughter—a lying, scheming cheat. Willing to betray all notions of honor for money."

Arianna held her breath.

"A public trial could send her to the gallows for treason. As for your reputation, Lord Saybrook, and that of your charming young sister . . ." He shrugged, and then added in a lower voice, "Then there's the case of the murdered man, with a number of witnesses who saw you with a knife. One could reasonably suspect that you were desperately trying to cover up your wife's betrayal."

Saybrook's response was a bark of laughter, though Arianna had noted a tiny flicker in his eyes at the mention of Antonia. "And what of *your* reputation, Grentham? A bumbling fool who can't sniff treason when it's right under his nose? By all means, make that public. We shall see who suffers most from the revelation that the dead man is one of Napoleon's elite Grenadier Guards."

Grentham stiffened.

"Ah, hadn't your lackeys gotten around to discovering that?" said Saybrook. "It appears Henning was far more thorough in his examination of the body." He too used a pause for dramatic effect. "Your experts will find it hard to deny that a serrated knife, and not my blade, cut the Frenchman's throat."

The minister's nostrils flared as he drew in soundless breath.

The tall carved bookcases, lined with heavy leather-bound volumes, seemed to muffle any ambient noise. The silence was deafening.

A draught finally caught the edge of the papers, stirring a tiny flutter. The whisper broke the tension.

"I'm willing to be magnanimous," said Grentham slowly. Saybrook made a rude sound.

"I shall offer you a way to avoid scandal." He stood and brushed an imaginary wrinkle from his trousers. "Go to the Peace Conference in Vienna and unmask this traitor—assuming he exists—once and for all. If you do, the personal transgressions of your family will remain our little secret."

*"Vienna?"* Surprise shaded the earl's voice. He considered the suggestion for a moment and then shook his head. "Subject myself and my wife to the rigors of traveling through a war-ravaged continent, only to dance through a gilded maze of intrigue and skullduggery? I think not."

"You would rather destroy your family?" demanded Grentham harshly. "It would, you know, no matter whether you are innocent."

"You know the truth, and yet would let the real enemy go free in order to persecute me?" retorted Saybrook. "Sod you. Go public and be damned." His mouth curled in contempt. "I wouldn't have thought you would sink so low as to allow a purely private, petty grudge to take precedence over the good of the country, Grentham. But be that as it may, we shall see who suffers most."

The minister looked torn between the desire for revenge and the commitment to duty.

*Ah, I know how you feel,* thought Arianna wryly.

"You would dare to challenge me?" snarled Grentham.

"We would both come away from a duel bloodied—but as to who would suffer a mortal wound . . . well, if I were you, I would not be so sure of your muscle. You have made a good many enemies who would be only too happy to see your entrails fed to the Tower ravens."

It was not just the glitter of malice that caught her eye. The flash of molten anger could not quite hide a glimmer of something else.

"Enough!" she suddenly exclaimed. "The two of you sound like snotty-nosed schoolboys who think they can prove their manhood by scrabbling in the mud."

Saybrook and Grentham fell mute.

"Go ahead and bloody each other's noses if it will make you feel happy. But it's clear to me what is going on."

Her husband drew his dark brows together.

"Lord Grentham needs our help, but he is too proud to ask." Locking eyes with the minister, Arianna moved to the table and set the book down next to the documents, forcing him to turn ever so slightly. "It sticks in his craw to admit that we are the only ones he can really trust to take on such a difficult endeavor. As you pointed out, Sandro, his department is likely harboring a very clever spy. I don't think Mellon's aide Kydd is the mastermind. He's been recruited by someone else. The question is who. And the problem is, the minister cannot give an answer."

Grentham had gone white around the mouth during her speech. Now he looked at her with pure loathing.

*Oh, I've been given the evil eye by far more duplicitous bastards than you, milord.* Summoning a careless shrug, she went on, "So, much as he hates it, his best chance of catching the culprit is by enlisting us to do his dirty work. Once again, I might add."

Saybrook nodded slowly. "As you see, Grentham, my wife is an uncanny judge of human nature. She sees things that others miss."

The minister answered obliquely, which in itself was an admission that she had hit on the truth. "I don't give a rat's arse if she can scry the future in a crystal ball. Will you go to Vienna?" he demanded curtly.

Saybrook didn't reply right away.

*Vienna.* Common sense warned against doing another deal with the Devil. But on impulse, Arianna decided to throw caution to the wind. Not out of any love for Grentham. The truth was, she had always wanted to see the city's fabled sights. As a little girl, she had spent hours curled in her father's lap as he had regaled her with tales about Europe's most romantic cities. Vienna—the crossroads of East and West. A melting pot of cultures, with rich history, exotic splendors . . . and sumptuous cuisine.

"The Emperor of Austria is very interested in science, and is said to have one of the most magnificent collection of botanical books in the world," she pointed out. "I am sure it would have some unique treasures concerning chocolate, given his country's historic ties to Spain."

The earl's scowl lessened a fraction.

"And our desire to see the collection would provide a perfect cover for a trip to the city. It's known throughout the *ton* that you are working on a book, and my interest in chocolate recipes is no secret either. We are considered odd. Unconventional and uninterested in the usual jockeying for power and privilege. So it will be easy to appear detached from all the political intrigue." In the reflection of the leaded glass, she saw that both men were watching her intently. "And yet your title and pedigree will assure that we are invited to dance attendance on the parties surrounding the Conference. Which would allow us to pursue our own agenda—that of catching the traitor and stopping whatever murder is planned."

Saybrook looked thoughtful. "An interesting suggestion."

The minister maintained a stony face, but a telltale pulse of flesh, just a hairsbreadth above his starched shirt point, betrayed his inner emotions.

*Yes or no.* The final decision was up to Saybrook.

"There is, of course, the question of the murder here." The earl met Grentham's gaze. "For which I am under suspicion."

"As you have pointed out, the evidence of the knife

wound seems to indicate your innocence," replied the minister tightly. "The inquest will no doubt return a verdict of assailant unknown."

"Very well," announced Saybrook after a long moment. "Seeing as you are in danger of making a royal cock-up of this business, we'll go and do your department's work for you, Grentham." His voice turned slightly mocking. "But let us not make a habit of it."

As the minister took a moment to square the documents, he speared Arianna with yet another daggered look.

Arianna felt a quiver of outrage. Rather than mentally cutting up her vital organs, the ungrateful lout ought to be expressing his gratitude. "You might say thank you," she muttered.

Grentham ignored the sarcasm. "We have no time to waste in formulating a plan."

"Starting with the documents." Saybrook folded his arms across his chest. "What do you suggest we do with them?"

"Why, copy them and put the originals back in the book," answered Grentham without hesitation. He was in command of himself, any hint of emotion banished by the intensity of crafting a trap for the enemy. She felt a twinge of unwilling admiration for a man who could so be single-minded in his purpose.

Life as a hunter. But surely the chase must grow tiring at times.

"Dare I hope that your wife managed to extract them without doing too much damage to the marbled papers?"

Thrusting aside her musings, Arianna smiled sweetly. "I am very good with a knife."

"Excellent. Let us hope your skills with a glue pot are equally sharp." He gestured at the cabinets built into the far wall. "I would imagine there are some bookbinding supplies here. Find what you need and smuggle the items back to your rooms—I need not remind you that secrecy is of the utmost importance."

"As you so kindly pointed out, sir, I am no stranger to

scheming," replied Arianna, any feelings of sympathy for the minister quickly dispelled by his insufferable arrogance. "It goes without saying that Davilenko must think he has outwitted us by getting his hands on the book."

"In this case, truth will serve our purpose well," said Saybrook. "I shall make a show of displaying the gift that my wife chose to celebrate my birthday. It will be easy enough to leave it lying around in one of the parlors."

"You think he'll take the bait?" asked Arianna.

"He has no reason to think that we know anything about the hidden documents," said Saybrook. "If I were him, I'd seize the opportunity to recover them. There's a good chance he has not yet admitted his initial failure to his contact—conspirators are very unforgiving of any mistakes—so my guess is that the plot will proceed as planned."

"Let us hope so," said Grentham brusquely. "For your sake."

"And for yours," countered Saybrook. "If I were you, I would not forget about the murdered stranger. Does not the fact that a former French Grenadier took dead aim at me set off any alarm bells?"

Grentham laughed softly. "Indeed, it's quite alarming to learn that Imperial Guards are such terrible shots."

Arianna muttered something in Creole that wiped the smile off his face.

"There are legions of half-starved former soldiers roaming the streets, both here and across the Channel," added the minister. "And most are willing to commit violence for a handful of coins. Perhaps someone doesn't like you."

"I can, of course, think of a few." They stared at each other, and the space between them seemed to crackle with invisible sparks. "But if I were you, I wouldn't be satisfied with such a glib answer."

Arianna could no longer keep quiet. Gesturing at one of the study tables, where a sheaf of fresh paper and several sharpened pencils lay on the blotter, she said, "Shall I draw you a diagram, milord? An unknown French operative loose in your department, a *Grognard* assassin." She sketched an imaginary line through the air. "Even a lackwit can see that they are likely connected. The question is, was the soldier aiming at my husband, or was he hired to shoot Rochemont. It would help our investigation immensely to know the answer to that question."

She paused, aware that her heart was drumming angrily against her ribs. All the talk had exacerbated her frustrations. She much preferred action to endless debate. "Surely your minions can manage to track down the truth while we occupy ourselves with the other conundrums. I am assuming that your resources are more extensive than ours—though quantity does not, of course, mean quality."

"Be advised that you rouse my wife's ire at your own peril. As you know, she doesn't suffer fools gladly." Saybrook's mouth twitched. "So, Grentham, are you going to pursue that lead?"

"No," answered the minister with a sneer. "As I said, I shall see that the coroner's inquiry rules death by unknown assailant, so you need not fear for your own neck. As to how and why the Frenchman came to have his throat cut, I'm leaving it to you and your motley Scottish sawbones to figure it out."

"Your confidence in our abilities quite takes my breath away," said the earl.

The minister dismissed the comment with an impatient flick of his hand. "Your uncle must also be dealt with."

"What would you suggest?" asked Saybrook warily.

"That you tell him nothing," replied Grentham decisively. "Mellon must not betray any hint that Kydd is under suspicion. Keeping him in ignorance is the best way to assure he does not make a slip."

Saybrook gave a grudging a nod. "On that, at least, we are in agreement. He has no experience in subterfuge."

"As opposed to the two of you." Grentham was clearly savoring the chance to reseize the offensive.

"We shall have to come up with an excuse for leaving here early," mused Arianna. "One that won't rouse his suspicion that anything is wrong."

"On the contrary, Lady Saybrook. You must not rush off in a pelter," replied the minister. "It's imperative that Davilenko have no reason to be alarmed either. And don't forget, your husband will have to appear at the inquest to give testimony on the circumstances of finding the body." The flash of teeth was not meant as an encouraging smile. "You can accomplish nothing in Austria until Kydd and the English delegation arrive, so use your time here to be sociable—spread word that all the talk of Vienna has sparked an interest to see the Emperor's library."

An astute suggestion, conceded Arianna.

"Once in Vienna, you will, of course, need to draw on your full arsenal of sordid skills," Grentham went on. "I suggest that you, Lord Saybrook, handle the mundane surveillance and the searching for evidence." The scudding sunlight lit hot and cold flickers of silver in his gray eyes. "While you, Lady Saybrook would be best used . . ."

Tapping a finger to chin, he pursed his lips. "Let me think . . . Ah, of course. You would be best in putting your God-given talents to work in seducing every last little intimate secret from Kydd. As I recall, you have no trouble making yourself comfortable among *Chlorella vulgaris.*"

A warning growl rumbled deep in Saybrook's throat.

"Yes, I studied a bit of botany too—enough to know the Latin name for pond scum," said Grentham nastily. Returning his attention to her, he continued. "Or perhaps your husband is afraid that your loyalties might not be as strong as they should be. After all, yours was a marriage of mere convenience—convenience for you, that is. As I see it, the earl has not profited by much, other than a warm body in his bed." A pause. "Or do you not sleep together?"

"Why not ask your spies?" said Arianna coolly, willing her blood to keep from coming to a boil. "I am sure they have been crawling like rats along the roof slates and window ledges of our town house."

Grentham began gathering up the papers and carefully folding them along their original creases. "My informants need not go to great lengths to gather quite a bit of interesting information about your habits. Take, for example, the rather attractive woman that the earl meets with every Thursday afternoon for several hours."

Arianna blinked.

"Oh, come, Grentham. If you are looking to dig up dirt on me, you had better tell your lackeys to use a shovel and not a teaspoon," drawled Saybrook. "Do you really think you have shocked my wife?"

*No, it's not a shock,* thought Arianna. *Merely a ... surprise.*

In an instant, the minister's spiteful sneer turned a little tenuous. But he covered it by taking up his dove-gray gloves from the table and slipping them over his well-tended hands. "I'll leave you to put the bait back together. And be advised that I shall expect a full report once you've coaxed Davilenko to bite."

Arianna was tempted to cram the leather-bound volume down Grentham's spiteful throat. With any luck, half of his perfect pearly teeth would be knocked to flinders.

As the door fell shut on the minister's parting words, Saybrook expelled a harried sigh.

"Pompous prick," growled Arianna through clenched teeth. Stalking to the storage cabinet, she began rummaging around for a glue pot and brushes.

The earl remained silent for a long, awkward moment. "About what Grentham just said," he began haltingly. "The lady in question is a botanist, a spinster who belongs to—"

"For God's sake, Sandro, you owe me no explanation of your life. Pray, do not make further mention of it."

"I ..." He looked at her uncertainly.

"It is of no concern," said Arianna sharply. The sudden clench in her belly was not jealousy, she assured herself, but merely anger at Grentham for his malicious games. "Come, we have work to do."

The book lay on the side table by the rosewood cigar case, a spill of candlelight catching on the gilt lettering stamped on the spine. A faint skirl of smoke wafted across the ceiling rosette as the lone figure in the smoking room rose from the corner armchair.

A puff of breath blew out the tiny flame, leaving the room shrouded in slanting shadows cast by the flickering moonlight. Footsteps crossed noiselessly over the carpet— the only sounds were a brief whisper of leather sliding over smooth wood, followed by a soft hiss of triumph.

Dark on dark, the shadows shifted as the clock began to strike the midnight hour. And then the door closed quietly, leaving the empty space enveloped in blackness.

The next morning dawned cloudless, the last vestiges of the squalling storms having blown through during the night. Saybrook rose early to join the Spanish diplomats for breakfast, while Arianna avoided the public rooms downstairs, choosing instead to invite Henning to share a repast in the sitting room of her suite.

"Vienna," muttered the surgeon, in between bites of kippered herring. "Do ye really think it's wise to get tangled in Grentham's web of intrigue again?"

"The strands are already twined around Charles," Arianna pointed out. "You know Sandro—he wasn't about to leave his uncle at the mercy of that spider."

"I say the minister was bluffing. He would have been hard-pressed to prove any wrongdoing on Mellon's part."

"Perhaps," she replied. "But the document would have been damaging, and Sandro is very protective of family." A bit of toast crumbled between her fingers as she recalled his reaction to Grentham's mention of Antonia.

So, the minister knew about Saybrook's sister. It wasn't overly surprising, given that Grentham's job was to know all the sordid secrets of the *ton*. Clearly the subject had been discussed between the two of them before, but the earl had not seen fit to tell her of it. Too personal? Arianna tried not to think of the other female mentioned by the minister. Given her own conflicted musings on independence, she could hardly complain.

"Not hungry?" asked Henning, eyeing the pile of crumbs

on her plate with wry amusement. "If ye have lost yer appetite, then things must be even more serious than I thought. Are there any new discoveries ye haven't told me about?"

"N-no. I'm merely trying to digest all that has happened. Like you, I have no illusions as to the dangers of being drawn into Grentham's world. But Sandro is, as you know, not intimidated by a challenge. Quite the contrary, in fact."

"Ye are getting to understand him rather well," murmured the surgeon.

*Am I?* Arianna was not quite so sanguine, but the earl's return forestalled any further discussion of her husband's inner workings.

"So, did the rat bite?" inquired Henning.

"Indeed, it appears that he swallowed the bait in one gulp." Saybrook handed the book to Arianna. "But perhaps you should check more carefully, just to be sure."

She quickly carried it to the escritoire, and opened the back cover. "Yes," she said, running a magnifying glass along the inside edge of the binding. "It's been reglued, and the bulge is definitely gone."

"Then I think we can safely assume that mischief and mayhem is still afoot," said the surgeon.

"You make it sound too poetically pretty," groused Saybrook. "Rather call it treason and terror."

*Ugly words,* thought Arianna. *Ugly deeds.*

"The inquest is to take place at noon," Saybrook informed them. "There's no need for you to attend, Baz. I think we can trust Grentham to keep his word about arranging the verdict. The announcement of death by unknown assailant will keep my neck intact for a bit longer."

"Only because it suits the bastard's purpose to have you free to do his dirty work," replied Henning.

"We offered," Arianna pointed out. "Or, more precisely, *I* offered."

The surgeon waggled a brow. "Bored with the life of an indolent aristocrat, are ye now, lassie?"

She smiled. "A little, I suppose. Not that I would have

chosen to have Sandro shot at and Mellon enmeshed in this tangle of treachery."

"Oh, our laddie will have it all sorted in two shakes of a lamb's tail." Henning allowed a last twitch of cynical mirth before turning serious. "Have you given any more thought to the letter you deciphered?"

Saybrook poured himself a cup of tea. "I've been mulling over the part that says, *'I've been appointed to the English delegation and our contact in Sx is also in place.'* At flush blush, the letters 'SX' would seem to mean the Kingdom of Saxony, whose ruler is currently being held a virtual prisoner by the Russian Tsar," he replied. "But I have a feeling that nothing is going to be as it seems in this affair."

"I don't understand—how can the Tsar hold a fellow ruler prisoner?" inquired Arianna.

"Because nobody is stepping up to give him a good kick in the arse," quipped Henning.

"Russia wants to remake the Baltic region," explained her husband. "The Tsar wishes to create new borders for Poland, and the tiny Kingdom of Saxony is standing in his way. So its king is enjoying the Tsar's hospitality for the moment. It's all very polite, of course, but let's just say that any decision to leave would prove awkward."

Arianna made a face. "I shall need to assemble a reference library in order to keep all the rivalries and alliances straight."

"Ye have another week to gain firsthand knowledge of all the petty quarrels and hatreds simmering on the Continent," said Henning with a cynical snort. "But of course, there will be plenty more to learn of, once you reach Vienna."

"I suppose that I might as well start with Rochemont," she mused. "The Aggrieved Adonis will likely want a good deal of sympathy for the injury to his perfect looks."

Henning tossed back another dram of whisky—his fourth—and rose. "Seeing as you've no further need of me at present, I'll be heading back to London. I have patients with real ills to treat." His hands flexed, setting off a sharp cracking of his knuckles. "And arrangements to make for doing some digging up north."

"Do be careful how you slide your spade into the auld sod," cautioned the earl. "We don't want Kydd—"

"To feel that someone is starting work on his grave?" suggested Henning. "Yer pipes keep whistling the same tune, laddie. I understand the need for secrecy."

"It can't be repeated too often," said the earl.

"The person I have in mind for the job can be trusted."

Saybrook seemed satisfied with the surgeon's answer.

"I'll send word for our carriage to be made ready," she said. "Along with a basket of food for the journey." She eyed the empty glass. "And another bottle of the marquess's best malt."

"You'll knock off all my rough edges with such luxuries, Lady S," said the surgeon with a sour grin. "I fear I'll turn quishy as boiled oats."

"I don't think there's any danger of your Highland flint going soft," she replied.

"None of us can afford to lose our edge," said Saybrook, his eyes turning opaque. "Or let down our guard for an instant. I suspect the coming months are going to test our mettle in ways we can't yet imagine."

# 10

## From Lady Arianna's Chocolate Notebooks

### Dark Chocolate Flan with Chili, Cinnamon and Pepita Praline

*Butter for pan*
*¼ cup pepitas (hulled toasted pumpkin seeds)*
*1⅓ cups granulated sugar*
*6 tablespoons water*
*1 cup whole milk*
*1 cup heavy cream*
*1 teaspoon mild chili powder (or to taste)*
*1 inch-long piece cinnamon stick*
*2 whole black peppercorns*
*½ star anise*
*5 ounces bittersweet chocolate, finely chopped*
*4 large eggs*

1. Preheat oven to 325 degrees. On a rimmed baking sheet lined with nonstick liner, buttered parchment or waxed paper, spread pepitas close together in a single layer.
2. In a medium saucepan over medium heat, com-

bine 1 cup sugar and 6 tablespoons water. Bring to a simmer, stirring only until sugar is dissolved. Continue to cook, tilting pan occasionally to distribute heat evenly, until a caramel of a deep amber color forms, about 15 minutes.

3. Working quickly (before caramel cools and hardens), pour half the hot caramel into a 9-inch loaf pan, tilting pan to coat bottom and a bit of the sides. Pour remaining caramel over pepitas, using an offset spatula to help spread caramel if necessary. Let both pans cool completely. When pepita praline is cool, break into 2-inch pieces.

4. Meanwhile, in a large saucepan, combine milk, cream, chili powder, cinnamon, peppercorns and star anise. Bring to a simmer over high heat; reduce to medium and simmer 5 minutes. Let stand, off heat, 15 minutes. Return to a simmer, turn off heat and whisk in chocolate until smooth.

5. In a bowl, whisk eggs, remaining $1/3$ cup sugar and the salt together. Whisking constantly, slowly pour hot chocolate mixture into eggs until fully combined. Pour custard through a fine sieve into caramel-coated loaf pan. Place loaf pan in a deep roasting pan. Add 2 inches hot tap water to roasting pan. Cover roasting pan tightly with foil; prick foil all over with a fork.

6. Carefully transfer pan to oven. Bake until flan is lightly set but still jiggles when shaken (lifting foil to check), about 1½ hours. Transfer loaf pan to a wire rack to cool to room temperature. Refrigerate flan at least 4 hours or overnight.

7. To serve, run an offset spatula along sides of pan to gently release it. Turn onto a serving platter and top with pepita praline; serve in slices.

Yield: 8 servings.

The fortnight finally over, Arianna breathed an inward sigh of relief as she followed the procession of baggage being carried up the steps of their London town house. The inquest, the interminable fugue of privilege at play had put her nerves on constant edge.

*The pop of champagne, the clink of crystal, the fizz of laughter . . .*

And it was, she reminded herself, just a prelude of what was to come.

The idea was exhausting. And at the same time strangely exhilarating. *As if that makes any sense.*

Her mouth quirked as she looked up at the stately marble columns and graceful pediments of the entranceway.

*The polished knocker, the imposing oak paneling, the well-oiled efficiency of the servants opening the portal to the perfectly polished interior . . .*

Perhaps life had become too comfortable, too predictable, admitted Arianna.

She slanted a glance at Saybrook as he greeted the footman who appeared to take his satchel of books. The change in him, however subtle, had not escaped her eye. The spark in his eye seemed a bit brighter. No—perhaps "intense" was a better word. Scholarship, for all its cerebral challenges, could not light that indescribable burn.

Along with wariness, and worry about the upcoming battle, Arianna sensed a thrum of anticipation pulsing through her husband's blood. Steel versus steel—strength against strength. The prospect of matching mind and body against a clever enemy was not intimidating. It was intoxicating.

Saybrook had once told her that danger was like a drug. She smiled as the truth of his words tickled down her spine. Oh yes, he liked his studies, but risk, like chocolate, was also a stimulant to the senses, and loath though he might be to admit it, the earl missed the taste of it.

"Welcome home, milady," intoned their butler, a tall, grizzled Spaniard whom she privately thought of as Don Quixote.

*Home.* She was still getting used to having a grand residence and servants to cater to her comforts. Her father had never lingered in one spot for very long . . .

"Allow me to take your books and your reticule," said the butler, his English vowels as soft and curling as his silvery goatee.

"*Gracias*, Sebastian." Saybrook added his cane and overcoat to the servant's outstretched arms. "I see you have been studying the book on codes," he said to Arianna.

"It's absolutely fascinating," she responded. "Certain things still puzzle me, of course, but as you said, the basic logic has much in common with mathematics. I've been making a list of questions—"

He laughed. "I noted how entranced you were with Becton's treatise during the journey."

"Yes, well, you seemed busy with your own work," she answered. "So I didn't want to disturb you."

"I was reviewing my notes on the present alliances, and all I can say is that if European politics is based on any rational system of order, it eludes me," replied Saybrook ruefully. "I swear, there is no rhyme or reason to the bumble broth of intrigue."

"So you think that we are stepping out of the frying pan and into the fire?"

"Tensions will be coming to a boil in Vienna, and it will be our job to see that England doesn't get burned." The earl tossed his gloves on the sideboard. "I would welcome your opinion on some thoughts that have come to mind concerning our strategy. Shall I order a pot of chocolate to be brought to the library?"

"You've whetted my appetite—how can I resist?"

With all the other distractions swirling around the case, Grentham's comment about the other woman, along with the awkwardness of its implications, had been forgotten. *Or at least relegated to some deep, dark recess of the mind,* thought Arianna. State treason took precedence over any private worries of personal betrayal.

His smile sent a slight lurch through her insides.

No—not betrayal. That was unfair, she reminded herself. They had neither made nor demanded any promises of fidelity. The church vows had been a mere formality.

"Ah, excellent," said Saybrook, brushing an errant lock of hair from the nape of her neck. "I was hoping that I could tempt you, despite the lateness of the hour."

"G-give me just a few moments to freshen up. I shall meet you there shortly."

Her toilette refreshed, her gown changed, and her thoughts reordered, Arianna entered the library feeling somewhat revived.

"Ah," she murmured, after savoring a long sip of their cook's special brew. "I missed Bianca's chocolate."

"As did I." Saybrook hooked the hassock with a booted foot and drew it closer to his favorite chair. "When one is used to spices, everything else tastes rather bland." He added a splash of Spanish brandy—a hotter, rougher spirit than French cognac—to his chocolate before propping his feet up in front of the blazing hearth and exhaling loudly. "I'm sorry that you've been dragged back into my private conflict with Grentham."

"Let us not trade recriminations," she interrupted quickly. "I couldn't resist baiting the minister during the opening reception, so it's quite likely that his venom is directed at me. Assuming, of course, that he isn't the serpent responsible for trying to poison the government."

Saybrook set down his cup. "Before we go on, perhaps we ought to clear the air."

"Of brimstone and gunpowder?" joked Arianna, watching a twisting plume of smoke rise up from the burning logs.

"Of innuendos and speculation," he replied.

Within the dark irises of his eyes, the reflection of the flames was like pinpoints of molten gold.

"Sandro," she began, only to be silenced by a flick of his hand.

"No, let me speak." He straightened, the slope of his broad shoulders steeling to an unyielding edge. "Grentham spoke the truth. I do make regular visits to a lady who lives in Charlotte Street, off Bedford Square. But it is not for any prurient reason, as was his unspoken suggestion. She is . . ."

Arianna sipped her chocolate, watching him through the fringe of her lashes.

"She is an Original, to use common cant." He heaved a harried sigh. "Though in truth there is nothing common about Sophia Kirtland."

He paused, as if waiting for some reaction. But Arianna, warned to silence, decided to take him at his word.

Clearing his throat, the earl continued. "Miss Kirtland has never been married—she is a spinster, a distinction she holds proudly, having little desire to surrender her independence to—as she so colorfully puts it—a dolt whose ballocks would likely be more active than his brain. Which is to say, she has no high opinion of men in general. Nor women, for that matter."

Arianna was careful to keep her expression neutral.

"As you no doubt gather by now," he went on, "she is eccentric. Acerbic. Opinionated." A fresh splash of brandy sloshed into his cup. "She is also the most brilliant scientist I know. I met her at a lecture on chemistry at the Royal Society some years ago, and engaged in a most interesting disagreement over the speaker's conclusions. We corresponded while I was in Spain, and over time, we became . . . friends, for lack of a better word." He drank deeply, avoiding Arianna's eyes. "Given her outspoken views, Miss Kirtland would not be overly welcome in Polite Society, even if she sought to fit into the social whirl. She lives as a recluse, surrounded by her books, her Egyptian cats and occasional visits to a small circle of equally unconventional thinkers. However, I think she's a little lonely, so I make a point of visiting her every week."

Arianna carefully aligned the sugar teaspoons on the tray, waiting for him to go on.

"Bloody hell," said Saybrook. "When I asked you to hear me out, I was not meaning for you to mimic the Sphinx."

"As you ought to know by now, I tend to take things to the extreme."

"I trust that does not mean you are contemplating cutting off my *testiculos* with a rusty knife."

"I am not crazed, merely curious," she replied. "Is there a reason you never mentioned this before?"

It may have been a quirk of firelight, but his cheeks seemed to turn a shade redder. "I . . . I suppose I feared that you might ask to meet her."

*"And?"*

"And that might have proved awkward," answered the earl reluctantly. "Miss Kirtland did not approve of my marrying in haste."

"In that we think alike," quipped Arianna. "Was the lady unhappy because she had designs on your person?" Not wishing to sound overly cynical, she omitted any mention of his title and money.

"God, no. It's just that as she does not bother to temper her tongue, I worried that she might say something . . . offensive."

Arianna burst out laughing. "Me? Offended?" she gasped in between chortles. "My dear Sandro, whatever were you thinking? On the contrary, I can't imagine anything more interesting than to be insulted by a brilliant female scientist."

His jaw unclenched ever so slightly. "She can be prickly and sarcastic."

"So can I."

"Yes, well, sometimes in chemical experiments, when one puts two volatile substances together, they don't react according to the textbook description but blow up in your face."

*True,* Arianna conceded. Strong-willed people often clashed despite shared interests. Still, his halting explanation had piqued her curiosity. Was Sophia Kirtland pretty? Strangely enough, that was the first question that popped to mind. The thought surprised her, but on a moment's reflection she decided it was a fair thing to wonder. Clearly the earl was attracted to unconventional females who weren't afraid to be different.

*Individuals who dared to defy the rules.* Sandro himself did not feel bound by many strictures. Save, of course, for his rigid sense of honor.

She shifted uncomfortably, heat tickling over the fire-kissed side of her body, while the shadowed half felt chilled to the marrow. All at once, the awareness of her utter lack of formal schooling seemed to press against her flesh. Did Sandro regret the fact that his wife did not possess a classical education, and could not discuss books and arcane scientific texts with him?

*Damnation.* Arianna forced herself to push such questions aside. There were enough hidden secrets to uncover without delving any deeper into how her husband felt about the erudite stranger.

"I appreciate your candor, Sandro," she said. "And consider the matter closed."

He looked faintly relieved.

"We've more pressing problems to deal with."

"Correct," he intoned. "*Not* that Miss Kirtland is a problem for us in any regard, Arianna."

*So you say, and I've no reason to doubt your word.* She accepted the statement with a nod.

There was an awkward pause, unspoken questions shadowing the silence. Saybrook cleared his throat, a tacit signal that in his mind the subject was closed.

"However, since we are being candid, might I ask something about another female?" she said quickly.

His face betrayed a spasm of surprise. "There is no other—"

"Antonia," she said. "I could not help but notice your reaction when Grentham mentioned her existence. Is she, perchance, a part of the reason you and the minister are constantly at daggers drawn?"

Her husband drew in a deep breath. "He threatened to blacken the name of an innocent girl in order to keep me under his thumb during our first investigation. I told him I would kill him if he ever harmed her, so yes, I suppose you could say that there is a lingering enmity over the matter."

"Is that not something I should have known about?"

That question elicited a harsh exhale. "At the time, we didn't know each other well enough for me to confide such a secret. Then"—he looked up—"you had enough to worry about in trying to fit in with Polite Society. I wished to protect you from yet another trouble."

*Protect.* Arianna allowed a tiny smile. "I am unused to anyone trying to shield me from the sordid realities of life."

"I know that," he replied softly, and yet the force behind the words took her by surprise. "We both have old habits that must begin to adjust to a new relationship."

"True," she acquiesced. "No easy task."

His mouth quirked up at the corners. "I fear that nothing we face will prove easy over the coming months."

"No," agreed Arianna. "But like you, I don't find a challenge intimidating."

Saybrook held her gaze for a moment before taking up a slim leather folder from the tea table and methodically shuffling through the papers inside it. "Then let us begin formulating a plan of attack. As I said, I have been thinking . . ." He withdrew several sheets and placed them side by side on the polished wood. "There are going to be a bewildering array of issues and alliances raised at the congress in Vienna. Now that peace reigns over Europe, the powers that defeated Napoleon want to fix the political and social problems caused by over a decade of constant warfare."

He pursed his lips. "But rather than try to sort through it all, and run the risk of becoming hopelessly entangled, we must choose our battles, so to speak. What I'm suggesting is that we decide on the most likely enemy, and draw up an offensive strategy. I know from experience that unless we are disciplined and focused, we will end up blundering around, and simply shooting in the dark."

"And if we are wrong?" she asked.

"We have limited time and resources, so there is only so much we can do in any case."

"I don't suppose we can count on Grentham and his department for much assistance."

"No," he said decisively. "For obvious reasons, I think it best to keep our own activities as much a secret from the minister as we can. There are certain ways in which he can help us, but I shall have to be extremely cautious in how I look to leverage them."

"Mr. Henning thinks him capable of treason," mused Arianna.

"Like many Scotsmen, Baz is suspicious of any English government official, especially one involved in state security."

"Do *you* think Grentham a traitor?" she pressed.

The earl shrugged. "It doesn't matter what I think; it matters what I know. And right now, I have no information one way or another to indicate whether Grentham is involved in this sordid scheme. So until I know more, I shall err on the side of caution."

"And yet, caution calls for going slowly," she pointed out. "Time is not on our side."

"True. The odds are against us being able to figure out the target and stop whatever murder is being planned in such a short time," agreed Saybrook. "But we have a clue—or clues. We simply have to use logic and probability to narrow down our choices, and then hope for the best." He looked up from the pages. "That is not to say we won't improvise in the heat of battle, but it's best to have a strategy in mind when embarking on a campaign."

*Interesting.* Arianna could see the earl's military experience reasserting itself. He was sitting up a little straighter, speaking a little more forcefully. "How would that be decided in the army?"

"A general would call a staff meeting. He would listen to his regimental officers and review the intelligence reports from units like mine, taking care to study the facts and weigh the options. On top of all that, a good leader, like the Duke of Wellington, knows the importance of understanding the character and motivations of the opposing commander."

She thought for a moment. "So when all the fancy uniforms and gaudy medals are stripped away, it all comes down to human nature."

"Yes."

"So, we should start by making a list of what we know about Renard. He's extremely cunning . . ." She paused to take up a pencil and her pocket notebook. "Extremely bold."

"Extremely confident," added Saybrook. "To the point of arrogance. And that fact should work in our favor. Hubris tends to make someone underestimate his opponent."

"Hubris will also make him want to strike at a grand target, not some obscure official," mused Arianna.

"I think it's safe to assume that Renard aims to do something dramatic. So we must consider his motives, and who he is aligned with." He carefully sharpened a quill with his pen knife and dipped the fresh point into the inkwell. "Talleyrand seems the most likely. He too is an extremely clever man, skilled in dissembling and a master of political manipulations. Together they make a formidable force."

"So do we," she said softly.

"Indeed." The firelight caught the subtle quirk of his lips.

Arianna wasn't sure how to interpret the response. It seemed shadowed by a hint of hesitation. But then again, the flames were a dancing kaleidoscope of colors and her imagination was already overstimulated.

"Intuition and luck proved stronger than cold-blooded calculation during our previous encounter with Renard," said Saybrook. "So we were fortunate enough to beat him at his own game. However, we must be mindful that he and his employer are, for lack of a better term, professionals at deception and duplicity. And likely they have a very strong incentive for ensuring that their plan is a success."

"So do we," repeated Arianna stubbornly. "They are acting on purely selfish desires, while we believe that thwarting their plans will avoid suffering and bloodshed for a great many people. So, in essence, it is a fight between good and evil."

Another little movement tugged at his mouth. "I thought you considered yourself far too pragmatic to believe in absolute principles like good and evil."

"As you see, you are a bad influence on me," she quipped.

Her husband's laugh was a low smoky rumble that echoed the crackling of the coals. "Forgive me." And then, in an instant, the flicker of humor was gone. "Fighting these dirty wars against dangerous adversaries was not part of our bargain, Arianna. I've very mixed feelings about involving you—"

"Come, give me a little credit for having the ability to make up my own mind," Arianna cut in. "I'm not some meek mouse of a wife, who wouldn't dare display her own teeth and claws."

"Your abilities, both mental and physical, are most certainly not in question," he replied tersely.

"So?" she challenged.

Saybrook stretched out his long legs and appeared to be contemplating the tips of his boots. Arianna poured another cup of chocolate, only to find the brew had gone tepid.

"So, very well," he finally answered. "I will take you at your word."

*Words.* Somehow their clarity had become clouded by nuance.

"Thank you," said Arianna, a little more forcefully than she intended.

Turning away from the light, the earl drew an envelope from the leather portfolio. The ornate seal was, she saw, already broken. "Charles is having a reception later this week for the English delegation going to Vienna. He's still a bit perplexed by my sudden desire to see the Emperor of Austria's book collection, but he is used to my odd quirks by now, so I'm sure he doesn't suspect any ulterior motive."

If her husband felt any guilt over the deception, he kept it well hidden.

"It's the perfect opportunity to renew your acquaintance with David Kydd." He offered her the invitation. "It would be helpful if you whet his appetite for a more intimate friendship."

*Ah, well. I did ask to be fed to the lions.*

"What man can resist the flirtations of a beautiful woman?" her husband went on. "That Kydd has a taste for games of betrayal might make the opportunity even more alluring to him. It would also afford a chance for Baz and me to pay a private visit to where he lives and search his rooms."

"An excellent suggestion," said Arianna coolly. "I will make every effort to turn him sweet." She flicked a quick look at the pearl-white card and its elegant engraving, then dropped it casually on the side table. "As Grentham said, I do have the lack of moral scruples to be comfortable dangling myself as bait."

The earl rose, and crossed the distance between them as swiftly and silently as a stalking predator. "I don't know what you are thinking, Arianna . . ." His hands grasped her shoulders, his lips feathered against her brow. "But be assured that you are very special to me." He kissed her, a long, lush embrace that ignited a spark of liquid heat deep in her belly.

Damnation, their bodies were eloquent enough in expressing their physical attraction. Would that their brains communicated half so well.

"I won't allow any harm to come to you," he murmured, slowly lifting his mouth from hers.

*Noblesse oblige?* Or was it some more primitive passion?

Her mind was too tired, her emotions too tangled to delve any deeper into such questions tonight.

Touching a finger to his lips, she said, "Suffice it to say, we'll both do our best, Sandro. Other than that, don't make promises you can't keep."

# 11

## From Lady Arianna's Chocolate Notebooks

### Chocolate Angel Food Cake

2 cups sifted superfine sugar (about 1 pound)
1⅓ cups sifted cake flour (not self-rising)
1½ cups egg whites at room temperature (10 to 12 eggs)
¾ teaspoon kosher salt
1½ teaspoons cream of tartar
1 teaspoon pure vanilla extract
½ cup coarsely grated semisweet chocolate

### For the glaze

½ pound semisweet chocolate chips
¾ cup plus 1 tablespoon heavy cream

1. Preheat the oven to 350 degrees F.
2. Combine ½ cup of the sugar with the flour and sift them together 4 times. Set aside.
3. Place the egg whites, salt, and cream of tartar in the bowl of an electric mixer fitted with the whisk

attachment and beat on high speed until the eggs form medium-firm peaks, about 1 minute. With the mixer on medium speed, add the remaining 1½ cups of sugar by sprinkling it over the beaten egg whites. Beat on high speed for a few minutes until thick and shiny. Add the vanilla and continue to whisk until very thick, about 1 more minute. Scrape the beaten egg whites into a large bowl. Sift ¼ of the flour mixture over the egg whites and fold it very carefully into the batter with a rubber spatula. Continue adding the flour in 3 equal additions, sifting and folding until it's all incorporated. Fold in the grated chocolate.

4. Pour the batter into an ungreased 10-inch tube pan, smooth the top, and bake it for 35 to 45 minutes, until it springs back to the touch. Remove the cake from the oven and invert the pan on a cooling rack. When cool, run a thin, flexible knife around the cake to remove it from the pan.

5. For the chocolate glaze, place the chocolate chips and the heavy cream in a heat-proof bowl over a pan of simmering water and stir until the chocolate melts. Pour the chocolate over the top of the cooled cake to cover the top completely and allow it to drizzle down the sides. If you have chocolate glaze left over, you can serve it on the side with the cake.

The moon hung low, a thin crescent of pale light barely visible through the dark turrets and rooftops looming above the narrow alleyway.

Saybrook chafed his gloved palms together and inched a bit closer to the twines of ivy wreathing the recessed gate. "No sign of movement here," he whispered, peering out toward the empty street. "How about you?"

"Nothing," replied Henning. He turned up the collar of

his dark coat. "You're sure Lady S can keep Kydd occupied for the evening?"

"She's promised to ply him with champagne and feminine flatteries," replied Saybrook as he set to work on the lock.

"The man would have to lack a pulse if he didn't respond to yer wife," said the surgeon. "If anyone is capable of squeezing the most intimate secrets from a man—"

"Thank you, but you may dispense with a detailed description of the process," snapped the earl.

"Jealous, are ye, laddie?"

"No." Several faint metallic clicks, barely audible above the rustling of the leaves, and the gate sprung open. "Now, stubble the talk and stay close. Kydd's rooms are on the second floor. The live-in servants are quartered up by the attics, and should all be asleep by this hour, so we ought to be safe enough."

Slipping through the opening, they followed the narrow cart path around to the coal cellar, where a tradesmen's entrance was set beneath the eaves. It too yielded to the earl's picklock, allowing them entrance into the back of the lodging house. He led the way through a narrow passageway, which brought them around to the front entrance. From there they climbed quickly to Kydd's rooms.

Closing the door behind him, Saybrook eased the bolt home. The quarters were small, as befitted a single man of modest means, and neater than one might expect.

"Empty," announced Henning after taking a peek into the bedchamber. "By the by, how did you know which set of rooms was his?"

"Grentham provided me with the information." The flare of the candle's wick caught the earl's fleeting smile.

"You and the minister are becoming bosom bows, eh?"

"I don't expect to be suckling at the tit of friendship anytime soon," quipped Saybrook. "Let's just say that for now, we both recognize the benefits of sharing information."

"Have a care that you don't swallow a swill of his lies."

"Never fear." He lifted the light and surveyed the sitting room. Its furnishing were Spartan—a large desk, pushed to one side of the window casement, a round table and four straight-back chairs, a worn leather armchair facing the hearth, a battered sideboard with one door hanging slightly askew.

The only extravagance was the handsome set of book-shelves, filled with various volumes. Most were the usual student's assortment of cheap, secondhand editions. But among the tattered spines were several sets of fine leather-bound books.

"Nothing out of the ordinary," murmured Henning, making his own survey. "A neat, modest abode, with nothing to excite any suspicions."

"Indeed." Saybrook continued his slow pacing around the perimeter of the room. "Let us start with the desk, though I doubt we'll find anything incriminating there."

"Not unless Kydd is a complete fool," answered Henning. "Put yer candle out before it leaves a telltale drip of wax. I'll light the lanthorn." He raised the shutter and ran the beam over the blotter.

They worked their way methodically through the papers, taking care to leave no signs of their snooping. No purloined dispatches, no copied correspondence was in the pile, and the locked drawer yielded only a few small banknotes.

"Mr. Kydd seems to lead an exemplary life," observed the surgeon, after carefully readjusting the angles of the pens on the blotter.

Saybrook made no answer. He was already circling the table, his gaze intent on the bookshelves.

"See something, laddie?"

No answer.

*"Hmmm."* Henning joined him in studying the spines. "The expected assortment of French philosophers... political theorists... American revolutionaries... well, well, well. What have we here."

He pulled out a slim volume and thumbed to the title page. "*Pride and Prejudice*, a novel in three volumes by the author of *Sense and Sensibility*." A fleeting grin. "I wouldn't have expected our friend to have a taste for such vulgar reading."

"Actually, Arianna thinks it a most engaging book," murmured the earl. "As do I."

"I confess, I enjoyed it immensely too." Henning flipped through the rest of the pages and then slid it back into its place. "What do you suggest? Shall we search through all of them to see if anything is hidden within the leaves or bindings?"

Saybrook continued to stare thoughtfully at the shelves. "We don't have time for a thorough examination of them all. We shall have to make an educated guess . . ."

*Tap, tap, tap.* He ran his fingers along a row of leather-bound spines. Pausing, he took down a book.

"Alasdair MacMhaighstir Alasdair," read Henning as Saybrook made a search through the pages. "The Clan-ranald Bard is perhaps the most famous of our Gaelic poets."

*Tap, tap, tap.* The earl's next choice was a volume by William Dunbar.

"Auch, I see your logic," said the surgeon. He plucked a worn edition of Robert Burns poetry from the center of the top shelf. "*Hmmph*. Nothing tucked away in here."

"No, but let us see what we have here." Reaching into the recess, Saybrook retrieved a small chamois bag that was wedged in behind the Burns book. Untying the drawstring, he carefully emptied the contents into his palm.

*A silver badge.*

"There are some papers as well," he said, handing the bag to Henning. "Have a look."

The surgeon fished out several crudely printed pamphlets. "They are in Gaelic." He took a moment to read them over. "The usual blather—arise ye Celtic warriors. Now is the time to seize your freedom." His mouth pinched to a grimace. "Both are signed 'the Dragons of St. Andrew.'

Which is a secret society much favored by the more radical-thinking university students."

"Bring the light closer, Baz." Saybrook ran a fingertip over the silver badge, tracing the carved details. "An odd sort of Celtic cross . . ."

"Look closely," said the surgeon. "It's fashioned from a claymore—a traditional Highland sword." He slashed a finger across his throat. "Which is designed for naught but war and killing."

"An Italian poniard would be a more appropriate weapon for Kydd, given his current propensity for stabbing his friends in the back."

"I'm sure he doesn't see himself as a duplicitous monster, but rather as a noble patriot." Henning's scarred knuckles tightened on the lanthorn. "'Ah, freedom is a noble thing!'" he read from the radical pamphlet. "'Freedom all solace to man gives' . . ." Looking up, he sighed. "That John Barbour poem is inscribed on the stone marking where Robert the Bruce's heart is buried."

"I fear your countryman is as naive as he is idealistic. Treachery is a dirty business, no matter how poetically it is phrased. But no doubt he would march happily to the gallows, thinking himself a martyr to a glorious cause, rather than a dupe to a clever demagogue."

Henning shook his head. "Daft bugger, to keep such incriminating stuff in his own rooms."

Taking a pencil and small notebook from his coat pocket, Saybrook quickly made a detailed sketch of the badge. "Let me refold the pamphlets and put everything back in its place," he said, after tucking the two other items inside the bag.

The rough newsprint crackled in reply.

Saybrook fixed his friend with a searching look. "Baz, I know your feelings on democracy and the rights of every man, but this Dragons of St. Andrew Society is dangerous. Preaching treason and armed rebellion will only result in the deaths of many young Scotsmen, whose intellect and passion could be put to far more effective political use."

The surgeon responded by reciting a few stanzas from a Robert Burns sonnet.

Undaunted, the earl pressed on. "We need to know specifics—the ringleader's identity, and whether, as I suspect, he is working with any foreigners. I would handle it through my own channels, but you know how clannish the Scots are. An outsider hasn't a prayer of getting answers to any questions."

"Auch, I know that," said Henning unhappily. "I'll send another messenger north. My cousin is in a position to know this sort of information, and he'll trust that I'm asking for a good reason." His voice tightened a notch. "Lies, manipulations, betrayals—why is it that I feel as slimy as Kydd?"

"Don't," counseled Saybrook. "There is a right way and a wrong way to achieve worthy goals."

"Right and wrong," growled the surgeon. "Is what we do for the higher good? God knows." An oath rumbled under his breath. "I bloody well don't."

"I don't claim to be a deity, Baz. But I've made a choice and can live with it. Can you?"

Henning swore another oath. "Would that the damnable matter didn't cut so close to home. I have friends and family who wuddna agree with what I'm doing—especially my young nephew, who's just begun his university studies. But ye know my sentiments on violence, so I really don't have a choice, do I, laddie?"

"We *all* have choices, and most of the time they are damnably difficult ones."

Henning grunted and turned for the bedchamber. "Let us finish our search, in case Kydd chooses to leave the party early."

Repressing a flutter of nerves, Arianna ascended the stairs and entered the drawing room. *Steady, steady.* Deception was in her blood, she reminded herself. It would soon uncoil and come to life, like a sleeping serpent suddenly roused by the heat of a freshly kindled flame.

"Lady Saybrook, I appreciate your coming, despite Sandro's indisposition." Ever the attentive host, Mellon quickly approached and bowed politely over her hand. "I hope that his war wound is not giving him trouble?"

"No, no, it's simply a stomach discomfort," she replied. "I expect him to be fully recovered by morning."

"Perhaps you ought to reconsider traveling to Vienna," he suggested softly. "The trip will be a long, grueling one, and the city itself will be aswirl in the pomp and pageantry of the Peace Conference."

*Meaning that I will stick out like a square peg trying to squeeze into a round hole?*

Keeping her thoughts to herself, Arianna responded with a smile. "Sandro is quite set on seeing the Emperor's private library. You know how serious he is about his work."

"Ah, yes—his chocolate book." Mellon looked faintly bemused. "I was, of course, happy that the subject provided him with sustenance during the dark days of his recovery." Saybrook had, for a time, sunk into a state of deep melancholy after being wounded in the Peninsular War. Chocolate had helped wean him from a dependence on opium.

"But perhaps he ought not push himself too hard," he continued, after a fraction of a pause. "Given all he—and you—have been through in the past year, it might be wise to wait until things are calmer on the Continent before undertaking such a journey."

A tactful suggestion—but then, Charles Mellon was ever the consummate diplomat.

She decided to respond to his counsel with a slight challenge. "That is sage advice, sir. But you know that beneath his outward stoicism, Sandro is a man of deep feelings. He is not really happy unless he is fully engaged in a pursuit that engages his passions."

The corners of Mellon's mouth quirked upward for an instant. "It appears that you understand my nephew well."

"It may not seem so on the surface, but the earl and I have much in common."

He nodded thoughtfully. "So I am learning."

Their private exchange was interrupted by the arrival of several Prussian diplomats.

"Please excuse me," murmured Mellon.

"Of course. I shall find Nora and pay my respects." Moving away, Arianna sought out Mellon's wife, who welcomed her with a warm hug.

"Arianna, how delightful to see you!" Unlike her husband, Eleanor Mellon had never kept her niece-by-marriage at arm's length. "Do come meet some of the other guests."

It was some time before Arianna could disengage herself from the round of greetings and seek a moment alone in one of the shadowed alcoves of the drawing room. The muted clink of crystal punctuated the soft serenade of a string quartet. Sipping her champagne, she watched the mingling of the different delegations weaving an intricate web across the polished parquet.

*Chance or design?* The question of how to interpret the pattern was one that would only grow more pressing in the coming days.

Narrowing her focus, Arianna began searching the crowd for a glimpse of David Kydd.

The Scotsman was across the room, half hidden by the leafy fronds of the decorative potted palms that flanked the entrance to the side saloon. He and Mellon were deep in conversation, and as befitted the pairing of mentor and protégé, the younger man was listening attentively.

*A disciple showing deference.* Head bowed, expression rapt, Kydd looked convincingly natural, which was no easy task. It took discipline, practice and a certain innate natural talent to perfect the art of deception. *And passion.* It helped to have some inner fire burning in one's belly.

Yes, Kydd was an excellent actor and played his role well, she reflected. He was good at presenting a false face to Society.

*But I wager that I am better.*

Switching skins was something that had, over the years, become second nature to her. She had learned to slip seamlessly into a role—saucy wench, streetwise urchin, temperamental cook, rich widow . . .

Setting aside her empty glass, she smoothed her silken skirts into place and stepped out from the alcove.

Mellon looked up at her approach. "Ah, Lady Saybrook, do join us. I am sure that Mr. Kydd would far rather converse with a lovely lady than with me."

Arianna gave a light laugh. "La, I fear you have placed the poor man in a very awkward position. Whether he says yea or nay, he is forced to offend one of us."

"It's good practice for a diplomat," answered Mellon with a smile.

"Ah, but why must I choose?" said Kydd lightly. "To have both Beauty and Wisdom by my side is the best of both worlds."

"I think Mr. Kydd is quite ready for the challenges of Vienna," Arianna said. "The Peace Conference promises to be an exciting opportunity for any aspiring diplomat, Mr. Kydd. Are you looking forward to being part of the delegation?"

"Very much so, Lady Saybrook," replied the Scotsman. "The whole of Europe is to be redrawn and the decisions made will have a lasting effect on world peace. As Mr. Mellon has kindly pointed out, through hard work and diligence, an individual has a real chance to influence the future and write a new chapter of history."

*With ink or blood?* The decoded letter seemed a clear enough answer of his intentions.

"Well said, lad. It will be a challenge," responded Mellon. "But I have great confidence in your ability to think on your feet."

*What a pity that Sandro and I intend to knock him on his arse.*

"Speaking of which, I see that Major Lowell is about to kick up a dust with Rochemont, so I had better go intervene." He made a face. "Why is it that military men—my nephew excepted—have so little tact?"

"Because rather than mincing around with words, as we

do, they are used to slashing their opponents with sabers," suggested Kydd, a glint of humor flashing in his blue eyes.

"Sharp lad," said Mellon, giving a quick nod of approval, rather like a proud papa, before moving away to forestall any explosions of temper.

Arianna felt a sudden, searing flare of anger rise up in her gorge, knowing how hurt and disappointed Mellon would be when the treachery of his protégé came to light. But she hid its heat behind a cool smile.

"What a great compliment that the Foreign Office has placed such trust in you. But then, Charles cannot speak highly enough of your abilities."

A breath of air stirred the palm fronds, the soft rustling sending a shiver of bladelike shadows ghosting over his face. *Black and white, blurring to an infinite range of grays.*

The leaves stilled, and as he turned into the glow of the nearby wall sconce, the candlelight gilded the choirboy curl of his smile. "I shall do all I can to justify Mr. Mellon's confidence in me."

*Oh, yes, he was good.* The flickering flames added to the illusion, creating a soft, shimmering halo behind his rose gold hair.

A part of her could almost admire his brazen lies. She knew what it was like to have one's head and heart in thrall to an abstract idea. In her case, it had been the desire for revenge. Thank God that Saybrook had helped her see the folly of that obsession before it had destroyed her.

"As I said, he has the utmost faith in you," replied Arianna. Looking up through her lashes, she watched for any subtle signs of guilt in his expression.

Kydd's smile stretched wider. "I appreciate your telling me that, Lady Saybrook."

His response reminded her of her real purpose in seeking him out. *Enough of my own mordant musings.* She was here to flirt. To flatter. To seduce a traitor into betraying his own dangerous secrets.

"But of course." A flutter of lashes. "I think you know how much I admire your intellect."

The pulse point at his throat quickened, the telltale twitch barely visible beneath the starched folds of his cravat. "There aren't many ladies who are interested in talking about ideas."

"There aren't many men who can make abstract theories and complex philosophies come alive." Arianna lowered her voice to a husky murmur. "Unlike so many others here, you never are dull or dry."

A faint flush of color ridged his cheekbones. "I'm honored that you think so."

"Enough so to tell me some of the things you hope to accomplish?" she asked.

"With pleasure, Lady Saybrook."

"Excellent. And be assured that I look forward to pursuing such subjects with you in Vienna."

As intended, the statement took Kydd by surprise. "You are coming to the Conference?"

"Not precisely." Arianna signaled to one of the footmen for two glasses of champagne. "Saybrook is anxious to study the Emperor of Austria's collection of rare botanical books, and a fellow scholar has arranged an invitation. I daresay he will spend most of his time in the library. But I hope to take in the sights of the city. There is, you know, an old adage about all work and no play . . ."

She paused to draw in a mouthful of the sparkling wine. "I do hope that your schedule will permit you to attend a good many of the festivities. Saybrook often finds his chocolate books more interesting than people."

"Parties are, of course, part of diplomacy," said Kydd slowly. "And the ones planned for the Conference are expected to be sumptuous beyond imagination."

She let a gurgle of laughter well up in her throat. "Oh, but I have a *very* wild imagination."

He smiled and raised his crystal flute in salute. "A toast to those who dare to let their minds soar free of constraint."

*No matter the danger of flying too close to the sun?* The glorious wax-and-feather wings of idealism were no match for such heat and fire. *Smoke and ashes.* The fall would not be pretty.

"As you said earlier, the Conference offers a unique opportunity to shape history. I take it you have some ideas of your own on how to rebuild a new Europe, based on modern ideals," prompted Arianna.

Kydd responded carefully. "I am only a junior assistant to Castlereagh, but I hope to influence some of his positions."

He was no fool. It would be a prolonged game of cat and mouse, and for the moment, she was content to do naught but purr. Only later would the time be right to unsheathe her claws.

"Please, I'm interested in hearing what you think is important." In her previous life, she had learned that knowing an opponent's hopes and his dreams was a powerful weapon. One that could be wielded to great advantage.

Her request drew a chuffed laugh. "Only if you agree to stop me if I start to bore you."

Arianna crossed her heart. "You have my solemn promise."

"Well, in that case, we must be wary of Russia . . ."

# 12

## From Lady Arianna's Chocolate Notebooks

### Chocolate Coconut Cake

*3 cups sugar*
*1¾ cups unsalted butter, softened*
*2½ teaspoons vanilla extract*
*8 large egg yolks*
*1 12-oz. can evaporated milk*
*1½ cups roughly chopped pecans*
*1 7-oz. package sweetened shredded coconut*
*4 oz. German's Sweet Chocolate, chopped*
*2 oz. unsweetened chocolate, chopped*
*½ cup boiling water*
*2 cups flour*
*1 teaspoon baking soda*
*¼ teaspoon kosher salt*
*1 cup buttermilk*
*4 large egg whites*

1. Combine 1½ cups sugar, ¾ cup butter, 1½ tsp. vanilla, 4 egg yolks, and evaporated milk in a 2-qt. pan over medium heat. Bring to a simmer; cook

until thick, 12 minutes. Strain through a sieve into a bowl; stir in pecans and coconut; chill frosting until firm.

2. Heat oven to 350°. Grease three 9-inch round cake pans with butter; line bottoms with parchment circles. Grease parchment; set aside. Put chocolates into a small bowl; pour in ½ cup boiling water; let sit for 1 minute. Stir until smooth; set aside. In another bowl, whisk flour, baking soda, and salt; set aside.

3. In a standing mixer, beat 1¼ cups sugar and remaining butter until fluffy; add remaining egg yolks one at a time. Add chocolate mixture and remaining vanilla; beat until smooth. On low speed, alternately add flour mixture and buttermilk until just combined; set batter aside.

❧

"**B**ravo, monsieur, bravo."

Arianna didn't have to turn around to know who had come up behind her. The Comte of Rochemont's silky voice was unmistakable.

"The enthusiasm of youth is always so . . . energetic," he added, moving smoothly to stand by her side. "*Mon Dieu*, I confess that I feel exhausted just listening to such eloquence."

Kydd's jaw tightened.

"I find Mr. Kydd's ideas very thought-provoking," said Arianna.

Rochemont winked. "I can think of far more interesting ways to provoke your thoughts than to prose on about politics, Lady Saybrook." He gave an exaggerated look around. "Your husband is not here, is he?"

"No," she replied.

"Thank God. I have suffered enough violence at his hands." Rochemont rubbed meaningfully at the trace of a bruise on his brow. "The earl is a very dangerous man," he said to Kydd. "A *sauvage*, as we say in French. Why, he knocked me to the ground during a grouse shoot at the Marquess of Milford's house party. I fear that the rock may have left a permanent scar."

"A *sauvage*?" repeated Arianna. "That implies a primitive wildness, a lack of discipline. Saybrook is a highly trained soldier. His quick reaction probably saved your skull from being blown into a thousand little pieces."

"*Alors*, I cannot think of why the shooter would have been aiming at *me*," he replied innocently. "It was your husband who was nicked by the bullet. Had he thrown himself in the opposite direction, I would not have suffered such a cut." The comte made a face. "The mark is still there, despite my valet's daily treatment with a slab of raw beefsteak."

*Ass,* thought Arianna.

"Yes, I heard about the disturbing incident from Mr. Mellon." Kydd's mouth twitched. "Perhaps you would not have had a face to disfigure, Lord Rochemont, had not the earl knocked you down," he suggested.

Rochemont expelled a low *hmmph*.

"I am sure you do not wish to be rude to Lady Saybrook, sir—" said Kydd. But before he could add any further chiding, he was called away by Mellon to escort the newly arrived Prussian envoy and his wife to the card room.

The comte rolled his eyes as the Scotsman walked away. "A bit too earnest, isn't he?"

Arianna regarded him over the rim of her wineglass. "Mr. Kydd seems to believe very strongly in his ideas. You think that is a bad thing?"

"*Ca depend*—that depends," answered Rochemont. "He's a puppy, and in their exuberance, puppies are easily led."

*An interesting observation.*

"My husband's uncle has great regard for Mr. Kydd's intellect."

"Ah, well, who am I to argue with such a distinguished diplomat." He lowered his voice to a silky murmur. "But let us leave politics to the men who find such discussions stir their blood. *Moi*—I prefer to talk of other things."

Arianna repressed a laugh. *Good God, do most ladies find such ham-handed flirtations flattering?*

"Such as?" she inquired, deciding to play along for the moment. He was, after all, going to be involved in the upcoming Conference, and despite his professed laissez-faire attitude toward politics, he had a lot to gain or lose from the negotiations, depending on how the new French King viewed England and the émigré community in London.

"Oh, take a guess," he said.

"I'm not very good at parlor games," she replied.

*"Non?"* His laugh had a teasing effervescence, like a mouthful of champagne tickling against the tongue. "I have a feeling you would be very good at anything you put your mind to, *madame*."

*"Oui?"* She held his gaze. "How so? The fact is, you hardly know me."

"Ah, but I am, with all due modesty, a very good judge of women—"

"I daresay there isn't a modest bone in your body," interrupted Arianna.

"Ha! You see! You have a certain spirit . . . a je ne sais quoi . . ." His chuckle stilled. "The truth is, you intrigue me. I sense hidden facets . . ."

A chill skated between her shoulder blades. "What makes you say that?"

Rochemont pursed his lips and subjected her to a lengthy study. "You have an aura of mystery about you. I find it very intriguing."

"You are mistaken, sir," she said softly. "As I told you before, ladies are allowed little opportunity to do much of interest."

"Assuming they obey the rules," he pointed out.

"True." The comte, she decided, was not quite as frivolous as he appeared. It would be wise to remain cool—but not *too* cool. A closer acquaintance could prove useful, especially if he was the prey referred to in the decoded document. Keeping an eye on him might allow her to see what wolves—or foxes—were stalking his steps.

After another sip of her wine, Arianna asked, "You think society can function without rules?"

"Ah, now *that* is a question we could discuss all night."

"I had the feeling that you prefer to spend the midnight hours engaged in activities other than talking."

He laughed again. "Conversation with you is so stimulating, Lady Saybrook."

"Be that as it may, I shall have to cut this one short. I see Mellon is about to ring the supper bell, and he has asked me to partner Mr. Kydd."

"Lucky dog," said the comte. "I console myself with the fact that I overheard you tell the puppy that you will be traveling to Vienna after all. I hope that we may continue to get to know each other better there."

"We shall see," murmured Arianna.

"I will take that as a yes."

"Does that mean you never take no as an answer?" she asked.

"I am so rarely asked to," was his response.

*A man used to getting what he wants.* No doubt Vienna would be filled with such hubris. *Power, pleasure, privilege*—a volatile mix if ever there was one.

As Saybrook had said, they would have to dance a very careful *pas de deux* through the ballrooms of the Austrian capital—one small slip and the intrigue could ignite, like gilded gunpowder—a burst of flame, a sudden death, shattering of hopes for peace at last.

The ormolu clock showed the hour to be well past midnight when the guests began to drift out to the curving staircase and down to the carriages waiting in Grosvenor Square.

"Thank you for keeping Kydd company, Lady Saybrook," murmured Mellon. In the candlelight, the tawny glow of his port reflected the mellow tone of his voice.

From what she could tell, the evening had gone well,

with cheerful toasts to camaraderie and cooperation punctuating the convivial dinner conversation.

"He sometimes grows a trifle impatient during these affairs," Mellon went on. "But I'm sure he will learn that they are important. Diplomacy depends on personal relationships, not just government policies."

"It was my pleasure," she replied, watching the Scotsman take his leave. She had done her job—Saybrook and Henning should be done with their mission. "I find him quite interesting."

*For reasons I can't describe.*

"I hope you were not too bored. I know these gatherings are not to your taste either."

"There is much that I must grow accustomed to, sir," said Arianna carefully. "If I appear to move slowly, it is because I do not want to make a misstep." *And fall flat on my arse.*

Mellon took a long sip of his port before answering. "A careful assessment of any situation is, in my opinion, always wise."

The conversation felt a little like moonlight and mist, silvery swirls of subtle nuances blending and blurring into one another. Dancing in and out of shadows, never quite touching.

Angling her gaze to meet his, she asked, "Is it also your opinion that one should ask for help if that situation is proving hard to sort out on one's own?"

His expression remained neutral. "My opinion is that it is not a weakness to ask for help. In my work I've come to realize that new perspectives on a problem can often be of great help in spotting a solution."

"A wise reply," she said softly. "But then, I expected no less from you."

Swirling the last of his wine, Mellon lifted the glass and watched the ruby-dark liquid spin in a slow, silent vortex.

Arianna asked herself whether she was making an error of judgment. Perhaps it wasn't her right to share family secrets . . .

*Ah, but I am family,* she reminded herself.

Drawing a deep breath, she made her decision. "Given your sentiments, I am hoping that you might consent to help me with a very delicate situation."

His expression remained polite but his eyes turned wary.

God only knew what he expected—a confession of murder. Or infidelity?

"It concerns . . . Sandro's sister."

Mellon cleared his throat with a cough. "I fear you are confused, Lady Saybrook. Sandro has no sister."

"Actually, he does. Though whether she is a legitimate sibling or simply the late earl's by-blow lies at the heart of the problem." Arianna went on to explain Saybrook's surprising discovery among his father's papers concerning the young lady currently boarding at Mrs. Martin's Academy in Shropshire. "Her name is Antonia, and she is registered as the daughter of a Spanish noble—a purely imaginary one, according to the letters left by Sandro's father. He chose to disguise her identity while he decided how to make public his secret marriage to another foreigner—and a commoner at that."

Mellon expelled a harried sigh. "I confess, you could knock me over with a feather. My brother spent a great deal of time in Catalonia, but he never breathed a word about having another family."

"Sandro was equally shocked," replied Arianna. "His father's notes revealed that an Englishwoman has been set up with an annuity, and acts as Antonia's guardian. The woman knows the truth of the girl's birth, but has told her that Sandro is a distant relative. For now, he lives with this charade, but I know he would very much like to acknowledge the truth and see that she takes her rightful place in English Society."

A furrow had formed between Mellon's brows. "Assuming she has a rightful place."

"Yes, that is certainly part of the problem." Arianna paused. "As is the fact that I am just as much a foreigner to the Polite World as Antonia. I should like to see her accepted by the *ton* regardless of her birth, but I have little idea of how to go about it. Aunt Constantina, of course, will be a great asset, for I am sure she will relish the idea of orchestrating a debut Season. I—I am hoping you might consent to give me advice as well. Things like whose favor it is important to curry, which hostess has the most influence."

"Forgive me, but aren't these the sort of activities you loathe?"

"I have done a great many things in my life that I did not wish to do, sir," she replied. "That did not prevent me from doing them very well. When I set my mind to something, I can be very stubborn." Her lips quirked. "As you have no doubt noticed."

He acknowledged the quip with a tiny nod.

"It would mean a great deal to Sandro. Though he keeps his feelings well hidden, I know that the matter is eating at his insides." Though she considered herself good at reading people, she was having trouble trying to gauge Mellon's reaction. For a skilled diplomat, masks were like a second skin.

*A fact that she must not forget during the coming weeks.*

"So, I was also wondering if, given your connections in the government, you might also consent to make a few discreet inquiries into your brother's affairs while we are away in Vienna," she went on. "It would be of enormous help to know whether there was indeed a marriage to Antonia's mother, and whether England would recognize it as legal." Arianna kept her eyes on his face. "I would like to surprise Sandro by making it possible for Antonia to come live with us when her school term is over next spring."

Mellon gave a rueful grimace, the first overt show of emotion he had allowed. "You know, I couldn't in my wildest dreams have imagined any greater shock than this news."

*I am afraid that you will soon have to confront an even worse nightmare,* she thought to herself.

"But yes, of course I can make some inquiries."

"Thank you," she said simply. "I'm very grateful."

"And I, in turn, am happy that you took me into your confidences." He stared meditatively into his port. "I assume that for now, you wish to keep this a secret from Sandro."

*Secrets.*

She nodded. "I think it would be best."

"You may count on my discretion."

A short while later, Arianna stepped into the night and walked the short distance to where her carriage was waiting. Shadows flickered over the pavement as the mist-dampened darkness dueled with the bright blaze of the town house torchieres, mirroring her unsettled thoughts.

There was much to think about. Kydd, Rochemont, Mellon . . . How ironic, she mused. Only a short time ago life had seemed a bit flat.

If it was a spark of danger that she craved—that frisson of liquid fire pulsing through the blood—the coming few weeks promised to leave every nerve ending tingling with its burn.

Lifting her face to the breeze, she inhaled and held the cool air in her lungs for a moment, waiting for the sudden pounding in her ears to subside. Ahead lay the unknown, and that should be frightening to any proper lady of the *ton*.

A tiny gust tugged the corners of her mouth upward. *Ah, but I'm not a proper lady, am I?*

"I trust your evening went well?" Saybrook stepped out of the shadows and opened the carriage door for her.

"Very well. And yours?"

"Baz and I made some interesting discoveries." He offered her a hand. "Come, let us return home without delay, and I'll explain it all over a cup of late-night chocolate."

The pale stone of the Horse Guards rose up like a square-shouldered ghost from the tendrils of morning mist. Despite the earliness of the hour, a troop of mounted soldiers emerged from the stables and wheeled into formation for their parade ground drills.

His boot steps melding with the muffled beat of hooves and jangling of metal, Saybrook mounted the side stairs and made his way through the warren of corridors to Grentham's office. He had spent the previous day and half the night following up on the information found in Kydd's rooms, so the urgent summons from the minister had not been a welcome sight at the breakfast table.

"How kind of you to respond so quickly," said Grentham, his voice dripping with sarcasm. "I would offer you coffee, but I assume you only drink the mouth-fouling sludge that you and your wife find so fascinating."

"You mean spiced chocolate?" replied the earl. He sat down without invitation. "Try adding sugar. Perhaps it would sweeten that sour phiz of yours."

"You're awfully generous with your *bon mots*, Lord Saybrook. Would that you were half as forthcoming with information," snapped the minister. "You were supposed to come by *yesterday* with an update on your visit to Kydd's rooms." He tapped his fingertips together. "I am tiring of giving you everything that you want and getting nothing in return."

"You wish a bon-*bon*?" Saybrook arched a brow. "Very well. I've discovered an interesting lead on how to learn more about Kydd's clandestine political activities. Which in turn may lead me to whoever recruited him."

Grentham waited.

The earl began buffing the chased silver knob of his walking stick on his sleeve.

"I don't find you amusing, Saybrook."

"I didn't come here to entertain you by jumping through hoops."

The locking of their eyes produced a near-audible click. Both men tensed, as if they had heard the hammer of a pistol being drawn to half cock.

"In all honesty, Grentham, can you blame me for being less than eager to reveal my plans or my sources? Based on our previous investigation, I have good reason to have little confidence in you and your lackeys. It would seem that

Renard, a French fox of a traitor, is still running tame in your own department. Until he is trapped, it would be foolhardy to be too forthcoming." Saybrook crossed his legs. "I'm pursuing the matter. What more do you need to know?"

Thinning his lips, Grentham countered with his own question. "That is all you intend to tell me?"

"Yes."

"The information will not be shared with—as you so delicately put it—my lackeys." A pause. "Or is it that you still suspect me?"

Saybrook's cool smile grew a touch more pronounced.

"You are balanced on a razor's edge, you know," said Grentham. "Teetering between triumph and disaster."

"So are you," retorted the earl. "Don't waste your breath trying to blow me over the edge. I did not come here to waste time in bluster or bravado." He stared for a moment through the tall windows overlooking the blue-coated riders, watching the raindrops form into sinuous snakes of water that slid down the glass. "I have been thinking over strategy, and I am concerned about a fundamental weakness in our plan."

Grentham leaned back in his chair and steepled his well-tended hands.

"It has to do with Davilenko," Saybrook continued. "Replacing the documents in the book may have fooled him into thinking that the treason is as of yet undetected. But he's not stupid, and our appearance in Vienna might appear too much of a coincidence. I am not sure—"

"I've already anticipated that problem, Lord Saybrook." The minister allowed a self-satisfied smile. "Davilenko has been dealt with. He won't be making any waves, so to speak, in Vienna."

"Might I inquire how you are so certain?" asked the earl.

Grentham's expression pinched to a smirk. "Unlike you, I shall not indulge in childish hide-and-seek games. Davilenko met with an unfortunate accident on his crossing to Calais on the way to the Conference. The ship encountered a patch of rough weather, causing him to lose his footing on deck and fall overboard."

Saybrook lifted a brow.

"Alas, the poor fellow drowned before the crew could fish him out of the water—and even the meticulous Mr. Henning, had he been there, could not have found evidence to the contrary." The minister lowered his voice to a deceptively soft murmur. "Water in the lungs leaves no telltale bruising, you know."

"Ah. Thank you for the warning," drawled the earl. "I've assumed that travel abroad is fraught with peril, but I shall be extra vigilant."

"It's always wise to be on guard," replied Grentham. "One never knows when Fate will strike, eh?"

"Indeed. I will take care, especially on the journey home," muttered the earl. "For some reason I have a feeling that getting to Vienna will not be as difficult as returning."

"Prevailing weather patterns in the Alps," said the minister with a perfectly straight face.

"That would explain it." He spun his stick between his palms. "Anything else, milord? Much as I enjoy exchanging social pleasantries with you, I've better ways to spend my time."

Grentham's nostrils flared, but he covered his annoyance with a sarcastic smile. "Let us hope so. It would be a pity to see your uncle's reputation sunk into a stinking cesspool after all his years of stalwart service."

The only answer was a whisper of wool as the earl brushed a wrinkle from his trousers.

"One last thing," added the minister. "Before he fell overboard, Davilenko did confess to the ship's captain that he had made no mention to his superiors of his temporary loss of the hidden documents. So as of yet, the conspirators have no reason to suspect that anything is amiss. Until, of course, you or your wife muck things up."

"Anything else?" repeated the earl

Grentham took a moment to inspect his pristine white cuff before answering. "It was Davilenko who you spotted sneaking into the woods. He had arranged through a local contact to have the French Guard take a shot at you, but he confessed that the man threatened to expose him unless he paid more money. So he slit the fellow's throat when your pursuit caused a moment of distraction."

"Who was the local contact?" demanded Saybrook.

"Davilenko claimed not to know—it was arranged by leaving a letter at a prearranged spot." A nasty smile. "And I believe him. Captain Leete is quite proficient at carrying out his duties."

"I thought your man left no evidence of trauma," remarked the earl.

"Oh, come—surely you know there are far more sophisticated ways of drawing out information than resorting to physical violence."

"Thank you for the enlightenment. It quite brightens my day." Saybrook rose. "I do have another request of my own. I take it you have routine dossiers compiled on Talleyrand, Tsar Alexander and Metternich. I would like to read them before I leave for the Continent."

Grentham gave a brusque nod. "Come back this afternoon. You'll find that their reputation as rapacious rakes is well deserved. So I should keep an eye on your wife, if I were you." He opened one of the document cases on his desk and began reading through some papers. "She seems to enjoy the company of dissolute men."

"Unlike most of the pompous prigs of the *ton*, I don't find an intelligent, clever female intimidating." Saybrook curled a mocking smile. "Indeed, I find it quite attractive."

The minister didn't look up. "If I want a sonnet on sex, I'll visit a brothel."

"Which one do you prefer? I hear the Grotto of Venus is much favored by gentlemen who need help in rising to the occasion of having a spot of fun in life."

"I suggest you remove yourself from my office, Lord Saybrook." Grentham picked up a pen and made a notation in the margin of the document. "While your *pego* is still attached to your person."

\*   \*   \*

Arianna crossed off another item from her list as two footmen carried a large brass-latched case down to the entrance foyer. "Good God, you would think we were moving home and hearth to Cathay," she muttered, surveying the growing mound of baggage with a baleful grimace. Saybrook had warned her that they might be away from home for as many as three months—and maybe longer. It was now the middle of September, so that meant they might not be home before the new year ... which suddenly seemed very far away.

"How many trunks are still upstairs, Juan?"

"A half dozen more, madam."

She let out a sigh. "I fear that come tomorrow, we shall need a camel caravan."

"The baggage coach is designed to handle a heavy load," said the footman tactfully.

*Yes, but I am used to traveling light.*

"There is a chest of books to be fetched down from the library," called Saybrook as he came down the stairs.

"Is all of this really necessary?" Arianna arched a skeptical brow as she read the first page of her list aloud to him.

"We have a role to play," Saybrook reminded her. "Several, in fact."

"You have a point," she said, surrendering her protests with a rueful smile. Among the trunks of fancy clothing and fine furnishings was one that contained theatrical face paints and false hairpieces, along with a variety of disguises. "Maybe more than several."

When she and the earl had first met, she had been masquerading as a French chef. A *male* French chef who had ended up being the prime suspect in the poisoning of the Prince Regent. "Monsieur Alphonse" had disappeared into thin air. But the situation in Vienna might very well require a new persona to come to life.

"It's best to be prepared," her husband said, as the footmen headed off for another load. "Mixed among my botanical books are a number of volumes on cryptology."

"I look forward to more lessons during the journey," she replied.

"There will be plenty of hours." He glanced at his pocket watch. "My uncle has invited us for a farewell supper. In the morning, we shall leave at first light to catch the tide at Dover."

"So, the wheels are finally spinning into motion."

"Yes." He fixed her with a searching stare. "No regrets?"

Arianna shook her head. "I confess, I am probably anticipating the challenge more than I should be."

The subtle shift of his mouth was nearly lost in the soft light of the wall sconces. "As am I." His lips suddenly possessed hers in a swift kiss. "Though I hate dragging you into danger."

"I would be kicking and screaming if you tried to leave me behind."

"I know. Not that it makes me feel any less guilty."

"Grentham has a grudge against me too," Arianna pointed out. "I'm probably safer with you than I am staying here in London on my own. You know my ungovernable temper—I can't seem to resist needling him whenever we meet."

"Arianna . . ."

She turned away before he could go on. "Ah, look! Bianca has sent up a sample of the new confection I found in your grandmother's notebooks." Taking the tray from the maid, she added, "There is a pot of chocolate as well. Let us retreat to the parlor and enjoy a respite from the chaos."

"Speaking of Grentham," said Saybrook, toying with his spoon as a plume of steam wafted up from his cup.

"I hope that duplicitous bastard hasn't turned you up sweet," growled a voice from the doorway.

Arianna looked around, a smile wreathing her face. "Mr. Henning! Do come join us." She offered him a plate. "The praline is made with Marcona almonds, a specialty from Spain."

The surgeon bit into one with an audible crunch. "I shall miss your treats while you are away."

"We shall hurry back," she said drily. "And with any luck, we will bring some new recipes back with us."

"Assuming Grentham doesn't sink your ship," said Henning darkly. He had been told the previous evening about Davilenko's demise. "Watch your arse, laddie."

"I shall depend on you to be the eyes in the back of my head," said the earl.

Henning made a strange face. "Alas, I fear my orbs will be turned elsewhere." He withdrew a letter, much stained from travel, from his pocket and tossed it on the table. "My sister has just sent urgent word to me—my nephew has gone missing from his studies at the university and she fears that he's the victim of foul play."

"I'm so sorry," Arianna said.

Saybrook took longer to reply. "I take it she gave a more detailed reason for her fears."

"Aye." The surgeon looked grim. "Angus had apparently been recruited by a group of fellow students to join a secret political society."

Arianna felt her throat go a little dry.

"The Dragons of St. Andrew?" asked Saybrook.

"Aye, the very devils, as I just discovered." replied Henning. "The lad was made head of the pamphlet committee—a bloody dangerous job, given the recent military crackdown on dissent—and his friends admitted that they haven't seen him since he was summoned to attend an urgent late-night meeting." His hands clenched into fists. "This is no longer an inquiry that I can entrust to someone else. Like you, I am readying myself for a trip. Desmond has promised to tend to my patients, so I shall be leaving for Scotland tomorrow."

The earl thinned his lips.

"Auch, ye need not look guilty, laddie. It seems that Fate had decided I was going to be dragged into this tangle, whether you asked me or not."

"Fate," repeated Saybrook. "Or some other sinister force?"

"Who else other than Grentham knows that Mr. Henning is involved in our investigation?" mused Arianna aloud.

"A good question," replied her husband. "An even better one is who else other than Grentham knows that an investigation is taking place. Davilenko supposedly took that secret with him to a watery grave."

"You aren't thinking fish have ears?" said Henning cynically.

"No, I'm thinking rats have tongues," answered the earl. "And it looks like it's up to us to smoke the vermin out of the woodwork."

# 13

## From Lady Arianna's Chocolate Notebooks

### Honey Chocolate Chip Cookies

2¼ cups all-purpose flour
1 tsp. baking soda
½ teaspoon salt
1 cup (2 sticks) unsalted butter, softened
1½ cups white sugar
3 tablespoons honey
2 eggs
2 teaspoons vanilla extract
2 cups bittersweet chocolate chips, or chopped bittersweet chocolate

1. Preheat oven to 375° F. In a small mixing bowl, mix together the flour, baking soda, and salt.
2. In a large mixing bowl, cream together the butter, sugar, honey, eggs and vanilla; gradually add the dry ingredients until a dough forms. Stir in the chocolate.
3. Drop 1-tablespoon portions of dough onto cookie sheets lined with parchment paper; bake for 8–9

minutes, rotating the cookie sheets after 5 minutes.
Cool on a wire rack.

The brick warming her feet had gone cold and the blankets had slipped as the coach lumbered through a tight turn in the downward-spiraling road. Would her body ever be the same? Arianna shifted on the seat, trying to find a comfortable position. Every bone and bit of flesh felt bruised from the bumps.

They traveled hard, pushing at a bruising pace through France and across the Alps. The snowcapped peaks, rising majestically against a brilliant blue sky, had taken her breath away. She had never seen anything like it.

"This second coded letter is proving devilishly difficult to decipher," muttered Saybrook, setting aside his notebooks with a sigh. "If you can tear your gaze away from the scenery, perhaps we should go over a few things, now that we are getting close to Vienna."

Despite the chill, her skin began to tingle. "Tell me more about the main people we are going to encounter. The ones who are likely involved in the conspiracy, unwittingly or not." The names were of course familiar, but she wished to commit the details about their strengths and weaknesses to memory.

"Let's start with our prime suspect," said Saybrook. "Ah, but where to begin with Charles Maurice de Talleyrand-Périgord?" The earl pursed his lips. "Some of this you already know, but it bears repeating."

She nodded.

"He was born the eldest son of an ancient aristocratic family, but because of a lame leg, he was pushed into a Church career while his younger brother was anointed the heir of the family. Through the influence of his relatives, he rose to become a bishop, even though his faith was, shall we say, lax. Indeed, he quickly established a reputation for wit and charm in the drawing rooms of Paris—along with an appetite for fine wine, sumptuous cuisine and beautiful women."

"So, he is not a saint," observed Arianna.

"Hardly. A cat, perhaps, seeing as he appears to have nine lives. But most of all, he is the consummate diplomat—a master of manipulation, though to give the devil his due, he's a brilliant statesman, and his views on world politics have much to admire."

"Then if he is our enemy, he is a formidable one," she said.

"Very," agreed Saybrook. "To say he is clever and conniving is an understatement. You have only to look at his career to see he has an uncanny instinct for survival. Through the influence of friends and his own natural abilities, he managed to serve as a trusted advisor to the *Ancien Régime*, the Revolutionary fanatics, Napoleon and now the restored French monarchy."

"Does he believe in *any* abstract principle?" she asked.

"Aside from pleasure and plumping his own purse?" Saybrook shrugged. "God only knows. It's well known that Talleyrand lined his pockets with bribes throughout his career—not to speak of his double dealing with the Russian Tsar in '08." He blew out his cheeks. "I think we can assume that for the Prince—in 1806 the Emperor granted Talleyrand the title of Prince of Benevento as a reward for his services—his own personal objectives are sovereign."

Arianna took a moment to consider all she had heard. Talleyrand was cold, calculating. In her past life she had matched wits with many clever, unscrupulous men, but the thought of facing off against the Prince of Benevento sent a shiver snaking down her spine.

"A formidable opponent," she repeated. "It's hard to imagine that anyone else is orchestrating this plot." Carefully keeping her eyes on the passing mountain landscape, she added, "Now, tell me about the others."

Saybrook thumbed through the pages of his notebook. "Prince Metternich, the Austrian Foreign minister, is equally astute in the art of political negotiations. For the last decade, he has, by all accounts, been remarkably good at protecting Austria's interests despite its daunting military defeats. And like Talleyrand, he's known for his charm and smooth social graces." A pause. "He also shares the Frenchman's taste for seducing women."

"I may have to return to my old habit of wearing a knife strapped to my leg in order to defend my honor," said Arianna lightly.

"It might be a wise idea." Her husband did not crack a smile. "Arianna, these men are used to getting what they want. Yes, they prefer to use charm, but don't be deceived that they will graciously take no for an answer."

For a long moment, the only sound inside the coach was the clatter of the iron-rimmed wheels over the flinty rocks.

"I've seen enough of deceit and depravity not to make such a naive mistake, Sandro," she answered.

The hazy half light seemed to accentuate his troubled scowl. "I have every respect for your formidable skills, my dear. And yet, I cannot forget that without my intervention, they would not have protected you from a horrible death."

"We have gone over all of this. I understand and accept the risks, Sandro," Arianna reminded him. "What else should I know about Metternich?"

He hesitated, and then gave in with a grudging sigh. "At the upcoming congress, he will be intent on creating order and stability on the Continent. He's enough of a realist to realize that means peace with France, so he will be open to Talleyrand's ideas. My guess is he's more concerned with the mercurial Tsar of Russia, who looms as a large and unpredictable power to his east."

"I see," she said. "And Alexander? Is he really as bad as the picture painted in the English press?" The Tsar had recently paid a visit to London, and had earned scathing criticism for his arrogance and boorish manners.

"The Tsar is a complex person," replied Saybrook. "He's a strange mixture of conflicting characteristics. He was greatly influenced by his grandmother, Catherine the Great, who had him tutored in the liberal ideals of the Enlightenment. After coming to the throne, he championed the idea of sweeping social reform in Russia. But as of yet, little change has really happened. A part of him is very autocratic and intolerant of criticism. He has a mystical side—some would call it messianic—and believes that God has chosen him to be a spiritual leader."

"And thus all should obey his commands?" remarked Arianna.

"Precisely," said her husband.

"Men like that are . . . dangerous," she mused. "Are the reports of his amorous exploits true?" Gossip about the Tsar's rapacious pursuit of women had been a popular subject in London during his recent visit to England.

"Alexander wants to feel loved," answered Saybrook somewhat obliquely. "He flirts shamelessly and seems to feel that a woman's physical surrender is an affirmation of his worth."

*An astute assessment.* The earl was a dispassionate judge of character, an ability that sometimes left her feeling a little uncomfortable.

*How does he see me?*

Tucking the fur-lined carriage blanket around her middle, Arianna leaned back against the squabs. It was, she decided, a question best left unspoken.

"I hear he is called the Angel," she said, affecting an air of nonchalance to hide her uncertainty. "Is he handsome? I only caught a glimpse of him from afar when he was in Town, so it was hard for me to judge."

"In his youth, he was considered ethereally attractive." Saybrook's expression finally betrayed a hint of humor. "But of late, he has been partying so hard that it is said he has put on a good deal of weight, so that a messenger had to be dispatched back to Moscow for a new set of uniforms."

"Ah—a glutton for pleasure? Perhaps I can ply him with chocolate and coax some useful tidbits of information out of him."

"Perhaps." He turned pensive. "He and Talleyrand were

close in the past, so it's possible that he is in some way involved in this intrigue. However"—he ran a hand along the line of his jaw—"I think that we will find Talleyrand at the heart of this conspiracy. Of all the men coming to Vienna, he is the one to fear most."

"Come, open your eyes, Arianna. You should not miss seeing your arrival in Vienna."

*Vienna.*

She shifted against the squabs and brushed a palm over the fogged window glass. "Vienna," she murmured softly, now wide-awake as they rolled over the majestic stone bridge spanning the Danube River. The currents swirled, quicksilver flickers of sunlight dancing across the dark water.

" 'The haunt of the Hapsburgs is famous for its parks,' " read Saybrook, quoting a passage from the guidebook they had purchased in London. "According to this, we should be passing the Augarten at any moment."

The coach lumbered past a vast swath of Baroque gardens, formal lawns and shaded walkways. " 'The flowering landscape is designed in the French style,' " Saybrook continued. " 'And its avenues are lined with stately chestnut, lime, ash and maple trees. Within the grounds are dining and dance halls for the public, as well as a grand palace.' "

"Interesting," she murmured, trying to read the elaborate inscriptions above the gate.

The earl seemed to be enjoying his role as tour guide. As they rolled toward the center of the city, he thumbed to a new section in the book. "The walls of the old medieval town were said to have been built with ransom money from Richard the Lionheart."

The horses circled a large fountain, and then they were bumping over the cobbles of the narrow, twisting streets.

"Look up and you will see St. Stephen's Cathedral." Saybrook pointed out the soaring limestone cathedral with its Romanesque towers and intricately patterned tile roof. "Its main bell is one of the largest in Europe and was cast out of cannons captured from the Muslim invaders in 1711."

"East versus West," she said. "I daresay we will see our share of modern-day conflict."

The earl regarded the weathered stone for a moment before nodding.

Arianna still felt a little like a wide-eyed child as she looked out at the elegant storefronts and the streets crowded with wealthy merchants and regal aristocrats. "Is every royal in Europe here?" she asked, watching a procession of gilded carriages drawn by prancing horses.

"I doubt that any of them would wish to miss being part of such a glittering glamorous spectacle."

"Ha." Her laugh turned into a yawn.

"We are headed to our rooms now—not that we will have much time to recover from the rigors of travel," apologized her husband. "We are invited to attend a soiree tonight given by our British envoy, and I think it best we begin work without delay."

"No rest for the wicked."

"Indeed, every night there will be drinking, dining and dancing until dawn."

"Not to speak of other activities," added Arianna.

"Intrigue never sleeps," said Saybrook.

"Let us hope that we are allowed a few hours of respite from time to time." She yawned again. "A splash of cold water and I shall be ready to hunt a fox."

The earl cracked his knuckles. "Or slay a dragon."


"The party is being held at Lord Castlereagh's residence on the Minoritenplatz, which is close by," said Saybrook, as he stepped into Arianna's dressing room an hour later. "The evening should end early, for Her Ladyship's entertainments are thought to be rather dull."

"I would probably doze through a performance of whirling dervishes," admitted Arianna. She arched her neck, so her maid could thread a seeding of pearls through the topknot of curls. "*Gracias*, Theresa. And thanks to you and

Juan for putting our quarters in such perfect order so quickly."

*"De nada, señora."* Her maid performed one last adjustment and then quietly withdrew from the room.

"The entertainment will not be nearly so lively," said Saybrook as he moved through the candlelight to perch a hip on the edge of the dressing table. "There will be no dancing. For Castlereagh, conversation is the center of attention, which is why we are going out of our way to make an appearance."

"I shall try not to be tongue-tied with fatigue."

Her quip drew a faint smile. "Not only is it polite to pay our respects, but hearing the latest gossip will give us a good idea of the lay of the land, so to speak." Flexing his shoulders, he rose. "Are you ready to go down to the carriage?"

It was only a short journey through the smoke-scented night to the residence of Lord Castlereagh, the head of the British delegation.

"Ah, Saybrook. I wasn't aware that you and your lovely wife had arrived." Castlereagh greeted them with a polite nod. "I trust that your uncle is well?"

"Quite. Though I daresay a part of him regrets that he is not here taking part in the negotiations."

"Tell him that there is an old saying . . . Be careful what you wish for." Castlereagh quirked a slight grimace after bowing over Arianna's hand. "I fear that the talks are going to drag on far longer than anyone anticipated, and to what end, I would not hazard to guess."

Saybrook made a noncommittal sound.

"Be grateful that you have come to enjoy the splendid cultural treasures of the city, rather than be mired in the mud of international politics. But I won't rattle on about such boring matters—Mellon assures me that you have no interest in diplomatic wranglings." Castlereagh gestured discreetly to a lady standing by the tea table. "My wife will be happy to introduce Lady Saybrook to her friends while I take you to meet some of my fellow diplomats. Several of them share your interests. Von Humbolt is here, and as you know, he is a serious scholar . . ."

It was nearly an hour before Arianna could gracefully withdraw from the circle of chattering ladies and join Saybrook in perusing a set of botanical prints hung by the side parlor.

"Did you know that the Countess of Sagan is called the Cleopatra of the North?" she murmured, accepting a glass of Tokay wine from one of the passing footmen. "And her rival, Princess Bagration, is known as the Beautiful Naked Angel because she wears only low-cut white dresses made of thin India muslin."

"You see what a font of interesting information these parties provide," he replied with a cynical smile. "Both ladies are vying to establish themselves as the reigning hostess here. They look to attract the most influential men and then parlay that power into gaining their own objectives."

"In that they are no different than the opposite sex. The male leaders have come here to preen and prance around in their bejeweled and bemedaled finery, hoping to forge alliances and trade favors," Arianna pointed out.

"True. The ladies simply negotiate without the formality of written treaties, but are no less skilled at getting what they want." The earl assumed an expression of cynical detachment. "The countess and the princess both reside at the Palm Palace, so word is that people will be watching with great interest to see who turns left and who turns right when entering the courtyard."

Arianna touched the rim of the faceted crystal to her lips. "And then there is Anna Protassoff, who allegedly served as the 'tester' for the guardsmen whom Catherine the Great chose for her bedmates." She made a wry face. "Perhaps that explains why the Tsar has such an appetite for sex—he must have inherited his grandmother's lust along with her throne."

"Do you know how Catherine the Great is supposed to have died?" asked Saybrook. "The rumors involve a horse, a scaffolding and . . ."

He stopped abruptly as one of the English diplomats and his wife joined them in the alcove. "My dear, allow me to introduce you to Mr. Repton and his wife. They are friends of Charles and Eleanor."

"How delightful to meet you at last, Lady Saybrook," said Mrs. Repton. She flashed a smile, though her tone implied a faint criticism. "La, I was beginning to wonder if you were merely a will-o'-the-wisp."

"His Lordship and I lead a very quiet life in London," Arianna said.

"Oh, well, it is *not* quiet here!" Mrs. Repton assured, ignoring her husband's warning cough. "There are parties every night—balls, musicales, soirees! It's so hard to choose, though often we attend two or three."

"Indeed," replied Arianna.

The other lady took it as a cue to elaborate. "You must be sure to visit the salons of Lady Sagan and Princess Bagration." Mrs. Repton lowered her voice a notch. "Both ladies are reputed to have slept with Prince Metternich. Of late, however, the Tsar of Russia is said to be pursuing the princess."

"Alexander chases anyone wearing skirts," muttered Repton, trying to stem his wife's garrulous chatter.

His wife went on, oblivious to the hint. "Everyone is betting on how long it will take for him to slip between her sheets," she confided. "The men are equally outrageous . . ."

Arianna listened politely. *Cluck, cluck, cluck*—the lady was a hen-witted goose. But as Saybrook said, gossip could be very useful, and clearly Mrs. Repton liked to gabble.

"It is hard to imagine how anything serious is supposed to be accomplished here," she remarked, when the descriptions finally came to an end. "It seems that all people are thinking about is drinking, dining and dancing one's latest lover into bed."

Mrs. Repton gave a titter of laughter. "Oh, it is *quite* shocking all the things that go on." She clicked open her fan and cooled her cheeks. "Now, allow me to offer a bit of guidance on where to go in order to see and be seen. Lord

Castlereagh holds this soiree every Tuesday evening, so you must be sure to stop by."

"Monday is Metternich's night," offered Repton. "And of course Friday belongs to the Duchess of Sagan and her rival across the courtyard. As for the other evenings, there is no lack of entertainment, but I daresay you will discover that for yourselves."

"Oh, do be sure to visit the Apollo Saal." Lady Repton clearly considered herself a font of knowledge on Viennese life. "You can waltz all night in the indoor gardens, which are decorated with faux stones and fairy tale grottos."

"Thank you," replied Saybrook. "Now if you will excuse us, we should probably be taking our leave. We are tired from traveling and wish to be rested for the Emperor's ball tomorrow night."

"Oh, that is definitely an evening not to be missed," exclaimed Lady Repton. "It is said that the state dinner will include three hundred hams, two hundred partridges and two hundred pigeons, not to speak of three thousand liters of olla soup."

The mention of food set Arianna's stomach to growling. "I have heard that the Viennese appreciate fine food."

"It's tolerable, though they don't know how to cook a proper joint of beef," answered Mrs. Repton with a slight sniff. "For a special treat, you must try to garner an invitation to one of the French Minister's dinners. He has brought the renowned chef, Monsieur Carême, with him from Paris to serve as his personal cook. Word is, the banquets are sumptuous—especially the pastries."

Now *that* interesting tidbit was certainly food for thought.

"Sounds delicious," said Arianna.

"Talleyrand is a connoisseur of decadent pleasures," said Repton, his face tight with disapproval. "And if we aren't careful, he will gobble up power and influence that rightly belong to Britain." He made a face. "After all, *we* were the victors, and he served the Corsican Monster."

"I am sure that our government will be keeping a close

eye on the French," replied Saybrook. "And that it will be vigilant in defending all that was won on the field of battle from diplomatic intrigue."

"Well said, sir. Well said," enthused Repton. "Your noble military record is well known. It's a pity that your uncle could not have convinced you to follow in his diplomatic footsteps. Whitehall could use more men like you."

"I'm afraid politics don't interest me," demurred the earl.

"A man of action, no doubt." Repton signaled for a footman to refill his wine. "Ha—too bad there are no wars left to wage."

Arianna watched his soft, fleshy hands cup the glass. *Oh, how easy it was to spout such sentiments when you have never smelled the throat-choking stench of fear, of blood, of death.*

"There are always battles to fight," said Saybrook softly. "But I, for one, am not unhappy that words are the weapons of choice these days."

Covering his discomfiture with a cough, Repton nodded. "Just so."

Without further ado, the earl bid their new acquaintances' adieu, and wasted no time in escorting Arianna out to the stairway.

"God save us from narrow-minded fools," he muttered through his teeth.

"I would rather that the Almighty help us with a far more dangerous threat," remarked Arianna. "However unwittingly, his wife was actually of some help tonight." As she drew in a breath, she could almost taste a hint of sugar wafting in the smoke-scented air. "A connoisseur of cuisine with a fondness for sweets . . . I think we must contrive to meet Monsieur le Prince Talleyrand without delay."

"That shouldn't prove difficult," said Saybrook. "Castlereagh just informed me that your other admirer, Comte Rochemont, is residing at the Kaunitz Palace as part of the French delegation. His family connections with the restored French King accord him such rank and privileges, though Talleyrand is not overly pleased with the arrangement."

"However, it suits our needs perfectly," she replied. "I see that I will have to encourage the attentions of both Rochemont and Kydd." *Even though there is an old adage about burning the candle at both ends.* "And yet, I must take care not to ignite a rivalry between them."

"On the contrary," said her husband. "Jealousy will likely work in our favor. A man vying for the attentions of a beautiful woman will often allow passion to overrule reason."

*Passion.* A powerful, primitive force.

Saybrook's expression betrayed no emotion. Cool. Calm. Controlled. She had never met anyone so in command of his feelings. The only hint that he was not so detached was the slow, silent flick of his lashes, shadowy specters of black obscuring his chocolate-dark eyes.

"I shall do my best not to embarrass you by stirring talk of my scandalous flirtations," said Arianna slowly. "An unhappy wife, seeking amusements elsewhere—"

"Is nothing out of the ordinary," he interrupted. "Dalliances are *de rigueur* for the *ton*. Any speculation on your amorous activities will be lost in all the gossip about the royal transgressions."

"How very lowering to know that I merit so little interest," she quipped.

"Let us pray it stays that way." Saybrook took her arm—possessively, or so it seemed. "The less our unknown adversary has reason to turn his eye on you, the better."

# 14

## From Lady Arianna's Chocolate Notebooks

### Chocolate-Almond Italian Cookies

2 tablespoons unsalted butter, for greasing
½ teaspoon baking powder
1 tablespoon lukewarm water
1¾ cups finely ground plus 2 tablespoons roughly chopped almonds
1½ cups plus 2 tablespoons flour
1 cup sugar
2 tablespoons chocolate chips
1 tablespoon cocoa powder
1 tablespoon extra virgin olive oil
½ teaspoon kosher salt
½ cup Strega or Galliano liqueur
⅓ cup coffee, at room temperature

1. Heat oven to 325°. Grease 2 parchment-lined baking sheets with butter and set aside. In a small bowl, whisk together baking powder and 1 tbsp. lukewarm water until dissolved, 20 seconds.
2. Combine ground and chopped almonds, flour,

sugar, chocolate chips, cocoa powder, oil and salt in a large bowl. With a wooden spoon, vigorously stir in the baking powder mixture, liqueur, and coffee to form a wet dough.

3. Divide the dough into 1-oz. portions. Using your hands, roll dough portions into balls and transfer to prepared baking sheets spaced about 1 inch apart. Bake until set, about 30 minutes. Transfer cookies to racks and let cool to firm before serving.

"**A**nd here we are back at the Hofburg Palace." David Kydd offered his arm to Arianna as they waited to cross the busy street. "Though here in Vienna, it is simply called the 'Burg.'"

"I still am amazed at how big it is," said Arianna, placing a hand on his sleeve. It had proved easy to engage the young diplomat as her escort for sightseeing. For the last week they had been meeting almost daily to explore the city's splendors. "I've been told that the main courtyard was designed as a jousting field."

"Yes, monarchs always wish to awe their subjects," replied Kydd with a wry grin. "Some of the visiting rulers of Europe are here as the Austrian Emperor's guests," he went on, as they passed into the massive courtyard. "Tsar Alexander is quartered in the Amalienburg wing, while the King of Prussia is in the old Schweizerhof section."

"Thank you for serving as such a gracious guide," she replied. They had spent the morning visiting the Belvedere Palace and the coffeehouses of the Prater park while Saybrook worked in the palace library. "I enjoyed it very much . . ." She deliberately added a tiny sigh. "But now, I'm afraid it's time for me to go meet my husband."

"It was my pleasure, Lady Saybrook," said Kydd. "Perhaps tomorrow you would like to see the famous zoo."

Arianna smiled. Her thinly veiled complaints about the

earl's selfishness and neglect seemed to be bearing fruit. The Scotsman's reserve was melting, and he was growing warmer in expressing his sympathies. She in turn was becoming increasingly vocal in expressing admiration for his political ideas. With just a little coaxing on her part, their conversations were turning more and more to mutual criticisms of the aristocracy and its arrogant assumption of entitlement.

"I would like that very much."

Kydd inclined a small bow. "Until tomorrow, then."

Arianna quickly entered the palace and requested that one of the Imperial footmen lead her through the maze of corridors to the library wing.

That Kydd saw her as a kindred soul stirred a slight twinge of guilt—until she reminded herself of how he had betrayed Mellon.

*If one lives by the sword, one must be prepared to die by the sword.*

Speaking of which . . .

Rochemont added yet another twist to the tangle of truth and lies. Biting back an unladylike oath, Arianna turned her thoughts to her other admirer. The comte was becoming more aggressively amorous. A *billet-doux* had arrived for her just after Saybrook's departure from breakfast. Along with a flowery—and rather racy—love poem, it contained a last-minute invitation to join him in dining with Talleyrand that evening.

The suggestion was that she might consent to serving as dessert after the meal.

*Sugar and spice.*

Arianna felt her mouth pinch to a cynical smile. Unlike Eve and her rosy red apple, she must somehow manage to dangle temptation in front of a hungry male without allowing him a bite.

"This way, madam," intoned the footman, his voice holding a note of faint reproach for her lagging pace.

Quickening her steps, Arianna followed him through

several more turns before coming to a set of iron-banded double oak doors, their panels black with age.

"The Botanical Room," announced her guide, as the oiled hinges swung open without a sound. "His Lordship is working in here."

Glass-globed wall lamps cast a softly flickering glow over the sherry-colored paneling and carved acanthus leaf moldings. Framed by the decorative woodwork, towering bookcases rose up from the parquet floor to the painted plaster ceiling.

Looking around from one of the Italianate work tables set along the bank of leaded windows, Saybrook took an instant to blink away a look of intense concentration. He brushed a lock of his long hair back from his brow. "How did your morning walk with Kydd go?"

"I think I am moving forward," she said. "He is becoming increasingly vocal about his frustrations with the British government and its rigid notions of superiority. I'm fanning his feeling of discontent with my own rantings about the oppressive tyranny of Society. With a few more hints about how much I long to strike a real blow against the Old Order instead of simply talking about it, I might get him to confide in me."

"Excellent, excellent." And yet the earl looked strangely pensive.

"That's not all." Arianna took the gold-embossed invitation out of her reticule and placed it on the table. "Rochemont has invited me to a dinner party hosted by Talleyrand tonight—*sans* you, of course."

"Let us hope the Prince serves up some useful information along with his chef's decadent nougat desserts. I am growing damn tired of watching him start to salivate every time you enter the room."

*Was there an odd edge to his voice?*

Oh, surely he didn't think that she was *enjoying* her role as taunting temptress.

Suddenly defensive, she stiffened, recalling Grentham's

nasty innuendos. *Your wife enjoys the company of dissolute men.* It was true that in her first investigation with the earl, she had also played the role of wanton jade. Not because she took any pleasure from it, but because it had been the only way to bring about justice.

But perhaps he was tiring of her unorthodox skills. Most men wanted wives who were . . . respectable.

*Which I am decidedly not.*

"That reminds me—I'm famished," said Saybrook, seemingly oblivious of the subtle change in her stance.

"No doubt because you dined on naught but tea and toast this morning." Arianna glanced down at his jumbled work papers and realized that he too must be feeling frustrated. He had been working like the devil to decipher the remaining coded letter, but it did not appear that he was making much headway. The sheets were covered with cryptic squiggles and scrawls, all scratched out with slashes of black ink. "I take it that your work is going slowly."

Although they were alone in the room, the earl lowered his voice to a taut whisper. It was well known that the Burg's magnificent walls possessed an uncanny ability to see and hear through wood and stone.

"As I've said before, finding the key to unlock our conundrum could take weeks. Months. Years." He tapped a long finger to a set of small leather-bound books hidden beneath the illustrated folios on *Theobroma cacao.* "I found several obscure Renaissance texts on cryptology in the Mathematics Room. They contain some interesting new permutations to try, but . . ." He flexed his shoulders. "Let me finish this one section and then we'll walk to the Café Frauenhuber for some refreshments."

Her own moodiness forgotten, Arianna was quick to agree. "Take your time. I noticed that one of the galleries along this corridor has a lovely collection of chocolate pots on display. I shall wait for you there."

Saybrook nodded vaguely, his attention already back on the diabolical little string of coded letters that he had copied into his notebook.

Leaving the earl to his solitary struggles, she quitted the room and began to retrace her steps. The Emperor was generous in allowing access to his priceless collections of art, as well as his rare books and maps. She passed by a gallery of Quattrocento Italian art and one of classical coins before turning into an airy room devoted to decorative Limoges porcelain.

The Spanish princess Anne of Austria had introduced chocolate to France in 1615 as part of her wedding trousseau—and judging by the beauty of the vessels on display, her new subjects had enthusiastically embraced the new beverage.

"Exquisite," murmured Arianna, leaning in so close that her breath misted the glass case. All worries dissolved for the moment as she stood in rapt study of the small treasures. The pots showcased a dazzling variety of elegant designs, their delicate colors and gold leaf highlights set off to perfection by the black velvet backdrop. Most were crowned by a distinctive pierced lid, which allowed the handle of a *molinillo* to protrude.

"Exquisite," she murmured again, captivated by the elegant simplicity of a pot formed in the shape of a swan.

"Not as exquisite as you." Rochemont's silky whisper caressed the nape of her neck. His breath was warm, and yet its tickle raised a prickling of gooseflesh along her bare arms. "Though I confess," he went on, "the curves have a certain voluptuous shape that makes my mouth water."

Arianna felt his hand graze her hip. Willing herself not to flinch, she waited a moment before drawing back from his touch. "Why, sir," she drawled. "Clearly you have a taste for fine things."

"Yes." He placed his palms on the glass and slanted her a sly look. "I'm insatiable when it comes to sampling the best."

Arianna reacted to the innuendo with a carefully calculated smile. "Oh? Then you must be looking forward to this evening. I hear that Monsieur Carême is a true artist with food."

Her teasing provoked a sinuous smile.

"Imagine butter and cream, meltingly warm in your mouth." Rochemont kissed his fingertips. "The French have a way of creating sublimely sensual pleasures, Lady Saybrook."

*As well as grimly horrific wars.*

The comte made a face. "*Alors*, perhaps too much so. Poor Carême is very unhappy that the King of Wurttemberg just lured away his sous-chef, leaving him shorthanded for the duration of the Conference."

A sudden tingle started to snake down her spine.

"Indeed?" replied Arianna. Hot and cold, hot and cold—men like the comte were tantalized by a challenge. "Then perhaps his performance will not rise quite as high as promised."

Their eyes met for a molten moment before she deliberately looked away.

"Like all Frenchmen, Carême will have no trouble performing at his peak for a beautiful lady." Rochemont sidled closer, his soft leather boots stirring nary a sound on the thick carpet, until they were standing thigh to thigh. "I am looking forward to introducing you to a sinfully seductive experience."

"I appreciate your kind offer to keep my wife amused while I attend a meeting of scholars tonight, Rochemont." Saybrook could move as lightly as a prowling panther when he so chose. "However, might I ask that you unglue yourself from her skirts so that she might accompany me to tea."

The comte smiled, though a telltale ridge of red on his cheekbones betrayed his pique at the interruption. "But of course," he replied. Bowing to Arianna, he said, "Until later, *chérie*."

The earl didn't react to the blatant endearment.

Emboldened by the silence, Rochemont tauntingly added, "Don't spoil your appetite."

---

"A toast." As the servants cleared the platters of viands and sauced vegetables from the dining table, Talleyrand raised a wine goblet, his bejeweled fingers winking like brilliant bits of fire in the fluttery light of the gold candelabras. "To friends old . . ." His lazy, lidded gaze fixed upon Arianna. "And new."

The crystalline clink of glass rang out over the muted chink of silver and porcelain.

"A divine meal. Absolutely divine." The Russian attaché leaned back in his chair and blew out a satisfied sigh. "Carême is a God of the Kitchen. I don't suppose the Tsar could trade you a province for his services, eh?"

"A country perhaps," replied Talleyrand lightly.

Everyone laughed.

"I swear, Carême is more valuable than my entire staff when it comes to melting old enmities and solidifying new friendships," murmured the envoy from Bavaria.

"Indeed. I have told Paris that I don't need secretaries, I need saucepans."

More laughter.

The Prince took a sip of his Burgundy wine. "And how did you enjoy the chef's menu, Lady Saybrook?"

"Superb," she replied in all honesty. "I have never had such a magnificent meal."

"It is not quite over. I have heard that your husband has a scholarly interest in *Theobroma cacao*, so I asked Monsieur Carême to create a special chocolate confection in your honor."

At the flick of his finger, the door opened and a pair of liveried footmen marched in, bearing an enormous platter between them.

A collective gasp greeted the elaborate pastry.

"He is a master of what we French call *pièces montées*," explained Talleyrand, a smile taking shape on his sensual mouth. "A form of edible architecture meant to surprise the senses."

Arianna felt her jaw drop ever so slightly as the servants set the creation down on the center of the table. Formed of molded chocolate, marzipan and sugar, the towering creation stood nearly two feet high and was a replica of Westminster Abbey.

"Chef studies architectural books for his inspiration," Talleyrand went on. "He chose a London landmark in your honor."

"You see, *chérie*. I promised you a treat," whispered Rochemont. "I have some influence with the minister, and so . . . *voila!*"

Someone let out a little moan as a knife sliced off a piece and set it on Arianna's plate.

"Art is meant to be savored," said Talleyrand as the servant added a dollop of nougat and meringue to the pastry. "Enjoy."

The room went silent, save for the crunch of spoons cutting through the sugary chocolate and almond paste.

Talleyrand tasted a small bite, his smile stretching wider as he watched the expressions of bliss form on the faces of his guests. Setting aside his serviette, he tapped his perfectly manicured fingertips together. "Does it meet with your approval, *madame*?"

"Carême deserves his reputation as a genius," she replied. "I wonder . . . might I get the recipe?"

"Perhaps you had better ask him yourself." The Prince's eyes lit with a twinkle of unholy amusement. "I consider myself a skilled negotiator, but I've yet to extract such privileged information from him. Carême guards his culinary creations more carefully than most countries do their secret alliances. But the appeal of a beautiful lady may win a concession." A lazy wink. "He is, after all, French."

"I would at least like to thank him for such an ambrosial treat," said Arianna.

Talleyrand lifted a hand to summon the servant stationed by the door. "Ask chef to come—"

"Actually, might I see him in the kitchens?" She accompanied the request with a flutter of her lashes. "That is, if you don't mind me spying on your territory. I am curious as to what sort of graters and molds he uses."

"Seeing as the Peace Conference is all about creating international accord and harmony, I give you my blessing to look around my palace to your heart's content, *ma-*

*dame.*" A clap set the spill of creamy lace at his cuffs to dancing in the buttery light. "Send Monsieur Jacques to escort Lady Saybrook to chef's inner sanctum."

A plume of steamy air wafted up the stairwell, its warmth redolent with the spicy scent of caramelized sugar and roasted cacao nibs.

Arianna breathed in deeply and smiled, the sweetness stirring old memories of—

*"Non, non, NON!"* The pained shout from the main kitchen was punctuated by the whack of a cleaver. "You must never *grate* ginger! It must be *minced*!" *Whack, whack.* "Like so!"

"Perhaps this is not the best time to ask chef a favor," she murmured to the under butler who was accompanying her.

"Monsieur Carême possesses a ... very sensitive nature," replied her guide. "And delicate nerves. It is difficult to predict what will, and will not, upset him."

"Ah." She nodded sagely. "You mean he is a tyrant, prone to tempestuous tantrums."

The under butler did not bat an eye. "Precisely, *madame.*" He stopped in front of the half-open door. "Would you mind terribly if I allowed you to, *er*, introduce yourself to *Le Maitre*? I have not yet had my supper, and if he blames me for the interruption of his artistic genius, I might very well have to go to bed hungry."

Arianna repressed a wry grin. "Not at all. I am experienced in dealing with temperamental chefs."

Looking grateful, the man bowed and hurried away.

"Into the frying pan—or is it the fire?" she murmured to herself.

The door yielded to her touch and as she crossed the threshold, she was immediately assaulted by a swirl of delicious smells.

Hearing the swish of her silken skirts, Carême whirled around. With the cleaver still clutched in his fist and his toque falling rakishly over one eye, he looked a little like a demented pirate about to commit unspeakable acts upon anything within arm's reach.

*"Mmph,"* he grunted, eyeing her finery. "You have taken a wrong turn, *madame.* The withdrawing room for ze ladies is *up* ze stairs and to ze left." The information was accompanied by a shooing gesture of the steely blade. *"Bonsoir."*

Arianna stood her ground, inwardly amused by her first sight of the celebrated chef. "Forgive me for intruding on your *atelier,* Monsieur Carême. I know that great artists dislike any disturbance of their creative process. But I couldn't resist coming to offer my humble admiration for your prodigious talents."

Like butter placed in a warm pan, Carême's scowl was softened by the egregious flattery.

*"Merci, madame."* The cleaver dropped a notch. "Not everyone understands how difficult it is to turn food into a form of art."

"One of the ingredients is, of course, genius," she murmured.

*"Oui, oui,* zat is true." The chef preened. "Also the freshest meats, fruits and vegetables. Prince Talleyrand understands this, and never quibbles about the cost of my supplies."

"Might I have a quick tour of your kitchens?" asked Arianna. "I should love to see what it takes to achieve perfection."

His smile was turned even rosier by the overhead rack of hanging copper pots. *"Alors,* I rarely allow anyone to see my works in progress. But for you, *madame,* I shall make an exception." With a Gallic flourish, Carême turned to the chopping table. "Follow me."

For the next quarter hour, Arianna was subjected to a lengthy explanation of stove temperatures, proper chopping techniques and the merits of iron versus copper for cooking. Prompted by her questions, the chef also revealed that the recent defection of his sous-chef had thrown his well-ordered kitchen into disarray.

"I should like to slice out his liver for leaving me in the

lurch," grumbled Carême. "Zat is the thanks I get for teaching him some of my special secrets?" His hand flew to his heart. "I am hurt."

"How disloyal," she agreed. "Was his specialty pastries?"

"*Oui*," answered the chef. "Thanks to God, my helpers with meats and vegetables are devoted to me. Zat part of the meals shall not be affected. But as for my desserts . . ." He blew out a mournful sigh. "I shall have to work very hard to see that they don't suffer."

"Speaking of desserts, I don't suppose you would consent to give me the recipe for tonight's creation. My husband adores chocolate."

He pursed his lips. "Ask me almost anything else, *madame*, and I should be happy to oblige. However, my recipes I share with no one—not even Prince Talleyrand."

"I understand," said Arianna. She had expected no less. But it didn't really matter. She was leaving with exactly the information she had come for.

"*Merci* for that," he responded. "Some ladies resort to tears. And much as I hate to see females cry, I never yield to such ploys."

"Don't worry. You will never see me trying to use weeping to make men surrender their secrets," Arianna assured him.

*I prefer other weapons.*

"Once again, I thank you for the tour. It was very enlightening."

"You are most welcome, *madame*." Carême bowed. "Come again some time."

"Thank you. I will."

*And sooner than you think.*

# 15

## From Lady Arianna's Chocolate Notebooks

### Chocolate Caramel Tart

#### For the crust

1½ cups flour
¼ cup plus 1 tablespoon Dutch-process unsweetened cocoa powder
¼ teaspoon kosher salt
10 tablespoons unsalted butter, cubed and softened
½ cup plus 2 tablespoons confectioners' sugar
2 egg yolks, preferably at room temperature
½ teaspoon vanilla extract

#### For the caramel

1½ cups sugar
3 tablespoons light corn syrup
¼ teaspoon kosher salt
6 tablespoons water
6 tablespoons unsalted butter
6 tablespoons heavy cream
1 tablespoon crème fraîche

## *For the ganache*

½ cup heavy cream
4 oz. bittersweet chocolate, finely chopped
Gray sea salt for garnish

1. Make the crust: Heat oven to 350°. Combine flour, cocoa powder and salt in a medium bowl and set aside. Using a handheld mixer, cream the butter and sugar in a large bowl until mixture is pale and fluffy; mix in yolks and vanilla. Mix in dry ingredients. Transfer dough to a 9-inch fluted tart pan with a removable bottom and press dough evenly into bottom and sides of pan. Refrigerate for 30 minutes. Prick the tart shell all over with a fork and bake until cooked through, about 20 minutes. Transfer to a rack and let cool.

2. Make the caramel: In a 1-qt. saucepan, whisk together sugar, corn syrup, salt and 6 tbsp. water and bring to a boil. Cook, without stirring, until a candy thermometer inserted into the syrup reads 340°. Remove pan from heat and whisk in butter, cream and crème fraîche (the mixture will bubble up) until smooth. Pour caramel into cooled tart shell and let cool slightly; refrigerate until firm, 4–5 hours.

3. Make the ganache: Bring cream to a boil in a 1-qt. saucepan over medium heat. Put chocolate into a medium bowl and pour in hot cream; let sit for 1 minute, then stir slowly with a rubber spatula until smooth. Pour ganache evenly over tart and refrigerate until set, 4–5 hours. Sprinkle tart with sea salt, slice and serve chilled.

∽

The branch of candles had burned down to small stubs, leaving the study shrouded in deepening shadows. Arianna heard the faint *scratch, scratch, scratch* of a pen before she could make out the shape of broad shoulders and bowed head hunched over the desk.

"Still at work, Sandro?" she asked softly.

Saybrook turned, his profile limned in the guttering flames. Fatigue shaded his features, along with some darker tautness that she couldn't quite identify. "Yes, there was another idea I wanted to test, but it's been a wasted effort." He put down his pen and massaged his temples. "Perhaps I have lost my touch. I used to have some skill with codes."

"Don't be so hard on yourself." Arianna came up behind his chair and began to knead the knots at the base of his neck. "When you were on Wellington's staff you had a cadre of trained intelligence officers to help you. And yet you've told me that attempts to decipher a captured code failed more often than not."

His muscles slowly relaxed beneath her probing fingers. "I suppose you are right. But I can't help feeling that I am missing some key element that is staring me right in the face."

"Why not let me have a try? I've none of your skills, but I have been studying the principles, and maybe a fresh set of eyes will see something you've overlooked. There is, after all, such a thing as beginner's luck."

Saybrook reached back and caught her wrist. "I would be grateful for your help, but it can wait until morning." He pressed her palm to his cheek, and beneath the rasp of his whiskered skin, she could feel the strong, steady pulse of his heart.

After all the duplicity and deceptions of the evening, its warmth was immensely comforting. She blinked as the sudden, salty sting of tears prickled against the back of her lids.

"Is something wrong, Arianna?"

She shook her head. "Just tired."

He gave a wordless growl and turned his face to brush a kiss to her fingertips. "How did your dinner go? I'm rather surprised that you are back at this hour. Didn't Rochemont try to spirit you off to some secluded love nest? Or was he worried that in the process of wrestling you into his carriage he might scratch his pretty face?"

"He's still complaining about your knocking him down on the rocks. I suspect that he thinks it was a deliberate attempt to mar his beauty," answered Arianna. "As for seduction, it was likely on the comte's mind, but Talleyrand demanded his attendance at an after-supper strategy meeting. And though it was obvious that he wished to refuse, he didn't quite dare to defy the Prince."

Saybrook let out a long breath. "So, another night wasted on frivolous entertainment."

"Not exactly."

Her husband must have heard the note of suppressed excitement in her voice, for he slowly sat up straighter and edged his chair around to face her. "How so?"

"I think I've come up with a way to gain access to Talleyrand's household—to be part of his intimate, everyday routine so to speak, which would allow me to spy on both him *and* the comte."

"Arianna, there are limits to how far I am willing to go for the good of my country." Her husband's voice turned dangerously soft. "So if you are about to suggest that you become the mistress of one of those lecherous Frogs, put the idea out of your head. Immediately."

"No, not a mistress." She couldn't hold back a grin. "A chef."

He blinked.

"Carême's pastry sous-chef has deserted him, throwing plans for the elaborate dinners into question. Think about it. Since we arrived, we've been hearing how Talleyrand brought his chef from Paris to serve as a secret weapon of sorts. His intention is to win support for the French objectives here at the Conference, using butter and sugar rather than muskets and cannons."

She paused to let him digest what she had said. "So, if an experienced chef with a talent for creating sweets appeared and inquired about a position, don't you think the chances are good that Carême would snap him up?"

*"Him,"* repeated Saybrook thoughtfully. "You are suggesting that Monsieur Alphonse—"

"Makes a miraculous resurrection," she replied with a note of triumph. "Though to be safe, he will have to assume a new name. Given that Renard was involved in our last investigation, he might remember Lady Spencer's erstwhile chef."

*"Hmmm."*

That he didn't dismiss the idea out of hand was encouraging.

"What about Kydd?" he asked carefully. "And, for that matter, Rochemont? Posing as a chef may be a clever cover, but we can't put all of our eggs in one basket."

"No, not with the fox running free in the henhouse." The dying candle flame seemed to turned a touch redder, a taunting reminder that their enemy had eluded all their attempts to catch him. "I've thought this through and see no reason why it can't work. I won't have to give up my flirtations with Kydd. I will simply have to pick and choose which party invitations to accept. One of my demands will be that I only work three days a week for Carême. I've checked—that's the number of diplomatic suppers that Talleyrand plays host to, so I believe the chef will accept the stipulation."

"So you are suggesting that you light the coals under two different pots and see which one boils first?"

"Things shouldn't become too hot for comfort. As you know, I have some experience in plotting these sorts of things," replied Arianna. "To cover my occasional absence from the ballrooms, we'll put out word that my health has turned delicate—ladies are always plagued by a variety of maladies. As for Rochemont, he's no longer so important to dally with, now that I'll have direct access to Talleyrand's residence and servants."

Saybrook took his time in replying. As he drummed his fingers on his papers, she could almost hear the gears whirring inside his head.

*Like a carefully calibrated military chronometer, the*

*earl's mind always seemed to work with exquisite precision in analyzing every detail of information.*

"You have a point about Rochemont. He would no longer be needed as a source of information." Her husband raised his eyes from his papers. "In any case, I was already beginning to think that he was turning into more trouble than he was worth. His attentions are growing more heated, and a man of his hubris is not likely to accept no for an answer."

"True," conceded Arianna. "Push might have come to shove if Talleyrand hadn't demanded the comte's presence at an evening meeting." She thought for a moment. "I think the Prince did it deliberately. Those lazy, lidded eyes don't miss much."

"Which is why I am reluctant to agree to your plan. Of all the men here in Vienna, Talleyrand is the most dangerous," said Saybrook. "Never, *ever* underestimate him."

"I don't," said Arianna quickly. "But it's not as if he spends a great deal of time in the kitchens. He comes to consult with Carême each morning on the day's menu. Other than that, he keeps to the upper floors of the palace. I shall demand to start work at noon and leave before midnight. Remember, chefs are allowed to be eccentric, and Carême is rather desperate for expert assistance. I believe he will swallow any reservations and hire me on the spot."

The earl pursed his lips.

Pouncing on his hesitation, she hurried on. "It's a golden opportunity, Sandro. Imagine—I shall have daily access to our main suspect's lair, with plenty of chances to poke around."

"How—" began Saybrook.

"I've already thought of a perfect excuse—I shall start making chocolate bonbons to leave in the bedchambers each night. And demand that I deliver them personally because my artistic sensibilities demand that I arrange the plate myself."

"Damnation," growled Saybrook. "How do you think I feel, allowing you to take all the risks while I sit here in the cozy comfort of my book-filled room, fiddling with pens, books and this maliciously maddening scrap of paper?"

"In this case, a chance to unmask our unknown enemy has appeared, and only I can seize it. We must be pragmatic, Sandro, and not let it slip away." Threading her fingers through his tangled hair, she combed the dark strands back from his brow. "Reason must always overrule emotion—isn't that what you always tell me?"

"Then I am a God-benighted bloody fool," he insisted.

"I wish you were." Understanding the flare of frustration, Arianna tried to use humor to defuse the moment. "Then I would have a far easier time leading you by the nose."

As she had hoped, Saybrook allowed his mouth to quirk upward. In their earlier investigation, they had quarreled—and rather vociferously—about whether she was using her feminine wiles to manipulate him.

"I—"

"Let us not argue over this. I am sure your turn to jump into the fire will come soon enough." Arianna leaned in and pressed her lips to his.

After several long moments, he broke away with a rough whisper. "*Dio Madre.* I suspect you are trying to lead me not by my nose but a far more primitive appendage."

Arianna answered with a throaty laugh. "Oh, that would be awfully low of me."

"Yes, and you've just finished telling me that you have no scruples about stooping to *any* ruse."

"So I did." Her arms slipped around his shoulders and drew him close. "Aren't you glad of it?"

"You know what I think?" Rising in one swift, smooth motion, Saybrook lifted her easily into his arms. "I think that my brain is far too tired to wrestle with any more intellectual conundrums."

After all the cloying colognes and decadent kitchen smells, the faint citrus scent of his shaving soap was like a breath of fresh air.

"So I suggest we defer all further discussion of conduct, codes and cunning criminals until morning."

The papers crackled. *"Hmmph."* After wiping a smudge of flour from his nose, Carême shuffled to the next page. "The Prince Regent, eh?" His eyes narrowed. "What did you cook for him?"

"A number of dishes, but his favorite was a tower built of sweet chocolate bricks," answered Arianna without hesitation. "Surrounded by a moat of Chantilly cream and port-soaked cherries."

*"Edible* chocolate?"

"Yes, like Monsieur Debauve of Paris."

"Bah, Debauve has no imagination," grumbled the chef.

"He deserves some credit for the concept," countered Arianna coolly. A show of backbone was imperative if she was to have the freedom that she needed to poke around the premises. "But I agree, his creativity can't hold a teaspoon to yours."

Carême gave a grunt but his frown faded slightly. Turning to the chopping block, he picked up a paring knife and then whirled around with a flourish. *"Alors*, what is the recipe for *crème anglaise."*

Arianna was just as quick with her reply.

*"Hmmph."* Carême tapped the blade to his palm. "Your accent is odd, Monsieur Richard. I can't quite place it."

"I was raised in the West Indies," replied Arianna truthfully, then quickly added a few embellishments. "My mother was English and my father was French, so I had an unorthodox upbringing. We were very poor, so I learned at an early age how to fend for myself. Cooking is one of the skills I acquired in the islands, and I found it to my taste."

A tendril of steam curled through the brief silence. "One last question. Why do you want to work for me?"

"A man has to eat," she quipped. "I find myself in need of funds. And since I must work, it might as well be for a genius of cuisine."

The chef considered her reply for what felt like an age. Had she misjudged his temperament? She gave an inward sigh. *Ah, well, too late to cry over spilled milk—*

"Eggs and butter are here in this larder. Sugar and flour are kept in the west pantry, along with nuts, cacao paste and the other pastry supplies." Carême tossed her an apron and a wooden spoon. "Come, there is no time for dallying. The Prussians are coming for supper, so let's get to work."

# 16

## From Lady Arianna's Chocolate Notebooks

### Chocolate Sauce

½ cup half-and-half
1 cup sugar
2 oz. unsweetened chocolate, chopped
2 oz. bittersweet chocolate, chopped
8 tablespoons butter
2 egg yolks, lightly beaten

1. Heat half-and-half and sugar together in a heavy saucepan over medium-low heat, stirring until sugar dissolves. Add chocolates and butter and whisk until smooth. Set aside to let cool briefly.
2. Stir in egg yolks and cook over low heat for 3 minutes, stirring constantly. Set aside to let cool slightly.

❧

Gold, glitter and glamour.
Everything in Vienna was done to sumptuous excess, thought Arianna as she and Saybrook approached the

entrance of Metternich's palatial villa on the Rennweg the next evening. Elegant carriages filled the surrounding streets, the plumed horses prancing in place on the stone cobbles as the richly dressed crowd squeezed its way through the ornate iron gates. The Austrian minister's Peace Ball was one of the most anticipated entertainments of the Conference, and it was clear that he had spared no expense on the extravaganza.

*Tonight I shall waltz in silk and satin amidst the flaming splendor of the garden torchieres, while come morning, I will once again don boots and breeches in order to dance from the fire into the frying pan.*

"Eat, drink and be merry, for tomorrow you join the un-washed masses who serve these gluttons of pleasure," murmured Saybrook, his caustic wit sharpened by the fact that he still had misgivings about her masquerade.

A week ago, they had hammered out the details of the plan over a long, leisurely breakfast. And so while Monsieur Richard toiled in the subterranean kitchens of the Kaunitz Palace, the Countess of Saybrook had become increasingly prone to headaches, causing her to cry off from several prominent parties. *Two birds with one stone.* Her absence had allowed her not only a chance to spy on Talleyrand but had also garnered further sympathy from Kydd.

The young Scotsman already envisioned himself as a he-roic knight fighting for noble ideals. A damsel in distress seemed to appeal to his notions of honor.

"Then get me some champagne," she replied, seeing a footman passing by with libations.

Saybrook plucked two glasses from the tray and handed one to her.

"*A su salud,*" he murmured in Spanish, raising the cut crystal in ironic salute. The pale liquid glowed like molten gold in the torchlight, its sparkling effervescence mirroring the countless diamond-bright stars overhead. "May we spin through this whirling dervish dance of deception without a stumble."

The tiny bubbles of the wine prickled like dagger points against her tongue.

*Deception?* She had played so many different roles in her life that at times, she wasn't sure who she really was. Luckily, Monsieur Richard was a persona who was as comfortable as a second skin.

"Don't worry. I'm on firm footing in the kitchen," answered Arianna. "All is going smoothly."

His gaze remained riveted on the heavens, as if he were having a silent conversation with Ursa Major and Orion. *Or perhaps he was offering up some sort of a prayer to the pagan constellations.* "How fortunate that Carême was so impressed with Monsieur Richard's impeccable credentials as a skilled pastry chef."

Her lips twitched. "The letter of recommendation from the Prince Regent of England was most impressive."

Her husband possessed a number of interesting talents, as she was slowly discovering. One of which was an expertise in the forgery of letters and seals, learned as part of his military intelligence skills.

Saybrook chuckled and then drew her aside as a line of heralds, resplendent in gold-threaded livery, trumpeted the arrival of yet another royal. "The King of Wurttemberg," he muttered as an enormously fat man toddled by. "It's said that a special half moon has been cut in one of the Emperor's dining tables to accommodate his girth."

"Good God," said Arianna through her teeth after slanting another look around. "In some ways I sympathize with the radicals of the French Revolution. The amount of money that is squandered by the aristocracy on personal vanity is . . . obscene." The torchieres danced in the swirling breeze, the towering tongues of flames gilding the crowd with a golden glow. "Let us hope that this Peace Conference can right some of the more egregious inequities of the old social order. Merit should matter more than birth."

"I couldn't agree more," murmured Saybrook. "But much as I sympathize with democratic ideals in principle, I can't condone murder as a means of achieving those goals."

Arianna nodded, their bantering mood disappearing along with the last swallow of champagne. *No mere mortal has the right to play God.*

"So we must set aside our personal dismay at the extravagant excesses and concentrate on stopping Kydd and his cohorts from carrying out their plan."

"In other words, keep my focus on the mission," she said.

"Much as I hate to say it, the real goal is to keep Kydd's focus on *you* for tonight," responded Saybrook. "Despite the new plans, you must continue to try to win his trust."

"Yes, I know." She watched the shifting patterns of colors, the hues blurring and blending as the guests moved in and out of the light and shadows.

"I've been thinking about the code you showed me this morning. You said that it's not necessarily more complex than the one you solved at the marquess's estate, just different, correct?"

Saybrook confirmed her statement with a gruff nod. "I made a lucky guess concerning the key word. Intuition tells me that we're still looking at Vigenère Square, but a new key word has been used to make it even more secure." He made a face. "It could be anything."

"The individual who wrote it might well use a word that has some personal significance. Something like a battle cry, a motto, a hero."

The earl's gaze sharpened. "Possibly."

"Do you think Kydd wrote it?"

He thought for a long moment before answering. "Hard to say. Again, it's possible. I'm assuming that the codes I cracked were meant for whoever is in charge of the assassination plot. The unsolved one may well be for the head of the whole conspiracy." His hand tightened around his empty glass. "But the damnable truth is, it's all mere conjecture. So far, my guesses have all come up empty."

"You need more information to work with," said Arianna resolutely. She didn't like to see his face pinched in such a brooding uncertainty. "Time to go flutter around

Kydd and see if I can get him to share some of his innermost secrets."

"I don't see how he can keep from acting the hungry cat with a canary," said Saybrook, darting a sidelong look at her plunging neckline.

"Actually, I feel a little like a drab English sparrow flitting among a flock of regal Birds of Paradise." She smoothed the heavy silk of her gown over her hips as she made another survey of the crowd. "My London plumage pales in comparison to the Continental styles."

There was no denying that the ladies who had flocked to Vienna from all over Europe were elegant in the extreme. The colorful crepe outer dresses were complemented by a whisper of pastel satin underneath. Sleeves were long and edged with lace, or short poufs of silk paired with long white gloves. On this particular evening, the ladies had been asked to wear blue or white, the colors of Peace, and in the twilight, the rippling of silks and satins created a sparkling sea of ocean hues. Gold and silver embroidery accentuated the effect, as did the profusion of precious stones and pearls.

"The Count de Ligne has described the ladies as looking like brilliant meteors when the dancing begins," murmured Saybrook.

Arianna could well imagine it to be true. "Yes, they must spin by in a blinding blur of light."

"Illusions," muttered her husband, unmoved by all the finery.

"The gentlemen are equally dazzling," she pointed out. "Look at all the gold braid and gaudy medals. Good God, if they all were such magnificent warriors, why wasn't Napoleon exiled to Elba years ago?"

He gave a mocking laugh. "Yet another question to add to our growing list." Squaring his shoulders, he turned for the main walkway. "But enough worrying. We must appear to be enjoying ourselves."

Passing through a stone archway, they entered the building that Metternich had constructed specially for the celebration. Encircled by classical pillars, the wooden building was crowned by a dome that soared high overhead.

"Shall we stroll out to the gardens?" inquired Saybrook. "Royalty will be dining inside, while the rest of us will partake of a supper under the stars."

Arianna followed, calming her flutter of nerves with a few deep breaths. *Steady, steady. I've played enough roles not to have stage fright.* Most of the other guests were probably just as much imposters as she was.

The estate gardens were no less magnificent. Countless lanterns lit the winding walkways, the flickering flames illuminating the formal plantings and marble fountains. White tents dotted the grounds, and beneath the shimmering silk, servants dispensed Tokay wines and champagne. Several orchestras were tucked discreetly behind hedges in different parts of the estate, the lilting notes of the violins echoing the faint trilling of the nightingales.

At the crest of the sloping lawn stood three classical faux temples. Moonlight dappled over the pale stone, its silvery glow swirling in tandem with the troupe of ballet dancers performing among the pillars.

Mesmerized by the fairy tale splendor of the scene, Arianna stood in rapt wonder, drinking it all in.

"Look—there's Kydd," said Saybrook.

His whisper jarred her back to reality. "Shall I stroll over to see him while you make a show of picking one of the plumed Birds of Paradise to flirt with?"

The opening chords of a Mozart sonata drifted through the greenery. "It would be best if he thinks we are not in harmony with each other," answered her husband. "I shall meet up with you later."

She turned, but the touch of his hand held her back for just a moment.

"Be careful. For all its veneer of civilized splendor, Vienna is a jungle—a jungle where predators are always on the prowl."

"Lady Saybrook." Looking up at the sound of her steps

on the graveled path, Kydd appeared upset, though he quickly covered it with a tentative smile. "How lovely to see you." After glancing around, he added, "Are you . . . alone?"

"I've been abandoned by my husband," she answered. She gave a curt wave at the sparkling lights of the main lawns. "He met several Spanish ladies of his acquaintance and they wished to be at the center of the festivities."

"Quite a spectacle, is it not?" remarked Kydd, sounding distracted. On edge.

"If you enjoy watching the rich revel in decadent pleasures," she said softly.

He studied her face for a long moment. "Would you care to take a stroll to a quieter part of the gardens?"

"Please," she murmured, accepting his arm. "I would much rather converse with a friend than cavort with strangers." Her slippers slid lightly over the stones. "I do hope that I may consider you a friend, Mr. Kydd."

"Yes, of course, Lady Saybrook." His voice grew taut. "I'm honored that you ask."

They walked in silence for a bit, the noises of the party fading until the only sound was the breeze ruffling through the leaves of the tall boxwood hedge bordering the path.

"It's so peaceful here, now that we're away from the crowd." She sighed. "I hate these gatherings with all their false laughter, false flatteries and false promises."

He nodded. "Believe me, I know how you feel."

Arianna paused and looked up at the heavens. *Careful, careful—one false move and I will ruin everything.*

Expelling a sigh, she turned her head slightly to meet his searching stare. "Do you?"

Kydd blinked.

"You speak so eloquently about noble principles. I—I come away from our talks feeling inspired by your idealism. And yet . . ." She deliberately let her voice trail off.

A glimmer of starlight ghosted over his profile, catching the tiny, telltale tic of his jaw.

*Oh, the folly of youthful passions,* she thought, suddenly feeling old as Methuselah.

"Lady Saybrook, may I ask you a personal question?"

At her hesitation, his pale skin darkened in embarrassment. "Forgive me—"

"No, please. Of course you may."

He cleared his throat. "Why did you marry the earl?"

"I take it you have heard that ours was not a love match."

Kydd shifted uncomfortably. "Mr. Mellon does not indulge in gossip. But I couldn't help overhearing several private exchanges with Lord Saybrook in which he voiced reservations about the match."

"I can't say that I blame him." Arianna let her tone go a little rough around the edges. "I was caught up in a scandal—please don't ask me to explain—and so was the earl. I had precious few choices." She shrugged. "As you know, females have little control over their destiny."

"I did not mean to stir painful memories," he said haltingly.

"Don't apologize." A tentative smile softened her expression. "Your company has been a source of comfort to me. It is very heartening to be able to converse with someone who shares similar beliefs."

"I *do* share them," assured Kydd. "I haven't betrayed my beliefs by working for the Foreign Office."

*No—just your country and the honorable man who nurtured your career.*

"I am not at liberty to say more," he whispered. "But I am working to effect real change, and create a better world for the future."

Arianna greeted his words with a tremulous sigh. "Oh, how I admire you. A better world— I shall look forward to that."

Kydd relaxed slightly. "Change is not easy, but there are goals that are worth fighting for. However . . ."

Suddenly alert, she held herself very still, hoping that he would go on.

"However . . . I am having some second thoughts about how to achieve my aim."

"Would it help to talk about it?" she asked softly. "I cannot promise to have all the answers, but sometimes simply expressing your doubts aloud helps to clarify your feelings."

"You—you are very kind. I can't tell you how fortunate I feel to have a friend I can trust."

Arianna looked away, repressing a twinge of guilt by reminding herself that Kydd and his cohorts were planning a cold-blooded murder.

"I can't help but wonder . . ." Shuffling his feet, he abruptly offered her his arm. "Shall we continue along this path?" He gestured at a shadowed stretch of gardens up ahead. "A display of fireworks is planned for later, and as Herr Steuer is famous for his pyrotechnics, it promises to be spectacular. The rockets are being set up near the North Gate, so we shall have a better vantage point from up close." His hand tucked a fold of her shawl more securely around her shoulders. "There is also going to be a balloon ascension to top off the entertainment."

"That sounds very exciting."

As they moved off at a leisurely pace, her mind began to race. Kydd was coming tantalizingly close to revealing his secrets. She didn't want to risk making him suspicious, and yet surely there was some way she could take advantage of his current mood.

*Information—Sandro needs specific details, not vague hints that merely corroborate what we already know.*

Arianna thought for a moment, and then a gleam of light from behind the thickets of greenery sparked an idea. "Oh, look! They are beginning to inflate the balloon." Looking up at the sky, she added, "Sometimes, when I stare at the stars, I let my imagination soar."

Kydd tilted his head upward.

"You may think me foolish, but I like to think of the words that inspire me. Ones like 'hope' and 'dream.' "

"It's not foolish at all, Lady Saybrook." He moved closer—so close that she could smell the warm scent of his bay rum shaving soap.

"What words make your heart sing?"

"Freedom," he answered without hesitation. "Equality. Democracy. Courage. Independence."

"All very noble sentiments," she murmured, making careful mental note of them as possible key words. It was a shot in the dark, but as Saybrook said, luck and intuition were major weapons in a code breaker's arsenal.

A wry grimace tugged at Kydd's lips. "You probably think me a pedant, to always be talking of principles and abstract ideas."

"Oh no, not at all." *Keep talking, keep talking.* "I want to hear all about what thoughts, what dreams are important to you."

"Dreams," he repeated. "I should like to see Scotland truly free, and in control of its own destiny. But at what cost?" Gravel crunched softly under his boots. "In a short while, I have a meeting in which I shall have to decide . . ."

His voice trailed off in a harsh sigh.

He seemed to be teetering on the edge of a precipice. Did she dare give him the last little nudge?

"You sound uncertain," she said cautiously.

"I confess that I am. For the longest time, I was so sure that I knew what was right. And now . . ." Kydd raked a hand through his hair. "But enough of politics and philosophy." His mood seemed to be veering wildly, from reflective to reckless in the blink of an eye. As he stepped closer, Arianna heard a different sort of intensity grip his tone. "Let us spend the rest of our time together enjoying each other's company."

The moonlight tipped his golden lashes with the flare of fire. He was leaning in, his breath hot on her skin. In another instant his mouth would capture hers.

*Distraction. Diversion.* Was there a way to deflect his advances without destroying his trust?

Deception was a dangerous game to play. Her husband

understood that, thought Arianna as she steeled herself for Kydd's kiss.

*BOOM!*

A sudden explosion ripped through the shrubbery, throwing up a shower of fiery sparks and burning leaves. The force of the blast knocked Arianna to the ground. Dazed, disoriented, she rolled to her knees and tried to shake the terrible ringing from her ears.

Flames shot up from the shattered hedge, forcing her to scramble back from the searing heat. A series of rapid-fire pops released plumes of colored vapors into the fire-gold glow, adding a mad, macabre beauty to the scene.

The wind swirled, driving the danger closer.

"Mr. Kydd!" she croaked, trying to see through the cloud of acrid black smoke.

On getting no response, she pulled her shawl up to shield her face and started to crawl forward along the edge of the gravel. "Mr. Kydd!"

Was that a whisper, or just the crackling of the branches?

Choking back a cough, Arianna felt her way over the soot-streaked grass. Above the roar of the fire, she was vaguely aware of shouts and the pounding of running feet. But they sounded very far away.

Her eyes began to water and the sour stench of gunpowder made it difficult to breathe. *Damnation—*

Another loud bang rent the air.

As she flinched, her hand grazed against a booted foot. Grasping the heel, she gave it a shake. "Mr. Kydd." The blast must have knocked him senseless. "Wake up, wake up. There must have been an accident with the fireworks. We must move away from here."

In answer, a pair of hands grasped her roughly around the waist and dragged her back from the raging fire.

"No! Wait! Put me down!" she protested as she felt herself lifted from the ground.

"For God's sake, stop squirming," ordered Saybrook. Gathering her in his arms, he stumbled down the hill and slid behind the shelter of a marble folly. "Stay down," he growled, covering her body with his. "The rest of the explosives could ignite at any moment."

"But Mr. Kydd—"

"Mr. Kydd is dead." Soot blackened the earl's face. Limned in the red glow of the burning bushes, he looked like the Devil's own shadow from hell. "And you are bloody lucky to be alive."

"Drink," commanded Saybrook, placing a large mug of brandy-laced chocolate in her hands.

"I don't need a posset." Arianna nestled deeper into the armchair of their parlor and heaved a sigh before taking a sip. "I'm not about to fall into a maidenly swoon of shock."

The warm, potent drink did, however, taste ambrosial. Closing her eyes for an instant, she savored its soothing sweetness. Gulps of water had already washed the smoky grit from her throat, but the sour dregs of fear still lingered—more than she cared to admit.

"Are you sure you aren't hurt?" asked her husband. He had taken advantage of all the confusion and chaos of fighting the fire to slip away from the estate unnoticed.

"Just a few bumps and bruises." She rubbed at a sore spot on her shoulder and winced. "But my wits were certainly wandering. Thank God you thought to whisk us away before anyone realized that I had been with Kydd at the moment of the accident."

Saybrook's scowl deepened as he plunged the poker into the hearth and stirred the coals to life. "*If* it was an accident," he muttered. After seeing her to the safety of their carriage, he had returned to the grounds for a quick surveillance. "Steuer's foreman was adamant that all possible precautions had been taken around that section of the fireworks. He's known as a stickler for safety and claims that it would have taken an act of God to set off the canisters of gunpowder."

"Or a far less Divine Being."

Their eyes met over her mug.

"You noticed nothing suspicious in the area?" he asked after a long moment.

Arianna shook her head. "My attention was all on Kydd. He was oh so close to confiding in me. I think he was having second thoughts about his involvement . . ." She swirled the chocolate and watched the dark liquid form a silent, spinning vortex. "In any case, I still might have learned something important from the interlude. I got him to talk about words that had special meaning for him, thinking you might try them as keys for the code."

"Clever thinking," he conceded. But if anything, his expression grew more troubled. He moved to the sideboard and poured himself a large glass of brandy. Which he proceeded to down in one swift swallow.

"Sandro, is something bothering you?"

"Other than the fact that my wife was standing a scant foot away from a man who had half his skull blown to bits?" he shot back.

A chill snaked down her spine. "Gunpowder is a volatile substance. It could have been an accident."

"The metal fragments I found embedded in his flesh were a thin gauge steel," he said flatly. "The canisters are made of heavy lead."

"So you think someone deliberately tossed a bomb to kill him?'

"And most likely you. I had only a quick look, but it appeared as if the killing arc—the spread of the lethal fragments—was thrown off. Perhaps he moved at the last moment and it struck his back instead of his chest."

Arianna felt herself go pale.

"What?" he asked softly.

"Yes, Kydd did move." She hurried on, hoping he wouldn't ask her to explain. "But if what you suspect is true, why the big explosion? Wasn't the assassin risking his own life by setting off such a conflagration?"

"He may have inadvertently dropped a lucifer. Or he may have planned to cover his crime by making it look like an accident, then set his fuse too short." Saybrook lifted his shoulders. "There are many ways in which a plan can go wrong."

*A not-so-subtle warning.* But then, her husband did not appear to be in much of a mood for nuances.

"Arianna, this masquerade you have undertaken—"

"If you are about to order me to abandon our plan, you may save your breath."

"It's too dangerous," insisted Saybrook.

"I beg to differ. So far, there has been no hint of trouble. We both know that most people see only what they expect to see—and no one in his wildest dreams will imagine that Monsieur Richard is a female."

"Talleyrand is a threat. He misses very little."

"I agree," said Arianna quickly. "I am taking care to stay well out of his sight when he comes down for his daily meeting with Carême. It's not difficult. Kitchens are smoky or steamy, and there are a number of storage pantries, all of them dark." Recalling their first encounter, she essayed a note of humor. "And if push comes to shove, I am rather skilled in using a carving knife to defend myself, as you have reason to know."

He did not crack a smile.

"Sandro, unless you wish to abandon the effort and leave Renard to execute his murderous plan, we cannot walk away from the opportunity to gain access to Talleyrand's palace," she reasoned. "That both the Prince and the comte are in residence makes the chance even more important. With Kydd dead, it's our one—our only—lead."

He looked as if he wished to argue.

She had held her best weapon until last, when his defenses had already been battered. "But if you wish, we can pack up and return to London. That will, of course, mean having to admit to Grentham that we failed to track down the traitor."

Saybrook drew in a harsh breath. And then let it out in a mirthless laugh. "You are utterly remorseless."

"And unscrupulous."

Perching a hip on the arm of her chair, he touched his palm to her cheek. "Ruthless," he murmured.

"Heartless," she responded.

His hand slid down to just above her left breast. "Oh no, you have a heart. You simply keep it well guarded."

The heat of him seeped through the singed silk of her gown. "That is rather like the pot calling the kettle black."

"So it is." His eyes had a strangely molten glow, perhaps from the burn of the brandy. "I hate being in the dark, Arianna. It makes me feel helpless to protect you."

"I don't expect you to," she whispered.

"That has no bearing on what I expect of myself."

*How to answer?*

Looking away, she watched the play of shadows on the far wall. "I won't take any unnecessary risks."

"Liar." There was no heat behind the accusation. Indeed, he said it with a reluctant smile. "Of course you will."

"No, truly. I have no desire to stick my spoon in the wall just yet. So I shall be careful."

"I suppose I must be satisfied with that for now," said Saybrook. He turned to the hearth and began to bank the glowing coals. A hiss of smoke rose from the crackling sparks.

"But that may change."

# 17

## From Lady Arianna's Chocolate Notebooks

### Chocolate Marshmallows

*Canola oil, for greasing*
*1½ cups sugar*
*¾ cup light corn syrup*
*¼ cup honey*
*1 cup water*
*3 tablespoon unflavored powdered gelatin, softened in*
*½ cup cold water*
*¾ cup Dutch-process cocoa powder, sifted*
*2 tablespoons cornstarch*

1. Grease an 8-inch x 8-inch baking pan, line bottom and sides with parchment paper, and grease paper. Grease a rubber spatula; set aside.
2. Combine sugar, syrup, honey, and ½ cup water in a 2-qt. saucepan over medium-high heat. Bring to a simmer; cook, without stirring, until syrup reaches 250° on a candy thermometer. Remove from heat; let cool to 220°.
3. Meanwhile, bring ½ cup water to a boil in a small

saucepan. Place bowl of gelatin over boiling water; whisk until gelatin becomes liquid. Transfer to the bowl of a stand mixer fitted with a whisk; add ½ cup cocoa powder. Add cooled sugar syrup to gelatin; whisk on high speed until mixture holds stiff peaks, 5–6 minutes. Pour mixture into prepared pan; smooth top with oiled spatula; let cool until set, 5–6 hours.

4. Combine remaining cocoa powder and cornstarch in a bowl and transfer to a strainer; dust work surface with mixture. Slide a knife around edge of pan to release marshmallows; remove from pan. Dust cocoa mixture over top. Using a slicing knife dusted with cocoa mixture, cut marshmallows into forty 1½ inch squares. Toss marshmallows with remaining cocoa mixture.

Yield: 40

❧

"**D**amnation, damnation, damnation." Saybrook balled the sheet of paper and lobbed it into the fire. "Would that you hadn't taken your bloody secrets along with you to the grave, Kydd."

He stared at the coded document. "None of the words Arianna wrested from you work, which leads me to believe that, as I suspected, you were but a pawn on this diabolical chessboard. So . . ." *Tap, tap, tap.* His pen drummed an impatient tattoo on the desk. "Who is moving the pieces around the board? There has to be a clue that I have missed. But for the love of God Almighty, I can't figure out what it is."

Another bout of scribbling.

Another crumpled missile arced into the flames.

"If only Baz were here," muttered the earl. "He is always willing to bat ideas back and forth, no matter how outlandish they sound."

Slapping a fresh sheet down upon the blotter, he dipped

his pen in the inkwell. But before he could begin to write, a clatter of footsteps on the stairs distracted his concentration.

"What in Hades . . ." Uttering a fresh string of oaths, Saybrook set down the quill. "Jose knows that I'm not to be disturbed. Whoever the arse is, it sounds like he is intent on waking the dead."

The earl was half out of his chair, intending to ring a peal over the miscreant's head, when the door flew open.

Saybrook sat back down with a thump. "Well, well, speak of the devil."

Basil Henning looked even more disheveled than usual. Unshaven, bleary-eyed, hair standing out from his head in drunken spikes, the surgeon looked like a wild Viking sailing in on the North Wind. His clothing, never very tidy to begin with, looked as if it had been slept in for days on end.

"Ye look like Hell yerself, laddie." Henning glanced around as he unwound his ragged muffler and tossed it on the sofa. "I don't suppose ye can offer me a dram of good Scottish whisky to wash the travel dust from my throat."

"You will have to settle for French brandy or Hungarian slivovitz," answered the earl.

"Hmmph. A paltry offering considering all the hardships I've endured on your behalf." The surgeon dropped into the armchair by the hearth. "Brandy, if I must," he added. "Where's Lady S?"

"Working," replied Saybrook with a grim smile. "But first questions first." He quickly poured a glass of the requested spirits and brought it over to his friend. "You are supposed to be in Edinburgh. So why in the unholy name of Lucifer have you journeyed to Vienna?"

"Not for the chocolate *mit schlag* or the cream cakes," quipped Henning. He gave a quick grimace before tossing back his drink. "I've uncovered some important information."

"Your ugly phiz is not an unwelcome sight, however there *is* such a thing as a diplomatic courier. You could have asked my uncle to forward it."

"Knowing that Whitehall is as leaky as a sieve?" Henning shook his head and made a rude sound. "No, I didn't dare trust anyone but myself to bring the news. It's too explosive."

The air crackled with tension as the surgeon rose abruptly and went to refill his glass.

"Well, go on," growled the earl. "Or do I have to hold a flame to your arse?"

"You should be kissing my bum," retorted the surgeon. "I've gone through nine circles of hell to get here in time to warn you."

"Of what," asked Saybrook through clenched teeth.

"That in your hunt for the elusive Renard, you and Lady S have been following the wrong scent."

"Is there anything else that you wish for me to do, Monsieur Richard?" The scullery maid finished drying the last of the copper kettles and hung it on its hook. "I'm done with my regular tasks, so unless . . ."

"*Non*, you may retire for the night," replied Arianna gruffly. "I wish to sort through the cacao beans, and check the inventory of spices before I leave. Monsieur Carême tells me we have several very important suppers scheduled for next week, and I must be prepared to perform up to his standards."

The girl shuddered. "Be prepared for him to whack the flat of his cleaver to your bum. He gets *very* bad tempered when we have important guests to serve."

"Ha! He shall have nothing to complain about." Arianna twirled her false moustache. "My pastry skills are far superior to his."

"Yes, so you have told us." The maid turned away, not quite quickly enough to hide a snigger. "More than once."

Arianna had made it a point to be obnoxiously arrogant. She didn't wish to encourage any overtures of friendship from the other kitchen servants. "You shall see, *chérie.*"

"Don't forget to latch the pantries and close the larders. Otherwise, *Le Maitre* will roast you over the coals in the morning. I warn you, he's already in a foul mood, on account of all the fuss surrounding the visit of some fancy foreigner."

"What foreigner?" asked Arianna, her senses coming to full alert.

"Dunno. It's all very hush-hush," answered the girl carelessly. "I overheard the Prince's secretary telling the butler that it's supposed to stay a secret. Talleyrand wants it to be a big surprise for that fancy party, the Carra ... Carooo ..."

"The Carrousel?" suggested Arianna. At breakfast that morning, Saybrook had made mention of the upcoming gala, an elaborate re-creation of a medieval joust that promised to outshine all the other Conference entertainments for pomp and grandeur.

The girl shrugged. "Yeah, that sounds about right." Her expression pinched to a grimace. "Imagine spending a king's ransom to prance around in swords and suits of armor. I swear, these rich royals are dicked in the nob."

"Queer fish," agreed Arianna. She allowed a slight pause before asking, "You are sure they didn't mention the visitor's name? I should like to think of a suitably special dish to impress him."

Another shrug. "I think it was a military toff—a General Something-Or-Other. Water ... I think mebbe his name had something te do with water."

Hiding a twinge of frustration, Arianna gave a curt wave of dismissal. She waited for several minutes, giving the girl ample time to gain her attic room, before taking the sketch of the palace floor plan from her pocket and unfolding it on the worktable. Saybrook had found the architectural plans in the Burg's library and had made a rough copy. Tonight was the first opportunity to put it to use.

It was, she guessed, just a little past midnight. Talleyrand and his advisors, along with his niece, had left an hour ago to attend a party given by Dorothée's sister, the Duchess of Sagan. They would likely be gone for at least several hours, providing a perfect chance to have a look around upstairs. The only slight complication was Rochemont. Since the day after the Peace Ball and its explosive ending, the comte had been sequestered in his room, sending word that he was too ill to rise from his bed.

But by this time of night, he would likely be fast asleep, and the sketch showed his bedchamber was at the end of a long corridor, overlooking the rear gardens.

The risk of being seen was slim. And besides, she would have a plate of chocolate bonbons to serve as an excuse.

*I will just have to chance it.*

She studied the plan for a bit longer, making a few last notations in pencil, and then put it back in her pocket. Between the breakfast list posted in the butler's pantry and Saybrook's handiwork, she now knew exactly who slept where, and which rooms were used for the delegation's official work.

The thought of entering Talleyrand's private study sent a frisson of heat tingling down to her fingertips. Or was it a chill?

*Dangerous.* Arianna didn't need reason to remind her of the consequences should she be caught in the act of riffling his papers. She was dealing with cold-blooded killers. Two men lay dead because of their involvement in this intrigue—three if one counted Davilenko's demise at the hands of Grentham's men. No mercy would be given.

"I can look out for myself," she whispered, her flutter of breath blowing out all but a single candle. Taking up the pewter stick, she angled past the massive cast iron stoves and into the back passageway. A tin of her buttery cinnamon-spiced chocolates was tucked away in the pastry pantry. A sprinkle of golden demerara sugar would top off . . .

The thump of the main kitchen door being thrown open was followed by the scuff of boots on stone.

On instinct, Arianna extinguished her light and stood very still.

A pot rattled, followed by a low oath.

*Rochemont?* What the devil was he doing down here? she wondered. If he were hungry or thirsty, he could have woken his servant. The comte did not strike her as a man who lifted an elegant finger to perform everyday tasks for himself.

Curious, she crept out of the pantry and inched forward in the darkness until she could steal a look through the passageway opening.

*"Merde!"* Rochemont cursed angrily as he fumbled with the top of a heavy crock. His hands lacked their usual grace, for oddly enough they were clad in bulky gloves.

She frowned, noting that he looked dressed for going out into the frosty night. *A sudden recovery?* It was not so strange that he might crave company after several days of being bedridden.

Save for the fact that he was so intent on opening a container of bacon fat.

*"Merde,"* he muttered again, the lid slipping from his grasp and clattering against the stone counter. Shifting his stance, he clumsily stripped off his gloves.

In the glow of his lamp, the white gleam of the bandages stood out like a sore thumb. After hurriedly unwinding the linen strips, Rochemont dipped a finger into the crock and with a low grunt began to massage a dollop of grease over his singed knuckles.

Arianna held back a gasp. She had enough experience working in kitchens to recognize burnt flesh when she saw it.

The comte flexed his hands. Seemingly satisfied, he quickly replaced the lid and rewrapped the bandages.

Ducking back into the pantry, Arianna crouched behind a flour barrel as he hurried past her hiding place. A moment later she heard the bolt thrown back on the tradesmen's entrance.

*A rasp of metal, a groan of oak.* And then all was silent.

In the cramped space, the thumping of her heart seemed to echo loud as cannon fire against the rough wood walls. Arianna drew in several calming gulps of air and made herself think. The burned flesh had brought back a searing image of Kydd's lifeless body. Dear God, was it possible . . .

But to confirm her suspicions, she needed some evidence, some proof.

*Thump, thump, thump.* Her pulse had slowed to a more

measured beat—which seemed to be drumming Saybrook's warning into her head. *Careful, careful, careful.*

Yes, she had promised him that she wouldn't take any risks, but in the heat of battle one must seize the moment and be unafraid to improvise.

"I'm sorry, Sandro," whispered Arianna. As a concession to prudence, she relit her candle and quickly assembled a plate of chocolates. If caught, they might serve as a plausible excuse. Rochemont's Adonis looks had no doubt attracted the eye of both sexes. Monsieur Richard could always act the part of love-struck admirer.

Moving swiftly and silently up the stairs and down the long corridor, she made her way to the comte's quarters. The door was locked, but a steel hairpin, hidden beneath her frizzy wig, made quick work of releasing the catch. Drawing the door shut behind her, Arianna paused for a moment to survey her surroundings.

The silvery shading of moonlight was just strong enough to illuminate the opulent furnishings, the gilded chairs, the Baroque pear-wood desk set by the bank of mullioned windows.

*Hurry, hurry.* Crossing the carpet, she set to work riffling through the papers on the blotter. She had no idea how long she had to explore. It was imperative not waste a second.

The pile proved to be nothing more than a handful of ornate invitations, a bill from a boot maker, and a memo from Talleyrand's secretary regarding the upcoming schedule of diplomatic suppers.

"Damnation." Her search of the drawers also yielded nothing suspicious. One was locked, but it turned out to hold only several unopened bottles of expensive cologne.

Arianna tried to decide where to look next. She had already eliminated the set of painted bookcases flanking the hearth. Searching through the volumes would take far too long. As for the dressing table, it was doubtful that Rochemont would hide any correspondence among the silver-backed brushes and hair pomades.

Unless . . .

A wink of silver drew her closer. The box, fashioned from dark rosewood and rimmed in precious metal, sat between the shaving stand and the tortoise-framed looking glass. Opening the top, she saw it contained the usual male fripperies—several carnelian watch fobs, a gold stickpin highlighted by a large, liquid-blue topaz, and a gold signet ring, its crest worn with age. The items lay atop a velvet lining, its midnight black hue accentuating the richness of the jewelry.

She was just about to snap the lid shut when a curl at the corner of the fabric caught her eye. Taking up the stickpin, she gently lifted the edge, revealing a hidden paper.

Her heart hitched and began to thud against her ribs. Easing it out, Arianna felt a spike of triumph as she saw the writing was in code.

*The cunning, clever fox has finally been run to ground.*

And then Reason quickly reasserted control, and the surge of savage elation gave way to disciplined detachment.

"Sandro needs to see this," she whispered. He had explained how having two examples of a code greatly increased the chances of deciphering it.

Hurrying to the desk, she found paper and pencil. Holding her breath, she transcribed the sequence of letters, taking care that the low light and her own suppressed excitement did not draw a mistake.

Shoving the finished copy into her pocket, Arianna set to work eliminating all traces of her visit. *Rochemont—or Renard—mustn't suspect that his lair had been searched ...* She shifted the inkwell and pens a fraction to the left ... *He was no fool ...* Rechecking the drawers, she made several minute adjustments ... *Not a hair could be out of place.*

All that remained was to replace the incriminating code back in the box, exactly as she had found it. "The top of the page aligned with the left corner," she reminded herself, edging back the velvet—

From the depths of the first floor came the sound of voices in the entrance hall.

Stilling the shaking of her hands, Arianna forced herself

not to panic. *Two minutes,* she gauged. *Maybe three before anyone could reach the bedchamber door.* Paramount was to slip the code back in place. And then . . .

The paper eased into position.

And then . . .

Boot heels clattered on the marble stairs.

*Improvise!*

The footsteps were now in the corridor and coming on quickly.

Snatching up the jewelry, Arianna dropped the box on the floor. A wild sweep of her hand sent the glass bottles sailing helter-pelter. A kick cracked the leg of the Rococo chair.

Shouts of alarm echoed from outside.

Racing to the desk, she knocked all the carefully arranged items to the carpet.

The locked latch rattled. Fists pounded on paneled oak.

Arianna flung open one of the leaded windows and scrabbled up to the ledge just as the door to the room burst open.

"Stop! Thief!"

A short jump landed her atop the slanting roof of the bowfront window directly below. Slipping, sliding over the slates, Arianna dropped to a crouch and caught hold of the carved cornice. She swung over the edge and grabbed for one of the decorative columns that graced the lower facade of the building. A bullet whistled past her ear and slammed into the limestone overhead, sending up an explosion of pale shards.

"No shots, you fools!" It was Rochemont who called the order, his voice taut with fury. "After him on foot—take the stairs and cut him off in the garden. Whatever you do, don't let him get away!"

The fluted stone scraped her palms raw as she slid to the ground. Giving silent thanks for her earlier surveillance of the grounds, Arianna whirled around and sprinted along the line of the privet hedge, making for the gate that she knew was set in the far right corner of the garden wall.

A door slammed somewhere on the terrace and suddenly there were footsteps peltering in pursuit.

\* \* \*

"Stop sneaking a peek at the clock, laddie. The hands have moved naught but a tick since the last time ye looked." Henning closed the folder of Saybrook's notes. "Which, by the by, was only a minute ago."

"She's never been this late before," said Saybrook.

"Something must have come up," replied the surgeon.

"That's what I'm afraid of," came the earl's gloomy retort.

Henning ran a hand through his hair, the gesture doing little to smooth the spiky tufts. "Don't worry. Lady S is exceedingly clever and resourceful."

"She is also exceedingly unconcerned when it comes to her own safety." Saybrook scowled. "And now that you've brought the news that Rochemont is a duplicitous viper, I have damned good reason to be worried."

"Laddie, if I thought she was in danger right now, I would be urging you on with a red-hot poker. But be reasonable. You've told me that she's been a week working in the kitchens and has had no trouble so far, eh?"

Saybrook conceded the point with a wordless shrug.

"So there's no reason to think tonight will be any different."

"Damnation, Baz. If you would tell the details, I could decide that for myself." The earl sounded tired. Frustrated. And a little frightened, despite the Sphinx-like stare. His face appeared carved out of stone, but his dark chocolate eyes simmered with anxiety.

"I told you, I'll explain it all when Lady S gets home. It's a long story and I'd rather tell it only once," replied Henning. "And as soon as she is here, we can also have a council of war about how to continue." The surgeon wagged a warning finger. "But don't have high hopes that she will want to abandon the masquerade. We still don't know how all this ties together, and Lady S isn't one to leave loose ends hanging."

"Bloody hell," swore the earl softly. "Why is she determined to take such dangerous risks?"

"I might ask the same of you," countered his friend. "And I suggest you think of an answer that does not include any mention of women being the weaker sex. Unless, of course, you want your ballocks served up for breakfast by your lovely wife."

"Don't remind me of cooking, if you please," muttered the earl. He rose and slowly circled past the hearth to the sideboard where he paused to uncork a bottle of port. "May I pour you a drink?"

Henning pursed his lips and then demurred. "Nay. I think I'll keep my wits about me."

Saybrook set the glass aside and resumed his pacing.

"Ye know, in all our battles together, I've never seen ye this on edge." A pause. "May I ask you a personal question, laddie?"

The earl's growl was nearly lost in the scuff of his boots.

"I'll take that as a yes," said the surgeon. "I was just wondering—have ye told Lady S that you love her?"

"I . . ."

Henning waited.

"I . . . she . . . Bloody hell, Baz," groused Saybrook. "She knows that."

A brow winged up in blatant skepticism. "Women are odd creatures. Unlike some of Nature's other creations, they do not always absorb things through osmosis."

"Since when have you become such an expert on the female sex?" snapped the earl.

"Don't bite my head off. I am merely offering an observation. And in fact, I'll add another one. Sometimes people feel compelled to take risks in order to win the regard of those they admire. Especially if they perceive that regard to be uncertain in the first place."

The earl's jaw clenched, drawing the skin tight over the sharp edges of his cheekbones. Candlelight dipped and danced over the angular planes, the fire-gold skitter not quite strong enough to penetrate the shadows.

Bowing his head, he resumed his silent marching.

After several long minutes of listening to the same

*thump, thump, thump* cross over the carpet, the surgeon chuffed an exasperated grunt. "Auch, you are more twitchy than a cat crossing a hot griddle."

The steps halted.

"If you can't sit still, perhaps we ought to take a stroll toward the Prince's palace. I've heard that Vienna is a dazzling sight at night, so I might as well take a peek through the windows at all the fancy people at play." Henning crinkled his nose in disgust. "Along with the rest of the Great Unwashed, I won't likely be invited to be on the inside looking out."

After a moment of thought, Saybrook asked, "Have you packed a decent coat?"

"One without acid burns or blood stains?" Henning made a face. "I believe the charcoal gray will pass muster."

"I'll have my valet bring you a starched cravat. And he'll have orders to brush the worst of the wrinkles from your noxious garments, so don't kick up a dust."

"Why?" demanded the surgeon.

"You just reminded me that there is a soiree going on tonight at the Duchess of Sagan's residence, and Talleyrand is said to be attending. Rather than sit here and stew over what Arianna is up to, we might as well pay a visit so you can get a firsthand look at the Master of Manipulation yourself and give me your impressions."

"You think he's secretly working for Napoleon instead of the newly restored king?" asked Henning.

"It wouldn't be the first time he has betrayed his employer," Saybrook pointed out grimly. "So it's only logical to assume that he and Rochemont are in league to destroy the balance of power here with their assassination plot. But who and how is proving perversely difficult to decipher."

"Patience, Sandro. And perseverance," counseled his friend. "All it takes is one small piece of the puzzle to fall into place for the picture to become strikingly clear."

"Then let us go look for that elusive clue," snapped the earl. "Before yet another body ends up in the grave."

# 18

## From Lady Arianna's Chocolate Notebooks

### Horchata with Chocolate and Pumpkin Seeds

*1 cup long-grain white rice*
*½ cup blanched almonds*
*½ cup pepitas (pumpkin seeds)*
*1 vanilla bean*
*1 2-inch piece cinnamon bark*
*2 oz. dark brown sugar*
*1½ oz. very dark chocolate*
*5½ cups water*
*Additional ground cinnamon and sugar, to taste*

1. Grind the rice, almonds and pepitas to a coarse powder (a coffee grinder works well here) and pour into a large bowl. To the powder, add the seeds from 1 vanilla bean and cinnamon bark. Pour in 3½ cups water, stir, and cover the bowl with plastic wrap. Let sit overnight.
2. The next day, pour the watery rice and nut mixture into a medium saucepan and warm it over a low

flame. Stir in 2 oz. dark brown sugar, 1½ oz. chopped very dark chocolate, and 2 cups water, mixing until all is well combined. (You may wish to add more cinnamon and sugar.) Once the liquid is even in color and just barely simmering, remove the saucepan from heat and let it come to room temperature. Then pour the contents into a large bowl, cover, and let chill for at least 3 hours.

3. Once it has cooled, strain the horchata—which should be a milky, dappled brown—through a fine-mesh sieve and into a pitcher, taking care to press the last bits of liquid from the rice and seed solids. If some nutty kernels make their way into the pitcher, don't worry; they will only enhance the drink's wonderfully thick texture. To serve, pour over ice cubes and garnish with a piece of cinnamon bark.

❧

The narrow alley twisted through a tight turn and plunged down a steep incline, the looming press of dark buildings making it impossible to get her bearings. *Left, right—which way was home?* She was now on unfamiliar ground, running blindly in a cat-and-mouse race to elude her pursuers.

A slip on the cold cobbles sent her careening into a stretch of wall, the force of the blow momentarily knocking the wind from her lungs. Bracing her bruised hands on rough brick, she sucked in a gasp of searing air. Pain lanced through her side, sharp as a stiletto, and her heart was hammering so hard against her ribs that she feared the bones might crack.

*Life as an indolent aristocrat has left me soft as Chantilly cream,* she thought wryly. In the past, she had often outrun angry men, laughing all the way as she left them choking on her dust.

At the moment, however, the situation wasn't remotely amusing.

A shout—far too close for comfort—echoed through the blackness. Shoving away from the wall, she turned away from the sound and set off again at a dead run.

"What's the commotion?" asked Henning, pausing as a well-dressed man burst out of an alleyway up ahead and skidded to a halt.

"Footpads, perhaps," said Saybrook. He didn't sound overly sympathetic. "With all the drunken revelries, the rich make an easy target for thieves at this hour of night."

"Have you seen anyone on the run?" demanded the stranger as they approached.

"Not a soul," answered the earl. "What's the trouble?"

"A robbery," answered the man curtly.

"Your purse?" inquired the surgeon.

"A slimy little slug from the kitchens has stolen jewelry from the Kaunitz Palace. But never fear . . ." The man's expression stretched to an ugly smile. "If he hasn't escaped this way, it means we have him cornered. The only place he can run is into the Burg's royal gardens, and once he's there . . ." His fist smacked into his gloved palm. "He's trapped like a rat."

Saybrook and Henning locked eyes for an instant before the earl asked, "What's the miscreant look like, in case we spot a suspicious person."

"Plump, with straggly brown hair and moustache," came the clipped reply. "And the fat bastard is faster than he looks."

"We'll keep our eyes peeled," promised the surgeon.

The man was already hurrying away.

"*Merde,*" added Henning under his breath. "We—"

Saybrook cut him off with a sharp shove. "Stubble the noise, Baz, and follow me."

From behind the dark, ivy-twined garden wall, the Hofburg Palace rose in fairy tale splendor, the soaring, stately archways and fanciful domes painted with a pale pearlescent glow in the soft moonlight. Silvery mist from the nearby river swirled over the dark foliage, the ghostly tendrils dancing in time to the orchestral music drifting out from the ballroom of the Amalienburg wing.

It would have been quite romantic had she not been running for her life, thought Arianna as she made a flying leap and caught hold of a sturdy vine. Like bird dogs driving a hapless grouse toward the waiting guns, her pursuers had spread out and forced her up against the rear of the imperial gardens. There was nowhere else to flee—save to scramble straight up and then down.

Her boots hit the damp grass with a muted thud.

*Now what?*

Taking cover under a low-hanging holly bush, she pulled the downy pillow from inside her shirt and shoved it deep within the prickly branches. A change in profile might help throw them off the scent. She wished that she could peel off the false hair and whiskers—sweat was making them itch like the very devil, but she dared not divest herself of her male camouflage just yet.

Cocking an ear for any sound of the hellhounds, Arianna crawled out of her hiding place and after a brief hitch of hesitation started to weave her way in and out of the foliage, heading for the glittering lights.

*In for a penny, in for a pound.*

It was too dangerous to go back. Retreat would leave her far too exposed and vulnerable in the midst of hostile territory. If she could somehow sneak inside the palace, there was a good chance that she could take shelter within one of the countless rooms and then drift out with the crowd when the dancing ended near dawn.

Rochemont and his cohorts would likely not want to make too much of a fuss over a simple robbery—assuming her ruse had worked. Even if they suspected a more sinister motive, they would not want to draw attention to their own malevolent plans. No, the dancing—a private ball given by the Tsar of Russia in honor of his sister's arrival in town— would not be disturbed. The Frenchmen would bring in reinforcements and prowl the perimeter, waiting to pounce.

Well, it would not be the first time that her persona of slippery chef had to escape capture by a superior force. Her lips quirked. What with his previous appearance in London, the elusive Monsieur Alphonse-Richard-Chocolat was fast becoming one of the most wanted criminals in all of Europe.

Digging a hand into her pocket, Arianna cast the purloined fobs and rings into the bushes. Better not to have incriminating evidence on her person, in case she was stopped by a guard. With luck, she could brazen her way past any trouble.

*Distraction, dissimulation . . .*

Lost in thought, Arianna was careless enough to stray through a thin blade of light. It was only for an instant, but a hand shot out and caught her arm.

Swearing, she tried to twist free, jerking up her knee to strike her assailant between the legs.

A hand clapped roughly over her mouth.

"Stop thrashing," hissed her husband, just barely dodging the well-aimed blow. "And stop trying to make me sing like a puling soprano."

The fight drained out of her. "Sandro! How did—"

"Never mind that now. Stay silent and follow me. When we get close to the palace, do exactly as I say."

Arianna pressed close to his side, grateful for the sudden warmth radiating through his overcoat. She fled wearing naught but her dark kitchen smock over her work clothes, and it was only now that she realized the night had turned chilly with the first hint of frost.

"There is a door set on the outside of the left archway— do you see it?" whispered Saybrook as they cut behind a line of rhododendrons to shield their movements from the formal terrace overlooking the gardens.

She squinted into the swaying light of the torches and nodded.

"There are two uniformed soldiers standing guard there. I am going to distract them, but we can't count on having more than a few seconds. When I say 'God save the King,' shoot for the door. It's unlocked and Baz is just inside. I'll join you shortly."

*Baz?* Arianna knew better than to ask—about that or any of the other questions that were jostling inside her head.

"Stay behind the marble urn up ahead. From there you have a straight line to the doorway. Remember, on my signal, run like the devil."

She squeezed his arm to indicate her understanding and then dropped to a crouch, her cheek pressing up against the cold stone.

Her body reacted to the loss of his touch by sending a shiver coursing down her spine.

Saybrook mounted the shallow steps a trifle unsteady on his feet. "Lovely night for a dance, what ho," he announced in a slurred voice.

The two soldiers, a sergeant and a corporal in uniforms of the Austrian Imperial Guards, moved out from their station by the main set of glass-paned doors.

Saybrook gave a drunken wave. "No, no, not looking to partner you fine fellows." A stumble. "Ladies. I'm looking for the ladies."

The guards exchanged amused looks. "Sir, you will have to go around to the front entrance," said the sergeant. "We are under orders not to admit anyone through these doors. The Tsar is very particular about keeping out uninvited guests."

"Quite right, quite right. No riffraff." The earl sketched a clumsy bow that nearly landed him on his arse.

Arianna hadn't realized that her husband possessed such finely honed thespian skills.

"Sir." The sergeant caught hold of Saybrook's elbow and pulled him upright. "You must circle back to the front of this wing. Just follow the gravel path."

"Eh?"

"Drunk as a lord," said the corporal. "What a pity he didn't bring *us* a bottle."

Saybrook made a slight retching noise in his throat.

"Bloody hell, if he's going to puke, let's have him do it off the terrace," grumbled the sergeant. "Else we'll probably be ordered to mop up the mess."

"Jez . . . jez show me the way, and I'll be right as rain," said the earl with a fuzzy grin.

The sergeant darted a look through the doors, before nodding at his comrade. "Take his other arm, and let's be quick about it."

"God save the King," warbled Saybrook as he lurched into his escorts.

Arianna took off like a shot and sprinted over the short stretch of tiles as fast as she could.

The door cracked open, and closed just as swiftly.

"Quickly!" Henning hustled her down a side corridor and through the first door set in the dark mahogany paneling.

The cramped windowless space smelled of beeswax, lamp oil and tallow tapers. A closet for the lighting supplies, decided Arianna after another sniff. The faintly sulfurous odor had to be lucifer matches.

"No offense, but Monsieur Richard is not nearly as attractive a character as your urchin boy," whispered Henning.

"Perhaps with a hair trim and a shave?" she quipped, brushing the lank wisps of scratchy hair from her cheek.

"And a bath." The surgeon stifled a chuckle. "Your clothing reeks of burned bacon and garlic, to put it mildly."

"Yes, well, a less than fastidious concern with my garments discouraged my fellow workers from seeking a closer acquaintance."

"I don't blame them." He shifted slightly. "We shouldn't have to be in here too long. Sandro seems to know his way around the place. He brought me here through the side saloons without a hitch, so I daresay he'll make his way back here in a trice. This part of the Amalienburg is not being used tonight."

"A stroke of luck," said Arianna. "Speaking of which—"

"Auch, let's leave the questions until later, lassie. There's much to discuss, I grant you, but for now, let's devote our attention to getting you out of this coil." He inhaled through his mouth. "Not to speak of that disgusting disguise."

"Have you any idea what Sandro has in mind?"

"Nay, but I'm sure he is putting together a plan as we speak," replied the surgeon. "The laddie's brain box seems to function even more efficiently during the heat of battle."

Arianna felt the tension suddenly melt from her bones. Over the years, she had learned to be tough and to trust only herself in the fight for survival. That she now had—as Saybrook once jokingly quipped—someone watching her arse was a source of surprising comfort.

*Am I growing soft?* Strangely enough, Arianna found she really didn't care about the answer.

"Yes, so I have noticed," she murmured, her breath barely stirring the air.

They both stiffened and went very still at the sound of approaching footsteps.

*Click, click, click.* The martial strides stopped by the door.

Arianna blinked as a sliver of light struck her eyes.

"We must move fast." All slurring was gone. Her husband's voice carried a sharp note of command. "I spotted Rochemont entering through the main gates. It's imperative that he see . . ." His hand drew her out from the closet. "I'll explain as we go along." To Henning, he said, "Baz, your part is done. Leave by the same way we came and return to our quarters. We'll meet you there shortly."

Henning snapped a silent salute.

Saybrook had already started down the dimly lit corridor, his grip keeping her close to his big body.

"Shouldn't we be trying to make our way outside, and slip away under the cover of darkness?" whispered Arianna.

"Not the best strategy, under the circumstances," he replied. "I've got a better idea."

His words were a welcome relief. Her body ached, her brain was muzzy, her resolve had gone a little weak at the knees. She was happy to let him take charge.

At the turn, Saybrook marched her through a doorway hidden discreetly in the decorative paneling, and up a flight of steep stairs. Then they were in another corridor, the glass-globed wall sconces illuminating a parfait of painted pastel colors highlighted with touches of gleaming gold.

"Good God," she whispered.

"This section of the Amalienburg was designed for the old Emperor's sister," said Saybrook. "Which explains the extravagantly feminine decor. The Tsar has quartered some of his female relatives here."

Arianna was still not sure what he intended.

"One ... two ... three ..." he counted under his breath. "In here."

He hurried her through a sitting room and into a large bedchamber swathed in a confection of frilly silks and satins. "Strip off your clothes."

"Sandro, I'm not sure this is the moment for amorous activities."

"It's said that anger adds an edge to it."

*Was he angry?* It wasn't as if she had deliberately disobeyed his admonition to avoid danger.

"But you're right." He threw open the armoire and sorted through the selection of fancy gowns. "Here—try this. I'm assuming a corset can be found in one of the drawers. Don't bother with stockings, or other fripperies. We just need to create a façade, if you will."

Arianna kicked off her boots and shed her smock. "You aren't worried that the rightful owner will suddenly appear?"

"The Baroness of Saxe-Gothe is currently taking the waters at the spa town of Baden, so we should be safe enough," said Saybrook. More rummaging produced a set of slippers to match the gown. "If disturbed, we can always claim we were simply playing prurient games."

"You seem to have thought of everything." Save, perhaps, for the choice of female from whom to purloin clothing. Apparently the baroness was molded along the lines of a petite porcelain doll for it took a fair amount of wiggling for Arianna to squeeze herself into the lady's corset.

"Is there anything you can do to adjust the lacing? I think I'm in danger of popping out of these cursed whalebone stays."

Saybrook did some fiddling with the strings, which seemed only to pinch tighter around her bosom. "I can't breathe," she complained.

"Breathing is not necessary. All you are required to do is smile and simper." He helped slide the gown over her head and stepped back to assess the effect. "Not bad. A few inches short, but it can't be helped." Gesturing at the dressing table, he added, "Fix your hair as best you can. Nothing fancy. I don't intend to linger long."

Peeling off the false mustache and wig, Arianna unbound her tresses and shook them out with a sigh of relief. "Perhaps you had better tell me what you have in mind."

"Rochemont and his cohorts have chased Monsieur Richard here," answered the earl.

"How did you know that?" she interrupted.

"Baz and I met one of his men in the street. I put two and two together and decided I had better come and check if my addition was correct."

"Mmmph." With her mouth full of hairpins, she could do no more than grunt.

"If Rochemont is Renard, or merely working for him, he may be aware that I was involved in investigating the Prince Regent's poisoning. That incident involved a chef, so if I were him, I'd be thinking long and hard about the coincidence of having kitchen trouble here in Vienna."

Her mouth went a little dry.

"So I think it imperative that people see the Countess of Saybrook here tonight, in all her feminine glory. The timing should quell any suspicions that Rochemont might have. Like most people, he will assume that it would take an act of God—or black magic—to effect such a transformation."

"Rochemont . . ." Arianna quickly jabbed a few fasteners into the hastily formed topknot and threaded a ribbon through it. "So you already know that Rochemont is the enemy."

He nodded. "Baz discovered some key information in Edinburgh. He refused to explain it all until you are present. But yes, he said enough to indicate that Adonis's outward beauty masks an inner rot."

"Damnation, we *do* have much to talk about," she murmured, taking up a comb to put the finishing touches on her hair.

"An understatement, if ever there was one." Saybrook began to gather up her discarded clothing.

"Wait!" she exclaimed, catching his reflection in the looking glass. "There is a paper in the right pocket of the breeches. I went through a great deal of trouble to ensure that you see it."

"Ah."

She saw him tuck it away.

"I thought you weren't going to do anything risky," he said softly.

"Please don't ring a peal over my head. I didn't intend to, but when the unexpected arises, one is sometimes forced to improvise."

"Improvise," he repeated. Opening one of the bureau drawers, he buried the chef's clothing beneath a pile of petticoats. "Well, we are not quite done for the night. Are you ready for one more adventure?"

Arianna drew on a pair of elbow-length kidskin gloves to hide her scraped hands. "But of course."

"At last! I finally meet the lovely countess in the flesh."

Arianna silently cursed her bad luck. Of all the rakes and roués dancing through the Austrian capital, His Imperial Highness, Tsar Alexander of Russia was perhaps the most blatant.

"And what lovely flesh it is," he added in silky murmur as he lifted her gloved hand to his lips.

"Your Majesty is too kind."

The Tsar gave a lascivious wink. "I hear that the earl is

writing a book on the history of chocolate. But really, why would he spend his hours in the Austrian Imperial Library studying moldering old documents when he has a wife that looks good enough to eat?"

"Ha, ha, ha." His entourage laughed at the witticism.

"You would have to ask him," answered Arianna with a provocative pout. She knew that she looked as though she had just tumbled out of bed. *So I might as well play the role to the hilt.* A saucy sway of her hips set her skirts in a slow swirl, the froth of lace and ruffles kissing up against the Tsar's polished evening pumps. "When we are together, we don't discuss his work."

Alexander ran the tip of his tongue over his plump lower lip. In his youth he had been called "the Angel" for his blonde good looks, but his dissolute lifestyle was turning his body to fat. "Boring stuff, work," he announced, drawing another round of titters from his friends. "Come have tea with me, madam. I promise there will be no talk of books or manuscripts." An exaggerated wink of his bright blue eye. "Ha! I will keep you entertained in other ways."

"I look forward to it," she replied.

"Excellent!" He bowed slightly and offered his arm, setting off the chink of gold on gold as his myriad medals brushed up against one another. "We shall discuss the details while we dance."

"Alas, I seem to have twisted my ankle during some vigorous activity earlier this evening," Arianna flashed a coy smile. "My husband was just about to take me home."

"Lucky man," murmured the Tsar. "When you are fully recovered—"

"Are you ready, my dear?" Saybrook, who had been conversing with one of the English military attachés, turned and placed a proprietary hand at the small of her back. "Forgive me, Your Majesty, but I must get my wife to bed. If an appendage is left to swell, it can turn very painful unless properly treated."

Alexander nodded—a little hungrily, thought Arianna.

"Do take care, Lady Saybrook. I look forward to meeting again when you are able to perform all the movements required of . . . the waltz."

*Men,* she thought wryly. No matter how civilized and sophisticated they were, rivalry to impress the opposite sex often brought out the most primitive instincts.

Saybrook waited until the porter had brought him his overcoat and they had moved out to the entrance portico before saying in a low voice, "I saw Rochemont by the refreshment table watching your exchange with the Tsar."

"Let us hope he comes to the conclusion that the light-fingered chef was simply one of the many petty criminals who have come to Vienna to profit from all the wealthy people gathered here for the Conference."

Their breath formed pale puffs of vapor as they hurried down the line of carriages to their waiting driver.

"We may have won a skirmish," observed Saybrook, draping his coat around her shoulders. "But I am damnably worried about the outcome of the war. We may now have a better idea of who our enemies are, but the truth is, with Kydd dead we have lost our only real lead. So, barring a stroke of luck, I fear we are fighting a nigh impossible battle in trying to stop them."

The door clicked shut, throwing his face into shadow. "If only . . ." he muttered, sounding tense and tired. "If only I could break the damnable code . . . if only we knew their target . . ." His breath released in a harsh sigh. "If only I didn't feel as if I was waltzing in damnable, dizzying circles."

Arianna settled back against the squabs, the slight movement drawing squeals of silent protest from her bruised body. And yet, despite the aches and scrapes, she managed a grim smile.

"I can't say for sure, but my own merry dance tonight may have led me to a bit of luck." She winced as she rubbed at the back of her neck. "I trust you have that scrap of paper tucked safely in your pocket."

# 19

## From Lady Arianna's Chocolate Notebooks

### Chocolate Spice Cookies

½ cups (7 ounces) unbleached, all-purpose flour
½ cup unsweetened cocoa (not Dutch process)
1 teaspoon ancho chili powder
1 teaspoon cinnamon
½ teaspoon cayenne pepper
¼ teaspoon cloves
¼ teaspoon fine sea salt
1 cup unsalted butter (2 cubes), at cool room temperature
1 cup sugar
2 egg yolks, lightly beaten, at cool room temperature
finely grated zest of 1 large orange
1 teaspoon espresso powder, dissolved in 1 teaspoon hot water
1 teaspoon vanilla extract
½ teaspoon orange oil (or 1 teaspoon orange extract)

1. In a medium mixing bowl, sift the flour, cocoa, chili powder, cinnamon, cayenne pepper, cloves, and salt together. Reserve.

2. Using a stand mixer fitted with the paddle attachment, cream the butter and sugar together thoroughly, about 3 minutes.

3. Add the egg yolks and continue beating until creamy.

4. Add the orange zest, dissolved espresso, vanilla, and orange oil, and incorporate.

5. Add the flour mixture and mix very briefly, only until incorporated.

6. Divide the dough into 3 equal portions and flatten each portion to a ½-inch thick disk on a sheet of plastic wrap. Seal the plastic wrap around each portion of the dough and refrigerate for at least 4 hours, or preferably overnight. (The sealed dough can be refrigerated for 2–3 days if necessary.)

7. Remove one portion of dough at a time from the refrigerator so that the dough stays cold while you are working with it. With a floured, cloth-covered rolling pin, roll the *well-chilled* dough out thinly (¼-inch or less) on a generously floured pastry cloth. Cut out shapes with cookie cutters.

8. Arrange on a parchment-lined baking sheet, decorate with clear sanding sugar if desired, and bake at 375° for 6–8 minutes. Watch closely to prevent cookies from overbrowning. It is difficult to tell when these cookies are done because color is not a cue.

9. Remove from the oven and cool on wire racks.

10. When completely cool, store in airtight cookie tins in a cool, dry location.

❧

"*Slàinte mhath.*" The brandy in Henning's glass cast a swirl of fire-gold patterns over his rugged face. "I was beginning to get a bit worried about you two," he said as Saybrook and Arianna entered the parlor. "Pour yourselves a drink and let us toast to dodging disaster."

"Amen to that," said the earl. He chose port.

To Arianna's eye, its dark ruby richness was uncomfortably close to the color of blood, but the sweetness was soothing on her tongue.

"*Slàinte mhath,*" she repeated, moving to the hearth and warming her hands over the dancing flames. A wrapper of finespun merino wool had replaced her purloined finery, and between the soft fabric and the flickering fire, the lingering chill was finally dispelled from her bones.

Saybrook sunk into the armchair facing the surgeon. "Much as I appreciate your peculiar sense of humor, Baz, I would appreciate it if you would stubble the clever remarks." A grunt rumbled in his throat as he shifted his long legs. "And cut to the bloody chase, now that Arianna is here."

"I've missed you too, laddie," drawled Henning, lifting his glass in ironic salute.

The earl responded with a rude suggestion.

"And you, Lady S." His tone turned a touch more serious. "You are a feast for sore eyes. Indeed, it warms me from my cockles to my toes to see you standing in one piece."

She returned his smile. "It's good to see you too, Mr. Henning. Ignore Sandro's snarls. You know he's always in a foul temper when he's hungry. I'll fetch a plate of chocolates from the kitchen to sweeten his mood."

"I don't want chocolate," growled the earl. "I want information."

"And you shall have it, just as soon as I return with some sustenance," said Arianna. She had come to understand that his barbed exchanges with Henning were part of some arcane masculine ritual of friendship. By the time she came back with the confections, the needling would be done and they could get down to business. "Besides, I am famished, and you know that I think better on a full stomach."

"Given your ideas of late, perhaps I should be quaking in my boots," retorted her husband.

"Ha! You may have to eat those words."

A short while later, the sultana-and-almond-filled chocolates consumed, the glasses refilled, Henning sat back and cleared his throat. "Well, now, it seems we are to have another one of our councils of war. Shall I start it off? Sandro has been pestering me for hours to explain why I am here."

The earl gave an impatient little wave.

"Don't rush me," retorted the surgeon. "It's a long and complicated story. But I shall try to keep it short."

"Do," growled the earl.

"As you know, I headed north to Scotland on the same day you left for Vienna. When I arrived in Edinburgh, my nephew was still missing, so . . ." He shifted uncomfortably. "I haven't spoken much to you about this, but I've kept up ties with a group of old friends who espouse the idea of independence from England. The Crown brands their ideas sedition, while I . . . I support many of their aims, even if I don't agree with some of their more radical efforts to achieve them."

"*Dio Madre*, you need not explain yourself to us," said Saybrook. "I guessed as much, and respect your choices."

"Auch, I know that, laddie, and am grateful. But this is about more than me and my personal feelings." He blew out his cheeks. "Suffice it to say, I'm trusted enough in the underworld of Scottish patriots that people are willing to talk." The air leaked out slowly. "And what I heard made my hair stand on end."

Saybrook was staring down at his glass, a habit that hid his dark eyes.

"We know that Whitehall has long suspected that the French have had agents in both Scotland and Ireland, looking to encourage unrest—and perhaps even rebellion," continued Henning. "And of course they are right. Money has been funneling in from the Continent for years. Most of it has been spent to buy loyalty from the locals, who in turn use it to support their families." He looked up, the harsh shadows accentuating the lines that furrowed his face. "Poverty is rampant, for many of the English lords treat their Scottish tenants as a lower form of life than their hounds or horses. That's why I've turned a blind eye on what was going on."

"But with the war over and Napoleon exiled on Elba, it seems that the threat should be over," said Arianna.

"You're right, lassie. The threat *should* be over," replied Henning. "But the more I delved beneath the surface, the more it became apparent that friends and foes were not what they seemed—which is why we have been chasing the wrong scent in our hunt for Renard."

"Let me guess," said Saybrook slowly. "You're about to tell us that conceited coxcomb, Comte Rochemont is, in truth, a cunning conspirator who has spent years betraying both the Royalist cause and Britain, correct?"

"Correct," confirmed Henning. "For nearly a decade, the duplicitous bastard has been running a network of *agents provocateurs* for Napoleon in Scotland. I was away on the Peninsula for some of those years, and then living in London. So I've kept at arm's length from the activities, and never knew the identities of the men in charge. Had I paid greater attention to what was going on in the North, I would have also learned that Rochemont wielded an iron hand within his fancy French velvet glove."

"That would explain Rochemont's many so-called hunting trips across the border," mused Saybrook. "Under the guise of a frivolous sportsman, he was overseeing his network."

Henning made a face. "Aye. And it seems he ran a clever operation. Recruits were flattered and stroked. Those who showed intelligence and idealism were brought up through the ranks and assigned ways to weaken England. All very comradely, right?" The sardonic laugh couldn't quite cover the pain in his voice.

Arianna felt her throat constrict.

"Except those who disagreed with the methods or tried to resign were beaten into line by Rochemont's henchmen," Henning went on. "Or they simply disappeared."

"I am sorry about your nephew, but you cannot blame

yourself, Baz," said Saybrook softly. "You have read history—from the very first, rulers and demagogues have always found it easy to seduce young men with fire in their bellies."

"I should have had my eyes and ears open. Then I would have been able to counsel Angus," said Henning bleakly.

"Yes, and he would have ignored you," countered Arianna. "When you were his age, would you have listened to your elders?"

The surgeon frowned, and then crooked a grudging smile. "No, I would have told them to go to hell."

"There, you see." She set down her glass. "But before we go on about Rochemont's past, I think you had better hear what I have to say about tonight."

Her husband looked at Henning and then gave a gruff nod.

Arianna quickly detailed what she had seen in the kitchen.

"His hands were burned?" said Saybrook.

"Yes," she answered without hesitation. "Which has to mean he killed Kydd. Any other explanation seems absurd."

"But why?" mused Saybrook.

"He must have suspected that Kydd was having second thoughts. And perhaps he feared that things were getting too cozy with me," she said.

Her husband took his time in answering. "Perhaps. And yet, an assassin, be it Rochemont or one of his cohorts, could not have known that you and Kydd would be walking that way."

"A good point," said Henning.

Arianna thought back over her encounter with the young Scotsman. "Kydd was quick to suggest we walk that way," she said carefully. "He hinted that he had an important meeting. He was nervous and on edge, so I would guess that he had a rendezvous planned with his killer for later in the evening."

"Pure speculation," the earl pointed out.

"As is your guess that someone lobbed a bomb at us with the intention of murdering both of us."

"The evidence of a lethal metallic sphere—what we in the military called a grenade—is inarguable," said Saybrook. "How it came to explode by Kydd's head is, I grant you, not something we know for sure."

"There are too damn many unknowns in this bloody case," muttered Henning. "One would almost think Grentham manipulated you into taking this assignment because he was sure you would fail."

Arianna swallowed hard, the lingering sweetness of the wine turning sour on her tongue.

"Another speculation," said Saybrook curtly. "We could sit here and spin conjectures all night. What facts are we missing?"

Her head jerked up. "I—I was just getting to that. After Rochemont went out, I decided to have a look around his quarters. Hidden inside his jewel case was a coded letter."

A sound—a snarl?—vibrated deep in Saybrook's throat.

"For God's sake, give me a little credit for clandestine conniving," she snapped, feeling a little defensive. "I was exceedingly careful about leaving no trace that it had been tampered with. I made a copy and put the original back exactly as I found it."

He leaned back and folded his arms across his chest. "Then how did you come to be chased within an inch of your life by the comte and his hellhounds?"

"As it happens, I heard him returning and knew I didn't have time to put his desk back in order and escape. So I threw some things around, including the jewel case, and pocketed the baubles to make it look like a robbery."

Without further comment, Saybrook extracted the paper from his pocket. Slowly, precisely, he unfolded the creases and began studying the contents.

"Bravo, lassie," said Henning. "Perhaps your clue will help us figure out what Rochemont and that bastard Talleyrand are up to. I don't know what new mayhem the two of them are planning together. But mark my words, I think we'll find that Talleyrand is at the heart of all this. He just *has* to be."

The earl kept on reading.

Arianna bit her lip, uncertain whether to feel angry or guilty. Had she been stubbornly reckless simply to prove her independence?

Tearing her gaze from his profile, she forced a careless shrug. "One other thing. It may mean nothing, but one of the kitchen maids mentioned that Talleyrand is expecting a special guest for next week's gala Carrousel, and apparently it's a matter of great secrecy. According to her, the person is a general, however she didn't remember his name . . ." Her brows pinched together. "Save for the fact that it has something to do with water."

"A general," repeated Henning. "That's hardly a notable personage these days. After a decade of constant wars, they are as common as cow dung."

"Water," she mused, then repeated the word in several different languages. "Anything strike a bell?"

Henning shook his head.

Preoccupied with the coded letter, Saybrook didn't answer.

"Sea . . . Spring . . . Creek." Each elicited a negative response from the surgeon, so she abandoned the effort. "Perhaps something will come to us later. In any case, it's likely not important."

At that, Saybrook grunted, showing that he had been listening, if only with half an ear. "We've enough word games to occupy our attention." He rose and went to the desk to fetch his notebooks, which contained the other coded document. "It's been a long day. Why don't the two of you get some rest."

"What about you?" asked Arianna.

Saybrook picked up a pencil. "I want to work for a while longer. Now that I have two samples, I might see something new."

"Can I help?"

"I don't know." His temper sounded dangerously frayed.

Arianna was about to retort when all of a sudden, she spotted the uncertainty in his eyes.

*He's not angry at me—he is angry at himself.*

"Don't be so hard on yourself, Sandro," she whispered as Henning bid them good night and headed off to the spare bedchamber on the floor above.

"Ah, yes—it's only a matter of life and death," he replied, his voice sharp with sarcasm. Unknotting his cravat, he tugged it off and tossed it onto the sofa. "Sorry," he muttered after expelling a low oath. "This whole damnable mission has me feeling as if I am dancing on a razor's edge."

"While playing blind man's bluff," she added.

A ghost of a smile flitted over his lips. "With two grenades in my outstretched hands, the fuses cut short to explode at any moment."

"Is that all?" She waggled a brow. "And here I thought you were trying to do something difficult."

He laughed.

"Come, get some rest."

"I will." His gaze had already slipped down to the papers. "I'll just be a little while longer."

Arianna woke several hours later, her mind too restless to sleep any longer despite the bone deep fatigue of her body. A hazy gray glow had begun to lighten the horizon. Clouds hung low in the pewter skies, heavy with the promise of rain.

Stifling a yawn, she pulled on her wrapper and padded out to the parlor.

The candles had burned out and in the murky shadows, she saw that Saybrook had fallen asleep in his chair. Tiptoeing across the carpet, she stood over his chair and watched the steady rise and fall of his breathing.

"Sandro." The word was a whisper that barely stirred the air. She pressed a palm lightly to his unshaven cheek, feeling the rough stubbling of his skin, the faint thud of his heart. Shadows, dark as charcoal, hung in half moon smudges beneath his closed eyes, and the hollows in his cheeks made his face look even leaner.

When Arianna had first met her husband, he had been thin as a cadaver and living on a diet of laudanum—a pernicious mix of liquid opium and precious little else. It was a wonder that he had survived the dangerous web of intrigue that had first drawn them together.

*Actually, it's a wonder that either of us survived.*

Grentham . . .

No, she would not think of Grentham. The tangle of deceptions and betrayals was twisted enough here in Vienna. If the threads, once unknotted, eventually led back to the inner sanctum of Whitehall, they would deal with that when the time came.

Slipping the coded papers out from beneath Saybrook's sleep-slack fingers, Arianna carried them over to the desk.

"Patterns, patterns," she murmured to herself, feeling a bittersweet smile tug at her lips on recalling her late father's admonitions.

*See the patterns and you see the logic, poppet,* he would always say. *Then it's simple to solve the problem.*

Oh, what a sad disappointment she must have been for him. Here he had passed on his gift for mathematics, only to have his own flesh and blood refuse to join him in a business partnership of manipulating numbers into profits.

Resolutely setting aside such distracting thoughts, Arianna smoothed out the two coded sheets. The past could not be changed, but the future lay here under her gaze, waiting, waiting.

Waiting for a look to unlock its secrets.

She began counting the frequency of individual letters within the seemingly meaningless string of gibberish. As Saybrook had pointed out, having two examples should increase the chances of cracking the encryption.

Her pencil point tapped against the blank sheet of foolscap she had set between the two coded messages. *Tap. Tap.* For the next hour she worked in methodical silence, save for an occasional tap, drawing up grids and testing her hunches.

*Damnation.* Frowning in frustration, she sat back for a

moment to rub at the crick in her neck. If only the letters were numbers, she thought. Equations seemed so much more straightforward.

"Speak to me," she crooned, hoping to coax some stirring of inspiration from her own muzzy brain.

A tiny draft curled through the window casement and tugged at the corner of the paper she had found in the chocolate book. Arianna was about to press it back in place when another gust lifted it higher and a ray of early morning light skimmed across the page.

The wind blew again, and the paper fluttered anew, forming a soft, creamy curve that brought to mind the shape of a ship's sail. *A bizarre flight of fancy, stirred by fatigue?* Arianna wasn't sure why the momentary image triggered a sudden thought.

She closed her eyes and pictured Rochemont's desk. The polished pear wood...the fancy pens...the crystal inkwell...the single leather-bound volume prominently positioned on the leather blotter.

*The Corsair.* A wildly romantic poem by Lord Byron.

She had thought it odd, for Rochemont didn't seem the type of man who read poetry. And yet, the ribbon bookmark had been set at a certain page of Canto II, and a word in one of the stanzas had been underlined with several bold slashes.

*Demons.*

It had stuck in her mind because it had seemed such a strange choice to highlight.

"Demons," she murmured aloud.

At the sound, a prickling of gooseflesh raced down her arms.

No, the idea was absurd—a figment of an overwrought imagination.

But as Arianna tried to dismiss it, a niggling little voice in her head reminded her that Sandro always stressed the importance of intuition. Trusting a hunch was key to solving conundrums.

With rising excitement, she pulled out a fresh sheet of

paper and quickly drew in a rough Vigenère Square. Using "Demons" as the key word, she worked through the conversions. It was a slow, tedious process, but when she was done, the result was no longer gibberish.

After checking and rechecking, Arianna was sure she hadn't made a mistake.

Setting down her pencil, she hurried over to give his shoulder a shake.

"Sandro, wake up! I have something to show you."

# 20

## From Lady Arianna's Chocolate Notebooks

### Arianna's Special Brownies

*16 tablespoons unsalted butter, plus more for greasing pan*
*8 oz. bittersweet chocolate, cut into ¼-inch pieces*
*4 eggs*
*1 cup sugar*
*1 cup firmly packed dark brown sugar*
*2 teaspoon vanilla extract*
*½ teaspoon fine salt*
*1 cup flour*

1. Heat oven to 350°. Grease a 9-inch x 13-inch baking pan with butter and line with parchment paper; grease paper. Set pan aside.
2. Pour enough water into a 4-quart saucepan that it reaches a depth of 1 inch. Bring to a boil; reduce heat to low. Combine butter and chocolate in a medium bowl; set bowl over saucepan. Cook, stirring, until melted and smooth, about 5 minutes. Remove from heat; set aside.
3. Whisk together eggs in a large bowl. Add sugar,

brown sugar, vanilla and salt; whisk to combine. Stir in chocolate mixture; fold in flour. Pour batter into prepared pan; spread evenly. Bake until a toothpick inserted into center comes out clean, 30–35 minutes. Let cool on a rack. Cut and serve.

⤸

Henning let out a low whistle as he read over the deciphered messages. "The two of you make a formidable team."

"It was Arianna who came up with the solution," said Saybrook. "I merely helped her apply it to working out the second message." He gave a wry smile. "Though I suppose that I deserve some credit for knowing she would be brilliant at this."

"Let us not start celebrating quite yet," she cautioned. "We can't forget that while we have worked out the text of the actual messages, we have yet to figure out what it all means."

Henning grunted in assent. "Aye, it's still cryptic." He pursed his lips in a wry grimace. "We had better order up a big breakfast, seeing as you claim to think better on a full stomach."

Arianna suddenly found herself craving a steaming cup of coffee and hot muffins studded with chunks of sweet chocolate. "I've a better idea. Let us go down to the kitchen, and I'll tell Theresa that I will take charge of the cooking." Given the need for secrecy and security concerning their activities, they had brought their own trusted household servants with them to Vienna. "The aroma of sugar and spices is an added stimulant to my brain."

"Far be it from me to object," said the surgeon, patting his bony ribs. "Your shirred eggs with peppered cheese are ambrosial."

"I'm hungry too . . ." Saybrook gathered up the papers. "For a solution."

"I shall try to serve up some inspiration," she quipped.

A short while later, the sound of the kettle whistling on the hob punctuated the sizzling of butter in the frying pan. Platters of sausages and fresh fruit, freshly baked rolls, and steaming pots of cinnamon-scented chocolate and rich, dark coffee crowded the work table.

"Delicious," murmured Henning, forking up another mouthful of *omelette aux champignons*.

Saybrook pushed back his plate, and cleared a place for his papers. "Try to devote an equal amount of enthusiasm to the problem at hand, Baz."

"I'm chewing over the possibilities, laddie," retorted the surgeon. "Read us the messages again."

The earl picked up Arianna's transcription. "The one that was hidden in the chocolate book reads, '*K's use to us will end in Vienna. Too risky to allow him to return to England. Removing the pawn from the board must be your first move.*'"

"So Kydd's death was planned from the start," mused Arianna. "I confess, I feel a bit better knowing that I was not the cause. I know he was a traitor, but I'm sorry he was murdered. He wasn't evil, merely misguided. Men far more devious than him manipulated his passions to their own advantage."

Saybrook's jaw tightened for an instant and then released. "Nonetheless, he would have hanged for his betrayal."

"There is one thing that I've been wondering about the messages hidden in the chocolate book," said Arianna. "Wouldn't it have set off alarm bells that they didn't reach Vienna."

"Not necessarily," replied her husband. "It's always assumed that some of the messages won't make it through. Davilenko was likely just one of several couriers. I would imagine that copies of the document stolen from Charles, along with duplicates of the coded notes, were dispatched with other carriers. And much as I hate to give the devil his due, Grentham arranged Davilenko's death to appear a plausible accident, so it would be unlikely to raise suspicion."

Henning had stopped eating. "I, too, have a question. Do you plan to expose the secret society in Scotland?"

"Rochemont's cohorts must be rooted out, Baz. As for the other Dragons of St. Andrew, I shall do my best to see that they escape England's lance."

The surgeon nodded curtly.

Arianna touched his sleeve. "Your nephew—"

"It's too late for him. I'm assuming he's been murdered by Rochemont and his bloody bastards." Henning fingered his knife. "Though I haven't the heart to say so to my sister. God knows, we'll likely never find the body." The blade drew a tiny bead of blood, more black than crimson in the muted light. "It will add to her pain not to be able to give the lad a decent Christian burial."

"I'm so sorry," she whispered.

In the shifting shadows, the surgeon's craggy face looked as bleak as a storm-swept chunk of Highland granite. "So am I, lassie. So am I." He curled a fist. "Which is why we must crush these men before they harm anyone else."

Saybrook cleared his throat. "The second message is what will help us do so, Baz. The plan is spelled out here in black and white. We just have to be clever enough to read between the lines."

"'*While the Kings watch the Queens, the Knight to Bishop, Q 4,*'" recited Arianna. She had already committed the brief message to memory. "'*And when the Well runs dry, the Castle will be ours and the Bee will once again rule the board.*'"

Henning made a face. "It seems to indicate a chess game of sorts." He looked at the earl. "Can you make any sense of it?"

The earl stared up at the ceiling for a long moment, watching the thin plumes of cooking smoke snake along the age-dark beams. "Knight to Bishop Q 4 seems the clearest message. In chess, that means the knight knocks the bishop from the board." His lashes flicked slowly up and down, like the silent swish of a raptor's wings, and with his forefinger, he started to sketch a pattern of imaginary squares upon the scarred tabletop. "And Q 4 is one of the center squares, so it might be a metaphor for doing the deed in the middle of a gala entertainment."

"Yes," agreed Henning. "That seems a reasonable guess."

"So, a bishop is the target," said Arianna, feeling a little like a round peg whose contours didn't quite fit into the hard-edged outline. "That blows all of my theories to flinders. I had assumed from the very start that a politician or a royal was the intended victim." She broke off a piece of bread, but merely crumbled the crust between her fingers. "I'm more confused that ever. How the devil is religion linked to England's security?"

"Good question," muttered Henning. "I haven't a clue."

A hiss of steam swirled up from the stove. Arianna took up the kettle and silently fixed a fresh pot of coffee.

"The bishop," muttered Henning "The bishop. The bishop."

Saybrook started to refill his cup.

"The bishop."

"Good God." A splash of scalding coffee suddenly spilled over Saybrook's fingers.

Arianna whirled around from the stove.

"Talleyrand," said her husband. Shaking off the drops, he slapped his palm to the table. "Damnation, how did I not think of it before now. As a young man, Talleyrand was appointed the Bishop of Autun through his family's influence." A trickle of dark liquid seeped through the cracks of the oiled wood. "A notorious nonbeliever, he quickly abandoned the Church for politics, but still . . ."

The three of them exchanged wordless looks.

It was Henning who glanced away first. "You think Talleyrand is not the mastermind of all this but the *target*?" he asked with some skepticism.

"Yes, actually I do," answered the earl slowly. "Indeed, when one looks at it from that angle, the pieces of the puzzle begin to fit together."

"Nay, I dunna see it, laddie," said Henning stubbornly.

"The Prince is perhaps the most crafty, cunning mind in all of Europe. It's hard to imagine him as a victim."

"Oh come, as I pointed out earlier, you have studied history, Baz," countered the earl. "How often have the mighty, however brilliant they be, fallen to an assassin's blade or bullet? Only God is omniscient—assuming He exists."

The surgeon scowled but had no retort. Instead he muttered, "Go ahead then—convince me."

"Very well, let's start from the beginning," said Saybrook. "Davilenko had the misfortune to meet Arianna in the bookshop, where his regular exchange of secrets was so rudely interrupted. However, he recognized Arianna at Lord Milford's shooting party and saw a way to salvage the situation. I suspect that the *Grognard* was brought in to create a diversion. Whether he killed me or simply wounded me didn't matter—in the confusion, someone could steal into our quarters and retrieve the hidden codes."

"And we know that someone did try to enter our rooms," Arianna pointed out. "The man posing as a servant with the starched cravats."

"Yes, but you say Grentham's operatives confirmed that Davilenko hadn't told his superiors about the book's loss," argued Henning. "How did he arrange for the *Grognard* to take a shot at you? And more to the point, why would he risk shooting at Rochemont?"

Saybrook mulled over the question for a bit. "From my experience, I know that the leader of a clandestine network keeps his identity a secret from his minions. My guess is Davilenko had a way of communicating with the network if he needed assistance, but had no idea that Rochemont was part of the group—"

Henning snorted.

Ignoring the interruption, Saybrook continued, "I'm assuming Davilenko was clever in his own way, so it wouldn't have been too hard to think of a lie to cover the need to shoot at me."

"Then why was the *Grognard* murdered?" demanded the surgeon.

"That's the one point that puzzles me," admitted the earl. "But wait a moment before you assume that smug smile."

Henning thinned his lips.

"Do you deny that Kydd was recruited through the Scottish secret society? Which, by your own admission, was run by Rochemont."

Henning gave a grudging grunt.

"You've also been told by your sources that the funding for these revolutionary groups came from Napoleon."

"Aye," admitted the surgeon. "My old friend told me that he had made several secret trips to France for the cause, and had met with the Emperor personally."

"So we know the link between Rochemont and Napoleon to be fact, not conjecture." Saybrook leaned back and steepled his fingers. "Which, as Arianna pointed out so sagely last night, raises the key question—what possible reason could Rochemont have for continuing his efforts to undermine England?"

"The Royalists aren't aware of his betrayal," suggested Henning. "Now that his former master is out of power, Rochemont offers them a way to foment trouble in Scotland, and as a weak England is always in the best interest of France, the new King agrees to fund it. *Voila!*" A snap of his fingers punctuated the exclamation. "The comte keeps his bread buttered on both sides and ends up looking like a hero."

"I think that the French King is far too worried about consolidating his power at home to be funding unrest abroad," said the earl. "No, I'd be willing to wager my entire fortune that the money is still coming from Napoleon."

There was a moment of utter silence, save for the *drip, drip, drip* of the spilled coffee, before Arianna whispered, "So you think that the Emperor is planning to seize back his crown?"

"Yes," said Saybrook. "That's precisely what I think."

Henning shifted uncomfortably in his chair.

"The French King is weak—the real political power in

France right now is Talleyrand," insisted the earl. "And while we've assumed that Talleyrand is the force behind this plot, it would mean that he's gone back to working for Napoleon, the leader he betrayed in '08."

"A not unreasonable assumption, given that the Prince has switched sides more often than a lady changes her ... hair ribbons," said the surgeon. His voice, however, lacked conviction.

"I know, I know," said Saybrook impatiently. "But when I analyze the plot, nothing quite fits together with Talleyrand as part of Napoleon's inner circle. It's only when we see him as Napoleon's *enemy* that it starts to make sense. If the most able diplomat in all of Europe is a loyal servant of the new King, he presents a formidable opponent to any plan to take back the throne."

Arianna watched tiny beads of condensation form on the spout of the abandoned kettle. "You make a convincing argument, Sandro. What do you think, Mr. Henning?"

The surgeon's chin took on a mulish jut.

"One last point," offered Saybrook. "The second part of the message we just decoded—'*And when the Well runs dry, the Castle will be ours and the Bee will once again rule the board*'—appears to hold the key to everything, correct?"

"Aye, I'll grant you that," replied Henning guardedly.

"You've been cajoling me to sharpen my old skills at cutting through conundrums, so how about this? The castle is, of course, a chess piece, and I think we can all agree that it symbolizes the bailiwick—or, if you will, the country—of the King and Queen. As for the Bee, it's well known that Napoleon adopted it as his symbol when he became emperor. With that in mind, the meaning of the phrase seems obvious."

"*Hmm.*" Henning made a rueful face. "I concede that the Castle and Bee reference seems to indicate that Napoleon is planning to escape from Elba and reseize the throne of France. But you still haven't completely convinced me that Talleyrand isn't part of the plot." His jaw took on a pugnacious tilt. "Can you explain to me what the devil 'Well' means?"

The earl's mouth quirked up. "As a matter of fact, I think I can."

But before he could go on, Arianna suddenly straightened. "Well—Water! The serving maid mentioned that a secret guest is coming for the Carrousel. A general."

"A general," repeated Henning. All of a sudden, his eyes widened.

"Yes, and I ask you, who is the only general whose military genius rivals that of the former Emperor?" said Saybrook. "Who is the only man Napoleon might fear on the field of battle?"

*"Wellington,"* whispered Arianna.

"Wellington," repeated the earl, a note of grim satisfaction shading his voice. "Napoleon has beaten every Allied commander he's faced—only the Russian winter put his army in retreat. But Wellington has bested the *crème de la crème* of the French generals. He, too, is undefeated on the battlefield." His fingers began to drum a martial tattoo on the tabletop. "It would be a clash of Titans. And if I were Napoleon, it would not be an opponent I would want to face."

The surgeon's low whistle took on a tinny tone as it echoed off the hanging pots.

It had not yet died away when Saybrook delivered his *coup de grace.* "At the moment, the duke is serving as our government's ambassador in Paris. But according to a comment I overheard Castlereagh make this afternoon, he is coming to Vienna for a private meeting with Talleyrand and Metternich to discuss France and the future balance of power in Europe."

Arianna's palms began to prickle.

"For now, it's being kept a secret so the Tsar of Russia can't stir up any opposition among the other delegates," Saybrook went on. "Alexander and the Prussians will be invited to attend, but as the talks are not part of the official Conference agenda, Wellington will avoid all the regular balls and banquets. His only public appearance will be at the Carrousel, where he will watch the display of medieval martial skills from Talleyrand's box."

"'When the Well runs dry,'" recited Arianna. "You think Rochemont means to assassinate Talleyrand *and* Wellington."

"I do," replied the earl. "Europe's greatest statesman and Europe's greatest soldier—it would eliminate the two most dangerous obstacles in Napoleon's path to recapturing his past glory."

"By the bones of St. Andrew, you just might be right, laddie." Henning blew out his cheeks. "So, how do we checkmate the Bee and his murderous bastards?"

"Chess is all about strategy, Baz. Knowing what moves our opponent is planning gives us an advantage but we shall have to play our pieces very carefully to turn that edge into outright victory."

"Ye needn't lecture me about the importance of strategy," groused the surgeon. "I am well aware that chess is considered a metaphor for war. But tell me, what game are we playing with this so-called Carrousel? I take it the event is to feature real-life knights, but what are the details?"

The earl crooked a rueful grimace. "The Festival Committee has been planning the evening for months, and from what I've gathered, it's meant to be the crown jewel of the Conference entertainments. Several aides have spent days in the Imperial Library poring over the accounts of past tournaments, so we can assume that the pageantry will be a dazzling spectacle."

"Which will only make things more difficult for us," grumbled Henning.

"Perhaps," said the earl. "And yet, it may also work in our favor. Rochemont is likely counting on the blaring trumpets, the flapping banners and the colorful procession of champions to cover his dastardly preparations. We can take advantage of the same confusion."

The surgeon chuffed a noncommittal grunt.

"It's to be held in the Spanish Riding School, which has

a large indoor arena designed for equestrian maneuvers. All the surrounding columns will be decorated with armor and various weapons from the Imperial Armory's collection," continued Saybrook. "At one end, they are building a grandstand for all the sovereigns—complete with gilded armchairs, I might add. At the other end will be a balcony for the twenty-four *Belles d'Amour*—the Queens of Love."

Another sound slipped from Henning's lips, this one far ruder than the last.

"*Dio Madre*, Baz, if you are suffering from gout or gas, kindly pour yourself a medicinal draught of whisky."

"Sorry," muttered the surgeon. "The antics of the aristocracy never cease to give me a pain in the gut."

"Well, stubble your stomach's sensitivity if you please. All of Europe will be hurting if we can't figure out a way to beat Rochemont at his own game."

"Sandro, that begs the question . . ." Arianna finished riddling the stove and dusted the soot from her hands. "Why not simply tell Talleyrand and Wellington what is planned and ask them to stay away?"

"For a number of reasons," answered the earl. "First of all, it's imperative to catch Rochemont in the act. Much as I hate to admit it, the evidence against him is flimsy enough that I don't think he can be charged with a crime." His gaze angled up, just enough for her to see the simmering anger in his eyes.

"You mean because I'm the only one who has actually uncovered the coded documents. The book, the hidden paper in the jewel case—it's my word against his and most government officials will believe a titled gentleman over a lady whose background is, shall we say, somewhat uncertain."

"That sums it up in a nutshell," said her husband tersely.

"Bloody bastards." It wasn't clear to whom Henning was referring. She assumed it was everyone who moved within the exalted circles of the *ton*, that special place where wheels turned smoothly within wheels, greased with the drippings of privilege and pedigree.

The earl signaled the surgeon to silence and went on. "Secondly, I want to catch his cohorts. I'm not convinced Rochemont is Renard—there is a weakness about him, despite his cleverness. So if there's a chance to catch the real fox, I don't want to miss it." He tapped his fingertips together. "And thirdly, being intimately acquainted with Wellington, I know exactly how he will react if I suggest a retreat from the enemy. He'll look down that long nose of his and tell me to go to the Devil."

"*Men,*" murmured Arianna with a slight shake of her head. "In this case prudence ought to override pride."

"It won't," said Saybrook flatly. "Trust me, you could light a barrel of gunpowder under his bum and he wouldn't budge—" He stopped abruptly, the rest of the sentence still hanging on the tip of his tongue.

Arianna had been sweeping the dark grains of crumbled toast into a neat pile but her hand stilled.

Henning straightened from his slouch.

"Gunpowder," repeated Saybrook.

"Medieval knights did not have gunpowder," Henning pointed out.

"Thank you for the history lesson, Baz. But I'm not suggesting they are going to ride in dragging a battery of cannons behind their warhorses. However . . ." Picking up his notebook, he thumbed to the center section and read over several pages. "The preliminary drills will include the *pas de lance*—riding at full gallop and tilting at rings hanging by ribbons—as well as throwing javelins at fake Saracen heads and displaying prowess with a sword on horseback by slicing apples suspended from the ceiling."

"An apple is the same size as a small grenade—like the one used to kill Kydd," said Arianna softly.

"An interesting observation." The earl added a notation to the page.

"How would he ignite it?" asked Henning quickly.

"For the moment, let's not discard any idea," said Saybrook. "No matter how outlandish it might seem."

"Fair enough," replied the surgeon with a solemn nod.

"You're right—we need to keep an open mind about how they intend to do the murderous deed. We know they are devilishly clever, so we must be too."

"I suggest we backtrack for a bit, and go through the whole program," offered Arianna.

"Right." The earl took a moment to consult his notes. "Twenty-four gentlemen have been chosen to be a knight in the extravaganza. All are from prominent titled families— Prince Vincent Esterhazy, Prince Anton Radziwill, Prince Leopold of Saxe-Coburg-Saalfeld, to name a few. As I mentioned, twenty-four highborn ladies have also been invited to be a Queen of Love. Metternich's daughter Marie is one of them, as is the Duchess of Sagan, Dorothée de Talleyrand-Perigord and Sophie Zichy. Each will carry her knight's colors and sit in a special section"—the earl's voice took on a note of sardonic humor—"where she will cheer her champion on to glory."

"With any luck, several of the idiots might manage to kill themselves," quipped Henning.

Saybrook grimaced. "Not likely. Though it's been dubbed a medieval joust, the participants will be wearing snug hose, fancy velvet doublets and plumed hats decorated with diamonds rather than awkward and uncomfortable armor."

Arianna stifled a snicker on imagining the absurdly elaborate spectacle.

Her husband's brows waggled in silent agreement. "Oh, it gets even better. At precisely eight in the evening, there will be an opening procession, complete with squires toting shields, and pages waving banners. Our noble nodcocks will follow their minions, mounted on black Hungarian chargers. They will gather in front of the sovereigns and give a flourishing salute with their lances. Then the games will begin." He paused. "After the pageant, there is a banquet for the guests of honor scheduled, but that need not concern us. Talleyrand and Wellington have already indicated that they do not plan to attend."

"How many spectators are expected?" asked Henning.

The question prompted a harried sigh from the earl. "The official guest list has around twelve hundred names. But judging by all the forged tickets that have shown up at other events, I think we can expect double that number."

"A horde of onlookers, a gaggle of Love Queens, a troupe of prancing knights in bloody velvet, a skulking pack of vermin looking to commit murder . . ." mused Henning. His chair scraped back as he shifted and helped himself to another sultana-studded muffin. "I take it you have some ideas on how to spike their guns, metaphorically speaking, that is?"

"As a matter of fact, I do." Saybrook turned to a fresh page in his notebook. "Arianna, perhaps you could brew up a pot of your special spiced chocolate. We may be here for a while."

# 21

## *From Lady Arianna's Chocolate Notebooks*

### *Chocolate Peanut Butter "Bullets"*

*2 cups sifted confectioners' sugar*
*¾ cup smooth peanut butter*
*4 tablespoons unsalted butter, melted*
*½ teaspoon vanilla extract*
*¼ teaspoon salt*
*6 oz. semisweet chocolate chips*
*½ teaspoon vegetable shortening*

1. Put sugar, peanut butter, butter, vanilla and salt into a mixing bowl and beat well with a wooden spoon. Roll peanut butter mixture into 1-inch balls and transfer to a wax-paper-lined cookie sheet in a single layer. Freeze until firm, 15–20 minutes.
2. Melt chocolate and shortening in a small heat-proof bowl set over a small pot of simmering water, stirring often. Remove pot and bowl together from heat.
3. Working with about 6 peanut butter balls at a time, insert a toothpick into the center of a ball and dip

about three-quarters of the ball into the melted chocolate, leaving about a 1-inch circle of peanut butter visible at the top. Twirl toothpick between your finger and thumb to swirl off excess chocolate, then transfer to another wax-paper-lined cookie sheet, chocolate side down. Slide out toothpick and repeat dipping process with remaining peanut butter balls and chocolate, reheating chocolate if necessary.

4. Freeze "Bullets" until firm. Smooth out toothpick holes left in peanut butter. "Bullets" will keep well sealed in cool place for up to 1 week and up to 2 weeks in refrigerator. Serve at room temperature or chilled.

❧

"**D**amnation, I still don't like this."

It was the next evening, and in the smoky light of the carriage lamp, Saybrook's face looked even more forbidding than it had the previous day, when the preliminary plan had been drawn up. Shadows accentuated the chiseled angles, but made any hint of expression impossible to discern.

"I know you don't," intoned Arianna, using her best Voice of Reason. "But we all agreed that Rochemont must have no reason to think that his devilry has been discovered. If I suddenly turn cold and start to avoid him, it will stir up his suspicions. Besides, you need me to keep him distracted for the next few hours."

The seat suddenly shifted, a rasp of leather and wool rippling through the swirling shadows as her husband turned and braced an arm on the squabs. "Yes, I know that cold logic dictates that we proceed on a certain course. But at the moment I am not talking about reason, I am talking about emotion."

Arianna didn't quite dare meet his gaze. She remained in awe of his ability to be so in command of his feelings.

*Calm, controlled.* And yet his voice seemed to crackle with an intensity that made her feel a little uncertain.

*A little uneasy.*

"Arianna, look at me."

Reluctantly, she raised her chin a notch. When she had first met him, her immediate impression had been that his eyes were an opaque, impenetrable shade of charcoal black. She had, however, quickly seen that she was wrong. The depths of their chocolate brown hue reflected a range of subtle nuances, from dark brewed coffee and molten toffee to fire-flecked amber at moments like now, when his passions were aroused.

"Danger lies all around us, coiled like a serpent," he said slowly. "And ready to strike without warning."

"I'm always on guard," she assured him.

His expression softened, in a way that defied description. "I know that. And I'm not sure whether I take comfort in the fact, or whether it makes me want to gnash my teeth and howl at the moon."

"The moon is playing hide-and-seek," she quipped, indicating the silvery scudding of clouds just visible through the window glass.

"So are you," he said softly. "Always dancing in and out of black velvet shadows. Sometimes it feels you are as far away as Venus or the North Star."

"Sandro, I . . ." Arianna hesitated. "I have learned from experience to be careful. Sentiment . . . can make one weak," she whispered.

"It can also make you strong." He closed his hand over hers and held it for a heartbeat before slowly releasing his hold. "So much is unknown and unresolved about this mission. But be assured of one thing: I will never, ever allow any harm to come to you."

*A rash, reckless promise.* Nobody could make such absurd assurances.

And yet the words sent her heart skittering against her ribs.

*Thud, thud, thud.* To her ears, the sound seemed as loud as gunpowder explosions.

Saybrook was silent for a moment longer and then reached up and framed her face between his hands. "Earlier this year, a friend recited one of Byron's new unpublished poems to me. I committed it to memory because it reminds me of you."

Arianna heard his soft intake of breath. "She walks in beauty, like the night; Of cloudless climes and starry skies; And all that's best of dark and bright."

*Dark and bright.* She sat very still, mesmerized by the glimmer of sparks swirling in the shadows of his lashes.

"That is indescribably lovely," she stammered.

"Yes, isn't it?" His kiss, though swift, took her breath away.

Reaching up, she twined her fingers in his long hair, savoring for a fleeting instant the silky softness against her skin.

"I love you." The whisper, like the embrace, was like a quicksilver sear of heat, imprinting itself on her skin. On her heart. On the terrible tangle of nameless fears that dwelled deep, deep inside her.

Just as quickly it was gone.

"Never forget that." Pulling back, he added, "I shall see you later," and then disappeared out the door before the carriage had rolled to a halt.

Moonlight played over the empty spot on the seat.

Arianna chafed at her arms, but strangely enough, her bare skin did not feel chilled by the night air.

*Perhaps because as Sandro said, I am more a creature of the Moon than of the Sun.*

But much as it was tempting to linger alone in thought, she reminded herself that she must slide into her third—or was it fourth?—skin and make ready to act out her role for the evening.

An aristocratic wife, bored with the tedium of married life. A jaded lady, tempted to play naughty games.

Drawing on her gloves, like a warrior of old donning his gauntlets for battle, she assumed a martial frame of mind.

*Mano a mano.* Saybrook had learned that Rochemont

would definitely be there tonight, so the upcoming encounter promised to be a cerebral fight with the enemy. One on one, stripped down to the bare-bones clash of will against will.

The comte would observe that she had come alone to the ball. Her mission was to keep him occupied until midnight. Feint and parry, that was all. But if given an opening, she was determined to seize the offensive and see if she could maneuver him into making yet another mistake.

One that would leave more than a mere scratch on his diabolically perfect face.

Snapping her fan open and shut in rhythm with the melody of the pianoforte, Arianna sidled up to one of the colonnaded archways of the Redoutensaal—the main ballroom of the Hofburg Palace.

"Why, Lord Rochemont, where have you been? Is it true that you have been unwell?" The sonata, a prelude to the upcoming set of dances, played softly over the smooth marble, its notes muffled by the swirl of silks and satins. "Or have you been deliberately avoiding me?"

The comte turned as she tapped the sticks lightly against his sleeve. He was wearing his customary smug smile— along with a pair of dove gray gloves that did not fit quite as smoothly as usual. "I was kept abed . . ." he answered, allowing a fraction of a pause before adding, "by a slight indisposition and not some more *interesting* companion."

She arched a brow at the provocative comment. "La, how boring."

"Boring, indeed." High overhead, the massive crystal chandelier blazed with a hard-edged brilliance, the creamy white candles catching the pearly glow of his smile.

*The smile of an angel, the soul of a serpent.* The palace was filled with glittering illusions, Arianna reminded herself. Medals hiding cowardice, gems masking poverty, crowns covering betrayals.

*Ah, but I too am wearing false colors.*

Light gilded the curl of his lashes, Rochemont leaned

closer and offered her arm. "I find myself in need of physical stimulation after such a prolonged period of inactivity. Come, partner me in a dance."

The pianoforte had given way to the flourishing sounds of the violins. A waltz had begun, and already the vast expanse of polished parquet was crowded with couples spinning through the steps. Skirts flaring, baubles flashing, they lit up the ballroom with jewel-tone flashes of color.

The comte shifted his hand on the small of her back, pulling her a touch closer than was proper. After glancing around the room, he asked, "Is your husband here tonight?"

"No," replied Arianna. "He has decided that such entertainments are too frivolous for his liking."

Through his glove, she felt a pulse of heat. "And you do not share his sentiments?"

Pursing a pout, Arianna released a sulky sigh. "I find that his scholarly obsession has become"—dropping her voice, she whispered—"exceedingly boring."

The caress of her breath against his cheek provoked a flash of teeth. "So the bloom is off the rose of marriage?"

"Let's not talk of marriage," said Arianna, casting a casual glance at the sumptuous surroundings. Slowly, slowly—to lead him in circles was a carefully choreographed strategy, but she knew she must not rush her steps. "Oh, look. Is that the Duchess of Sagan standing by the punch bowl? What a magnificent gown."

Rochemont waggled a lecherous grin. "I daresay her bevy of admirers are not admiring the stitching or the silk." His glove dipped down to the swell of Arianna's hip. "The man holding her glass is Prince von Windischgratz. It's said he's replaced Metternich as her latest lover."

The duchess tittered over something the handsome officer whispered in her ear.

"Look how Metternich stands in the corner, making calf's eyes at her." The comte gave a grunt of contempt. "What a besotted old fool."

"Affairs of the heart seem to be far more important than affairs of state here in Vienna," quipped Arianna.

"Oh, it's not the heart that is motivating most of the pairings." Another lascivious leer as his thigh brushed up against hers. "It's a different bodily organ."

She looked up at him through her lashes. "Isn't it against the rules of Polite Society to make any mention of anatomy in the presence of a lady?"

"Oh, yes, it's strictly forbidden." They twirled in a tight circle. "Does it offend you, Lady Saybrook?"

"Perhaps my sensibilities are not quite so refined as they should be."

He led her through a few more figures of the dance before speaking again. "A pity about Mr. Kydd. The two of you appeared to be close friends."

"As you were saying about anatomy . . ." She let the suggestive remark trail off. "Poor David—he was amusing up to a point, but I confess, his prosing on about politics was beginning to grow tiresome." A tiny pause. "Dear me, that sounds rather coldhearted, doesn't it?"

Rochemont looked amused, which was what she intended.

"I am, of course, sorry that he fell victim to such an unfortunate accident," she added. "How very unlucky for him to have been in the wrong place at the wrong time."

"Fortune is a fickle lady," said the comte carelessly. "She did not choose to smile on him."

"And what about you, Lord Rochemont?" murmured Arianna. "How does Fortune favor you?"

His boudoir laugh was low and lush as fire-warmed brandy. "I have always been lucky with ladies."

"Oh?" She curled her mouth in a teasing, taunting challenge. "Have you never suffered a defeat?"

"No, never," replied the comte. "I—"

But before he could go on, the music ended and a booming voice intruded on their tête-à-tête. "Ah, Lady Saybrook, you have yet to come visit me!" The Russian Tsar snatched her hand from Rochemont and lifted it to his lips. "Our delegations may be at odds over politics, but that is no reason for us to avoid being friends on a personal level, eh?"

"Your Majesty is most magnanimous," responded Arianna. "But then, you are known as a Champion of Peace."

His rosy cheeks flushed with pleasure at the flattery. "*Da*, I love peace!" A wink. "Though perhaps not quite so much as pretty women."

*And judging by his growing girth and the recent drawing room gossip, his appetite for pleasure was growing more rapacious by the day,* thought Arianna sardonically.

"I am giving a private party next week," Alexander continued. "In the interest of bringing our two countries closer together, I command that you come."

"Well then, I dare not disobey."

The comte shifted his stance, seemingly impatient to escape the Imperial shadow. "*Alors*, France is also anxious to promote international harmony. So I am sure you won't object if I escort Lady Saybrook away from the crush of the crowd and fetch her a glass of champagne."

The Tsar did not look pleased at having his flirtations cut short, but Rochemont was already nudging her toward the grand central staircase that led to the upper galleries.

"Pompous buffoon," he growled, taking two glasses of wine from a passing waiter. "He struts around as if God has anointed him the world's Savior."

"I've heard that Alexander has a mystical side, and thinks that the Almighty speak directly to him," mused Arianna as she looked up at the folds of red and gold velvet draped over the balconies. A profusion of exotic flowers were woven around the gilded balustrades, their petals perfuming the air with a heady sweetness. Surrounded by such sumptuous displays of pomp, privilege and power, she could begin to see how a mere mortal monarch could delude himself into thinking he was a deity.

"Yes, he has some charlatan fortune-teller babbling nonsense in his ear about Divine Destiny," replied Rochemont.

"You don't believe in such notions?"

His sinuous mouth snaked up at the corners. "I've a far more pragmatic view of life, Lady Saybrook. I believe man makes his own destiny."

*As do I.*

"An interesting philosophy," said Arianna, deliberately catching his gaze and holding it for an instant before starting up the carpeted steps.

"Does that frighten you, Lady Saybrook?"

Arianna chose her words carefully. "Not particularly." She lowered her voice. "I was not raised amid the pampered luxuries of the indolent rich. I've had to make my own way in the world, so I have a—shall we say—more practical understanding of what it takes to survive."

Quickening her steps, she crossed the landing and found a secluded spot at the far end of the balcony railing.

Rochemont joined her a moment later. "You intrigue me." He ran his gloved knuckles along the line of her jaw. "From the first time I saw you, I sensed you were different. Tell me, why were you so cool to me at the Marquess of Milford's party?"

"The climate in England was decidedly chilly at that time, especially with my husband and his disapproving uncle clinging like icicles to my skirts."

"So, you married the earl for money?" asked the comte.

A sardonic sound rumbled in her throat. "Really, sir, I didn't expect such a naive question from you."

"So the climate has thawed, so to speak?" he said.

"I find Europe much more to my liking. I may linger here for a while. I have always wanted to visit Paris."

"A city renowned for its *joie de vivre*," replied Rochemont. "We French have made an art out of appreciating beauty and pleasure. I think you would enjoy yourself there."

"And what of you sir?" asked Arianna. "Now that the war is over, do you plan to return to Paris?"

His mouth curled into a scimitar smile. "Most definitely."

"Will you be taking a position in the new government? I

have heard my husband mention that your service to your country during Napoleon's reign will likely be rewarded."

"I believe that my loyalty will be recognized." His mouth took on a sharper curl. "Perhaps we shall soon be waltzing in the ballroom of the Louvre."

"Perhaps," replied Arianna.

*But I wouldn't wager on it, if I were you. The only dance I wish to see you perform is the hangman's jig on the gallows of Newgate.*

From one of the side saloons, she heard the faint chiming of a clock. An hour until midnight. Surely with just a little more fancy footwork, she could maneuver him into making a slip of the tongue.

With a soft *snick*, the lock released.

"Stay close," cautioned Saybrook. "And tread softly. According to my source, there are no guards posted, but let us not take a chance." Easing the heavy iron-banded door open, he quickly squeezed through the sliver of space and then signaled Henning to follow.

The creak of the closing hinges seemed unnaturally loud as it echoed through the cavernous interior of the Spanish Riding School. The earl froze, but the faint spill of starlight from the high windows showed that the vast rectangular arena was deserted. After a moment, when no challenge rang out from the gloom, he released a pent-up breath and started forward.

Sand crunched under his boots as he ducked into the shadows of the low planked wall rimming the equestrian arena.

Henning glanced back but saw that their tracks were lost in a pelter of other footprints.

"Work began yesterday to prepare the place for the Carrousel," whispered Saybrook. "Our steps won't be noticed." He stopped to get his bearings, then pointed to the far end of the building. "The storage rooms are there, next to where the tack is kept for the horses. Uniforms and banners, along with the various draperies and cushions, are kept in a row of small chambers running along the left corridor. The armory sections will be on our right. We'll start there."

"Ye seem to know yer way around," murmured the surgeon.

"I found the architect's plans for this place in the library." The earl paused by one of the massive columns to cock an ear for any sound of movement up ahead. Looking up at the soaring arched ceiling and the magnificent chandeliers hanging down from the central beam, he added, "It was designed by Josef Emanuel Fischer von Erlach in 1735, and is quite a splendid work of art."

"I'll take your word for it." The surgeon eyed the bristling display of medieval weapons that hung just above their heads. "Though all I see is an ode to man slaughtering his fellow man." Armor, swords, pikes and crossbows—an arsenal of old decorated the arena in honor of the upcoming Carrousel.

The earl took one last look around. "Come on."

They entered the storage section of the school through another set of locked doors. Saybrook veered to the right, and took a small shuttered lanthorn from inside his coat.

"We can risk a light in here," he said. A lucifer match flared for an instant. "I had an interesting chat with one of the Austrian officers in charge of arming the participants in the pageant. All of the weaponry for the martial displays of prowess is being kept in the old munitions chamber." The pinpoint beam of light probed through the darkness, revealing a wrought iron gate guarding an oaken portal black with age.

*Snick. Snick.*

"If I didn't know better, I'd actually think you were enjoying this, laddie," said Henning as he carefully drew the door shut behind them.

"Bloody hell." The earl grunted as he lifted the lid of a massive chest and peered inside. "My wife is at the heart of the danger, dancing with a depraved murderer in another part of the palace while I am merely tiptoeing around the fringes of the action." Metal scraped against metal. "Trust me, I am *not* in a jocular mood, so kindly stubble the humor and help me shift these crates."

"Lady S is more than a match for any miscreant, Sandro."

Another grunt, followed by several words in Spanish that made the surgeon blink.

"Any idea what we're looking for?" asked Henning once they had sorted through the assortment of polished broadswords and jeweled scimitars.

Saybrook was standing by the rack of lances, methodically running a hand over the lengths of varnished wood. "Not precisely," he answered. "My gut feeling tells me that they won't try to strike at Talleyrand and Wellington with a simple blade or lance. The odds are against the chances of killing both men outright, not to speak of the fact that the attacker would be sacrificing himself. The chances of escape are virtually nil."

"So?" prodded Henning as he moved over to a tall wooden cabinet and unfastened the latch.

"So, I suspect that Rochemont has something else in mind. Something he considers a surefire method of success." The earl finished fingering the decorative hilts and hand guards. "No hidden gun barrels, no concealed triggers—not that I thought that a likely possibility." Perching a hip on one of the sword crates, he made a slow, silent survey of the room. "Let us keep searching, Baz. I may not be certain what we are looking for . . ." In the murky shadows, his expression appeared grim as gunpowder. "But I'm sure that I'll recognize it when I see it."

# 22

## From Lady Arianna's Chocolate Notebooks

### Chocolate-Rum Imperial Drink

½ gallon milk
3 whole star anise
2 sticks cinnamon
Zest of 1 orange
5 whole allspice berries
6 tablespoons brown sugar
½ lb. bittersweet chocolate
1 cup aged dark rum
Whipped cream

1. Combine milk, star anise, cinnamon sticks, orange zest, allspice berries and brown sugar in a large, heavy saucepan over medium heat.
2. Scald milk, stirring to dissolve sugar. Lower heat and cook 10 minutes. Remove from heat; steep 10 minutes. Strain into a large pot.
3. Heat gently, then add bittersweet chocolate and dark rum. Whisk briskly until chocolate dissolves, about 5 minutes. Serve topped with whipped cream.

Setting her hands on the railing, Arianna leaned out and watched the crowd below forming the figures for a Hungarian *csárdás*.

Rochemont came up behind her and placed his hands on her bare shoulders. "Have a care, Lady Saybrook. That's a little dangerous. What if you lost your balance?"

"Oh, but what fun is life if you don't take a few risks?" She turned into him and made no protests as his palms slowly slid down her arms. "All these balls are becoming tiresome. I am looking forward to the Carrousel. I hear it is going to be quite a display of pomp and pageantry."

"Having some knowledge of the arrangements, I can promise you that the evening will be unforgettable."

Arianna looked up at him through her lashes. "Alas, Saybrook has refused Lord Castlereagh's offer of tickets. He wishes to work." A coy flutter. "While I wish to play."

His gaze seemed to sharpen.

"I don't suppose I could ask you to take me as your guest?" she asked. "As the head of the French delegation, your Prince must have a private box."

"Indeed. It is in a place of honor, right in the front row," replied Rochemont. "Unfortunately, the seats are all taken, for Talleyrand has a special guest coming."

"Oh?" Arianna assumed a petulant pout. "Who?"

"It's a secret," said the comte is a low voice.

"I promise not to tell."

"Perhaps . . ." The soft leather of his gloves slid down her bare arms. Turning, he drew her into the shadowed corridor leading to the side saloons. The sound of muted laughter swirled in the smoke-scented air, its music melding with the faraway melody of the violins. "Perhaps I could arrange a favor, Lady Saybrook. But tell me, what are you willing to give me in return?"

"That would depend on how special the favor is," she countered.

"What would you say to being part of the pageantry?"

The slithering sensation on her skin had nothing to do with his touch. "You could arrange that?" she asked. "I've heard that the program has been worked on for months, and that every detail has been carefully planned. Surely the organizers won't allow a last-minute change."

"True. However there *has* been one change concerning the presentation of the grand prize to the winning knight. Due to the importance of the Prince's guest, Von Getz, the secretary of the Conference, has appointed me to be in charge of arranging a slight variation to the original ceremony."

*A change to the ceremony?* Arianna felt her pulse begin to quicken. "That must have cost you a fortune—it's said that von Getz's influence does not come cheap."

"The secretary likes money—but he also has a weakness for chocolate bonbons." Rochemont smirked. "Monsieur Carême recently hired a pastry chef who created some unique treats. No matter that the man turned out to be a criminal and was forced to flee when we caught him robbing the palace. There were enough of the sweets left that I was able to assemble a very sweet bribe."

Nearly overcome with the insane urge to dissolve into giggles, she managed to keep a straight face. "How clever of you."

A rough laugh, and suddenly Arianna felt herself shoved deeper into the alcove between the archway colonnade. Cold marble kissed against her back as the comte pivoted and pressed his body against hers. "I'm clever at a great many things, Lady Saybrook. Including seducing a woman into my bed. You've led me on quite a chase, but I sense that I'm getting close ..." His lips were now hovering a hairsbreadth from hers. "Close enough to taste triumph."

Touching her fingertips to his chest, she forced a fraction more space between them. "I was under the impression that men like the thrill of the hunt."

"We like the thrill of the kill even more—metaphorically speaking, of course," replied Rochemont.

"Of course." Arianna met his gaze without flinching. "So, what part do you have in mind for me?"

"It's been decided that Talleyrand's guest will present the prize to the champion, instead of the Austrian Emperor. I've been wondering just how to orchestrate the ceremony, and then it suddenly occurred to me that you, my dear Lady Saybrook, would be the perfect person to carry out the trophy," explained Rochemont. "What say you? Is that a sweet enough enticement?"

"Oh, yes," she said.

*Oh, yes.* Did the fox think he was pursuing a helpless rabbit? Ha! She intended to lead him right into the snapping jaws of Saybrook.

A low, feral sound rumbling in his throat, he sought to capture her mouth.

She evaded the embrace with a sly turn of her cheek. "*Tut, tut,* my dear comte. You'll have to wait until late night hours after the Carrousel. A smart lady never lifts her skirts until she has been paid in advance."

Rochemont allowed her to slip free. "You drive a hard bargain. Lady Saybrook." He brushed a wrinkle from his sleeve and patted his cravat into place. "I shall expect you to come to me then—and to make the experience worth my while."

"You may count on it being unforgettable," replied Arianna, her voice a silky, smoky whisper. "I perform at my best with men like you."

"Nothing." Henning grimaced as he put the papier-mâché head of a snarling Saracen back in the cabinet. In the wavering light, the grotesque teeth seemed to gleam in mockery. "Twenty-four of the bloody grinning Infidels, and not a single suspicious hinge or hollow space that I can make out."

Saybrook shook the head he was holding before placing it on its rack. "I agree that they appear harmless—the layers of paper are so thick that the space left inside isn't big enough to hide much of a threat."

"Ye think Lady S's suggestion that they are planning to use some sort of gunpowder bomb is bang on the mark?"

"Actually I do," answered the earl. "Rochemont's burned hands are too much of a coincidence to dismiss. Besides, the other alternatives are too hit or miss. Even if they convinced one of the knights to charge Talleyrand's box with scimitar flashing or lance lowered, the chances of him killing both men aren't very good. Wellington is, after all, a man much experienced in war. He won't sit there like a petrified pigeon waiting to be slaughtered." Vapor rose up from the stone floor in slow, serpentine swirls. Chafing his hands together to ward off the chill, Saybrook watched a ghostly tendril wrap itself around the metal lantern. "No, a man as clever as Renard would choose a more reliable method."

"Think of the *Grognard*," said Henning suddenly. "If I were Renard, I'd put a marksman in the crowd. Be damned with a bomb—a well-aimed bullet and the deed would be done in a flash."

Saybrook shook his head. "I might agree if it were only one target. But two?" His fingers twined and tightened together into a fist. "No, there are too many variables working against gunfire. Even with the crush of the crowd, a rifle would be hard to smuggle in. And then there is the time it would take to reload."

"A brace of pistols," suggested the surgeon, loath to give up his idea. "They are easily hidden inside a coat, and at close range it would be hard to miss."

"It won't be all that easy to get close to the section reserved for the dignitaries," argued the earl. "It's possible that one of the diplomats has been recruited to be the assassin, but still . . . the first shot would set off a panic. In the chaos, aiming a second shot would difficult, even for a battle-hardened soldier."

"Bloody hell, Sandro. If you're so convinced it's a bomb, how the devil is Renard going to deliver it?" He scowled. "And then detonate it? We've gone over the weaponry with a fine-tooth comb."

"I don't know," admitted Saybrook. "Let's move on to the costume closets."

"A bomb isn't going to be concealed in a button," groused Henning.

The earl picked up the lantern from its perch on the rack of lances. "The Carrousel is tomorrow. It has to be here, Baz. A clever assassin would ensure that there wasn't a last-minute mishap in bringing it into the building. So I mean to go through every stitch of—"

The scudding beam caught the folds of an ermine-trimmed cloak draped over a stool. Dark as midnight, the spill of lush fabric was almost hidden by the corner of storage cabinet and the rough-hewn moldings of the door.

"What's that?" he asked.

Henning gave a wordless shrug.

Saybrook hesitated for a moment, eyeing the square-cornered shape. "Let's have a look."

"Auch, we'll be here all night if ye mean to poke through every bit of cloth."

"Have you a more pressing engagement?" quipped the earl as he swept back the cloak to reveal an ornate brass box.

The gleam silenced the sarcasm hovering on Henning's lips.

"It's locked," said the earl after trying the lid. The steel probe reappeared from his pocket and made quick work of the catch.

The surgeon crowded close, straining to see over Saybrook's shoulder. "What—" He blinked as a flash of burnished gold momentarily blinded him. "What the devil is *that* doing in here?"

"I believe it's the Champion's Prize," replied the earl.

Henning gave a low whistle as he watched the earl struggle to lift a large ornate eagle from its nest of purple velvet. "That bird must be worth a bloody fortune. Why, it looks to be made out of solid gold."

Saybrook set the statue on the floor. "It's heavy," he agreed. "But there's something odd . . ." Squatting down,

Saybrook surveyed the intricate workmanship from several angles. "Baz, point the beam here . . ." He indicated a spot under the half-spread wing. "Hmmm."

*"What?"*

Sliding a thin-bladed knife from his boot, the earl pressed the point to an emerald set discreetly in the precious metal.

*Nothing.*

Henning released a whoosh of air.

The sharpened steel moved to the ruby. Again, nothing stirred, save for the faint rasp of the surgeon's breathing. It was only when the blade pricked against the pale peridot that the *objet d'art* came to life. The gem clicked a quarter turn to the right and sunk into the sculpted feathers as the eagle emitted a strange whirring sound.

The taloned feet rose half an inch out of the large round malachite base, revealing a hidden mechanism. Reversing his knife, the earl tapped the tiny lever with its hilt and sat back on his haunches as the top of the stone gave a shiver and a hairline crack appeared around the middle of the orb.

"Well, I'll be buggered," muttered Henning.

The eagle tilted forward with the top half of the base. Inside was a hollow interior, and nestled like a egg within it was a shiny metal ball. It too was hinged.

Saybrook gingerly nudged the lid open. And uttered a soft oath.

"Christ Almighty, don't touch anything," warned the surgeon. "Move over, and let me have a closer look."

"Gladly," replied the earl drily, edging over to allow Henning a better view of the glass vials, looped wires, and brass discs that were neatly embedded in a dark granular substance.

It was a rather lengthy interlude before the surgeon spoke. "Hmmph."

"Would you care to amplify on that statement?" asked the earl.

"In a moment, laddie." Flattening himself to the stone,

Henning checked the contraption from a few different angles before giving another grunt. "Ingenious. I saw a recent scientific paper from the University of St. Andrews describing a chemical experiment on fuseless explosions, and the accompanying diagram looked almost identical." Another slight shift. "And I had heard that Sir Humphry Davy was conducting some private work on the subject at the Royal Institution. However, I thought it was still in the theoretical stages." Pushing up to his knees, the surgeon dusted his hands. "Apparently not."

"Does that mean we should theoretically be running like the devil?"

"No, no. We're safe." Henning pointed out a thin brass rod welded to the inside of the lid. At its end was a small ring. "Right now the vial of acid is missing so there is little danger of the bomb going off."

Saybrook eyed the elaborate coil of wires and disks as if it were a serpent ready to strike. "How does the cursed thing work?"

"Oh, very cleverly," responded the surgeon, scientific enthusiasm overriding all else for the moment. "A glass vial of acid, designed with a tiny hole in the bottom, is inserted in the ring. When the top is closed, the liquid will drip onto this bit of wax here . . ." His finger indicated one of the disks. "Once it burns through—and that rate can be pretty much calculated in a laboratory depending on the thickness of the wax—it will allow the acid to touch the mercury fulminate percussion caps here"—he pointed again—"and spark a tiny explosion. From there, the fire will travel down the cordite-soaked twine wrapped around the wires to gunpowder, which has been specially corned to increase its volatility . . ."

A short technical explanation followed on the force generated by such a tightly contained explosion.

"So, what you are saying is that this bird is deadly enough to fell two people in one fell swoop."

"Hell, yes," said Henning. "Anyone within a half dozen feet will be blown to Kingdom Come."

"Don't sound so bloody cheerful about it," snapped Saybrook.

"No need to get your feathers ruffled, laddie. I'm counting on you to make sure the eagle will have its wings clipped, so to speak."

"Right." The grim lines of worry etched deeper around the earl's dark eyes. "It seems we have two options. We can disarm the thing now. Or we can wait and catch the miscreant in the act." He pondered the dilemma for an instant before adding, "A damnably difficult choice, for I would like to have unassailable proof that Rochemont is behind this."

"Perhaps we can do both." Henning fingered his stubbled chin. "There can't be any overt sign that the bomb has been tampered with. But if we are able to slip a thin piece of steel between the wax and mercury fulminate percussion cap, that will prevent the acid from setting off a spark."

The lanthorn's beam started a slow, undulating dance around the room. It flickered over the crates, the rack of long lances, the massive storage cabinet . . . and then darted back to the jousting weapons. A soft, silvery glow glimmered against the varnished wood. Each of the pommels was festooned with an elaborate design of hammered metal and studs of semiprecious stones.

"Will silver do?" asked the earl.

"Aye," replied Henning.

The blade slid out of his boot. "Let's get to work. Come tomorrow night, the comte is going to find that his high-flying hopes of throwing Europe into chaos have been plucked of their last, lethal feather."

Arianna took another turn around the room, her agitated movements impelled by a volatile crosscurrents of emotion colliding inside her. Impatience. Uncertainty. Anger. All churning with the ferocity of a storm-tossed sea.

Oh, be honest, she chided herself. Fear was the foremost force, spinning in a tight vortex that left her stomach lurching against her ribs. Strange how frightening a simple word could be. Strange how it could provoke such a visceral reaction. Fire sizzled up her arms. Ice slid down her spine.

"Love," she whispered, the single syllable feeling so very, very foreign on her lips. *Love.* A part of her feared making herself vulnerable. *Dio Madre,* she had spent half a lifetime hardening her heart against its hurt. A father who loved brandy and the allure of money more than he did his own flesh and blood. She had forgiven him—but she had also vowed never to let its pain wound her again.

That she felt safe and secure in Saybrook's arms had her feeling confused. Conflicted.

Fighting against devils like Rochemont felt like second nature, while wrestling with her own inner demons seemed to sap her of all strength.

*Should I surrender to trust?* Her mouth quirked. That felt a little like donning a blindfold and stepping off the edge of a precipice.

"I suppose that is what is meant by a leap of faith," she murmured. And yet, she never trusted in anyone but herself.

*Sandro was just as guarded, but he has taken the first tentative stride . . .*

Arianna spun around as the earl and Henning entered the parlor. "Thank God you are safe—I was beginning to imagine the worst," she said.

Henning hurried on to the sideboard and poured out a generous measure of brandy. "For once, I think even your colorful mind would fall short of the task." He drained his glass in one swallow.

*That didn't sound good.*

She looked at her husband and noticed several new cuts and scrapes on his hands. "I've some interesting news, but I think you had better go first. Did you run into trouble during your search?"

Saybrook made a wry face. "That depends on how you define trouble." Waving off the surgeon's offer of a drink, he dropped into the nearby armchair and ran a hand through his hair. "No, we did not have any problem entering the Spanish Riding School. Nor did we encounter any guards."

Her clenched hands relaxed ever so slightly.

"And in fact, we discovered how Rochemont means to kill Talleyrand and Wellington. It's a bomb—a diabolical bomb."

"Aye," chimed in the surgeon. "For it's likely to reduce them and a good many people close by into fragments of flesh no bigger than mincemeat."

"Good God," intoned Arianna. "But I thought you said a bomb would be unlikely, given the smoke and smell of a burning fuse—"

"This bomb doesn't need a conventional fuse. It's a brilliant piece of chemistry," said Henning. His face pinched to an unhappy expression. "Like mathematics, science can be used for good—or for evil."

"How—" she began.

Anticipating her question, Saybrook was quick with an answer. "Another bit of cunning. It's hidden inside the Champion's Prize. I'm not sure how he means to arm the infernal thing. Timing is critical, but somehow I am sure he has that worked out. Someone is going to serve as his pigeon, offering the Eagle to Wellington for the special presentation."

"That would be me." She sat down rather heavily on the arm of his chair and let out a little laugh. "And here I thought I was being so clever, teasing him into allowing me to be part of the ceremonies."

"He asked you carry the Eagle?" In contrast to the expressionless ice of his face, her husband's voice shivered with molten fire. "He's a dead man."

"Sandro . . ." she began, then fell silent as their eyes met.

"We've sabotaged the bomb, but still, on second thought, I prefer not to take any chances," Saybrook went on. "I'll need to catch him in the act of trying to arm it with the acid, and then . . ."

"And then prevent him from carrying out the dastardly deed," said Henning blandly. "An excellent plan. Any ideas how we're going to do it?"

"Yes, as a matter of fact, I have."

Arianna felt his big hand clasp hers in a hard, possessive hold.

"To begin with, Arianna is not going anywhere near the Spanish Riding School."

His gaze glittered in challenge.

After a long moment, she looked away.

"Thank you for not arguing," said her husband softly. "As for you, Baz, I want you positioned by the rear gate a half hour before the Carrousel is scheduled to begin, while I ..."

Arianna listened in silence. It was a good plan.

But she had a better one.

# 23

## From Lady Arianna's Chocolate Notebooks

### Chocolate-Ginger Muffins

2½ cups all purpose flour
1 cup plus 2 tablespoons sugar
2 teaspoons baking powder
½ teaspoon baking soda
½ teaspoon salt
1 teaspoon ground nutmeg
1 cup oats
6 tablespoons butter, melted and cooled
1 large egg
¾ cup yogurt
½ cup milk
½ teaspoon vanilla extract
1½ cups chocolate chips, dark or semisweet
¾ cup candied ginger, finely chopped

1. Preheat oven to 375°. Line a muffin pan with paper liners (I simply buttered my silicone muffin pan).
2. In a large bowl, whisk together the flour, sugar,

baking powder, baking soda, salt, ground nutmeg, and oats.

3. In a medium bowl, whisk together melted butter, egg, yogurt, milk and vanilla extract until smooth. Pour into dry ingredients and stir just until no streaks of flour remain. Stir in chocolate chips and candied ginger.

4. Divide batter into prepared muffin pan, overfilling each muffin cup so that the batter slightly rises above the top of the pan.

5. Bake for 20–25 minutes, or until muffins are lightly browned and a toothpick inserted into the center comes out clean.

6. Cool on a wire rack. Serve slightly warm. Makes 12 muffins.

❧

*A*h, well. *It is not the first time I've ignored an order*, thought Arianna as she crouched in the shadows and tucked her breeches more securely into the tops of her boots. *And likely not the last.* No matter that Saybrook's display of pyrotechnics on learning of her foray would no doubt put the famed Steuer fireworks to blush. Lucifer could light up all of Hell and she would still crawl through the burning sparks and flaming cinders to be part of the action.

Rolling her shoulders, she gave a mental salute to the earl's expensive London tailor, who despite his initial reservations, had crafted a sturdy set of dark masculine garments for her that fit like a glove. No rustling lace, no whispering silk—a predator had to move sleekly, silently through the night.

A carriage rattled over the cobbles, causing her to duck deeper into the murky alleyway. Arianna quickly squeezed through the sliver of space and then hesitated as she reached a gap in the buildings. A left turn would take her directly to the Spanish Riding School, while a right turn would lead to a more circuitous path past the Amalienburg wing of the Emperor's palace.

*Risk and reward.* She patted her empty pockets, loath to face off against a dangerous enemy with naught but the slim knife in her boot. Saybrook had taken his pistols with him, leaving her bereft of gunpowder and bullets. But she knew from the Russian Tsar's garrulous boasting that he possessed a pair of deadly accurate dueling weapons, recently purchased on his visit to London.

*And of all the pompous party-goers, Alexander was sure to be at the Carrousel.*

The chiming of the astrological clock echoed through the courtyard of the Amalienburg wing as Arianna edged around the towering fountain and peered up at the pale stone facade. Lights blazed in the windows of the first-floor salons, but on the floors above, where the Tsar was quartered, all was dark.

A side entrance for servants yielded to her hairpin, and it took no more than a minute to gain access to Alexander's sumptuous suite of rooms. All was quiet, and in the corridor leading to the monarch's private chambers, the gilded moldings gleamed in silent splendor, lit by only a single wall sconce flickering on the far wall.

A thick Turkey carpet muffled her cautious steps. *Thank God for Alexander's hubris.* In his blatant flirtations with her, the Tsar had described in detail exactly where his bedroom was located. With luck, the royal valet would be enjoying a well-deserved rest from the rigors of dressing his monarch . . .

Arianna froze in her tracks as one of the sky-blue paneled doors cracked open.

A shuffle of bare feet, a querulous mutter, and then the flutter of embroidered silk as a portly figure padded into the dimly lit passageway.

*Oh, bloody Hell.*

Blinking the sleep from his eyes, Tsar Alexander lifted his candle a touch higher, suddenly aware of a shadowy intruder just steps away from his person. With her hair knotted at the nape of her neck and a black knitted cap drawn low on her brow, Arianna knew that she must appear an ominous threat.

To his credit, Alexander did not cry for help. Assuming a pugilist's pose, he swung a meaty fist at her face. "Scrawny scoundrel! How dare you invade my private quarters."

Arianna easily dodged the clumsy blow and caught hold of his cuff. Whatever his other faults, Alexander was no coward. "Your Highness," she began, only to find an elbow flying at her face. She twisted away just in the nick of time, but her hold on his dressing gown pulled the Tsar off balance. He teetered on one foot for an instant and fell backward, landing on his Royal rump with an audible thump.

*"Merde."* They both swore in unison.

"My apologies, Your Highness," added Arianna, making no attempt to disguise her voice.

Alexander's eyes widened as his gaze traveled up the length of her legs. "You make a *very* attractive boy, Lady Saybrook," he murmured, regarding her snug breeches with obvious approval. "Is this some new English game of seduction? It's quite diverting, however I think that I prefer you dressed in frilly feminine attire." A leering wink. "Or nothing at all."

"I'm afraid this is not a social call, Your Highness," replied Arianna, wondering what the consequences would be for lashing a hard kick to the Imperial jaw. She couldn't afford to waste time in flirting. "I need a favor, but not one that involves sliding between your sheets."

"How disappointing." He patted his plump stomach and sighed. "However, I confess that I'm not feeling very frisky this evening, so perhaps it's for the best. My physician has ordered complete quiet and bed rest for the next few days."

"What a pity that you must miss the Carrousel. It promises to be quite a colorful spectacle." Arianna offered a hand to help him up. "I'm here to ensure that the hues don't include blood red."

His expression sharpened slightly. "Indeed?"

"I need to borrow your dueling pistols—the ones you purchased from Joseph Manton on your recent trip to England."

"My Mantons?" His jaw dropped. "But they are far too dangerous for a lady. They have hair triggers and are deadly accurate—"

"Which is precisely why I need them," interrupted Arianna. She smiled sweetly. "*Now*, if you please."

The curt command rendered him momentarily speechless. The weapons were not only frightfully lethal, but frightfully expensive.

"*Why?*" he finally sputtered.

"I haven't time to explain, but a cadre of conspirators is seeking to throw Europe back into chaos. Saybrook and I intend to stop them."

As Alexander shifted, she began gauging the distance between her fist and his chin. On second thought, a knee to the crotch might be a more effective way of rendering him immobile—

"Wait here." He was lighter on his feet than she expected. Stepping over the still-smoking candle, he disappeared into his bedchamber. Arianna heard a drawer bang, and then he was back, brandishing two perfectly matched pistols. "I wouldn't lend these to just anyone, but you strike me as someone who knows how to handle them." The burnished walnut butts were smooth as satin against her hands as the Tsar passed them over. "However, be forewarned that if you lose them, you will have to pay a forfeit. A rather large one."

"Agreed, sir." Arianna slid them into her pockets. "But I don't intend to lose either your weapons or my virtue—or the battle against a traitorous bastard."

"Ye are sure ye don't need my help, laddie?"

"We've been over this, Baz. It's best that you stay here." After a quick look at the time, Saybrook handed the surgeon his pocket watch. "The pageant is scheduled to last just over an hour. If I am not back by a quarter to nine, force your way to Talleyrand's box. Wellington will recognize your ugly phiz, and as we agreed, I sent him a note this afternoon informing him that if you appear, he is to follow your instructions without question."

"Aye, I know the plan." Henning listened to the music drifting out from the palace. "But I still hate playing second fiddle. You are the one waltzing into danger."

The earl ignored his friend's grousing. "If things go badly awry, I am counting on you to get Arianna safely out of the city," he went on in a low voice.

"That goes without saying," answered Henning.

"Not that I expect any trouble." *Click, click.* Saybrook checked the priming of his pistol. "With the metal strip in place, there is little danger that the bomb will go off. In any case, I'll be hiding behind the cabinet and will apprehend Rochemont before he puts the acid in place."

"What if he has an accomplice?" demanded Henning.

"You think I've gone soft from all my wife's sweetened chocolate and can't handle two adversaries?" countered the earl.

"I'm simply warning you to stay on guard for the unexpected. We both know that when on a clandestine mission, it's always a good idea to have someone watching your arse."

The earl's chuckle formed a pale puff of vapor in the night air. "Seeing as I have no intention of allowing either you or Arianna to ogle my bum tonight, I'll have to trust that I have eyes in the back of my head."

The surgeon didn't smile. "I'm serious, Sandro. Be careful. Renard and his pack of varlets are utterly ruthless."

"As am I, when I have to be." *Click, click.* The hammer slid to half cock. "Save me a swallow of your Highland whisky."

Thick as saddle leather, the earthy smells of horse and sweat filled Arianna's nostrils as she crept along the row of empty stalls. The Hungarian stallions had been led to another part of the stables to await the final preparations for the Joust, leaving the area near the storage rooms dark and deserted. The only sounds were the creak of a loose gate and the faint scrabbling of cat hunting through the straw. Looped reins and silver-studded bridles hung from the dark beams, forcing her to keep her head down to avoid tangling in their web.

Saybrook had been adamant about keeping her away from danger, but what if he needed help? Her plan was simply to watch his arse. If all went well, he would never know . . .

Bent low, she suddenly saw a twitch of lamplight dart through a small gap between the planking and the floor. Edging into one of the storage alcoves, she held herself very still and cocked an ear to listen. Someone was moving slowly and stealthily along the row of stalls on the other side of the wall.

"You are late," came a curt whisper.

Arianna inched closer to the rough wood.

"Be grateful I'm giving you a moment of my time." It was Rochemont speaking, and he sounded angry. "I'm the one who has done all the planning, and taken all the risks. Why should I suddenly take orders from you?"

"Because I carry this." A crackle of paper, followed by the clink of metal.

"Then I suppose I have no choice but to accept your authority, seeing as you bear his badge." Rochemont's tone had turned petulant. "Does that mean Renard is here in Vienna?"

The other man gave a humorless laugh. "If he wished for you to know that, he would tell you."

"So, that means you aren't him," said Rochemont quickly.

"Jumping to conclusions is dangerous, *mon comte*."

*So, the man was the comte's superior*. Arianna tried to catch a glimpse of his face through the crack, but the angle afforded naught but a view of highly polished Hessian boots and a hint of biscuit-colored breeches.

"Renard has survived by being clever and cautious as a fox," the other man went on.

"I'm tired of toiling in the dark," protested Rochemont. "From now on, I want to know who I'm dealing with."

*So do I.* Biting back an oath, Arianna balled her fists in frustration and looked around.

"Is that a threat, comte?"

A hesitation. "*Non.* Call it a request. If I succeed, I think I will have earned enough respect to merit it."

"Succeed, and then we shall discuss further reward. As I recall, you've been paid quite handsomely for your efforts."

Spotting a prick of light in a knothole, she reached up and hoisted herself onto one of the iron saddle racks, taking care not to make any noise.

"What is it you want to say?" demanded Rochemont sullenly. "I'm in a hurry."

"Yes, well, that is what I wish to discuss. Renard wishes for me to deliver a few words of caution. He is concerned that you are becoming a bit reckless. First the *Grognard* marksman with his throat cut, and then Mr. Kydd with his head blown to flinders. Both deaths were a touch too dramatic for his taste."

*Damnation—too late.* The man had turned, and all Arianna could spy through the small hole in the wood was a dark head, half hidden by the upturned collar of a caped coat.

"I can't be held accountable for what happened to the *Grognard*," retorted Rochemont. "It was agreed that Davilenko was too untrustworthy to know of my role in Renard's organization. Apparently the Russian worked through his local contact to arrange a diversion involving the wounding of Saybrook—why, I am still not sure. The poxy bastard nearly killed me instead." The comte ran a hand over his smoothly shaven cheeks. "Davilenko told my local contact that the *Grognard* threatened to implicate him in the shooting if he didn't pay more money, so he slit the fellow's throat instead." Again, a fraction of a pause. "I warned you that Davilenko was a loose cannon, but his accident has solved the problem. Any secrets he had are now buried with him in a watery grave."

"And Kydd?"

"That was my initiative, and nobody questioned whether it was anything other than an unfortunate accident," protested the comte. "Indeed, you and Renard ought to be glad that I can improvise so cleverly. Kydd was experiencing a belated attack of conscience and was on the verge of confessing his betrayal to Lady Saybrook."

"Ah, yes. The countess and her husband." The other man was silent for a moment. "Another concern."

Rochemont let out a nasty laugh. "She is naught but a slut, who likes to play games with men. Oh, she may put on airs now that she is married, but I happen to know that before she coaxed an offer out of the earl, she was involved with a rakehell crowd of reprobates." He paused. "The earl, I agree, is another matter."

"A former military intelligence officer is not someone to take lightly," agreed his superior.

"I'm aware of that," snapped the comte. "From the start, I've pursued his wife in order to keep abreast of the earl's activities."

"A-breast," repeated the other man coldly, adding his own inflection to the word. "Renard fears that perhaps you have allowed yourself to become distracted from your primary duties. Your predilection for whoring is becoming, shall we say, excessive."

"Is it?" jeered Rochemont. "You will soon see that I'm thinking with more than my pego. I suspected that the earl was using his wife to sniff around me, so in another hour, she will be joining Talleyrand and Wellington in a rather untidy grave."

His companion was silent for a long moment before replying, "Don't make a mess of this, Rochemont. Or Renard will be most unhappy."

The lamp flickered as a shutter slid shut, narrowing the

beam to a thin blade of light. "Enough talk, then. Let me get on with my preparations," muttered the comte.

"We shall meet later, at the appointed rendezvous." A boot scraped over stone. "Assuming that you don't fail."

Through her spy hole, Arianna watched Rochemont and his superior move off into the gloom and split up.

Dropping down lightly into the straw, she made up her mind without hesitation about who to follow, and cut through a connecting passageway to pick up the stranger's trail. Saybrook had been adamant in his demand to deal with the comte alone—and so she would take him at his word. In a *mano a mano* match between the two men, she had every confidence that her husband would prevail.

As for the comte's superior, it was imperative she learn his identity.

Weaving her way through the gloom, Arianna darted past the granary and paused for an instant to listen. *Chuff, chuff*—was that the soft crunch of straw underfoot up ahead?

As she slipped out from behind the wooden post, her hand brushed against a groom's smock hanging from a peg. On impulse, she tugged it on over her coat, and then added a battered leather hat beneath it. The fit was a trifle odd—it must have been some sort of practice headgear for the knightly games, for the top half of the crown was filled with a thick feather padding. But the brim shadowed her face, and the loose canvas overshirt helped further disguise her figure.

Given her quarry's aristocratic London accent, he was likely part of the English delegation.

*But who?*

Shadows wavered and rippled in the dim dribble of moonlight coming in through the corner windows. Arianna slowed, straining to make out any shapes in the darkness up ahead. The ambient sounds of the stable made it hard to distinguish footsteps . . .

The strike came from behind, quick as a snake. A shovel

smashed down on her head, sending her sprawling to the ground. Half stunned, she caught the glint of metal cutting through the air and managed to roll away from a second blow aimed at her spine.

Pain shot through her skull, but thanks to the padded hat, it was still in one piece.

*But that will end quickly if I don't gather my wits.*

Moving with a cold, calculating precision, her assailant slid a step sideways to gain a better angle and came at her again. No words, no hesitation, just a ruthless determination to land a lethal hit.

She coiled like a hedgehog, waiting until the very last instant to kick out. Her boot heel buckled his leg, and he dropped to one knee with a grunt, the shovel slipping from his grip.

Twisting out of reach, Arianna scrambled to her feet and kicked it away. Her assailant was back on his feet as well, and circling slowly to force her deeper into the storage alcove under the hayloft. Clearly he was no stranger to back-alley fights—his movements were calm and deliberate. Indeed, a fleeting flicker of moonlight showed that he was smiling.

*A formidable opponent.* But then, she had faced other hardened, hell-bent rogues before and survived. Brains over brawn, she reminded herself. Saybrook would never forgive her if she were to stick her spoon in the wall after disobeying his command.

He turned slightly, giving her a quick view of his face. *Good God—so there was rot at the very heart of England's aristocracy.* Lord Reginald Sommers, senior aide to Lord Castlereagh, was the younger son of a prominent duke.

Beneath Arianna's smock, the pistols bumped against her hips. *Tempting.* However, forcing his surrender would be all for naught. Without proof of his perfidy, her accusation would likely fall on deaf ears. As for a shot, that might ruin Saybrook's chances of catching Rochemont in the act.

*Think, think.* Instead she drew her blade from her boot and made a quick feint.

Lord Reginald drew back a step. He was no longer smiling. "Why were you following me?" he demanded, then repeated the question in halting German.

"*Geld,*" replied Arianna. *Money*. With luck, he would believe this was robbery gone awry.

His shoulders relaxed slightly. "*Geld,*" he repeated. "Unfortunately, you've just purchased your own demise. I can't afford to let you live." He too had a hidden sheath, and out slipped a knife twice as big as hers. "Boys shouldn't go up against men."

*And men shouldn't underestimate women.* Arianna had no intention of crossing steel with him. As long as Lord Reginald remained ignorant of her real identity, she held the upper hand. A trap could be set to catch him at treason.

But first she had to escape.

He made several quick probing jabs.

Arianna retreated, drawing him along with her. The wall was at her back. But so was a small ladder leading up through an opening to the loft. She had also spotted a bench with an open bottle of liniment perched on its edge.

"Tsk, tsk. A wrong move, boy," drawled Lord Reginald. "You're now right where I want you."

Grabbing the bottle, she flung the stinging liquid at his face, then bolted up the ladder rungs as fast as she could. A quick jerk, a hard heave and the ladder landed alongside her.

Lord Reginald's vicious oath reverberated in the darkness below. "Bloody imp of Satan, I'll cut your guts into garters." His fingers grasped the edge of the opening. A big, muscled man, he apparently meant to hoist himself up and finish the job.

*A wrong move, Lord Reginald,* thought Arianna, slamming her boot down and feeling bones crack under her heel.

Still he came on.

As his snarling face appeared in the opening, she spun around and sprinted to the open end of the loft, where a thick rope for hauling the bales of hay was looped through a pulley attached to the ceiling beam. Catching hold of the iron hook in midstride, she jumped, giving silent thanks for the vagabond years spent sailing around the Caribbean. Her momentum swung her in a wide arc, the rope held taut by a bracket anchored to the wall.

Arianna landed hard on the stone floor, the impact knocking the wind from her lungs. Breathless, she took a moment to recover. Ahead of her, the corridor was only a few steps away . . .

With a muffled roar of rage, Lord Reginald snagged the rope with one hand on its swing back and launched himself into the air.

*Oh, bloody hell.* Staggering to her feet, Arianna whipped out her knife and slashed the rope just above its knot.

A low whistle of wind was followed by the fleshy thud.

She turned to see his body lying crumpled in a heap behind an iron anvil. Creeping close, she gingerly nudged him face up.

*If you live by the sword, you must be prepared to die by the sword.*

Swallowing hard, Arianna couldn't help but recall one of Henning's favorite aphorisms as she stared at Lord Reginald's own knife protruding from his chest. Strange, but she felt no real remorse. The man was a cold-blooded murderer who had planned to plunge Europe into chaos. Be damned with pity—he was no longer a threat to peace.

But was Rochemont still a force to be reckoned with? She stripped off her smock and checked the priming on the Tsar's magnificent pistols. It was high time to locate Saybrook and find out.

# 24

## From Lady Arianna's Chocolate Notebooks

### Austrian Marbled Coffee Cake

*17 tablespoons unsalted butter, softened*
*1¾ cups flour*
*2 oz. semisweet chocolate, preferably 54%, roughly*
*chopped*
*2 tablespoons dark rum*
*3 tablespoons cornstarch*
*½ teaspoon salt*
*½ cup confectioners' sugar, plus more for dusting*
*2 tablespoons lemon zest*
*1 tablespoon vanilla extract*
*5 eggs, separated*
*1 cup sugar*

1. Heat oven to 325°. Grease a dark metal 1½-qt.
   *gugelhupf* mold or bundt pan with 1 tbsp. butter.
   Add ¼ cup flour and shake to evenly coat the inside of mold. Invert and tap out excess flour; set
   mold aside. Set a medium bowl over a 1-qt. saucepan of simmering water. Add chocolate; melt. Stir
   in rum and set aside to let cool slightly.

2. Sift together remaining flour, cornstarch and salt; set aside. In a bowl, beat remaining butter, confectioners' sugar, lemon zest and vanilla using a hand-held mixer on medium speed until mixture is pale and fluffy, about 2 minutes. Add egg yolks one at a time, beating after each addition. Add reserved flour mixture to butter mixture in 3 additions, beating to combine after each addition. Set batter aside.

3. In a large nonreactive bowl, beat egg whites with handheld mixer on high speed until frothy. Sprinkle in sugar and beat to form stiff, glossy peaks. Whisk ⅓ of egg whites into reserved cake batter to lighten it. Using a rubber spatula, fold in remaining egg whites to make an airy cake batter.

4. Fold ⅓ of the cake batter into the reserved chocolate mixture to make a chocolate-flavored batter. Spoon half of the remaining cake batter into the buttered mold. Spoon all the chocolate batter into mold and top with remaining cake batter. Using a butter knife, swirl the chocolate batter into the cake batter to create a marbled effect. Smooth the top. Bake until a toothpick inserted in the cake comes out clean, about 55 minutes. Transfer cake to a rack; let cool. Unmold cake and dust with confectioners' sugar.

❧

It was quiet, the shadows still and solemn, like sentinels standing silent guard on the storage room.

"Perhaps a little *too* quiet," said Saybrook under his breath. He flattened himself against the cabinet and ventured a look at the doorway. The latch was reset, the cases untouched, the Champion's Prize aligned exactly as he and Henning had left it the previous night.

"So why do I have an odd feeling that something is not right?" The earl frowned, the lines of anxiety deepening around his eyes as he looked around the room. But before he could answer his own whispered question, a key turned in the lock, the metallic click echoing like cannon fire off the suit of parade armor propped in the corner.

Rochemont entered. He appeared agitated, and after fumbling with the bolts, he merely shouldered the door shut and hurried to the center of the room. Swearing, he put down his lantern, peeled off his crimson gauntlets, and carefully pulled a small silver case from inside his ceremonial surcoat. The bandages were gone, but the comte's elegant hands were still swollen and scabbed. Another oath rasped from his lips as he worked the lid open.

Saybrook could just make out the contours of a slim glass vial nestled on a bed of red velvet.

Setting the box aside, Rochemont dragged the metal case containing the Champion's Prize out from its spot by the cabinet. Another key, another procession of clicking noises, and the top lifted. The comte sat back on his haunches and muttered something in French. Rather than remove the ornate eagle from its nest, he rose abruptly and approached the cabinet.

The earl held himself motionless.

Rochemont rummaged around inside for a bit, then returned to his work spot and propped a trio of medieval broadswords against a stack of wooden boxes. Each of the three hilts was festooned with a different color of semiprecious stones—reds, greens, blues—and he spent several moments contemplating how they looked next to the gold-threaded splendor of his embroidered doublet. The blue seemed to win the duel, for he edged it a bit apart from the others.

Exhaling softly, Saybrook watched as the comte shifted his body into the ring of lamplight and set to work.

*One step, two steps*. The earl's soft-soled shoes moved noiselessly over the smooth stone. The eagle was now perched on one of the wooden boxes, its burnished gold wings mirroring—

In a blur of motion, Rochemont snatched up his sword and flew around. Steel clashed against steel, the force of the blow sending Saybrook's pistol arcing into the gloom.

"Poxy half-breed," snarled the comte. He lunged again.

Hemmed in by the crates, Saybrook had little room to maneuver. Throwing up an arm to deflect the blade, he spun away and leaped over a low bench.

"I was warned to be wary of your military skills, yet it seems you are naught but a bumbling fool," taunted Rochemont, brandishing the point of his weapon at the gash on the earl's wrist.

"I'm a bloody fool," agreed Saybrook, ignoring his wound. "I should have put a bullet in your verminous brain. But unlike you, I am not a cold-blooded murderer. I'll allow justice to take its proper course."

"Justice? Good God, what a quaint notion!" The blade slashed, but cut only air.

"You'll have to be quicker than that," said the earl.

"Oh, never fear. I'll gut you like a pig, and though I would like to prolong the pleasure, I *will* have to make it fast."

"So you can murder Talleyrand and Wellington?"

Surprise spasmed across Rochemont's face. "How did you—"

The distraction was just for an instant, but Saybrook seized his chance and ducked under the broadsword and dove for a gap in the crates. A twist and a roll brought him within arm's reach of the other swords. Bouncing to his feet, he hefted the ruby-colored weapon. "Ah, red. How apt, don't you think? Seeing as your blood will soon be spilled unless you surrender now."

"Never!" said Rochemont. "I've trained for years with Lavalle, the best fencing master in England! I'll slice you into mincemeat." Despite the show of bravado, he looked a little shaky as he slid into a sidestep. Sweat began to bead on his brow.

"Trust me, a fencing parlor is not the same as a field of battle," said Saybrook. "And a broadsword is far heavier than a foil." He cut a few practice swipes with the long blade and flashed a small smile. "Indeed, it's much closer in weight to a cavalry saber."

Flickering patterns of light and dark danced across the comte's face.

Saybrook edged forward, a quick flick slicing off a section of Rochemont's fancy sleeve. "Come, shall we test our skills?"

The sweat had turned from beads to rivulets—tiny snakes of moisture glistening against the comte's pale skin. He reversed his lead foot and with a quick feint tried to slide his blade up under Saybrook's guard.

A flick of steel parried the thrust. "Not bad," murmured the earl. "But you will have to do far better."

The next lunge was just as easily deflected. As was the following flurry of slashes.

"I never did like the combinations that Lavalle teaches to his students. Unless one executes them perfectly, they leave one vulnerable to a *croisé*," said Saybrook calmly, his blade forcing Rochemont's sword high before darting a quick jab that drew blood on the comte's shoulder.

Rochemont staggered back, his breath now coming in ragged rasps. He tried a *passata-sotto*, an evasive move designed to duck under an opponent's blade, but the earl saw it coming and countered with another thrust, this one scoring a gash along the comte's cheek.

His bravado suddenly crumpling, like a Montgolfier balloon whose silk had suffered a lethal puncture, Rochemont let out a shriek and scrabbled sideways, swinging his sword in a flailing arc. He cast a wild look at the glass vial, which was standing serenely on its box, untouched by the violence.

"Oh, you may forget about the acid," said Saybrook pleasantly. "I'm not going to let you near it. And even if I did, your clever little bomb has been disarmed."

Panic turned Rochemont's face a ghastly shade of pale green. "It—it wasn't my idea." He swallowed hard, his arrogance dissolving into a sputtering of fear. "I . . . was forced against my will to cooperate. They have one of my family held hostage in France."

"Who is 'they'?" asked Saybrook, drawing a touch closer.

"Lord R-Reginald Sommers is my superior," replied the comte.

"Is he Renard?"

"I—don't know," said Rochemont. "Truly!" he added, seeing the earl's brows wing up in skepticism. "Renard has never revealed his identity."

"Then tell me what things you do know," demanded Saybrook. "This assassination is meant to make it easier for Napoleon to return to France?"

Rochemont wet his lips. "Yes."

"Who else is working with you here?"

The comte rattled off the names of a Saxon margrave and a Russian officer on Tsar Alexander's staff.

Saybrook pressed on. "How do you contact Renard in London?"

Rochemont stumbled against a stack of supplies as he retreated, knocking a box to the floor. "I—"

"Monsieur le Comte?" Yielding to a fisted rap, the door sprung open. "Is anything amiss? We heard strange noises—"

"Seize this madman!" screamed Rochemont, pointing at the earl. "He's trying to murder the guests of honor!"

The two Imperial Guards recoiled in confusion as the comte shoved past them and took off down the corridor at a dead run.

Saybrook vaulted a stack of crates.

"Halt!" Recovering their composure, the burly guards moved to block his path.

"Out of my way." The martial note of command was unmistakable.

One of the guards drew his rapier. "Sir, I must ask you to—"

The earl's blade slapped aside the sword point. "Fetch reinforcements," he shouted. "Then follow me in pursuit of the real villain."

Somewhere off to her right, Arianna heard a clatter of commotion. The pelter of running steps, a rumbled shout.

*Sandro.*

She plunged into a narrow passageway, the darkness forcing her to go slowly. Slowly, damnably slowly. In contrast to the soaring, stately spaces for the equestrian performances, this part of the stables was a maddening maze of stalls and cluttered storage areas.

Holding her frustration in check, Arianna paused to peer around the next turn. An archway loomed up ahead, its opening framing a set of iron-banded double doors, large enough for a horse and rider to pass through. Creeping closer, she saw that they led out to the side courtyard of the Riding School. And from there to the city park beyond its gates, she thought, recalling Saybrook's map of the area.

Sheltered by the shadows of the arched stone, Arianna halted again to get her bearings. Which way to turn? The shouts had died away, leaving her uncertain of what to do next. Retreat and return home?

But before she could make up her mind, Rochemont came racing into view, legs churning as if the Hounds of Hell were in hot pursuit.

*Bang. Bang.* Slamming his shoulder into the paneled doors, the comte yanked at the latch, but the bolt wouldn't budge. Spotting a large wrought iron key hanging from the decorative molding, he reached up to snatch it down from the bracket. Escape—escape was at his fingertips.

*I hope that Alexander was not exaggerating about the deadly accuracy of his prized pistols.* Drawing a steadying breath, Arianna took deliberate aim and squeezed off a shot.

*Bang.*

He wasn't. Through the skirl of blue-gray smoke, Arianna saw the key explode in a whirl of spinning shards.

Rochemont recoiled with a scream as a sliver of metal gashed his cheek. Blood spattered over his fancy doublet, and with his face contorting in fear, he looked like a demented demon. A veritable spawn of Satan.

Kicking, swearing, he threw himself once more at the unyielding oak. But on hearing Saybrook's stentorian shouts coming closer, the comte left off his efforts and fled.

"That way!" she yelled to her husband, pointing to the passageway Rochemont had chosen.

The earl shot her a surprised look, but didn't slow his

loping stride. "I'll deal with you later," he called. "Go find Henning."

Arianna pocketed the spent pistol and pulled out its loaded mate.

"Ah, well. In for a penny, in for a pound," she muttered, then set off after her husband.

The six Hungarian chargers snorted and stomped their massive hooves at the sand-covered stone, the vaporous puffs of breath silvery against the burnished black coats. The soft swoosh of the silk trappings was punctuated by the jangling bits of gilded brass and polished crystal adorning the bridles as the grooms struggled to keep them grouped in a tight line, allowing the other horses for the pageant to be led into the staging area from the outdoor bridle path.

A squire patted the plumes of his velvet hat into place while another adjusted the girth of his knight's mount. One of the heralds blew a low practice note on his trumpet, setting off another rustling of restless energy.

"A quarter hour," intoned the master of ceremonies after consulting his jeweled pocket watch. "Our noble cavaliers will be arriving in a quarter hour."

Banners fluttered in the breeze blowing in through the open gates. An air of expectancy swirled around the saddling arena as the participants jostled to take up their assigned positions.

A figure burst out of the main walkway, the crimson satin tails of his surcoat trailing behind him like tongues of fire.

"What the devil . . ." The master of ceremonies stared in slack-jawed shock as the flash of red streaked past him. "I've not been informed of any change in plan."

"Out of my way!" The shrill shout rose above the confusion. Swinging the flat of his sword, Rochemont knocked down a groom and scrabbled into the saddle of the horse nearest the gate. The big animal whinnied and reared as the comte slammed his ceremonial spurs into its flanks, then shot off in a blur of flame-tinged charcoal and disappeared into the night.

"Stop! Stop!" wailed the master, waving a helpless hand as Saybrook sprinted toward the gate.

The earl veered around one of the startled grooms, and with a lithe grace grabbed the saddle pommel, speared the stirrup with his boot and vaulted lightly onto the back of the biggest charger. "Move aside, lad," he ordered, fisting the reins in one hand and quickly bringing the powerful stallion under control.

The horse danced through the gates and then surged forward, muscles rippling, nostrils flaring, hooves kicking up clods of damp earth as it shot down the bridle path.

Ornate copper torches lit the way, blazes of bright gold against the darkness. Up ahead, the pale stone of the palace rose like a ghostly specter out of the evening mist.

"Damnation," muttered Saybrook, urging his mount into a gallop. "If the dastard cuts through the side courtyard and reaches the main gates, he'll have a good chance of escaping."

In answer to the flick of leather, the stallion thundered through a tight turn and began to gain ground on the comte.

Rochemont was sliding from side to side, his big sword flailing as he fought to keep his seat in the saddle. Hearing the drumming of pursuit, he cast a desperate glance over his shoulder. His jaw fell open. His mouth moved, but any sound was swallowed in the wind.

Spotting an opening in the wrought iron fence, Saybrook guided his horse through the gap and cut through a series of zigzag turns. A low wall loomed up ahead, its frieze of gilded spikes a daunting hurdle for the big-boned charger.

"Up, up, on my signal," murmured the earl as he squared his horse's head and gave a light tap to its lathered flanks.

The stallion gathered its powerful legs and soared high. Horse and rider hovered for an instant in the air, a dark avenging angel silhouetted against the night, before thundering back to earth.

Saybrook was now neck and neck with his quarry. Ignoring the panicked kicks from the comte, he edged his horse sideways and forced Rochemont's mount off the path to the Imperial gates up ahead. Hooves skidding and sliding over the smooth cobbles, both chargers rumbled through a narrow archway and into a side courtyard.

"You might as well surrender now," called Saybrook, calmly reining his sweat-flecked mount into position to block the only avenue of escape.

Rochemont darted a desperate look around at the regal stone façade rising up on all sides. "Out of my way," he screamed, brandishing his weapon high overhead.

Steel flashed in the moonlight as Saybrook gave a mock salute. "Alas, your skills with a sword don't have me quaking in my boots. But if you wish for another clash, by all means come at me. I shall be happy to slice open your traitorous throat."

The comte's horse pranced nervously over the stones.

"If you promise to let me go, I'll tell you all I know." Rochemont's bluster gave way to a wheedling tone as he circled into the shadows of the courtyard's center fountain.

"You're in no position to bargain," countered Saybrook. "I want Renard's name, and you don't have it."

"I lied," cried the comte. "In fact, I have proof of his identity."

"Proof?" repeated the earl.

"Come here and I shall hand it over."

Saybrook's low laugh was nearly lost in the splashing of water. "Do you think me a gudgeon? Throw down your sword and come out. If what you say is true and you help us apprehend Renard, the government may agree to spare your life."

"W-will you drop your weapon as well?"

"That's a fair request."

A moment later came the ring of Rochemont's steel falling to the cobbles. "Now it's your turn, Lord Saybrook."

"I'm a man of my word," he called, letting his sword clatter to the ground.

*Clack, clack.* Iron-shod hooves echoed the metallic sound.

Saybrook placed a hand on his pommel.

*Clack, clack*—the equine steps quickened to a hard trot as Rochemont rode out from the gloom. A long pitchfork protruded from under his arm, the stout length of oak topped by a menacing crown of prongs.

"You *are* a gudgeon," cried the comte, spurring his horse forward. "Let the joust begin!"

Saybrook reacted with martial quickness. Kicking free of the stirrups, he hurled himself to the cobbles and spun into a tight, twisting roll, causing Rochemont's desperate lunge to miss by a hair. His hand shot out to seize his fallen sword, and in the same smooth motion he sprung to his feet and ran to block the archway. "Don't be a fool, Rochemont. In a fight to the death, you won't come away the victor."

Swearing a savage oath, the comte yanked his mount around as he sought to regrip his weapon and charge again. Hands tangling in the reins, he lost momentary control of the pitchfork and the points raked across the other charger's flanks. With a foam-flecked snort, the animal reared, lashing out wildly with his forelegs.

Spooked by the sudden melee, Rochemont's mount shied sharply, throwing the comte off balance. He swayed and then tumbled from the saddle, pitching headfirst in between the panicked horses.

"Damnation." Ducking under a flying hoof, Saybrook grabbed hold of Rochemont's surcoat. A bruising blow caught him hard on the ribs, but he held on, even as he fell to his knees. "Keep your head *down*," he warned, trying to haul the other man to safety.

But Rochemont lifted the pitchfork, intent on launching one last spearing attack. An evil grin split the comte's face ... an instant before a thrashing kick crushed his skull.

Saybrook slowly levered to his feet.

"If you live by the sword ..." An out-of-breath Henning skittered to a stop beside him and eyed the dark pool of blood welling over the stones. "You must be prepared to die by the sword."

"I'm afraid your favorite aphorism is falling on deaf ears," said the earl drily.

"Sandro!" Lowering her pistol, Arianna edged around the surgeon and touched a hand to her husband's dirt-streaked cheek.

"I suggest we all save the soulful sighs until later," counseled Henning before she could say anything further. "In this case, discretion may be the better part of valor. The threat is over. If we leave now, the authorities will have a devil of a time ever piecing together what happened here tonight." He shuffled his boot back from a trickle of viscous black. "Which I daresay is what our government would prefer."

Saybrook nodded grimly. "I agree. However, there is the matter of the Champion's Prize. Much as I respect your scientific skills, Baz, I would rather not have that infernal bomb brought anywhere near Talleyrand and Wellington. God knows, we've worked hard enough to keep them safe—I would hate to see all our efforts go up in a cloud of smoke."

"Don't worry, laddie. The eagle has had its talons removed."

"How?" demanded the earl.

Henning took his arm. "Lady S, kindly grab yer husband's other wing and help him fly."

Saybrook scowled but allowed himself to be hustled through the archway.

"In answer to yer question, I heard the commotion and crept into the storeroom after you gave chase to the comte," said the surgeon. "I removed the guts of the bomb and dumped the gunpowder in one of the fountains. The brass gears and bearings have been smashed with a farrier's hammer. As for the acid . . ." Henning removed a vial from inside his coat. "If you don't mind, I kept it. I'm curious to analyze the exact composition of chemicals."

"You were told to wait out in the main courtyard, away from trouble," muttered the earl.

Henning shot a sidelong glance at Arianna. "Yes, well, as you see, I'm not very good at obeying orders."

A glint of starlight flashed off the fancy pistol as she waggled a return salute. "Neither am I."

*"You,"* growled Saybrook. "You, too, have a good deal of explaining to do." His eyes narrowed. "Beginning with where in the name of Hades you got that weapon. It's one of Manton's special models, if I'm not mistaken, and worth a bloody fortune."

"It's a long story . . ."

Arianna carried a glass of brandy over to where Saybrook lay stretched out on the sofa. He had listened to her account of the evening with surprisingly few interruptions. But on seeing his expression, she guessed that the silence was about to end.

"I expect that it's time for one of our jolly little councils of war, eh?" Henning clapped his hands together in anticipation. "But we had better make it quick, before I tend to my patient's injuries and dose him with laudanum."

The earl made a sour face. "It's naught but a few bruises." He was, however, looking a little pale as he quaffed a swallow of the brandy. "So, Rochemont's superior here was Lord Reginald Sommers?"

"You were acquainted with him?" asked Henning.

The earl pursed his lips. "Only in passing. His father is, of course, a prominent peer—and well liked, I might add—which helps explain Lord Reginald's position on Castlereagh's staff. But he had done nothing to distinguish himself from the crowd of other gentlemen who frequent the gaming hells and brothels."

"You think he was Renard?"

The earl mulled over the question for a moment. "No. Something in my gut tells me that the cunning fox is still running free."

"Call it an instinct for survival," said the surgeon. "So, we may have guarded the henhouse on this night—"

"But a dangerous predator is still on the loose," finished Saybrook. "However, we are beginning to pick up a scent. The government should start sniffing out the details of Lord Reginald's life and acquaintances. Combined with the information you acquired on Rochemont's activities in

Scotland, Baz, they should be able to narrow the field of suspects."

"Especially as we now know for sure where his loyalty lies," said Arianna.

"Napoleon," said Saybrook. And yet he didn't sound entirely convinced.

"You don't agree?" she asked.

"We can't dismiss the possibility that his—or her—only Master is money."

*The glitter of gold versus the fire of abstract ideals.* It was, she mused, an age-old conflict. One that had consumed countless lives.

Arianna fetched herself a glass of port, and settled into a cross-legged seat on the carpet, close to her husband's head. "A mercenary rather than an idealist?" She thought for a moment about David Kydd and felt a slight pang of regret at the terrible waste of passions and intelligence. "You're right of course."

"That's a conundrum for the coming days," remarked Henning. "I have a more mundane question about the present. We now have three deaths to explain. And while I don't give a fig about leaving the Austrian authorities to chase their own tails, our government is going to have to offer some sort of explanation." He rubbed at his jaw. "To wit, what do you propose to tell your uncle about Kydd? And what should the duke know of his son's treason? Or Talleyrand and the émigré community in London about Rochemont's perfidy?"

Saybrook shifted his shoulders in a cynical shrug. "Remember, I am not in a position to make the final decision. But I would advise the Powers That Be to say nothing about the conspiracy. It serves no purpose. The parties involved are dead—there is no need for anyone to know of their betrayals."

As he lifted his wineglass, Arianna watched the candle flame refract off the cut crystal, sending shards of light winking in all directions.

"The fewer people who know the truth, the better,"

went on her husband. "Let Renard wonder just how his well-laid plans went so awry."

"Cat and mouse," quipped Henning.

"Yes. A game that is growing far too familiar." The earl's gaze found hers. "As is the one of masquerades."

Her chin rose a fraction. "I play it rather well, don't you think?"

Saybrook met the challenge with an unblinking stare. "It's not your skills that I'm questioning. It's the fact that I asked you to stay out of harm's way and you didn't."

"Seeing as I was dressed as a male, it could be argued that I didn't actually ignore your request," she murmured. "You made no mention that a London street urchin was to stay away from the action."

He tried to look angry but a telltale twitch crept to the corners of his mouth. "For someone who claims to have little regard for formal academic training, you parse philosophical points with the skill of an Oxford don." He eyed her snug black breeches and lifted a brow. "And by the by, those look far fancier than your original urchin rags from Petticoat Lane."

"Yes, and they are far more comfortable," she said. "No wonder you gentlemen are willing to pay Weston an arm and a leg for his services as a tailor."

Saybrook's chuckle dissolved into a cough. Grimacing, he raised himself on his elbows. "I—"

Henning quickly rose from his chair and placed a hand on the earl's chest. "Don't move until I get a few bandages wrapped around you, laddie. I think you have a few cracked ribs."

"Speaking of bones, I'm going to break every last one in Grentham's body when we get back to London," growled the earl. "I swear that this is the last time that any of us risk life and limb to do his dirty work."

# 25

## From Lady Arianna's Chocolate Notebooks

### Devil's Food Cake

15 tablespoons butter, softened
1½ teaspoons baking soda
¼ cup boiling water
2½ cups flour, sifted
½ teaspoon salt
2 cups light brown sugar
2 eggs
1 cup buttermilk
6 oz. unsweetened chocolate, melted and cooled slightly
6 cups confectioners' sugar
½ cup heavy cream
¼ cup unsweetened cocoa
2 teaspoons vanilla extract

1. Preheat oven to 325°. Grease two 8-inch round cake pans with 1 tbsp. of the butter and set aside. Stir together the baking soda and ¼ cup boiling water in a small bowl and set aside.
2. Whisk together flour and salt in a medium bowl and set aside. Combine 8 tbsp. of the butter and

the brown sugar in a large bowl and beat with an electric mixer until fluffy. Add the eggs one at a time, beating briefly after each addition. Working in 3 batches, alternately add the flour mixture and buttermilk, beating briefly after each addition. Add the baking soda mixture (stir before adding) and chocolate and stir to make a smooth batter.

3. Divide the batter between prepared pans and bake until a toothpick inserted in the middle comes out clean, 35–40 minutes. Set the cake pans on a rack to let cool.

4. While the cakes are cooling, make the icing. Melt the remaining 6 tbsp. butter and transfer it to a large bowl. Add the confectioners' sugar, heavy cream, cocoa and vanilla and beat until well combined and fluffy, about 2 minutes. Set aside.

5. Loosen the cakes from their pans. Place 1 cake on a large plate and spread top evenly with about 1 cup of the icing. Top with the second cake and use the remaining icing to spread over the top and sides. Serve immediately or refrigerate until ready to eat.

Grentham leaned back in his chair, his gunmetal gray eyes focusing on the far wall of his office rather than meeting Saybrook's gaze.

Arianna waited for a moment and then, matching his deliberate rudeness, twisted around in her chair. Rain pattered against the mullioned windows, the watery light blurring the details of the gilt-framed painting that the minister appeared to be studying.

"Turner's seascapes are far more interesting," she commented. "But then, I suppose that one must have some artistic imagination to appreciate them."

*Tap, tap, tap.* Ignoring her barb, the minister continued to drum his fingertips together in echo of the passing shower. After allowing the silence to stretch a little longer, he finally spoke. "You mean to tell me that Talleyrand and Wellington were the intended targets?"

"Yes," replied Saybrook.

"And you think the assassination attempt was all part of a plot that indicates Napoleon is planning to break out of Elba and retake his throne?" Grentham's inflection on the former Emperor's name added an extra measure of sarcasm to his tone.

"Yes," said the earl.

"I've heard no such whispers from my sources in Europe," sneered the minister.

"It is not my problem that your sources have their heads wedged up their arses," retorted Saybrook. "If they were so competent, you wouldn't need me—or my wife—to clean up the mess they make of things."

Grentham's nostrils flared, but he was quick to cover his anger with a mocking smile. "In case you have forgotten, England has an official observer stationed on the island precisely to prevent the former Emperor's escape. His monthly reports say that nothing is out of the ordinary."

"Perhaps you ought to send in another set of eyes," suggested Arianna. "As well as consider the purchase of a pair of spectacles to help sharpen your own vision." She folded her hands in her lap. "Blindness is often a problem when a man approaches his dotage."

"My friend Henning knows a very skilled lens maker," offered Saybrook.

The minister's face turned an ominous shade of puce. "Oh, yes, the two of you possess such a clever sense of humor. You are going to need it where you are going."

"More threats?" Saybrook sounded bored.

A mocking smile. "Good heavens, no. Simply a statement of facts. The choice of what to do about them will, of course, be entirely up to you. But given your absurdly fierce sense of loyalty . . ."

Determined to end the verbal duel between the two men before it turned truly ugly, Arianna intervened. "Get to the point, sir."

"The point?" Grentham's gaze turned to her. "The point is, Mr. Henning's nephew is in a British military prison in the Highlands. A rather cold, isolated place, with precious few comforts." He made a low clucking noise. "Indeed, I've heard that few survive more than a short incarceration."

"We heard he was already dead," said Arianna quickly. "Killed by Rochemont's henchmen for wishing to resign from the group."

"As luck would have it, the lad was apprehended by my operatives, who were tipped off about a secret meeting. Unfortunately the others escaped, but thanks to me, young Mr. MacPhearson is still alive." A deliberate pause. "For the moment."

"You bastard," growled Saybrook. "You know he's innocent. The lad was but a pawn, manipulated by lies. He's no threat to England."

"What I know is that there is still a French spy loose within our government," countered Grentham. "Root him out once and for all, and then we can negotiate." A pause. "There is still the matter of Mellon's reputation."

"Just as there is the matter of yours."

"True. But in this case I think I shall call your bluff. If you go public, I shall suffer some temporary embarrassment, but I daresay I shall survive. But Mellon would almost certainly be ruined." *Tap, tap, tap.* "As for Henning, and his Scottish kin . . ."

The earl clenched his jaw. "The lad goes free now rather than later?"

The minister gave a tiny nod. "I'm willing to be magnanimous. That is, if you agree to pick up Renard's trail in St. Andrews and follow it until you bring him to ground once and for all."

Arianna met his gaze as Saybrook muttered a curt assent.

*Fire and Ice.*

"Pack plenty of warm clothing." It was Grentham's turn to toss out a taunt. "The north of Scotland is quite chilly at this time of year."

# AUTHOR'S NOTE

Much of the action in this book takes place at the famous Congress of Vienna, which convened in the fall of 1814 in order to reorganize Europe after Napoleon's exile to the isle of Elba. The gathering, an unprecedented convocation of rulers, influential diplomats and their entourages, was meant to be a grand ending and a grand beginning—the movers and shakers were looking to close the book on the strife and upheavals of the Napoleonic Wars and begin a new chapter of world peace. (In many ways, it was the precursor to the United Nations.) Countless books have been written on the complex negotiations and their ramifications—Henry Kissinger wrote his PhD thesis on the Congress—so I won't attempt to delve into its nuances. Suffice it to say, it was an extraordinary attempt to consider a vast range of issues, both political and social, and to structure a "balance of power" to ensure that there would not be another world war. For those of you interested in an an overview of both the people and the politics, I highly recommend *Vienna, 1814* by David King and *Rites of Peace* by Adam Zamoyski. In addition, *Talleyrand*, the classic biography by Duff Cooper, provides a fascinating look at the era.

Many real people play minor roles in the book, for the cast of colorful real-life characters at the Congress of Vienna makes truth appear stranger than fiction. Prince Metternich, the powerful Austrian Foreign Minister, was a savvy negotiator, a polished diplomat—and a rakish lady's man. Prince Talleyrand, the worldly and sybaritic French Foreign Minister, was perhaps the most brilliant—and cunning—statesman of the era. He really did bring the famous chef Antoine Carême to Vienna with him, not only for his own pleasure but to butter up potential supporters of French interests over sumptuous dinners and desserts. (At one point he wrote to Paris and wryly said he needed more saucepans, not more secretaries.) And then there was Tsar Alexander I of Russia. It seems he was also determined to seduce every female within arm's reach. One of my favorite anecdotes involves him seeing the wife of a prominent diplomat at a party. As she was alone, he sidled up and asked if he could occupy her husband's place for the evening—to which she replied coolly, "Does Your Majesty take me for a province?"

I have tried to stay true to their character in my story, and all the descriptions of the parties and the Carrousel are based on actual events. However, I have taken a few liberties with history. The Duke of Wellington was indeed serving as Great Britain's representation in Paris at the time, and later replaced Castlereagh as the head envoy at the Congress of Vienna. But my having him make a secret visit to confer with Prince Talleyrand in Vienna is pure fiction, as is my elaborate assassination plot and the chemical concoction discovered by Saybrook and Henning.

I hope you have enjoyed the history behind *The Cocoa Conspiracy*. For more fun facts and arcane trivia, please visit my Web site at www.andreapenrose.com. I love to hear from my readers and can be contacted at andrea@andrea penrose.com.

Turn the page for a sneak peek at
Lady Arianna's next adventure in the
upcoming Lady Arianna Regency Mystery.

Coming in Fall 2012 from Obsidian.

A jolt of the coach bounced the open book in her lap, rousing Lady Arianna Saybrook from a fitful half sleep. Wincing, she shifted against the leather squabs and flexed her aching shoulders, trying to loosen her knotted muscles as the wheels hit another frozen rut.

*Hell—this was truly the Devil's own journey.*

Though instead of rolling through fire and sulfurous brimstone, they seemed to be entering a bleak realm of ice and frigid vapors. With each passing mile, the landscape looked more and more leached of all color.

Touching her numb fingertips to the page, she couldn't help but wish that the handwritten recipe for hot Spanish chocolate might transform from ink and paper into a large pot of steaming, spice-scented liquid. Despite the fur throw wrapped around her, she was chilled to the bone by the damp cold seeping in through the creaking woodwork.

And the weather looked to be turning worse.

December was not an auspicious time to be traveling from London to Scotland. *Not that there had been any choice,* Arianna reminded herself with an unhappy sigh.

Peering out the windowpane, she saw that large flakes of snow had begun to fall, smudges of dull white against the grim grayness of the windswept moors. A shiver skated down her spine. There was something about the dark, desolate surroundings that stirred a prickling of unease.

Her two companions, however, appeared untouched by worry. Alessandro Henry George De Quincy, the fifth Earl

of Saybrook—and her husband of little more than a year—
was slumbering quietly on the facing seat, his long legs
wedged against her bench to steady himself against the
bumps. Basil Henning, his good friend and former military
comrade, was not quite so peaceful in repose. His raspy
snores were growing louder by the minute.

But then, Henning was always a little rough around
the edges—stubbled chin, wrinkled clothing, irascible
temper . . .

A clench of guilt squeezed at her chest. He wouldn't be
forced to make this miserable trek if it hadn't been for his
loyalty to her and Saybrook in their previous adventures.

"Damn that bastard Grentham," swore Arianna under
her breath, tucking the wrap tighter around her middle.
The government's Minister of State Security was renowned
as a ruthless, manipulative master of intrigue. Most people
feared him, and didn't dare to challenge his authority.

*But not me.*

"He is not a good man to have as an enemy," she acknowledged in a wry whisper. A fact that hadn't stopped
her from sticking a needle into his puffed-up vanity on several occasions.

She had won those skirmishes. But as for the war . . .

Another lurching bump. And then all went very still.

"Why are we stopping?" she asked.

Saybrook came instantly awake. Leaning close to the
opposite window, he brushed a hand to the fogged pane
and squinted into the swirling shadows. "Perhaps a tree has
fallen across the road."

Henning was slower in opening his eyes. "Auch, or perhaps a bloody rein has snapped, or a spoke has cracked," he
grumbled, rubbing at his unshaven chin. "There are a
hundred—nay, a thousand—things that can go wrong on
these miserable rutted roads of Yorkshire."

"Thank you for the cheery note of optimism, Baz,"
quipped Saybrook.

"If you want sweetness and light, you should have
headed south, and caught a ship to the balmy shores of

Catalonia," retorted his friend. The earl was, in fact, half Spanish, a fact that only added to his reputation for eccentricity among the Polite Society of London. "Heaven knows, we would all be far more comfortable there than in this godforsaken wilderness."

"I'll step outside and see what the problem is. If there is an obstacle blocking the way, Jose may need a hand." Saybrook buttoned his overcoat and, after a hint of hesitation, eased the carriage pistol from its holster by the door before reaching for the latch.

Arianna frowned. "You expect trouble?"

"It is always wise to be prepared—"

*CRACK!*

One of the windowpanes suddenly exploded in a shattering of silvery shards.

"Get down," ordered the earl calmly as he ducked low and shoved the door open with his shoulder. "Arm yourselves. The dueling pistols are in a case under the chess set, Baz, while the cavalry weapons are in my valise. You guard the left while I reconnoiter on the right." And with that, he rolled out into the gloom.

Henning's sleepy scowl vanished. Like Saybrook, he was a battle-toughened veteran of the Peninsular War. The bullet did not spark panic, merely a short, sarcastic laugh.

"Ah well, we did ask for things to get a bit warmer." His lips pursed as he pulled out the rosewood box and checked the priming of the sleek pistols. "Here, you had best keep one of these fancy barking irons, Lady S. You've already proved you know how to use it." The matched pair had been a gift from the Russian Tsar, who had professed his undying admiration for her marksmanship during their recent stay in Vienna, when her shot had saved—

*Be damned with old enemies—there were new ones to face.*

Arianna took the pistol and then slipped a sheathed knife from her reticule and pushed it into her pocket. The long, slim blade was deceptively dainty looking. Its steel was lethally sharp.

"There is something to be said for possessing an unlady-like expertise with deadly weapons," she replied.

Henning's chuckle died away in the sound of splintering wood as another bullet smashed through the casement. "Stay here and keep low." He crawled over her tangled skirts and unlatched the far door. "I'll go cover Sandro. Whoever is out there is in for a rude surprise."

She watched his boots disappear and then counted to ten before following after him.

Cold spiked through her as she hit the ground and slithered into the shelter of the spoked wheel. The light, gray and grainy as gunpowder, was fast fading behind the weathered clefts of granite, leaving the narrow road through the ravine shrouded in shadows.

Squinting, she tried to bring the hazy shapes into focus. Sounds were just as muffled—all she could hear above her pounding heart was the nervous snorts of the horses and the rush of a nearby mountain stream tumbling down through the rocks.

*Damn.* Arianna drew in a deep breath and held herself very still. No sign of movement up ahead, no stirring of—

A scuff—and then a step, coming from the rear of the carriage.

Easing back the weapon's hammer to full cock, she slithered forward for a better view.

*Swoosh, swoosh.* The faint whisper of wool brushing against leather. A moment later, the dark flutter of a greatcoat, skirling around a pair of well-worn boots.

Not those of her husband or his friend.

Arianna tightened her grip on the butt. Her hands were so cold that she could barely feel any sensation in her fingers.

"Ha." With a low hiss, the stranger dropped to a crouch by the wheel and raised a rifle. "I see you now, behind that rock," he muttered under his breath. "One . . . two . . ."

"Drop your weapon before I count to three," said Arianna, moving the pistol to within a hairsbreadth of his temple. "Or you are a dead man."

His jaw twitched in shock.

"In case you are wondering, I'm an excellent shot," she went on. "Not that any aim is required at this distance to blow your skull to Kingdom Come."

Snarling a low savage oath, he tried to swing around, but the rifle barrel knocked against the iron rim and went off with a deafening bang.

At the same instant a sharper shot rang out, and a gurgle of blood spurted from the man's jugular as the earl's shot tore open his throat. He pitched forward and fell face down on the hardscrabble ground, a viscous black pool quickly spreading over the snow-dusted stones.

Wrenching her gaze up from his sightless eyes, Arianna spotted Saybrook moving along a ridge of rock.

"Sandro—behind you!" she cried in warning as a second silhouette rose from the murky shadows, too close for her to dare a shot.

The earl whirled and lashed out a kick that caught his assailant's knee, knocking him to the ground. The man rolled out of reach and sprang to his feet, flinging a rock at Saybrook's head. It missed by a hair, the echoing ricochet sounding like gunfire in the swirling wind.

"Bloody hell, Jem—what are you waiting for! Shoot the bastard," cried the assailant, whipping a hand up from his boot and cutting a slash at Saybrook's chest.

"He's got a knife, Sandro," called Arianna.

"Yes, yes, don't worry," he responded, parrying a thrust with a quick flick of his forearm. "Stay where you are."

Ignoring the order, she edged along the side of the carriage, alert for any other sign of movement. *Where was Henning?* she wondered. *And what of their coachman?* A low groan from the driver's perch seemed to indicate that Jose had survived the first attack.

Question, questions—but they would have to wait.

A flurry of wild thrusts had forced Saybrook back several steps, giving her a clearer shot at his assailant.

*"Tírate al suelo,"* she called to him in Spanish, ordering him to duck down.

"Aim for his knee and not his heart," called her husband. "I want him alive for questioning."

"Jem!" cried the assailant, his voice turning shrill.

A shot rang out from somewhere on the other side of the coach, followed by a scream. One of the horses whinnied in fright, spooked by the flash of fire.

"Ye'll be getting no help from Jem." Henning's voice rose above a wispy plume of gunsmoke.

"I suggest you throw down your blade," said Saybrook to his attacker. "The lady is a crack shot."

"As if any bloody female could hit the broad side of a barn," jeered the assailant, but he sounded a little shaky.

"Oh, I assure you, my wife is no ordinary female."

Arianna angled the pistol's barrel a fraction. "I'll aim a touch high. If I miss, it will hit his cods rather than his knee. Either way, he won't be walking very steadily for quite a while."

Her sangfroid seemed to spook the man. Cutting a last halfhearted jab at Saybrook, the man suddenly turned and bolted for the tangled wildness of the looming moor.

*"Dio Madre!"* She was about to pull the trigger and drop him with a shot to the leg when her husband took off after him. Cursing her flapping skirts, she scrabbled up to the top of the ledge and followed as fast as she dared.